The England's Dreaming Tapes

by the same author

The Kinks: The Official Biography
Up They Rise: The Incomplete Works of Jamie Reid (with Jamie Reid)
The Faber Book of Pop (with Hanif Kureishi)
Time Travel
England's Dreaming: Sex Pistols and Punk Rock
Teenage: The Creation of Youth, 1875–1945

The England's Dreaming Tapes

JON SAVAGE

faber and faber

First published in 2009
by Faber and Faber Limited
Bloomsbury House, 74–77 Great Russell Street, London WC1B 3DA
Published in the United States by Faber and Faber Inc.
an affiliate of Farrar, Straus and Giroux LLC, New York

Typeset by Coppermill Books, London
Printed in the UK by CPI Mackays, Chatham, Kent

A CIP record for this book
is available from the British Library

ISBN 978-0-571-20931-6

10 9 8 7 6 5 4 3 2 1

Contents

Introduction

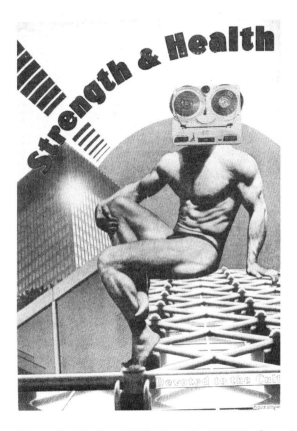

Montage for *The Secret Public*, December 1977 (Jon Savage)

All of these interviews were taped in 1988 and 1989, during the research for *England's Dreaming: Sex Pistols and Punk Rock* (London: Faber and Faber, 1991). At that time punk was only a decade old. Very few people were interested in the period, and so the interviews I got were at once vivid and untainted by layers of myth and historiography.

The starting-point for the book was the story of the Sex Pistols, an unlikely tale of how four ill-assorted youths transcended their shoddy beginnings to become the starring players in a great pop drama, one of the best ever. During 1976 and 1977 punk became a national and global event – it had politics, scandal, violence, weird clothes, radical aesthetics, kinky sex and hard, hard rock.

The musicians were only the start of it. Between 1975 and 1978, dozens if not hundreds of waifs and strays, dissidents, intellectuals, gays, thugs, suburban weirdos and, eventually, teenage rock fans were drawn into the Sex Pistols' orbit. It was a time of rapid movement, when you could meet the most extraordinary characters and see the most extraordinary events.

One way to unlock this time compression was to keep the focus fairly narrow – the Sex Pistols and London punk, with a detour into Manchester – and then go as deep as possible. That meant talking to as many people as I could, and finding out what they thought and felt that they were doing at the time. Punk was a leap into the dark, born out of mutual recognition. So how did they transform themselves?

Once I'd finally got hold of the four original and living Sex Pistols and Malcolm McLaren, I went on to speak to members of The Clash, The Damned, Siouxsie and the Banshees, the Buzzcocks, Subway Sect and X-Ray Spex, to name but a few. Then there were the journalists, the record-label owners and the faces, the people whose presence and appearance helped to define the period.

In the end, I talked to about one hundred people. I could have talked to many more, but as in any book, there has to be a cut-off point. Otherwise it would have been an endless work-in-progress. Some interviews were just to clear up a particular point or illuminate a moment in time; others were more general, and set up trails that were impossible to follow up – the subjects of other books.

Each interview started with the question: 'Where were you born and raised?' From there on, most interviewees loosened up to the point that when they got to talking about 1976 and 1977 they were relaxed, and settled into being themselves. The comparative lack of other histories meant that there was less time to spend in refuting other claims and other versions of the story.

About one tenth of all the material was used in *England's Dreaming*, so the idea of compiling the tapes afresh seemed like a good idea. Because of the long lead-up into the punk period, there was a lot of unused material about 430 King's Road, late-sixties radical politics and the early-seventies pop mood. There was also a lot of extra detail about the Sex Pistols' career.

Rather than compile a narrative of chopped-up quotes, I have arranged the interviews into themed chapters covering the shop, the group, New York and so on. Some interviewees – Roberta Bayley for instance – knew McLaren at different times in his life. There is a loose chronological thread, however, culminating in a chapter about punk's lost boy, Sid Vicious.

Even so, only about 60 per cent of all the tapes are included here. All the featured interviews have been edited for sense and libel, and there are others that have been omitted completely, for reasons of space, repetition and the book's internal logic. I intend to make these other interviews – which include a chapter about North America in 1977 and 1978 – available online.

Looking back through the transcripts has been a fascinating experience. Some of the people are dead – among them Joe Strummer, Nils Stevenson and Anne Beverley. Some are untraceable. A few are still part of my life. I'd like to thank everyone who was interviewed for the original book, twenty years ago now. Here they are, speaking in their own voices – in many cases, first-time fresh.

CHAPTER ONE

The Shop: 430 King's Road

John Paul Getty III and Jordan in SEX, early 1976 (Kate Simon)

Towards the end of 1971, Malcolm McLaren and his partner Vivienne Westwood took over the running of 430 King's Road from clothing designer and retailer Trevor Miles. The name of the new shop was Let It Rock, to showcase McLaren and Westwood's obsession with teddy–boy clothing and 1950s culture.

The shop – and the clothes – went through various permutations until 1974, when it was renamed SEX, and fetish wear was sold alongside original, confrontational fashions. It was at this time that a young clientele of disaffected outcasts began to frequent the shop – some of them were budding musicians.

The group that they formed – 'Kutie Jones and his SEX PISTOLS' – was first named in the famous SEX T-shirt-cum-manifesto 'You're gonna wake up one morning and know which side of the bed you've been lying on'. The Sex Pistols were formed out of the SEX shop to promote the SEX clothes, and so 430 King's Road became the seed-bed of London punk.

Malcolm McLaren

Sex Pistols' manager, cultural catalyst, punk impresario and self-proclaimed 'swindler'. Interviewed in New York, summer 1989. During this period McLaren was living with Lauren Hutton and undergoing psychotherapy. He always has the rant of the moment, and so he begins by talking about his family, and in particular his relationship with his brother, Stewart Edwards.

It's really weird, you just don't stop thinking about it. You end up spending a long time trying to fit it all together. It upsets you, and you start piecing together who you are and what makes you do the things you do. It was all that that somehow led me to concentrate on sorting myself out. It was something I'd never bothered to do before; basically, I tried to grow up.

How did you and your brother Stewart get on as kids?

I think he must have felt pretty bad, cos I was basically a child brought up by a grandmother in an environment that he was kept away from. I was protected. In some respects, I was lavished upon and he was starved. If he looked from my perspective, I could never go out and play, I had to stay inside with my grandmother. He was allowed to have friends, because she didn't care about him. He was allowed to run amok.

I suppose at the same time he must have felt, because we had an unloving, uncaring mother, and a father who was never talked about, that we never ultimately believed fathers existed. We had no idea what family unity was. We grew up a bit dotty, ill-equipped to deal with the real world. But my grandmother had such a strong alternative world, dominated by her, that I could exist by creating my own in the same fashion.

Stewart had to get married to create a real world for himself, cos

7

that was what his friends had. He got married to the first girl he met, just as I fucked the first girl, got her pregnant and ended up living with her for fifteen years. I got married too, but I wouldn't allow the normality to grow around me completely. I did at least in my own fucked-up way create an environment that I could run wild in. I did try. Stewart couldn't do that.

He was sacrificial, and I only think now that he to some extent resents it, but has accepted it. He was a brilliant academic. He had an incredible appetite for information, golloping down encyclopediae, and I always looked up to him cos I was the most dreadful student, I refused to learn anything.

From the day I entered school, the worse I could be, the better I liked it. I was the bottom of the heap and proud of it. In fact it was difficult to become the bottom of the pile. I was such a snob, really fucked up in those schools. Refusing to learn anything, refusing to listen to any kind of authority, and refusing to wear the uniform in the way it was meant to be worn.

I would go to great effort, picking the badge off the blazer and sewing it back on upside down in perfect position. I spent an entire evening doing that, in front of my grandmother, who would only praise me for sewing so brilliantly! She thought it looked good. I was encouraged to be awful, except in my grandmother's eyes. My brother didn't have that, and he didn't have a mother or father.

What was the stepfather like?

Mentally deficient, to be perfectly honest. A sweet soul, though I was brought up to absolutely loathe him by my grandmother, and to think of my mother as an older sister gone bad. It was something I repeated in the relationship with my own son later on, and you don't even know it until somebody comes along and opens the door to all your secrets.

I don't have any fear of the future. Most people would hate me for it, because it's so irresponsible. Do you think I think more than a few hours ahead of me? To be frank, Jon, I don't. It's a dreadful attitude, the attitude of a spoilt brat. Never worry about anything. Always do exactly as you like. So I did.

That's why I can play cat and mouse. It's my cruelty, that I take delight in it. I could have been a really cruel general in Napoleon's army, a major strategist. I'm learning it all now. I'm quite happy about it, to be one of those refined grown-ups that I detested all those years, as long as it doesn't take away your sexual libido. That's the only thing I dread.

I've been totally programmed, conned. I don't mind. I didn't used to understand why people didn't want to be exploited. I love to be exploited. I'm waiting for a girl to come in here and exploit me. I'm happy to be manoeuvred and used. I don't even mind being abused, a bit. It's a recognition that you exist.

The English hate the idea of it, that's why they can't stand success, because success comes with abuse. It comes with being exploited and used. They're so fucking conceited as a race, they can't stand the humiliation. Most races don't mind it. At the end of the day, you'll find they fuck a lot more too because of it. It's the abuse that they adore.

Here we make it such a special practice behind closed doors at a certain price. Movies like *Scandal* trying to pretend that they're sexy are a joke. To see the pathetic portrayal of Stephen Ward, who must have had something more in his blood, and if he didn't, god help England. He came across as a tragic, pathetic figure, as soon as you saw that goddamn ugly face of John Hurt's that doesn't have an ounce of rebellion on it. I hated the movie for that.

At the time I worked for three weeks as a filing clerk in an accountant's office in Devonshire Street, next door to Stephen Ward's osteopathic clinic. I used to throw the files in the bin, and they fired me, but in the three weeks I was there, the milkman used to tell me what went on, it was like a Norman Wisdom film. So one day I plucked up the courage to press the bell, pretend I had the wrong address, just to sneak about.

Of course I couldn't get any sense of anything. It was amazingly straight, but he had very fashionable clothes and sunglasses. He was incredibly handsome. Nothing like John Hurt. He was a man about town, nothing like they portrayed. I don't think he had that kind of a relationship with Christine Keeler at all. I don't believe it for a minute. I think Christine Keeler was basically pissed off because he didn't fuck her. That's all.

9

He was gay, man. End of story. He was a fabulous gay dandy. Although he may have matured, as often gay boys do, with fag-haggy girls, which probably Christine Keeler was.

I doubt MI5 was together enough to kill him in those days. I think he felt very betrayed by his snobby friends. He didn't kill himself for Christine Keeler, I think he killed himself because he couldn't have those friends again. Snobbery is frightening, man, it kills everybody.

Look, I don't care what people think about my grandmother. If she was a perverted lunatic, maybe so. The tirades I got from my mother about my grandmother before she died. My bloody mother accused my grandmother of the same thing that Johnny Rotten accuses me of. She was 'the evilest woman in the world'.

She was nothing of the sort. She was a woman who created her own world, and everybody else had to live in it, or live without it. Her world was far better than the world we live in, it had a lot more soul and passion. It was a world that was fairly inventive, but that had brilliance, it shone, and I felt for it, because it was the world that I was protected by.

*

[*Phone call – another tack:*] You know, Chrissie [Hynde] is like a younger, American version of Vivienne Westwood. They're a similar type: hard, focused, and very stubborn. Which is great, really, although I can't talk to her that well. They think of me as some real horrible macho man.

Vivienne reminds me of Mrs Thatcher, that same dogmatism.

That English, petit-bourgeois, 'up North' shopkeeper mentality. Napoleon always said we were a land of shopkeepers. I don't know whether that's derogatory these days, or whether it's a great idea, but it's true.

Was she always like that?

You know, you can never tell when you're under the sheets with someone. At the end of the day, I do feel that there was something amiss with Vivienne. I think she was a wonderful person to know and to enjoy her company at times, but I was the brat, the one that wanted to be loud and wild. I always felt inhibited in her presence. That was my hangup, something I didn't grow out of until after the event.

You were younger when you met her.

Six years younger.

Where did you meet her?

I knew her younger brother really well. She was running away from her husband, and she came to live in a house I was sharing with her brother and a bunch of others, American draft-dodgers who were all going to film school.

I was studying music, believe it or not. And drama. My grandmother always had visions of my being an actor, and at a very early age, back in the mid-sixties, I think I'd been to one art school before, for about three months, and I lived in a hotel and my grandmother supported me. Basically I was going to continue being supported by my grandmother if I took the idea of drama seriously.

So I enrolled at a drama school and there I also took piano lessons, studying Bartók. Anyway, I shacked up in this house, because a distant friend from Harrow Art School had this house that possibly I could live in, and this friend turned out to be Vivienne Westwood's brother, and Vivienne came to live there, to my shock and horror, at that time, because I hated the idea that girls should come and inhabit this house.

It was boys only, as far as I was concerned, and girls coming in made it all look dreadfully slimy. I brought her to tears, every single day, and she had this little kid, which I also hated and loathed, and I brought him to tears as well. This turned out to be Benjamin Westwood.

I almost persuaded her to leave, but because of her northern stubbornness, it defeated that end, and instead, three or four weeks later I decided to feign sick. Curiosity at the thought of being inside a woman's bed – even though I was twenty-one, god knows why I didn't think about it before.

I decided I would try this out on Vivienne, and it was very slow and uncertain. She was a schoolteacher, and I felt that I was in bed with one. There was something harmlessly perverse about the whole notion, of this spoilt brat being in bed with a schoolteacher. I slowly discovered Vivienne Westwood's sexuality, and everything that turned her into a woman. And fucked her.

I think finally, again with horror, I had to deal with the fact that she was pregnant. That was something my grandmother never forgave me for. We were going to get her an abortion, but then she persuaded me, and I think I almost persuaded myself, that it was a better idea to have the kid, and we did, and that was Joe.

From then on, I kept going back to live with my grandmother, and going back to live with Vivienne, backwards and forwards for three or four years, until I lived with Vivienne and left art school, and started in fashion. The thought of being in movies hadn't dawned on me then. The thought of being sartorially cute was something I was constantly aware of. Very vain, and being constantly English, being able to emulate whatever character one so chose.

At that time for me it was Elvis Presley, and a blue lamé suit was something I just had to have made. I forced Vivienne to learn how to cut trouser patterns in order for me to wear this costume. I did it on the King's Road and ended up having my own shop.

Is that when you changed your name?

I changed my name just before that, because I finally had to go and get a proper passport, and I had to go and get my original birth certificate, which proclaimed me McLaren. Not a name that I ever knew. This was somebody who was once mentioned, at an early age, but was quickly thrown out of any conversation.

It was only later on that I decided to find out more about this McLaren. I did figure out that he did, or at least his father did, actually come from Scotland. I know he served time in prison, he was a thief that basically was promoted by my grandmother, who enabled him to steal cars during the war, to paint them up, change the number plates and re-sell.

Cars were a very scarce commodity in those days and my grandmother ran a roaring trade on the black market, and he became the only culprit, and did a term in prison, which my grandmother quietly rubbed out of her life. When he came out, he wanted to commit great sexual and total destruction on the household, as a result of which I popped out of my mother. Then I think he ran off.

My mother has just died, four weeks ago. Luckily I went to see her on behalf of this private detective that I hired, who had persuaded me that the only way to get the truth that wasn't going to cost an absolute fortune was to go and see my mother. So I went and confronted her and got certain truths out of her. I was going to go back and see her more, cos I hadn't seen her for twenty-five years, but she died, that was it. A lot was lost with her. But I think I would have felt pretty awful if I'd put it off any more.

I think when you're older you do have to get your relationship with your parents sorted out.

You can't seem to go on without it. You may, as I did, close that door and just reinvent yourself, but suddenly the door flies open and you've got to go back in there and sort all that rubbish out.

I saw your son Joe recently. He can't seem to figure it all out.

I think the reason he can't figure it all out is that Vivienne is making him draw sides, rather than bring it all together. Whenever I'm over here I try and contact Vivienne. I want her to come out with me and Joe. She won't do that.

Why is she like that?

I suppose you have no right, at some point in this world, to leave a woman who had reached forty. But I wasn't her age mentally or in love with her as she thought I should be. She was the first girl I ever made love to, and maybe in medieval times that meant you had to stay with her. But I didn't know what it is to love somebody, to have a relationship and make it work.

I'd come from a closeted environment, so completely cut off from the world I had never grown up. The Sex Pistols was as much a part of my teenage years as anything else in my life. As a teenager I didn't live out that part of my life, except under the aegis of my grandmother. It wasn't until I reached the age of twenty-five or twenty-six that I even understood what it was. I was doing it much later on down the line. I don't have the mind of somebody my age.

13

I think Vivienne is still bitter over the fact that I left her. Nobody left her. Vivienne left everybody, threw everybody out. Vivienne always had the last word. Always got what she wanted.

Where did that moral authority come from?

I don't know, its just something that she personally feels, that she is the person whose point of view has been made because she's done all the research on it, and everybody else's point of view is completely irrelevant, because she knows the answers. I never understood that, and it used to make me laugh.

Sometimes I'd get really angry with her, because she could be stubborn about things that I couldn't be stubborn about. I felt that was because I came from London, and we can't get worked up about anything, because we're far more decadent as people.

Vivienne is not decadent, she is righteous, Christian and puritan. Her parents were upright church-going people and looked at me as a Jew and an alien, both at the same time. Vivienne was attracted, because I gave to her a world of culture that she didn't possess outside of the Christian church and Sunday School. At the end of the day, Vivienne had an intelligence and the demand for that, to make it part of her world.

She has a brilliant feel for culture, but absolutely no sense of humour about it all. You must be able to laugh at yourself. If you can't do that, it's difficult to expect people to take notice of you. People don't want to feel as if you're harbouring grudges when you're talking about things you care about. They'll never believe what you say, they'll always doubt your intentions.

Vivienne used to teach in Sunday School. When I first met her she went to church every Sunday. I couldn't believe it. When we used to rehearse with Johnny Rotten, on Sundays he would never come down until very late, right. He was at confession, for at least six months. Even after we made 'Anarchy in the UK', with his mum. Vivienne got on like a house on fire with John Rotten. I never. I was always suspect.

Didn't you spark off, you and Lydon, at some point?

Never, never. I had an eye, and my eye saw his ability to create image

14

around himself, personality, in the shop the first time. I knew he had something, it was just a gut feeling. Just as I knew Jones had something. But I never could feel comfortable in his presence because I felt this dreadful Catholic guilt, this masochism.

Ultimately he got off a little by Paul Cook beating the living daylights out of him. Jones pulled Cook off of him, otherwise John would have been a hospital case. He turned around to Paul and said, I admire you for that, I really do. We all looked at him, we couldn't believe what the group had inherited here.

At the same time, he wrote brilliantly. He couldn't have written anything better, he needed Vivienne's incantations, whatever they were, regarding anarchy. He needed me and my more perverse attitudes. He needed the confidence of Jamie that he was doing right. I never gave him that confidence.

Jones saw everything was working, so John was cool and one of the lads, but not before he told Jones he was a member of a Hell's Angels gang. All Rotten had was this sixth-form intelligence, and even that was borrowed, from John Gray. John Rotten's ideas for the Sex Pistols were all borrowed. None of them came from him. He didn't even want to be called the Sex Pistols, he wanted just to be called Sex.

I couldn't understand why he was so terrified of getting on a stage with that name. It was only Jones that loved it, and Cook thought it was reasonable but was looking for something more normal-sounding. Being a genuine sixth-form character, Matlock sided with John. I wasn't having it, I was in control and I wasn't going to waste my time with a bunch of Herberts going out with a name like Sex, I wasn't going to allow it. I was out to sell lots of trousers.

Rotten was a good boy. If we were rogues – and I particularly was a rogue – it was because we were genuinely concerned with being irresponsible and being part of what we felt was a good idea. He was never sure it was a great idea to hate everything else. He loved Captain Beefheart. I didn't even know what Captain Beefheart sounded like, but it was enough to think that he was part of the sixties.

But he projected that hatred very well.

Yes, he took on the act. We would never speak to him otherwise. You do realise that the group left him at least twice before the group carried on together. I was agreeable to it because I couldn't think of anybody else who was good enough.

When was this, just before you signed?

No, just before we actually played, when we were courting the idea, rehearsing. We had one rehearsal and none of them showed up because they thought he was a cunt. Right there, first day. They never liked each other, never liked him. I liked Jones, Jones didn't mind me. I quite liked Cook but to me, he was a bit boring. I brought Matlock into the group and used him. He was an anchor of normality. He had a certain intelligence that I thought could be used to get Jones and Cook to construct songs.

Rotten never had an ounce of musical ability. Whatever he said, he was just an arrogant little shit who thought he knew everything. He hated their music, he hated rock'n'roll. Literally hated it. He wanted it all to be fairy-like, like the sixties. Captain Beefheart. He wanted to be reggae, cos that was in that week. He was a fashion victim in the true sense, a musical fashion victim.

He didn't have the focus that Jones and Co. had. They were going for the tradition of mutated, irresponsible, hardcore raw power – Iggy Pop, New York Dolls, MC5, bits of The Faces. They knew where their musical scene was. He hated all those groups. You can see it now: Camden Comprehensive, Captain Beefheart weekend, round the back with mum's brandy. Pathetic.

Whereas Jones was bonking birds on the King's Road where he could, nicking records and cavorting with as much sartorial sense as he could muster. A whole different sensibility, and far more sophisticated than Rotten. More sense of rock'n'roll. Rotten had no sense of rock'n'roll, how could you when you went to Catholic church on a Sunday?

He was to shut up, do as he was told and write this. And he was given the political line, if there was one. Here's the poster, 'Blank Generation', copy it. He came up with 'Pretty Vacant', and it was Matlock who coined that phrase. Write a song about the Queen. I think that came from Vivienne originally. 'Anarchy' was the word we kept using.

I don't remember talking to him about politics at all. I must have done, because I think in those days I was probably more overt about politics in pop music, mostly because we all hated what was on the TV. That's what brought us all together.

The song 'Eighteen' I had on the jukebox. 'Eighteen' and 'School's Out'. Rotten liked them, but he thought they were a bit mindless. He thought being mindless was a good pose. He was terrified of being in a group, of having to announce himself. I knew there was a star there when I saw him blow his nose, cos he was so terrified of the audience, and this was a way to hide his embarrassment and shyness.

I knew people would see that vulnerability and go for it, and they did. It was those elements that made him. We knew he couldn't sing, that he had no sense of rhythm, but he had this charm of a boy in pain, trying to pretend he's cool. That was the most accessible thing. You knew all the girls were going to just love him. I thought they could be the Bay City Rollers. That was my head, I was so out of it.

To think he would be the alternative to the Bay City Rollers. Dour and tough and the real thing. A genuine teenage group. For me, that was anarchy in the record business. That was enough for me, I didn't need to sell anything else, they were like young assassins. That was the best selling point. The rest was cream on the cake that rose with the tide, and not something I necessarily promoted. I did promote 'Pretty Vacant' as an idea, but it took on a life of its own.

It was a wonderful controlled accident . . .

. . . as all great things are, really. We knew when we went round to John's house, and he was, you know, good. But Jones was so fucking bright, he had this ability to walk on the wild side and be in control. He always said, don't expose Rotten, cos if you expose his shortcomings, the whole thing would blow up.

Sid was dim, he could be a bit stupid.

People say that Sid was quite bright.

Put it this way: he wasn't bright enough to stay alive. He was dragged through the mire by someone he would have left if he'd had any sense. Sid would probably would have been alive if he hadn't met her. She led him to kill her, and she led him ultimately to kill himself. That is his mother's fault.

17

His mother was dangerous, she was unnerving from the first time I went to meet her. She was dealing him dope from day one. This was before going to America. Early days, she was bad news. He was a little boy lost and his mother had no real sense of care for him, other than what she could obtain for herself.

It was the first time I'd ever been with a mum of a rock'n'roller who right from day one was totally into it for what she could get out of it. I'd never seen that in a mother. It was weird. I'd seen Rotten's mother, and she wasn't really interested in it, but her son was happy about it, so that was okay. She was proud of him.

I think the reason Sid is such a myth is that he went right into it.

He did what every fan would love to think they could do. He became immortal by doing that. There's nothing mythic about John Lydon; he got rid of his myth, which was John Rotten, he revealed to the world that he was a god that wasn't really meant to be. His line is that the Sex Pistols was my group, I did it, McLaren's the evilest man in the world, Sid was nothing more than a fuck-up, Jones was stupid. He quite liked Paul, cos he gave him a good hiding. It's stupid.

Robin Scott

Fellow student with Malcolm McLaren and Jamie Reid at Croydon Art School, where Scott participated in a sit-in inspired by the évènements in Paris, May 1968. He was the first to get involved with the music industry, releasing an album, Woman from the Warm Grass, *in 1970. Wary, he has clear memories of the radical currents of the late sixties and early seventies.*

What was Croydon like then?

It wasn't like part of Greater London, it was like nowhere else. The Saturday-morning market in Surrey Street was a fantastic place. It was like somewhere in the Caribbean, and full of corruption and intrigue round the edges of the market, all very fascinating. I used to go down there on nicking sprees, in and out the pawn shops and down the baths. The swap shop had Nazi memorabilia and stuff like that, it was really lurid but an exciting playground.

Was there any subcultural activity? Teddy boys?

That was a bit earlier. Malcolm is a bit older than me, and he was probably more conscious of it. He had an older brother like I did, and my older brother was a teddy boy and I think Malcolm's was, so he had all these sentimental connections, but I don't remember much about teddy boys at all, I remember Purple Hearts and The Who down in South Croydon.

When did you go to art school?

'67. Straight into a vocational course in painting, which was where I met Malcolm. At that point I had been out in Kent living with my family for about six years, and I recognised that although I liked the countryside, if I was serious about painting I would have to get back into the flow of things. By the time I went to Croydon it was too late

19

for me. Apart from the relationship with Malcolm and the ensuing sit-in period, which was very stimulating . . .

My course was full of people who had broken some ground in some way or were mature students. It was pretty broad in its possibilities, but rather vague, we were left to our own devices, and that was attractive to me. There was not much teaching; the presence of people like John Hoyland and Barry Fantoni and various other people, Bruce Mclean was there. Painters in their own right, it was an obligatory role for them. Bread and butter.

That was probably the one aspect of the college's image that inflamed the situation at the time. We felt that their role was pointless, and the existing walls between authority and the students should be torn down, that's what the basic manifesto was. I suppose Hornsey had more grievances than we did, but we were in a very apathetic situation and boredom was the main complaint. It was time to test the system, see what the limitations were.

Had you already met Jamie and Malcolm?

I met Malcolm within days. I was in my studio with a couple of girls, and maybe another guy, and Malcolm arrived a bit late. As I said, we were all left to our own devices; they'd check us out, see what we were up to, but there was no syllabus or anything like that. I was doing some graphic work, very precious. I was biding my time.

It was very quiet in the studio. After about a week, Malcolm arrived, he came from Harrow, and there was no communication at all, then I remember a guy called Popplewell who attempted to strike up a conversation with us one by one. Finally he came to me and he asked me if I was colour-blind. The colours I was using made him think I was colour-blind.

So what I did, I started leading him along, pretending I knew I wasn't when in fact perhaps I was, and this got rather comical and the other students were drawn into it, sniggers going round the room. Finally everybody just broke out laughing. It was at that point that I befriended Malcolm.

Jamie didn't come in until later. He was down the other end. I suppose we'd managed to break down all that nonsense in our studio, but down there it was all very precious. He was very preoccupied

20

with being a painter, very serious about what he was doing, whereas I grasped that here was a situation where anything was possible, to have a good laugh, without taking myself too seriously.

I didn't feel attracted to Jamie at first, he was too deep really, for me, not on my wavelength at all. But I appreciated that he was attracting attention with his work, he was thought of as a serious student, he had credibility in that sense. He played the saxophone, he used to take over the common room and make a hell of a din every lunch hour.

I thought that was all that was interesting about Jamie. Then came the sit-in and he became very politicised. His father was in the printing trade, he was affiliated with some movement, and Jamie became very proud and started banner-waving at that time, and I think that's when he became closer to Malcolm.

When did the sit-in occur?

It was 1968, it must have been the summer term. It was documented in *The Times*. Malcolm and I were orchestrating the whole bloody thing between us, and we finally went down to the annexe at South Norwood and barricaded ourselves in there, and we would keep everybody informed and wind them up at the same time, and hopefully maintain an hysterical situation within which we could pump out these press releases.

We had all these telephones, and these bits kept appearing in *The Times*, and eventually they asked me to go on this BBC TV programme, *Town Round*, to account for what was going on down at Croydon, answering these ridiculous questions.

How did the sit-in occur, from your point of view? Was it a question of responding to Hornsey?

There were a number of emotional confrontations with the staff, who didn't have a clue what was going on. They didn't associate it with any political unrest or anything like that, they felt perhaps there were a few upstarts who wanted to cause a bit of mayhem. It was unfortunate for them, cos they had a very comfortable situation there. It was annoying for them, but at the same time they were prepared to listen and have some kind of audience with us.

Once we'd got into the annexe, we bolted up the doors and said we're not going home. We put up a sort of sixth-form manifesto about tearing down the partitions. Most of the demands were directed at the staff; it didn't go beyond that, we weren't looking to do anything constructive like affiliating ourselves with any political or educational objectives. It was very provincial. It was almost like a fashionable thing to do.

Eventually we couldn't keep the doors closed and not have some kind of discussion with the powers that be, so we had to form committees and all that bloody nonsense. I was singled out to represent the student interests in the body, and to go and confront the staff. I said, 'I'm just not interested in doing that, I don't even know whether I represent the students' interests.' But time was running out, people weren't sleeping and we had to get out.

The fun was over, it was a weekend picnic. I don't think Malcolm's intentions were any more serious either, because when it came to the crunch, having anything constructive to say or do, or to put forward any constructive replacement for the problem, or the prevailing attitudes, he had nothing to say. Indeed, when the opportunity arose to actually change the system, or do anything about Croydon School of Art, he was gone, he fucked off.

All the time he was creating a position for himself elsewhere, at Goldsmiths. It was the other Malcolm coming out . . . the little boy lost, who was really just wanting to settle down and do his work, and 'Can you find me a place cos I think it's getting a bit rough at Croydon?' Whereas as time went on, the excitement was wearing a bit thin with me, I was getting impatient with the whole set-up.

Where were you living while you were at art college?

I was living with a girlfriend I met at Croydon, and I remember when Malcolm had just met Vivienne, she was teaching then. Malcolm was Malcolm Edwards then. I don't know what was going on, but he was having trouble getting a grant at Croydon, and maybe that was another reason why he wanted to go to Goldsmiths, that he had more credibility on a degree course and could therefore get a grant. He was switching names and stuff . . .

Vivienne appeared warm and in a sense I suppose more practical and maternal and stable, and I think those were the attributes which attracted Malcolm. She was a teacher in Brixton or somewhere. Then she was pregnant with Joe, and she got a place in Stockwell, I remember going to a party there. I suppose she was breaking out then, they were making some jewellery and flogging it up on Portobello Road. This would have been before the sit-in.

The only person Malcolm seemed to trust was his grandmother. Vivienne to a certain extent helped him wean off that strange relationship with his grandmother, but he had the archetypal, screwed-up artist's childhood. It's always the way, anyone who's at all interesting has to go through that painful imprisonment with some fucked-up people we call our parents.

What did you do afterwards? Did you leave Croydon at that point?

Well I got on that TV programme *Town Around*, and thought I was a star, a sit-in star. I was plonking around on a guitar, and I thought I'd write a topical song. I called them back and told them I'd got a song, and I was doing that for the next year, writing these songs for all these magazine programmes, it was all nonsense but I got paid pretty well. It had an element of excitement. I'd ring them up with an idea, and if they liked it I'd come in and sing it live.

In a year I did about ten or twelve, for the *Today* programme, *Town Around*, *Scene South East*, *Late Night Line-Up*. Then I was doing *John Peel* and *Late Night Line-Up* on the same night, and someone asked me had I got a record out. All this exposure and I didn't have a record out, so he said 'Do you want to make a record?' So I made a record in a day at this studio in Chelsea, with a group called the Mighty Baby, who were formerly The Action.

So then I started drifting off into the music scene. The next time I met Malcolm he was doing this festival at Goldsmiths College, and he asked me to do something with my group. I saw him a bit around that time, and I lived with Malcolm and Vivienne around that time, I think that was his last year. So whilst I had been doing these topical songs on TV, he had stuck it out there and established a relationship with Helen Wallington-Lloyd.

Was Malcolm interested in the fact that you'd got involved in the music industry?

Probably. I'd worked my way back to stay with my parents in Seaford. Malcolm appeared and stayed for a few days, met my parents and my elder brother,who was living a rather strange existence, travelling round in a caravan with his wife and first child, and Malcolm managed to meet the whole family. He seems very interested in families, perhaps because he has this very unsuccessful model. We all do that, him more than anybody.

Anyway we spent a bit of time together and he wrote a letter saying he was starting this shop, and if I could put forty quid into it I could come in on it. I said no, but I want to come back and live in London with you, so that's what we did. I said I didn't want to get involved with the shop, but I said, I've got this idea for a song, and did he want to put some money into that? He wasn't interested. There was no crossover at that point.

His interest in music was connected with rock'n'roll really, and the teddy-boy thing; for him it all died with the likes of The Beatles and the Stones. He wasn't interested in anything after that. So he started it up, and after it had been going about a year he asked me if I wanted to work with him and I said okay, what the hell. So I came in and I got a car and we used to go up North and look for materials and stuff, generally.

Was it only materials or did you find old clothes, original teddy-boy stuff?

No, we usually went down to Chinese Den to have the suits made up. I got heavily involved in the shop until one day I said, 'I don't know how you can afford to live, Malcolm, but I can't on what you pay me', and I knocked it on the head. Then Vivienne said, 'You shouldn't have left, you were going to be a partner and everything', but it was too late.

Was there anyone else involved in the shop in those early days?

Not really, it was just the three of us. I enjoyed working there, but I wasn't interested in the business, I just wanted the general excitement, that's all, the craziness of it all.

What sort of clientele was it?

There were some really hardcore teds that came down, but they were disappointed, I think they sensed that it was a posture rather than real authentic sentiment. Malcolm got hold of some interesting records, he was trading them. That element was coming in, the musical aspect. A lot of tourists would come down. The audience that you were thinking of, they hadn't arrived.

After that I didn't really have any further contact for a while, then Malcolm showed up again. He came up to the flat, with Paul and John, and he said, 'I just want to introduce these guys, I'm thinking of starting a band.' I think he was looking for advice. I remember thinking that they were young, and he obviously was thinking like an impresario. Then he got back to me looking for somewhere to rehearse. Obviously picking my brains.

I remember having a coffee with him on the King's Road in '76 and he had this name, the Sex Pistols. 'What do you think?' I said 'Fine, what are you going to do with it?' Then they started rehearsing and he said, 'Come down and listen to them', but I didn't have too much faith in the idea, and I never went.

How did you see the relationship between Malcolm and Vivienne?

I always saw Vivienne as the woman behind the man; she was largely responsible for much of the drive and many of the ideas which Malcolm had. They had a relationship which was about educating each other, and in the death throes of that relationship they were both claiming responsibility for certain ideas, because they had become one, it was difficult to know who was who.

The reason she had to be confident was she was doing all the bloody work back at the flat, and she knew she was holding it together. I admired Vivienne, I thought she was and still is a great person, much more prepared to commit at an emotional level and admit one's vulnerability. She was very supportive and she was happy for Malcolm to be the centre-piece in a conversation, when she had just as much to say.

Malcolm saw the possibilities in her ideas, and was happy to have a line and go on repeating himself silly. It could get a bit exasperating. He would pick up something he'd heard and decide he liked it, and he would use it all the time. He was very tenacious and wouldn't tire, he would carry on in the face of adversity, preaching whatever ideas had been generated between them, but Vivienne was crucial.

That's what I felt looking from the outside. I know he was attracted to her for that very reason. She wasn't always great to me when we were living together. One time she said, 'I want you to go, Robin.' 'Why?' 'I don't think you're part of the revolution.' God! She was bound up in that rhetoric at the time. Little did she know that nor was Malcolm committed to the revolution. Malcolm was committed to himself, and she took a long time to realise that.

Malcolm knows very well how to capitalise on other people's imagination. He has this ability to be a catalyst and to have tenacity with a particular project, to the point where he's not bothered about anyone else being exhausted and falling by the wayside or getting hurt, he just has this ability to plough ahead, and it could have gone in any direction, it didn't have to be a group, or music or fashion.

He would stay up all night at things, drive himself into the ground, because he obviously saw something at the end and it wasn't money. He'd like money, he knows what it can do, he's not stupid, but he's motivated by being the centre of attention. He doesn't know what kind of attention is going to make him happy. What impressed me more than anything else was the energy and staying with it.

What did you think of what happened to the Sex Pistols, the way they became a national obsession?

I felt that punk was the death throes of hippy idealism really, hippies dressed up as bulldogs. They weren't materialistic. They were nihilistic, perhaps, but wanting to create chaos in the same way as that generation of '68 wanted to tear down the barriers and create a new society. They were the younger brothers and sisters of the generation of '67/'68.

Helen Wallington-Lloyd

South African émigré and close friend of Malcolm McLaren since the late 1960s. For a time in spring 1976, the Sex Pistols' office was in her Bell Street flat. Interviewed at her then home in West Hampstead, London, Helen was outrageous and camp. Best known for her appearance in The Great Rock'n'Roll Swindle *as Helen of Troy, her wider input into the early Sex Pistols has never been fully acknowledged.*

You were at Goldsmiths, weren't you?

Yes, in the late sixties. I was brought up in Johannesburg, South Africa. We left because there was no culture down there. In '67 I was in New York, just before the summer term at Goldsmiths, and the last people to show their paintings was Malcolm and me. That was the days of flower power and bells and all that, but Malcolm had this peaked cap, a long Army & Navy coat, miles too big for him, newspaper rolled up under his arm, smoking Woodbines.

But he asked me what I'd do if I didn't get in. I said, 'I'll go to San Francisco and join the hippies' – something like that. 'What would you do?' He said, 'I'd go and cause a revolution.' I was so sheltered in South Africa; although the Mandela thing had started, you didn't hear about revolution.

Were you bored there?

I wasn't bored cos it's a beautiful country, and I was doing my art. I had friends. My brain wasn't sophisticated enough to be bored. I went off to America and came back to go to Goldsmiths, and saw Malcolm, and he goes, 'Oh hello, you got in!' We stuck together. He was strange, he'd say, 'What you being so precious about? Don't tickle the canvas, you're more important than the canvas.'

He was very restless, he'd been expelled from a few colleges beforehand, where he met Jamie Reid and Robin Scott. He was an

27

agitator. He loved art, but he only went there because of the grant. He didn't want to make pictures for people to buy. He wanted to instigate something, and be an imp. An itch in somebody's knickers. The things he used to say to the tutors: 'Fucking rubbish!'

How did they react?

Ever so English, reserved, polite. I think they quite liked him. I was so closeted and he seemed like the person who would free me. He wasn't nice or patronising to me, he treated me like anyone else. I'm Jewish, and he was Jewish, or half-Jewish. His grandmother brought him up. She was wonderful.

Did you meet her?

Yes. She thought I was twelve years old, like a little kid. She gave elocution lessons. His grandmother was quite ugly, she was a tear-away. She wasn't the nice Jewish girl, she had devilment in her. He loved his grandmother. He couldn't stand his mother.

What did you think of Malcolm's friends?

Jamie is a blubber, he's got no flexibility, he's a bloodsucker, like Robin Scott. They used to come round and suck Malcolm's blood. I couldn't understand what he wanted those people for. Malcolm had so much spunk.

What was Fred Vermorel like then?

Fred was really weird. He's very hard to get to know. He'd come in, and Goldsmiths was basically a teacher training college, and the art department was way out across the green. He'd just come in and just stand there. He was hanging around. This was the days of Danny Cohn Bendit and Tariq Ali and all that.

Did Malcolm go to Paris, or was that one of the myths he put about?

I think he did, actually. I don't know how involved he was, but he did go, and that gave him the feeling that he should do something here.

Even if he wasn't at the riots, the feeling in Paris must have been very exciting.

Sure, the young people were becoming citizens, and they could say what they wanted to be taught and how. Malcolm loved that, because it was changing things, it was new and challenging. But Malcolm doesn't think about people's needs, he forgets people have to bleed, eat, shit, and they like a pat on the back, or something. He would take things that people said, and say that he said it. I don't think it was intentional, he just doesn't think.

He needs a lot of people around him, doing different things, and he needs to feel not threatened. He needs to feel that people are there because they want to be there, and not to stick a knife in his back. And that they've got something to give, or say, which he wouldn't think of, and which he would use. I think that's great, cos you can't do everything on your own. Although he should have thought about me . . .

So how long were you at art school with Malcolm?

Three years. I left in about 1971. There were always sit-ins and festivals. Malcolm organised the first festival at Goldsmiths, during the summer term. Malcolm never took his diploma. There were debates at the students' union, and Malcolm used to put things in terms they could relate to, because he's not an intellect. He had a more ducking-and-diving kind of life.

Do you remember the Oxford Street film that he did?

I was helping with it. We used to do projects together, we'd take over a space with string and ridiculous things. I lived in Marble Arch then and he used to come and stay with me. He wanted to show how the façades in Oxford Street change in a minute. It was hard to do a film like that, particularly if you've got no film-making experience, because with façades, there's no core to it. Too amorphous, you could never make an end.

Malcolm always liked Hogarth and Dickens. He knew lots of things about London's history, he was mad keen to live in Bloomsbury. Little things like that. How people lived, and what they had to pretend. But the Oxford Street film, what was shot was the changing façades and the type of clothes that Take Six made.

It was about creating a need for people to buy something. If they

29

didn't buy things, there wouldn't be anything. It was like advertising, if you didn't have something, that was it, you weren't hip. That and the fact there was just a straight street with no trees and nowhere you could sit, no bars, you had to go inside, the Wimpy, not relaxing like in Paris, where you could sit and just watch people.

A very interesting subject, but very hard to film. It had to do with life, in the end.

How did he get involved with teddy-boy clothes?

I think it was to do with when he was a young kid, he loved the music, Gene Vincent, Eddie Cochran. And there was still teds around. The bootlace ties and the beautiful shirts.

He hated hippies. 'Make love not war', it was so passive. It was awful, because they were so elitist, you'd walk in a room and it would be dark with Indian things hanging on the wall. Everyone sitting there stoned and silent, as if they were meditating or on a different plane, and if you came in loudly or wanted to talk you were looked upon as really gross and uncouth and insensitive.

I think Malcolm can't take drugs, he's so way out anyway, a space cadet. In a sense he's right because drugs become a way of life. Clear thinking was what he wanted to be into. A joint would make him passive. The teddy boys were looking for action, anything going. They weren't into sitting in dark rooms smoking pot. And there was the romantic thing. Malcolm is ever so romantic, he needs people with warmth.

When the shop started, I had become a fag hag. I was finding Malcolm a bit one-sided, and somehow I was like his sidekick all the time. One time he burned a Greek flag, which I couldn't understand. He said it was a sign of fascism.

Which clubs did you go to?

Le Duce, Masquerade, Yours and Mine, Sombrero, Chaugerama's, the Piano Bar, the Pollo Bar. The Boltons, where I met Derek Jarman for the first time. Malcolm was there too, with Vivienne. She had come out of the woodwork, with Malcolm's kid. After then I went to South Africa for a year or so, cos my husband was in prison, and Malcolm was working with the New York Dolls.

30

Was he really their manager?

Their manager ran away and Malcolm just walked in, without any contract or anything. He ended up a real nutcase. Thunders was amazing. He's got something, charming and relaxed, he's not hung up, but that awful Jerry Nolan, he was horrible. Arthur Kane was an alcoholic, I never met him, but Malcolm used to tell me about having to prop him up.

Malcolm liked Syl Sylvain, he was closest to him. I don't know about David Johansen. Malcolm just thought he could make this total mess into something. Glam rock was very much the thing. They were a total mess, their whole foundation was really rocky. But that gave Malcolm the taste, he was the media man. He never stayed in one thing. He made clothes, he got into writing songs, he's a bit of an arty-farty.

When I came back from South Africa I got divorced, I was starting over again. And Malcolm was the only one I felt at home with, I trusted his instinct. That's when he told me about the band. He had long hair, and he was talking like an American. He was wearing leather jeans and stuff, and he said, 'I've got this band, called the Sex Pistols.' Glen was working in the shop. He was very nice to me, always smiling, but he didn't interest me, he was nice wallpaper.

When did you first meet John?

We went to some pub, and I met Johnny and some of his mates. Sid wasn't there, he was in remand. Johnny looked amazing. Mohair jumper. He looked like a young Albert Steptoe. Very queenified. Always moaning. Being obtuse, always contrary. He's very bright. I know a lot of Irish people and they're so hung up. And he comes from a real heavy family. Live by their wits. He's terrified of being beaten up, of blood.

From what you were saying, John was quite creative

Yes, he had definite opinions about things, and he would voice them, loud. I'd look at him and think, 'What has Malcolm got himself into?' To me, the English working class of that time were quite threatening. Nudging each other about poofters and blacks and yids, anything. John was a bit like that, very suspicious of middle-class

31

people. I spoke to his mother on the phone. She asked me, 'What is this Malcolm McLaren really like? Do you think he's for real, is he thinking about the boy?'

John always talked in opposites. His mother used to say, 'He's a funny boy, talking in opposites.' I think with Malcolm it was narcissistic, they looked so much alike. Both Aquarians, the same bone structure, they've got those eyes, and they're absolutely fearless of other people's opinions. They're hard. Obviously different things in their backgrounds made them different, and also they had the gift of the gab, they'd come up with the most bizarre innovations.

Malcolm loved Steve Jones, because Steve had warmth. John Lydon was cold, and so was Paul Cook in his aloofness. I think John liked Malcolm basically, in the beginning. Perhaps as a father figure, or as a mirror of himself. And to Malcolm, John was this younger version. Malcolm's got this thing about youth. When you're young, you're fearless, you can do things. That's what Malcolm wanted.

Jordan

In many ways, the first Sex Pistol – before anyone else, Jordan wore the SEX clothes in the proud, confrontational manner that McLaren and Westwood envisaged. Between 1974 and 1978 Jordan was the front woman of 430 King's Road, the most photographed and the most imitated. Interviewed down near her home on the South Coast of England, Jordan was very generous with her time.

I went to ballet school in Eastbourne, I started when I was about four and carried on until I was about eighteen. I know every dancer says they would have liked to have gone to the Royal Ballet School, but I had a really bad car accident when I was fifteen, smashed my pelvis in three places, and that put a stop to that.

When you were growing up here, was it solitary or did you have friends – or did you get a bad reaction from people?

I don't remember any of my friends being embarrassed by the way I looked, you would think that would be the first reaction. At school, I was very strict about my lifestyle, and I had a few very close friends. I was also quite tough, I used to protect other schoolmates who were having trouble. I would be called upon to beat somebody up after school, on behalf of somebody else.

How did you get involved in the shop?

I wore a skirt in Brighton one day and someone asked me if I'd bought it at Let It Rock in London, and I'd never heard of the place. It was an original fifties skirt, with musical notes done in gold filigree. I asked them where this shop was, cos I thought if I'm making this stuff up myself down here, scraping around, why not go up there and see if they've got anything to sell me direct, rather than search around for things. So already I was working on a parallel, before I'd ever heard of them.

33

It must have been '73 to '74. I went up there and it was closed. The next time I went, someone was putting up this big pink sign saying 'SEX' on the door, and I went in and I was floored. I saw the manager, Michael Collins, and I was pushing myself, I really wanted to work there. I was working in Harrods at the time, selling designer stuff. Velvet jackets and things like that. I never heard any more.

I left Harrods and I got a call one afternoon from Michael Collins saying could I come and help for the afternoon. He was really desperate for someone, and that afternoon sort of blossomed, and I was there for seven years. It wasn't even a try-out, I suppose I just fitted. It was really based on how you looked. It was pretty important how you looked then.

I had a pink and red Mohican haircut at school. When Mia Farrow had her hair cut short it was quite unusual, and I stole that idea, and I saw an interview with Keith at Smile, and I took all my pocket money and went and got a Mohican hairstyle. Short but not shaved, and long and bright pink here, with two red tails coming down the back. I must have been very naive cos I went to school thinking it would be all right, but it wasn't.

Where did you used to buy your clothes on the South Coast?

I used to go to these second-hand shops, and I found this place that sold original fifties shoes, never been worn, they'd been stocked away somewhere, all size 2 or 3, and I had a size 2 foot, so I got all these great shoes, turquoise leather slingbacks, the original ones with the elastic running around the inside. That was in Brighton.

Did you always go to Brighton for amusement?

Yeah, I went to a lot of discos there. I cut my teeth on Brighton, it's quite an outrageous place, always has been. If you could hold your ground in Brighton and people knew who you were, then you were somebody. When I came up to London I went to the Masquerade Club in Earls Court, a gay club, very outrageous even by today's standards.

It was difficult for a woman to get into those clubs, the male gay scene was very insular, and the only way you got in was by how you looked. If you looked crazy and outrageous you were all right, you weren't a straight girl going down there for a laugh. It so happened that I liked good dance music, and the only places you could get that was those gay clubs.

Can you remember what they played?

Things like 'Rock Your Baby', 'Rock the Boat'. Lots of Bowie. I was a big Bowie fan, and a big Rod Stewart fan before that. Big Roxy fan. Probably the best concert I ever went to was the Bowie and Roxy double bill at the Rainbow. I've still got the original Roxy badges from that. Pink with blue writing.

What were the boys wearing at the Masquerade?

The wedge haircut, high-waisted Oxford bags.

You were going there while you were working at Harrods?

Yeah, I got away with murder at Harrods, cos I used to wear green foundation and stuff, I don't quite know how I kept my job there, now I think about it. I think because I did ballet for many years, it gives you a sense of physical confidence when you've done a tight discipline like that. Apart from that, I liked to treat myself like a painting. I didn't consider that people would be offended or outraged by it. It really never crossed my mind.

It's got to do with the way you carry yourself and the way you walk. If you slouch and look like that, people think you're a tramp. But if you carry yourself right, that's style, the way you carry yourself.

Who was working in the shop when you started?

Michael was there, Vivienne came in now and then. Malcolm was away in New York, with the New York Dolls. He didn't know of me being employed till he phoned the shop one day and I answered the phone. When he came back we introduced ourselves, but he wasn't involved with my employment at that time.

That must have been the very early days of SEX. I don't suppose Vivienne was designing very much then?

A lot of things were still drapes, beautiful fifties petticoats with bows on, a few sort of lamé things, creepers, penny loafers, the remnants

35

of Let It Rock, and the vinyl and rubber wear. There were some leather trousers. The shop became quite famous for them, because our leather trousers were better than anywhere else.

The impression I get is that in the early days there weren't many kids hanging about, it was quite a specialised business.

That's right. There were a lot of teddy boys for their drapes. Whatever Malcolm and Vivienne have done, they've done properly, and there were certain dress codes that had to be strictly adhered to, they wanted certain things out of their clothes and Vivienne could provide that, so you were guaranteed a certain clientele if you kept your standards up.

But nothing really broke until *Honey* magazine came in and did a tiny little piece with a picture of an ordinary girl wearing one of those I Groaned with Pain T-shirts on, with a split across it, and gently gave the impression that it was a place to go and see. That there was this shop with rubber walls and chicken wire, and that it was worth going to see the shop and the shop assistant, which was me. I think the quote was, 'If you don't want to buy, just go and look.'

Weren't the teds put off by the leather gear?

Not really, but then the rubber men who came in weren't put off by the other stuff. Never was the shop just one thing. I know the rubber men did want privacy, they were very introverted about their fetish, but if you've got a certain amount of decorum you can get away with it. The rubber men were a mixed bunch, we had regular customers who would have things made to order for them, whole rubber suits, which were very expensive.

There was a rubber screen there, and there was this terrible kerfuffle once when someone was putting on these rubber pants, knickers, briefs, behind it – a woman, I think it was – and we could hear this terrible slapping against flesh and her elbow bashed the screen, and the screen came over, and the shop was quite full, and there she was with these pants halfway up her legs. She screamed. We had to go out of the shop cos we were laughing so much.

You'd get people coming in wanting personal attention, or wanting you to try the things on, which is all very suspicious. I used to make Vivienne do that. The first thing you learned in that business, they didn't really mind being told what you thought. That's why they came back; if something looked terrible on someone, we said so.

Did you get any famous people coming in? Was the Reginald Bosanquet story true?

He came in, yeah, he bought a pair of leather pants. He lived just round the corner, used to pop in all the time. He bought me a bunch of flowers once, we were in the florists at the same time, he said, 'You look so beautiful', and he turned to the assistant and said, 'Give her a bunch of whatever she wants.' He wasn't shockable.

When we had the Cambridge Rapist T-shirts in, and they found out that the Cambridge Rapist wore one of those zip-up masks, Michael Collins was absolutely convinced that one of our regular customers was the actual rapist. He phoned the police up, and it wasn't him at all. They found out later that his was a home-made mask. People were very offended if you wore a Cambridge Rapist T-shirt, I got a lot of trouble on the buses at that time.

When did that stuff start to come in?

We had those Vive Le Rock T-shirts. I don't know if this is true, but Malcolm made all those T-shirts for one of those Wembley teddy-boy concerts and worked out that one in three people would buy them, when in fact in was more like one in thirty. So he was stuck with all these T-shirts and he made them into pants. We had thousands of them, they lasted for years.

What about the square T-shirts?

That came from the Valerie Solanas book [*SCUM Manifesto*]. Those were really one of the first T-shirts that were later to be seized, that the police found so offensive. I remember the original artwork coming into the shop for that. Then there was the American footballer [T-shirt]. The real T-shirt boom came after the Sex Pistols came along. That was the vehicle to sell the band.

I was interested in the way the designer stuff slowly took over from the original two specialised codes, teds and rubber, then slowly this other stuff coming in, which I suppose was Vivienne getting more into designing?

37

Also the kids were getting more into rubber, and the shoes which were a major feature, the stilettos, the high court shoes were very popular. Once you got that market, you had another market for selling clothes; the teds weren't an ongoing thing.

Malcolm was trying things all the time, wasn't he, to see what went? Teddy boys, rubber wear, a bit of this, a bit of that. Diversify, my boy.

Oh yeah. But Vivienne could always rationalise what she was doing, she could always make it into some political statement about the world as it is today. Me and Michael really just sold the clothes, I wasn't interested in what was behind them. You can go on and on, can't you, about what's in someone's mind, and why they designed it. The customers didn't want to know that.

It seems like a mixture of accidents and planning to me.

I don't think I've ever seen two people interact so well as Malcolm and Vivienne making a garment. Many times I'd see them around their flat discussing a particular design together, and even though Vivienne had done so much of the groundwork, Malcolm would give that little touch to it that made it work. They had a great relationship, their minds worked well together. I could never quite see either of them designing on their own, put it that way. It caused a lot of arguments too.

You also did specialist sex stuff, didn't you?

All that rubber gear, yeah, I did whole sessions with all that on. *Dressing For Pleasure*, that was another film that I – and Malcolm – was in. Malcolm was very self-consciously flicking through the racks of rubber pants.

Vivienne tends to be a bit school ma'am-ish . . .

You couldn't have said anything more appropriate. Vivienne was a teacher, and she has never ever lost that attitude, of teaching and wanting to teach. That's why people like Debbi and Tracie who were so young, they were the perfect vehicles for Vivienne to sculpt, to teach, to nurture. She is the perpetual teacher.

What was Malcolm like before the band started?

38

He used to work in the shop sometimes. He was such a laugh. He used to pretend he'd given us our wages when he hadn't. We used to make clothes to order, and once I'd ordered a pair of vinyl trousers, and somebody came in and their trousers weren't ready, and he told me to take mine off and sell them to somebody! We used to have huge rows: 'I'm not taking my trousers off!' 'You take 'em off!'

And what was SEX like in the King's Road at that time? Was it very different from everything else?

Absolutely. I know the King's Road has always been such a chameleon-like place, it's never stayed the same for more than six months. I don't remember when BOY came along, but they were the poor cousins to the SEX shop.

Were you aware of Acme Attractions?

– and Don Letts? Yeah, we despised him.

What about Jeanette?

Jeanette? God, that takes me back. All those people were terribly in awe, Jeanette was completely in awe of me and Michael. She used to follow me around like a little lost doll. You were the bee's knees when you worked in that shop, you had The Look. I'm not talking about the clothes, just The Look.

When did you start growing the beehive? In the early pictures it's still quite low, isn't it?

Yeah. I think I already had the beehive when I went for the job. I had that done at Ricci Burns in the King's Road. That got wider and wilder, that was all through the SEX Shop. And all the vinyl and rubber. I used to bend over and lacquer it all, and then mould it like you would a sculpture. A lot of people used to ask cos they could never get it quite the same.

I was interested in the idea of making yourself into a sculpture, an artwork.

If you got a really good hairdresser and you could tell them what you wanted, like I could, and be persistent, you got what you wanted in the end. I had people up till twelve o'clock at night in hairdressers, calling up the old-style hairdressers who did ballroom dancers, saying, 'I am at a loss what to do next.' At one stage I used to sculpt it and then cut it. It looked useless the next day, but great for one night.

I remember thinking you were like the mirror image of Mrs Thatcher, there was a doppelganger thing going on, you were bringing all the repression that Thatcher symbolised out, which is why you got such a reaction.

I probably felt the same as you, because at one stage I used to wear twinset and pearls with all the geometric make-up and slides. That's the ultimate diversity. At one stage I used to wear Pierre Cardin outfits with my hair like that, to have the two things on one body, really, and it worked really well.

What did you think of the swastika?

I suppose it was the ultimate shocking symbol. We got banned from an all-night club, The Candy Box. John and Sid and I all got memberships for it, an all-night place for people who worked in clubs to go to. I went down there with a swastika shirt on, and somebody took offence, there was an argument, and that was the end of our memberships. I just liked the shirts, and I didn't really understand Vivienne's argument for the swastika.

What was her argument?

That it was shock value, demystifying the symbol. Like I said before, you can rationalise something to the point where it becomes ridiculous. I just looked at things on an artistic basis, and I thought the swastika armband fitted on the anarchy shirt. I thought it looked nice, that's all I thought. It didn't worry me, I haven't got any taboos about those things.

The particular person who had a fight with me about it at that club was my age, and I said, 'What the hell do you know.' 'My grandmother and grandfather were killed by the Nazis.' 'But what do you know?' I got very annoyed by this attitude towards the swastika, people being so touchy about it. It's all stories handed down – handed down twice by then, it was history.

40

What did Malcolm think about the swastika?

Malcolm was in awe of the symbolism. Not just the swastika, but a lot of artefacts from that era that were extremely beautifully made. The Nazi youth badges. They were extremely rare; I had one, an original enamelled Nazi youth badge. A triangle split up with the swastika in the middle. A lot of rings and things like that.

Were they for sale in the shop?

I don't think so, cos they were originals. Certainly the youth badge he gave me was an original. I just couldn't believe at the time that people could be so touchy, all that time ago. We all know what happened, this was my attitude, and we all knew it was wrong, and to all intents and purposes there was no Nazi Party now. There was this genius who was also a loony, Hitler, and it's all out of taboo, I thought, by that time.

The whole shop started with one taboo and spread out to all taboos.

It's a corny old term but it was like bringing people out of the closet, and by making things standardised, not making them feel apart any more. But you get the feeling that those rubber people really wanted to be apart. When the kids took over, a lot of the rubber guys felt worried about it. It was very difficult to get hold of that rubber wear. Mail order was the only way, really.

Did Glen work at the shop ever?

Glen did work at the shop for a little while, we had these stand-ins when somebody was on holiday. Sid worked with me for a little while. He was useless as a shop assistant. He used to be so scruffy. I used to take real pride in the way I looked when I went to work. I kept the job because of the way I looked and because I could do the job. If I was no good at selling I don't think I would have been there very long.

Was your job partly to weed out the people who weren't enthusiastic or committed? People tell stories about going along there and being terrified.

Yeah, people were terrified of coming in. I'd heard reports from people who later became friends, that people wouldn't go in because of me, that I wouldn't say anything to them, I'd be horrible. It was just my attitude. I thought I looked better than anyone else. I was very introverted, I know people thought I was an exhibitionist, but I was pretty stand-offish. I know I looked very intimidating. By that time I'd built this reputation for myself.

You just wore on the train what you wore in the shop?

Yeah, and I didn't wear a coat or anything. I lost my flat in Sloane Square, Drayton Place, so I had to come back to Seaford and commute. I had a lot of trouble when I did it but there we are. What did I expect. The reaction was mixed, sometimes I'd get on a train and all I had on was stockings and suspenders and a top, that was it. People say it must have taken guts, but if it needed guts to do it, you wouldn't do it. The fear part didn't come into it.

Some of the commuters loved it. Then you'd get ladies who'd say I was corrupting their son, and would I move, and I'd say 'Well, you were here last, you move', or I asked the boy, 'Am I corrupting you?' I even got the whole carriage once, 'Put your hands up if you think I'm corrupting this boy!' And everyone laughed, nobody put their hands up, the woman was absolutely furious, she went red with rage: 'If I wanted my son to go and see a stripper on a train, I'd go and pay for him to see one!'

Some of the men got rather hot under the collar, paper on the lap. There was absolutely nowhere you could go where people wouldn't say something. It was just too blatant for them. People up on scaffolding would shout, there'd be tourists running, trying to get photos. This is long before it all burst, taking pictures of punks and what have you. I threw a camera out of the train one day. I know that German tourists are renowned for it, but they are really rude.

What other sort of things did you wear?

I used to go to work in that vinyl leotard and fishnets, and once in just fishnets and those big mohairs with satin padding at the front. Turquoise. I had a little tennis skirt with tennis racquets up the side, very very short. I went to a party that Lady Ann Lambton

42

had for Andy Warhol, and I stuck some black fringing on them.

So when did the kids start to come and hang around the shop, and who were they?

Well, Marco Pirroni came in early on, I suppose the kids from Bromley were quite early. A few gay black guys. There was a bloke, Amadeo, who used to be the DJ down the Sombrero. The Sombrero was another one of our hang-outs. This was a long time after the Masquerade, which just outraged itself eventually, it was closed down cos it was a public nuisance. Pete Burns used to come in; he'd buy a lot.

When were you first aware of this supposed band? Were you aware of Steve and Paul, and Glen?

Malcolm took me to somewhere in Shepherd's Bush to a big old rehearsal studio – Hammersmith, Riverside – and they were just called QT Jones then, it was Steve and Paul and a guy called Wally. I went down there and saw them rehearse. They were very rock-'n'roll. Status Quo.

There was John Gray and John and Sid, did they come in individually?

No, they used to hang around together, they were very groupy in those days. Sid used to come in. He was a very serious man, very concerned about his position in life at that time. Quite conservative. And John used to be there. He was always a bit negative about most things. He used to argue just for the sake of it. He did remind me years later, he saw me wear a safety pin once and that's what gave him the idea. They were admiring really.

The good thing about the shop was that people didn't have enough money to buy what they really wanted. But they used to just hang around, like the old 2i's [coffee bar], I guess, from the old Tin Pan Alley days, where Tommy Steele used to hang out. The shop became a bit like that.

Did Chrissie Hynde work in the shop?

Not while I was there. She might have helped out before I got there. But Chrissie and Viv fell out quite badly, didn't they. And that rubbed

43

off on me, cos Viv didn't want her in the shop, and I had to eject her one day.

Did you often have to do that?

Only people who were shoplifting. I had face-to-face arguments with people in the shop, the T-shirts aren't as good as they used to be. We used to have the Road Rats come in, those biker guys, try and knock things off. I actually chased somebody up to the Fulham Road once, on my own. I didn't know what I was going to do when I caught him. We had knife attacks as well, a skinhead came in and drew a knife on me and Michael. All sorts of things.

So were you aware of the Sex Pistols getting together?

Yeah. I do actually remember auditioning Johnny Rotten. I know it's a story that's probably been twisted through time, but I remember him standing by the jukebox and being asked to do something – and him saying he could only play a violin, out of tune. I distinctly remember him saying that.

Weren't they formed to promote the clothes, pretty much?

Well what came first, the chicken or the egg? The clothes were a pretty important part of their make-up, but also a lot of things were sold because of them. Initially, I think they were just a vehicle, I don't think truthfully Malcolm knew what was going to happen with them.

They played at St Martins. Did you go to that?

Yeah. I can't remember a thing about it, but I know I was there.

Didn't you actually perform with them?

We did that Andrew Logan party, and Malcolm came rushing up to me saying, 'The *NME* are here!' He was really excited. It's funny to think of it now. 'The *NME* are actually here. Do something, Jords!' He wanted them to get a bit of outrageous publicity. He said, 'Take your clothes off, girl.' And I said, 'Naw, I'm not going to.' He said, 'Go on, we haven't got much time.'

I said, 'I'll do it if John says. If John knows, and we can do some sort of act. I'll do it if John rips them off!' Which is what happened.

I jumped on stage and John ripped my clothes off; and that was all for publicity. Malcolm asked me to do it and I did it, after a bit of persuading. It was funny, actually, he broke the zip on the back of this polo-neck leotard, and a pair of Manolo Blahnik shoes!

What did the audience think?

Well as you know, the Andrew Logan crowd were pretty unshockable, so we were in good company to do it, but they used it as a poster, and I think it did appear in *NME*.

Did you go to Paris to the Chalet du Lac show?

Yeah, me and Vivienne went together. It was a scream. If you can imagine me and Viv turning up at Gatwick, at the wrong terminal, miles away, not a hope, didn't know what we were doing. Nobody knew we were turning up, it was supposed to be a surprise. It was really exciting. And going to discos – Malcolm and Vivienne and the Sex Pistols and I went to a really straight disco. They were jiving, we were! Me and Malcolm dancing together, I remember that.

Did you ever go up on stage with them again?

Malcolm asked me to go to that *So It Goes* show, to lend a bit of ambience. Tony Wilson – who I have since realised is a very nice man – turns up with clogs on to greet us, there was another band on wearing blue satin suits, big lapels, all the kids were drinking tins of Coke, and you've got Clive James, who's a terrible Australian straightie, being terribly huffy, so we just waded in. I called him a baldy old Sheila. And John just called him Bruce for an hour.

They got my back up because they wouldn't let me wear this swastika armband, right, there was the biggest do about it. They eventually put a piece of sticky tape over it. But our backs were up, that's why the performance was so good. Those were the days when you could actually take advantage of that situation. Nils ripped all the buttons on my 'Anarchy' shirt open. The band were just really pissed off.

We'd already had an argument with this group Gentlemen, they said they liked bands like Joni Mitchell, and you can imagine what John said, 'You fucking arsehole.' They all started wading in. We

45

realised we were like fish out of water, but there was definite ability there to make the whole show work for us. Peter Cook was on that as well, and he was great.

Do you remember any other gigs?

We had a party at the El Paradise. It was typical. Malcolm gets this club, doesn't let the people know what's really going on, they had to clean the place out it was so filthy. There was no drinks licence. It was run by a load of Maltese guys. Michael and I decided we'd do this punch, made of all this booze together, and we found people were disappearing through the night, they were just collapsing basically. It was 40p a mug, this stuff, and it was really potent.

People kept coming back for more. It was really awful. The stage was tiny, with these chintzy curtains. Round the back there was this notice, there were fines that they gave the strippers for doing things wrong on stage, if you were two minutes late – it was just a strip club. Anyway, halfway through the evening these Maltese guys turn up to check that we weren't selling alcohol, cos the licence was lost, and they were really not very well-in-the-head people.

Michael and I screamed out, 'Drink the evidence', and about five of our friends and us drank the lot. I think we had the best night ever, but people just collapsed. But it was typical Malcolm, not letting these guys know what was going on. They probably thought it was a folk group in there or something.

You were really on hand when there was some sort of event going on.

Yeah. I went to the 100 Club a lot. There was great rivalry at that time, cos the BOY crowd were very much into The Clash, and we were the elitists, the Sex Pistols bunch, and we very much frowned on The Clash and a lot of the other bands that were around. I'm not purist about it, but there was nobody as good as the Sex Pistols, nobody else had a chance of vying for the top position.

Where do you think that 'goodness' came from?

It came from the lyrics in the songs. Most of those punk groups started preaching, and I don't think people want to hear a sermon set to music. The Sex Pistols never preached, they made statements.

They made them tough, they accused, and they hated and irritated and they got up people's noses, but they never told you what you should do.

A lot of the other bands got high and mighty about themselves. And of course it came from the attitude and the clothes, but mostly it was a vital combination. John Rotten, really.

Where do you think John got that gift, that he had?

It's hard to say. He was a sceptic, but incredibly, underneath it all he was a very shy person, he wasn't what I would call a sexual creature. He was very tentative about his sexual persona. There were all these girls after him and I don't think he ever thought of doing what most bands do, which is to pick up lots of girls. Sid was like that too; until he met Nancy he was quite naive, really. Neither John nor Sid was sexually mature. Totally opposite to Steve.

Because of John's naivety, because he was such an innocent, there were connotations, we used to make jokes about it. Sid had more of a physical presence than John, who was a diminutive figure really. He didn't see himself as attractive in any way, I suppose, if you were to ask him. He didn't want the trappings of a normal person. He was John Rotten, and much the same as myself, I didn't go out with anyone either, the image was everything, in a way.

When he stayed at my flat he used to take his trousers off in bed, he didn't like to show his body. Whether he felt insecure, or insufficient, one never knows. When he performed, it was never masculine, was it. It was postured.

It was similar to yourself, although obviously you were more feminine.

People were scared out of their wits of me. Absolutely. I would have people write to me, adoring letters, I could do anything with them, I could kick them around the floor, they'd be my slave for life, but nobody would say it to my face. I never got anyone saying they'd like to take me out.

But you didn't want it, did you?

No, because I exuded that . . . leave-me-alone-ness. It wasn't a sexual thing, it was something that enticed people.

47

That was the thing about the Sex Pistols, the fans would have done anything to get to them, like Nancy for instance, came over to England to catch a Sex Pistol. I found a postcard in my kitchen. She was writing home: 'I've got a Sex Pistol.' It didn't matter who it was, John, Sid. She made a play for John first and got nowhere, but it could have been anyone. She came over with that specific goal.

Was Sid a bit of a poser? Did he buy a lot of clothes?

He was a very adaptable person, he'd make a lot of things out of what he already had. Better than all of them. John would need someone to tell him what to do half the time. But Sid was very imaginative. Wearing garters outside of his jeans, I remember that very well.

And he had a padlock over his willy. Very symbolic.

That's right. I think Nora was the best person for someone like John, and Nancy was the worst person for someone like Sid. If you're not a sexual creature and you have your first sexual encounter with someone who's going to have a hold over you, you hope it's going to be a nice person. Nora was a nice person.

As far as you could see with the band in '76, with the record companies and Grundy and everything, what was the interaction between all the people involved?

They had a little place in Denmark Street, and there was a lot of fashion discussion; I know that much, because I remember John talking with Malcolm about his clothes. It wasn't just, wear this and do it.

But they couldn't stand each other's company for very long, it seemed to me. They were from quite different backgrounds. There's Steve: we went down to Dingwalls and somebody gave him some coke, and you've never seen such a kerfuffle in your life. He wanted someone to go home with him, he felt so ill. He was thrown in at the deep end. None of them were lads, as such. Steve was a lad as far as the girls go, but they were quite diverse characters, you couldn't quite see them going out together. We haven't mentioned Glen much, but he was an odd character. He used to wash his feet all the time, he had this thing about his feet.

48

As soon as the music industry got involved, it became rock'n'roll. Is that a fair comment?

I think the most laudable thing about the Sex Pistols was that their image was formed before the record company got hold of them, and that Malcolm had that very clearly mapped out. Had they not been at such an advanced stage of formation, the record company might have turned out different. I think they held themselves very well, when you consider the pressure of a major record company.

I know how desperate a record company is to make it their idea, and the Sex Pistols came out of that really well. There's not many who do. Artistic control is a difficult thing to keep when someone else is paying. It took great fortitude on Malcolm's part to keep them as they were intended to be. There are ways a record company has of nurturing a band away from its manager, if they think it's to their advantage.

Did you go to any of the concerts after Grundy? Screen on the Green, the second time? The first time Sid played with them.

That was crazy. One person that really needs a medal is Roger [Austin, manager of the Screen on the Green]. He was constant through all of that, he was a benefactor, and someone who didn't want any recognition for it either. He got badly beaten up on the boat, you know, by the police. Smashed him over the head. I found him wandering around later.

I was objective about their performances, I didn't say something was a great performance when it wasn't. There were times when it didn't work. A lot of it involved the audience, John couldn't work with an audience that wasn't feeding something back to him. They had this distance from the audience, but there had to be some sort of buzz going on with the audience for it to work.

Can you remember any concerts that weren't good?

It was touch and go on the Jubilee boat trip. There was a big do that night. John wasn't in the mood to do anything. He was fed up, here was this anarchist group, the Sex Pistols, with people like Richard Branson coming to see them, and record company people, poshes on the boat that he didn't think should be there. He got the hump that

49

night really badly, he thought half the people on the boat shouldn't have been there, it should have been fans, real people. The Slits, for instance, got left on the quayside.

It was spelling disaster, so he started to play up. Then Steve started to do all the singing, which got John even madder. Cos John wasn't singing the words, Steve was doing it. There was a lot of stick that night. John was very rude to Vivienne that night. You got this feeling that it had started to snowball too quickly. I think Vivienne went and kissed John and he just pushed her away.

Boat parties are always a bad idea anyway, cos you're stuck on this thing, you can't take a walk. We were going up and down the river endlessly, and there was lots of speed on board. I remember people with bags of speed.

There was free drink for the first hour or two as well.

The atmosphere on that boat was really edgy, not fun.

I know John was really not into it. It's amazing it got going at all.

I thought their performance was really good though. In the end.

It was, but John was furious, that was why. He just got to the limit.

What happened then? Was there a fight?

As the boat was coming in to moor, someone said the police had been called, and they came on board, and they said for it to stop, and we all screamed for them to carry on, and they carried on for as long as they could.

When did things start changing with the band? Do you think they got more rock'n'roll?

They did, yeah. I think the problem was when Sid emerged as the heart-throb in the band. That's where it started to go wrong, John felt insecure about the situation.

I think Sid would have had a great career as a singer in his own right, he had a lot of charisma. *Never Mind the Bollocks* was a bit one-paced. It's all too much at one go, it needed something to break it up.

50

Did you go and see them on the SPOTS [Sex Pistols On Tour Secretly] tour, or the final tour, Brunel?

No. I just thought there was doom coming, after the boat trip.

John was being really obnoxious to everybody. It was the star trip, and him thinking that everything had got too commercial. I don't think he could quite handle it. Nobody quite believes how difficult it is to carry on something like that. Anyone can sing, if you've got a good voice, but to sing with conviction, those sort of powerful words every night, words that were black and white, not clouds and rolling hills. I think he'd lost it by then, he'd lost the need to do it.

John was a softy in some respects. He couldn't look after himself. If someone came up to him and said they were going to beat him up, he'd run. When that thing broke and they were holed up in Chelsea Cloisters, John and Sid and I were walking down the street, somebody just gave John a funny look and he was off like a shot. He's got a really unfortunate way of running, too, with his feet open. Most unphysical.

It must have been a lot of pressure for John, being the figurehead.

Yes, they were the bad boys in the eyes of the public, and so easily recognised. Nobody could have that sort of control again. Nobody has ever had that sort of coverage. Every paper in England had them on the front cover in a very short time. When they were holed up together, when they started to have trouble in the streets, and the general public turned on them, they were easily recognisable.

John and I got trapped in a taxi by somebody, a middle-aged man bashing on the door. Malcolm got them a flat, just off Chelsea Cloisters. They called me up one night and asked me to come over. There was Wobble and John and Sid. An outsider's impression was that they couldn't play, they didn't give a damn, they were just rebels; and I went round there and Sid was practising the bass. He really wanted to be a good bass player.

But if you went to the cinema with him, he was totally unruly. I went to see a film with him, and he just screamed and shouted all the way through it. He didn't care about people shushing him and looking at him. It wasn't a question of him plucking up courage either, to be a punk, he just was.

51

Was he at all disturbed? Or vulnerable?

I think he was a vulnerable type. I think that's what killed him in the end, his vulnerability.

Alan Jones

Early SEX assistant and part of early punk iconography, thanks to his appearance in the famous group photo that appeared in the June 1976 Forum article about SEX. Also part of the shop's history after he was arrested in Piccadilly for wearing a SEX T-shirt. An important witness of the strong gay influence in early punk. Deliciously indiscreet.

I come from Portsmouth – Southsea. I moved to London in '69 to become an assistant trainee manager for Sainsbury's supermarkets. I lasted exactly four months, got a job with Gear of Carnaby Street, and never looked back really, whisked around the circuit. I moved around a lot, I lived everywhere on the 31 bus route. I used to live round the corner from SEX, with an actress friend. Anyway, that's how I got to know Malcolm and then Vivienne . . .

I used to go to Let It Rock when it first opened, and I got talking to Malcolm just in passing. We had a lot of stuff in common really, we both liked fifties music, and I still have the Marilyn Monroe EP that he sold me. We struck up conversations, and once you're used to buying things from a certain store, you go back. It fitted the image I liked at that time. The gay scene was pre-Village People.

That was when they were doing the straight ted stuff? Was it mainly teds who came in the shop then?

Always. It wasn't trendy at that time, but it was the image that I liked for myself, being on the gay circuit. You wore tight jeans, it worked. At that time we're still talking glam rock, and it was all long hair and sweaters tied around the necks. The stamping grounds then were the Catacombs and the Masquerade in Earls Court, that's where I would be parading around.

When they changed into Too Fast to Live, Too Young to Die – can you remember what they had in the shop then?

I remember wearing a T-shirt with fringing, the sort you get around cowboy hats on seaside piers, purple. It sounded a bit faggy, but it was quite contemporary, fifties by way of the early seventies. Also the red tight trousers, and before that there were blue ones, typical ted stuff.

You worked at the Portobello Hotel?

I just drifted into that really. It was important for me, cos every star known to man was coming through those doors. My most famous story about the place was when I was wearing complete Nazi gear, when we all started wearing swastika armbands, and this group of German tourists checked in, and walked straight out again! Filed a complaint to the manager, who fortunately thought of me as part of the atmosphere.

What sort of people did you get passing through before punk?

I remember Maria Schneider. *Last Tango in Paris* was just about to open. She'd come over to promote it. Had a great time with her and her girlfriend. The ex-Turtles, Flo and Eddie. Abba stayed once, that was a thrill for me, cos I still love them. Patti Smith, Nico, Mick Jagger, Carly Simon. They were having a raging affair, her and Mick Jagger, and we were all being ultra-discreet about it.

Did you ever work in the shop at all?

Yes, for nine months. I was on the dole, living with a prostitute in Notting Hill. The deal was, she'd come down from Leicester, I let her have my apartment – slum! – and she would use that to bring back her tricks, and she would give me 20 per cent of her money, so I was on the dole, making money from her, and I was moonlighting with Vivienne.

There was me, Jordan, Debbi Wilson and Michael, and we would do on and offs. Tracie O'Keefe was there, too. That was just as it had turned into SEX. One of the major things I remember about working at the shop was Vivienne being visited by the tax people. When they walked in she said, 'Quick! Make it look like you're customers', and we were wandering round trying to look nonchalant.

Everyone was paid off the books. And Malcolm and Jordan used to augment their wages quite a lot out of the till, as well as Michael. I don't know why Vivienne trusted him as much as she did. He must have made so much money over the years out of that. For my sins, all I ever took was a pair of boots. I have a big problem with doing that sort of thing.

I remember when we moved into the rubber gear, we'd have all the sleazy old men coming in, pretending they wanted to have a look at the stuff, and they were desperate for either Jordan or Debbi to sort of . . . try it on. You know, could you . . . model it for me, and it was obvious they were just going to jerk off behind the screens.

So in the early days was it mainly pervs and a few kids? Presumably the teds melted into thin air.

They did, as soon as Vivienne moved into the early punk, Village People stuff, the wrist bands and the chains and things, which I loved, that's when they went off.

Was one of the first things you started wearing the T-shirt with PERV written out in chicken bones?

I had four major things. There was the porno story, I had the one with SEX written diagonally across it, I had the very first nude little boy T-shirt, which was a purple T-shirt roll-neck, and the PERV T-shirt. Leather trousers and the accoutrements – the spurs, the dog collar – I wore at one stage. I had earrings then, but I stopped wearing them when everyone else did.

Oh, the other thing was that woollen thing with the plastic gloves and zips, with Nazi emblems all over it and a swastika armband.

What sort of a reaction did you get?

Very bad, actually. One particular incident, I was visiting a friend in Notting Hill Gate, and this guy in front of me turned around and says, 'It's disgusting, I can't believe you're wearing this', and our stock remark at that time was, 'We're here to positively confront people with the past' – it was something that Vivienne and Malcolm told us to say, so we did. And he followed me down the street and ended up hitting me very hard. I staggered into my friend's place, and from that time on I turned my armband around.

Another time, I went to the opening night of *A Chorus Line*, and I wore one of the 'Anarchy' shirts, and the manager came along and said, in front of the whole audience, 'AS MANAGER OF THE THEATRE ROYAL, DRURY LANE, I OBJECT TO WHAT YOU'RE WEARING AND I WANT YOU TO LEAVE'. And I said, 'I'm sorry but I'm not going to, I've paid for this ticket and I want to see this musical.' He went away, but it caused a lot of bad feeling around me, and my friends would say to me, 'When the fuck are you gonna learn?' But at that time, I didn't care.

Was it just a wish to shock?

I wonder now, why I did all that. Vivienne and Malcolm would like to think that we were part of this global consciousness that was springing out of the streets of London. I was in that group because I loved the clothes and I wore them, and I liked the people I worked with. There was no political content for me, and I don't think it was for anybody else. When I heard people at the time talking about that, it seemed like lip service and it still does. Nobody really believed in Malcolm and Vivienne's vision.

Did they?

Oh, they did. Malcolm to a lesser degree, but I think Vivienne is one of the most amazing minds. The ways she thinks of things – askance conventionality, she always comes up with a twist on what you'd expect. She's incredible like that. Everything she said made sense, and it's not that I didn't believe in it, it just wasn't anything to do with what I wanted to do, which was go out, have a good time. That's what it was all about.

Often we used to stand outside the shop door, waiting for coach parties to come along. They'd stop at the zebra crossing and we'd walk out and they'd go . . . ! Jordan was amazing, she pushed it to the limit, and got away with it. She always looked marvellous, I loved her for it, still do.

Do you regret wearing the swastikas now?

No, no not at all. It didn't bother me. I saw it as a fashion, I never saw it as making a statement for or against anything. That was the first time I realised how people must be noticing it. Jordan and I would play a really good game. We'd go on the tube and sit opposite each other, and it would be packed, and we'd talk to each other really loudly and say the most outrageous things. 'Oh, what a great orgy last night', sort of thing. For no reason.

Were the rubber customers driven out by the kids?

I don't think so. I've come across that sort of thing before. If people are really into that sort of thing, I don't think they could care less who's around or not. It adds to the sleaziness of it. Like the proverbial guy jacking off on the tube . . .

Did they do that in the shop?

Yeah, a couple of them did. Jordan used to complain about having to clean down the changing-room curtains. It used to get really hairy though, on Saturday afternoons, cos Vivienne was in the firing line of the Chelsea football supporters. Every Saturday the windows would be broken, she'd replace them and put metal guards up, it didn't make any difference, they would still get smashed, and we would still stand at the back of the shop.

Why was that?

The sheer up-fronted-ness of what she was trying to do. I got that in spades when I was arrested with the T-shirt with the cowboys.

Tell me about that.

It was after I'd left the shop. I went with my best friend, a Norwegian guy, to SEX, to see what their new stuff was. It was the day they had just brought out the Cowboy T-shirts. I bought that and the Cambridge Rapist T-shirt. I wore the Cowboys T-shirt, blue jeans and whatever, and walked along King's Road, got to Piccadilly Circus and these two plain-clothes policemen came up behind us and said, 'Ah what you wearing here', blah blah blah. I hadn't noticed, but my friend said everyone was looking at us as we went.

They said, 'Will you accompany us to Vine Street police station.' My friend was mortified cos he was working illegally, didn't want to know. They looked through the bag, and they said, 'You must be some sort of pervert to wear something like that.' I said, 'I'm not, how dare you, this is just fashion.' Apparently it was the day after

Johnny Go Home had been on the TV. But please, I did not look like a rent-boy, hustling in Piccadilly.

But I phoned Malcolm and told him what had happened, and he said, 'Alan, we're going to do everything we can, we'll get you a really good lawyer, you're going to get off.' What happened? Fuck all. I ended up going to court on my own, not knowing what to do, and in the end I pleaded guilty. Nicholas de Jongh was there, and he came to me afterwards, said, 'What did you do that for?' But what else could I do? If Malcolm had given me the backup, which he promised, it would have been fine.

Didn't they also raid the shop?

Yes, but I wasn't there. They took a lot of the T-shirts away. I was in the wrong place at the wrong time.

Can you remember this picture of you all? [published in *Forum*, July 1976]

I wasn't working in the shop then. Vivienne called me and said to come down. We all did that for a laugh. Except it wasn't really a laugh. It was all right. You can imagine what this sort of rag would say: 'More ass, more tits.' And like idiots, we did. You know, I always hated Chrissie Hynde. She was there only to be seen with that sort of crowd. I've never liked the Pretenders as a result of that. I thought she was a real old cunt. Couldn't stand her.

Anyway, I went off to the hotel, and it was about the time that the Pistols were ready to perform. As I was working nights at the hotel, they'd all come over, and I can't tell you the times it would end up with everybody in the lounge, harassing the other guests as they came in. Jordan would be sat there all night, and the boys would come in cos I'd give them free booze, food from the restaurant.

Were you aware of when Lydon came on the scene?

I always fancied Glen, so I took more notice of him than anyone else. I just remember John being there. I was never close with John the way I was with Steve and Paul, cos of my connection with Nils Stevenson at that time, Nils and I are old friends.

The hardcore group was about twenty people, and we would all

58

meet up at Louise's and that was the only time we would ever talk to each other. I knew Viv Albertine from The Slits by face and name only, I never ever spoke two words to her, but I must have gone out with her about twenty-eight million times. When she was Sid's girlfriend.

I got to know Sid very well towards the end, in fact him and Nancy used to stay here, cos I'd moved in here at that time. The place was empty, I had no furniture, and he'd come in and say, 'Ah, fabulous place!'

Did you know Sid before Nancy?

Yeah, he used to hang around the shop. I liked his dry sense of humour, he was very funny. We all knew he was taking drugs and stuff, but I never saw all the aggression and violence, never. My vivid memory of Sid was him wearing Durex outside his trousers. And the padlock round his neck too, which he lost the key to, and could never get off.

When did you first see the band?

I didn't see the very first one at the college, but I saw everything else after that. I still think their very best performance was the first time at the Nashville. It was a little club atmosphere, everyone knew each other. I remember John sauntering on and going, 'Oh hi Debbi, hi Alan, hi!' It sounds a bit elitist but it was nice. That was the one I took Caroline Coon along to, and she started promoting it quite heavily.

From then on it was all a bit of a blur, except for the Screen on the Green, cos I was on acid. And the El Paradise, where they asked me to DJ, and all they did was slag me off all the way through, cos I didn't have any time to get any records together. All I ended up playing was 'White Punks on Dope' and 'Thoroughly Modern Millie'. And a lot of Annette's songs.

What was the Screen on the Green like?

Wonderful. Packed out. I got there really late cos I'd had a really heavy night the night before, still on this acid. Caroline in the corner, with that guy Jonh Ingham. I was sitting there with safety pins through my tie, which was very designer, even though that hadn't been coined at the time. And Siouxsie down the front with that ever-so famous topless outfit that she wore. Severin and all of us there. The Buzzcocks were good then, and that was fun.

I'll tell you when it all stopped for me. The day of the boat party was the day I said, enough is enough. I was on the boat and Vivienne was hanging over the side having a piss through her trousers. I said, 'Why don't you take them off?' 'Oh no, I can't be bothered.' They were white muslin ones she had, and for the rest of the day she had piss-stained trousers on.

And as soon as we got surrounded by the police, and the ensuing hysteria when we docked, and everyone was being filed off and being hit, and running off in all directions, and filed into the vans, and I stepped back and looked and I thought, this is it. I don't want to know any more.

Why was that?

It had just gone beyond. It wasn't because other people were joining in, in fact a couple of months later I remember being surrounded by punks on the tube and they were slagging me off, and I just got up and said, 'Listen, if it wasn't for people like me, you wouldn't be dressed like that.' That sort of shut them up. But I just stopped. It was getting to be a drag. It was fun until then.

Chrissie Hynde

SEX assistant for a brief while in 1974, then part of the small pool of outsider musicians who went to form almost all the major punk groups. Born and raised in Akron, Ohio, Chrissie moved to the UK in 1973, before undergoing a complex odyssey that resulted in the formation of the Pretenders in 1978. Interviewed at her then home in Maida Vale, London. Unstoppable once she gets started.

I met Malcolm in 1973 probably, maybe 1974, walking around the shops with Nick Kent. We went into this particular shop, it wasn't called SEX at the time, nor Seditionaries. They had all this teddy-boy gear, and being American I'd never seen anything like that. It was called Beneath . . . something about the paving stones . . .

When I worked there it was called Fashion Must Wear Clothes, but the Truth Loves to Go Naked – can you imagine? – on the sign outside the shop in spray paint. When you went in, it was set up like a gymnasium, with foam rubber on the walls, and racks and things to climb up on. There was all these feminist slogans written on the walls. This is when I worked there, not when I first met Malcolm. They were excerpts from the *SCUM Manifesto*.

The great thing about their clothes was that they were the antithesis of fashion, and it really appealed to me, being saturated with these Virgo qualities, all that attention to detail. I was obsessed with detail. I'd see someone wearing a shirt with a pocket flap which didn't have a pocket – I would wonder why they put it there. Fashion had become very much about little flourishes.

I came from Ohio, where it was still like J. C. Penney stuff, and in there, they had like a square of T-shirt material, sewn there and there so you could stick your arms through it, and it was stamped with an excerpt from the *SCUM Manifesto*. I was going around wearing this stuff, a rubber skirt, fishnet stockings, and all these brilliant shoes.

It was the first shop I'd ever seen where I thought, 'I could wear this gear exclusively, never go to another store.' It was so hip and well thought-out. Vivienne had designed this brilliant raincoat which I really loved. The raincoat was like nylon, with a real big skirt, a belt. They reprimanded me for wearing blue jeans, which was the kiss of death in their eyes. They hated nostalgia.

I left the *NME*, I wanted to leave because I'd split up with Nick Kent, and also, I wasn't really a journalist, I was only trying to make a quick buck. I was working illegally, and someone said, because I was so opinionated and had a big mouth, 'Why don't you write for us?', and I became Chrissie Hynde of the *NME*, which I really didn't like.

The scene was so bad in '73/'74, there was nothing to write about. All you could say was, 'This is crap, next please' – that was how my singles reviews went. The turning point was when they asked me to write a piece looking back on The Velvet Underground, and I thought, why always looking back? I thought working in the shop seemed so much more happening than looking back on the past, and I just left the *NME*. They couldn't believe it.

It didn't last very long, but it was quite an experience. Steve Jones used to come in, he was this young boy they had taken under their wing, who had a lot of trouble with the law, a bad family life, whatever. He used to come in in the mornings, sweep the floor for me, keep me company, then at the end of the day he would fix the grilles up on the wall for me, sweep up, and I'd say goodbye and he'd go on his way. He was about seventeen.

One day, Nick Kent came into the shop. Malcolm was there, we were just closing up. I don't know if Nick thought I'd been with someone else, he was hanging out at Granny Takes a Trip, up the road – not the enemy, but kind of old-school, not associated. Nick took off this belt he was wearing, which had big coins on it, real cheap and nasty, and started whipping me with this belt, and I ran into the dressing room, and Malcolm hid behind the counter. I still have a scar from it.

He left, and Malcolm closed the shop, and I think the next day they said, 'It's too confusing when you're working here, you'll have to go, we don't need you any more.' I'd been fired before, so I was used to that, but what I thought was funny was the idea that it was 'too confusing' when I was there, and he was the anarchist who loved confusion.

What were they like then, those two?

They lived in this place in Clapham, Nightingale Lane. It was a council flat, and Vivienne had Ben and Joseph, the younger boy, who was their son. I was very close to Viv, we used to be really buddy-buddy. I always talked about getting the band together, maybe she would play keyboards. We used to go to The Roebuck after work.

I remember walking from the shop back to Clapham with Malcolm, it was a fair walk, a couple of miles, talking about what rock'n'roll needed. I don't know what my angle was. I thought it was definitely going to be a female thing next. We had Elvis, we had The Beatles . . .

I split, because I met a guy in the shop who really impressed me, a sort of French hippy vagabond, a two-bit criminal sort, very good shoplifter, helped me a lot. Out of the blue I got a call from him in France. We're getting a band together, would you like to be the singer? Which of course was always my thing, which I secretly wanted to do, but never really talked about it to anyone.

So, I wanted to get out of the country at that time, cos I'd been fired from the shop, so I went. I think I went around three record companies that day – you know, Chrissie Hynde from the *NME*, I think I got about 40 albums, all I could get, sold them at Cheapo-Cheapo, and I got a ticket to France, and that's where I was for the next six months.

What was the scene like there? There was a French tie-up with the punk thing, wasn't there?

I think Viv came over to visit at one point. I was staying at this woman's house, who was looking after this transvestite who was a big star in a well-known cabaret. She said I could stay there. She and I were going to do the singing in the band, and there was a scene there. They were very tuned in to what I would call the original punk sound of the sixties.

I went to Marc Zermati's place, the Open Market, and they had ? and the Mysterians records. I was impressed, because this is what I was looking for when I first came to England, and I hadn't found it. All the guys were in cowboy boots and motorcycle jackets, very American in a way that wasn't really American. I always keep in mind that 'connoisseur' is a French word, and they were connoisseurs, they knew more about all that than the Americans or the English.

Did you actually form a band there?

I tried to form a few bands, but I got so frustrated. Everyone was doing 'Johnny B. Goode', playing all this amazing Rolling Stones stuff, but they didn't know who Mitch Ryder and the Detroit Wheels were . . . I went back to Cleveland at that point.

That's when you were playing in that soul band?

Jack Rabbit, yeah.

Can I ask why you came to England in the first place?

I just wanted to leave America, I just bought a ticket and came. I felt so uncomfortable with the American way of life. I didn't want to buy a car so I could get to work to pay for my car. I didn't want to fall into that trap. I wanted to see the world. I thought, I'm white, I can get a passport, let me go. I went to London because of The Beatles and the whole thing, but also because at least I could speak the language . . . well, I thought I could speak the language! I learned a whole different language when I got here, in more ways than one.

Was there anyone else in that early period, anyone eventually involved in the punk thing, who came into the shop, or was Steve the only one?

I can't think of anyone else, actually. Steve was like this jailbird who they took under their wing, and he befriended me.

Anyway, I got frustrated in France because no-one understood. What I found out once I started to make the band was that I wanted to play the songs that were my roots: 'Louie Louie', 'Hang on Sloopy'. Nobody really understood that, so I made what was a big sacrifice to me, to leave a place where I was really happy, working in France, to go back to Cleveland for six months, then I drove out to Tucson, Arizona, with some people who were going there.

Then someone I'd met in France called me after I'd been about a week in Tucson, totally frustrated, with the heat and everything. He said, we're starting a band, we want you to be the singer, I'll send you a ticket. So I went back, this is my second instalment in France, and that's when I took a trip back to London and met Bernie Rhodes, who was doing T-shirts for Malcolm.

While I was in Cleveland, Malcolm had called me and said he was starting up a band called the Love Boys and he wanted me to front it as a boy. Not singing, not playing guitar, but fronting the thing, as a boy. I think it was going to be Richard Hell and Sylvain Sylvain. At that point I was learning to sing, locking myself in the closet, singing Candi Staton songs and stuff, so I said no.

Malcolm has a reputation for being very tight, but he did offer me a ticket to get back to England, but I turned it down. I ended up back in France, and came back to London at that point, and that's where I met Mick Jones and that band he had then [London SS]. I don't know what it was, I just had this intuition. I left everything I had going in France at that time, and came back to London, and got set up in a squat.

When I got back, Malcolm had finally got this band together called the Sex Pistols, and I saw them a few times. Of course, Steve was in the band. The first time I saw them was maybe Andrew Logan's party, maybe a college gig, I can't remember. There was probably about five people in the audience, but it was amazing to me, I was very taken with it.

So I ended up back in London for 1976, and I tried to get a band together, in various incarnations. I just felt like I was there, you know. This is it. I was probably loaded, and I'd been travelling all over the place, but seeing them, I felt that London was the thing, something was going to blossom and happen there, so I gravitated back to London.

Didn't Malcolm try to help you at that point?

While the Sex Pistols were getting off the ground, Malcolm was going to manage me in this band. We had a meeting one night on Lisle Street, in a Chinese restaurant, and talked about it for a long time. He said he'd met this great kid drummer, and he had these other people. We met this guy named David Zero, whose real name

65

was Dave Letts, who later changed his name to Dave Vanian. I thought he looked like an Alice Cooper thing.

Later on we went to a store called Nostalgia or something, a little clothing store in Covent Garden, to see this blond guy called David. Malcolm's vision of this thing was that there was a blond singer, very effete but not gay, who didn't want to be in a band, who didn't want to sing at all, but Malcolm dragged him into it. That was very Malcolm, he didn't care about the music. He wasn't very musical himself, as such. He was just into personalities.

This David Zero was really into being this thing, so we had the black one, the white one, and they were the singers. I was supposed to just play guitar, not sing at all. He said he'd met this guy at a party who was going to be the drummer, who turned out to be Chris Miller, later Rat Scabies. And it sort of came to fruition.

I was supposed to marry Sid Vicious, so I could stay in the country, when originally I was supposed to marry John. He agreed to do this, and then they did the Bill Grundy show, and they got very famous, and I was desperate to stay in the country to get my band together. I couldn't really approach John because he was famous all of a sudden. I mentioned to Sid, you know, what about our thing, he said, 'Oh, I'll do it, but I'll have to be paid.' I said, 'Okay, I'll give you £2.' He said, 'Okay, done.'

Patti Palladin drove me over to pick up Sid from his mum's council flat, because he needed his birth certificate, and he was underage, and he was with this girl named The Wig. They were into a squelching session while I was trying to sleep. The three of us were on this mattress on the floor in my place in Clapham, and I kept saying, 'Come on, you guys, leave it out.' I kept getting elbowed – everyone was so skinny!

Sid lived by the scruff of his neck, you know, he was like a greased pig, getting hold of him and his birth certificate. Patti had to drive him back to my place, and finally holding him down in my bed while he was getting up to all sorts. Then getting to the Town Hall, and it was closed. I remember standing there, like in a cowboy film, and there it was, closed for the holiday.

There was that whole thing about how The Damned was formed because the band I was going to get into was called The Masters of the Backside. That was a Malcolm name. It was very interesting about Bernard and Malcolm, I saw these two sort of Jewish competitors, when they could have been working in a team.

When I finally came back to London I was going to do something with Mick Jones, but he called me one day and said, 'Look, there's this guy Bernie who really wants to manage us, I want you to talk to Bernie.' 'I don't want to talk to Bernie, I want to talk to you, I'm in a band with you.' And he goes, 'Well, all right. Well . . . he has this idea that you won't sing at all, you'll just play guitar and you'll be way in the background, and it's going to be called School Girls' Underwear.'

Like I'm going to be in a band called School Girls' Underwear. Everything Bernie did seemed to be a sort of pale imitation of what Malcolm was doing with the Sex Pistols. I said, look, that's it.

Mick introduced me to this kiddie, very artistic, who he thought looked amazing. That was Paul Simonon and he was a pretty boy, but pretty boys were never my forte. He had mock-ups of album covers he'd done for Alex Harvey. He was very good, but it seemed everyone was into Mott the Hoople, but I was two years older, and into Bobby Womack, and it just wasn't my scene, I felt left out.

But I had driven a lot of these people into their thing, I felt instrumental. I remember cutting Mick's hair, there are so many things. Riding on the bus, his gran making us beans on toast, turning Mick into a vegetarian. The formation of The Damned. Getting together with these guys who were going to be the Johnny Moped band . . .

It was a very London thing. At that point, the original punk thing had nothing to do with drugs. I remember Sid saying, 'What can we do tonight?' We'd be standing outside a call box in Tottenham Court Road. 'We could always go to our mummy's house and smoke hippy drugs.' So, we'd go over to his mum's flat in Kilburn. She was with this twenty-six-year-old guy named Charlie.

Sid would look through the letterbox. We'd be on the twelfth floor, or whatever, and he could see her in there with Charlie, and we'd have to walk all the way back down the stairs, and he'd call, 'Mum, is it okay if we come up?', and we'd go back up, and they'd be sitting on the sofa, both wearing kaftans, so we could smoke 'hippy drugs'. His mum rode a motorbike.

It was weird for me because I was like halfway, I'd sort of bridged the gap. The interesting thing is how it affected people who were outside of it. When I finally got in a band, it was with non-Londoners. At that point it was because I couldn't really cut it on the London scene, I was a little bit too worldly. Most of these people had never left their council flats.

I didn't fit in, so when I met people from Hereford, a kid who was five years younger than me and was into Eric Clapton . . . People on the punk scene didn't give a fuck about Eric Clapton, but I met some musical people, who weren't really into punk, but somehow we bridged the gap together. That's how the Pretenders got together.

CHAPTER TWO

New York

Punk magazine issue 3, April 1976 (John Holmstrom)

Although it's easy now to detect many other influences, in particular sixties mod culture, the biggest single inspiration for British punk came from New York. A genuine outbreak of teenage anarchy, the New York Dolls gained a small but dedicated following after they appeared on British TV's The Old Grey Whistle Test *and outraged presenter Bob Harris.*

The link between the Dolls and the Sex Pistols was explicit. McLaren was fascinated by them, and sought to reproduce their chaotic ambience in the UK. He also took inspiration from the scene that evolved around CBGB's in New York's Bowery, where the Patti Smith Group, Television, The Ramones, The Heartbreakers, Blondie and Talking Heads played from 1974 on.

Although very disparate, all these groups shared a stripped-back, black-and-white aesthetic, with delinquent, symbolist and pop flourishes. The new style was given its name – punk – by its own house magazine, run by John Holmstrom and Legs McNeil. The links between London and New York, although riven by quarrels and misundertandings, were very close, and run from the beginning of the Sex Pistols story right through to the end.

Sylvain Sylvain

New York Dolls founder, writer and guitarist, interviewed in 1988. A rock star on his uppers when I met him at his then home – a walk-up Manhattan flat right on 6th Avenue in the 30s. But Sylvain was very gracious and forthcoming about the group that had made him, at that time, very little more than a faded legend. A true gentleman.

I was born in Egypt, Jewish parents, and moved to the United States in 1961, when I was about eight. We weren't allowed to emigrate to New York, we had to move to Buffalo [NY] or Detroit, or these kind of places, and my father picked Buffalo for some reason. It was a hard life, cos the winters up there are really bad. And coming from the desert, to the snow belt.

It was incredible, very brutal, immigrant workers – Italians, plus the Irish, plus the blacks, and these were the days of segregation. There was an all-black school and an all-white school, and the white school was brand new and had white swimming pools, and the black school was the old white school. I went to an all–white school. It was very strange, but there's a big class system there.

It was the early sixties in America, and I loved all the twisting records that were coming out of New York – the 'Peppermint Twist' and all. My older brother had all those records, and the girl groups. They were the cool ones. We moved to Brooklyn, and it was The Four Seasons, and more girl groups, and that's when I fell in love with The Ronettes and The Shangri-Las.

Were the Dolls formed straight out of high school?

My parents moved out of Brooklyn into Jamaica, Queens, a better neighbourhood. I met Billy Murcia there. When you're an immigrant, you've got to be cooler than every other American, you had to come in and take over. I had a lot of girlfriends at school, and I guess I was

71

competition. His brother came up to me and said, 'My brother's gonna meet you at three o'clock. To fight.' Then they showed up, and I knew Billy already, I said, 'That's your brother?'

We became real close friends after that, and we went into a clothing business together, we used to make sweaters, we used to sell to Betsy Johnson. Me and Billy had bands all along. The Young Rascals and Jimi Hendrix and The Vagrants were big influences for us. Roger Mansour, who was their drummer, was just like me, from Egypt, Jewish parents.

We were going to New Town High School, and you'd get attracted to other people who were cool. You clique together. Johnny Thunders would come over to Billy's basement, where we had all the equipment, and we got a band together, me, Billy and Johnny for a while. We were learning together. Johnny didn't even smoke a joint at that stage; he took downs, but he wouldn't smoke a joint.

Johnny was really straight, he had this girlfriend Janice, and no-one could have looked better than them. You can see him at The Rolling Stones concert at Madison Square Garden, the one they made the movie at, *Gimme Shelter*. You can see Johnny in the third row.

He was such a Rolling Stones fan. We all were. The Beatles, early American rock'n'roll and the girl groups. Those were our big influences. Back then, the nasty ones were The Rolling Stones and The Doors. That was the true rock'n'roll, it's got to be rebellious in one way or another. That's what rock'n'roll is, when it drives you so wild you cannot fucking help yourself.

So how did you find David?

We moved into Manhattan, don't forget in those days it was easy to get a place. We used to rent lofts in SoHo for two or three hundred dollars a month. You could ride your bicycle around them, they were so huge, you could live there, carry the band, and this one's gotta sell pot, and this one's doing artwork, and this one's making sweaters to bring in some money, and that's what we did.

David was a New York theatre guy, the Ridiculous Theatre. He was in that clique but he had his bands on Staten Island. He was more like an activist. He would do things, like stand on a pole in St Mark's and try to get everybody to go to a precinct on 5th Street and get some schmuck out of jail that just got arrested for smoking pot.

David was that kind of a person, a believer. He would stand up and try to make things happen.

I discovered the name, the Dolls. I didn't know it meant pills, I didn't know about *The Valley of the Dolls*, I just thought it sounded good. Then there was the fact that we were flamboyant, wearing make-up. If you were influenced in any way by the best of the late sixties, you had to have sex appeal. Before we started, me and Billy used to put on make-up just to go down to the supermarket, shopping. Getting dressed up to go shopping, it was fun to do that.

Johnny was very serious about his clothes, always had to have everything pressed. He was a very serious Mod. I was more funky, and when it came to spandex jeans, I was one of the first ones that was making them, with the fringes and all that stuff. To me, it was more like the fifties gold lamé. I ripped that off. I was sick and tired of wearing bell-bottoms, it was a rebellion against that.

Was there a crossover with the Warhol scene?

We played Max's Kansas City, and the Warhol stars would hang out there in the back rooms. There were these small theatre things, and we'd play in these lofts, The Angels of Light was one of them. Art, rock, theatre, drag queens, very flamboyant. But not violent. There were orgies and scenes, that was the thing. Sex was free. Everyone had great fun with it. Sex is a drug too, the best. We tried it with as many people as we could, but we weren't gay.

But you didn't mind being thought of as gay?

We used it . . . maybe David tried it, I certainly tried it, but I'm not gay. I wasn't worried about it. If I saw a good-looking kid, what the fuck's wrong with that? The significance of things is what's important, and that's why the Dolls never made it in America. You can be a lot of things. Today maybe you can be gay, but you can't be communist. We certainly tried that too, but art takes all forms. I cannot stop doing what the government tells me to stop doing.

How did you take off?

In England, this guy Roy Hollingsworth gave us five pages in *Melody Maker*, and we became stars overnight there. We were playing the

Mercer Arts Centre over here, and we couldn't even fill 150 people in the place, and we'd go home with less than twenty dollars in our pockets. Suddenly we were having our pictures taken by Leee Black Childers.

We went over to England to play with Rod Stewart, we opened at Wembley Pool for him. We did a Kevin Ayers show, we went to Leeds and all these kind of places. And Billy Murcia died from taking too many Mandrax, and drinking, and being with people who couldn't help him when he got in trouble. That was a shock for me.

Did you go to Malcolm's shop on that trip?

Malcolm wasn't around on any of those trips. At that time there was a shop called Paradise Garage where that shop is today. He had a kind of wholesale rock'n'roll gear business, which was called Let It Rock. I met him at the McAlpin Hotel [in New York], cos I used to make clothes also, so you'd get all these invitations to go to boutique shows, all this kind of shit. In those days, if you were weird, you had a boutique show. This was summertime, '72 or '73.

Malcolm had this little room where he sold his clothes with Vivienne. I still have one of their ties, one of those forties ties with snow scenes on them. Ice-skating, satin. They were making teddy-boy suits. Johnny got one of the jackets, blue with a black velvet collar. We loved to dress up. Here in America, nobody gives a shit about clothing. But in Europe, somebody will go, 'What the fuck are you doing with those crazy pants.' That might get you to be cool.

But that's how I first met Malcolm. As far as I knew then, he didn't have a shop. Later on, Paradise Garage was gone, and he had Let It Rock, before it became SEX. We went in there of course, he was the best in England at that time. Also he was very lucky. Over there you can create something and make it happen. It's a smaller scene, you still have crafts people who can actually make the stuff.

Malcolm and Vivienne thought that the Dolls were exactly what rock'n'roll should be in those days. And we in turn felt the same about them, they had the hottest shit going. When we went back to England for our first big tour in 1973, they would come with us wherever we went. They knew all these clothing people in Paris, like Jean Castelbajac, and we'd all mix together. We went to the best places, met the best people, had the best fun.

74

So why did the first album not sell? That was your big one.

The cover blew their asses. The cover wasn't my idea. The photographer was a fashion photographer, a friend of mine. He's still quite important in New York. I got worried that the Dolls had such a reputation, but I gotta do what I believe in. If it bugs you cos I'm putting nail varnish on, I'm sorry, tough shit. How's it gonna hurt anybody?

But when they try to hurt you for it, that's what killed the Dolls. When we put out records, nobody bought them. The only thing you have is the kids to support you. What else do we have? The business sucks, every day there's a new guy, somebody gets fired, and this one takes the job, and there's so much politics. They love music, deep down inside, but the formula is what dictates.

Mercury were the only company that didn't pass on us. When we came back after Billy's death we were a big smash, it got us a lot of publicity. We were living this lifestyle, everybody wants to see a movie, and we were giving it to them. You don't think, one day I'm going to be a big star. Now, kids come out of school and they think, now I've gotta become a big star. They do whatever they have to do.

What did you do when you went to tour the Deep South, places like that?

We had the same sets, all the way through. You'd come into town, and each town would have its own teenage TV show. It would be, 'Johnny Thunders is going out with this girl tonight! Ding!' They don't have those kind of shows any more. But we were still popular, but we never really got accepted, to the point where people would buy the records and keep you going to the next stage.

We were always the rebels, the drag queens, all the rest of it. The band America did not know what to do with. That turned on Malcolm even more. He always liked the rebel, the underdog.

You had Leiber and Krebs as managers?

Yeah. L&K were like a bank. They went on to manage Kiss. A group like Kiss can copy the shit out of the Dolls, there wouldn't be a Kiss if there hadn't been a Dolls, but they became so big, and still they don't matter. They don't make history. I can't pay my rent, but I made the history.

75

The only true manager of the Dolls was Marty Thau. When we first met Marty, he had a beautiful big house in Westchester, a Rolls Royce in his garage, gold records on the walls, he was working with Buddah Records, had a lot of hits, Melanie, and he came to see us and said, 'Either this band sucks, or they're the greatest fucking band in the world.' That was the other thing too. We were the worst, but we were also the best.

Leiber and Krebs came up and said, 'These Dolls are spending too many champagne dollars, and we don't even have advertisement dollars, you're going to have to put up half of what we put up.' At that point he put up his house, that's how much he believed, just to keep this thing going. We needed a lot of support, we were playing all over, the Michigan Palace in Detroit, the Hollywood Bowl, 17,500 capacity. That's huge for a band that's never been accepted.

We went up and we came down, playing shit clubs every night of the week just to keep the money coming in. The '74 tour was when we were strongest. After that, we were back down again. And it fell apart. Marty Thau lost his house, his cars, everything, down on the street, literally broke. Johnny was really sick in those days, he'd got into junk, and Jerry had hepatitis, it was heavy heavy drinking. Basically it was falling apart.

I remember having a meeting with Marty, myself, David and Malcolm, cos Malcolm was in New York, to sell some clothes and to get away from Vivienne. This was 1974 going into '75, it was SEX now, not Let It Rock. All of a sudden Malcolm was there in New York. He was staying right around the corner on 20th Street. He had a friend with an antique clothing store on 22nd Street. He was making the SEX clothing.

Marty always put his heart before the business, and he was very upset by what had happened, he was devastated, and he went into his own private depression. But Malcolm and I were close friends; Arthur [Kane] was the one we convinced, we took him uptown to the detox centre. David had problems, he wasn't doing anything. Everybody was getting more and more stoned out.

Malcolm said he could get this loft in 23rd Street, from his friend who gave him the apartment. The loft used to belong to this black group called Mandrill who were breaking up, and it had studio walls and everything. We checked it out, and he said, 'I'll sell some clothing, we'll get the money together and we'll get it.' 'Fine, let's go.' That was the exchange right there.

I said to the group, 'Look, this guy's the only one who's trying to help us, he always believed in us. So he's got no experience of how to run a band, doesn't know anything about the music business, but he's into us. What more could we ever want.' I always said, 'This guy has a lot of power. He believes. He has that freshness, which is very attractive. To have so much excitement about rock'n'roll.'

Jerry said, 'This guy's a little British wimp.' When you shoot junk, it makes you very macho. The significance of sticking a needle in your arm being like having sex with another man, if you know what I mean. A lot of junkies have that hang-up. Johnny hates gays, he's so afraid he might like it. They hated him, though they loved his clothing and everything. They loved the kids in London, they were cool, not like the assholes we had to play for in Middle America.

Malcolm was never formally our manager, he declared himself our manager after he went back to England. He was our personal friend, but we never discussed sharing royalties or anything. Never signed one paper. It never became that. First we put Arthur Kane in rehab. Then we set up a tour down South to make some money. He didn't have money, his investment was no more than maybe eight hundred dollars. This was early '75.

We went on tour, shows in Florida, and sure enough, after two or three shows, Johnny and Jerry had had enough, they couldn't get their drugs, that was part of the problem, but the relationship between David and Johnny was getting worse and worse. They just didn't give a shit. Anyway, those guys came back home, it was over. Me and Malcolm remained friends, cos it was more than music.

The Sex Pistols were supposed to be my band. He said he had these kids hanging outside my store, they'd love to play with you, not like this fucking asshole David Johansen, and I believed him. But I got stuck in New York and I was broke, then Bob Gruen and his wife came to me, and they brought up a tour, to go to Japan, we were going to make thirty thousand dollars, more money than I'd ever heard of.

Malcolm got really mad at me. I'd given him my guitar, signed the thing so he could get it through British customs, but I went with

77

David, and he wrote me, said, 'I don't trust David, he's a bastard.' It is true, David is out for himself. Malcolm is an Aquarian, and I am too, and I don't like that kind of quality in mankind. I made mistakes, but imagine, if I'd been in the New York Dolls and the Sex Pistols I would really be nuts by now.

Leee Black Childers

*Heartbreakers manager, MainMan employee, Stooges manager. I first
met Leee when he was with The Heartbreakers, a job calculated to
drive a weaker man into the ground. The life-story of this legendary
pop-culture maven would make a great book, illustrated by his many
wonderful photos. Leee was involved with almost all the major players, and talked about them freely.*

I was born and raised in Kentucky, near Fort Knox, where they keep
the gold and the soldiers. Very suburban. Football games, cruising up
and down the Dixie Highway, drinking beer and yelling at each
other. A suburban middle-class upbringing. This is the fifties and the
very early sixties. A lot of doo-wop, The Supremes and Smokey
Robinson, but otherwise real gingerbread stuff, Frankie Avalon,
Fabian, stuff like that.

It was an easy life, and very cool. In the fifties they gave you
tests, and they would tell you what you would be happiest at in
your future life. You'd be asked, 'Would you prefer to associate
with a) intelligent people, b) honest, hardworking people or c)
flamboyant, self-destructive people?' So of course I put flamboyant, self-destructive people. I answered every question with the
most outrageous choice, and the result was that I should be a taxi-
dermist.

But I began to get restless and crazy during the sixties. It was like
that scene from *Billy Liar* – all you have to do is stay on the train, and
the train will take you away from it all, and there is no going back.
Once you've got away from suburban life, you can't live it.

I went by way of San Francisco, and the first rock band I ever worked
for was Big Brother and the Holding Company, and I picked them, they
didn't pick me. I went up to them and said, 'You need anybody to do
anything? I'll do it.' They were brilliant, everyone was nice then. Only

Lou Reed wasn't nice then – 'Get some herb tea for us all, please.'

They were all strange. Janis, bless her heart, was probably the most down-to-earth of them all. She talked about early rock'n'roll a lot. I worked for them sporadically, I'd show up, and they'd go, 'Hi, come on in', and I'd do things, and sometimes I'd just hang around. You never really got paid then either. A little money here and there.

What did you do when you got to New York in the late sixties?

I moved into the Village, instinctively, and hung out on Christopher Street instinctively, and this was my first exposure to drag queens. They would create wigs from eight or ten wigs sewn ingeniously together, not always the same colour either. They would wear twelve pairs of false eyelashes, one on top of the other, until their eyelids looked like shutters going up and down, mini-skirts, shoes that went clack-clack-clack on the pavements – and they were illegal of course, it was illegal to dress as a woman if you were a man.

Was homosexuality illegal then?

Various aspects of it were. There were things you could do behind closed doors if you were a consenting adult, and other things you couldn't do. But this was a law about masquerading, which was meant to stop people holding up banks, as if any of these girls, if they held up a bank, could have gotten away with their wigs and heels. Still, they were often prosecuted under that law.

So I got to know them, which wasn't easy cos they were so paranoid. If you didn't want to fuck them or buy or sell drugs with them, they were suspicious of you. They fascinated me, so I had to come up with a reason, so I chose photography. I would say, 'I am a photographer, could I take pictures of you?' And they would be thrilled. They never asked questions. I got some great pictures, and that's how I met Holly Woodlawn and the Living Theatre.

It started about the time that Jackie Curtis had her first wedding, on a rooftop on the Lower East Side, and that's where I met all the Max's Kansas City people. Warhol was there. I had my camera, I was pretending to cover it for something or other. Andy said, 'The reception is at Max's back room, come in my car', so suddenly we were all in the same room and Andy saw the value of using them. That's when the Theatre of the Ridiculous had its most brilliant period.

At one point I found myself living in a one-bedroom flat on 13th Street with Jackie Curtis, Holly Woodlawn, Rita Red, Rio Grande and Jayne County.

I know the MainMan period has been well covered, but I just want to ask whether you think Bowie took a lot first from Warhol, and then from Iggy?

He had been taking long before Warhol entered his sphere. Bowie always says his great talent is for finding other talents and taking what is worthwhile from them. He considered it moral on the grounds that they weren't going to make proper use of it anyway. Warhol created the same possibilities, but he didn't take, he allowed a lot of things to happen around him.

David did it in reverse. He created a situation where people could be creative, and then took the best of it, but didn't give the credit or the support that should have followed. To him, if he was creating a situation where people were having fun, eating well at times, travelling well at other times, and they were fool enough to expose their ideas to him, and their fashion, and sometimes their music, he didn't consider it wrong to take it, he considered it payment.

Iggy isn't a dumbo by any stretch, which a lot of the people who got taken by David were. Iggy knew he was being taken and was perfectly willing to pay the price, and has triumphed in the end because of it. He was able to come back and use David's name and influence and money, to keep himself going past the point where he probably would have self-destructed had he not done.

When I was working with Iggy, by all logical standards, that should have been the end. '73. He was being wildly destructive with drugs, musically, and on the streets. He was taking knives and stabbing himself, stuff like that.

Where did all that come from?

Iggy was doing that from what I saw from early on. I saw him immediately he came to New York cos Danny Fields brought him to New York and Danny let everyone know that he had found this great star, so we all went to the first show, on 73rd Street. It wasn't a very big room, but boy, what a turn-out. The whole of Max's back room, a lot of record-company execs, a lot of pressure for any young artist to come and perform to.

He went way beyond what was necessary to completely flabbergast the audience. Nobody could believe it. Some of the most outrageous people were there, and he left them all with their mouths hanging open. The early Iggy stuff was very spastic, very Three Stooges – ha-ha – slapping his face so hard his feet would go from under him, pushing his nose up to his eyes and pulling his eyes down, making horrible faces at the audience.

We all went away going completely crazy. The next night he was down in Max's, and Nico was there. Some of the early superstars were stand-offish, and it didn't bother him one bit, he went straight for the most famous person he saw in the room which was Nico, and started this big affair, carried on publicly in front of us for weeks.

What had happened to him by the time you took him on?

All kinds of things. Poor Danny Fields had been dragged over the coals – drugs, drugs drugs. Iggy has a brilliant mind and a really good heart, it was strictly drugs. He got into a situation that he couldn't possibly control, and Danny being a really nice man and an innocent, much as he wouldn't say it, couldn't control it either. Iggy killed the things that loved him the most, and tortured Danny until Danny had to give it up.

Then he started on the Johnny Thunders syndrome, a series of sucker managers with a bit of money which he screwed them out of as fast as he could. In that way David was a big saviour for Iggy's career. It was David who insisted to Tony DeFries that they take him on and do an album. David wasn't altruistic, he knew that by producing Iggy he would get out of being perceived as a bit fey.

He wasn't being taken seriously the way he wanted to be. He went for Lou Reed and Iggy and he got both of them. He chose them to give him the street credibility as a musician that he didn't have. He was more like Leo Sayer at that time. The difference between the two was that Iggy was perfectly willing to play the game, and Lou wasn't the tiniest bit interested in being a touchstone for anyone.

Did you come over when Iggy came to England?

No, I was working at *16* magazine then, I was the protégé of Lisa Robinson, so I got told a lot of what was going on. Tony Zanetta was over for Iggy's debut at the Scala, so I got a lot of reports on it, that he was totally out of control, and no-one knew why David or Tony DeFries was having anything to do with him. No-one knew why good money was being thrown away on this ungrateful jerk.

Tony DeFries in his extremely middle-class way got him an extremely nice little house to live in, which he almost completely destroyed, brought to the ground, scandalised the neighbourhood and left the country in disgrace, and that's when I saw him again, when I was on tour with David, and Tony said, 'Oh Leee, would you go to Detroit today and meet Iggy at the airport and make sure he's comfortably ensconced in a hotel there, and come back.'

So I went and met him at the airport, and of course the other side of him, which he never lost, and which he could turn on when he wanted to, was the great, extremely well-mannered gentleman, and that's who walked off the plane – out came Prince Charles. 'How nice of you to meet me, how lovely to see you.' He was given the whole MainMan treatment – a bungalow at the Beverly Hills Hotel.

He ended up living there for about three months. During that period he was alternately well and badly behaved. We were all on tour, so we left him there. Tony sent me back there to find him a house, cos he was costing so much money, and I did, and then, surprise surprise, I had to live there with him. He was wildly, horribly out of control. He was out for what he could grab.

What did you think of *Raw Power*?

Some of it was good, some of the images, 'Search and Destroy'. It was so heavy-duty Iggy, he was getting in touch with what people thought he was. He was learning what people wanted, and he was refining it into what was him. At the same time he was being extremely physically self-destructive. He had been playing around with scratching himself, but that's when he started stabbing himself with steak knives that would catch under his ribs.

But that's the problem you get yourself into when you're in show business. 'If he did that last time, what's he going to do now?' People came not for the music but for the antics, and he started throwing up on stage. So he really got himself frantic, he began to stab himself, and it was horrifying.

How did you get involved with the New York Dolls?

This is attributable to Roy Hollingsworth, one of the first rock-journalist stars. A good writer and a good man. He was posted to New York and I had come back to New York and had gone to work at 16 magazine. He called Lisa Robinson and said, 'I have to find a photographer to work with for *Melody Maker*', and I met with Roy and we got on straight away. It was he who said there was this group who are supposed to be really weird, 'Let's go. I'll interview them, you photograph them.'

It turned out that I more or less knew Johnny Thunders already, cos he went to Max's, and had that huge mane of hair then. No-one knew him, he was very sullen and wouldn't talk, but everyone watched him, and assumed it was a wig. We went down to this loft on the Bowery, and it was the very beginning of the New York Dolls and they are some of the photographs I'm most proud of. They were totally irreverent, totally crazy.

To my mind, they were much more interested in being irreverent than Iggy was; Iggy was physically irreverent, they were mentally irreverent. They did it with their clothes and make-up and attitudes. David Johansen was more cerebral, he could speak your language. Iggy would go from one to the other, Gentleman Jim or the Dead End Kid. David J was both at once, and to my mind in a more creative way.

Did you see a new generation of people coming up after the Dolls?

No, I guess I should have, but I didn't. The Dolls were playing at the Mercer Arts Center, which actually fell down. That's when Jayne County had her first group, but I didn't look upon it as a new movement in rock'n'roll at all. I looked upon it the way I looked upon the Theatre of the Ridiculous, it was the same people – more as an art movement. Shortly thereafter, when Patti Smith started up, I still looked at it as a theatrical thing, a poetry thing.

When I first became aware of it was when I was touring with Mott the Hoople, and the most beautiful bleach-blond boy was in the audience, and Mott the Hoople had this thing where towards the end of the show, I would pass among the crowd with napkins with invitations back to the hotel written on them. My instruction was to give them to the most beautiful girls in the audience.

On this night, I think it was the Palladium in Los Angeles, of course I gave one to this boy, who was also wearing pink lipstick, so he came back, and in the morning Ian Hunter came in and looked at this boy and said, 'My god, you did better than any of us!' The boy was Richard Lloyd.

I really liked him, and about a month later in New York he came up and said, 'I've just formed a group called Television, you should come and see it.' So I went. It was in a loft, and it was very rough, very weird, but very different. That's the first time I realised that the thing I was thinking of theatrically could in fact become rock'n'roll. I loved Television from that time on.

What was different about it?

The whole thing. There were elements of New York Dolls, Warholian elements, a lot of fifties Beat poetry elements, but for the first time I was reacting to it as a rock'n'roll show, as opposed to a be-in, a happening. Gradually, on the heels of it came The Ramones, and suddenly there was a real new weird scene. No-one thought that anyone would get signed, certainly not the groups.

What did you think of The Ramones?

I didn't take them seriously at all, but they were irresistible. It never occurred to me that there was an idea of it. It seemed instinctual to me, what they were doing. It was all too funny to think about it being thought about. It just seemed to be happening. It was where we wanted to be. I met so many people who became lifelong friends at Ramones gigs.

Did their velocity inspire other people to speed up?

Oh yeah, very much so. The first time they got a gig at the Bottom Line. They might have been supporting Bruce Springsteen or someone much more mainstream, and you could see the Bottom Line audience holding on to things, like they were on a rollercoaster.

85

I worked in theatre with Patti Smith, early on, and loved her. I remember that Patti and Robert couldn't get into Max's cos they looked too crummy, but they didn't care, they'd just sit on the kerb out front. They'd talk to people coming and going. Seemingly naive.

She started out being support act to Gerard Malanga's poetry readings. Her stuff was personal, very entrancing, and she read in a galloping cadence. Even in Beat days they didn't especially do that then, the accepted way to do it was in a respectful fashion, not in a performance fashion. You were supposed to be listening to content. But she became a sensation as a poet, people were packing into her readings.

Then Lenny Kaye, a journalist, who was entranced with the rhythms, talked about giving a guitar counterpart for it. They did that for a few months, and finally there was this penthouse in a cheap, flea-bag hotel on 43rd Street that did poetry readings, and she got up and sang 'Speak Low', with Lenny playing guitar, and people went crazy. That was it, there was no going back. If ever there was an example of public demand, that was it.

Where did the gay element come from?

She had a huge gay thing in her life, as well as in her poetry. We all did, those who were gay and those who weren't. It would have been impossible not to. Max's was actually listed in the gay guides as mixed gay. This was never the intention, although it was true, but it wasn't a gay bar. But because of the people who went there, drag queens, Andy Warhol, Patti was living at the Chelsea Hotel, so she was around thousands of gay influences, she became a good friend of Janis Joplin. Janis was very into the gay scene.

Wasn't the CBGB's scene more macho?

No, it may have appeared that way, cos in rock'n'roll, bands were made up of men. But you could hardly call The Ramones macho, they didn't behave so. Television didn't appear so, and weren't. One of Blondie's first gigs was to play the music for a Jackie Curtis show called Vain Victory, an extremely gay show. I'm not saying that members of Blondie's band were gay. It didn't matter to them.

Did The Heartbreakers worry about that?

86

Oh no. Entirely the opposite, they flirted with it constantly. David Johansen used to flirt with it. Johnny Thunders adores the company of gay men. And flirts uncontrollably. In those days, in New York it would have been perfectly ridiculous to have entered into that society and expected not to be surrounded all the time by gay people. Gay people ran all the clubs, restaurants, bars. Gay people ran all the taxis. And they made up most of the audience.

When *Punk* magazine started . . .

There was a huge, huge fight going on with *Punk* magazine over that, until they backed down. Very ill-advisedly, Legs McNeil and John Holmstrom wrote a few things about Wayne County and others, and it created a huge war. They tried to present it as a war between Max's and CBGB's, but that didn't work, because too many of the popular bands of the time were on the other side of the war.

Plus a lot of the bands they tried to champion, like Blondie, would have no part of this anti-homosexual number. And John Holmstrom remained a gentleman throughout it all. They did something they thought would be cute and outrageous, and it didn't work, it hurt the magazine in circulation and certainly in estimation.

People like Richard Hell jumped in on their side because he thought it was funny, not because he believed it. He thought it would make trouble. There are a lot of stirrers in New York and Richard is very much one. That's fine, especially when you have a growing scene, for a little while it's fun to have a feud. People create them on purpose to create interest.

There was a furious exchange of letters between *Punk* and the *New York Rocker*, then it resolved itself at CBGB's, I think at a Wayne County concert, where Peter Crowley and Legs and John Holmstrom hugged and kissed, and it was kind of like the old punk–ted war, more a war in other people's minds than it ever really was.

Tell me about The Heartbreakers.

I'd been working with David Bowie until '74, when things went insane, and myself and Cherry and everyone left. I went to work for Robert Stigwood; that was brilliant, but almost too much for the system to bear. Bloody Marys the minute you woke up. I was working

87

on the relaunch of the Bee Gees. I was heading in the wrong direction for me, so I stopped.

So I was going to be a writer and photographer, Lisa Robinson's support, and I was doing all right. No-one thought the punk scene would turn into a real rock scene. So the idea of writing about it and supporting myself was remote. I faced a future of photographing heavy metal bands and stealing nights away to see the music I really liked, when Johnny Thunders said one night, 'We need a manager, will you manage us?' He wanted me and Tony Zanetta, the two of us to do it. Tony said 'Brilliant, let's do it.' I said, 'They're hopeless junkies, they're completely self-destructive, their catch phrase is "See them before they die" – you want to get involved with a band like that?' He said, 'Yes, the music is great.'

Was Richard Hell still with them?

Yeah, they were still doing *Blank Generation* and stuff. The feud was raging between Johnny and Richard, who was the star of the band, that sort of number. But we decided to do it, and I told Johnny, 'Yes', and it was at that moment that Richard said, 'I'm out of this band.' I remember once a very straight, CBS News journalist was in New York and I took him down to CBGB's, and he said, 'I'd like to do something on this, can you introduce me to somebody?'

I brought Richard Hell over. Richard had hair sticking in every direction, his lips were so chapped, his skin was blotched, he had sleepers in both corners of both eyes, bits of dirt and filth here and there, his clothes were ripped, and he sat down opposite this West-Coast journalist, and neither of them could believe they were sitting at the same table as each other, and the journalist ran in total panic.

Did Richard start that look?

Absolutely, he gets complete credit for all of that. He didn't make it up, though, it came out of his lifestyle. It's how he ended up looking because of the way he lived. He didn't care to smarten up for anyone else, he got out of bed and that's the way he looked. He safety-pinned his clothes together, the whole look, years before anyone, except of course Jackie Curtis, but she did it out of style.

Jackie Curtis, one day in 1969, had taken some old curtains, safety-pinned them around her into a makeshift evening gown, ratted her hair straight up in the air, covered her face with glitter and smeared with make-up, and laughed and said, 'One day everyone will look like me!' And she was right!

When did you first become aware of Malcolm and Vivienne?

I met Malcolm in Max's when he came over for that short, strange managing deal with the Dolls. I remember him spouting a lot of strange communist stuff that didn't interest or convince me. I went away saying to Wayne County, 'I don't know who this guy is, but I hope he's got a lot of money because he seems pretty much a jerk.' But he was not jerky, because he managed to pull out before they robbed him of whatever money he did or didn't have.

The next time I even heard the name was when he called me up. I don't know how he got the number. He told me he was managing the Sex Pistols and would The Heartbreakers come and tour? I didn't remember him from that earlier meeting at all, and I had never heard of the Sex Pistols, but I was dying to go to England.

I was also dying to get The Heartbreakers out of New York where they were on the 'See 'em before they die' circuit. They were taking a lot of drugs, playing the same clubs over and over. They always did well, they had big audiences and their music was brilliant at that time, but it was a dead end. Up to Boston, down to Washington DC. I thought, if I can only get them to England, that will solve everything.

So I asked Johnny, I said we'd had this offer to come to England, and Johnny remembered him. He said, 'Malcolm is crazy, we don't want to do that.' I said, 'England, we get to go to England', and so Johnny said, 'Okay'. I hadn't been managing The Heartbreakers more than about six weeks when we were on English soil.

You walked straight into mayhem, didn't you?

Oh yeah, I asked Lisa Robinson if she'd heard of the Sex Pistols, and she said, 'Yeah, I think they're some kind of crazy, Ramones-like group', and I thought, okay, that's fine. I thought we'd go over and maybe get a record deal. There was no way we would ever get a record deal in America, because what record company is going to sign a band that is going to be dead the next day?

So we got here and Nils Stevenson met us. First of all we had no work permits, which we had been promised. Nils had this new-born-bird haircut and was in one of those huge fluffy Seditionaries sweaters, and I said, 'Oh, you must be Sophie.' I had never seen this look before, to me he looked like a fairly plain girl. So he got all crazy and said, 'No, no, no no, I'm Nils.'

The whole band were there to meet us, the Sex Pistols, and it was quite late at night, and we went to that Hamburger Disaster place on Fulham Road, and they said they'd done a TV show, but they said the guy was fucked up and they told him where to go, that was all they said about it.

The next morning, Jerry Nolan, who never sleeps, he's like a bat, he woke me up at about six or seven in the morning, and covered my bed with newspapers. Our reaction was what Jerry said: 'How are we gonna top that?' It was only later when we went into our rehearsal at the Rainbow, and we began to talk with The Clash, that we realised we were in the middle of a much more dangerous controversy.

Malcolm loved it. He was in glory, the more days he could sustain these headlines, the happier he was. By the time we were at rehearsal, the first day, he was crowing to me, anyway. I did detect moments of weakness as all the shows were being cancelled, but I wasn't so sure myself, cos my concern was, are we going to play? Malcolm by that time was saying, 'It doesn't matter if we never play.' Now I see that it wouldn't have mattered, but at the time I was wondering where the next hamburger was coming from.

Were you getting money from the Sex Pistols or EMI?

Certainly not from EMI, we were meant to be getting money from the Sex Pistols. Malcolm in his cagey way had never defined it, certainly not on paper, he just said you'll be well taken care of. This of course depended on how well taken care of *he* was, and there wasn't any money in his camp then either.

We always got fed, usually in hotels, usually far more expensive meals than we would have chosen if we had the money in our pock-

et, but as for pocket money, for the whole band it would be sometimes £20 per week, through the month of December. That's fair
enough.

**When you saw the English groups, were there any similarities with
the Stooges?**

I went crazy, I called Cherry Vanilla and Jayne County and said, 'Sell
the furniture, get over here quick.' What we were doing in New York
at that time wasn't apparently getting anywhere; it had been a cosy
little scene, poor people enjoying the music. Here, because of the way
your media works, it was a whole lifestyle, actual fashion, make-up,
everything, besides the music.

I couldn't believe what we'd landed in, I was beside myself. A lot
of it was very derivative, visually, from what I'd seen recently with
Richard Hell and people. I couldn't help feel that it had been going
on a long time previously in New York, certainly The Ramones had
brought it over very recently, but they never looked that way exactly.
But it didn't matter, because it was refined, it was a lifestyle.

Was there an anger here that wasn't in America?

The anger was only here. There is a lot to be angry about in America,
a lot of injustice and poverty, but it has never been successfully allied
to the arts in any way. Whereas here, a whole rock'n'roll movement
was enshrined with the social injustice, in a way that could not have
been separated from it. In the sixties there were protest songs, in the
fifties there was rebellious rock'n'roll, but it was never like the punk
thing here.

What did you think of the Sex Pistols when you first saw them?

What I thought about the Sex Pistols and The Clash was always the
same. We had dinner with them the first night, I didn't think any of
them were cute, and that's basically the way I've always worked
things out. If someone is cute, I get interested. But the next day at
rehearsal I began to watch, and what I thought was, what a shame. I
was wrong, extremely wrong.

On that first full day, I thought they had the music all wrong, their
attitude was all wrong, and although I hadn't heard the phrase yet, I

felt they had no future. I was a part of commercial rock'n'roll and I thought, this ain't gonna work at all. Paul Simonon I thought was cute, and he was real trippy and smiley in those days. Other than that, the others were unsaleable. I thought, you'd never get these mugs in a magazine, they're horrible looking.

Did you still think that when you saw them play?

No. I hate to agree with Lisa Robinson on this, but she looked at the line-up and what she saw was, The Damned had already pulled out. She saw the Buzzcocks, The Clash, The Vibrators and the Sex Pistols, in that order. She said, The Clash are totally brilliant. The Sex Pistols' stuff seemed then, and still seems now, technically brilliant but far too negative for me to deal with.

I thought The Clash were a nice combination of the Pistols and The Heartbreakers. I became a great Clash fan. They performed bottom of the bill for that whole tour, what little there was of it, without the tiniest rumble. They were treated very shabbily, not purposely, but by the time the money filtered down to them there wasn't any left. They put up with it, because they wanted to play their music.

What did you think of England? Was it different to the England you had seen in '71?

Extremely so. It became the England I fell in love with. Before, I had moved in celebrity circles, then I was always here with Bowie or Mott the Hoople, and this was my first time to live here. While there was the feeling of danger in England, there was no reality of danger, at least to me, on the streets of London in '76 to '77. The bands and everything was like New York, taken into a liveable situation. I was able to live in the realm that I enjoyed.

What about touring?

The first tour was so weird. The first date was cancelled, we were shoved into the hotel with our jackets over our heads while photographers tried to take pictures of us, then we were locked in our room. There was a code to get our meals into our room. To me that was the most exciting thing I'd ever done. As you recall, it was a freezing winter, there was a lot of snow, so it was shivering on the bus while they tried to find us a hotel.

When we started to actually tour with The Heartbreakers, I found touring in England far superior to touring America. Less distance between gigs. England is a rock'n'roll country, and you have that in your favour before you ever walk in the door. They are interested in what's going on. American kids are not interested. They have to be slapped into some sort of interest. American kids change costume from gig to gig.

English kids are into what they go for, it's their whole life. It's what they eat, how they study, what car they drive, the car they steal. It's part of their life. That's how it was with me, even when I was a teenager, but I never knew. I had fantasies of having sex with Fabian, stuff like that. I dreamed of dressing for living in a movie, but in America you're not allowed to live your fantasies.

You fitted straight into the gay-manager mode. Larry Parnes, here I come!

Very much so. I never knew about Billy Fury and Marty Wilde and all that. I certainly knew about Billy Idol, he was one of the first people I met, Sheila Rock introduced me. I said, 'Oh my god, is this one going to be a huge star!' I was right.

What was their attitude to sex?

English people are more secretive. These kids were very affectionate, very demonstrative. I can't tell you how many times I slept in the arms of Sid Vicious. Although we never fucked. It wasn't important to me and it wasn't important to him, but we were really affection-ate, and that I liked. I never pushed it any further with Sid, or with any number of other people, cos it wasn't important.

I've since found out that a lot more of it was going on than I thought. I thought of myself as older, and I didn't want to be a bad influence on them. Talking later to Steve Jones, I learned that there was a lot more kinky sex going on than I would have believed at the time.

Meanwhile the bad drug influences I had imported were moving helter-skelter as fast as they could, wrecking their lives in a far worse manner than I could have.

They really brought smack in, The Heartbreakers?

Sure they did. It was a very innocent scene, sexually, drug-wise, socially, and it changed extremely fast. There was a constant supply of drugs. I ceased to be manager and instead was the interceptor of the drug dealers, they came from everywhere.

We were put into a bed and breakfast in South Kensington, the morning that Jerry Nolan showed me the newspapers. That night, two girls showed up that I took to be groupies, and having been brought up on the MainMan school, I looked for a way to eject them, reasoning that we could barely afford to feed the boys, let alone extra mouths. I was met with such resistance from The Heartbreakers that I got suspicious.

They were dealers, they were there in twenty-four hours, and they looked like the little girls in *Blowup*. Wide-eyed, string-haired girls who looked for all the world like groupies. From that day on, until the last day I saw Johnny Thunders, that was my main problem, intercepting drug dealers. It wasn't a solution, but it was the only thing I could do in that situation. You can't cure him.

You got involved with record companies pretty quick?

As fast as I could. I had come here in the hope that we'd get signed, because there was no hope in America. What I didn't have was connections, or any knowledge of how English record companies work. The only company I had ever dealt with in this country was RCA, with Bowie, and so I went to them first, and they threw up their hands in horror at the prospect of The Heartbreakers.

We were living in this house in Regent's Park with Sebastian Conran, and I had no idea then what the name Conran meant, and the house seemed to me like a hippy crash pad. Now I realise we were probably living in some brilliant, fabulous mansion. Anyway, we couldn't stay there and I went into The Ship in Wardour Street and ran into an old friend from Bowie days, and he was living next door to The Ship, and he said I could move in with him.

I said to him, 'I have to get a record company right away, or else we'll have to go back to America, and then there's no hope', and he said, 'Track is just down the street, they'll love it.' He took me down there and introduced me to Danny Secunda, and I fell on my knees

94

right there and went, 'Please sign us!' He said, 'When are you playing next? 'Manchester', and he came up, and after the gig he just said, 'Fine, we'll sign you.'

Since then we've had a lot of other interest, Malcolm begged me not to sign with Track, he wanted to set up an umbrella company that would cover us all, of which he would be the head. Who knows what the result of that would have been, probably a disaster, probably riches for him and heartbreak for us. But I stuck with Track because they had done it so quickly and easily.

I quickly realised I was involved with madmen, but I didn't mind that. They were throwing what looked like lots of money at punk, they supplied all the rehearsal facilities for Siouxsie and the Banshees, they gave me a lot of money for Sid, for The Flowers of Romance. They were doing what Miles Copeland was doing, only Miles hung in there for a little longer, and he made a fortune out of it. Track thought it was going to be sudden, like The Beatles.

But The Heartbreakers were hardly The Beatles, and money was disappearing at every step, and Sid didn't appear to be sane, and neither did Siouxsie, and they just decided not to throw any more money at this bunch.

The meetings were quite surrealistic. I would go for fifteen or twenty minutes sometimes, not having any idea what they were talking about. I'd be listening hard, too. They'd be talking revolutionary stuff, crazy stuff, looking at each other and chuckling, laughing, and I was thinking, I hope I can catch on to this conversation soon, this is incredible.

How did you meet Sid?

Christmas Day, 1976, we were at Caroline Coon's, all down in the basement, and they were flaming up the Christmas pudding or something, which I wasn't familiar with, and I was feeling displaced and weird, very melancholy, and drifting down the stairwell I heard Jim Reeves. Am I hearing this? This is what's being played at home right now, by my family.

So I went up to this little room, and there was this one person sitting there listening, and I sat down. We listened to the album till it ended, and I was crying, and I looked up, and he was crying, and I said, 'Hi, my name's Leee', and he said, 'Hi, my name's Sid.' Of course I had heard of Sid Vicious. Oh my goodness, this is the great, dangerous Sid Vicious sitting on Christmas Day, crying to a Jim Reeves album.

We know he had a psychotic side, we know he was crazy and self-destructive, but he was also a very sentimental person.

Did you ever go and see his band, The Flowers of Romance, rehearse?

Oh yeah, they would have done fine. There was Keith Levene, Sid and I don't remember who else, I'm sad to say. It was a combination of Ramones and Sex Pistols. Very much the 1-2-3-4 syndrome. If Sid had kept himself together . . .

Were they doing speed, or had they started taking smack by then?

Sid wasn't taking anything until Nancy Spungen got here. It became one of those weird, perverted English relationships that I have since found out are very common. This father/son, I love you very much, why don't I sleep with you and kiss you, but not fuck each other relationships. This is not very common in America, but very common here.

I was with him a lot through the days of The Flowers of Romance, up until he joined the Sex Pistols, and then I wasn't around him nearly as much. Malcolm became the father figure. He was totally innocent of any drugs then. He popped some pills and stuff like that, but we were all doing that, but that was nothing when you're with The Heartbreakers. No needles. I'd say nothing went in that way until Nancy showed up.

Certainly The Heartbreakers brought heroin to the punk scene in England. Nancy brought it to Sid. Almost typically, he was reluctant to do or even to think about that kind of stuff, when The Heartbreakers were around, he wasn't interested. Suddenly when Nancy came, bang. That was the power of love. Her world was smack.

I told her, I saw her on the day she arrived, I ran into her in the little alley that runs from Carnaby Street to Regent Street, and she came running up and said, 'Hi', and I just said, 'Go away. Leave England.' I'd known her for years in America. She was a total junkie prostitute. That doesn't mean I didn't like her, I liked her fine, she was okay. She hung around Max's, she fucked for drugs, she'd give people drugs if they would fuck her, all combinations.

She had a scene with Richard Hell?

Oh yeah, and Jerry Nolan. Dee Dee Ramone, and frankly anyone who would do it. She didn't mean any harm, but with the added menace of drugs, and she would actually give drugs to a boy if he would fuck her.

Although I wasn't keeping Jerry really pure, I was keeping him on the drum kit, and the last thing I needed was Nancy Spungen, with her bag full of drugs, so I literally told her, 'Go away, leave this country now. Over my dead body you will see Jerry Nolan.' And she turned around and she walked away. She wasn't hurt, it was just an incident, it wasn't personal at all.

Almost immediately I heard that she had found Sid and hooked up with him. A cold chill ran down my spine when I heard, and from that day on, Sid was no longer the person that I knew. He was still very affectionate toward me, but you could tell that you weren't really there any more.

What happened with The Heartbreakers?

It was the old syndrome, taking the money that's on the table, rather than playing it cool and collecting later. Johnny is a big victim of that, and Jerry Nolan is even worse. The deal complicated it. For those days it wasn't bad, it was £60,000 advance and escalating rapidly from that, but the deal was complicated. We were not financially equipped to wait it out, so we began to take advances against our advance.

That put us in the impossible situation of using up our money in dribs and drabs, rather than having our £60,000, which we could then have used to get equipment and establish ourselves, which we needed to do. Part of the budget was £5 per person per day, which was chump change even then. I had worked that way with David Bowie, but with Tony DeFries it was open-ended, and with Track we were eating up the money we were going to need very soon.

By the time the deal was consummated, we were already in debt. £60,000 isn't much when you have Jerry Nolan demanding a double candy pink drum kit, and I said, 'Why do you need two of everything?' 'If we're going to be professional, I'll need two of everything, so if something should break, it can be replaced immediately.' As soon as he got two of everything, he sold one of everything. Sold a whole drum kit, to get drugs.

So between that and Johnny's amazing bills, by the time the deal was signed, there was negative money. That not only disillusioned me, but it made them crazy, and now even the £5 per day wasn't forthcoming – once the deal was signed, no more £5 per day. So now we were contracted to a record company that wasn't willing to give us any money of any description, and quite understandably, cos we hadn't shown we were going to come up with anything.

As a record, the album stunk. All the rest of the money was spent on that. The way to record that kind of music was to go in, do it, and get out again. The Clash did it, and The Adverts, who were the most brilliant example of it. That song, 'One Chord Wonders', is a great song, and brilliantly recorded. Instead, Johnny and Jerry wanted to spend all this money on it, and it could never be drilled into their heads that it was their own money they were spending.

We went into the studio down by the South Bank, and it was over-recorded, for weeks and weeks, and when the bills came in, the bills included the whisky, the cocaine, all that stuff, on the bills from the studio. All the engineers were getting constantly stoned. I'm saying it was out of my control, I'm not saying I did all that could be done. It was like Iggy, you get to the point where you just don't care.

Maybe if I'd turned over a few amps, maybe if I had screamed, maybe I could have achieved some kind of improvement in the situation. But at that point, I didn't care. I'd go down, cos it was my job to be there, I'd sit there in the living room of the joint, and watch TV for twelve hours while they basically did nothing. Overdubbed and overdubbed, and the sound of the album was like mud.

And then, they were all so stoned, they said, this is great, let's put it out. The result was a very predictable disaster, when I think at that point they were doing the greatest songs in the genre. Even greater songs than The Clash's songs. Irretrievably wrecked.

Is that what split the band up?

No, Jerry Nolan split the band up. He wanted it split up and he used the album as a handy crowbar, and away the band went. He always wanted the band split. Who knows why – because he's crazy. Every gig we did, the last thing you'd hear before they went on stage was Jerry Nolan saying, 'This band sucks, I think we should break up. This is our last gig.' I don't know why.

When did you get involved with the punk–ted thing?

It happened very arbitrarily. Gail Higgins had gone off to New York to visit her family, and we were living there on Holmes Road in Islington, and I was all alone. I took out the *NME* and found a Darts gig. I knew I could get in for free, and I knew the Darts were a teddy-boy band, and to me teds were just this glamorous image.

By that time I had heard Billy Fury albums and to me it seemed quite fabulous, and I had a motorcycle jacket and I quiffed my hair up and away I went to the gig on my own. I loved the dancing, it wasn't like anything I had seen in America, it was Hollywood's version of rock'n'roll. Gail got back a few days later and I raved to her about what I had discovered, and we went to a couple of gigs, and we began to know some of the kids.

It was always in dim lighting, and the kids never saw that my black hair had an electric-blue streak through it, until the time when we went to see Shakin' Stevens, and between the movie and the concert, the lights came up, and all the teddy boys gasped in unison.

They didn't have a go at you, the teds?

Oh yeah, but not physically. Verbal insults, and for some reason a lot of them had water pistols, and we kept getting shot with water pistols, which I've never seen before or since. We didn't dare go out in the streets, we were safe in the theatre.

Where do you think the aggressiveness between punks and teds came from?

I think it came from the teds, because of the mods and rockers thing. The teds were very idle at the time, and suddenly the newspapers were full of punks. I'm not saying the punks wouldn't hit back, but if I were to guess who threw the first brick, I guess the teds did. They were on a waning scene, and they didn't like that, and it was their tradition to have a war.

Roberta Bayley

CBGB's door person and scene photographer, with many credits including the cover of The Ramones' first album. Interviewed at her home near St Mark's Place, NYC, she was very generous and forthcoming. Having moved to London in the early seventies, she had experience of Malcolm McLaren at two very different stages of his life. She also photographed the Sex Pistols' final, US tour.

I was born in Pasadena, California, near Los Angeles. Moved to Seattle, and from the age of seven to seventeen lived in the suburbs outside of San Francisco. Marin County. When I was seventeen I moved to San Francisco. Then when I was twenty-one, I went to England for a couple of years, '72/'73. Then I came to New York in '74. I was mad on The Beatles and then everything that came after it, The Rolling Stones, The Kinks, Gerry and the Pacemakers.

Is that one of the reasons you wanted to go to England in the end?

Yeah. I had that very strongly when I was fourteen or fifteen. I'd gone over there once for six weeks when I was still at school, and it felt like you'd lived there, listening to all these Kinks records. Anyone who had an English accent, you just thought they were great. Any types, an English accent was cool. And there was this country where everyone was English, what a great place to be!

I must have had this idea in back of my mind that I was gonna be involved in the pop world. Then I got there, and it was a pretty dead time. The radio was pretty good; Bowie and Marc Bolan were on Top 10 radio then, and they had those little shows, Charlie Gillett, and all those people were playing American music. Pub rock was happening then. I went to see Kilburn and the High Roads and a couple of other bands.

Were Kilburn and the High Roads good?

Well, I'd met Charlie Gillett by then, and I thought they were just so weird. They had two crippled guys in the band, a black guy, a midget, I mean Ian Dury was totally bizarre, evil, threatening. They seemed pretty good to me. I hadn't seen a band I'd really liked in four or five years, since I'd left California.

Do you think John Lydon picked up any of his things from Ian?

Yeah, that's Ian's contention. He had that way of leaning on the microphone. For Ian it was for balance, and it was his evil thing. Just the way he would dress, he'd have all these scarves tied around him. He had all these weird bits and pieces. I don't know for sure, but I know Malcolm came along to a gig they did in the middle of Regent's Park. Ian knew Malcolm then.

At that time everyone was going around looking for what was happening. I'd always have my own group. In Frisco you'd go and see Quicksilver and Jefferson Airplane and everything, but the Flamin' Groovies were like my personal group. You'd go and see them everywhere they play, and you'd get to know them. They were the sort of group that was on your level.

They were a total anachronism in San Francisco. No-one liked them except their own fans, they didn't fit into the scene, they never got above third on the bill, Bill Graham hated them. They were outcasts. But they were the people who turned me on to liking music from the fifties. The drummer had actually seen Elvis in the fifties. This was unheard of, and he'd also seen The Beatles live, when they played in Washington.

Did you see the Stooges?

Yeah, that was something else that the Flamin' Groovies turned me on to. After Bill Graham left, their management took over management of the Fillmore, and they put on the shows there for about a year, and they did bring all these bands that were equally despised in San Francisco: Alice Cooper, MC5, Iggy and the Stooges – who couldn't get arrested in San Francisco because they weren't psychedelic, they were heavy rock bands.

I think I saw the Stooges all three nights, cos the Groovies opened up for them at the original Fillmore. I wouldn't say I got the music, exactly, but I was fascinated by Iggy. It turned out when I asked him about it in '76 that he was drugged out the whole time he was in San Francisco, LSD or whatever, the whole time. He caught every disease imaginable to man, living in a commune, the demise of the love thing. He was this monster, but with his silver clothes, and no shirt, he was incredible-looking, like from another planet.

No-one was in the audience, it was two dollars to get in, the place was practically empty from what I recall. It wasn't a very fashionable thing in San Francisco. The Velvet Underground came and they just got trashed, nobody wanted to know about them. Iggy was standing up there on stage by himself, with this huge feedback, the rest of the band had left the stage, and he was just doing these poses with his back to the audience, and I just thought, wow, that's really great! Who could get away with this? What is it?

Then I saw him later in London.

King's Cross?

Yeah, it was really crowded and hard to see, but everyone in the world was there, there was a big buzz on that. Iggy walked out into the audience. He was hitting himself in the face with the microphone, and bleeding. I remember that. I thought that was pretty strange, he'd whack himself on the lip and get his lip to bleed, to have a little blood drip down his chin. This was a freak show. I wasn't thinking of it in terms of music.

Can you describe how you met Malcolm?

I used to work in this restaurant in Langton Street called the Chelsea Nuthouse, I was a waitress. Malcolm and Vivienne used to come and eat there and they would always talk to Americans. I knew this guy Jerry Goldstein who was friends with Malcolm, and Malcolm gave him a job in the store, but he couldn't start work for two or three weeks or something, so I took the job.

I didn't work there more than a few weekends and days. But even in the brief time I worked there, these people would come in, Marianne Faithfull, Jimmy Page, The Kinks. It was just between being Let It Rock and Too Fast to Live. The drape stuff then was a cool thing cos nobody else really had it. But they were starting to get into bondage stuff, leather mini-skirts with little chains.

What were they like then?

Vivienne didn't spend much time in the shop. She was very nice, strong. Malcolm was interested in all these weird things, I found him really fascinating. He'd have all these political ideas. Gene Krell came by one day, and said, 'Picasso died', and Malcolm just said, 'Oh, good.' That was my first exposure to anybody saying something really outrageous, just what he felt. I'd never been exposed to that type of attitude; it was a shock.

Malcolm was starting to get real fed up with the teddy boys. They had these redneck attitudes, he wanted to change the shop for that reason. He dreaded the weekends cos all these yobs would come down. Later I got a letter saying he was changing the name of the shop and there was going to be white mice in the window and a sign saying Modernity Killed Every Night.

Was Malcolm confident then, or was he still trying things out?

He seemed really spacey and a gentle person, then, he still has that side to him. I don't think he had strong ideas then, he was in a formative stage. He was still trying to make money, selling his shoes and stuff. I remember seeing him sometimes at CBGB's, and I guess that was when he got involved with the Dolls. It was '75 when that red leather thing came out.

How did you get involved with CBGB's?

I met Richard Hell at CBGB's, and went back to San Francisco, came back to New York, lived with Richard for a few months and that's when Terry Ork asked me if I would do the door at CBGB's. They felt that to have a woman at the door was better. That was when the take at the door was twenty dollars, maybe forty.

What sort of criteria did you use about whether to let people in, or did you just let anybody in?

I let people I knew in, when there was a list. My thing was, it was two dollars and you should just pay it, cos all the money went to the band

and my boyfriend was in the band. That's all they made. CBGB's had its own crowd that would always come there, like the Hell's Angels, so of course you would let them in. Basically there was nobody there at the time, so it was no big thing. We would make maybe thirty dollars.

Then it moved up when Patti Smith started playing. The big big night was Patti Smith and Television, and we made about three hundred dollars at three dollars a head, and then it was decided that it was getting too big, we'll have to get a professional to do the door. Hilly asked me to come back when the CBGB's festival was happening and they were having seven nights a week of punk rock, which was '76, and I just started working every night.

How did the CBGB's scene develop?

It didn't take that many people to make it unbearably crowded. But people started having records out and articles written about them, and the word of mouth. CBGB's was the only place besides Max's for bands to play, and you either played one place or the other. So on certain nights that was the place to be. But it got too crowded to have any fun.

When did New York City go bankrupt?

That was around '75. That was the turnaround period. '76 was when things started being better in New York. *Saturday Night Live* and CBGB's and stuff all started happening around then. Then, you could live for pretty much nothing, you could have a little job where you worked for two days a week, still support yourself and go out every night and have fun. You can't do that any more, you have to have a job where you make a lot of money.

Can you tell me about the Ramones cover?

I wasn't trained as a photographer, I was faking the whole time. I'd bought a camera only a few months before I took that Ramones picture. I was fine in natural light. This was for a session for *Punk*, and they were whingeing and whining, then when their album came along they hired somebody and paid them two thousand dollars and did this photo session and the pictures were awful, the worst pictures you ever saw.

So they were desperate and they called me and they paid me a hundred and fifty dollars for this for the album cover. It was over round the corner from CBGB's cos Arturo Vega, who worked with The Ramones, had a loft there. We just went down 1st Street to some vacant lot. There's one sequence where Dee Dee steps in dog shit and he's trying to scrape it off the bottom of his shoe. One reason I think they used that picture was it made Tommy look almost as tall as Joey. Everybody has tried to copy this shot.

Can we talk about the Sex Pistols' US tour; how did you get on to it?

Tom Forcade of *High Times* was very interested in the Sex Pistols and felt they were the most culturally important thing going on, and also felt that way about *Punk* magazine. He was our distributor at that stage. So he was helping *Punk* and starting to put punk things into *High Times*. He put Debbie Harry on the cover, John Lydon on the cover, everyone at *High Times* was freaking out, in total rebellion, they thought he'd lost his mind.

The Sex Pistols were coming, they weren't playing New York, everyone was pissed off, then John Holmstrom calls me up and says, 'I'm going on the tour', and I was of course really jealous. He couldn't tell me anything about it, who was paying, how he was doing it. Then I got a call in the middle of the night saying, 'You're leaving tomorrow for Texas for the Pistols tour. Don't ask any questions, your first-class ticket will be waiting for you at the airport.'

I just threw a few things in a bag, not realising I would be gone for two weeks. I got on the plane the next day and went to Texas. I got there, and everything was weird and secretive. John was going, 'We've got to find the Pistols, they're hiding.' They were trying to keep the Pistols away from the press, so John and I spent the whole time trying to find what hotel they were in, it was really strange. We went to the gig, the soundcheck.

That was Randy's Rodeo in San Antonio, the most insane show, all these rednecks throwing bottles for the whole show, and that's when Sid hit the guy over the head with his bass. You definitely felt there was going to be a riot or something. There were very few people there who cheered for them, it was definitely Texans who had come down to check out what this shit is, these macho guys . . . and there were all these weird people selling safety pins, nobody knew what punk was. It was totally strange.

Had you seen the Sex Pistols before?

No. I thought they were amazing, but I wasn't getting up close, even to shoot pictures. I thought, this is too frightening. Then we got in with them, we stayed in the same hotels they did, we were the only journalists there. There were a lot of British journalists at that particular gig, from all over, like Fleet Street, but they disappeared after that.

Somehow every place we'd go we'd find out what motel they were staying in, I don't remember how. Along with Bob Gruen and Joe Stevens we were the only other people who were travelling with them the whole time. Even the other journalists were staying in better hotels than they were on tour. It got to the point they knew who we were, we were a little bit older, but kind of their age. We gave them copies of the magazine.

Everybody was really wary of everybody. Lydon and Sid were travelling on the bus, and at that point Paul and Steve started flying with Malcolm. They got tired of being on the bus. The whole thing was really bizarre. We had no idea where our money was coming from, we had no cash, we had a credit card which was charging up a huge amount – which was of course mine.

Tom Forcade is saying, 'Don't worry about it'. He was lurking in the background. He was making the film, *D.O.A.*, but trying to pretend he wasn't making that. He had a secret film crew who were pretending they were a news crew, sneaking into the gigs and filming, cos nobody wanted it filmed. They were managing to get footage – and thank god, cos that's the only stuff left of that tour.

The gigs were totally bizarre, they were playing places like Tulsa. People were driving from long distances cos they weren't playing in major cities, so when they were playing in Texas, people had driven from LA, cos they knew they wouldn't get a chance in San Francisco, it would be cooler to see them at San Antonio, or something.

Do any of the concerts stand out?

Randy's Rodeo. I liked the Tulsa show, it was a really cool place, it was very beautiful, it was snowing. Most of the shows it was difficult to see, but I think that was the one where I could see really well. I think I have lots of photos from there. Some it was impossible to see, and Winterland was just a nightmare. At no time did I have any idea what was going on.

Did the Pistols?

They were on a different thing from us. To me, I was on a secret mission and I didn't know what it was. To them, it was probably more normal, they were just doing gigs, having less and less fun. Sid was getting drunk all the time and he would never talk to Lydon. Steve and Paul were just bored. They were going round the radio stations and picking up girls, but I think they were in over their heads, and they had no protection.

There was no-one there saying, c'mon guys, it's okay. I don't think anyone except John was intellectually advanced enough to see it the way Malcolm saw it. I don't think Malcolm gave a shit, he was throwing them to the wind, saying, won't this be an interesting sociological experiment, but he wasn't being very protective of them as people.

Was he getting fed up with it as well?

It wasn't causing the stir that he had wanted it to, although I don't know what he expected. Maybe the whole thing had just got boring. You go on a tour, it becomes hotel, this, that. They didn't reach the media, they were still doing that 'Punk rock comes to town' jokey article. America is a big place to try to make an impact. Not at all like England, where some little thing can get huge headlines in all the papers, this was something on the entertainment page.

What was the Winterland concert like?

That was the night they tried to keep me out of the concert for being a CIA agent. Paul Cook had given me my tickets and then they said, 'The band doesn't want you to see the show.' They met us at the door, threw us out of the soundcheck. Once again, we couldn't work out what was going on, something to do with Tom Forcade but we couldn't figure what it was. Then it was like a regular rock concert, it's just a big city and a big venue.

107

In a way it was exciting, cos it was the Sex Pistols, but there wasn't any challenge, there was no danger, everybody was there because they wanted to see them. So it was different to the other shows, where it was fifty-fifty.

They never played a major concert in England. That was so strange, it was probably the first time they had seen their success.

I'm sure they could have played the Hollywood Bowl; in New York they could have played the Garden. The Pistols really made a mess of things. Breaking up was such a good idea, even if they didn't do it for all the reasons we could have wished they did it, but it was the best thing they could have done. It would have gotten awful if they had carried on. Sometimes with a group, no matter how much you like them, the best thing they can do is break up.

Do you have any memories of Sid?

I was sitting around with Sid at the soundcheck and he said, 'I wanna be like Iggy Pop and die before I'm thirty', and I said, 'Sid, Iggy is over thirty and he's still alive, you got the story wrong.' At that point every drink would be a completely different drink.

I just sort of goaded him into dropping his trousers, he was say-ing, 'I wanna give you one', or something like that, and I was like, 'Oh get out of here.' So he was doing this for my benefit, and of course Joe Stevens steamed in and was stealing my shot, and I do have the picture after that where he's trying to get his trousers up, and his willy's hanging out. There, he's Mister Punk Rock, and a minute later . . . poor Sid.

John Holmstrom

Co-founder of Punk *magazine and noted graphic artist. Working for* High Times *when I talked to him about the origins of the magazine that gave punk its name and launched Legs McNeil on the world. He had clear and definite opinions on the differences between New York and London, as well as an eyewitness view of the Sex Pistols' last tour.*

I was raised in Connecticut, the same home town as Legs. I came to New York in '72, to go to the School of Visual Arts, on 23rd Street. Chris Stein went there, Keith Haring went there. I went there to learn cartooning. Comic books more than strips. Robert Crumb, *Mad* comics, particularly Harvey Kurtzman. At SVA I studied under Harvey Kurtzman and Will Eisner. In two years I went from being someone with very little ability to getting my first jobs.

How did *Punk* magazine start?

I spent the summer of 1975 doing this movie, *The Unthinkable*, with Jed Dunn and Legs out in Connecticut. It was a gangster comedy, very forgettable. Legs was also making a movie about the mentally retarded. I told them about the music scene going on. I'd just bought the Dictators record. Joey Ramone used to go to their gigs all the time, and The Dictators were one of the first groups I read about in *Creem*.

When did The Dictators get going?

About '74. They were a big influence on The Ramones, but then when we came to bring out *Punk*, they'd already broken up. They were the first people I wanted to put in the first issue.

Weren't The Ramones like an edited version of The Dictators?

That's a good way to put it, same influences, mid-sixties music with a twist, modernised. Coincidentally, they both did versions of

'California Sun' on their first records. The Ramones were going to do Tommy Rose's 'Sheila', I would have loved to have heard that. The hippy thing had turned rock into a mellowed-out sound, we wanted the fun and the liveliness back. We weren't trying to be grim at all. I thought punk was fun.

How did the name come about?

Creem was my favourite magazine at the time, it was pushing Iggy and the MC5. Lester Bangs would use the term 'punk rock' to describe this early-seventies music, and something like *Who Put the Bomp* would use the term to describe the garage bands of the sixties. A magazine called *The Aquarian* would use the term to describe what was going on at CBGB's.

The word was being used to describe Springsteen, who was on the cover of *Time* and *Newsweek* in the same week in '75, and to describe Patti Smith, and the Bay City Rollers, and AC/DC when they were in England, Eddie and the Hot Rods . . . It was pretty obvious that the word was going to be very popular, so we figured we'd take it before anybody else claimed it.

Legs thought of the name and I thought it fitted what we wanted to do, it had so many different meanings. *Happy Days*, the TV show, the fifties, leather jackets. I wanted to strip rock'n'roll of all the bullshit. During the sixties, rock'n'roll became acid rock and folk rock and it got political, until it became really horrible in the early seventies, classical rock, rock operas, and we wanted to get rid of all the bullshit.

We figured 'punk' was the name that would express that very easily. But we had people coming up saying, 'What is punk rock? What is this new kind of rock?' We tried to explain to writers that it was getting back to the old sound, but the writers didn't like that, they wanted punk rock to be a new scene. English punks did what the writers wanted, they were media-savvy, they got the fashion look, made a hybrid of what we were doing.

But you had groups with names like 'Television' in the States . . .

But it wasn't tailored to be commercial or anything. Television was very anti-commercial. To me they had intellectual pretensions, we weren't too enamoured of them, they were a writers' band and I never liked music that was tailored to rock critics. What I wanted to do was promote basic rock'n'roll. Like The Ramones. They were the most basic group.

How did the magazine get started?

Legs and Jed and I decided to work together, and within six months or so of leaving art school, we were starting the magazine. In October of '75. It was all based on *The Dictators Go Girl Crazy!* and the scene at CBGB's, which I was aware of but Legs and Jed hadn't been; the first time they went was when we went to interview The Ramones in November '75.

And Mary Harron came with you as well?

Yeah. Legs came to New York when he dropped out of high school, I put him up and he got a job with this film company called Total Impact, and they would allow people to eat and sleep there in return for working on their films. Mary was a cook there, a very good cook.

Presumably CBGB's had had some press already?

Creem mentioned it, and *Village Voice* had done a big story on the New York Rock Festival. I think we were the first official feature, it was about the third time The Ramones had ever been written about. Danny Fields told us that it was because of our article about them that they got their record contract, and Blondie told us the same thing, cos of us and *New York Rocker*, which came out a few weeks after us, covering the same groups from a pure music perspective.

Where did the idea for the cartoons come from?

It was to publish my work. I went to the underground press while I was at school, and they basically told me look, if you want to get your work published, do it yourself. I talked Jed into it and we took it from there. Originally I wanted to do more of a comic book and less of a magazine, but once we decided on a music publication, we figured we'd run serious features.

So were The Ramones and The Dictators influenced by cartoons?

Johnny Ramone would always wear cartoon-logo shirts. They had Arturo Vega doing their graphics, and he was more of a minimalist artist. We didn't like a lot of that stuff. I think The Ramones were more tuned to fine art. The Dictators were funny, but I don't know if they were influenced by cartoons, but everybody read underground comics, they were a big thing.

That market had crashed by about '74, the market was saturated, and it looked like the underground comic scene was ending. I wanted to see something new happen in comics, but punk didn't get into comics; we were about it. I think we accomplished it with our comic-strip interviews. Roberta was very good at taking photos for these things. For some reason, she has a simple photographic style, her work was very casual.

Was the first Ramones album a big event in America?

It was big on the scene. But the reaction against it was horrible. People taking one look at it and throwing it in the trash. Record people and radio people saying I'll never ever play this group. The resistance to what we were doing was astounding. I was just trying to bring out a nice little fun magazine, and the reaction against it was incredible. We liked it, but everybody else hated us and hated The Ramones and everything we were doing.

What did you think of the English punk scene?

What I disliked about the London thing, everybody wore scowly faces and extreme fashions and were angry at the government, and we weren't. One of the big clashes between New York and London came about because our distributor, Rough Trade, were buying from us really cheap and then marking up the prices incredibly. As soon as it was out here, it was out there, but they were charging lots of money for it.

The fanzine revolution in London, where they were all xeroxed and cheap and not professionally printed, was a reaction to what our distributor was doing to us. We got a bad name in England as a result, a lot of resentment and hostility, which I didn't really understand.

So about the Sex Pistols' US tour – why did you decide to go and cover it?

Tom Forcade talked us into it. He went along to make the movie, *DOA*. It all happened because Lech Kowalski came to talk about making a movie on the tour. An hour later they were in a helicopter on their way to Kennedy, making a movie. That's the way Tom was about things. He loved the idea of making a movie about a Warner Brothers rock group, especially the Sex Pistols.

He was the publisher of *High Times*, and later he shot himself. I'm investigating the story now, because there's a lot of rumours around about whether it was an accident or a set-up. During the tour, I was watching Sid try to kill himself all the time, always breaking bottles and scraping himself. I mentioned once that Sid Vicious was the most self-destructive person I have ever seen, and Tom said, 'No, he's not, I am.'

How had he got involved in punk?

He was into the MC5. *High Times* got its name from the MC5 album where they're rapping away about high society, meaning drugs. Tom was very savvy. Ninety per cent of the people around him hated punk, they figured we were against everything they stood for. Tom figured that if this was the new youth movement, he wanted in on it. Also he liked the music, which a lot of those hippies didn't.

He instantly gave us all kinds of support, and asked for nothing in return. He had done *High Times*, which was instantly successful, he was making a lot of money and wanted to share the wealth, and I think he saw us as his children, almost. Shows how smart he was. Especially, you would figure, the publisher of a magazine like *High Times*. Stupid drug use, indiscriminate drug use.

He put Johnny Rotten on the cover of *High Times*, I don't have a copy of the issue, it's very rare, but everybody who worked there signed a petition to talk him out of doing it, but Tom insisted that *High Times* reached punks.

Where did you pick up the Sex Pistols' US tour?

Memphis. Tom called me into the office, we were all set to go see The Ramones that night – they'd just released *Rocket to Russia*, we had all these seats in the front row – and Tom calls up and says, 'Hey, just saw the Sex Pistols last night, they were great.' I'm killing myself, but I said, 'Really?' 'Yeah, you should come down and see them.' 'Great, how am I gonna see 'em?' 'I got a ticket waiting for you. Just talk to my secretary, come on down here.' Wow!

So get the ticket, rush home and throw a few things in a suitcase, fly down and see the show in Memphis. I showed up an hour or two after they were supposed to go on, and a riot had just happened, they're not letting anyone in. I was totally confused, standing there with a suitcase, looking at broken glass and police sirens and people wandering all over the place, very angry.

I get in and I'm listening to Alice Cooper, *Killer*, the first side, and I go to someone, 'Great record', and they go, 'Yeah, but they've been playing it over and over for three hours.' Everybody's pounding on the floor, there'd been a riot cos they'd sold too many tickets and had to turn people away, it was pandemonium. The Pistols went on, and they weren't very exciting.

I looked for Tom but I couldn't find him. I ended up walking towards the hotel and met Lech Kowalski, who I had incidentally met while he was talking to Tom in his office with a bunch of film equipment, a couple of cameras. He went up there with the equipment, and he gave me some money. I had gone down there with my last ten dollars, I didn't have any money to get to the hotel.

The next morning, Tom wanted to talk to me. I thought I was going back, but he brings me into a limo and lays out his master plan: he's going to make the movie, I'm down there to do the book on the tour, do the greatest issue of *Punk* anyone's ever seen, and we're going to make so much money that it's going to make everything happen.

He said how Warner Brothers were holding the Sex Pistols against their will, and he saw Sid Vicious get beaten up by the bodyguards the night before, so he wants to go out and get them some bicycle chain belts, so the Sex Pistols can get away from their bodyguards. He wanted to be their manager, basically. He felt they were on the same political wavelength, he really liked what they were doing. Tom was one of the original Yippies.

So why did punk not have the impact in the States that rock music had had in the mid-sixties?

The reason it didn't happen like it did in London was geography. This is a giant country, and I think a lot of the country picked up on the conservative end of the hippy thing, which was typified by the culture of the early seventies – the Grateful Dead, the Allman Brothers. I think there was some government tinkering, too. They didn't like what happened in the sixties and they wanted to make sure it didn't get resurrected with punk.

I heard that Carter said during a jazz concert or similar on the White House lawn that he wanted to stop punk. I know once we got involved with Forcade we were under surveillance. We had trouble with our mail which continued until the magazine's demise. I don't have any proof, but it was generally a lot more difficult to get things done.

So, was there FBI on the Sex Pistols tour?

I heard rumours that there were, but I think some of them thought that Forcade was FBI, the Pistols didn't like him. They didn't figure out that he had us on the tour. Forcade had told us not to let anyone know that we were involved with him at any time. He was very paranoid. He was not a nice guy. He was very moody, and at times he appeared sinister. But he was a genius at getting things done.

What happened after Memphis?

Tom got me a three-piece western suit with boots, the whole bit. And he got the belts for the Pistols, and for us, in case anybody messed with us, he called up some bodyguards to follow him to New York in case Warners gave him a hard time, then we got on the plane and hit the next stop, which was San Antonio. That was the best show. We spent a day chasing round trying to get an interview with the Pistols, but it was almost impossible to get to them.

In San Antonio we met with Malcolm, and Roberta had come down with us by then, and she knew Malcolm and we had dinner together. He was telling us his plan for the tour, which was brilliant. I was asking a lot of questions, like why tour the South, why not the North? I think Malcolm and Tom must have had a lot in common, I get the feeling Malcolm put the Pistols off on a personal level, they didn't listen to him any more.

But if they'd stayed together they would have been giant. He would have broken them, and punk rock, in a big way. The Damned and some other groups had come over before the Pistols, but he spoke of creating an environment where the Sex Pistols philosophy would thrive. He knew if they came down to the South, it would be much rowdier audiences, that there might be a violent episode that would get the band some press.

I think Malcolm had an antipathy towards the New York scene, possibly due to his experiences with the Dolls.

At the time they did say they wanted to play New York, they wanted to finish the tour at a place like Madison Square Garden. They just didn't want to play CBGB's. They didn't want to be associated with that, which was right. But their idealism was their undoing. They wanted to stand for too many things that they didn't really believe in.

What was your impression of the members of the band?

John was busy being nasty to everybody. Sid was a nice guy, a little out of it. Paul and Steve we hung around with a bit, they seemed like nice people. But I didn't form strong impressions. Touring is such a disorienting experience, we were always on the move, there was always something to do, there was always trouble with bodyguards and security. It was the most stressful, crazy two weeks of my life.

What happened with Warners? Weren't they flying Paul and Steve around, while John and Sid went in the bus?

That was a big problem. The Pistols were all pissed at Malcolm, cos he was flying everywhere, but he wanted the Pistols to stay on the bus so they could see the country, or something. Then somehow Steve and Paul got on the planes, but I heard Sid and Johnny wanted to be in the bus; they liked their travelling party, they were getting along great with the bodyguards. Sid needed somebody to watch him all the time.

Noel Monk was the bodyguard. He was creepy, such a fascist. They were spending a lot of time with those guys, I think they thought they were new friends. But once they broke up, they couldn't even talk to those guys. I think they found they weren't such great friends. They were horrible to us.

116

So what did you think when you saw the Sex Pistols?

I think the San Antonio gig was one of the best I ever saw, if not the best rock'n'roll show. It was insane, there were bottles flying everywhere. They were responding to the audience. That was the one where Sid hit the guy and the lights went off, I thought there was going to be a riot. The Pistols rose to the occasion. It's captured a bit on the *DOA* film. But I wish they could have shown more of that, no matter how bad the filming was. They were amazing.

It was very hostile, but if you wanted what punk rock was supposed to be, this was the ultimate show. They got the audience into it too. The incident with the guitar happened very early on. There was a great headline: 'Pistols Win the San Antonio Shoot-out'. It was like that. The audience seemed ready to kill the Sex Pistols as soon as they came out. Who are these punks from England? Let's go down and show them what Texas is about. Malcolm had mentioned this as the place he wanted, he was hoping there would be this kind of incident. They were throwing full beer cans at the Pistols. I saw Sid take a full beer can right in the mouth, and he took it and dared them to throw more, and they realised they were for real. Then they started throwing things for fun. Johnny got a pie in the face. After the show you couldn't see the stage for the beer cans piled on it.

I've never seen such a mess, and the Pistols loved it, they came out and talked to the press for the first time. I think the only time they came they talked to people. They were under rein for the first two shows. Under a lot of scrutiny, and if there were any riots they weren't at Atlanta. The Sex Pistols didn't throw up or kill anybody, and by the time they reached San Antonio, a lot of people dropped off the tour and they were themselves.

The next show was great too, at Dallas. That was where Sid got hit on the nose, and was bleeding. They were hanging out talking to people before the show in Dallas too, things had loosened up. Then it got tight, in San Francisco. Tulsa was in the middle of nowhere, there were all these Jesus freaks outside, there wasn't a big audience, it was a cold, snowy night.

Then they played San Francisco, which was the worst show on the tour. No energy, the sound was terrible. Malcolm had lost interest, he

117

felt they'd become just like Led Zeppelin, a group with an uncritical audience, and there was nowhere to go but down.

Was there any difference between the Malcolm you had talked to in the weeks before, and the Malcolm you talked to in San Francisco? It sounds as though he got fed up with them very suddenly.

An awful lot happened on that tour, and there was a difference in everyone, it wasn't just him. There were so many hassles – with the hotel people, within the group, between Warners and the group. Tom Forcade wasn't helping things by making the movie. I'm sure they'd never done a tour where they had to deal with so much. Every time they'd get to a gig, they'd find a camera crew there, so they'd chase them out and find there were more cameras.

There were people recording off the sound board, there were so many hassles it was incredible. We were just trying to cover an event, but they weren't letting us cover the band, even though we were there all the time. They wouldn't let Johnny talk to anybody, Johnny would stay in his room, and Steve and Paul didn't really have much to say, and Sid was busy being Sid, and no-one was trying to keep him from killing himself.

There was also seemingly a rift between Warner Brothers and the bodyguards, cos the bodyguards had their own agenda for what they wanted the Sex Pistols to do, which was different from what Malcolm wanted them to do. The Sex Pistols were using the body-guards as a way to keep Malcolm away from them, and to keep other people away from them. It was a very political situation, and it was a shame it led to the break-up of the group.

Did you go backstage after the last show?

I didn't, Legs did. We could only get one person back, and I'm sorry we sent him, cos he just came back and said, 'Ah, it sucks back there.' Nobody was kissing his butt. But we ran into Malcolm right after-wards, and Legs conducted an hour-long interview with him. That's when he started talking about breaking up the group, and how this wasn't the way he pictured it.

It sounds like everything was heightened. If most bands do a bad show, they don't worry about it. But it sounds like everything was

telescoped, and things that might have taken years to happen with other bands happened in two weeks.

Well, yeah, they were on national news. That tour was the biggest thing happening in America, in a way. During the tour we felt we were covering the first Beatles tour, their arrival was so heralded, but during the tour, very little news got out.

Do you think that was censorship or just lack of interest?

The censorship was happening when they wouldn't let them in the country, when they were supposed to play Pittsburgh. I think that was the federal government cracking down on punk, but the local thing was lack of interest.

That was a big problem for all of us; writers were either totally uninterested, or if they were interested, they'd write totally ridiculous things, emphasising the stupidest aspect of whatever it was we were doing. Some intelligent, thoughtful things were being done. I didn't like the way the Pistols played up the more ridiculous aspects of things, and they paid the price for it.

Why did punk rock die in the States?

The Sex Pistols broke it. If something happens in New York, nobody pays any attention to it in America, America hates New York. That's why it had to happen in London. America loves England, at least it did. The same way Jimi Hendrix had to go over to England before he could make it in America. When the Sex Pistols came over and did the tour and broke up, that was the official end of punk rock, because they were the only punk rock group in the world, according to America's perception.

Legs McNeil

Punk *magazine co-founder, figurehead – billed as 'Resident Punk' – and feisty chronicler of the New York scene. Despite the much-ballyhooed antipathy between the London and New York scenes, Legs is charm itself when I meet him just off St Mark's Place in Manhattan during the summer of 1989.*

I was born in Newhaven and raised in Cheshire, Connecticut. My father died when I was two months old, so we were on public assistance. It's a very pretty town, but back then it was post-war, slap up the buildings. I grew up in a Catholic ghetto. People would move in when they were on their way up, they'd live in it for five years then they'd get a raise and they'd move to a big house, but if you were Catholic, you had ten kids so you could never move.

You were at college with John Holmstrom?

John was older, he'd just graduated. I knew of him, he had long hair, he was a cool guy, and I was four years younger. We started hanging out when I was sophomore and he was out of school.

What were you studying?

Nothing. The thing is not to go to school. We made these films. John had this acting group, that was how we first met, he was into confrontational theatre. It was a good excuse to get drunk and do stuff. We were always doing things, cartoons, real dumb stuff, like making take-offs of Three Stooges movies, funny stuff. I'd made some movies for the State of Connecticut.

In high school I won this contest for making an anti-smoking commercial. They had this mixed-media class which I did pretty good in. I flunked everything else. The teacher was nice and they took some time with you. It was such an upper-middle-class town that if you were a dirtbag they really wouldn't care about you. I had dyslexia, so I didn't do very well at school, and if you didn't do well at school they just threw you out, which I did.

How did you get to New York?

They told me I wasn't going to graduate, they wouldn't let me take an exam cos I was drinking, so I left for New York the next day. John would write me these letters, saying I should come. He was studying under Harvey Kurtzman at the School of Visual Arts. In fact I got accepted for the School of Visual Arts, so I was planning on going to college, but since I didn't get my high-school diploma, I just came down and moved in with John.

And you'd started drinking already?

I started when I was thirteen, not as heavy as it would later progress.

What was happening in New York when you got there in 1975?

Remnants of hippies, people with high-heeled shoes and flares. The war in Vietnam ended, which I think helped punk a lot. If you were a kid, you grew up afraid that you were going to go, and it was a release, it was like a party. That happened in '75, it was the summer of Watergate, it was a time of change. Something was going to happen, it confirmed your feelings, this government sucks, Nixon's an asshole, which everyone knew, but Watergate confirmed it. Watergate was '74, the end of the war was summer of '75.

The only things you could be, growing up, was a straight guy, a jock, a greaser or a hippy, and we didn't want those options. I think that's why it exploded so much. Remember in '74 people were still saying, 'Man, you should have been at Woodstock.' Fuck you! You wanted to hear it but also, you had missed it all. You don't have anything to look forward to, so the reaction was, fuck you, we'll make something of our own.

Nixon resigned in August of '74, so then there was a real change, and we had Ford, who was a real klutz. No-one in New York had any money. That was when Ford said to the city, drop dead. But it was a great time to be broke. The record companies had lots of money and they'd throw parties for these disco acts every night. You could go out every night and drink for free. It was eating the record companies from the inside out. You'd meet everybody.

It was like The Beatles coming to America after Kennedy got shot, everyone was sad, then there was this explosion of joy. Perfect timing. Punk was real good timing. It's the mood of the country. People wanted to get back to the aggression, prove they weren't wimps, put on a leather jacket.

Where did that black leather thing come back in?

The Ramones. John probably has the date of when we went to see them, we were wearing these nerdy T-shirts and denim jackets, it was embarrassing. I worked for this hippy movie commune called Total Impact. That's where I met Mary Harron, she was the cook. She was wearing hippy skirts and stuff.

So where did The Ramones get that black leather stuff from? James Dean?

Yeah, Brando, *The Wild One*. I walked out the next day after seeing The Ramones and bought my first leather jacket. Nobody in New York wore black leather. They wore brown leather bomber jackets with fur collars, and we thought that was gay, you didn't see any at CBGB's. If you had a black leather jacket, the streets parted in front off you, it wasn't like now.

It was very threatening, black leather was aggressive. It was a return to the fifties, you know the Fonz? *The Lords of Flatbush*. The Fonz started on TV about '73. *Happy Days* was already into reruns by '75.

The Fonz was cool when it started?

Yeah, but then he became paternal. And in the first episodes he wore a windbreaker, cos it was too threatening for him to wear a black leather jacket. But The Ramones probably got it from *The Wild One*.

Tell me how you started the magazine.

We made this movie in Connecticut in the summer of '75, and John bought The Dictators album and we played it all summer. They wore black leather jackets on the inside cover. It was fun angst. Yes, everything sucks, but we're not going to do anything about it, and we're going to have a good time anyway. We'd all come from the same place; nobody had come from the city and had a hard life.

It was just so boring where we came from. Nobody starved; you had a fucked-up life, but compared to the rest of the world, it was a pretty good life. So on one hand you had nothing to complain about, but if you eat in McDonald's every day and your mother takes you to Howard Johnson's for your birthday, and you look at this corporate muzak world, something is going to explode.

The Dictators came from Co-op City in the Bronx, The Ramones came from Forest Hills, we came from Cheshire. We all had the same reference points: White Castle Hamburgers, Howard Johnson's, muzak, malls. And we were all white, which was also very interesting, there were no black people involved in this.

Why was that?

I don't know. There's always racism in this country, but I don't know how conscious it was. In the sixties, hippies always wanted to be black. And we were going, fuck the blues. Fuck the black experience, we had nothing in common with black people at that time. Unless it was black people who grew up in the suburbs, went to McDonald's, etcetera. There's a lot more now than there was then. There was no separation between middle-class black experience and being poor black. It was still the same.

Plus they were into disco and we weren't, there was a real separation. It was funny, you'd see guys going out to a punk club, passing black people going to a disco, and they'd be looking at each other, not with disgust, but isn't this weird that they want to go there, and them probably thinking the same about us. I don't know how racist that is. If you read Lester Bangs' article, about us being white noise supremacists, it's more about Lester than it's about us.

I was going to ask you about that, in connection with your band, Shrapnel.

I did that as a response to Vietnam. I made the mistake of thinking you could take a band and make them into characters, like actors. Which is what Alice Cooper did, but nobody separates the singer from the song, so when they sang 'Hey Little Gook' . . . I don't know why it's acceptable for you to say it in a movie and not in a song.

Punk was supposed to be dangerous, right? Well you already had The Ramones wearing black leather jackets, and soon everybody else was wearing black leather jackets and trying to be as obnoxious as hell. I thought, well, what's the most dangerous thing? The military. So you dress these guys up and sing how they love war, doesn't this make it a little more exciting? And confusing?

The Sex Pistols did the most confusing job on everybody, no-one knew who the fuck they were, they just went with it, and The Ramones too. All these external things that meant more than music, except for 'Anarchy in the UK'. Shrapnel came later, anyway, and it was a reaction to English groups, which I hated by then.

Why was that?

They weren't fun, there was no sense of humour. Plus The Clash had gone political. Don't you guys ever learn, do you always have to go left? In the stupid fucking commie dribble. You went to concerts and you went to demonstrations . . . and the rhetoric, you go through ten years, and the whole thing of being politically correct – we weren't ever going to be politically correct, we were going to have fun.

Which is what kids are supposed to do, they aren't supposed to be politically correct. What does a twenty-one-year-old kid know about anything? Basically . . . the Sex Pistols probably had the best sense of humour of any of them, right?

So how did you start _Punk_?

John Holmstrom was going to do a magazine, which I thought was stupid. But he said, if we do a magazine we can go everywhere for free, we'll get drinks, people will take us out, and we use that as a stepping stone to other things. To tell the truth, I didn't know how we were going to fill it up. John had this definite attitude. He wanted to call it _Teenage News_, which I thought was really stupid.

Now Lester Bangs had used 'punk rock' before, but I didn't read _Creem_, so I didn't know. So I said to John, 'Why don't we call it _Punk_?' He said, 'Okay.' We were driving, and John said, 'I'll be the editor', and Jed Dunn said, 'I'll be the publisher', and they both looked at me and said, 'What are you going to be?' 'I'll be the resident punk.' It was all decided in about two seconds.

So why did you choose that name?

On TV, if you watched cop shows, *Kojak*, *Beretta*, when the cops finally catch the mass murderer, instead of saying, 'You fucking asshole, I'll kill you', they'd say, 'You dirty punk.' It was what your teachers would call you. It meant you were the lowest, that you'd never get anywhere. It also meant a complete failure.

Wasn't there a sense in the whole punk movement, a sense of failure built into it, so if you became successful, you hit a real problem?

Yes, but everyone wanted success. I don't think anyone in The Dictators graduated from high school, I don't think any of The Ramones did. All of us drop-outs and fuck-ups got together and started a movement. We'd been told all our lives that we'd never amount to anything, that we never lived up to our potential, lazy idiots and all the rest. We're the people who fell through the cracks of the educational system.

Was it true that Dee Dee Ramone had been a hustler?

Oh yeah. On 53rd and 3rd.

What part did Arturo play in The Ramones?

Arturo had a loft next to CBGB's, and everybody hung out there, it was another clubhouse. He's a gay Mexican, and an artist, he did Day-Glo swastikas. Very right-wing, pop minimalism. He was the only one with an apartment, that was more important than his art.

Did he give The Ramones ideas, shape them a little bit?

I think he did. I don't know in what ways, it's hard to say what influences you get from somebody. Definitely right-wing overtones, but he was more philosophical than political; it wasn't, let's go out and start a youth movement about fascism, or anything. It was more, look at these guys, isn't it stupid? Everything was more of a reaction. It was cause and effect, rather than heavy-duty people sitting around dreaming up this stuff.

125

CBGB's was a very small and localised scene . . .

First of all we were really young, and if you read too much into it, you realise that there isn't much here, so fuck that. Why over-analyse, why not just do it? It was more emotional. When you went out in a black leather jacket, it felt good. You had to buy the jacket, you had to make that initial investment, but you had the sneakers, you had the jeans. I still have two pairs of tight blue jeans, two pairs of sneakers and two black leather jackets.

Going to CBGB's, drinking on the Bowery and staying out, you felt like coming home. I remember going to Studio 54 with Deborah Harry and everyone in Blondie and being refused. People hated us. What better way to get attention in New York? We were the coolest of the cool, there was something about knowing you were the coolest people in the world at that time. Plus you could get laid every single night.

Were you aware that the scene was developing?

I think everybody knew that we were on to something, when we put out *Punk*; it was Holmstrom's graphics, I think, that brought it together. We folded all the first issues by hand. I took Mary's two-page Ramones spread to the band. On New Year's Eve The Ramones and The Heartbreakers played this horrible little loft, they didn't get paid, and I brought them that, and you know you look at something and it's so right?

So you became the resident celebrity?

Yeah, I just did interviews all day, I got drunk and had people take me out to dinner all the time. John said, 'What do you want?', and I said, 'Just keep me in beer and cigarettes', and he said, 'Okay.' John was a very fair guy. I don't think he was a punk.

Did you get into lots of fights?

Me? I'd go down with the first punch, every time, and stay down. When you get hit, go down, close your eyes and pretend. I didn't like fighting. I remember one night at CBGB's this guy coming in wanting to fight, and there was three of us, Joey Ramone, some girl and me, and Joey threw these bottles and they would explode in front of the guy, so he'd have to step back, and he did it till he was all the way out the door.

The Hell's Angels hung out there. What are you gonna do, fight with the Hell's Angels? There was a guy with a hook, like the cartoons, and no matter how drunk I was, I'd see this guy with the hook and sober up immediately. They were serious killers, they'd throw people off the roof. You couldn't compete with that kind of psychosis.

I think they kept everyone from fighting. They used to do real damage to people, not like two guys slugging it out. They were mostly trying to get chicks, and they didn't stay late. They were pretty well behaved, considering how things might have been.

What was nice about CBGB's was there was always someone you could talk to. Everyone was pretty intelligent, for being involved in the scene. There were the art guys, and the hipster poets, and the strippers, it was the best place to get a girlfriend. All the strippers hung out, like Nancy Spungen.

What was Nancy like then?

A neurotic crazy Jewish girl from the suburbs, another fuck-up. She lived on 23rd Street, and we didn't have a shower in the dump, so we used to go around there to take showers. She was okay, she was kind of sad.

Was there a lot of drugs on the scene then?

A lot of heroin, which I wasn't aware of then. I was pretty naive. Hard drugs and alcohol. People smoked joints like cigars. It was very macho, pot-smoking! It wasn't, 'Let's get mellow.' It wasn't an acid scene. Maybe people took Quaaludes, I don't know.

What did it mean, that the City of New York was going broke? Did the quality of life deteriorate fantastically?

Nothing worked. There were no options. Then there was the *Village Voice* you could work for, which is still the worst newspaper in the world. You were always looking for cigarettes and a quart of beer, and a burger. There was garbage everywhere. New York always looks dirty, so the physical manifestations were the same, but what it affected was the people. Everybody wanted to find the party that night, constantly. There was this network, fifty hardcore people on the scene, and it grew.

127

So what happened with *Punk*?

All the bands went out on tour, and the bands that came up weren't as good. For me it was very lonely. We didn't make a lot of money, and then the Sex Pistols came over and turned punk into vomit and violence, so they kind of destroyed us. No-one wanted to take ads in the magazine – you say *Punk* and suddenly people think, Sex Pistols. Which was Malcolm's brilliance, he made them the premier punk band.

You went on part of the Sex Pistols tour?

I was there at the end. I was hanging out with The Ramones in LA, so I watched them come across America; as they toured, I watched the kids skin their heads, in that week.

The audiences at the Ramones concerts changed during that week?

Yes. It was overnight. There were scene-makers that went out there and got things started, but since LA is a big suburb, it's hard to be centralised. There isn't a Bowery; you couldn't just get in a cab and go down to CBGB's. The kids there got it off the TV, Telly Savalas saying, 'And next the fabulous Sex Pistols' on some award show. It was every five minutes. It was so weird.

Were The Ramones good at that point?

They were great. It was *Rocket to Russia*, and it looked like they were going to take off too, but then along came the Sex Pistols and ruined The Ramones too.

How did they ruin things?

If you wore a black leather jacket after the Sex Pistols you were punk, and punks were these horrible people who threw up on aeroplanes. There's that great thing in John's article about Malcolm keeping the press away, cos they make it up better, which is brilliant. You can't blame the Sex Pistols for Malcolm doing his job, but it wasn't The Ramones' style, cos they were a lot smarter in a way. They had a mystique, and the Sex Pistols blew away that mystique.

Were The Ramones pissed off by this?

Oh yeah, they hated the Sex Pistols.

I was there at Winterland, their last show, it was the worst rock-'n'roll show I've ever seen. The sound was terrible, the place was too big, nobody was having any fun on that tour, everyone was completely miserable, I just didn't want to be around them. I went backstage and watched them. Sid was sitting there going, 'Who's going to fuck me tonight.' I was really jealous that they were paying attention to Sid, but of course they were rock stars.

Really beautiful teenage girls, black leathers, prime fucking condition, and Sid didn't look like he even knew how to undress them! 'Who's going to fuck me tonight?' And this girl's saying, 'Don't I even get a kiss first?' Then there was Paul and Steve, going, you know, 'Who's got the can opener?' Looking like they could have been working a gas station and been happy all their lives.

And Annie Leibovitz there to take a picture, with her assistant, wearing a black leather jacket. *Rolling Stone* does a punk story! It was so pathetic. She wanted a picture of the whole band and nobody would get up. That was real funny. They never seemed to drop it. The Ramones would do that for the press, then they would drop it and have a good time, but the Sex Pistols didn't seem to know who to trust. All Americans were all Americans, there was no distinction.

What was John doing?

They finally got him in the bathroom. 'Is my hair all right?' Being an obnoxious asshole. You felt like asking them if they wanted to split for a beer, but the Sex Pistols never dropped the pose. Can you imagine if you hung out with Jerry Lewis all the time and he acted that goofy all the time? You'd say, 'Fuck you, Jerry!'

I didn't wanna be around them, that's all I knew. They weren't having fun, I just wanted out of there. The only funny guy was Malcolm. I told him he should go try and get Nixon re-elected. He said, 'Who are you?' But they were so obnoxious, so British. It seemed like they were into class and stuff, and punk wasn't about the class system, they were being totally arrogant without humour.

Punk had got very fed up with the English scene anyway, hadn't you?

When things like 'White Riot' came out we thought, hey, these guys are on our side, cos we felt so alone. They seemed to get it, but as time went on, they weren't being funny so we realised that they didn't get it. What are you guys doing? Why don't you have some fun with this?

Mary Harron

Punk magazine contributor, interviewer of both The Ramones and the Sex Pistols. Canadian, had lived in both the UK and the US. Visited the UK in autumn 1976 and was perfectly positioned to see the differences between the London and New York punk scenes. Very observant and thoughtful.

When did you start living in New York?

It was autumn of '75. I'd left Oxford that summer and I'd gone back to Canada and really hated it there, so I went to New York to go to Michael Zilkha's birthday party, and I fell in love with it then, and in October I packed up my stuff and took the train to New York. They used to have these room-and-board jobs, the *Village Voice* would have a list of them, and I got a job with a film commune called Total Impact.

They were making this unbelievably trashy hippy picture called *Getting Together*. It was on 14th Street and 2nd Avenue, which turned out to be a good area to be in, the Lower East Side. I was the cook, and I thought all these people were assholes, but one day I met this kid who had arrived for lunch or something, and it was Legs McNeil. I thought he was the only smart, sane person I had met. He asked me what I was really, and I told him I wanted to be a writer, so he said a friend of mine's starting a magazine called *Punk*.

I'd never heard the word before. Normally if someone's starting a magazine it would sound like some dumb literary effort, but *Punk* struck me as completely brilliant. It was early, and it wasn't associated with music to me. The word wasn't new to me, but it meant being a snotty kid, a person who stands around being obnoxious. It wasn't literary, it was an attitude, which in this awful exploitative hippy environment was quite sympathetic.

131

When were you at Oxford?

'72 to '75. I was sort of interested in music but I was intimidated by people who knew about it. I was editor of *Isis*, and I thought that music was something that boys knew about, and that modern serious music was things like Grateful Dead – that's what my friends liked. I liked music in the sixties up until about '68. I had a very pop taste, and I was embarrassed by it. I liked Joni Mitchell, Judy Collins, but I didn't feel included in it at all.

I did read *Rolling Stone*, I'd come to New York partly because at university I was in love with the New Journalism, and I was obsessed with Andy Warhol, and I did like The Velvet Underground. That was one band I did know about. I wrote a big thing in *Isis*, which I'm now very embarrassed by, a disapproving thing about Warhol. I was a little liberal. But I spent a summer reading about him and getting very fascinated by him.

What was wrong with being a liberal?

I just meant that I disapproved of what I thought was exploitativeness, amorality in Warhol. But I realise now that what attracted me about punk was that amorality. My mother and stepfather were very high-art people, brought me up in a very righteous art background. What I was looking for in my own liberalism was amorality, the honesty of saying, I'm not interested in morals, I'm interested in the truth, or whatever. There was something in this amoral art that you couldn't get anywhere else.

I never liked hippies, I was always cynical.

Were you not touched by '68?

Oh yes I was, but after that I wasn't. Hippy detritus I didn't like. I liked Woodstock when I first saw it. But by '70 it had gone off. You got so sick of people being so nice, mouthing an enforced attitude of goodness and health and niceness. The punk thing was wonderful and liberating and new, was an idea of smoking sixty cigarettes a day and staying up all night on speed or whatever.

Presumably there was nothing of that sort going on when you left England in 1975?

Nothing. In Canada, my brother-in-law was involved in the rock business, so I had some connection there. He explained to me about Iggy Pop. Anyway, one night, Legs said he would introduce me to his friend John Holmstrom. This may even have been the first time I met him, maybe the second. Legs had said you must see The Ramones, I'll take you to CBGB's, and I didn't know what either of those things were.

So I was finishing the dishes one night and Legs came in with John Holmstrom, and said they were going to take me out. I'd only been in New York a few weeks and it was winter, and out we went. We walked to CBGB's and Roberta Bailey was on the door and she let us in, they'd made friends with her, and Lou Reed was in the club! Andy Warhol was in the club the next time I went. So the one person I had heard of was actually there in the club.

We watched The Ramones and I had no idea whether it was good or bad, whether I liked it or not, except that it was completely extraordinary, I'd never seen anything like it. I couldn't believe people were doing this. American punk was very funny. The dumb brattiness: 'Beat on the Brat with a Baseball Bat' – this at a time when it was, what? – King Crimson. It was comic.

Punk magazine was totally influenced by *Mad* magazine, that's important to remember. There was a real bratty cartoon element, and yet you're in a real place, you want to do something real, so you're in a situation where they could be genuinely delinquent. It had an edge to it. And they looked dumb-smart, smart-dumb. I didn't make the connection immediately, but obviously there was the Warhol look, the black leather and dark glasses.

How big was CBGB's?

Half the size of Dingwalls. There was a very strong connection between what Americans called glitter rock and punk. People tell these stories about the New York Dolls, who would still be legendary figures and they would go down there. There were these girls, Nancy Spungen among them, who had been friends of the Dolls, who dressed in trash style, they'd have net stockings with rips in them, thrift-shop. All these girls dressed that way, but at that point the only new style was black leather jackets and shades.

133

In the era where it was a real small scene, it wasn't stylish in any sense. I would go there in jeans and T-shirts, and I didn't look particularly hip. Most of us didn't. Lester Bangs once said that you would expect, from the lyrics of people like The Velvet Underground, super coolness, and what you found was a lot of unhappy lost lambs. It had this incredibly homey feeling. Every time I went for about two years, I would walk up 2nd Avenue, past these sleazy hotels, and my heart would race as I got to the door of this little world, it was wonderful.

Legs is an amazing person. I was this rather shy middle-class sort of girl, and Legs was great cos I could always talk to him, and he would explain it to me. Legs was the mascot of *Punk* magazine, and although he was a bit of a pain in the ass, he epitomised dumb-smartness. I think it's the same as in English punk.

That's why I loved Warhol – he freed me from my terrible nineteenth-century upbringing. It's about saying yes to the modern world. Let's talk about hippy detritus – it was about saying no to anything modern. Unless you lived in a commune or some pastoral idyll, you couldn't enjoy anything about the society you lived in. Punk, like Warhol, embraced everything that cultured people, and hippies, detested: plastic, junk food, B-movies, advertising, making money – although no-one ever did.

Apart from Talking Heads, who were preppies and never said they were into money, they were the only ones who did make money. They had good lawyers and got good deals, everyone else got fucked. Their ethos was to be commercial. Nice middle-class boys and girls like Talking Heads understood money but they never talked about it. They were smart.

Who did you see at CBGB's?

Everyone. The Heartbreakers, Richard Hell, I had a huge crush on him, he was so brilliant. Actually they were terrible but Richard was good. Television of course, and The Ramones were always good, and Talking Heads as a three-piece. John Cale would play a lot. Patti Smith wasn't playing CBGB's any more although the band were always there. Blondie I didn't go to see in the early days. Suicide were great, they played the most wonderful version of '96 Tears'.

You were saying that one of the most punk punk groups was The Dictators. Can you explain?

They were basically a heavy metal band and they only ever did one good album, the first. You had to see them live, cos Handsome Dick Manitoba was one of the funniest performers I've ever seen. They were a kick-ass rock'n'roll band. Some of the dialogue is on the record: 'I don't have to do this, I have a trust fund'. It was very deadpan. 'Sometimes I look at my audience and I think, has science gone too far?' That embracing of suburban culture, and there was a lot of bohemian disapproval.

Hippy culture had gone very mainstream and taken over, and for the first time there was a bohemia that embraced fast food and all the rest. There was a lot of suburban surrealism in the humour and the graphics. They were more fucked over by the class system in England. In America, before the English punk injected politics, and everyone had to pretend to be something, it was more bohemian. Hardcore CBGB's wasn't that young. I was twenty-three and I was among the younger ones. Richard Hell was twenty-seven, twenty-eight.

I know it was a joke, but calling your band The Dictators, or Shrapnel ... Lester wrote about it very well, the toying with Nazi imagery ...

I would have arguments with people about this stuff. Some of these road managers ... Arturo Vega had some really nasty ideas. But Joey Ramone was a nice guy, he was no savage right-winger. The Ramones were problematic, they did hover on the edge, it was hard to work out what their politics were, the same with Handsome Dick. Andy Shernoff, who was the brains behind The Dictators, had quite right-wing politics, and everyone else was more bohemian-liberal and leftist. I don't think they were more right-wing than bands are today, it was putting the needle into liberals and hippies. Hating hippies was a big thing.

Why was it necessary to needle liberals?

It was considered hippy. Now we can see that they had a lot in common. But it was needling the older generation. It had this difficult edge, but it was obviously not the most important thing about it. That wasn't the main thrust.

135

How different was the CBGB's scene from the New York Dolls scene? Was it very different from glitter?

I'll hazard a guess that the New York Dolls scene was a punkier version of the scene that Roxy Music were attracting in London. People were attracted to the style and attitude, but the Dolls were much raunchier and more teenage in their following. They would collect a crowd of girls, groupie types who would follow them anywhere. They used to play a lot at the Mercer Arts place, which burned down about a year or two before CBGB's started.

CBGB's had been going for at least a year before I went there. Even though I came into it reasonably early, in late '75, even then I felt that I'd missed a whole era, which was when Patti Smith used to play there. The other early groups were Television, Talking Heads formed the summer before I arrived. Blondie were very early, they were very on-the-scene people.

Was it less gay?

Yes. Wayne County was there, but he was a hangover from that, and Lou Reed used to be around, and he'd just been through his *Trans-former* episode, so there was a lot of ambiguity, a lot of shades. It was more like a little clubhouse.

I'd been going there for about six months, and the first time I went into Cinemabilia, which was where Richard Hell used to work, and which was run by Terry Ork, who managed Television, and I bought something and took it up to the counter and he looked at me and said, 'Oh, you're a CBGB-ite aren't you?', and it was so great, it felt like you belonged to this world which no-one else was interested in.

Though that's not entirely true, it had cult media interest – but no mainstream commercialism. When someone got a record contract, that was very big news. That was part of the crusade. But if someone had told me that punk rock would take over the world, I wouldn't have believed it. It was just an amazing thing happening in a basement, I didn't think it could last, it was living moment to moment.

So why did it take over the world?

I remember hearing about this group, the Sex Pistols, in the late spring of '76, when I was going over to London; John Holmstrom

136

mentioned to me that there was a punk group in England now. This seemed very entertaining to us, and a sign that someone would care to imitate your home scene. I do believe that it had a lot to do with McLaren coming over and managing the Dolls. I think it had a huge amount to do with Patti Smith, and people forget that. The impact she had, and The Ramones.

What separated punk from glitter was not attitude particularly. There was a sense in which the New York Dolls were the last decadent, overblown, bratty side of rock'n'roll stadium rock. They were the young side of what was going on then. They were wild and sloppy. But there was something about punk that was very rigorous, I think. It was very New York.

It had an art element in it, always, even though it wasn't being done by people who were necessarily arty. Tom Verlaine and Richard Hell should have credit for inventing an aesthetic that was really new, that picked up on French things, and also on fifties American things. He was a great fan of Samuel Fuller and his idea for Television, he had a vision of a band on stage playing in front of a bank of black and white TV sets. Can you imagine that in '73?

There was something very, very modern about it. It was much more to do with the Velvets, I think, than glitter had been. It was the Velvets without the humanism, the while thing was more nihilistic. I didn't know what nihilism was, though I was an educated person. It took a long time to realise that this attitude was called nihilism.

In what way was it nihilistic?

There's a great interview with Richard that Legs did in *Punk*. It captured the attitude – not that it was an attitude that I particularly shared, I didn't feel that I didn't believe in love or humanity on any level – but I wouldn't have found it so fascinating if it didn't say something genuine, and obviously it fulfilled a need. People needed to say something that negative, there was something liberating about that negativity. It was so hard and cold, and glitter was the end of something, and this was a search-and-destroy aesthetic.

What was the relationship with Warhol? Ubiquitous?

Warhol defined the notion of the New York underground, through

137

the Factory. He defined the notion of people identifying themselves as stars, and changing identity, and extremism, and heroin. Drugs.

I think you could say he refined it – it's in the difference between British pop art and Warhol. And before, in the early sixties, you had the English pop managers, turning people into creations, like the whole Larry Parnes syndrome.

That's classic showbiz manipulation, with a modern slant on it, but what Warhol did was pick up on things that actually happened in the drag world, about people transforming identities, creating themselves as imitation movie stars; so making yourself into a star, into a new identity, was very Warhol.

That element was very strong at CBGB's, all these kids would come in, you'd see this exotic-looking girl and find that she came from Idaho, and she'd obviously been the one freak in her town, and she'd come in and said, 'Mmm, this is nice.'

It was possible to do that in New York then, cos it was still cheap to live in. Was there a sense that New York was a decaying city?

Yes, and that was nice. I remember standing at windows, looking out over the Lower East Side, and feeling that the whole city was infested, and crumbling, but wonderful.

Punk seems to have created order out of chaos.

It created something hopeful and exciting. It was paradoxical; the attitude was that you were bored, but you weren't bored at all. It was fun to say you were, I don't know why. I never adopted the punk persona, I didn't feel very credible.

It also seems that CBGB's punk wasn't very mod. English punks took great care about their appearance.

No, it wasn't very fashion-conscious at that point. Its mod equivalent was the California garage bands of the sixties. Let us not forget some of the bands that never made it. The Marbles, The Shirts, Tuff Darts. Lots of humour about those terrible bands. I think Monday was audition night, and it would be empty.

138

Was there much speed there?

I did diet pills, but I was just a wholesome little girl really. I didn't do heroin. You should probably talk to someone who did heroin, cos if you did it, there was a whole social world that you didn't have any access to if you didn't do it.

That was part of the nihilism as well.

Yes. There was nihilism in the atmosphere. Longing to die. This sounds pretentious, but part of the feeling of living in New York at that time was this longing for oblivion, that you were about to disintegrate, go the way of the city. Yet that was something almost mystically wonderful . . .

When did you encounter punk in England?

I came to London in August. I'd really come just to see my family. I'd just missed the festival at the 100 Club. John Holmstrom asked me to get an interview with Brian Eno, so I rang up Island Records, and they said fine, but why don't you come and see the Hot Rods – so I did, and had this terrible experience where I was backstage interviewing them.

I was wearing a Punk T-shirt and ripped jeans and they all got very excited by this, cos they were ripped, and they just attacked me, and ripped my T-shirt off while I was trying to interview them, and all this was on my tape recorder, and the story was repeated in *Sounds* that I'd actually been raped by these guys, which was hardly likely with the A&R man from Island there.

This was at the Marquee. Obviously I beat them off, and I was rescued by their A&R man, Howard Thompson, but it was very frightening on one level because there was something that I'd never felt with New York punk, which was very asexual, I thought. The music wasn't at all sexy, nor was our social scene. There was this real hostility to women actually, real working-class male aggro.

In them more than in the Sex Pistols, presumably?

Oh yeah, much more. That was very shocking, I'd never felt such a violent expression of it. At that point the Hot Rods were good, and they were quite popular, I don't know what got into them. Anyway, there was violence in the air, you could tell it was a different world.

In the punk scene, or in England as a whole?

Both. There was violence in the streets. I'd come from a place where it was dangerous, and therefore in your club, you don't want aggression and violence. Your club was an absolute sanctuary and haven where there was friendliness. I think I remember two fights in CBGB's, one with some Hell's Angels who came in. It was very tranquil. That's also very heroin, rather than speed.

Then I went to the 100 Club, where The Damned were playing, and I caught this amazing reaction cos I was wearing a Punk T-shirt, and they were incredibly interested in me. I thought The Damned were so dreadful – some ludicrous, pre-gothic thing. Music to me was about being minimalist – fast stage act, driving rhythm – or Television's guitar thing. Black, ironic lyrics. It certainly wasn't some nineteen-year-old painted up as Dracula.

Backstage at the 100 Club, something was really different; I saw these little teenage girls with swastikas, and my reaction was, I must tell John and Legs, they're taking all this seriously. They really have something to answer for, I must tell them, this is being done for real. To us it was just a cartoon, and these people mean it.

You think they got that from punk? Remember people were thinking it all over the world, there was a rise in fascism in England at that time.

I think it got its kick-start from New York, though. It wasn't a big deal. Punk didn't do much of that. I don't think punk really used swastikas much. But I did feel a nightmare coming to life, it was quite exciting. It was overpowering and disturbing, cos the world I was in was an adult, bohemian art scene, with the rock'n'roll side to it.

I was at grammar school in England, not a public school, and I was aware that there was a lot of working-class violence, a violent society, and all the stuff that my relatively genteel school . . . I had been just on the other side of it, and all my life I'd avoided this, this was really coming home to roost. It was sure at that time, something had been given permission to show itself, it was exploding out.

I think the things that English punk was playing with were very dangerous, but you had to judge by its spirit. When I talked to people like Mark P or the Sex Pistols, this was basically good, and the fans were sweet.

When I went up to Liverpool, I'd gone to the shop to see Malcolm and ask if I could interview the Sex Pistols. He was rather epicene. I thought he was evil. You know that party line about Malcolm, that he was exploiting our wonderful kids? I'm afraid I followed that, I should have talked to him more, but I was freaked out by meeting him.

It was a very intimidating atmosphere in that shop.

I'd never been a style person, and I think it would have helped if I had been one. I didn't see it as fashion.

He was offhand, he said if I wanted to, sure. I could go and see them up at Eric's in Liverpool, so I did, and I had my purse stolen at the station, so I had no money and no ticket, so I ran through the barrier, and hid on the train, and managed to make it to Liverpool. It was a half-empty club, and them doing what I thought was an incredible show, although they said it wasn't, with a lot of people kind of sneering, and little clusters of fans in rubber trousers.

Now I'd heard all about the Bromley Contingent, and I thought one of these girls was Siouxsie, and I went up and asked if I could interview them, and it turned out they were all local hairdressers and art students, wearing rubber clothes. They were very sweet and charming, nice kids who wanted to be different. They told me all about the difficulties of wearing rubber clothes, and how uncomfortable it was, and obviously for them it was self-expression.

What was the difference between the Sex Pistols and the groups you saw in CBGB's?

There was something electrifying about the mythology that they had already brought with them. They were chaotic, which I liked, I thought they were very good, and they had this big guitar sound, Steve Jones was very good, and Glen Matlock. It was wild, whereas everything had been much more proficient in New York. Much more controlled. There was a sense of chaos, and the New York scene was not about chaos, it was anarchy, nihilism.

141

But the Sex Pistols created a sense of, 'What the fuck is happening?' John Lydon being really insulting to the audience, which I thought was really funny. Very obnoxious. I went backstage. It wasn't that difficult, they weren't that well known, and I brought all these kids with me who wanted to meet the Sex Pistols; I just thought, oh well, it's all supposed to be about the kids, they should meet the fans. They sat with me.

The band were very amused that I was coming to interview them, they were good-humouredly determined to give me a bad time, except for Lydon, who was very nice to me, I think because I was mature-ish, young, and nice to him. The thing is, I was a girl, and I didn't come on heavy. I didn't try to be rude.

It was a wonderful interview. I was very impressed. The single biggest thing that converted me to English punk was talking to John Lydon. Incredibly intelligent and honest and clear-sighted. It had politics. American punk had no politics.

Why was that?

I think because they'd come out of a period that was so politicised. What were their issues? The whole country couldn't decide what was happening next. They had a liberal-ish government – it was Ford, going into Carter. They'd had Watergate, but that was over. The best thing to do was to not have politics, to disengage. In England, rock had not had its own political issues, and also had been very middle-class, and that's when I realised.

What was the attitude when you got home, to English punk?

At first they were very excited to hear about it. I'd been sending my pieces on, and everyone was thrilled about that. I'd sent the Hot Rods piece and that had come out, and to have somebody rip your clothes off during an interview was considered a bit of a scoop. And when the Sex Pistols thing came out I was the local heroine. Then that autumn the *Village Voice* asked me to write the first big piece printed anywhere, I think, in America, about punk.

I had a huge row with the editor about it and withdrew it, because they wanted to rewrite it and hack it around. It didn't come out for another four or five months, because I wouldn't let them rewrite it. I felt they were trying to make me simplify it and sensationalise it. Eventually Bob Christgau read it and said it was wonderful, and he published it, hardly changing a word. He tacked something on the end of it, which I didn't like. But when that came out, more than anything else I've ever written, that had a huge impact.

Where did the anti-English thing come in with Legs and John?

Jealousy, I think. None of them ever understood the politics of English punk. They thought it was middle-class English kids whining and complaining that they didn't have jobs or a future. Legs and John were lower-middle-class, but they didn't understand English pop at all, they thought it was an inferior copy, that it was whining, that it was communist, and that somehow it was stealing the thunder from America – which of course it did.

When English punk took off, no-one was interested in American punk. It had an image, it had teeth, it was genuinely hostile. I remember feeling that my whole attitudes to life, my middle-class liberalism, were being ripped apart. It sounds fine to talk about it now, but I came back feeling shredded. I didn't know what I believed in any more, and that was why it was so good. American punk had no moral authority.

CHAPTER THREE

Sex Pistols

Sex Pistols in taxi, April 1976 (Ray Stevenson)
L–r: Glen Matlock, Paul Cook, Steve Jones, Johnny Rotten

The original Sex Pistols in their own words, beginning with Warwick Nightingale, the fledgling group's guitarist.

Warwick Nightingale

Co-founder and guitarist of the Sex Pistols, sacked in 1975. Better known as Wally. Grew up in the same area as Steve Jones and Paul Cook, the Wormholt Estate to the north-west of London's Shepherd's Bush, where he was interviewed in 1988. Infamous as the sacrificial victim; withdrawn, angry, troubled.

It could have been anybody. Paul was in my class at school, Christopher Wren. Steve was in the lower class. I was born in Blythe Road – strangely enough, the same road as Aleister Crowley. Steve wasn't wanted at home. He got on with his mum, but he didn't get on with his stepfather at all. So he was hardly ever at home, he was out thieving, or he was in remand, or he was staying at other people's places. He lived at Stephen Hayes', the bass player who didn't play bass. Paul lived at Carthew Road, Hammersmith.

Christopher Wren had quite a big catchment area, then?

Yeah, before it joined up with the girls' school, Hammersmith County, there were over a thousand kids in the school. Something like twelve hundred. And it was hard. But I got through the first and second years, and by the third year I'd got it sussed out and I'd stopped attending. During the fourth year I hardly went to school. I hardly knew Paul, and he was in the same class as me. Steve was in the lower class, and his idol was Rod Stewart.

We went to Biba's one night and walked out with the sound system; we just put it in bags and out. Steve was the leader in thieving. It was all front. Or would have been, until I introduced him to music. Cos I was the only one who could play. None of the others would have formed a group. Paul was heavily into an apprenticeship as an electrician. Steve was going to be a petty criminal, as simple as that. Stephen Hayes just ended up being a punk.

Did you steal the gear and then form a band, or did you decide to form a band and then go out to steal the gear?

I suggested a group, I had a guitar and an amplifier, a Les Paul copy. I was into music, and after I left school I started to hang around with them, cos I liked Steve. He was funny and he could do things. He would nick cars. Things happened around him, he would make them happen. He liked being the centre of attention. I thought Steve would be a good front man. Then Paul wanted to be the drummer.

What was their relationship like then? Paul just hung around with Steve?

Yeah, he was a sort of yes-man to Steve. He wouldn't do too many jobs with him. He was a sensible sort of fellow. But he's always been a good friend to Steve.

Did you go to gigs? Did you ever see the New York Dolls?

Yeah. Because Steve was there we could always find a way to get in for nothing. It didn't matter if we had to tear a door down. We went to Wembley, The Faces and the New York Dolls – to get in there, we had to virtually rip this door down. We got in, got right down to the front, then went backstage, drinking all their drink in the dressing room – Rod Stewart just standing there – doing all their champagne, having a great time. They didn't know who the fuck we were. They just let us get on with it.

Can you remember what the New York Dolls were like?

We weren't really paying attention to them. They were terrible. We were waiting for The Faces. The Dolls looked good, outrageous. But that wasn't the reason they'd gone to the gig. At that time we were hanging out down the King's Road, and we got our clothes from the same shops that they got their clothes – Alkasura, Granny Takes a Trip. Steve would nick stuff out of the place, cos he wanted to wear the same clothes as Rod Stewart was wearing in The Faces. I don't know how he found out about these places.

But then we started getting in with all the people. There was a guy called Tommy Roberts, he had a shop called City Lights. We turned him over, we took every single bit of clothing that he had in that shop, shoes and everything, and brought it round here. This was where David Bowie and Bryan Ferry had their suits made. And we used to dress in all the clothes, and go down the King's Road in a stolen Jag, to the Drug Store, or The Bird's Nest or The Roebuck.

There was quite a lot of drugs around?

Oh yeah. We took mandies, but because we didn't live in the area we weren't into the coke scene. Then we used to go into Malcolm's shop, Too Fast to Live, Too Young to Die. He was selling leather gear, biker gear, studs. All the James Dean kind of thing. I bought that leather jacket you've seen in those pictures. I had money then, I was working with my dad.

What was the shop like?

Fifties furniture, T-shirts, it was different from all the other shops. It was Vivienne's shop, it wasn't Malcolm's. But we got talking to Malcolm, told him about the group. He thought it was strange. We told him what we did to Tommy and he couldn't believe it. All we were into was drink and taking mandies. We'd send Steve out to nick a motor when we wanted to go down the King's Road.

Did he ever get nicked for doing that?

Yeah, I did too, the day after we did the David Bowie job. We took the whole PA, every single one of their microphones. RCA were recording it too, so they were Neumann microphones, about £500 apiece. There was a security guard up in the sixth row, asleep, and we walked on the stage with a pair of pliers, snipping the wires. We nicked all Mick Ronson's gear. Prior to that, Steve had gone out and nicked a minivan to cart the stuff away in. Paul didn't want to go, so me and Steve did it.

So you'd decided to form this band and Steve went out to nick all the equipment?

Yeah. He was the main man for nicking the gear. The first guitar he got was an SG, then a Les Paul custom. I think he walked out of a restaurant with that one. Another time they nicked Ronnie Lane's briefcase. There was a hotel called the Warwick and we used to do the rooms, we got some really nice camera equipment. Professional gear.

So did the band come together when you'd got all the instruments?

Paul started to buy a set of drums. We were buying gear as well, trying to save money. It wasn't that fast, this was over quite a long period of time. We all got nicked one night trying to unload a vanload of gear into another van. We all got done for that. I can't remember what happened. We were all in the back of the van and the Old Bill came along and that was it. Bang to rights. I think I got a suspended sentence.

I don't remember ever going for drum gear. It was always guitars, amplifiers, microphones. We had an H&H six-channel PA, which we slaved up. I was using some strange amp, but it sounded good, with a 4x12. I'd bought an Ampeg 4x12, which they kept. We had about seven guitars. All top-notch gear, all the microphones from the Bowie gig.

Where did you rehearse first?

Beneath the Furniture Cave, King's Road. Right down the very end.

What songs did you play?

'It's All Over Now', 'Twisting the Night Away'. Small Faces stuff, 'All Or Nothing'. 'Sha La La Lee'. I remember Steve bringing round the first Queen album, and the Thin Lizzy song, 'The Rocker'.

Steve was singing?

Well, we couldn't really tell, because instead of pointing the monitors in, we pointed them out. For effect, as though we were doing a gig. We could hear the music okay, but we couldn't hear Steve enough to know that he wasn't a good enough singer. He really wanted to be like Rod Stewart, but there was something holding him back. He could play drums better than Paul at that time. He's naturally talented, rhythm. He had a lovely touch on the drums.

So it was you, Paul, Steve . . .

Jimmy Machin tried to play organ. Until we met Glen, it was Del Noones on bass. There was a guy trying to build up a recording studio in Lots Road but he didn't have the money, so we hired it for rehearsals after the Furniture Cave. That was when it started to get more serious.

How did Glen come in?

He started working at Malcolm's shop, and Malcolm put him on to us. He came up and auditioned here. He could play this riff from The Faces and we thought it was amazing, and that was it, he was in the group.

How did you get on with him? Wasn't he different?

He was grammar-school educated. He came from Greenford. He was art school. He wasn't posh, but he hadn't been around too much. He was the first one to get a car, pass his test and everything. He was different, he got his gear together; he wanted a Fender Bassman, and we nicked a Fender bass, a Precision, and we rubbed it down to the wood, and he got that. He bought the cab, and he eventually bought the Bassman top. Then we got down to rehearsals. That went on for a couple of years, the rehearsals.

Could you not find gigs?

We were just trying to get better. Don't forget they couldn't play. I was the only one who could play, and I was teaching them. Glen could play, but Steve couldn't play a note. I was trying to get them serious about it.

When did you get to play a gig?

We never really did, just a party. I've been told it was in a café, but all I remember is there were these kids we knew who were into taking cocaine, who had some nice little birds with them. They lived in Chelsea and their parents had a lot of money and were very hip, didn't mind them smoking dope and things like that. So that's the place I remember.

What did you play?

Probably three numbers: 'Scarface', 'Twisting the Night Away' and 'Can't Get Enough of Your Love', that's right.

Was Malcolm there?

No. Not the one I did, anyway. If there was another one, in a café, without me there, maybe he was at that. But he was popping up, and Bernie Rhodes was turning up.

So they were interested in you?

Yeah, but they weren't letting us know, they were playing it very, very cool. Malcolm is sharp. I admire the guy for how sharp he was, he was waiting for something he could exploit. It had the right story about it. He liked things like that, the fact that we nicked all the gear and the clothes, he thought it was funny, interesting. Then we started to get a group together and Malcolm went off to manage the New York Dolls for a while. He came back with a guitar, the white Les Paul, and then he got more interested.

Malcolm thought I was strange, I don't know why, but he said that one day: 'You're very strange.' He looks at things in a different way than other people do. I was too young to know what he was up to, and I think he knew I was going to be an obstacle. I didn't have as much style, I didn't bother about clothes the way they did. Style and attitude, I could have put myself across a lot better, but I didn't know that someone was going to take the group away from me.

Did the group have a name?

The first name was The Strand, after the Roxy Music song, then the Swankers, which was a joke. QT and the Sex Pistols was the original name that Malcolm came up with, and they didn't like it. I remember being round at Paul's, and Steve and Paul were saying about this name, which I liked and they didn't, funnily enough.

Was the shop called SEX then?

Yeah. I helped Malcolm make that PVC sign. There was a rubber bed in the shop, and he used to get this pervert coming in on a bike, used to buy the long women's lace-up boots with the heels. He used to have all the leather and bondage stuff. It got really heavy. There was a gay boy who worked there with Jordan, and I remember him showing a blue film with men, and I thought, ooh, how strange. That was in the shop. Not on public view, on a little editing machine, up against the wall or something.

The cheek of it was, after they'd got rid of me, Malcolm rang me up and asked me if they could still use the studio. I said, 'You've got to be fucking joking.'

Did he pay you for doing the sign?

Course not. They're a type, both of them. Malcolm and Bernie, it was like they never had money. I spent more money than they did.

When you were rehearsing, you were starting to write songs?

The first song was 'Scarface', which me and my dad wrote, and 'Did You No Wrong'. Those were the first two. Paul wrote the rough words to it, and I did the riff. Steve changed it slightly, one tiny section. They never did 'Scarface' after I left. It had a story written into the song, so it was too standard for what Malcolm wanted.

How were you thrown out?

I went to rehearse as normal. Me and Steve used to fall out by that time, he was playing guitar behind my back. He'd moved back home and nicked another Les Paul, a black one, and a Fender amplifier. I wasn't keen on the idea cos I wanted him to be the star, the front man. I was too naive to think that he wanted to take my position in the group, so I wasn't thinking along those lines at all.

I don't know what period of time it took them to decide that I was leaving and Steve was taking over on guitar. Malcolm realised he wasn't right as a singer. Why it happened I don't know. The things they said about me in the papers, they really slagged me off, I couldn't work it out. It was either pure guilt or envy, or something. It must have been something that turned them against me, cos I wasn't aware of it, and neither was Glen. Glen stuck up for me. I don't think even he knew about it.

It was a normal rehearsal at Riverside, and Malcolm was there, and they just said, 'You're not in the group any more.' That was Steve, and Malcolm backing him up. It was very hard. I didn't say anything, I was virtually in tears. Didn't cry, but I was so gutted that I didn't say anything. I even went for a drink with them that evening.

As far as they were concerned, it was no reaction.

It must have been Malcolm, that's all I could think, I didn't fit into his plans. He could walk all over me, he had a business, contacts. During those six months before that, they sussed that you could earn money at this, they could actually do it, which I knew from the word go. Afterwards I was so disgusted, they wanted to pick up the equipment, and I just gave them the keys, I didn't even go along.

Steve Jones

Sex Pistols' co-founder, writer and guitar hero. The group's secret heart, he was the main instigator of the Bill Grundy scandal and originated the phrase 'never mind the bollocks'. Interviewed at the office of his American manager in the Valley, outside Los Angeles, he seemed ill at ease. I thought he'd given me very little, but everything he said was completely to the point.

I was brought up on Goldhawk Road; down near there, Benbow Road. It seems so weird thinking of that now. Little streets, West Indian people and Irish people. Wild.

Were you a mod?

A skinhead, definitely a skinhead. Used to go to football matches and cause trouble. Never watched the game. Go on the rampage afterwards, down Shepherd's Bush market. I used to go to QPR, Chelsea, Fulham, any of them clubs, I didn't really support anybody.

Did you live with your parents?

I left them when I was fifteen or sixteen, and lived with Hayesy for a while, and round Paul's house for a while. Until the Pistols started, then I got my own place. But we moved over to Battersea when I was with my parents, and we lived there for a few years. I still kept going to the same school, Christopher Wren, in White City.

When I started going down to the shop with my friends, Jim Machin and Stephen Hayes, it was Let It Rock. I used to like it. There was the other shops, Granny and Alkasura, there was a couple of them where all the rock'n'rollers used to go, and Malcolm's was cool cos you could hang out in there, with the jukebox and the sofa and stuff, we just used to sit in there and watch people come in.

After a while I used to hang out with Malcolm, he used to go down to the Speakeasy. I used to go down there on a Friday night and wait for him to go down there, cos I couldn't get in, I was only seventeen or eighteen or so. I started driving him around to all these little tailors down the East End, cos he couldn't drive. I'd drive Viv's mini, getting all the materials.

How did the band start?

I knew Wally from school and he could play guitar a bit, and we'd go round his house, and we had the idea of the band. There was Wally on guitar, Paul playing drums, I was singing and Matlock was playing bass. I met him through the shop really, he used to work there Saturdays. I never really got on with Glen that much. I found him a bit poncified, he weren't one of the lads. He'd have liked to have been, cos I was a total fucking hooligan.

But he could play, he liked The Faces, we all liked The Faces at the time. Wally's dad was under contract to do this Riverside place up, and it used to be the BBC, and there was a studio in there, and we used that room to rehearse in.

What about the name QT Jones?

That was Malcolm's idea, when I was a singer. It's on the T-shirt with people he likes and people he doesn't like. The name's actually on there: 'QT Jones and the Sex Pistols'.

Did you play with either Wally or Lydon as the Swankers on the King's Road?

Yeah, with Wally, I was singing. Salter's Café, next to The Bird's Nest, opposite the fire station. It was a nightmare, I can't remember much about it.

Is it true that Malcolm helped you get out of Ashford at one stage?

Yeah, I was going back to court to be sentenced, and he did a big rap, a famous spiel, to the judge, and I got off. I don't know if it helped, what he said – about how he's got a career ahead of him and all sorts. That was for nicking, I'm sure.

All the equipment was stolen, of course, by me. Then Malcolm started to come down. He wasn't managing us or anything, he just wanted to get involved. He said, 'You've got to get rid of Wally' and I said, 'Well look . . . ' He said, 'You should play guitar', then we started auditioning singers at the same time. From the shop. We had a few idiots come in, and then Rotten came in, who I didn't really like at all, cos of his attitude, he seemed like a real prick.

How did you learn guitar, were you helped?

I just picked it up. I was living down at Denmark Street, I lived above there by myself for a long time, and I just used to take black bombers and play along to records, for hours on end. Iggy Pop's *Raw Power* and the New York Dolls. My fingers would be down to the bone. I picked it up real quick. I was using that white Les Paul that Malcolm got off Sylvain Sylvain, come back from managing the Dolls, he brought it back with him.

Who wrote those early songs?

Basically me and Glen who wrote the tunes, and we'd do some of them together. 'Anarchy' we collaborated, Glen wrote 'Pretty Vacant', 'Bodies' I wrote, 'Holidays in the Sun' I wrote, 'Seventeen' I wrote. 'God Save the Queen' was basically Glen's riff . . .

Wasn't there a point before you played your gig where Paul wanted to leave?

Yeah, he still had his job at Watneys, as an electrician, and he'd just passed his apprenticeship, and that was as far as his eye could see. I used to have to go down to his work and go, 'Come on, man, this is going to be great.' He says, 'No, nobody can play', which was true, he could hardly play himself. 'We'll get another guitarist or something.'

We had all these auditions for another guitarist, and he came down and sat in. They were all wankers who came down, and by that time we didn't need another guitar player, and I think he finally realised that. It was hilarious, these tossers would come down with all this gear, all these foot pedals and what have you.

Had you seen Rotten in the shop before?

Once or twice. He looked really interesting, there was something about him that magnetised you to him. He had all the punk stuff on,

157

that was nothing to do with McLaren, he had all the safety pins and everything, he had the I Hate Pink Floyd T-shirt and his hair was orange or green. He was wild-looking. His brothers were boot boys. So he came down and we tried him out. We did a couple of cover songs. 'I'm Eighteen'. He wanted to do it.

Was the story true about him miming in front of the jukebox?

Yeah. He wouldn't do it, he just fucked about in front of it. I started playing guitar, and three months later we did our first gig at St Martins College.

What was that first gig like?

It was fucking wild. I was so nervous I took a Mandrax. It was packed, it seemed like millions of people at the time, with Bazooka Joe, and when we started playing, the Mandrax was hitting me and I cranked the amp up. It was a 100 watt amp in a little room with no stage, and it was great. Everyone was looking at us, you could tell there was a buzz. Then they pulled the plug on us after about five songs, but the next gig, all that crowd was there again.

Can you remember the Logan party?

Yeah, that was pretty wild. I think that's actually on film. The Nashville was a good gig, and the couple we did after that were good as well. There was a gig where we opened up for that band Roogalator, that was a good one.

What about the Grundy thing, Steve? Were you pissed when you went in?

I was fucking paralytic. They put us in this hospitality room with this fridge with six bottles of wine in there. I downed at least two, I know that. And he was drunk out of his mind too, Grundy.

Were you wound up before you went in?

I wasn't wound up to give him a hard time, no-one was going to do that, but he started coaxing us out, so when drunk, the obvious thing to do is to have a go, you know? That was hilarious. It was one of the best feelings, the next day, when you saw the paper. You thought, fucking hell, this is great. We came out of Denmark Street and there's all these guys there from the daily papers, following us down Oxford Street to Dryden Chambers.

From that day on it was different, before that it was just music, and the next day it was the media.

It seems that you played your best gigs before Grundy.

Yeah, after that musically it became a nightmare.

What happened on the day of the A&M signing?

That was insane. I fucked a girl who worked at A&M, in the toilets. I was drunk out of my mind. We'd been up at about seven in the morning, doing the signing, then down to this press conference. By ten o'clock we were all pissed, and we had a fight in the limo. We was all getting stroppy with one another. Nuts.

Then you did some trips, to Berlin, Jersey . . .

We got banned from Jersey, they wouldn't let us in there, cos of the reputation. They wouldn't let us out of the airport. They called up the hotel and told them not to book us. We got out of there to a bar somewhere, then came back again. In Berlin we just went there for a week after Sid had that fight with Bob Harris down the Speakeasy, and no-one wanted to know us. It was fucking boring. Sid and Boogie [John Tiberi] had a car crash, they went into another car. It was boring, that time, the image took over.

You always got on with Paul better than the others?

Yeah, well me and Paul grew up together. Sid was all right, he was a laugh. He didn't care about anything. John was the only one you used to resent, he was a bit stupid sometimes. He'd let his trip go a bit too far, he'd do it with us, the band.

What did you think about the boat trip?

It was a stunt, that's all really. All I was interested in was getting my dick sucked and getting drunk. If we'd done a good gig and there was plenty of birds around I knew there was no problem. Or before the gig . . . I was just a sex fiend.

159

Did you have a good time on the SPOTS tour?

Yeah, that was real good, there was a lot of fans, queuing up around the block, and they went nuts when we played. It was like how it should have been, a band playing to an audience which dug you. Before all that we were playing good, but it was all these Northerners who didn't know what the fuck we was. There was a lot of trouble. But this was playing to people who wanted to come and see us.

What was Sweden like?

That was a laugh, it was just that everything closed at ten o'clock. Gorgeous crumpet though, knew everything. Not like English birds, all fat and sweaty, these were dolls, little blonde beauties.

They had this gang out there called the Raggare, this biker gang, a real pain in the arse. They used to beat up all the punters when they came out of the gigs. Idiots.

What about the last English tour you did?

We did two gigs in Huddersfield, one for the kids and one proper one. That's when Boogie was doing a porno movie of Sid, with Nancy sucking his knob, and he couldn't get his dick up for about an hour. But it was a good gig. It was good for the kids cos we were throwing pies around and stuff . . . but that bird Nancy was a pain in the arse, she had a weird vibe about her.

Why did the band split in San Francisco, Steve?

John wanted to carry on, he was saying, 'Let's get rid of McLaren.' I was sick of the band, I was saying, 'I'm gonna piss off with McLaren, I'm going to Brazil and do something with Biggsy', just to get away from that scene, I was sick and tired of it. My mind was made up, and Paul just followed. The American tour was what really done it, if anything. We weren't talking to one another, there was a lot of needling going on between the band. It was horrible. It used to be a laugh.

When we got back from Rio we were still poncing about making the movie . . . it was still going on and we were still getting dough, a little bit. But I was a miserable sod. All the excitement of the early Pistols, until we split up, and there was this big hole, and I just felt terrible, and smack just filled that hole.

Paul Cook

Sex Pistols co-founder, writer and drummer. Childhood friend of Steve Jones. The group's musical engine and heartbeat. Initially reserved, if not suspicious, he assented to two separate interviews in 1988. His clear memories were tinged with disbelief at the mania that the group underwent.

Where were you brought up?

Shepherd's Bush and Hammersmith. West London. The school I went to was called Christopher Wren.

What was it like growing up around there?

It was fun actually. Up to all sorts of mischief. There was so much to do, you had the whole of London to explore.

When did you first meet Steve?

Steve lived just round the corner from me. We went to the same school, but I knew him from before then. Steve lived in Benbow Road, I lived in Carthew Road, what's now called Brackenbury Village, a very desirable area. Just off Goldhawk Road. The whole area has totally changed. We went to different primary schools, but his mum sort of knew my mum.

He was always stealing bikes and stuff. One of my earliest memories was down in his basement, he was fiddling with these bikes he'd stolen, changing all the bits and pieces around on them.

I suppose even round where you were in Hammersmith was quite different from the White City estate?

Yeah, it was a lot rougher up there I suppose. We used to hang around a lot up there though, a lot of school friends lived around there. If there was a club going we'd go down there.

Was there much music around there?

It was all reggae at the time. Bluebeat and all that. Motown. I was never into rock music at that time.

When did the first idea of playing together come up?

A certain crowd of us was always into music and fashions, and that's how we got to be friends. Toniks, skinhead stuff. There was a guy called Wally, he was into playing guitar, and he lived round the corner from the school, and at fifteen or sixteen we were always round his house, and we slowly got into it that way. Steve was an expert thief, used to go round stealing a lot of the stuff.

Those stories about taking the mikes off Bowie at Hammersmith and all that were true?

All of them, yeah. It gave us somewhere to channel our energies, we knew what we wanted, you know? We knew we wanted a band, and there was no way we could afford to buy it so we stole it. Once we'd got all the equipment together, we'd rehearse every night at this derelict warehouse place down on the river.

Didn't Steve get Keith Richards' coat?

No, Ronnie Wood's. Steve found out where he lived, at The Wick. We used to go round there and get out of it, and one time Steve nicked some stuff.

Were there any other people who started groups, or were you the only people doing it?

We were the only ones. There were no bands about really. There was the pub rock scene, Ducks Deluxe and Dr Feelgood at the time, that was the only thing about which was local and you could go and see. There were always bands on at Hammersmith Odeon, so we'd always be drawn towards there in the afternoons.

Didn't you see the Dolls?

At Wembley supporting The Faces. They were the first band I liked, I suppose, cos they were so funny on *The Old Grey Whistle Test*. They were just anti-everything, lurching about, falling into each other on their platform boots. Really stupid, they weren't taking it too seriously, which was what I liked about them. We never imagined we'd end up doing it seriously, it just happened. It was a good thing to do.

Was there anybody else in the band? There was you and Wally and Steve.

There were other people who used to hang around but they just didn't fancy it at the death, you know?

When did you start going down to the shop?

Steve moved to Battersea, so he was always hanging around the King's Road, and we just felt drawn towards the shop, it was different to all the others down there. It was Let It Rock at the time. Those were the clothes we were into at the time, ted-ish. Flash. We got involved with Malcolm, though he didn't want to know at first, we told him we were in a band. He was involved with the Dolls at the time.

We kept pestering him. Steve wouldn't be working, you see, so he'd go in there quite a lot. I was working in a brewery in Mortlake, Watneys. Electrician apprenticeship. That was a drag, but I had to work, I suppose, to get some money. I stopped just before we signed with EMI.

Malcolm was sort of half-interested, cos he was getting into the music side of things as well as the fashion. By this time we had a rehearsal place down the King's Road somewhere, round the back there near Lots Road. Malcolm gradually got more involved. It was me, Wally, Steve and Glen by that stage, cos Glen was working at the shop.

We got rid of Wally, he wasn't right. It was hard to explain his attitude really. We were all having fun, and he was one of these don't-touch-my-guitar merchants, you know? We wanted to get rid of him. Malcolm did instigate it a bit, but we didn't need very much persuading.

Wasn't Steve originally going to be the singer?

He used to piddle about on guitar as well, but when he switched to guitar, it seemed totally natural, and then there was the search for a singer, which I'm sure you know all about.

Well, not in detail. But before that, when you started playing drums, were you just trying to play really simply?

I used to have a kit in my mum and dad's bedroom, drive all the neighbours wild, coming home from work and practising. Then we got the rehearsal place.

Was there anyone you modelled yourself on, or stuff that you liked that you wanted to play like?

Not really, I never had any drum heroes as such. I liked Roxy Music at the time, and I would always listen to what they were doing. Yeah, Paul Thompson wasn't fussy, but he'd try different things, you know. The whole band did, I suppose, and that's what made them stand out from the crowd.

Didn't you have a keyboard player at one point?

We did try out a few people, we had an idea about having a keyboard player, but we soon dropped that. That was when Malcolm really got involved, and helped sort us out really.

Were his suggestions good? Did he know what he was doing?

No! Nobody did really, it just all fell into place. It was just one of those things. John walked into the shop and he was perfect, you know . . . Glen was working in the shop and he was looking out for people. John came down one night and met us in The Roebuck, which was then like a throwback to the sixties, all those long-haired types . . .

What was John like at that meeting?

He was all right, he obviously wanted to get involved in doing something. I think he was quite thrilled that people were getting something together, and he wanted to be involved in it.

I'm sure he hid it a bit!

Oh yeah. I remember saying to him at the time how nothing was happening in music and how the whole youth movement needed something to get them going again. That was my view, cos after the skinheads, teds and mods, everything had been in a lull since about 1970, and this was 1975. Five years had passed.

164

Did he do the miming to 'I'm Eighteen'? Was that story true?

Yeah, that was really funny. Thought yeah, let's go for it. He was screaming away, jacket hanging off him, arms all over the place. It was quite a sight to see.

Hadn't you worked with Nick Kent?

He came down a couple of times. There's this fallacy that he was actually in the band somewhere along the way, that's rubbish. I suppose Malcolm brought him down to get in with him. Another way in the door, if you like, fancied himself as a bit of a guitarist, used to strum along a bit. Steve used to go round his house while he was learning the guitar, but there's no way he was ever in the band.

We did try a singer out, a bloke called Dave, just before John. A rocker, a really good-looking guy, with fair hair. But he was more of a model, you know what I mean? One of those types, and straight after that we got John, so there it was.

Can you remember when you got John?

It was in the summer, it was very hot. After that, things really moved, cos we were playing by November, so it must have been about July or August. We started rehearsing straight away.

Did you ever play a gig with Wally?

We played in this flat in King's Road once. These kids we knew, Chelsea kids, had a party one night and all the instruments were up there so we got up there, did a couple of numbers. It was quite funny.

How did the band get on in the early days?

I think there was a bit of a thing between John and Glen from the first, I don't know why that was. They both went to art college, maybe there was a rivalry there. But they used to hang around together at first, Glen would stay round his house, got to know each other, maybe that's when they fell out.

Didn't you try a second guitar player as well at one point?

Yeah. Steve New. We realised we didn't really need it, in the end. We were still learning, we couldn't really play.

165

Wasn't there a point there where you were going to jack it in?

I was, yeah. I thought Malcolm was bullshitting all the time, he'd say these things would happen all the time, and they never did. I suppose we thought we weren't good enough, and that was why we were going to get another guitarist. But really we were still learning, it was running before we could walk.

What were the early rehearsals like? Chaotic?

Yeah. We used to rehearse a lot though, every night straight from work to the West End, once we got the studio in Denmark Street. I think we realised we had to move fast, cos there was an undercurrent of all these people coming up, who were going to start bands. You could feel something was going to happen.

When we advertised for a guitarist Mick Jones turned up, just to see what was going on. There were other bands like that coming up, The Hammersmith Gorillas, the Count Bishops. They were mainly pub rock, and we didn't want to get into that really, but something was bubbling.

Who came up with the name, Paul?

Malcolm. It was totally Malcolm's idea. It was all to do with his fantasies about sex and violence. He's such a poser, Malcolm, he was into all that, whips and chains, the whole bloody lot. At the time, though, Malcolm was like another member of the band, he got off on hanging around younger people, feeding off the energy and that. Definitely. And causing a bit of mayhem along the way.

It sounds like in the early days everyone was really into it.

It was an experience for us. We started getting recognition instantly, you know? So we thought we must be doing something right.

What were the early songs you did? 'Did You No Wrong'?

Those were the songs that we did already, a few cover versions. People thought we did it cos we were into the songs, but we just didn't have our own numbers. A number called 'Through My Eyes'. 'Psychotic Reaction', we used to do that. 'No Feelings' was early.

Do you think Malcolm taught you a lot in that initial stage?

Not really, we were all pretty much our own men. We weren't his puppets, as everyone believed. He was like another member, he'd throw ideas in. Malcolm was a good guiding figure, though, obviously; when all the publicity started coming in, he knew how to manipulate all that.

John said Malcolm worked very hard in the first year, always on the phone and everything.

Once he knew something was happening Malcolm was totally into the band. That was when he started taking it away, he started thinking the whole thing was his. I could see that then. That was to feed his own ego, I think. It obsessed him in the end, that story, the film, he started to believe that was the way it was.

St Martins was the first gig, wasn't it?

Yeah. We carried the equipment across from Denmark Street, cos it was just over the road. It must have been a terrible racket, someone pulled the plug on us, there was a big fight and we left.

What were the college gigs like?

It wasn't very exciting, cos there'd be all these hippy bands on, and I don't know how Malcolm worked it, but we'd just turn up and there'd be a few people standing around watching. But it was all good practice for us. It was Malcolm's idea to do as many gigs as possible. You've got to practise, haven't you?

For Glen and you it was fairly simple, but what were John and Steve like at that stage?

They were pretty much on their own really. Everyone knew to stay together cos we were all pretty nervous. John was pretty stiff, but he'd have the verbals, if there was any barracking and that. We did loads of gigs around that time, I can't remember what they all are. When we'd do colleges, we turned up supporting somebody, East London somewhere, around Christmas. By then John handled himself so well on stage. He had everyone in stitches.

167

Can you remember which band you were supporting on that New Year's Eve gig?

They were one of the bands that were doing the circuit at the time, a joke band, I forget their name. We supported Shabby Tiger once, do you remember that band? Ho ho. I think they were a sort of Scandinavian rock band, they all had long hair and leopard-skin leotards, bleached hair . . .

Did you get better really quickly?

Yeah, improved really well. We found we had natural ability for some reason, which we found when we started doing records; playing back the tapes we thought, yeah, sounds great.

The Dave Goodman ones you did in July were really good. The Spedding ones aren't very good.

No, they were the first ones we did. Kept time all right though! They were just to see how we sounded.

So when did you start getting press? It was in February, wasn't it? The first one was Neil Spencer at the Marquee.

There was a little thing before that about a college gig in Chelsea. Georgie Fame, it was a massive do. We bumped into Kate Phillips and she put a little bit in the *NME*.

Didn't you have a big fight on stage?

That was at the Nashville. That's when all the publicity got hold of it, and the violence started creeping in. I don't know what caused that. I think everyone was just ready to go, and we were the catalyst. People just wanted to go mad, but we didn't instigate it.

How did it feel sitting behind the drums with all this going on?

I couldn't even get out and duck out the way, I was the mug at the back. The others could dance about all over the stage, run away, but not me.

Did Malcolm ask you to wear the clothes, or did he give you clothes to wear?

We'd always gone in there, to steal stuff or to buy it, and we carried on doing that. We had a few arguments about the clothes early on, but I don't think they ever told us to wear anything. In Let It Rock we didn't go for the classic stuff, the drapecoats or anything, we went for the more modern things, the zip-up baggy cardigans. The fashions then were so bad. It was still seventies flares and all that.

The early look of the band was really good.

Even when the punk thing started, the crowd that would come to see us were like normal working-class kids. They didn't dress up in all the gear. Maybe they wore a ripped jacket, normal V-neck jumpers, whack the hair up a bit . . .

You started getting the posers as well quite early didn't you?

Oh yeah, we always had those, the fashion lot trying to get in on it. We didn't mind. That's what was good about playing that Logan thing, it got us into that sort of crowd as well.

When did you start playing out of London?

Straight away. We'd travel out to Bromley, that's when Siouxsie and all that lot got involved, which they've never lived down ever since. Supporting all these horrible bands, but we made a lot of friends along the way. People were latching on to us.

We knew we'd started something, but it's like anything with the press; once they get hold of something, and it's news, and people want to hear it, they go mad on it. We thought it was funny, we milked it for all it was worth. If they wanted a story, we gave them one. They wanted something to write about, we'd give them something to write about. Whatever it was. Like after the Grundy thing, which sold papers, and the kids latched on to it; that was it, every story went. It fell right into our hands.

I've been told by several people that on the evening of the Grundy show, Malcolm wasn't in control as he says he was, he was actually quite freaked out.

He was, yeah, I remember that. And the next day. I've never seen him panic so much. The whole thing had blown up, and that was it, press banging on the door. We were rehearsing that day in Harlesden, we went from rehearsal to the studio and went out after the interview with Grundy, Malcolm got us into the car and off. We just went home, and woke up in the morning . . . there's all these press banging on the door.

We were still half asleep, walking down Oxford Street, all these press chasing us along to the office. 'What's happening?' – people were pointing at us down the road. We couldn't believe it, we was away then.

So Malcolm's real talent was to milk situations?

Yeah. He didn't instigate them, that was always our own doing. There was never any blueprint, as people believe that Malcolm sat down and planned it in advance.

I get the impression that Steve was one of the real instigators.

Steve was mad, ever since he was young he was looking for adventure and excitement, breaking the law to have a laugh. He started the Grundy thing. If the press were there and they wanted a story, he would always do something to please them. A real exhibitionist. Which is funny, cos he's quite shy by himself.

He was the main troublemaker. He thrived on it. Even on tour he used to steal off the bands we were supporting, anything. He'd always complain about Malcolm – he'd say, 'Malcolm is always going on about anarchy, but whenever I do anything, he always tells me off! He don't wanna know.'

What did the Grundy thing feel like when it was actually going on?

I was just sitting there, I didn't hardly talk at all. I didn't know it was going out live, people swearing and that, I just thought we were having a laugh. I just thought everyone was taking the piss and it wouldn't have been shown.

He was obviously drunk, wasn't he?

I suppose he must have been. If you look back on it, he seems a bit drunk, doesn't he? He must have been, cos he stirred it up. If he was a professional, he would have played it down and got on with the interview. He got annoyed and acted like a real amateur and stirred us up even more. No wonder he got the sack.

Was there some aggro before it started on air?

No, it was his questions that got everyone going. He obviously knew nothing about what was going on. Nobody did. Punk was just starting, and he was being his usual sarcastic self.

The Anarchy tour, it seems that Malcolm's plan was just to keep it going.

Yeah, it was. It was just to get more publicity. By then Malcolm had started to get into it, working out his jargon for everything. He was getting off on the publicity, the media, manipulating everything.

Where was that interview done, where he was in the front and you were in the back? He was talking for you?

That was somewhere up North, on one of the cancelled dates somewhere. He took over then, which was fair enough, they wouldn't have got much sense out of us, at the time.

You must have been under a lot of pressure at that point.

Yeah, there was all the violence stirring up. It wasn't just kids' stuff, it was nasty violence, people wanted to throttle us, I don't know why. It got worse and worse. It was really frightening, people don't realise, the atmosphere around that time.

When did that violence start, cos people didn't really hate you at the Grundy time did they?

No, it was after that, when stories started coming out about fights in the audience, and the band getting involved, which happened on one occasion, and the people who wanted a bit of that came down to the gigs, throwing abuse.

When did the group really start to have problems? Was it around that period, or was it still all right?

No, it was all right. We should have pulled together a bit more as a band, I suppose, and there was always different factions in the band; John was with his pals, and me and Steve with our pals, and there was Glen off again. By that time Sid was in. John wanted Sid to join so he'd have a bit of camaraderie. But they didn't get on once Sid joined, that was another faction there.

Was that because of Nancy, or Sid wanting to be a star?

Both. When Nancy got involved that was another problem altogether. There was always a bit of friction in the band, right from the word go, that was the make-up of it. Maybe that's what made it a good band. But things got worse, the relationships in the band got worse. But we didn't hate each other, as everyone thought.

I get the impression that Malcolm could have done something to help that, and he didn't.

That's right, he was a bad manager in that respect. Someone said to me once that he was a band-breaker, and it was true. It was in everyone's interest to get out of the way and hold it all together. We did go away to places like Jersey to get out of the way, and we went to Berlin for a couple of weeks, when we were on the point of signing yet another contract. That was fun, when we went away places and we were just together.

What happened in Jersey? Jamie said you were followed around by police the whole time.

That's right. Jersey police, and these Jersey gangsters trying to get in with us, trying to get us to do a couple of gigs. You could see pound notes in their eyes. Pathetic, really. We left there after a couple of days anyway.

Didn't you have a fight with John on that trip?

No, I don't think so. Had a fight with John up Denmark Street once, just a little scuffle, that's all. He was winding me up all day.

The best fight we had in the band was in the Daimler, going to sign the A&M contract at Buckingham Palace. The Daimler turned up at Denmark Street about nine o'clock in the morning, and John and Sid were in there already. I don't know how they managed to get them up that early. They were in bad moods, looking really wrecked. Steve got up in a bad mood, and the row started then, there was a big free-for-all in the back of the Daimler.

It was so funny. Sid's legs nearly got broken, cos Sid's legs were up on the seat and Steve fell on them. It was just one of those early morning things. It was really funny. I think Sid was drunk when he turned up in the morning, then we went on to a press conference at that sleazy hotel in Piccadilly, everyone was drinking.

Then we went to do another interview somewhere else, and they got slowly worse and worse, and that was it. That wasn't the reason we got thrown off A&M, it was to do with the fight down the Speakeasy, I should imagine. I'm not sure. I don't know who signed us even, cos we didn't really meet anybody. Malcolm was getting on with all that.

What happened in the Speakeasy?

It was just a fight between Sid and a couple of others, Wobble might have been there. There were a few of us. It so happened that there was someone to do with A&M who got injured. Bob Harris was there, but someone else got hurt. I can't say who done that, I don't know, I didn't see it. That was it, really.

There was a period around the Grundy thing when you weren't playing very well?

Well, the playing came secondary to the publicity then. You were always worried, with people throwing things on stage, that you were going to get hit. And all the gobbing, which we never started. Just general chaos surrounding all the gigs, there was no way you could concentrate on the playing, it was impossible really. People didn't seem to mind, they were just going mad.

What was the story about Glen leaving? He did leave, rather than being sacked, didn't he?

Yeah, that was because John fell out with him, more than anything. I don't know why, he was different from the rest of us, a different attitude, but he fell out with John mainly. It wasn't about power, taking control of the group, cos nobody was doing that really. Just personality.

173

Was Malcolm stirring it?

Of course. Malcolm stirs everything.

Maybe Glen was asking questions about what was happening to all the money.

No. I don't think he was. We were all too busy to worry about stuff like that at the time. That came later. We was doing all right.

You were on what, fifty quid a week?

Yeah, I think so. It seemed like a lot then. We had a good time. Going out, eating out. It was the best we'd ever done. Obviously there was money coming in but a lot of it was being spent as well. Malcolm was really frivolous with money. He used to spend other people's money, that was his problem. As if it didn't matter.

There was that period when John and Jamie and you got attacked.

That was the teds, basically. The reactionaries.

What happened when you got attacked?

I was walking along the Goldhawk Road with my girlfriend of the time, and there were these young teds, three or four of them, and I had teddy-boy shoes on, which was the order of the day. 'Oy, what you got those shoes on for, punk?' 'I like them, why?' And we walked on up to Shepherd's Bush Green, them following us behind. I knew they were going to go for us so I turned round and had a go at them, and that was it. I just got a bit of a hiding. I got hit with some metal.

It ended up in Shepherd's Bush station. I knew who it was, they were from round there. A couple of them got put away eventually, for other fights. And I've seen the others since, years later.

What did they say?

Nothing, I think they just felt guilty about it, I suppose. Four blokes attacking one. It was a nasty period. People were frightened to go out. We was marked, everyone knew our faces. There wasn't many punks around then. People think punks, leather jackets, chains, but then, punks were normal kids with scruffy hair, macs on and stuff like that. More like flashers than anything else.

What did you think when Malcolm tried to put that in the movie? Did you mind that?

Not really, cos it was all part of it. It did happen. I went out the next day, and somebody saw me, and they'd seen the headline in the *Standard*. I had some stitches in my head but I still went out, and people started to think it was a lie, that the stories were made up. And that we didn't play on the album. Everything, people were questioning everything.

Wasn't there a plan, when Sid came in, to get Glen to play as well, on some of the recordings?

Yeah, cos Sid was in hospital, with hepatitis or something. He came down, but Steve ended up doing the tracks. Sid did play on the album, on 'Bodies', 'Queen', a couple of others.

There was a big thing that Sid didn't play on the album.

Yeah well, if you go through a lot of bands you'll find that people don't play on their albums, and it doesn't really matter. What pissed me off was that people thought the rest of us didn't play. They thought it was Chris Spedding and all this stuff.

What was Chris Thomas like to work with in the studio?

He was good, I thought. Professional. He seemed to know what we wanted to sound like, anyway. There was a bit of tension sometimes, but I thought it sounded great, I still do, a lot of it.

How would you work?

Me and Steve would go in and do the guitar and drum parts, which is pretty unorthodox, it's usually bass and drums, but we knew the songs so well we could do it without the bass. And we got them done quickly. The studio thing was all right, really. John and Chris Thomas fell out sometimes, but that was just normal, really.

John's voice got better too, by the end.

Yeah, he was really into it. Everyone was, and you can tell, I think, from the album.

Did you ever record 'Belsen Was a Gas'?

No, it wasn't good enough. That was one of Sid's things, it wasn't really a Pistols thing. It was one of Sid's more morbid ideas. By then we weren't writing any new songs, for various reasons.

Did you rehearse 'Religion'?

No, there was an idea, John wanted to write a song about that, but never got round to it. We'd split up by then.

How did the split happen? Did it come from you and Steve?

That American tour was so heavy with paranoia, the whole tour. Malcolm wasn't helping, he was really paranoid, saying that people were following us around. And we did have to be careful; sometimes there were policemen with guns standing at the side of the stage while we were playing, two on each side. I got the feeling someone was going to get killed at any time, it was really heavy.

And there was that stupid film crew following us around. There's so many loonies in America just waiting to latch on to something . . . thousands of people came out of these little towns, to see us.

Did you get hit by stuff?

Tons of stuff thrown at us on stage, mainly cans, but dead rats, pigs' ears, stuff like that. Really sick.

It strikes me that you and Steve were holding the whole thing together musically, by that stage.

It was hard to play with all this stuff going on around you. Which is why some of it sounds so ropey. But I've seen some clips of that American tour, and it looks so exciting . . . so much tension.

All the band went on the bus at first, then you and Steve started flying, didn't you?

Yeah, bodyguards, that was another thing, Vietnam vets looking after us. John and Sid were obviously the most striking, they got the most attention and they needed more looking after, I suppose. Me and Steve could always go off and mingle.

But Sid was driving everyone mad, so me and Steve started flying

176

to the gigs, cos otherwise it was driving in the bus for ten hours at a time in the snow, ridiculous. By the time we reached San Francisco, we'd had enough of it all, and that's when the split occurred.

What was the last gig like?

It was all right. It was alien to us, cos we'd never played in such a big place. By the time we got there, we'd originally been booked to play a five-hundred-capacity place, but because of all the publicity it was the Winterland, six thousand people. By far the biggest venue we'd ever played. But we got away with it, people loved it.

Sid was really out of it on that gig.

He was on all of them, I think. I didn't see much of him, to tell you the truth, he was always off with these loonies who would latch on to him.

So on stage, you worked with Steve. What drums were you using?

Gretsch, I've had the same kit for years. Apparently the sound was very good at that one. Boogie was doing the sound. It was hard for us to say, cos we're on stage, obviously. You get different views of things. There was that famous line, 'Ever felt you've been cheated?'

What happened after that?

Me and Steve were at the Japanese hotel with Malcolm, and John was out of town somewhere. Malcolm had a word with John. Malcolm looked really ill at the end of that tour, it was just getting too much. We just said, 'I don't know how much longer we can carry on like this.' The problem was, we were due to tour in Sweden straight after, and nobody fancied it after America. We should have just cancelled it, rested for a few months.

There was no way that was going to happen, so we split up instead. Malcolm was trying to set up this thing in Rio, and we was into it. I was anyway, but John wasn't, and Sid OD'd somewhere in San Francisco. Some girl turned up crying her eyes out, and me and Steve rushed over there. Sid was laid out on the floor, the doctors had just got there, girl punks crying all round him. I thought, 'Oh god.' Then he was in hospital . . .

And then he OD'd again on the flight back to New York. He was totally out of control.

There was no way we could have gone on tour anyway, with Sid like that. We went to see John and he turned up with Joe Stevens, and we just said, 'We can't handle this any more, we're going to Rio, are you coming?' And he had a talk with Malcolm, and he didn't want to go, for some reason. So we went down there, and had a great time.

How long were you down there?

Nearly two months – six or seven weeks. Warner Brothers were sending us all this money just to get us out of America in the first place, cos we only had two-week visas and we had to be gone by then. They paid for us down there, first-class tickets, return. When Malcolm came down he was getting money sent from Virgin, and we started to make the film with Biggs. We were just messing around and relaxing.

Did you think about what was going to happen with the band?

Not while we were down there. We totally forgot about everything till we got back, and then it was totally depressing. Malcolm came back and started planning the film, which he always wanted to make. That was Malcolm's ego getting in the way. He knew nothing about making films. But we didn't really want to make the film then, it was too early. With all that trouble going on with the band, he wanted to make a film as well.

John definitely didn't wanna do it, and me and Steve didn't really wanna do it. John had got his lawyers involved already, slapping injunctions on everything.

When you got back you started recording, did you?

Yeah, we were going to get a band together with Eddie Tenpole, but Steve didn't really want to know, he was starting to turn to drugs.

When did that start?

When he got back, and nothing was happening. It was a wind-down, I suppose. All the bands were still going, but nothing great had come through after that. Everyone was bickering.

The next year you were going to get involved with Jimmy Pursey, weren't you?

Yeah, but that fell through after a couple of days of getting to know the guy. We didn't wanna know after meeting him. He thought it was going to be called the Sex Pistols and there was no way me and Steve were going to be called the Sex Pistols Mark fucking Two or something.

What happened with the first court case? Did you side with Malcolm at first?

Yeah, I suppose we did. I didn't study what was going on, but then we took a neutral position between John and Malcolm. In retrospect, we should have sided with John from the beginning, but we were still involved with Malcolm on the film. We weren't interested in court cases, we didn't get into it for all that. It wasn't in our make-up to sort business problems out. John hated Malcolm, he really wanted to take him on. John thought he was being ripped off, and there was this clash all the time.

Just before Sid died, me and Steve were going to fly out to New York to do an album with him, to raise some money for his court case. Some standards, and write some new songs. Sid was actually quite a good singer, a performer.

Did you play on 'My Way'?

I didn't, Steve did. They went to France and did it, I didn't go. But there was a plan that we'd start a new band with Sid as well, as the singer. He was a good singer. Steve got on with Sid really well, but even he couldn't, towards the end.

What happened after the court case? Weren't you very pissed off that all your royalties were going to ...

Yeah, especially as it took eight years to sort it all out.

And you got no money during all that period?

No, we were broke. We could have sat down and sorted it out, but it was all between John and Malcolm. Malcolm was really depressed after all that. There was a plan just before the court case where he got

179

the film and we got everything else, but the lawyers thought we should get everything. I don't think Malcolm could handle going through it all.

What sort of money did you eventually get out of it? A quarter of Glitterbest?

We all got a quarter of it, but there wasn't much left at the end of the day. It's amazing though, it's still making money, it's still selling, so we're still getting money coming through from it, but I didn't think we were going to see anything. The lawyers cost something like three hundred thousand quid.

Are the receivers still in charge of anything?

No, it's all in our hands now. Which makes a change.

What happened to all the stuff from the film?

We've got all that, all the out-takes. Haven't seen it, I must go and have a look at it sometime. It's up to us what we wanna do.

Glen Matlock

Sex Pistols' co-founder, composer and bassist. Often presented as the fall guy after he left in January 1977, he was in fact the musician with the pop savvy – the grasp of arrangement, melody and structure. The proof is in the pudding – the Sex Pistols wrote only four songs after he left. Two sessions, both at his then flat in Maida Vale, London; full of detailed memories once warmed up.

Where were you brought up?

The Harrow Road, a local lad, born in St Mary's. Then I lived in Kensal Green until I was about fifteen, up by the cemetery. When I was just starting to get it together to go out, it was a handy place to live, cos if you got a cab back it was about a quid then, or something. Then my folks moved out to Greenford, which is horrible suburbia, and on top of that it was like fifteen quid back, so I spent many a night on Acton Town station waiting for the first train.

You went to school in the Kensal Green area?

I went to St Clement Danes, which is next to Wormwood Scrubs prison. That's how I first came across Paul, cos I used to play football. Most of the guys came from around that area, Shepherd's Bush. I used to play five-a-side football, and we beat Paul's team in the final once. That was the first time I met Paul.

Were you always aware of pop music?

Oh yeah, I had a band at school. A rotten band, it was like learning to play, you know. I used to go to quite a lot of gigs. I was into the Small Faces and all that, then I went off it for while. I got into football and heavy-duty maths homework and all that. But then when I was about sixteen, I started getting interested again.

What was school like?

I wasn't a boffin, although I didn't do badly at school. I just went with the flow. I was always in trouble. Not heavy trouble, but half the time we used to slope off at lunchtime, come back about five past three, from the pub, and then school finished at half past three, so we didn't get a lot done.

Did you have brothers and sisters?

No, just me. Not my fault; not my mum's fault either, I was born by Caesarian section, I don't think she could have any more kids after that. I didn't like it. Even now, I consider myself a bit shy. I just like to go off on my own.

When you went out to Greenford, did you change schools?

No, what happened was I'd left school by then, and I went to art school, at St Martins, right in town, and I had to schlep it out to Greenford every day. I didn't like that, but I wasn't in a financial position to move away from home at that time. In the meantime I was working for Malcolm from when I was about sixteen, when I was in sixth form.

How did you get involved in that?

I'd heard there was a teddy-boy shop down there and I fancied getting myself a pair of creepers – and it was great, it was like my gran's front room, from the fifties. And I asked if they needed anyone to work, and the guy said, actually we might do, cos I'm leaving, I'll ask Malcolm. So I met Malcolm and he said, all right.

When you started at the shop, was it still Let It Rock, or Too Fast to Live, Too Young to Die?

It was just changing. We used to call it Let It Rock, but the sign said Too Fast to Live. It was lots of teds, basically. They were a bit of a pain. No, they were okay but really straight, you know. Just caught in a time warp. It was fun though, I enjoyed measuring people up for suits, getting into a bit of tailoring.

Was Malcolm mainly doing drapes?

Initially, then he started doing zoots, and there was two types of

182

clientele, there was the teds, who were just one big group with half-moon jacket pockets and all that, and when he started doing the zoot suits, the younger kids were coming in . . .

Did you think the clothes were good?

Yeah, it was good. Course, the stuff I really liked, the suits for seventy pounds, when you're getting seven pounds a day, there's no way you're ever going to get that together. Contented myself with a few pairs of Day-Glo socks . . .

Who else was working in the shop back then?

There was a bloke called Michael Collins, and a girl called Elaine Wood. It was a good job, the money was good, and we didn't open on Saturday till twelve, and finished at seven.

What was Malcolm like then, when you first met him?

When I first met him he was a bit offhand, cos I was pretty straight – you know, I was just there, working, there was no big deal – but as we got to know each other, he opened up a bit more. The thing I used to enjoy, Bernie Rhodes used to come in quite a lot, and we had a few discussions, he fancies himself as a statesman of the world. Bit like me being at art school at the time, getting into minimalism and all the different kind of art movements, dadaism and all that lot, and he was into art, so. Quite a few discussions. I found that a good way of opening up, cos they'd been through the whole sixties thing, they knew a lot of that World's End scene as well . . .

Now, St Martins is synonymous with all that Soho lifestyle. Was there much of that going on?

Yeah, we did, but it was all pubs and stuff, it was before it got gentrified. So it was a lot funkier. That was quite an eye-opener as well, being in Soho every day. Finding all the little coffee bars and that. Thinking, yeah, I'm a real bohemian! . . .

What were you studying?

I just did a foundation course, and I got accepted to do the degree in fine art, painting, but I didn't go, cos in the summer I decided to take

183

the Pistols more seriously. I strolled in on the induction day, the day I was supposed to start, and said, 'I don't want to do your daft art thing, I'm in a rock and roll band', and I thought they'd go, aaaargh! But they just went, 'Oh, all right then, we'll give your place to someone else.' I thought, is that it?

How did the band first come together?

As far as I know, well, I met Steve and Paul cos they used to come in the shop and try to nick stuff, and I had to stop them, didn't I? They came in quite a lot, and we got talking, and they had this band, and Steve was a right tea-leaf. They'd nicked all this equipment and didn't know what to do with it, cos it was too hot to sell, and one of their mates had the bright idea, 'Why don't you learn to play it?'

And they were like, 'Oh, yeah. Hadn't thought of that.' They had a band already with Paul's brother, called Strand, or the Swankers . . . the bass player wasn't taking it that seriously, and they found out that I was playing bass . . .

Were you still playing the bass at St Martins?

I'd been playing at school, just playing in my bedroom, trying to copy Ronnie Lane. In fact that was how I got the gig. There was this intricate bass part in a Faces song called 'Three Button Hand Me Down'. I know now that it had been overdubbed twice and all that, but I'd actually learned it as it was. My first audition with them, I went round to Wally's house, and he said, 'What can you play then?' 'Well I like The Faces. I know this one, "Three Button Hand Me Down".' Played it . . . 'You'll do!'

What sort of stuff did you play?

Oh, just jamming, Faces stuff. When 'Roadrunner' came out we had a go at that. 'Shake Some Action'. Steve was singing at the time. Tom Jones impersonation. But the biggest thing that really got the ball rolling was that Wally's dad was an electrician, and he got this contract to do up what is now Riverside Studios – not to do it up, but to strip out what wasn't needed. It cost Hammersmith Council like three million pounds then – and we got a set of keys cut!

There was this room in there that was the best acoustic room in

Europe, and we rehearsed in there. Paul worked at Watneys brewery, so we had a bar set up. It was like an Aladdin's cave, all this equipment around, and Steve was happy cos outside there's this dead end, and a couple of the local businessmen used it as their Lovers' Lane with their secretaries, so come half past seven or so, Steve would disappear for a bit. It took us a while to twig, but he was going out there and peeping in on them.

How did the three of you get on at that stage?

Alright. Steve was a funny bloke, a bit more streetwise than me. I was like the only child, so there was a bit of friction.

Did Malcolm know about your band?

It was him and Bernie, actually. We were badgering him a bit to get involved, but he realised that it was early days still. He said he didn't mind getting involved but he wanted us to get rid of Wally cos he didn't look right. He was a bit bolshy in his attitude as well. Then Malcolm went off to the States, and he was expecting to come back with another guitarist, and there was a bit of a furore, we didn't want to get rid of Wally cos he was all right. On top of that, his dad had this place where we could rehearse. But it all got sorted out. Steve had been learning guitar at the time. So we were a three-piece for a while, and we tried out a few different singers. Nick Kent came down and jammed with us a couple of times. A mates thing, through The Roebuck. He'd hang around there cos Chrissie Hynde was working there and he was after Chrissie, but he was in a bit of a state at the time.

He'd been going on to Malcolm, like, 'This is ridiculous, I'm having to write all the songs in this band, you know' – and it wasn't like that, he just jammed with us. So I remember going round to see him one Sunday. I walked in there and I'd never seen such a state, it was a tip. It was about midday, I woke him up and he went, 'Do you want a drink?' I thought he meant a cup of tea or something. 'What you got?' I said. 'I've got this', and he holds up a bottle of Kaolin and Morphine. So that was Nick Kent's involvement.

There was another bloke, called David, I can't remember what his surname was, used to come and hang around in the shop. But he didn't sing very well. There was somebody else too, not very serious, and then John arrived on the scene.

The group was called QT Jones and the Sex Pistols, wasn't it?

That was one of the names, but we never actually called it that. Malcolm came up with a few ideas. There was a few names floating around. The Damned was one of them. Kid Gladlove was another one. You got to remember that it was the tail end of the Biba thing. Obviously that would colour your judgement a little bit. Then the band was called The Pistols, and the shop was called SEX by that time. Malcolm came up with that. I think the QT was from the postcode where we were rehearsing was 4QT.

Steve came along one day looking pleased with himself. He'd nicked this bloke's briefcase, and it had five hundred quid in used notes inside. He said, 'You hungry?' I said, 'Yeah.' So we went into this pie and mash shop opposite the Hammersmith Odeon, and I had pie and mash, Steve had double pie and mash, and then we had the same thing again. And then Steve had another pie and mash after that. And we waddled off to rehearsals, on the proceeds of this felony.

Wasn't there an occasion when you took a bass back that they'd nicked?

Oh yeah. I went to flog this guitar. I didn't know it was stolen. All the music shops were opposite St Martins. The bloke said, 'We're just waiting for the bloke to come back for the valuation', and it went on for a bit, and I thought, hold on, something's wrong here. I'd never been in trouble before, I was just kind of curious.

Next thing, sirens. One of the blokes in there was all right, saying, 'Are you sure you want to sell this?' Giving me an opportunity, you know. But next thing, I'm being frog-marched out to the back of this blinking Rover. And all the tutors from St Martins all watching . . . I got done for receiving stolen goods.

Were you all wearing the shop's clobber at this stage?

Yeah, what we wanted. I was about the trendiest one at St Martins for a bit, I had one of those little Eton-collared shirts, creepers, zip

T-shirt, and one of those mohair sweaters, while everybody else at St Martins is in flares and dungarees.

So you'd been trying out various people. Why did Malcolm pick on John?

Because he looks hilarious, I think. I always thought he was a bit of a twit. Actually I still think he's a bit of a twit. There was a sort of rivalry between us and a shop called Acme Attractions. It wasn't heavy, but they were like, second division, and John was wearing a lot of things from there. Also he used to wear those horrible plastic sandals. I always thought that was the height of naff, anybody who could wear shoes like that must be a twerp.

He used to come in with Wobble, and a bloke called John Gray who was around quite a lot. I think Sid was around, but I wasn't that aware of him. I think they'd all met up at this college in Kingsway, an A level college, and they was all called John, so they invented nicknames for themselves.

Were you still working in the shop?

Yeah. It was just Saturdays, then I started working through the summer holidays. In fact when it was done up as SEX, I as good as made that pink sign. Didn't design it, but I made it.

Who did the graffiti on the walls?

Malcolm did most of it, I think. One of them said something like, 'Under the paving stones, there lies the beach', which I thought was great. Used it in a song. But Malcolm had nicked that from somewhere else.

How did you get on with Vivienne? Was she all right?

She was and she wasn't. I always found her a bit unnecessary, a bit too intense. On top of that, they were always, 'We're on a mission' and all that. I just thought it was a decent Saturday job with decent money – although I could see their side of it. Obviously it was their thing, and I was just a part of it. I think they both were into it.

But Vivienne was very absolute . . .

Exactly, to a point where it became a bit overbearing, you know. But I've seen her since a couple of times, and we've got on fine. Except I was at this party once, the Christmas before last, and she introduced me to some people she was with, and she was like, 'Oh this is Glen, he used to be my Saturday lad.' Pulling rank, you know. And she's very Thatcherite in a way.

When it was SEX, did people ever come in for the actual sex gear?

Oh yeah. People would be trying to nick stuff, and you'd go into the cubicle if they hadn't bought anything. A couple of times there'd be spunk all over it. There was one bloke used to come in, he was a real rubber mac fetishist, and he just used to come in and ask prices, and he was always wanking. He can't have had any pockets in his trousers. He'd ask the price of some rubber stockings or whatever, and you'd tell him, and he was, 'Ah . . . ah . . . AH! Okay, I'll come back then . . . ' If it wasn't so funny, it was horrible.

So how did the whole John thing come about?

He started coming into the shop, and Malcolm suggested him.

Did he have the short hair, even then?

Yeah, he looked much the same. Then we organised this rehearsal. Wally had gone by then, so we didn't have that other place. On top of that, the police were sniffing around as well. So we had this rehearsal down in Rotherhithe, a place called Crunchy Frog. Like a warehouse, a bit hippy dippy. We arranged to meet him down there but nobody turned up.

John wasn't too happy about that. I called up the next day to say sorry, and he was, 'Aw'll kill you. I will, I'll come round there with a hammer!' There we go.

Why was he putting all that on?

I don't know. I don't even know why he does it today. Cos he's a fucked-up Roman Catholic. Lots of the lyrics he was coming out with – 'waiting for the Archangel Gabriel', you know, and 'Anarchy': 'I am an Antichrist'. That's all part of the Catholicism in a way. I think he's a bit myopic about how clever he is . . .

Had you done a gig by this stage?

No, not until we got John in. We did do one at Tom Salter's Café. But we just got up and jammed, we didn't really have any songs. It was a complete abortion. I had the hump with Vivienne about that cos she was going, 'Oh, get up and play', and we didn't want to, cos we knew we didn't have it together enough. And then Vivienne was going, 'I think that's disgusting, terrible.'

Wasn't there a stage where Paul left?

That was after John came in, and we were rehearsing in Denmark Street. Everybody was leaving all the time. There was always a bit of friction going on. Which turned out to make it work, I think, for a little while. Except between Steve and Paul, who were always like Fred Flintstone and Barney Rubble.

Anyway, we got this Denmark Street place together. I saw an ad in *Melody Maker* and showed it to Malcolm, and he said, 'Call the bloke up, and offer the bloke a thousand pounds without seeing it.' I said, 'What?!' But I called up, and said, 'My mate says we can offer you a thousand quid without seeing it', and he said, 'I think we can talk business.'

It turned out to be Bill Collins – Lewis Collins' dad from *The Professionals*. He used to manage the Mojos and Badfinger, and because one of the band had topped himself, he was selling off the assets. He turned out to be a real nice bloke and a lot of help to us. And I don't think he got his money.

Didn't you audition a lot of people at one point?

We had auditions when John was in the band, in Denmark Street, we were starting on a more professional level then. Paul didn't want to give up his job at Watneys. He wanted to leave if we didn't get another guitarist, cos he didn't think Steve was good enough at that stage.

So we had a lot of auditions then, for a guitarist, and that's where Steve New came along. His girlfriend was his art teacher from school. He was fifteen at the time, but he said he was sixteen. He was great, his playing pissed all over Steve's playing at that time, and he was in the band for about a month, just rehearsing, but he wouldn't get his hair cut, so I had to give him the sack.

We rehearsed practically every day. Me and Steve were living there, and Johnny would come down in the evening, and Paul would come after work, and if anybody had any ideas, we'd work on them. It was ideal.

Did you get lots of ideas, being in the centre of London? It's a great place, Tin Pan Alley, with the music business . . .

Yeah, there was a lot of other things going on. With Bernie being around, we'd chat about this, that and the other. Malcolm had come back from the States and had brought back all these posters. In fact he brought back one which was a great help, which was a Television poster, from when Richard Hell was in the band, and it had all these great song titles on it, 'Blank Generation', 'Venus de Milo', and that's where we got the idea for 'Pretty Vacant' from.

It was like a collective consciousness, which sounds a bit hippy. I think that was the whole strength of it, actually. But then on the other hand, I remember writing 'Anarchy', I'm blowing my own trumpet here. John wrote the words for that, but the music side of it came from me. I'd been doing all the writing up to then, all the better stuff, and Steve hadn't been doing anything . . .

So when Steve New left, you'd been writing?

Yeah. One of the very first ones was 'Did You No Wrong', which Wally should have got a credit for, actually, but he never did. It was Wally's guitar riff.

How did the first gig come about? Was that St Martins?

Well Malcolm said, get some gigs together. I went to the Central School of Art, and asked Al McDowell and Sebastian Conran if we could have a gig, and he asked if we'd done any, and I said, 'No, it's our first one.' He asked what was the name, and I said, 'The Sex Pistols,' although we hadn't really decided. And Sebastian went, 'Oh yes, wonderful! With a name like that, we have to book you.' So that was that.

Then in the meantime this gig at St Martins came up. Al came along to it, and thought it was really funny . . .

What was the first gig like?

Pandemonium. We were supporting a band called Bazooka Joe, all those snotty kids from Gospel Oak and all that. The idea was that we were going to use their equipment, but they wouldn't let us use it at the last minute. So we had to go back to Denmark Street and trundle all the equipment through the crowds. Pushing a big bass amp isn't exactly fun. Then we set up and played for about twenty minutes and they pulled the plug on us. Although everybody enjoyed it, you know.

Can you remember what you played?

We would have played 'Pretty Vacant', 'Problems'. Might have done one of the Small Faces things.

What was John like as a performer at that time? Did you think it was working?

I don't think we even considered it. That was it, and that was it. I remember doing the gig at the 100 Club, and he was out of his box. He sounded abysmal. The band was all right, but he was singing the right words to the wrong songs. And I went up to him and said, 'John, you're acting like a cunt, get it together', and this was in the middle of a song, in front of a crowd at the 100 Club.

He says, 'Do you wanna fight?' And I said, 'Not particularly, I'm playing the bass, we're doing a gig.' And he stormed off the stage and up the stairs, and Malcolm went after him and he was outside waiting for a bus to go home. We're still playing. Malcolm made him go back and apologise to us. Which he did. That was a bit later on, our first 100 Club gig.

What was the Central gig like?

That was a very good one, one of the best gigs we did. It was only our second gig, though. We supported Roogalator. They'd already booked them, and it was supposed to be a double headline, but we went on first.

What guitar were you using at that time?

The one in those pictures. Steve was playing the guitar that used to belong to Syl Sylvain from the New York Dolls. Malcolm had brought some stuff back, cos he hadn't got paid. Bands starting out don't normally have that. As-good-as-new Fender twin. Steve had purloined the amps, but I bought the cabinet.

Where did you play next?

We did a gig at Andrew Logan's. That was great. It went down so well, we did the same set three times. And it was an amazing set, cos it was the set for [Derek Jarman's film] *Sebastiane*. In fact the pictures, you know the little handouts with the three of us, was taken at that gig. The one where Jordan's got her tits out. That was there.

Logan had designed all the stuff for Biba's, the kids' room, remember they had all the stuff from *Sleeping Beauty*? When it shut down, he got the stuff back. And so his bedroom, cos it was this big loft, was like Sleeping Beauty's bedroom, and the kitchen area was like plants, all these false trees, and there was people pissing up against the trees cos they thought it was outside.

Were people shocked by you, or did they like it?

I think they liked it. It was that arty crowd, they could see the funny side of it as well. Also we were playing pretty good. Chrissie Hynde was there. Derek Jarman.

We hadn't been doing a lot of gigging, but we'd been rehearsing all the time. This whole thing about us not being able to play and all that really used to get my goat up, cos we'd been working.

And you wouldn't have had an impact if you'd been shit, would you?

Exactly. But it was totally against anything else that was going on in London at that time. I can see why people thought it was a racket . . .

When did you start to feel that it was getting beyond just being a little band?

I think we thought that all along, I was pretty confident. We started getting press pretty early. I was sitting in this café in Kensington High Street, I'd just bought the *NME*, and there was this review of a gig at the Marquee, we'd been supporting Eddie and the Hot Rods, and I don't think they even mentioned Eddie and the Hot Rods.

That was an early gig. John smashed up the monitors, I think out of frustration, cos it was the first time he'd really heard his voice properly. It was the first decent PA we'd used. The PA company wanted to keep our equipment until we'd reimbursed them, but we got it back somehow.

Was the material changing, or were you just basically playing the same set at that stage?

We were adding to it, as new songs came along. I still don't think 'Anarchy' was around at that time. The first time we played 'Anarchy' was the Lesser Free Trade Hall in Manchester. We opened with it.

And were you writing most of the music?

It varied. 'Problems' was a four-way effort, it came out of a jam. John wrote the words. But 'Pretty Vacant' was my song, as far as I'm concerned.

Were there any songs written that you didn't use?

Not really. The sets were short, but that was the idea, to keep it short and sweet. That idea was floating around anyway, like The Ramones, even though we hadn't see them at that point.

Did the Ramones LP have an impact on you?

Yeah, I remember listening to it in the shop. Thunders reckoned we really copied the Dolls. I never consciously did it. Maybe Steve modelled his guitar-playing on it. But the chords that I wrote were more influenced by The Who and the Small Faces. That's where my inspiration came from.

Did you speed up, when you heard The Ramones?

We never played fast. There isn't one really fast Pistols record, if you think about it. That was the difference between us and the other punk bands. 'Anarchy' is strident, but because we weren't rushing through it, it gives it more power.

We played the Nashville a couple of times. Supported The 101ers. The night before, we'd seen them at the Acklam Hall, and we went up to Joe Strummer and said hello. Steve wanted a pee just before we were due to go on. And he just peed on the floor, because the curtains were shut. And Malcolm was operating the curtains, and he got the cue wrong and the curtains opened and there was Steve. People used to think we did that kind of thing deliberately, but it was just an accident.

What about the fight?

As far as I remember, somebody sat in Vivienne's seat while she was at the bar, and she had a ruck with him, and he was like, 'Tough shit.' Next thing, somebody else steamed in, and he was getting really horribly pasted. There was all these kids from West London who used to come in the shop, and I supposed they wanted to protect Vivienne, kind of thing, but it was like eight on to one, and we just tried to stop it.

Cos if there's a fight going on in front while you're playing, there's no way anybody's going to pay attention to you. As soon as there's a fight, nobody watches the band. And the next thing we know, in the *Melody Maker*, we're beating up the audience.

Were you all trying to stop it?

I really can't speak for the others, but that's the way I remember it. I think Steve just wanted to hit anything, boosh. For me it was a matter of principle that when you're on stage, you want people to take more notice of you than some cunt who's happened to sit in Vivienne's seat. I thought maybe it was Vivienne's fault in the first place, she shouldn't have been so stroppy.

Wasn't there a fight at High Wycombe as well?

We played at High Wycombe Town Hall, supporting Screaming Lord Sutch. It was a total abortion. Steve's mate, Jim, was trying to do the sound, pissed out of his head, and he didn't know anything about sound at all. Johnny smashed every mike on the stage, so there was nothing to even sing into, but it was Screaming Lord Sutch's PA, and all the other guys in the band were going apeshit, and Johnny just totally denied that he'd done it.

But everybody had seen him do it. 'No I didn't.' And Lord Sutch just burst out laughing, at the barefaced cheek of it all.

Were you getting a lot of adverse reaction?

People heckled, but they do that at gigs anyway. I dunno, it was my first proper band, I just thought, that's the way groups are, you know? I didn't know any different.

Who was doing your sound?

Dave Goodman, and Kim Thraves from the first gig we did at the Nashville. I think they went to Malcolm and said they wanted to get involved, and they had their own PA, and a van. I suppose they were quite good, I never really got to hear the sound. It was quite funny, they were two right hippies – especially Kim, had a little goatee beard . . .

There was a stage where you were just off in the van with Nils, weren't you, doing lots of gigs?

Yeah, there was one we did at Northallerton. We'd had a little bit of press by then. That girl Pauline turned up, from Penetration, with her boyfriend. They'd travelled quite a long way. They used to come to a lot of gigs. She was a nice girl too, had a great voice.

Anyway we got there, it was this little market town, and it was like a chicken-in-a-basket place. And this bloke, I'm not kidding, with a Tom Jones tux, gets up, and goes, 'All right ladies and gentlemen, they've come all the way from London tonight, please put your hands together, here for you in cabaret, the Sex Pistols.' And we was like, 'Whaat?'

That was the first one, then I think we went to Whitby Bay, and we couldn't find anywhere to stay, they took one look at us. We played this place, and they kept telling us to turn it down, they came up about three times, and in the end we were just larking about, pretending we was miming, like you'd do on the Hughie Green show, and this bloke comes up and says, 'No lads, it's no good, we'll pay you what you're due, but we just can't hear the bingo in the other room.' So we played about fifteen minutes of that gig.

Then we went off to another place and couldn't get there because the van wasn't powerful enough, and we had to get up this hill, and there was this long detour, miles around. There was seven of us in this Transit, and all the equipment, and the PA. Dave, Kim, Nils and the band. Imagine being in a van with fucking Rotten. One time their van had broken down so we hired this van, a Luton box van, there was no seats in it and only room for three people in the front.

We got the van at Denmark Street, loaded up, and drove for about four hours, right up to Scarborough or somewhere like that. The rain was pissing down, we were dying for a pee, hammering on the thing. Then we got out, when they finally heard us hammering on top of the cab, and we got out and we were right in the middle of the bloody Yorkshire Moors . . . there was fumes coming into the back from the exhaust. Before we really got going, there was no money coming in at all, I'd think myself lucky if I had a KitKat to last me a couple of days.

But by the time of these gigs were you living on what you got paid?

I can't remember where the money went, to be honest. We'd get bed and breakfast, and the petrol out of the gig money, and that was it. There wasn't a lot. But then when we were doing the Nashville and the 100 Club, I don't know where the money went. Also we had to pay for Denmark Street.

On a few of those early pics, you were wearing paint-spattered trousers.

The idea was to take the piss out of all that op art. The reason I did those trousers was I only had one pair and I was painting up Denmark Street, make it look a bit more homely and clean. I got a bit of paint on them and I thought maybe if I put a bit more on. I imagined one of Jackson Pollock's paintings, in the Louvre or wherever they are, with a shape of a pair of trousers cut out of them.

So did The Clash . . . ?

They ripped it off, yeah.

What was John like in the van?

He was asleep, most of the time. We did quite a few gigs. We played Eric's in Liverpool. And Dundee. That was our first time up North. That was quite good actually, Steve and Kim and Dave drove up with the gear, and we went up on the sleeper. It was great, going over the Tay, first thing in the morning.

And we checked into this hotel, the best hotel I'd ever been in up till then. They had all this fish, six different selections of fresh fish for breakfast. Same for lunch. Malcolm hadn't thought about extras at the hotel. And of course we were starving, I tucked into kippers for breakfast, smoked haddock, and that went on for a day or two and then Malcolm got the extras bill, and that was the end of extras in the hotel. Frankie Vaughan was staying in the hotel, there was all these women hanging out for him.

We did the gig at the university or the art college, and we just got pelted with glass. But they wanted an encore! I think they wanted to get us out so they could pelt us some more, but we were like hiding behind the door. I was talking to a couple of blokes after, they were saying, 'Great gig', and I said, 'Why did everybody sling stuff at us?' They said, 'We thought that's what you're supposed to do, we thought you'd like that.' With Scottish accents.

It must have been funny going to those places, cos outside London people were still wearing baggies . . .

That's not strictly true, there was some kids by then that were getting into it. Wearing plastic bags and stuff. One gig we did in Chester at a place called Quaintways I think, was full of Hell's Angels, and we were thinking, oh dear, but they really got into it, doing that rocker's dance, you know.

We went to France quite early on as well. It was a scream, that gig. Madness. Cos it was free to get in. This new club was opening, and nothing is free in Paris. So practically the whole town turned out for this new thing. It was jam-packed. And they'd only finished painting the place that morning. They had to carry all the chairs outside in the afternoon to get them to dry, and they weren't, and there's women in white dresses are getting up and they've got black chair marks all over them. They weren't too happy.

And they had this new glass floor, and I was kind of pogoing, just sort of stomping, and the janitor of the place is going, 'Oh, sacre bleu! The floor, monsieur', and I'm trying to play, and he's tugging my trouser leg, cos it's glass, with lights underneath. The more he did it, the more I did it, you know. There were some good pictures from that gig.

197

Malcolm forgot his passport. The manager. And the equipment didn't turn up because the carnet wasn't organised, nobody knew what a carnet was, so they wouldn't let the gear out. We did two nights. We got there, played Friday night, had Saturday off, played a Sunday afternoon gig which wasn't quite such pandemonium. People were there who wanted to see the band. Siouxsie turned up and Billy Idol, they all turned up in Billy Idol's Ford Escort van.

What was Malcolm's role through all this? He likes to present himself as a Svengali, but . . .

Malcolm's whole thing was being a situationist, except that the situation was presented by a lot of luck, really. But then he was good at making the most of it. The Bill Grundy thing, for example. We didn't go on there to deliberately swear. It just ended up that way, and it was perfect for Malcolm.

I think a lot of the time what he was doing was, he was mates with people at the *NME*, Nick Logan and all them, I think he was on the phone to them a lot, trying to create a buzz, though it might not result in an article directly then. Hustling.

Then there was the Screen on the Green . . .

Yeah, that was funny, I enjoyed that. The place nearly caught fire, cos Malcolm and Dave wanted to use some smoke bombs, and we thought it was hippy shit. So they said they wouldn't do it, but they let them off anyway. I think the fire extinguisher had to come out. The funniest thing about it was there was no stage there. We said The Clash could support us if they provided the stage, and built it themselves.

Was that one of The Clash's first ever gigs?

Their first gig was in Sheffield. A pub called The Black Swan. That was the first proper gig.

What did you think about all these other bands coming out, like The Damned . . . ?

There was two ways to think about it. The guys had been around. Mick Jones, London SS and all that, they'd come down, knocking around with Bernie. Ray Burns was around, and Rat Scabies. There was a coterie of people. I liked The Clash, actually, but they looked like a right bunch of herberts. It was good, because it created more of a scene, which gave everything a bit more weight; on the other hand, we regarded them as a bit second-division anyway.

The funniest thing, one night we went to the Speakeasy, and that band that used to play all the time, Gonzales were on. Albert King was in town, and he got up and jammed, he used the bloke's guitar and everybody was at the bar, and suddenly everybody went and watched. You never watched the band at the Speakeasy. And while the band was on, Steve went backstage and he nicked this pair of stack-heeled boots with moons and stars all over them, and wore them walking home.

I used to have this rubber suit that I wore on stage at the 100 Club, it was really hot, and you'd be standing there in a pool of sweat, cos the trousers were like drainpipes, and then trying to get the tube home. You didn't think to take a change of clothes, and you're sitting there steaming in this rubber suit.

What did you think of the press you were getting from Jonh Ingham and everyone?

I thought it was great, but I never liked the word 'punk'. I mean, today you accept it. But I just thought it was a bit of a naff word. But no, it really helped out. I can't really remember what I thought at the time, but looking back on it, it was pretty instrumental.

Did you genuinely think you were the best band on the scene?

Yeah, I mean, I think history has borne that out. The Clash were good, but they had a different slant on it, but The Damned and Subway Sect and all that lot . . .

Can you remember any really good or bad gigs that stand out?

I think the best one we ever did was the Babalu Club, in Finchley Road. It had been advertised on radio and all that. We thought it was gonna be really packed. It was a funny place to play. We got there and there was about thirteen people altogether, and that was including us. But we set up and played, to get paid, and put on a really good show.

The worst one was probably the 100 Club, when John stormed out and went to the bus stop while we were still playing. But that had its funny side to it. When you're playing, you don't think about it that way, you remember your surroundings. Early on they were good, we played the art schools. Chelsea was good, they were well equipped to put it on.

We did gigs supporting Doctors of Madness at Middlesbrough Town Hall, in the crypt. We were supposed to be using their PA but they wouldn't let us. All we had was these two Eliminator cabinets, which we used to use for small gigs, and two HH 200 watt amps which we thought we'd slaved up, but we didn't know how to do that properly. And this place held about two thousand people.

But it was great, we just blew them off the stage, just with sheer enthusiasm. We really had the hump with them, though. I think Steve nicked all the money from their clothes . . .

Did you ever sign a contract with Glitterbest, or with Malcolm?

Yeah, but only just before we signed the record contract. He brought in this management contract, from his solicitor, Stephen Fisher. I wanted to get legal advice, but nobody else was particularly bothered. John said, I hope you've read it, cos I'm gonna sign it, but if it's wrong, it's your fault. I had read it, and I wanted to argue the toss, cos he wanted 25 per cent of everything, which I thought was a bit strong. But nobody else was bothered to back me up. So we all signed it.

In the court case, John said he produced the contract after a gig, at two in the morning . . .

No, well, he might have done, but we had it for a couple of days. I remember sitting in Denmark Street, reading it. He agreed to do this, that and the other, and he had 25 per cent off the top. It wasn't a carve-up agreement or anything like that. As it happens, that 25 per cent, who knows, it's neither here nor there, really, cos there was never any accounts.

Were you involved at all in the record company negotiations?

No, that was going on while we were gigging. We were gigging quite a lot at that stage. It was sort of foisted on us, it was a bit of a surprise that there was a deal arranged. Chris Parry was interested as well. Polydor. I think the idea was we were gonna sign to them. We turned up to record at Kingsway Studios, and Malcolm hadn't told him we'd already signed to EMI the previous day, he was practically crying. Then the same thing happened to him with The Clash, then he finally got The Jam.

When you recorded the single for 'Anarchy', did that take a long time to do?

Yeah, we did it with Dave Goodman, it took about a week. I think it took so long because Malcolm was at the session, basically. The idea was to get the spirit of the live thing, but we were pressurised into getting it faster and faster and faster. We didn't really want that, we thought it was taking the character of the song away. We got the hump, doing it over and over again.

Then we went in with Chris Thomas, and did about six run-throughs while he was getting the sound together, and then we had it recorded. In fact, it's two takes; the first half is one take, and the second half is the other. In fact John turned up and said, 'I suppose you haven't even started yet', cos he thought we weren't playing well in the studio, but it wasn't our fault, we said, 'No, we're waiting for you to do the vocals.' We all just got on with it.

Then we went in a few days later and did some overdubs, and Chris Thomas reckoned that was it. Simple. I don't really like the other version, my idea about the song was it was a slow marching rhythm. More strident. But that was it really, we did a few other things while we were in the studio.

Was that when you did all that stuff like 'Roadrunner'?

That was at Wessex, with Dave Goodman. While we were attempting to do 'Anarchy'. Because we were in there so long, we didn't want to keep playing the same thing over again. In fact we went to another studio first, we started in Lansdowne Studios. Which was a fine studio, but it just didn't work there so we thought we'd try somewhere else. Dave was around for about two weeks, I think. But other stuff came out of it, like 'No Fun'. 'I Wanna Be Me' was recorded at Denmark Street, on the 4-track. And then it was tarted up somewhere else.

It seems that when you left, they lost the melody.

It's not for me to say, but there wasn't a lot after that. 'Bodies' isn't bad, I quite like that.

Can you remember anything about the Notre Dame gig?

That was for the TV. We'd just signed, and I wanted a new amp, and Malcolm wouldn't let me have one. I smashed my amp up at the end, so I'd have to have a new one. Then we decided we'd do an encore, So I had to plug directly into the PA, and I couldn't hear what I was playing. It was a good hall. It sounds funny, talking about the hall having good acoustics. People think, 'Oh the Sex Pistols wouldn't care about that', but we did.

Was Dave good with the sound?

As far as I can tell, but when you're on stage, behind the cabinets, you can't tell. Steve used to play with a phaser a lot, this little box. But I don't think it was that hard to get a good sound, we were reasonably tight. Paul had a good drum sound, and as I said before, we had decent equipment. There wasn't a lot of vocal harmonies or anything, it was direct.

Did you and Paul play closely together?

I suppose so, but we didn't really think about it, we'd been playing together so long. Two or three years.

What did you think of all the TV shows that you did then?

The *So It Goes* one was great. We did a number beforehand, as a warm-up, 'Problems', and I broke a string at the end, and they were worried about it going over time, because of the technicians' over-time rates and all that. And I'm sitting on the stage, cos I didn't have a spare guitar, putting a new string on, which takes a few minutes, and Tony Wilson comes over and says, 'Tell me, Johnny, why is it that you refused to do an interview?' 'Cos you're a cunt.'

And there's this big studio audience, two or three hundred people, and he just went bright red with embarrassment, and Clive James, who had a slot on the programme, got up thinking he was going to take control of the situation, and he was throwing all these questions at John, and John went absolutely mad. After that, we were clearing the equipment away and this older bloke came up, said, 'Were you in the band?' I said, 'Yeah.' 'Smashing, mate,' he said, 'it's about time somebody gave that guy a mouthful. The best thing I've seen on TV for ages.' It made my day.

Did they cut the version of 'Anarchy' that you played then?

Well, we finished the song, but I think they edited it to make it look even more chaotic than it was. I kicked over a mike stand at the end, you see it going over, and it landed right on top of one of those cameras. Oops. There's some good close-ups of my Anarchy shirt. But we didn't do a great deal of TV. After Bill Grundy.

Tell me about that.

Bill Grundy was in a right mood. What I've heard since was that he didn't want to interview us, not cos he thought we were loathsome and horrible, but because he didn't know that much about it. But also he thought he was the bigwig of the show, and he could call the shots. But the producer of the show said, 'No, you've got to do it.' And he had the hump about that. And he'd had a few drinks. He thought his position was being undermined.

While it was happening, Malcolm was behind the cameras, going, 'Oh no!'

What happened afterwards?

Well, I headed straight back to the green room to have another drink. But Malcolm just grabbed me, said, 'Come on, let's go.' There was a limo waiting outside and we all piled into that, and just as we pulled away, a Black Maria turned up with about half a dozen coppers. I suppose the switchboard must have been jammed, somebody must have called the police, and that was it. We were off then.

When you left the TV station did you think that something had happened?

Oh, something definitely had happened. But we didn't realise the consequences. We went back up to the rehearsals for the tour, except there wasn't much of a tour after that.

What happened the next day, when the papers came out?

We went into EMI. I got the bus in, cos I was living in Chiswick, and there was this bird who used to be one of the *Doctor Who* girls. I fancied her a bit, and she was half giving me the eye, kind of thing, but we never spoke again on the bus, but that morning, she gave me such a dirty look. I thought, oh, hang on, something's happened here. I hadn't seen the papers or anything.

What was EMI's attitude when you went in?

They thought it was funny, I think. All the people on the shop floor, as it were, wanted to hang on to us, they thought it was good for business. It was just the people on the top floor freaking out.

Did things change in the band after that?

What happened after that was we went out on this tour and we were hounded everywhere. We weren't getting to play. We were cooped up in hotel rooms, and it started to break down into factions a little bit. I think it accelerated something that was happening anyway. I was mates with Mick Jones at the time, and I used to room with Mick, and Steve and Paul were always together, and John was off doing whatever he was doing.

Was any of that tour fun?

Yeah, it was a laugh. In hindsight. But when you've got a gang of journalists trailing you in this coach, half a dozen cars chasing you over the Pennines, you just thought, silly bastards.

Did you stay on the coach the whole time, or did you come back to London?

No, Malcolm's attitude was we had to turn up and sit it out, kind of thing, so it looked like we were prepared to play. To come back to London would be to admit defeat. We did break it up a little bit, and we did do a few gigs: Leeds University; we went back to Caerphilly, that was a reorganised gig; we did Cleethorpes; and we went down to the West Country, to Plymouth, and we did an extra gig down there, cos it went down really well the night before, but because it was short notice there was nobody there.

There was only three bands on the tour then, cos we fell out with The Damned. The Mayor of some place wanted us to do a showcase just for him to decide whether to allow us to play, and we said, 'Fuck off, we're not doing that', and The Damned were prepared to do it, and we thought that was letting the side down. That was Jake [Riviera], I think, trying to get publicity for his boys. There was quite a lot of rivalry between Jake and Malcolm.

What did you do in the hotels when you couldn't play?

Just went out to the pub. At the Dragonara in Leeds was quite funny. The press came in and wanted to take some pictures, and they wanted us to smash something up, so there was this big potted plant in the foyer. Over that went. Then the press went to the manager, wanting a quote about our behaviour, and wasn't it disgusting. 'Oh, no', he said, 'I don't mind as long as they pay for it.' This was the *Sun*.

Another thing that made me think, with the gutter press, is when we went in for this interview after Grundy, we were larking around a bit, and they wanted us to get closer together for a picture, and Steve wouldn't cos he said, 'Johnny's got smelly armpits', or something, and I burped, as you do, and I said, 'Pardon me.' And when it came out in the paper, it was Johnny wouldn't sit close to Steve cos the guitarist had smelly armpits and the bass player just belched. Mostly I just remember silly little things like that.

Did the band start to come apart a bit from that point on?

Yeah, well it was tough doing that kind of thing, you know. I had trouble with my mum from that, cos I'd told her it was going to be on TV – you know, 'Ring round all the family, it's gonna be on TV' – and my cousin was watching, who was about seven at the time. I phoned up a couple of days later, test the water, you know, and I got a right earful.

There I was out on the road, and I'm getting my mum going, 'You don't think of us, why didn't you change your name', and all that. 'The girls at the gas board are all calling me Mrs Sex Pistol!' So on top of everything, I had all that going on every time I called home.

So what happened with 'Anarchy'? They pulled it?

Yeah, it went in at 27 in the charts, and the next week, nothing, they'd pulled it.

Were you aware of what was going on at EMI?

Not really, cos we were away, we did the Grundy show and then we were on tour. Incommunicado, really.

What were The Heartbreakers like?

I was really knocked out with them. They walked straight in and they were doing their soundcheck. We were rehearsing cos it was supposed to be a package tour, so we were doing change-overs, and running times, and they were doing 'Chinese Rocks'. And they finished and sat down and we introduced ourselves, and I was sitting next to Jerry Nolan. I said, 'I really like that one, "Chinese Rocks".' He said, 'Well, thank you.' I said, 'Well what's that one all about then?' He says, 'Heroin.' 'Oh, that's nice.' I didn't know, you know!

After the tour, I really had the hump. I wasn't getting on with John, at all. I thought he was just getting a bit big-headed. Well, totally big-headed. I'm quite an easy-going kind of bloke, and it was something I didn't really need. At the beginning we were doing quite a lot of writing together, and I'd stay at his house and all that, we'd go out for a drink. Slag the other two off, and I suppose they used to slag us off.

But I got increasingly pissed off, cos I'd go out to gigs and people would come up to me and ask, 'What's going on, Glen?' Offering to get us gigs. Obviously there was a certain amount of bullshit involved, but some of it was meant. And I was thinking, if they can do that, how come we can't get to play anywhere? I had the hump with Malcolm, cos I see myself as a musician, I want to play, there's no point in being in a band otherwise. I'd see it as being made to look like puppets.

Malcolm had a lot of power by that time. He was being quoted in the press all over the place. The last thing we did, we went to Amsterdam, played the Paradiso. We went to Rotterdam as well, and we got bottled there. Then we went back to the Paradiso, and that was the last gig I did with them. After that there was a bit of a lax period when nobody really knew what was going on. And they had the hump with me, cos I wasn't pulling my weight.

I had a talk with the three of them – Paul, Steve and Malcolm, not John. I told them, I hate John's guts by now, all that press thing had gone to his head. And it was getting a bit 'Johnny Rotten and the Sex Pistols', which I didn't like, but that didn't bother me too much. It was an amalgamation of a lot of things. On top of that, I was getting fed up with John's voice. The stuff I wanted to write wasn't really falling in with what the band could do, you know.

I liked to write melody, and I'd been doing it for about three years. So after that, I think Steve and Paul went away on holiday, and I started playing around with a few other people. And when they came back, I heard that they'd started trying Sid out on bass. And people were going, 'Aren't you worried?' I said, 'No, not particularly', cos I had the Rich Kids starting up by then.

Anyway, I had a call from Malcolm, who said, 'We've got to have a meeting, and I want you to go in there and kick down the door kind of thing, tell them you're the bass player.' And I said, 'To be honest, I'm just not interested any more.' He was a bit upset about that. Anyway, we had a meeting in The Blue Post, behind the 100 Club. And he said, 'If that's the way you feel, I'm sorry to hear it but fair enough.' And I said, 'No hard feelings, the best of luck to you', and he said, 'Yeah, and to you.' And the next day, or a couple of days later, the *NME* comes out, and he'd sent them a telegram and told them he'd sacked me. For liking The Beatles. I mean, I don't even particularly like The Beatles. It was pathetic.

Did you have to sign a release when you left?

Yeah. I got my share of what was left of the kitty, the money that we got from EMI, less what we'd spent on the tour. And I would get my share of the songwriting royalties, which is fair enough. But I said, 'What about stuff that I've played on', and he said, 'I doubt if there'll be anything else coming out that you've played on, we're going to re-record everything.'

I wasn't too sure about it, but I was skint at the time. He had a cheque sitting there. I was pretty green. I needed to pay the rent, so I had to sign it. About three grand. I wanted proper accounts, but there was none of that. It wasn't bad, but it was well short of a quarter share of £50,000, or whatever it was we got from EMI.

Why weren't you involved in the court case that was the four Pistols against Malcolm?

Well, I think I'd given up my rights by signing this paper. But I always got my songwriting royalties. I get a quarter share of those songs, I did a deal with Warner Bros. That's a separate thing.

So the stuff that was in the Glitterbest settlement wouldn't have been record royalties ...

Yeah, it would have been recording and songwriting royalties, because their share of the songwriting royalties was still tied up with McLaren. Because I'd signed the release, I dealt with Warners direct, so I was better off. So in a way, until that money is sorted out with the other guys, I've done the best out of it. But I'm chasing them for the stuff that has come out, that early stuff like 'Roadrunner', and 'No Fun'. I've never seen a penny of that.

What about the LP?

Not most of the LP, no, just the singles.

Did they get extra musicians in on the LP?

Actually, after I left, I was going to play on 'God Save the Queen', which used to be called 'No Future'. I went to the session, I was going to play bass on it, but there was a bit of animosity there, and Steve decided he'd have a go at doing it himself. As far as I know, Steve played the bass on it. I think a bloke called Andy Allen might have played bass on the LP. I'm not really sure.

What did the other two think about you leaving?

They must have been pretty concerned about it, after all they started the band in the first place. It was Steve and Paul's band, right from the get-go. I think they thought John was quite funny, and they could tolerate him. It was like water off a duck's back to them. Whereas it got my back up.

So did you stop all contact with the Pistols when you left in the February?

208

Yeah. Well, I used to bump into them. I couldn't care less what was going on. On top of that the Rich Kids were talking big money with EMI. We were getting a pretty good deal.

I always thought of the Pistols as two lines that came together and really worked for a while, then broke apart.

How long do you think it came together for?

I think the run-up to when 'Anarchy' came out, maybe that year.

Did people have a go at you in the street?

Not really, the people I knew, knew I was in the band. But I didn't stick out as much, like Johnny. All that happened later, after I'd left, after the boat trip and all that.

Can I just check which songs you wrote most of the music to? You wrote 'Anarchy'?

Yes, and 'God Save the Queen'. All of 'Pretty Vacant', except that John changed some of the lyrics in the second verse. 'Submission', me and John wrote the lyrics, I wrote the music. That was funny. We turned up at this rehearsal, at the Roundhouse, and there was this symphony orchestra there doing a live broadcast, and we were in the basement. We were making a racket, and they came down to tell us to turn it off. It was picking up on their mikes. And we wouldn't.

There was trouble going on with Paul at that time, he was thinking of leaving. We'd turned up at this rehearsal and Paul and Steve didn't turn up. So me and John went and had a drink in the pub opposite. I said, 'Malcolm's got this idea for a song.' John goes, 'Oh yeah, what's that then?' I said, 'Submission, about bondage and all that. Oh, gawd.' And John goes, 'How about a submarine mission?'

So really, it was just taking the piss out of Malcolm. We sat there and wrote the lyrics in about five minutes. Most of them, anyway. I like it, I think it's one of the best ones. I like the noise on it too, we did that at Denmark Street, it was Steve blowing into a kettle. I think Ray Stevenson's got a picture of Steve doing it.

'I Wanna Be Me' was a four-way thing. We'd work up a riff and change it around, and John would write the lyric. Same with 'Problems'. The music on 'New York' is mostly mine, John wrote about the Dolls. I thought the lyrics were good. I think 'I Wanna Be Me' was about Nick Kent. 'Did You No Wrong' was Wally's riff. 'Satellite' was mainly Steve's. The first three singles were mostly mine, the most focused and coherent.

Did you know Sid at all?

Reasonably well, yeah. He was all right. He came up to me once, down at the Roxy Club, just after I'd left them. I wasn't that bothered, I was doing what I wanted to do, he was a bit surprised. I offered to give him some lessons.

There was a side to Sid that was quite sweet, and there was a side that was violent. Do you think Malcolm put him into that role?

I think it had come earlier than that. Sid and John were pretty close mates, and when John got in the band and was getting the limelight, Sid felt a bit left out. I think it was his way of attracting attention. But then when he became known for that, I think he must have got caught up in it. He wasn't exactly in a healthy frame of mind, what with one thing and another.

Were there a lot of drugs about when you were in the Pistols?

Not really. I think John was into it, quite a lot. I certainly wasn't.

Do you think people got the wrong end of the stick, about the Pistols?

I think there were two distinct episodes. There was a real good rock'n'roll band, and then there was what happened later; the boat trip, Sid pegging it, all that, was a different thing, and to me, later, outside of it, it did look like a puppet band. That could sound like sour grapes. I think it created a precedent for the kind of media coverage that you get these days. People get taken apart. I don't think it happened to the same extent before that.

Johnny Rotten

Sex Pistols' singer, lyricist and front man – the voice and the face of a generation. It took a year of negotiation with John Lydon's then manager, Keith Bourton, to get an interview, but once the tape started rolling, Lydon was helpful and reflective – no attitude at all. Two sessions, over many pints, in the Warwick Castle pub on Portobello Road in London's Notting Hill.

Can you remember roughly what month it was that you started with the band?

It might have been August '75. It was summer.

So that would have been about three months before you played your first gig.

Yeah. They never turned up to the first rehearsal. Never bothered to ring me and let me know. I felt like a fool walking around Bermondsey Wharf, and it's dangerous down there, particularly the way I was looking at that particular time.

Were you still in your hippy gear then or had you cut your hair?

Bright green crop, I looked like a cabbage.

When did you cut your hair off?

About two years before, when my old man threw me out. In fact he threw me out because I got my hair cut. You see at the time, long hair was accepted, and I thought sod that, so I hacked it off and dyed it green. 'Out! Out, you dirty bastard, don't come back!'

So what did you do?

I went squatting with Sid. Hampstead. Not the posh end; those awful Victorian dwellings round the back of the station. Really

desperate people lived up there, it was awful. I liked it, it was better than home at the time, it wasn't winter. When winter came I
was on tour. I could never say life has been hard for me. I'm not
one of those people that wallows in misery – if I don't like a situation I'll do something about it.

**But I got the impression from what you told me before that your
family was quite stable and content . . .**

Yeah, apart from the fact that my old man never used to speak to me
to the day I left home. Then he suddenly started showing signs of
respect. 'Oh, you're a man now . . . ' he must have thought, 'that
damn wimp, I hate him. He'll never be anything.' I hardly knew my
old man till I left.

Isn't it funny how fathers are, unless you're obviously a lad?

It's like birds, they've got to kick them out of the nest at a certain age,
which I think is healthy and natural. I've no time for people who stay
at home.

How many were there besides you?

Three others. Martin, the youngest, moved to America; he was sick
of it here, and he was fast turning into an outrageous hooligan.
Now he's completely different. I'm beginning to have doubts, he's
the complete Californian.

Are you the oldest?

Yeah. Jimmy and Bobby are fairly solid about what they want.
Bobby wants nothing, Jimmy wants everything.

Were you always brought up in Finsbury Park?

No, we moved around a lot, for all kinds of reasons. I can't get to the
bottom of any of it. I don't know really where I was born. My birth
certificate was registered two years after I was apparently born. We
lived in Norfolk, Hastings, all over.

Did you like that moving around?

When you're young you don't care, it just means you don't have to go to school. I think it's important, yes. We lived on the ground floor of a place right on the sea at Hastings. It isn't there any more, the sea has washed it away. I suppose it was really squalor, but my memories of it aren't bad. Kids don't see the dirt and the peeling wallpaper. I was about four or five. Until I was about six.

We went to Norfolk for a year when I was about ten. Came back to London with an oo-ar accent, which didn't go down too well. I must have been about eleven. I don't really remember any of it, and I don't want to. None of it was romantic and brilliant, and no interest at all to me. I always wanted what I wanted right from an early age. I always lived outside of things, looking at things from a detached point of view.

I can remember my parents having parties and my brother Jimmy doing his soldier dance to some dismal Irish folk song, and I'd be sitting in a corner going, 'This is awful, they're not getting me to do that.' My old man never talked to me, but I never talked to any of them.

I used to hate my mother's clothes, she used to wear that crimplene stuff that was very fashionable then, a huge beehive hairdo, and the smell of the hairspray used to repulse me. And my aunts and all their friends. I remember the smell of sweaty corsets. And all the men had stinking armpits. I wasn't happy.

Where do the Lydons come from? Galway?

Galway's the old man, Cork's my mother. First generation. Part of my fantasy is maybe I was really born in Ireland. It's not much of a fantasy, I must admit; going back there now I want nothing to do with the place. The South is all right, I like the easy-going attitude. It isn't like the North. I've got relatives both sides of the fence there, Catholic and Protestant, and it's nothing to do with religion, it's just Mafia. Territory. Once the army goes by, the gunmen are at your door, you've got to give them money and that's all there is to it.

Did you see the Iggy Pop concert at the old King's Cross Scala?

Yes, it was really quite bad, there was just him and James Williamson playing the most dreadful out-of-tune guitar. He wasn't liked, in fact he was ignored. I liked it. He'd run around and he'd bash himself with the microphone. They only played for about twenty minutes, if that. It was no great memorable event. Nowadays, of course, everybody says they were there.

I mean, I've also seen Quintessence live.

I bet they were good.

Ha! Haargh! At the Oval. The worst experience of my life, we were right smack in the middle, and the PA at the back was out of phase with the stage PA, and you kept getting things double, and when the wind blew it was quadruple, and the sound whipped around the middle, like whipped cream. Terrible. The Faces were terrible, Rod Stewart was a complete idiot.

Is that who you'd gone to see, or The Who?

I'd gone to see no-one in particular. Oh yes, the Grease Band, I'd mistakenly thought I might like them.

What did you used to do in '73, '74? Stay at home and go out to gigs every so often?

Yeah. The Roundhouse was particularly good. I used to get in there for about two bob, cos the bouncers were quite friendly to me. I had horrible hair down to here. At fourteen that was quite rebellious. A jean shirt. No jackets. I could never wear those bumfreezer satin jackets, I was always too self-conscious about my fat arse. No skinhead-ism, never was into that, I was the freak of the neighbourhood. I had hob-nail boots painted bright green. And multicoloured suede boots. What a joke. Platforms.

Where did you meet Sid, John?

Hackney and Stoke Newington. I was there to do my O levels cos I was thrown out of school when I was about fifteen; part of the reason was because of my long hair. They'd ridiculously described me as being a Hell's Angel. Because I had a bicycle. I had to have a bicycle because they wouldn't give me a bus pass. The school was I think thirty yards within the three-mile limit, so you'd have to wear a leather jacket or coat in the rain: therefore, Hell's Angel.

214

What was the school called?

William of York. Absolute filth, a shit-hole. Catholic schools should be pulled down, they're wrong. They separate you from everybody else. The local normal schools would resent that, they'd think something special was going on there, so there'd be school fights. Every evening at four o'clock, the clash of cultures. Those are not friendly bus stops.

Did the school teach you anything at all, even on your own terms?

Hate and resentment. The religious classes were just excruciating. In the end I said I wanted to be a Muslim, just to get out of that class. It was rubbish. You're not allowed to question, you have to accept as a fact, you'll die and go to hell if you don't believe in the lightning rod of Jesus Christ Almighty and the sanctity of his virgin mother. What nonsense. Awful, hideous rubbish.

Did you read a lot? What did you read?

Mostly history, any kind of documentary book, biographies, and good novels. I couldn't stand science fiction though. Loathed it. Unreal. All this nonsense about ray guns that could do all kinds of shit. Asimov to me is a fucking bore. I loved *Fear and Loathing in Las Vegas*.

Taking five different drugs in the same weekend . . .

That's very much like being in the Sex Pistols!

So what happened to you between leaving home and you joining the band?

I don't remember a great deal of it, because I loved getting wildly drunk. It was good fun, it was freedom, but then responsibility rears its ugly head at a point when you realise you're flat broke.

Didn't you work at Cranks at one point?

Yeah, as a cleaner, when it was in Heal's. That's funny, isn't it? With Sid. If only those health-food hippies knew who was cleaning out their kitchen. What fun! I tell you, we cleaned it out in more ways than one. Night after night we stuffed our faces. Not the till, just the food side of it. We'd wait for the boss to go, and we'd run around Heal's trying out beds, cos there was no-one else in the building – it was a huge adventure playground.

It was quite nice, there was no time limit on when we had to finish, so we waltzed out of there at one in the morning. A dirty kitchen tonight. Such fun, the toy department. You couldn't actually steal anything, but you could use it all as much as you wanted. It was great. You remember *Night of the Living Dead*, where they're in that huge department store, that's what it was like, it was a dream come true. We'd move furniture, the way you'd like your house to be, whatever.

How long did that job last?

About six months.

What other jobs did you do?

When I was living at home I worked at a sewage farm. Killing rats in Guildford, and laying concrete with my dad. Huge amounts of money, for that time. Seventy quid a week was outrageous money. I was thrown out after that. The other job was in a shoe factory. What a farce.

The one job I really wanted, I went to the dole and said I wanted to work in a funeral parlour, and they would not take me seriously. I wouldn't declare my exam qualifications to anyone, I knew the jobs they'd bung my way wouldn't be what I wanted. Bank clerk and all that crap. Tedious, and a trap. There's no way out. You have to have your hair cut in a certain way, you have to wear that suit, and once you allow that to happen, you've lost it.

Did you squat anywhere else?

No, that was it, really.

What was Sid like?

He was a Bowie fan. He'd do silly things to get his hair to stick up, cos it never even occurred to him to use hairspray. He'd lie upside down with his head in an oven, so his hair would go rigid in the heat! Absolutely hilarious, he was. Sid was such a poser, a clothes-hound of the worst kind. *19* was the magazine he loved the most. Anything they told you to wear, he'd have to have it.

You called Sid 'Sid', didn't you?

Yeah, after my pet hamster.

And was he named 'Vicious' after the Lou Reed song?

No, apparently Syd Barrett used to call himself Sid Vicious. I can't remember where that came from, but I remember being told that and thinking, okay, that'll do.

Was he the first of you to go to the shop?

No. I went first. I was intrigued, they were doing something completely different from everybody else, and they weren't liked, which was absolutely brilliant. They were totally horrible people. Vivienne was the most awful old bag, and that really fascinated me, she just didn't give a damn about you. To buy anything in that shop was a real fight.

The shop was just stunning. The originality impressed me with Vivienne, her clothes were very very good. She's really mad. One of her best friends was Judy Nylon, and she had a row with her, and because I knew Judy, she wouldn't talk to me. That kind of pettiness was around all the time, you had to watch your step, cos Vivienne's a vicious lady. A killer. She's more than once tried to smack me.

When you started going to the shop, were there many kids there or was it just perverts?

Perverts. There were no kids, there was no scene. They were relatively new, because before that they used to sell to nothing but teddy boys. They were still trying to get rid of that stigma. I think that was where all that teddy-boy hatred of us began. They were the teds' clothes designers, and overnight they got rid of the drapes and put in rubber T-shirts.

I loved the rubber T-shirt, lock, stock and barrel, I thought it was the most repulsive thing I had ever seen! To wear it as a piece of clothing rather than part of some sexual fetish to me was hilarious.

Jordan was always friendly. Genuinely interested. She'd obviously seen us for what we were, which was silly little kids who hadn't got a clue.

217

So when you first went down to the shop, there was hardly anybody there. When did people start coming in?

A lot of the fashionables, Little Nell and the *Rocky Horror* lot, would always be around, but I wasn't allowed to know them. I was never introduced and they always looked at me as scum. Until of course the Sex Pistols started to take off, and then it was, 'Ooooh, Hiiii!!!'

Jones and Cook knew all these people, because Malcolm had taken them out all the time, but not I. I think they wanted me to be this mystery figure that they could hide in the cupboard and spring out like a jack-in-the-box. Close the lid when it's not needed any more.

From what you were saying, you didn't really get on with either Malcolm or Viv . . .

No, Vivienne was all right, but it was like holding a firecracker that could explode at any moment. I think Viv had some kind of respect for me, though. Definitely about clothes and things. The bondage pants was my idea. I thought it would be hilarious to have a kilt sewn on to a pair of trousers. They were incredibly stupid and wonderful, but they managed to offend everybody in the world. But now of course it's become another uniform, it's lost its individuality.

You must have enjoyed wearing all that stuff, it must have been great fun.

Yes, I like dressing up, I always have done.

What were you wearing then?

No flares. Hated flares, always have. Tank tops, god almighty. I had a black one with rainbow stripes. The patchwork jackets, the Budgie gear. I could never afford that, and I thought it looked silly, anyway. Those round collars, awful.

Did you used to enjoy going up and down the King's Road winding people up?

Yeah, not so much enjoy it. It was necessary. People were very stiff and boring then. Long hair was everywhere. I was bored with everything. What was there to do then, there was soul boys and the Roxy

Music kind of clothes then, and all that was naff, very weedy and not going anywhere. It's all very well dressing up, but you should be able to use these things to make deliberate statements. People think dressing up is enough, but it isn't. It has to come with an attitude, a direction, otherwise it's completely useless, vacuous.

Who did you used to go down the King's Road with?

Sid, and Wobble, and John Gray from school. I met Wobble at Kingsway – what a dump that was. We were in exactly the same predicament – outcasts, the unwanted – and we were all extremely ugly people, which helps. Good looks just creates vanity; it's a good thing to be ugly, it makes you harder. People thought we were sick, because we were unrelated to anything they could put a label on.

Are the stories about how you came to join the group true, that you were asked to audition when you used to hang around the shop and they spotted you?

Not hanging around the shop, although I did buy stuff there. It was Bernie Rhodes that spotted me, because he thought I looked bloody peculiar, with the spiky hair, and the safety pins, and everything torn, and an I hate Pink Floyd T-shirt. They thought that was stunning. All of that so-called image was out of poverty. There was no great master plan on my part or theirs that we got together. I was asked to mime to a jukebox, to an Alice Cooper record, 'Eighteen' and 'School's Out', which I did very well thank you!

Were you nervous at all?

Terrified. It never occurred to me that the music biz could be a place for me to vent whatever talent I had.

Who thought up the name, was it Malcolm?

Steve Jones. It used to be Cutie Jones and the Sex Pistols – that was Steve. He was also the one that called me Rotten, and the name stuck.

Was that because of the teeth?

Yeah.

Was there ever a group discussion about the name?

No, I liked that name very much, I thought it was hilarious. The word Sex had never been used in that blatant way before, and to put it on to a pop band was very funny. 'This'll have a few eyelids batting.' I thought it was perfect to offend the old ladies.

In the early days, how did you get on with the rest of the band?

Alright. I liked Steve and Paul very much. I still do to this day, particularly Steve, Steve is hilarious. He'll never change, and although he's a bit of a tea-leaf, I found Steve Jones to be one of the most honest people I've ever met. If you ask him something outright, he cannot lie to you. He will tell you exactly, and that impressed me. I hope that is part and parcel of my own make-up. That is essential. Life is far too short to be telling fibs. It gets you nowhere.

What about Glen?

Glen was a bit of a mummy's boy. The best musician out of the lot of us, certainly, but too bogged down into The Beatles. He wanted us to be a camp version of the Bay City Rollers. He wanted that kind of innocence, and I'm sorry, I was completely the other way, I saw the Sex Pistols as something completely guilt-ridden. You know, the kids want misery, they want death. They want threatening noises, because that shakes you out of your apathy.

Can you remember your first St Martins gig?

Yes, supporting Bazooka Joe. It was vile, they pulled the plug on us. I don't blame them, we were terrible.

So you were in this band, playing around, you were starting to gate-crash gigs – when did you realise the power that you had?

Not really, no. I don't think we ever did, till the day it stopped. We were so intensely disliked, there was no real audience for us outside of the 100 Club, that was it. Anywhere else, you were taking your life in your hands. We'd go up North and we'd be lucky to return. We played all sorts of weird places like Scarborough and Barnsley. A teddy-boy pub, of all places, in the middle of nowhere.

Whose idea was that?

Who was the manager at the time? Anything to pick up a fiver.

There must have been some point where you thought, yeah, I can do this, this is exciting.

Yeah, right from the start, when I was given the opportunity. Sod them, they're going to go off doing Small Faces covers and Who rip-offs, I don't care, I'll just write the songs I want to write.

How did you write songs at that stage?

A lot with Steve, we'd sit with an acoustic guitar and just thrash out ideas – no, no, no, yes, that'll do. Steve always had a set of the lyrics before anyone else. It was very little to do with the music then. I couldn't play a referee's whistle.

What was the first song you wrote?

Probably 'Problems'. I hated rehearsing, I couldn't stand it, so I'd hide in a corner. I'd write these little things and I'd crawl into a corner and mumble, hoping that no-one would hear. In those days, the only time the band heard what I was doing was live. That's when it dawned on Glen what 'God Save the Queen' was getting up to. He was furious.

Can you remember any fights on stage?

I remember a fight with Paul, but it wasn't really a fight. That was at the pub on North End Road. The Nashville. I decided to quit that night. They'd decided that I was an arsehole again. Over nothing at all, I suppose. It was actually highly enjoyable, and after the gig it was a huge laugh. What kept winding me up all the time was that I kept feeling left out of things. I didn't ever feel part of the band.

That was presumably just the nucleus of Steve and Paul, because Glen probably didn't either.

Yeah, Glen was off into his own trip. Looking back on it I feel quite sorry for Glen, because he really was humiliated time and time again.

By Steve and Paul, or by Malcolm?

By the three of them. And by me, although I'm pleading an injustice

221

here, at the same time I was delivering one to someone else. I was very insecure, and I thought, maybe that's the way to get in here. Then I stopped wanting people to like me and just get on with the serious job. And treat it as such.

Were you nervous?

Terrified. I'm very nervous before gigs, I can quite easily vomit with nerves before a gig. I still do to this day. But the minute I get on, it's quite different. I really enjoy the pressure. When I'm writing or making albums, I love the pressure. I've never been casual about my work. Hence the intensity, I suppose, that people keep seeing in me. Actually I used to bury my nerves in tons of alcohol.

Did you take a lot of speed as well?

Then, yeah. I loved the stuff.

Did that change you, do you think?

I'm normally a very slow person, and it made me more intense, but you get bored with these things, the thrill of it wears off.

Did it make you paranoid?

No. I'm naturally paranoid. It makes me feel better, but I haven't taken it in years. I could never do the pills, just the powder.

What was it like actually being on stage and playing in front of those hostile audiences?

I don't do things to deliberately antagonise people. I'm deadly earnest about what I'm doing, I think it's valid and necessary, but when an audience behaves badly to you, it does tend to make your work better. At that time I'd never known what a good audience was.

When did you start getting good audiences?

Never in the Pistols, I don't think.

The 100 Club?

Yes, I'd forgotten about those, but there again I felt bored that it wasn't going any further. It was too minuscule, too small. We could very easily have fallen in love with ourselves and stayed there and died the death, like the Small Faces. You've got to get out of there, you've got to preach to a wider audience.

You must also have been having a good time at some stage through the first year?

No, it was very tough. Very tough. Lack of money, being banned from everywhere, the riots – I mean we were hated. There was no audience for us. Don't let people lie about this. Everybody was stuck firmly up the arses of ELP and Yes.

What was it like going in that van to all those places up North?

Vile, horrible, a nightmare. No chance to relax, nothing. Nylon sheets. Mind you it's still the same now. It doesn't matter how posh the hotel is, it's still the same nausea. I've always found the cheap hotels to be better.

In the early days, one thing that a couple of people said about the Pistols was that there was quite a lot of discussion in '76 about politics. Is that true?

No, not with us. They left me with a free hand, and I naturally obliged, because that's how I felt. Not political anarchy, because I still to this day believe that anarchy is just a mind-game for the middle classes, but personal anarchy, which is quite different. Unlike most anarchists, we were offering an alternative. We were breaking down the structures but offering a clear new way. I don't think that's been fully understood.

What new way were you offering?

A much more honest and open approach, not hiding behind bullshit and imagery but attacking it all.

Who were you close to at that period? Did you see a lot of John Gray and Wobble?

I still do. Those are still my friends. I remember Malcolm saying to me once that he didn't think I should hang around with my mates, cos they were bad for me.

Why was that?

Because we'd think things out.

Did you discuss a lot of things with them?

Yeah, I like to verbalise about things, and if you're not going to get that out of the band you're working with then you're going to go outside. It's very important to have an interaction with other people. That's the only way you're going to know you're being wrong – when your friends say, 'That's a crock of shit, John.'

Somebody said that some of the Pistols, maybe not you, took acid at Louise's?

Oh yeah. Always at Louise's, it heightens the enjoyment. It was a naff club. That's when I used to hang around with prostitutes, who I think are the most open and honest people on this earth.

People like Linda [Ashby]?

Yes, and hundreds more. I never went out with Linda, I went out with her mate once, and she caught us and beat the living daylights out of me.

There was Debbi as well, wasn't there?

Yes, Debbi was funny, a bit like a pudding. Very nice person. I don't know what she's like now though, I haven't spoken to her in years except on the telephone. Do you remember her in [porn story] *Mayfair Was My Manor?*

She made it all up, and got a lot of money.

Of course. This is one thing that Chrissie Hynde used to do. One of Chrissie's jobs was to write letters for *Forum*, and I wrote a few with her. Used to just sit there making up this utter gunk and then buy it the next month and think, people are masturbating to this nonsense! Hilarious. It was a very pure time then, towards sex. It wasn't treated as something dirty. People took it as it comes. It didn't matter what your sex was, it didn't matter. It was very open.

Was the Paris trip fun?

Yes, it was very good. That's when Siouxsie Sue turned up in a swastika and was beaten up. For wearing swastikas, I thought they were quite foolish. Although I know the idea behind it, it was the same with Sid, was to debunk all this crap from the past, wipe history clean and have a fresh approach, but it doesn't really work that way. I used to wear Luftwaffe badges, upside down, but that's the most I'd do to that, so you can't associate me with Nazis.

Can you remember when you signed the contract with Malcolm?

Yes, it was at [Stephen] Fisher's office.

Did he give you plenty of time to look at it?

No. We had no independent lawyers. We were told, if you don't sign it tonight, there'd be no deal. Very shyster. At that age you're very naive, you don't think of these things. You just see: contract. Ouch, the big time. Record company. Money. You think of the hundred quid you're going to get out of it, not how for the rest of your life it'll be like an albatross around your neck.

How many per cent did the contract give Malcolm? Twenty?

No idea, I can't remember. I still have a copy of it somewhere. I've learned since to keep all these things, and read them with a fine toothcomb.

There were some wonderful lines in 'God Save the Queen'. How did you write, was it fast or did you write and edit?

In the kitchen at the squat, just like that. I thought about it for weeks and then it came out in one go. I still write like that. But how far can you take that kind of approach, really? You fast run out of subjects, you can only really say all that once, and then move on to new territory. I couldn't see the Sex Pistols continuing, cos if we did, we'd have been like The Rolling Stones, a parody of ourselves. It had to stop.

It's interesting that the only new songs after Glen left were 'Holidays', 'Belsen' and 'Bodies'. They're more sort of raps, aren't they?

No, I disagree. They were getting out of the politics area, which I wanted to do. I was being asked all kinds of stupid questions by the press, 'What are your political views?' I'm sorry, I won't answer that. I hate Thatcher, but so do most people. I hate left-wing politics as much as I hate right-wing. I can't vote for Jeremy Thorpe's Liberals, or any amalgamation therein.

Can you remember much about the boat trip?

My brother got arrested. I remember when we had got off the boat and Malcolm was on the boat, going, 'There he is, that's Johnny Rotten!' To the police! He wanted me nicked! And I slipped away magnificently! Yes, we all got away. Damned if I was going to be beaten up in the cells for publicity. Fuck that!

It was really tedious, it was like patting yourself on the back, playing to a captive audience who have to pretend they like you, one way or another. Selfish rubbish is what that was.

Did you do a lot of recording at Wessex? There was a lot of time spent there.

A lot of guitar overdubs. One song, I think it was 'Anarchy', there were twenty-one guitars. These was Steve's first time, but it was all of our first times, and there was one track left for the vocals, that was it. All I can presume is that Mr Chris Thomas didn't know how to bounce down, and neither did we. I don't think he was particularly interested. But I had to do my bit in one go. But twenty-one guitars, I couldn't believe the ego.

Were you recording the album after the attacks, or before?

All that was happening during those sessions.

Was the studio a safe place?

Yeah, but the local pubs weren't. It was very odd, cos it was Highbury, an area I was brought up in. But there's a huge element of that to it as well, that the working class hate you if it looks like you're making good, or getting out. They want to drag you back in. Then there's a ten-year period and suddenly they all think you're marvellous. Cos you've been around for a bit and the jealousies have been blunted. If you're born in the ghetto, don't be the first one out. They'll all follow if you open the door for them, but . . .

What do remember about being attacked in '77? What happened?

I was with Chris Thomas in a pub.

You'd just been recording?

Yeah, and 'God Save the Queen' was in the charts, and as we left for his car in the car park, we were attacked by a gang of knife-wielding yobs, who were chanting, 'We love our Queen, you bastard.' I mean normally I'd say they were National Front, but a third of them at least were black. There was all sorts.

Just lads out on a spree?

Yeah, just out for violence. I got some bad cuts from that. I got stabbed here, and it severed two tendons, so this hand is fucked for ever, and I'm left-handed. I can't close the fist properly. I'll never play guitar, there's no power to it. I jumped into the car and someone jumped in after me with a machete and cut me from there down to there. I had on extremely thick leather trousers at the time, thank fucking god, cos it would have ripped the muscle out and now I'd be a one-legged hoppity.

And of course Malcolm thought that was hilarious. Then Paul got jumped at Hammersmith, he got hit on the head with a hammer or something like that.

Jamie got his leg broken....

And all this time we had no money.

Were you on a wage, John?

Twenty-five a week, if that, but that was only when we had gigs, and we had very few gigs, so normally no money at all.

Did that change at all, or was it all the way through?

It was pretty consistent.

So how did you live?

Very, very badly; I was squatting. But you know, your face is in the newspaper morning, noon and night, and they're calling you all kinds of vile filthiness, and you still have to go home on the subway and meet a gang of drunken yobs who want to tear you apart, because they think you're a millionaire. People automatically associate your face in the newspaper with money, which is quite wrong.

Weren't you living in Chelsea Cloisters at some time or other?

Eventually, yeah, when we got thrown out of our other place.

Was the LP done over a long period of time?

No, it was all done pretty much at one go. I remember about twenty-five tracks were devoted to Steve's guitar, and I was given one track per song, and I'd better get it right first time. It was good, and I still follow that philosophy. If I don't get something right in one go, I'm never going to get it right at all. I can't be bothered to do vocals in bits and pieces.

I'm thinking of the vocal on 'Holidays in the Sun'. How would you work in the studio? Were you under pressure?

Yeah, I'd be sitting there all day, screwed up, dying of nerves, dreading the moment when I'd be called down, and with all that energy and adrenalin and fear, I'd just let rip. The most times I could ever do it would be four times in a row, and by then I'd be completely hoarse. I had to go home.

Was the ending of that song ad-libbed?

Totally. I don't think there's any great talent in what I do; I hit the nail on the head sometimes. If anything, that's when instinct takes over, none of it is premeditated. You can't work out those moments.

Did you like the album in the end?

It was too produced, too clean. It still sound like that now, too nice. It reminds me of a West-Coast record the way everything fits so nicely into place, all note-perfect. It isn't what makes you want to go back and listen to a record.

Did you try and work out any new material with the band, after *Bollocks*?

Yes. One particular song was 'Religion', which no-one wanted to touch. The only one who was interested was Sid, and he couldn't play the bass line. There's one picture from America where we're all sitting on the stage, and Sid's got the bass and I'm pointing and Steve's sitting behind. That was 'Religion', and they wouldn't touch it. 'It's vile, can't do that. People won't like us!' Ha-haa!!! Which is still one of my favourite songs. And that was it, it was a waste of time trying to get them involved with anything else. I started to write my own stuff independently from them.

It seemed to me that after the Swedish trip, the whole thing pretty much fell apart. Or were there other good bits? What about the secret tour, the SPOTS?

Some of it was quite enjoyable. The gig part was all right. The rest of it, the hotel rooms and the boredom was nauseating.

What about being banned and not being able to play anywhere, was that just a Malcolm hype?

I don't know about all that. All I knew was that Malcolm said we were banned, and it's since come to light that that wasn't quite the truth. If that's the case, then Malcolm overestimated his publicity angle quite badly. All it achieved was to make us and the audience extremely frustrated. It achieved nothing press-wise, because nobody really cared. Journalists are by nature bastards. This I know.

Can you remember much about that last tour of England before you went to the States?

I remember Brunel University being awful, it was hideous, a fiasco. We were in that big hall, which was jam-packed, nobody really knew why anybody was there, least of all us. I was very confused by the sheer popularity of it, and I thought, this is horrible, it shouldn't be like this. I'd seen us as a small, clubby band at that time, we were way ahead of ourselves. We didn't know how to cut it on stage, how to get past the first twenty rows.

Did you ever cut it on stage?

At the 100 Club, definitely, up North a couple of times, but not like that. Paris, difficult.

There's a couple of shots of you performing where you look absolutely exultant.

Well it's great fun to take the piss out of fans. Here's some more rubbish. The good gigs were when we were taking the piss out of ourselves, our situation. That didn't happen at Brunel; we were all terrified, there were too many people, we didn't know how to deal with it. And there was a real nasty mood in that audience, all trying to out-punk each other, and the fun had gone.

Sid was out of his tree, thinking he was god, because by that time Nancy was telling him he was 'the only star in this band'. The fact that Sid made no recorded contribution to any record didn't occur to him to be important.

What were the last gigs like at Penzance and Huddersfield and Newport?

Again, all right, but too big, they were missing the point of it. Sid was taking the fun away and it was nasty and stupid. When we went to America we fell apart. It was my idea to get Sid in, because I couldn't imagine him doing anything else.

He'd always wanted to be in the group, didn't he?

Yeah, he did. He got in, got into drugs, fell in love with his ego, and it was the end of him.

What was the American tour like?

Very bad. The same kind of thing. Not being talked to, being ignored, being stuck in my room with nowhere to go, nothing to do – very, very boring. It was awful.

Was it worse than on the SPOTS tour, and the Dutch tour?

Yeah, then we were more . . . not mates, cos we never have been. Very different, but . . . closer definitely, and when Malcolm tried to get into that manoeuvre, it all just fell apart. He destroyed it. They wanted to do what Malcolm wanted them to do. Malcolm would give it this, wahey, we're all mates, and he's an odd one, the outsider, and Sid's a loony.

230

They'd known Malcolm for longer, hadn't they?

Yeah, a lot longer . . .

What was the last gig like, can you remember, at the Winterland?

Very bad. Sid was misbehaving appallingly, no-one was talking to anyone. Steve and Paul and Malcolm flew everywhere, and ignored us, and all the time Malcolm was behind this, plotting and scheming and breaking things up. He couldn't control me, Malcolm, and that really upset him. He tried to get back at me in all kinds of ways – all kinds of lies. I would have thought it wouldn't have worked on me, feeding me bullshit like that. Oh ye of lesser faith!

So what happened at that Winterland gig, you were all pissed off with each other or just not communicating?

I wasn't talking to them, they weren't talking to me. I was just as bad as them, don't get me wrong. I have my faults too, my faults are really quite intense. There's a huge catalogue of complaints about me, this I know. But there just didn't seem to be any way of connecting it all, ever more.

'No Fun' at the end was extraordinary.

I meant it – no fun. 'Ever get the feeling you've been cheated?' Well I meant that from here, because I felt cheated. I knew it couldn't go on.

Can I ask you, while I think about it, about the first court case. Was it brought at your instigation?

Yes, all of it was.

You'd asked Glitterbest to produce some accounts?

Yeah. In fact they wouldn't even speak to me. Not only did they leave me stranded in America, but when I came back they wouldn't talk to me at all. That was the situation and the only way around it was the courts. Initially Malcolm threatened court action against me, then he claimed that the name Rotten was his property, and that was an impossible situation, and I was forced into court. I hate courts. But once I was there, I thoroughly enjoyed it.

It's a kind of theatre, isn't it? And once you're there, you've got to win.

Yes. I don't do things to lose.

When did you first ask Glitterbest for the accounts, can you remember?

Not the exact day, but as soon as I got back. I got no joy out of them at all. All of them, the whole staff wouldn't talk to me, it was ridiculous, really petty. A sort of, you're not in our gang any more, that kind of attitude. Because I didn't go to Rio, apparently. I wasn't even asked to go to Rio. The band didn't know that, they were told something completely different. They were told that I'd refused to go. Very sad. Everything was withheld from me, all monies, everything. It was a ridiculous situation. I was literally stranded. Enter Brian Carr [his lawyer].

What was the substance of your case against Malcolm? That he had misappropriated the money, or that he simply hadn't managed it properly.

He hadn't produced any accounts whatsoever, and I hadn't received any money. He was claiming that he owned the name and that I didn't deserve any money because I apparently broke contract, which wasn't true, so it went to court to prove exactly that. His initial case against me was absurd in the extreme, it was just character-slander, it was nonsense, pure fantasy. He called all kinds of weird and peculiar people to say all kinds of weird and peculiar things. Most unfair.

Then it went into the hands of the receiver?

Yes, and as you know, it took a hell of a long time to clear up, because even to this day there's not a proper settlement, and none of this should have gone to court in the first place.

Was there no way you could have sat down and sorted it all out at the time?

I would dearly have wanted that, and I asked for it time and time again, but the answer was always clearly and completely no. You're not getting anything, go away.

Why was there such bitterness?

Not on my part. There was bitterness on Malcolm's part, and his office, but not from the band.

The band just jumped, didn't they?

Yeah. It was all rather pathetic, and it should never have ended in such a dismal way. But there you go. Such is life. I was fully prepared, in all of this, that there would be no money for me. It did become a principle with me that I wouldn't be kicked in the teeth like that. I don't do it to other people and I don't want people to do it to me. There were some damn scandalous things being said about me.

Was Malcolm using the money that he got from the advances and the Sex Pistols royalties for the film purely?

As far as I know, yes.

He wasn't embezzling?

No, I don't think so. Malcolm likes to give the impression that he's a bit of a shyster, but he's more involved in his artistic ideas rather than any lust for money. And I hated that film, it was an appalling idea right from the start. But the final *Rock'n'roll Swindle* script was something I'd never even seen; I only saw the early ones, which were appalling.

I was disgusted by things like when they got that idiot American, Meyer, they spent something like £70,000 to go to Wales and slaughter a reindeer with a crossbow. Absurdness. They more or less wrote it as they went along. It was all too ridiculous, and as you know, the film ended up as the Ten Commandments According to the Ayatollah McLaren. Gross inaccuracy.

Did you shoot any film with Meyer?

No, none. What they did do was get an actor in to imitate me, but apparently they didn't use that. I remember they did auditions at the Rainbow for Johnny Rotten lookalikes, which was doubly insulting because I was living at the time at my parents' place in Finsbury Park, which is like a hundred yards away from the Rainbow.

Who paid for the original court case?

Me. I'm still paying.

Did you get any money from Virgin?

No, not a penny. No sport whatsoever.

And for the second?

No sport.

Who did costs go to?

Costs were shared by everyone. I could have fought it longer, but I just wanted it settled, stopped. Because Malcolm doesn't have a penny.

The figure quoted was eight hundred and eighty thousand, wasn't it?

Yeah. When you take costs out of that, and lawyers, and the receiver, and divide up what's left, that's nothing at all.

How much did you get each, roughly?

About a hundred before tax, and before my costs. My lawyers' fee alone is a hundred thousand.

You had so many people there, I couldn't believe it. Those guys charge about thirty thousand a day in court. Your QC was a killer.

Wasn't he good? He died, poor sod. He died the week after we came out. He was dying of cancer while we were in court.

What did you think of what was happening to Sid?

The point is, Sidney was not a violent person, he was utterly useless in that respect.

He must have got fucked up in that jail in New York.

God knows how Sid would have coped. I don't really want to know. I'm not going to ask his mother, or any of those people who made him sign bits of paper signing over all his monies to them. What a horrible situation he was put in. I wanted to help at that point. Me and Sid had fallen out, but not to any great extent. I wanted to go

234

over, but Malcolm put the blocks on that, and Sid's mum followed suit. She did what Malcolm wanted her to do.

Malcolm did care about Sid though, didn't he, in his own way?

No, not at all, couldn't care less. All Malcolm was interested in was turning him into a pop idiot. Propagating that myth about the music business being about people destroying themselves. Malcolm always wanted me to be that way, but it didn't work. He wanted me to hide in a cupboard and never be seen anywhere, be this mystery figure and not to give radio interviews, not talk sense, and not clarify a few situations, he wanted it all to be just a mess.

It would have been fine if Malcolm wrote the songs, designed the clothes, did whatever, but he did none of these things.

I understand that, but wasn't there a time, however brief, where you actually worked well together?

No, only that we'd feed off each other, because there was the animosity; anger is an energy, and that was quite useful, but he wanted to push himself as the main man by using Sid, and by slowly destroying Sid. If I was around, there was no drugs around Sid. If Malcolm was around – strange coincidence – Sid would seem to be well and truly fucked up. The implications are very clear.

CHAPTER FOUR

The City

The Westway with Clash graffiti, January 1977 (Jon Savage)

British punk began in London. In the mid-seventies, the capital was suffering the effects of a severe economic recession. Many inner-city areas were near-derelict, a desolation that paradoxically offered freedom and possibility. Young people without means could squat or rent very close to the city centre, an ease of access that fostered the rapid urban transits of the punk period.

From the early 1970s on, there was a cult, ground-level revival in basic rock music that encouraged the small pool of outsider musicians that eventually peopled the first punk bands. First there was pub rock, then Dr Feelgood, then a new generation of tough R'n'B bands like The 101ers and the Count Bishops. Street rock was in the air, and the competition was intense to get there first.

This chapter also deals with the experience of living in a decayed capital.

Roger Armstrong

Manager of the Rock On stall in Soho market. Along with Ted Carroll's parent shop in Camden and stall in Golborne Road, this was a major catalyst in the revival of roots rock. Many punk bands and fans bought their records there, holy relics of mania on 7˝. With Carroll, he also formed Chiswick Records, who released records by the Count Bishops, Johnny Moped and The 101ers. From Belfast, Armstrong is enthusiastic and expert.

I had known Ted Carroll for a long time. I was basically down and out, on the dole, living in a squat, and a mutual friend of Ted's and mine, Sylvia, found this market stall down Soho and only wanted it Thursday, Friday and Saturday, and wanted Ted to take it Monday, Tuesday, Wednesday. Frank Murray did it for a few weeks and got fed up with it, and then Ted came to me and asked me to do it, just three days a week. That was summer '74.

What were you selling down there?

Right across the board. The rockabilly thing was huge from about '72; The White Hart and the Lyceum on a Sunday night, it was wall-to-wall teddy boys. You had young kids coming in asking for 'graffiti rock'. They all had their copies of the *American Graffiti* album and they wanted more of it. That sort of image. American college. Straight-leg Levi's and creepers, slicked-back hair. The girls in the white dresses. These were thirteen-, fourteen-year-olds.

We were selling a fair amount of rockabilly. And the blues, of course, the blues punter goes on for ever. A bit of sixties soul, there was still a bit of a mod thing around. One of the biggest things was the New York Dolls, Flamin' Groovies, Iggy and the Stooges. We found they were available, and we sold them by the bucket-load. Also sixties garage, and Small Faces records.

One of the big things that kept us going as a stall was no-one else had thought of ringing up Decca and finding out what was on catalogue. Decca was the only one of the majors we had an account with. Things like Small Faces and Them albums were in catalogue! Hundreds of singles, Moody Blues EPs. They just hadn't deleted them. It was the old system where if a record dropped below a certain level of sales it was automatically deleted, and if it didn't, it stayed on the catalogue.

All these singles had been changing hands for a lot of money and we undermined the entire market, because they were actually available. They were the glory days when organisations were shipping in American cut-outs by the container-load – they didn't know what they were getting, they just got A TON of cut-outs. Ted would pay a little bit over the odds to cherry-pick. Armfuls of Jan & Dean albums . . .

Who was the clientele?

The blues bores, the rockabillies, and for the Dolls and Stooges and sixties garage stuff, what was to become the punk bands, and their hangers-on. Shane MacGowan was a big buyer, when he worked in a bank somewhere and wore a three-piece pinstripe suit with hair in his eyes. Joe Strummer used to come in occasionally. Brian James used to come through.

Then before the British scene got off the ground, you had the Flamin' Groovies, Ramones and Talking Heads, and I remember opening up one morning to find The Ramones waiting on my doorstep. Joey wanted to complete his Sweet singles collection. I'm sure there were a lot more that I don't necessarily remember. The ones you remember are the ones who once they join bands, still come in.

You'd obviously developed a very different clientele from the other stall and the shop.

Well, in '74 the shop hadn't even opened, that came later. Ted's stall had been going for a long time and had its own world. The Soho one was where we opened up that New York Dolls thing . . .

No-one has talked about what an important part second-hand record shops played.

That was it. Nobody was handling the sixties garage scene.

Did you think there would be some sort of English punk rock, before it happened?

I always regarded 'Keys to Your Heart' as one of the great crossover records. What had been happening was the Brinsley Schwarz, Bees Make Honey pub rock, R'n'B-based. The 101ers were coming slightly out of that, with a more ramshackle approach. They weren't pro musicians the way a lot of the pub rock musicians were. That was the first inkling for me that something was going to happen. It was recorded the end of '75, put out early '76.

A lot of the kids who were in the first punk rock bands were rock fans, so they would have heard a whole variety of music.

Oh sure, Captain Sensible was a huge Soft Machine fan. Heavy metal was a big influence. The Sweet and T.Rex. That was the music of their early teenage years, it was around anyway. The second-hand stalls gave them access to hear things they wouldn't have heard. There's a history of cover versions, from Flamin' Groovies numbers through to Standells and Chocolate Watchband and that kind of thing. It was a big place for playing stuff.

Was it just you and Phil?

It started as just me, then Phil came over from Belfast and I took him on, and when the Chiswick thing developed I took Stan Brennan on, and Stan and Phil did the counter scene, and I was running around doing the Chiswick label stuff. When it started I'd work the stall during the day and then maybe take a day off when we had someone in the studio. We used Pathway in Barnsbury.

Did you do The Hammersmith Gorillas there?

We did one there, and did the second one at Olympic, went big-time. Me in at the deep end, pretending to be a producer.

Where did they come from?

Jesse Hector used to hang round Ted's stall and tell him he had a band, and he looked so weird you had to believe him, with the big sidelocks and the funny crop on the top of the head. We decided, this guy was mad enough. I went to see them in rehearsal, they weren't even playing gigs. Away down near St Albans, in the back of a pub.

There were these three strange characters, and all of a sudden the band just exploded! This little guy on guitar just careered across the rehearsal room, about six somersaults, as if he was playing in front of twenty thousand people at a festival, and did this blinding set in front of me, an audience of one. You had to sign them, you had to do something with them.

They did The Kinks' 'You Really Got Me'?

They did 'You Really Got Me' for Penny Farthing Records in '73 or '74, which Jesse had brought in. It was actually a very good version. Then we picked them up and the first one was 'She's My Girl'. The publicity we got on them was ridiculous, front page of *Sounds* and everything. He really was one of the great performers then, he would do anything to get an audience going, and he always did it.

What happened to them?

Jesse flipped out. I remember one weird gig out of town, somewhere near Luton. There was a small audience, but some of the lads got rather enthusiastic. I think Jesse's foot slipped off the stage, someone tried to lift his foot and put him back on stage, and for the rest of the night Jesse went on about how somebody had attacked him on stage, and he got into cancelling gigs in the afternoon that they were supposed to play, and that was it, it all fell apart.

When did you first see the Sex Pistols?

Ted and I remember seeing Chelsea Art College, very very early. Malcolm rang us up and said come and see my new band. It must have been one of the first couple of gigs, there was maybe fifty people in the hall. I had an inkling that Malcolm was going to do something, cos we'd done all that T-shirt selling for him at Wembley, where I first met him, and Ted was flogging him rock'n'roll records for Let It Rock.

It was the only time I've ever been to that particular hall, and I seem to remember we went in the early evening and it was still light.

They were a total mess, but it was fun; Johnny just slagged the audience off, basically, and the audience slagged him off and threw things at him, and that encouraged him. But it was that college-kids level, it wasn't even on the level of playing The Hope and Anchor. It wasn't as if they were playing to people who would throw bottles and glasses at the slightest encouragement.

When did you see them again?

I remember distinctly the Screen on the Green, the first of those. The Buzzcocks and The Clash getting no fair crack of the whip on the PA whatsoever. Miserable little sound like a transistor radio, then the Sex Pistols came on and suddenly they switched the PA on. I think the others had been going through the monitors. I thought it was so funny, these people putting something new together, and here's the old tricks. That was the night Johnny knocked his tooth out on the microphone.

Did you suddenly see much of a change in the people at the market?

Yeah, I started getting teddy boys in setting fire to punks, literally. That was what was going on then, the teds versus punks stuff, and we were the melting pot for both, cos we were selling records to both. The day any punk record came out, they would bring it down to the stall, because it was one of the things of the time, your record had to be sold in Rock On first.

We shunted loads of 'Anarchy in the UK' on EMI, loads of them. We bought those as soon as they came out. Ted had a few contacts with people in real record shops, who had real accounts with real record companies, and we'd do exchanges with these people, and while people weren't ordering many of them, we were sticking in huge orders for the things. We were always aware that we could over-order by five hundred or whatever, and we knew we would sell them.

Malcolm was very aware of the importance of the collectors' scene.

Yes. It's where the whole punk scene came out of. You had with the sixties garage period certain records that fetched high money cos they were on red vinyl or spotted vinyl or whatever. Punk took that to extremes, records coming out in five different colours, and collectors would buy every single one of them. It was the first really instant collectors' scene.

Before that, collecting records was always retrospective. No-one bought new obscure sixties garage records because they thought, in five years' time I'll get a tenner for this. There was no real awareness of that. But punk was like that, possibly because the people involved in the scene were buying records in shops like ours . . .

When did you first think that something different was really happening?

Possibly the opening of the Roxy, in a way, was the real point, at the tail end of '76. It went from pubs to the first club of its own. That's when it first really came home to roost, that it had gone beyond a few lads in a couple of cities around the country, messing around. Those first two gigs, Generation X on New Year's Eve and The Clash on New Year's Day. I remember that Clash gig as definitely one of the best gigs I've ever been to in my life.

On New Year's Day, people don't even normally put gigs on, people are too hung over. Wall-to-wall punters, it got to the point where the band were leaning on the audience, who were leaning back on the band. They crashed into each other, and the band actually managed to keep a semblance of the songs going. Joe kept shouting, 'Is the PA all right?', and the crowd shouted, 'Fucking get on with it!'

The thing with the Roxy was you did get your suburban punks to that, they could get back at three in the morning on the milk trains, and you didn't get so much your West End middle-class kids, who actually had more difficulty getting home. So the Roxy was full of these kids from Luton and places like that. It was this weird mixture of the older crowd and your weird crew, your Steve Strange lot, then your suburban punks – a very strange blend of people.

Did you go to the final 101ers gig at the Nashville?

Probably. I remember the night Joe told me he was quitting the band, it was at The Red Cow in Hammersmith. I think it was a Jam gig, cos they used to play there relentlessly. I was at the bar and Joe came rushing up to me, and the first thing he said was, 'Have I done the right thing? I've left the band, I've quit them.' He was in tow with

Mick and Bernie, and he started on a whole rant about it not being the right music any more, this is the future.

I knew Bernie from the great King's Road triumvirate, him and Malcolm and Andy Czezowski. The tailor, the rabbi, the accountant. It was a funny little alliance, actually. They all got their band out of it, anyway.

Did you sign any punk bands?

We almost signed The Jam. We missed The Damned, we'd gone to see them early, one of the first Nashville gigs. Jake and Ted and me were all standing at the back after it finished, and we all looked at each other and said, 'That was great, somebody's got to sign them.' It was terrible, but it was great. I went on holiday shortly after that and when I came back I found that Jake had snapped The Damned up and was putting them in to do an album.

We also missed The Adverts, who had sent us a cassette, and by the time we responded they'd gone. In a way, we never did get our really big punk band, none of the top five or six. With The Clash and the Pistols, Malcolm and Bernie were adamant from day one they were going to majors, they weren't interested in the indie circuit.

There were quite a few A&R people in the majors who had to have their punk band. They moved very fast when they saw a bit of publicity. I don't know all the details of the CBS deal with The Clash, but by today's standards it was a hell of a contract, something like ten albums over ten years. That was the other aspect of it, they stitched them up quite heavily. They all were, except for the Pistols.

The Radiators from Space was my first big venture, I flew over to Dublin and produced their first single, 'Television Screen', which got a rave review in *Rolling Stone*, of all places. I kept that; it said, 'If all punk records are produced like this, it might go somewhere.' Funny how wrong people can be.

They were just Dublin lads, they came out of a band called Greta Garbage and the Trash Cans, a glam band. They latched on to punk very early on, they were the only true punk band to come out of Ireland, from the South. Later you had The Undertones, and the Boomtown Rats started a bit after, but they got out of town very fast, and came to Britain.

There were a few places to play, but there wasn't a live gig circuit particularly. It was the tail end of the Irish scene being dominated by the showbands. U2 may have been even too young to have seen the Radiators, they were very early. We got them over here very early. They came over for one tour, went back, and then moved over. We found them places to live.

Then there was that thing where somebody got killed at one of the gigs, knifed. It was traumatic, cos somebody from the *NME* was at the gig, and had photographs, and were going to run a piece on it. Rick Rogers, our press officer, rang them up and said, 'Please, don't run a big shock-horror story about somebody killed at the gig.' What had happened was there was a long-standing row between two kids, nothing to do with punk.

What about the violence at punk gigs? I always thought it was over-rated.

Totally. A lot of the violence I saw was generated by the bouncers and people like that. In a way, you couldn't blame them, cos the band came on, they had no experience of this kind of thing before, and suddenly these kids would start rucking, and they assumed it was a fight, and joined in. They were so loaded up with speed and beer they probably didn't feel anything.

I think the measure of how violent a scene is, if you as an innocent bystander who doesn't want to join in, do you get hit? You just weren't at punk gigs. If you wanted to get into the thick of it and have someone's elbow in your ear, you could, no problem. If you wanted to stay away from it, you could stand at the back and you were out of it. There was the occasional thing where people got a bit uptight and threw a punch, but there was never any serious heaviness. I always thought they were quite friendly.

When did punk start tailing off for you?

Late '77, early '78, it had gone, for me anyway. Where it tailed off, although it was probably a starting-point for the vast majority of the people who bought punk records, that's when your first-generation bands had either established or broken up. The Damned had broken up, the Pistols were in disarray by that point, The Clash were heading for the mainstream, the Buzzcocks were getting hits, and Siouxsie had finally been signed!

From there on in it was the second-generation bands, who were genuinely inspired by punk, rather than those who had been inspired by what we've been talking about, from glam rock through. It lasted a year and a half, as far as the core of the thing went. After that it was different. It was amazing, the short time-span it happened in. The Damned had been going as an act in '76/'77, then they'd broken up for a while and re-formed.

Punk happened fast, and the legend happened even faster, and along with that, the prices for the original records went through the roof. Normally it takes ten years for that to happen, this happened in two years. The truth is, when punk had its first fling, it didn't actually sell a lot of records. It wasn't a big-selling thing.

What it did, it got kids who were very young teenagers would gravitate towards it. I think your sense towards what's happening when you're thirteen or fourteen is very heightened. You're watching it from outside, you can't get into the gigs and you're dying to get in and do it. So as soon as you're fifteen, you're straight in there, and that's what happened, it got really big at that point.

Presumably a lot of these punk groups didn't have more to say once they'd cut their album or their few singles . . . or was it just that the time had gone?

It came and went so fast. You listen to the second Clash album, and they'd moved on; the Buzzcocks found their pop sensibility pretty early; and Siouxsie, with that swirling, almost psychedelic thing. They all went to the roots of whatever they'd got into it for in the first place. The bands that obviously suffered were the thrash bands.

Punk went pop. The Pistols had hits because of the hype, but hardcore punk was never commercially successful music, really. But by the end of '77, beginning of '78, you had people like The Police, people who had been around before punk, who had managed to get their hair cut and buy a pair of straight jeans, and they came out the other end, because what punk did create was a live circuit, which is what's missing now.

Joe Strummer

Inspirational Clash singer, the human face of punk rock and, after the Sex Pistols split, its biggest star. Co-writer of great punk-era London songs: 'London's Burning', 'City of the Dead'. He was at a loose end when I talked to him in 1988, in a tiny café just down from The Warwick Castle on Westbourne Park Road, London. Middle of the afternoon, nobody there. Strummer was very friendly, warm and expansive. We agree on a second date but it never happens.

I'd like to talk about where The 101ers started, where you played, what the arena was at that time.

I'd been on a busking tour of Europe with my friend Tymon Dogg, and when we came back he moved into the squat at 23 Chippenham Road. We were loose kind of people, we had two squats going, and one was at 101 Walterton Road, and the other was at Chippenham Road. Eventually we took over the whole area, cos 23 ran the local restaurant, that tea room, and we put the group together that everyone would go and see.

I always felt that in the cultural life of all those hundreds of squats around Elgin Avenue and Shirland Road, eventually our two squats were the lifeblood of the area, cos none of us were into heroin, or alcoholics, you know. We managed to be good. After I came back from that busking tour I moved into 101, more to get away from Tymon – you know when you've been very close to someone in very harrowing circumstances?

I continued busking in the underground, but it got too heavy when they started putting microphones and speakers in the tunnels, so I was looking for a way round it. I looked into the Elephant and Castle pub on Elgin Avenue and I saw this Irish trio playing, and I thought, I could do that! So I thought it would be a good way to get over the summer, I thought it would be an easier way of earning money than running from these transport cops down the tube.

This was '74. I went back to 101 and tried to put a group together. Big John was trying to learn the saxophone, and I got Patrick to play the bass, but we had no money or equipment. I borrowed a bass guitar and amp and speaker, and suddenly we were happening, we had a bass rig, which we set up in the basement; and we begged, borrowed or stole stuff until we had a drum kit, and I bought a guitar for £20, a Hofner.

After the right-wing coup in Chile we had a lot of refugees come over, and two of them moved into our squat: Antonio, who was a drummer, and the sax player, Alvaro. He was the only one of us who could really play. We had a group, but we learnt six numbers: 'Bony Moronie', 'Gloria', 'Route 66', 'Too Much Monkey Business', and two others.

We managed to get a gig at the Royal College of Art, where there was a Chilean refugee's art exhibition, we went down and set up our pathetic equipment, a mike stand that required two bricks to hold it up. There was like two people there, and we played our five or six cruddy rock'n'roll numbers. This Chilean guy came down saying, 'Get out of here, you're playing this imperialist rock'n'roll!' And I thought, blimey! – this guy's got a hard-on, and we split.

I said we should hire the room above the Chippenham as a club, but we were scared to do it, and this girl Ros physically dragged me over to the Chippenham one day and forced me to ask the landlord to hire the room on Wednesday nights. It cost a quid for the room. We called it the Charlie Pig Dog Club, cos there was a dog in the squat that was a cross between a pig and a dog. Then every Wednesday night we'd go up there, and charge 10p to get in, I leafleted all the squats in the area.

Soon we had quite a jumping scene, we'd learn a couple of numbers every week and add them to our set, and we learned standing in front of those gypsies and squatters and lunatics – you can't really learn unless you're playing to people. We were also doing gigs at The Brixton Telegraph. We did another Chilean benefit, and Matumbi were headlining and they lent us their equipment. I always thought how great that was, cos we were a really dishevelled-looking bunch of people, dressed in rags.

There were so many squats then, that's all gone.

There were streets and streets, a real community. There were certain areas that were being left to run down, the councils hadn't got it together. Elgin Avenue was because someone in the council had decided they were going to knock all these down, about a hundred fine Victorian terrace houses, and it was between deciding and them actually knocking them down that the squat culture flourished on that street.

To go back a bit, how did you get to be a busker?

I did that because Tymon Dogg, who was the musician of our community at that time, I went with him 'bottling' as it's called, because you're supposed to have a fly in a bottle in one hand and collect money with the other hand, and the musician knows that you haven't stolen any money if the fly is still in the bottle. It comes from Mississippi, that's why you're called the bottler when you're collecting. I used to collect for him.

I knew I wasn't any musician, I was already about twenty-one, and I never played, so I got a ukulele, and I used to play Chuck Berry songs on this ukulele. One day in Green Park, down in the tunnels, he said to me, 'Right, I've just heard there's a patch going at Leicester Square, you do this patch and I'll go off to the next one.' And suddenly there I was alone, for the first time in my life, and a thousand people came rushing past, and I was going, 'Sweet Little Sixteen, dingadingadingading'. I thought, wow, I'm playing, and there's no-one here to help me!

Did you get any money?

Yeah, we used to prefer what was called the loony shift, between ten and eleven or later in Oxford Circus or Leicester Square, where everyone is drunk, or out on the town, and they see a couple of ragamuffins, and they go, 'Heey, give 'em a tenner, I mean 10p.' So we used to earn somewhere between four and five pound an hour. Good money. There was a slight drawback cos some drunks would come through and they'd try it on; somehow the fact that you were defenceless down there always protected you, in the end.

So when did you leave school?

I left in June '70 at seventeen, and went to the Central School of Art in the September, and then by June '71, that was it. I applied to Stourbridge and Norwich and was refused by both. I remember coming back from Norwich I was apprehended on the train without a ticket with my portfolio, and slung off at this godforsaken place in the middle of nowhere, with this huge portfolio, so I dumped the portfolio in a skip and hitched back to London, and that was the end of my art career.

Did you not like it?

I was in boarding school, locked up really good for nine years, and all of a sudden you're staying at a hostel in Battersea, with no-one to say what to do, where to go. It was 1970, and there was drink and drugs, and by the end we were doing acid and I never went near the art school. It was a bit much for a young guy to handle. By the end of the year we'd moved into this rented house in Palmers Green, me and the most partying people on the course, we were getting really wild. We were examining the way to live.

Where did you go to school?

City of London Freemen's School. It's in Ashtead, about five miles south of Epsom. It was mixed. If it hadn't been mixed it would have been really hell. I ran away when I was nine. I didn't get very far. Me and this guy who was slightly older, Paul Warren, he said, 'Come on, let's run away.' I said, 'Yeah, let's go', and we left one Tuesday lunchtime. We were walking near Epsom and we saw this policeman and we knew it was the middle of school hours and he was bound to say what are you two doing, so we took this long detour.

While we were walking, the geography master came by in a car. He bundled us in, and back at the school this fascist guy was shouting at us, 'How dare you leave school without your caps!', and I remember thinking, what an idiotic question, we're running away, man, you don't run away with your cap on. It was only a couple of weeks after my ninth birthday. My dad was in the Foreign Office, so I think he was in Tehran, but the place they put me in was really horrible.

251

Before that, I hadn't been in England at all. I'd had a great life, in Egypt and Mexico and Germany. It was great. But suddenly it was like *Tom Brown's Schooldays*.

So what did you do after you left Central?

A dead loss, you know. A couple of the guys from art school who were as wild as I was, and like me hadn't managed to get in anywhere else, we ended up in a farm in Blandford in Dorset. We worked the hardest that year on the farm. Then we moved back to London and got a horrible flat in Harlesden where there were about ten of us living. We hadn't discovered squatting yet.

A lot of people were already squatting, but I got a job in an Allied Carpets warehouse, as a sign painter, which was quite a good groove for about three months, until they asked me, 'Are you going to get into this seriously', and I said, 'You must be fucking joking'. I was just doing it for money, to keep body and soul together, and as soon as I said that I was back on the carpet-cutting floor.

Then I came back one time after I'd been for a drink at the Memphis Belle with this girl I was friendly with from the local supermarket, and I arrived back at the flat and there was this police car outside the flat, and all our stuff was being thrown out of the window. Me and Tymon had found this black guy in the park, and being hippies, we'd invited him back to our place to live, cos he didn't have any-where to live.

As soon as the Irish landlord found out we had a black guy living in our flat, he bunged the cops a few quid to get rid of us. We'd all been evicted, a gang of toughs had rushed in, beat everybody up, slung 'em out. It was when I started to learn about what was justice and what wasn't. All our stuff was in the road and the cops were there, laughing at us.

Up to that moment I'd been doing it by the book. I actually had a copy of the '65 Rent Act on me, and I went along to the cop and said you can't do this according to section whatever, opened it up, and he went, 'Don't fucking tell me about the law, sonny Jim', you know? From that moment on, if we wanted a house we just kicked the fuck-ing door in. We wanted electricity, we just jammed wires into the company head. Bollocks.

Had you lost touch with your parents?

From the time I went to London they freaked out. Obviously I fell
out with my parents. But you know what it was like at boarding
school, you had to become somebody on your own at the age of nine,
and it's hard to get back. I suppose I resented them without being
aware of it. My parents were somebody I saw once a year from then
on. They were five thousand miles away in Tehran.

So after a few years I could see them at Christmas and in the summer, but for the first few years I saw them in the summer. And at half
term when all the other boarders were going, thank Christ we're getting out of here, for me sometimes we'd go to Scotland and stay on
my mother's farm. Pablo LaBritain was my friend at school, he was
the drummer in 999. Me and him were a deadly duo. He used to take
me down to his father's farm in East Sussex.

How do you get on with them now?

They're dead. When The Clash became really happening, my father
for the first time in his life was really proud of me. That helped. But
you can't really heal a lifetime's estrangement just because your
records are selling. It's not his fault, it's mine, I never really got off
my high horse. I didn't know I was sitting on it, but I realise it now.
Now, I'd be able to say to him, cor what a lot of shit we've been
through together. But we were touring Italy when he suddenly took
ill and died. I hate not having that final conversation with him.

So for eighteen months you squatted and had a good time?

Well no, I had another adventure. When we were slung out of the flat
illegally, I went to the Harassment Officer at Brent Council, I was the
only one of our group who really cared to follow things through. I
went to a hearing and they stitched me right up. There were these
eight law students up at the back and I remember screaming at them,
'I'm not something to fucking study, this is people who've been done
over.' They hustled me out.

Anyway me and Tymon were sleeping on this kitchen floor. I had
acquired a drum kit through a swap in my last year at school, and it
was in the garage in my parents' bungalow in Purley, and so I knew
a friend of mine had got into art school at Newport in South Wales,

253

so I hitched down there. I thought I might as well stay in this town cos I can't make it in London, it was too heavy, there was nowhere to live and so on.

I got the drum kit down to Newport and bartered my way into the art school group by swapping the drum kit. It was called The Vultures. We played the art school and the Kensington Club in Newport. We used to do 'I Can't Explain', 'Tobacco Road', R'n'B. I took jobs there, I was grave-digging there for three months during the winter of '72/'73. I was cutting grass on the Malpas estate. I was the king of the Flymo. But that fell apart after a while and I went straight into the squatting.

It was very organised then as well. Didn't you have a squatters' union?

Yes we did. Piers Corbyn. We had a lovely bit of paper printed: 'This premises has now been occupied' We knew all the legal ins and outs. You'd go in there, bang, change the locks, yeah. Property is nine tenths of the law, we were really organised.

So you had The 101ers, and this club which was jumping. What happened then?

They were going to close the boozer down, cos it was getting out of hand. The cops were coming down every week. Some gypsies started to move in. When we were living at 101, on one side of us we had a house full of junkies, and the council had been through ripping out anything – water, lights, smashing floorboards and so on. We'd go in there and rebuild them, the wires. That was on one side, these junkies lying there and on the other there was a gang of really terrible alcoholics, you know, those people who are usually in the park. God, the horrible fights and shit, it was the pits.

Eventually, I got Allan Jones from *Melody Maker* – I'd known him from Newport, he was a student at the college – to come to the Pig Dog, hoping that we'd get a bit of press, and he wrote four lines at the bottom of their gossip column. We took this four lines down to The Elgin and we showed it to the landlord, and he read it and said, 'Right lads, Monday then. I'll give you ten pounds.' That's when we got on to the circuit.

That's when the Pistols first came across me. Although we didn't realise it, we were at least playing very fast music. Those earlier pub rock bands disappeared up their own arseholes trying to play like Memphis sweet style, but we couldn't play at all, we knew how to bash the shit out of a number. By the time we hit The Elgin, it was Snakehips Dudanski on drums, Evil on lead guitar, me singing and Mole on bass.

When did Boogie [John Tiberi] come in?

After Boogie got out of prison, for some reason he was into the music, and he used to come down and say he could get us played on Charlie Gillett's programme. So we taped some music and sent it to him, and we all crouched round the radio in the squat at Orsett Terrace. Charlie Gillett goes, 'What's this, sounds like hundred-mile-an-hour race-along rubbish', and he didn't even play it, just dismissed it in half a sentence. What a crushing blow that was.

Tiberi had said he could get us on the radio. I was the one who christened him Boogie, cos the first time he came round the squat he was smoking Winston, and at the time a packet of Winston seemed rather glamorous, so I called him boogie after the John Lennon, Dr Winston O'Boogie, remember? When he pulled out his fags I said, 'You must be Dr Winston O'Boogie.'

With him and Mickey Foote helping us we started to become a real little operation. Mickey was a contact from Newport. He was attending the college of art. Him and Bernie Rhodes were a right little team for a while, after The Clash started. Bernie needs to have a lieutenant. There are few honourable men in these stories, but Mickey was one of them.

Did you meet the Pistols first, or Bernie first? How did it all happen? You're with The 101ers, you're doing well . . .

We're doing well, we've got a single out, but I got a feeling that we were invisible; we were working very hard, loading the van, driving up North, unloading, playing the gig, loading it up again, driving down again, unloading again cos we didn't want to get the gear nicked. We did twelve gigs in fourteen days in places like Sheffield, and we couldn't afford to stay up there, it was up and down every day. We were invisible, we weren't getting anything in the papers.

Then one day the Sex Pistols were supporting us at the Nashville, and that was when I first saw them. I walked through the corridor, and we'd done our soundcheck and in came these Sex Pistols people, I remember looking at them as they went past: Rotten, Matlock, Cook, Jones, McLaren, and coming up the rear was Sidney, wearing a gold lamé Elvis Presley jacket, and I thought groups in those days didn't talk to each other, it was extremely cut-throat. You fought for gigs.

But I thought I'd talk to them, and I said to Sid, 'That's a nice jacket you've got there, mate.' He looked at me and went, 'Yeah, it is, I got it down at Kensington Market.' Then I walked out on stage while they were getting their soundcheck together and I heard Malcolm going to John, 'Do you want those kind of shoes that Steve's got, or the kind that Paul's got? What sort of sweater do you want?', and I thought, blimey, they've got a manager, and he's offering them clothes! To me it was incredible.

The rest of my group didn't think much of all this, but I sat out in the audience, there can't have been more than forty people in the whole boozer, they did their set, and that was it for me. The difference was, we played 'Route 66' to the drunks at the bar, going, please like us. But here was this quartet who were standing there going, we don't give a toss what you think, you pricks, this is what we like to play, and this is the way we're gonna play it. Regardless of whether you like it or not. That was the difference.

Did Lydon say anything to the audience?

Yeah, he pulled out this huge snot-rag and blew his nose into it, and he went, 'If you haven't guessed already, we're the Sex Pistols.' Really, come on, you know, and they blasted into 'Substitute', or 'Submission', or something.

The material they were playing at first wasn't that different from what you were doing, was it?

No. They were doing 'Stepping Stone', which we did occasionally, but they were light years different from us. They were on another planet, in another century, it took my head off.

I understood that this was serious stuff, they honestly didn't give a shit. John was really thin, and kept blowing his nose between numbers. The audience were shocked. That's when I fell out with the rest of the group, cos after that I started going down to Tuesday nights at the 100 Club, it started happening there. That's when Bernie came up to me and said, 'Give me your number, I want to give you a call about something.'

I split the group up, cos Bernie called the squat and Dan Kelleher the bass player at the time pretended to be me. That's when I said, 'It's not happening.' Evil was wearing Hawaiian shirts, and I was saying, 'Look at what's happening, we've got to move with the times', and they thought I was going mad. They were probably right, but it was certainly more interesting than what we were doing. That was it, the last few gigs that we had booked, the Pistols took them over.

You were suddenly faced with the present. And the future, and you had to make a decision, it was an emotional thing. It was a case of, jump that side of the fence or you're on the other side. It sorted people out. That T-shirt that Bernie designed, Which Side of the Bed? Brilliant, but it was so clear.

What happened when you left The 101ers?

I was signing on at Lisson Grove and I was aware that there were these people staring at me on this bench, and as I was queuing I was thinking there was going to be a ruck. It was Paul and Mick and Viv Albertine, and they'd seen me, in the weeks that Bernie had pulled Mick and Paul out of London SS and put them together, and they'd seen me at gigs around the manor, and that's why they'd been staring at me.

I didn't talk to them, if they'd have come up to me, I'd have probably swung at one of them. Get it in first, cos when people stare at you that long, y'know, and Lisson Grove was the worst place on earth. I'd seen them but never met them. The next day or two I met him at Paddington and we drove to Shepherd's Bush to the squat where Paul and Keith and Mick and Viv Albertine were staying, and put the group together.

What was it like, that Davis Road squat?

Their squat was a bit nicer than the ones round here, it was above, there was an old biddy living down below, and the electricity was still in place. It looked slightly more like a normal home.

Didn't you play your first gig in Sheffield?

Yeah, the Mucky Duck at The Black Swan, supporting the Pistols. It was really funny. We had a number called 'Listen', which started in an ascending progression of a couple of bars. This began the set for some reason, and Paul had never played a gig in his life, and he got up, nervous, and went right up the scale. I wasn't much of a musician myself, and I was waiting for the D note or something, and he started to go up the frets one by one. It threw us right off, we all just collapsed laughing.

What were the Pistols like at The Black Swan? I get the impression they were really brilliant at those northern gigs in the summer.

They were brilliant, they were firing on all strokes. We had a sort of Roxy Music audience. The Pistols had had a few Jonh Ingham articles, right, that one in *Sounds*, but it wasn't a lot for people to go on. It was a Sunday and I remember being amazed that at least two or three hundred people turned up. Girls in leopard-skin overcoats, the tail end of that Roxy thing, sharkskin suits, that type of thing. They were very receptive.

That must have been the best time for them, cos they were beginning to find their audience and they didn't have all the hassle.

Yeah, they weren't expected to be Rotten. They were enjoying their music, and they were being very courageous too. Like, new numbers were coming up.

Did you talk to them much at that time?

Me and Rotten never got on. Couldn't be expected to, really. I got on very well with Glen and Steve. I still get on well with Paul. He's a nice geezer. But what impressed me with Steve, we'd have this game going where he'd come up to me with his guitar and go, 'What's that?' He'd be holding down a chord, and I had to look at his fingers and go, 'It's a C ninth.'

That shows that Steve had probably stopped nicking them and started playing them only a year before, and yet he could do much more exciting chords than I could, I was still into, just slide your fingers up and down like that. But Steve was already into jazz shapes and inversions, he really knew his fretboard. It was brilliant. And he got that sound, straight into a Fender twin reverb, no pedals, it was the way he hit it.

What numbers had you worked out for that first gig?

I suppose some of those ones that I can't identify, 'Listen', and a few of the Clash standards, I suppose we had about ten numbers.

Did you wear the paint-spattered gear?

Yeah, we didn't have anything else. It was cheap. All the stuff about Pollock was a bit of a veneer on it, cos what actually happened was Bernie rented that British Rail warehouse in Camden Town and we painted it, and we didn't have any overalls or anything, we didn't have any clothes at all. We got all covered in paint and we saw it was a good cheap way to put an image together, something to wear on stage. Paul knew something about Pollock, he'd just come from art school.

We didn't have the backup of the SEX boutique. By that time, Malcolm and Bernie had fallen out over the swastika armband, cos Bernie's mother was a Jewish refugee from the oppression in Europe, so it was close enough for him to take that seriously, whereas I don't know where Malcolm came from. It was messing with things they didn't understand. At the 100 Club when Siouxsie asked to borrow our equipment for her first gig, Bernie said 'No, not unless you take off that swastika armband.'

So the clothes were a bit like The Who, smashing up the instruments and then calling it auto-destruction.

Yeah, after the fact. But it was out of necessity. We had to adapt what stuff we could find in the second-hand shops, which was really horrible. We used to take jackets round to the car spray shop in the railway arches round the corner and saying, 'Okay Pete, give us a spray.' Then we got into stencils and stuff, I think Bernie got us into that.

How much was Bernie guiding you and packaging you?

Very much so, I would say. He said to us, 'Write about what's important.' He never actually said write about this or that, but he used to watch us rehearse and say this is good, this is bad. He was very creative, his input was everything.

Where did his ideas come from? He seems to have been like an old-style coffee-bar intellectual.

Right, he'd read all the books, knew all the trends. He probably suggested, after the Pollock business, looked at Jasper Johns, and we ended up stencilling words on. I never knew much about that situationist stuff, to this day, but he probably suggested that we write words on our clothing.

So the next gig you played was the Showcase?

Yeah, then a few gigs supporting Crazy Cavan at the Roundhouse and ULU.

How many gigs did you do with Keith Levene?

Six or seven, I'd guess.

There's a tape of the Roundhouse show with your chat . . .

The reason for all the chat was that Keith broke a string, he had to go find a string, put it on and come back out, tuned up. I don't know why we didn't just kick into the next number, that's what I'd do now, cos we had three damn guitars. After that gig Bernie was laughing. He said, 'Where did you get those old Johnny Rotten scripts from?'

He wasn't there for the Punk Festival, was he?

No, but at the Punk Festival the same thing happened. I used to always have a transistor radio with me. There was those cool pirate stations, you could flip between them. I was carrying a radio at the riot, cos I remember somebody tried to mug it off me. I didn't let 'em. But we didn't have spare guitars then, so I just switched on the radio and held it up to the mike.

Dave Goodman was hip enough to put a delay on it, and it happened to be a discussion about the bombs in Northern Ireland, and there were some journalists who couldn't believe that it hadn't been set up. It was pure luck. I suppose, instead of having something to say. It's just reminded me what that radio was about.

We'd decided, as a question of purity, that we were never going to say anything in between numbers. It probably only lasted a few gigs, but we'd stand there all solemn in between gigs, but then when someone broke a string . . .

Was that idea of being pure very important?

Yeah, we'd look at everything and think, is this retro? There's a picture there of the Chuck Berry is Dead shirt that I painted. If it was old, it was out.

Why did 'I'm So Bored with You' change to 'I'm So Bored with the USA'?

I'd gone to the squat in Shepherd's Bush, and Mick had this riff, and I thought he'd said, 'I'm So Bored with the USA', I jumped up, said, 'That's great. Let's write some lyrics.' He said, 'It's not that, it's "I'm So Bored With You".' But he agreed that USA was much more interesting. When Mick wrote it, it was a love song. But I thought it was more interesting, cos *Kojak* and all that stuff was big at the time. *Columbo.*

That lyric's not bad, even now, although it's caveman primitive, it says a lot of truth, about the dictators, 'Yankee dollar talk to the dictators of the world'.

So what was the Screen on the Green gig like?

The Pistols were brilliant that night. We built the stage, and *The Outlaw Josey Wales* was playing that day, and two of us were elected to sit there and watch the gear, cos our gear and the Pistols' gear was underneath the stage while the film was showing during the day. I remember sitting there watching *The Outlaw Josey Wales* about two and a half times through, and about the third time through, three black blokes shot underneath the stage, trying to grab some of the gear, and we leapt up and grabbed them, and hustled them out the back door, and they never got anything.

We weren't very good that night, cos we were exhausted from building that stage, we were up very early, unloading the scaffolding and building the stage. I remember how mean we were to the Buzzcocks, cos we were the London crews, and we looked at them, sitting in a row, thinking, you measly berks from the North, you know? There was no solidarity. Now I really like those Buzzcocks records.

It shows how mean we were, we didn't think of them as part of our scene. But they were very good that night, the Buzzcocks. That was the night that Charles Shaar Murray wrote that we were the type of garage band that should be speedily returned to the garage, preferably with a motor left running. I remember we were slightly pissed off by that.

Why did Keith Levene leave?

We were all on speed. Not that we could afford it that much, but our drug intake was financially limited. Our idea of a good time was scoring a lump of dope the size of four match heads. Now and then we'd get some blues, or a little bit of sulphate, but Keith was much more pro on the speed, sometimes I'd see him with a plastic bag of resiny balls, speed in a very pure form.

Keith began to lose interest and I lost my temper with him when he rang up and we were doing 'White Riot', he said, 'What you working on, the "White Riot" tune? Well, there's no need for me to come up then, is there?' I said, 'Make that never, man.' Bernie was quite shocked when he arrived at rehearsals and I'd sacked him. Keith was always a favourite of his, when he'd come to The Golden Lion that night, he'd come with Keith. I can see now that he was worried about losing control, cos we'd done something without him.

You had a hole to fill on the sound, didn't you?

Mick and Keith had a competition about who was going to be the lead guitar player, so Mick was quite pleased that Keith was sacked.

Did he write anything?

The chorus of 'What's My Name'.

What did it feel like doing those concerts? The Pistols weren't playing and you were coming up real fast, weren't you?

No, I don't remember noticing, we were just doing what came naturally, we had a group, we had a set, a will to perform. From that moment that the Pistols perceived us as a threat, out the window went punk solidarity. We still had solidarity on the Anarchy tour, but The Damned were kicked off the tour pretty sharpish. I can't remember why.

They decided to play for the councillors.

Thought crime! We had to audition to see if our stuff was decent. Imagine!

Tell me about the Notting Hill riot.

For some reason, we weren't that aware of the Carnival, but we knew it was on, so we went down to check it out. It was a lovely day. Me and Bernie and Paul, we were under the Westway on Portobello Road, and we were standing there, grooving to the reggae, and I can still see that Coke can. About twenty coppers came through in a line, and I saw this Coke can go over and hit one of them on the head.

Immediately, twenty more were in the air, and then the crowd parted to get away from the targets, and there was this whole line of cops crouching, swivelling this way and that, to see who they should attack, and the women began to scream, me and Bernie and Paul were thrown back against the wire netting as the crowd surged back. I thought we were all going to fall down into this bay underneath the Westway, but the wire held, and Bernie's glasses flew off.

I lost Paul and Bernie for a minute, and chaos was breaking out all over the Grove, and Ladbroke Grove was lined with rebels, and cop cars were speeding through, these Rover 2000s, and they were being pelted with rocks and cobble stones and cans as they came through, it was like a bowling alley. And I thought, fucking hell, and I ducked in The Elgin and said, 'Gimme a couple of drinks here!' And I downed one and took the second drink outside.

Standing there I saw Paul with one of those plastic cones, and a police motorcycle came bombing down the road and Paul slung this plastic cone across the road and hit the front wheel of the motorbike, but he managed to keep on the bike and carried on. Then it was like *Zulu*. The coppers started to come down from the north end of Ladbroke Grove in a line, and we started to chuck everything we could at them. Then the fight boxed into these six streets here, and we were boxed in with the rest of them.

263

Me and Paul were standing on Lancaster Road, and I hadn't really noticed that all the white faces had gone. Suddenly this young posse came up and one said, 'Yo man, what you got in that pocket there?', and I had this transistor radio, but I had this brick in the other pocket, and I said, 'Don't say that shit to me, if you're not ready to fight what the fuck you doing here?' And the posse like shrank back, cos I was shouting really loud, and eventually an old guy came up and said, 'Leave these guys alone.'

Then darkness fell and it got really ugly. We trudged off back to the squat, and Sid was there and we said, 'Sid, where've you been, there's been a most amazing riot', and Sid said, 'Come on then, let's go and look again', and we went back to have a look. By that time there was a crowd of like five hundred young black guys around the Metro Club, and we were walking up Tavistock Road, and this black woman leaned out of her window and shouted at us, 'Don't go up there boys, they're going to kill you.'

We said, 'Bollocks', but another black woman came out of a basement somewhere and grabbed us, and we could see there was these five hundred youth, the hard core of the hardcore, they weren't fighting, they were just standing, cos the police were regrouping. That was when I realised I had to write a song called 'White Riot'. Cos I realised it wasn't our fight. It was the one day of the year when the blacks were going to get their own back against the really atrocious way the police behaved.

That must have been one of the first recent urban riots.

I've never tried to set light to a car before, but there was a car flipped up on its side down on Ladbroke Grove, and there was a burning car already a couple of blocks away, and I was admiring it, thinking, what a lovely plume of smoke that car is making, and I had a box of Swan Vestas on me, so I approached this car, and two or three young black blokes came up, and we were trying to set this car alight. We never did get it alight.

Who took the pictures there?

Rocco McCauley. He's now a porn photographer, he lived in the squat at Orsett Terrace. I was living with Palmolive, we split up before punk really happened, but we had a Spanish connection and Rocco somehow came in there.

Did you ever go down to the SEX shop?

No, it was completely off my turf, I had no idea what was going on down there. I was in the hippy squat end of the scene.

By the autumn you had Subway Sect in there as well . . .

Yeah, they were Bernie's discovery. Vic was always very close to Bernie's heart, much more so than The Clash ever were. They were brilliant. Bernie used to tell me he'd get demo tapes and in the middle of a song he'd stop, and with the tape still running, he'd light a cigarette, smoke the whole thing and then carry on from where he left off. It's a Vic thing.

Yeah. I've got a good Rocco story there. He's Spanish, he comes to England, and he's learning that he wanted to be a photographer. The punk spirit inhabited him, and we were playing the ICA and he was taking photographs of us, and on the second number, he was just about to take a picture and this hippy jumped on stage and started idiot-dancing, and he put down his camera and went, will somebody get this hippy off the stage? What is this? I'm not taking a picture till this hippy gets off the stage!

The next day he found out it was Patti Smith, and he could have sold those pictures to the music press. To me, he was the purest man in the house, cos he wasn't going, 'Wow, it's Patti Smith.' Terrific. He didn't even know. He was seeing it true and clear: there was a hippy on the stage!

What happened at the Royal College of Art [on 5 November 1976, the Night of Treason show, which ended in a fist-fight between Strummer and members of the audience]?

There was a big fight, me and Sid waded in. After those bottles started coming over, we'd finished our set, we didn't stop, but I knew as soon as we finished I was going to go over there and get stuck in, I could see roughly where it was coming from. It was drunken, oldish students. But they were throwing glass bottles, they could have murdered somebody.

265

I put down my guitar at the end of the last number, went straight off the side of the stage and Sid had been really supporting us, and I stormed off the stage, through the swing doors into the auditorium, Sid was with me, and I saw this student with a beard that I'd recognised from the stage, and hit him so fucking hard, he went down, poleaxed.

It was all dark, and somebody was going, 'Hey', and I turned round and smashed this other guy in the face, and Sid was getting stuck in, and I looked round for the rest of the band, and they weren't there, and me and Sid went back after we'd sorted out these bozos, who were chicken and ran away, and I said, 'Where were you?' 'Oh, we got caught in the crowd, couldn't quite get through the glass doors!'

What about the Anarchy tour? What can you remember about that?

That was when the balloon went up. The Pistols were the hottest news in the country, the *Sun* and all those people were following them around, we were confined to the hotel rooms, gigs being cancelled everywhere, and places the coach would pull up there was a choir of religious people singing, like from the Deep South or something. I remember going down to the bar and bringing up a tray of pints, cos the Pistols definitely weren't allowed out, and they didn't want any of the musicians pumped by any of those gutter people.

We felt pretty small just then, cos the Pistols were front-page news and we were just nothing. We were bottom of the bill. The best time we had was in Bristol, we checked into this bed and breakfast, and I was so tired I fell asleep immediately, it was like four or five to a room.

Meanwhile Bernie and Malcolm decided that this wasn't really happening, and they walked over to the Holiday Inn and checked everybody in there, and everybody moved, but I was forgotten about. Eventually Debbi came and woke me up and brought me over. Good times were had there, they broke into the swimming pool at night, rock'n'roll madness. That was when Mickey Foote got the scar on his forehead, he got completely drunk and dived into the shallow end of the pool and split his head open on the tiles. He was staggering around laughing his head off, blood gushing everywhere. Madness.

266

What was the problem you were having with your drummer at that stage, Terry Chimes?

Terry wanted to join a pop group and get a Lamborghini, your average suburban kid's dream, right? And we used to have discussions, we were quite rigorous, and when he said this about the Lamborghini, it was heresy! We were laughing and jeering at him, and he took it very seriously, and one day he just didn't show up for rehearsals. He phoned up and said he quit. But he was cool enough to come and do the album with us, cos we'd rehearsed the numbers with him.

You had problems finding another one, didn't you?

Yeah, all the drummers that later became known in London, we rehearsed.

Who did you do the Roxy Club on New Year's Day '77 with?

A bloke called Rob Harper. Eventually he became the mentor of the New Hearts, and they dumped him, stabbed him in the back a good one. But he played a tour with us, the Anarchy tour, I think.

Did you feel that gig was in any way special?

It was special in that the club was opening, and we all felt good about that. But Johnny Thunders had just sold me his Gretsch White Falcon, because they were desperate to score.

When you did Harlesden, that was the first time you changed out of the paint-spatter stuff?

Yeah, that was when Bernie found Alex Michon, and her, Paul and Bernie began to design clothes for us. We all threw our bit in. First it was just a zipper here, and it grew into pockets and stuff. I think Bernie was probably repeating his SEX shop experience, that painting dead men's clothes wasn't really it, had gone as far as it could. We moved one step away again. That was the night the Buzzcocks wore their Mondrian shirts, really cool.

Can you remember much about the CBS negotiations?

Are you kidding? We went down to sign with Polydor, and the cab

267

took us to Soho Square instead, we were completely in the dark. We didn't know anything. Mick was the one who was sharpest about business, but we let Bernie handle everything. We were really the people we were supposed to be. What did we know about record companies and contracts.

When did you do the album, in March? You seemed to move away from personal songs to songs more about issues. Is that fair?

We'd got so involved in the lifestyle of the group that we no longer had lives to write about. I think Bob Dylan feels that today, being singer-songwriters, he hasn't really got a life to write about, it's too far removed from people's ordinary experience.

The Pistols didn't write much either after a while.

After they sacked Matlock, that was the end, because Matlock was the tunesmith. That shows how crazy they were; just because he liked The Beatles, they sacked him.

With the album, were you trying to write songs about specific things, rather than just write about yourselves?

'I'm So Bored with the USA' goes on about heroin coming back in body bags, soldiers becoming addicted, the way American foreign policy operated imperialistically – any right-wing bastard who wasn't a communist, they'd support, you know.

Did that come from discussions within the group?

Yeah, after these discussions, Bernie would say, 'An issue, an issue, we'll all fall down.'

But he never told you what to write?

No, he just said, 'Write about what's important, don't write about love', really. Write about what's affecting you, what's important.

To me, a really important thing was from seeing you, I had a particular image of The Clash, then you had that really good piece in the *NME*, with Tony Parsons.

The Circle Line interview.

268

That seemed to change it into something that was a lot more socio-logical, more to do with high-rise and tower blocks; how did you feel about that, did you feel that confined you?

No, when you're part of it, you're so close to it it's hard to get an overview. Sometimes I wished I could have a weekend off, not that there was anywhere to escape to, but when you're young and stupid, you don't think about anything. You just go straight ahead.

Adam Ant

Singer and frontman of Adam and the Ants, actor in Derek Jarman's Jubilee, *huge pop star in the early 1980s. He witnessed the Sex Pistols' first show, as a member of headliners Bazooka Joe. Interviewed at his then home in Primrose Hill, London; very helpful with research material, and extremely anxious to tell his story.*

I grew up on a council estate in St John's Wood. There was an adventure playground, a youth club where they played 'Band Of Gold' and all the Tamla stuff, and all you could be was a skinhead. At fourteen I was Sta-Prest out, V-necks, crew-necks, Royals, brogues, Harringtons, quite neat though, Crombies . . . semi-crop, side part, done at Andy's in Camden Town.

When did you first go down to 430 King's Road?

I'd seen the New York Dolls, first off when I went to see Rod Stewart at Wembley, and that was very much a turning point for me. This was 1972, before they did the *Whistle Test*. Johansen came on, black tights, black top, top hat; he looked just like Mick Jagger, fucking around. Arthur had a tutu with thigh-length pink patent boots, and everybody fucked off to the bar.

Soon after that I was in a rock'n'roll band called Bazooka Joe and the Rhythm Hot Shots, and I went in Let It Rock a few times and saw Malcolm. It was all second–hand petticoats and stuff, there wasn't too much in there, then later on when I went back they'd started to put some of the SEX stuff in the back, then it was SEX, with the scrolled door, when I clapped eyes on Jordan and Michael Collins, and the first thing I bought was a Cambridge Rapist T-shirt.

What was the atmosphere like?

It was different from any sort of shop anywhere, it had a very kind of

Tin Pan Alley, Soho feel to it, but it also had a lot of the artist Allan Jones, the whole connection there with the leather and rubber and stuff, which I picked up on heavily and which Malcolm had picked up. You could buy clothes in there that normally you would buy through the post.

Jordan was in there the second time I went. First time I went there there was nothing I was interested in. They had that big rock'n'roll festival that Malcolm was doing. The Killer T-shirt must have been at the end of Let It Rock, cos Malcolm had done that for the festival, and couldn't sell 'em, so he ended up making them into pants and knickers, that's what Jordan told me. That was the Vive Le Rock T-shirt with Little Richard . . .

Jordan had black make-up going all the way up like that, and she just looked like a rocker, but the worst, toughest, nastiest rocker's girlfriend that would stand on the corner and dare their boyfriend to go like a hundred miles an hour and pull up on a sixpence, and practically kill themselves. I think I just fell in love with her from day one, she was so good.

SEX, anyway, was quite scary to even go in – lots of pink, lots of leather, lots of rubber, it was almost like that feeling of going round Soho. When you got inside there was a jukebox going, I think they were banging out either 'Where Were You (on Our Wedding Day)' or a Vince Taylor song, something very strange they had on in there. There was graffiti, and then netting over the graffiti . . .

Can you remember what the graffiti was? Was it stuff from *SCUM*?

I think it was the *SCUM Manifesto*. There was the scroll door and two windows, lit – very shallow windows. In the right-hand side he had the Which Side of the Bed T-shirt and the London Leather Man torsos with some stuff on that, and some high-heeled shoes on it as well, bits and bobs. When you went in, on the right was the rack with all the clothes, then halfway down on the right was where Michael and Jordan were.

I think the jukebox was on the left at that stage, then more clothes down the left, and there was a separate section at the back, where there were black rubber screens for changing and there was the shoes there. Clothes-wise: Cambridge Rapist, Boys, Anarchy shirts, and odd ones which Marco got – a black T-shirt with little plastic pockets, studded with cards, yeah, there was a few Gene Vincent T-shirts.

When did you go to art school, '72?

Yeah, '72, '73. I went to Hornsey and did a foundation course, then I did graphics and worked with Roger Law who does *Spitting Image* now, and that was quite an interesting time. I met Danny Kleinman there, and I was impressed with Danny cos on the opening day, out of five hundred art students we were the only two that had crepes on. He had really long hair, but he was all in leather, which was quite rare then.

But it was the usual art school thing. They had a very interesting history of art course there that was useful for the history of erotic art. All I can remember from art school was I used to play the first two Roxy Music albums.

There was one other shop at the time that's just come to mind. I was living in North London at the time, going to Hornsey, I was living around Muswell Hill. Swanky Modes was starting up. That was the place where you'd get . . . in Bazooka Joe I'd wear teddy bear, fake leopard-skin jacket, black T-shirt, jeans rolled up, black lurex socks and crepes, which was basically a Roxy thing. Malcolm's thing was completely different.

I remember with Bazooka Joe, doing Camden Town, Joe Strummer was there, The 101ers went on and just got booed off, and Strummer looked really unhealthy. And we went on and committed the cardinal sin, doing a reggae version of 'Teenager In Love'. We were doing the gig and some ted had sent his wife down the front and she called me an arsehole, just waiting for me to retaliate. It was a very frustrating time for me as a musician.

What sort of songs would you play in Bazooka Joe?

We'd play a lot of instrumentals, 'Pipeline', 'One Hand Loose', Charlie Feathers numbers. We used to do 'I Won't Go Hunting with You Jake but I'll Go Chasing Women', which I think was a Jerry Lee Lewis song, and then our own stuff, an art-school set-up. For me it was like learning and playing the bass.

I first saw the Sex Pistols at their first ever gig, in November 1975, at St Martins College of Art when they supported us. I'll never forget that, I left the band that night; I thought fuck it, this is it, you know? They were fantastic. I distinctly remember seeing them.

They all came in together, the Pistols. John had really baggy, ripped-up pinstripe trousers with braces and a T-shirt saying something like 'Rock'n'Roll' written on it, with 'I Hate' painted over it. He looked fantastic. Jonesy was tiny, he had denims, white cap-sleeve T-shirt, baseball boots; looked like a young Pete Townshend, a white Les Paul Junior. He wanted to borrow our equipment so we lent it to him and it wasn't loud enough, so they went off round the corner and got an old Fender. Matlock had splattered trousers and white patent SEX boots with red laces, and a light pink leather top, a girl's thing. Paul Cook looked like Rod Stewart, like a little mod really.

John Lydon was picking his nose and eating sweets. He used to cough up big lumps of phlegm. I watched them play. I remember Malcolm standing at the front, orchestrating them, telling them where to stand. There weren't many there, maybe a dozen of their people, this was September '75. They did 'Seventeen', 'No Lip', 'Substitute', 'Whatcha Gonna Do about It' with the lyrics changed – 'I want you to know that I hate you baby.'

I remember him eating sweets, he'd pull them out and suck 'em and just spit 'em out, and it was the look. He just glazed over, he just lost interest in the whole thing. They were very tight, they could play, they'd been rehearsing. It was only John who hadn't learned how to make the voice last, but over a fifteen-minute burst he was very clear.

This was their first gig, they were very nervous, and at the end of their gig Rotten slagged off Bazooka Joe as being a bunch of fucking cunts, and Danny leapt from the front row, got hold of John, pinned him against the back wall and made him apologise. Danny hated them, the whole band hated their guts cos they couldn't play. In fact there was such a ruck that I left the day after.

What was it about the Sex Pistols that made them different?

It was the way they looked, they stuck together. They came in as a gang, not as a band, and they were abusing the instruments, turning it up. The St Martins show was a rehearsal for Malcolm and Viv. I came out of that gig thinking, I'm tired of Bazooka Joe, I'm tired of

273

teddy boys, and it seemed to me they were playing simple songs, that I could play. With the Sex Pistols, they were always above me and you had to aspire to imitate them.

How would you have placed John? As a genuine oddity?

John looked older than the rest of them, he looked really ill, but there was something intimidating about him. He looked fucking angry, between songs he'd go, 'Applaud louder', or something, you know? They'd face the back between numbers. And they didn't tune up, that was another thing I was impressed with. Jonesy was posing, swinging about, but I tell you what, I still maintain Jonesy's one of the best solid rhythm players. He's like Thunders.

Going on to that time you saw them at the Nashville. Around that time, the first Ramones album was released. Did that make any impact on you?

I bought the first Ramones album, and that was when I was first aware of the Pistols really growing, cos I went to see The Ramones at the Roundhouse with the Flamin' Groovies, who were considered punky. They were dreadful, they came on like The Rolling Stones. I loved the Ramones album, I thought they were wonderful. They came on and their equipment didn't work and there were a load of Pistols fans in the audience heckling. They gave out little baby baseball bats, with 'Ramones' on. But once they got the power on, they really delivered.

Don't you think that the whole of British punk sped up, the Pistols included, when they heard that album?

Oh yeah. I mean the whole idea with The Ramones was to try to get the set done in record time. They used to say, 'Oh, we can get it done in an hour now.' The energy level! Then there was The Damned, who I went to see at the Roxy, who I wasn't very fond of. Vanian looked good, but I think they picked up on it more than the Pistols.

My view of the punk thing was that all this stuff about dole-queue martyrdom and politics, that's all the Clash stuff. They did all that, and the journalists too, it was the only hook. The Pistols – they looked great. I knew that the clothes in SEX at the time were expensive. They were well made, but thirty-five pounds or forty guineas for a pair of leather trousers was a lot of money. The suede boots were thirty pounds. You really had to save for that stuff, you had to want it bad.

I remember it said on their handles, 'sartorial correctness' – it was expensive. The Pistols looked expensive, they had expensive clothes, and the idea was, 'We're going to fucking take your money off ya.' Tin Pan Alley, don't forget that about Malcolm, he's a fucking salesman. Malcolm is like Laurence Harvey in *Expresso Bongo*, and Larry Parnes, but also there's the artist and he's a very intelligent person. There was a lot of spiv about him, and there was a lot of spiv about them. They were like out to rob you.

So later on, when punk was like, Oh we wanna be like the audience, the Pistols were in a class of their own, cos their songs were noticeably slower; 'Anarchy' is not a fast song. It was sexy. Glen used to pump it. All the other stuff was like [affects Chelsea riff whine!] – but they were class volume. It was like the difference between riding a Harley Davidson and a fucking Honda 125 – that's what The Damned were! The Pistols chugged along – they always played slower live, but they sounded really good.

Through '76, did you go and see the Pistols a lot, after you saw them at the Nashville?

I saw them twice at the Nashville, and then the last time I saw them was on the boat trip. Marco Pirroni said something, I think it's true, that by the time they went on Grundy, a lot of it was over, and his definition of the end of punk rock was when they started to wear Doc Martens, and I agree with him. That was all the Clash shit, the DMs. The Pistols always looked great.

The boat trip was a fucking dead horse; Sid was out of his fucking tree, Wobble jumped somebody. But it was a good day out.

What did you think of them as characters? Did they change?

Jonesy was just a sex maniac, that's what he liked to do. Paul was always the one you could talk to the most. He didn't come across as too bright, but steady, a good solid drummer. I got to know John a little bit cos we went to the Rock Garden. John was one of these people who'll be your best friend for a night and the next time you see him he won't even know who you are.

Remember it was Jonesy who *was* the Sex Pistols, it was his band, he was the lout, he was the hooligan, he was the fucking Dickensian urchin that Malcolm's been trying to be all his life. Deep down I think Malcolm really wanted to be Steve Jones. He was very fond of Steve, and of Sid, but he can't give that over, because knowing Malcolm, he's not what his image is.

I've got Sid's psychiatrist's letter from the States, writing to Malcolm after Sid died. It's a really interesting letter, saying 'how much I knew that you cared for him', and everything.

He hated Nancy, he tried to kidnap Nancy once, took her to the airport. Everybody hated Nancy. Nancy got me beaten up by Sid, she told him I'd said he couldn't play the bass – which wasn't true, and that wasn't the point anyway. I actually told him he was really good, he was doing all right, and he was like a little kid, you know? I was sleeping round at Jordan and Linda's one night and sleeping on this couch in the kitchen, and I woke up and it was Sid.

'Hello Adam, I hear you've been talking about us.' 'What?' I think he must have been out of it cos he didn't hurt me, he just whacked me in the face and tried to give me a going over, but he must have been out of it, he wasn't too strong. The next day he was really sorry. The last time I saw him was outside Dingwalls, he looked really pathetic.

His eye was cut, cos he'd gone into Dingwalls and picked on a marine by mistake, and this marine had smashed his face in. He was bloated, he was spotty, he was ugly, Nancy stunk. Linda wouldn't let her in the flat cos she stunk so bad. Jordan was a good friend of Sid's and she said he was a really charming guy, and bright – and he was. It was very sad . . .

What did you think about the film *Jubilee*?

Jordan was managing me, Jordan was in the film, the Banshees were in the film, The Slits were in the film. I always liked The Slits, they were like the baby sisters of the Pistols. It didn't seem to do any harm doing it, and Jordan said do it, so we did it, but we got paid about a fiver, they ripped us off. Derek's all right, but it was all a bit *Rocky Horror Show*.

There's a great bit in the film where you're on the roof and you crack up.

That was about the fifteenth take, cos they couldn't stop me laughing. The actors were dead straight, and they were doing this punk rock, Clash thing, and I couldn't keep a straight face because the dialogue was so fucking corny about punk rock, and I couldn't handle that at all.

I looked at *Jubilee* again recently and I thought your performances with the band were good.

They were hectic, it was a hectic time, I'm just glad I wore the stuff; it's one of the only times they were used in a film, the '77 bondage stuff. It was nice, the clothes were good. I dislocated my knee during that performance. There were a lot of people standing around with cameras, they were very scared of the group in a way. Pandemonium . . . I think it stands up.

Did you think at the time of the boat trip that the Pistols were all over, that it was just a stunt?

It wasn't the same. John had become very unfriendly. I was going to give him a pair of these boots that I had as a present, riding boots that I'd inscribed for him. He'd once given me a gold safety pin – people used to give each other clothes and that – and he didn't wanna know. Jonesy was out of it. They were very unhappy. Sid, actually, was the only one making an effort on the boat. He was the only one really trying to make it good.

The ironic thing was when they started out they said fuck guitar solos and all that, and drugs was a part of all that, so it wasn't motivated by drugs; they were motivated by some kind of energy, very narcissistic, in an early-Elvis sort of way, it was real London. Sham 69, that was the end of it. I saw him on stage shouting, skinheads are back, skinheads are back – and they wonder why there's British Movement at their gigs. It was awful.

Tony James

*Founding member of proto-punk band London SS with future
Clash guitarist Mick Jones; later formed Chelsea and Generation X.
Co-writer of one of the greatest punk songs about London, 'Day By
Day'. Conscious of his position as one of the very early adopters.
Interviewed in Maida Vale, London, after his success with Sigue
Sigue Sputnik; articulate and precise.*

I was born in the same ward of the same hospital as Steve Jones,
Queen Charlotte's Hospital in Goldhawk Road, Shepherd's Bush. I
grew up in Fulham. Then my parents moved to Twickenham, so I
lived in uptown West London. I went to Hampton Grammar School,
then Brunel University. Maths and Computer Sciences, which I got a
first in. Before I went, I was playing in various groups.

The first thing you want to do when you go to grammar school is join
a rock group, you can meet more girls that way. I was in a group that
did basically Bowie covers and blues. I saw the New York Dolls supporting Status Quo at Imperial College, and Mott the Hoople, all those
gigs. The same background as Mick Jones. I was playing bass. I went to
university basically to get a grant so I could buy an amplifier. During the
last two years at university I was in London SS with Mick Jones.

How did you meet Mick?

I met him at The Fulham Greyhound, at some sleazy gig, and we read
the same magazines and things, and we've been best friends ever
since. Twenty million people came in and out of that group. We were
looking for a singer and another guitarist, and we'd advertise every
week. We never really found them. They didn't have the right attitude, and they didn't look right.

It was still quite Lookist at that point. We wanted 'singer, drummer,
guitarist into New York Dolls, MC5, Stooges, Mott the Hoople,

Rolling Stones'. They were the key groups. Originally London SS was a long-haired group, like a London New York Dolls. Girls' shoes. Bernie Rhodes became involved in London SS, we met him at a Deaf School gig, supported rather ironically by The 101ers at the Nashville.

I'd just bought one of those Which Side of the Bed T-shirts from SEX, and this twerpy little bloke in a flat hat was standing next to us, and I said, 'Would you mind standing over the other side of the room, cos you're wearing the same T-shirt as me, you're crowding me.' He said, 'Listen, you cunt, I fucking designed this T-shirt.' 'Oh yeah?'

We got talking. 'Actually, a friend of mine's putting a group together called the Sex Pistols. Interesting. You might like 'em.' We saw him a few weeks later, and Bernie says, 'I wouldn't mind managing you.' Because Malcolm had a group, he wanted a group.

He said he'd meet us in The Bush on Shepherd's Bush Green, the worst place you could possibly go, looking like we did, like the New York Dolls. Bernie opens his bag and slaps this huge swastika on the table in the middle of this pub, and says, 'If you're going to be called London SS, you're going to have to live with that.'

He did have good ideas, I must say. We needed somewhere centralised, where the group came from, like a café where we could hang out, and we found the Praed Street Café in Paddington, which was our manor, this was the place, we used to hang out there every day, and we used to interview all the people who answered our ads in the café. That gave us a base.

Bernie found a rehearsal place in the mews around the back of the café, and we had all these brilliant posters from sixties films stuck around the room. Mick was at art school, but by that time I think he was working in a bookshop in Camden Town. So we put these ads in. We did have a long letter from someone claiming to be the world's number one New York Dolls fan, saying, 'I'm your man'. He sent a picture and we didn't like the look of him, but of course it turned out to be Morrissey.

We auditioned a variety of people. Brian James turned up, and we quite liked him. He was from Crawley, though, which was hinterland, but Bernie never really liked him. But we started working with him, and he brought this mate of his down, called Chris Miller, who took his shirt off while he was drumming with us, and bugger me if he didn't have scabies! I remember Bernie putting pages from the *Guardian* all over the seats in the room where he'd sat, in case he caught something.

We thought he looked like a rat, and Mick and I used to call him Rat Scabies behind his back, thinking it the most derisory name we could possibly give him, and the next thing we saw him in a pub on the King's Road with this T-shirt that he'd made himself, saying Rat Scabies, with this hideous picture of a little rat on it. He adopted the name, which we'd thought up as a term of derision.

Thousands of people now claim to have been in the group. We did make recordings at that time, covers of MC5 numbers, and we did 'Protex Blue', which we wrote then and which later turned up on the Clash album. We made the tape and Bernie brought Malcolm down, and we played him the set we'd worked out, and I taped it all, along with Malcolm's comments. Among other things, Malcolm said, 'Get rid of Brian, he's no good.'

Meanwhile they'd introduced us to Glen and Steve and Paul, and they used to come down and hang out. At that point they had very short hair and we had very long hair. There was a time just before we met Bernie when we went into the shop and asked Malcolm to manage us, and he said to come and see him in Denmark Street; and we trooped down there and found these blokes sitting around in black T-shirts and very short hair, who were the Sex Pistols.

We hated the idea of getting our hair cut. Long hair was still a symbol of rebellion, rather than short hair. It took a long time and loads of persuasion from Bernie and Malcolm to have short hair. We didn't talk to them much at the time, only to Glen and Paul, who were and still are regular guys. They were really good cos they could play 'Substitute' properly.

Why was it called London SS?

It was just a name that Mick had kicking around. There's nothing simpler for shock value than Nazism, drugs or dodgy sexuality. It was naive, for what happened later with the National Front. It would have been a hideous monicker to have been lumbered with.

Bernie said once, 'I hate all these Mott the Hoople songs, you lot are obsessed with rock'n'roll and the *NME*', and banned us from reading the music papers. And he gave us a reading list. He made us buy *Spare Rib* and *Gay News* in our local newsagents, to embarrass us.

Why did London SS fall apart?

London SS never found a singer. Chrissie Hynde came and went, as did loads of other people. I don't think Bernie ever really liked me, cos I was clearly middle class. It just wasn't happening, and Mick and I drifted apart for about six months or so.

One day Bernie said, 'Why don't you write a song about anarchy?' We weren't really sure what he meant. We wrote a song called 'Rockets For Sale', about buying hand-launched missiles in Selfridges. He liked that one.

Did you see the Sex Pistols when they started?

Oh yeah, at Chelsea Art College. We used to see them at the Nashville all the time. I thought they were the best group I'd ever seen. They were King's Road, we were Paddington. There were the two factions. We must have auditioned everyone who was into that scene at one time or another, and a lot of people who turned up in those later groups had been seen by us.

Mick started playing with Keith Levene and Chrissie Hynde, and Sid Vicious was living in the squat in Shepherd's Bush. Meanwhile I answered an ad in *Melody Maker* that wanted a guitarist into The Who and Small Faces, a Bromley phone number, and I went down there with a borrowed guitar, which I couldn't play at all, and there was William Broad. We got on terrifically.

This might have been slightly before the Pistols played gigs. We started playing together, and Billy was hanging out with Siouxsie and Severin. Siouxsie came round that first day. Almost at the same time, we both went for an audition with a group that the Acme Attractions people were putting together, Chelsea. That was with Gene October; it was going to be Billy Idol on rhythm guitar, Marco Pirroni on lead guitar.

Did you go to the Ramones gig and all of those?

Everything. At the beginning, we felt that we were the only people that knew what was happening, and no-one ever believed that it would be bigger than cult. All the groups we liked were cult groups, the idea of being in the charts never occurred to us. The Stooges and the MC5 weren't big groups, they were cult groups. If it's really happening, the general public don't like it. So when it exploded, it certainly caught us by surprise.

I was in a Chinese restaurant with Malcolm one time and he said, 'You watch, the Sex Pistols will be in the Top 10, this is going to be the biggest thing ever', and I just said, 'Don't be silly.' The whole grisly story, and it bloody well unfolded, just like he said.

Chelsea played the ICA, supporting the Genesis P-Orridge art exhibition. That was the first gig we ever played; we just set up in a corner and did 'Ready Steady Go' and 'Your Generation' and a couple of covers, 'Under My Thumb', things like that. That was Chelsea. It was weird, we felt happening, cos in all the books I read, happening groups always played at art shows. I read all the books that set out the myth of rock'n'roll, and I believed it all.

Then what happened was just as Billy and I were getting pissed off with Chelsea, Gene said he knew a place, Chaugerama's, where we can do a gig. He knew the owner. So we went down and booked a date, changed the name to the Roxy Club, built a stage and invited loads of journalists down. Meanwhile, we got rid of Gene October and played as Generation X. Andrew Czezowski was somehow involved.

We already had a gig set up as Chelsea at the London College of Fashion, so we decided to replace Gene with another guitarist, with the gig two weeks away. Ten days before the gig, Billy went to a party in Fulham and saw Derwood playing, but he had really long hair. We rehearsed him every night for a week, and on the Friday night, he still had long hair and flared trousers. We were begging him. The afternoon before the gig, he says, 'Okay.' We took him down to a hairdresser's and had his hair cut off in the nick of time.

Andrew Czezowski was the manager of Gen X for the first few weeks. He started to run the Roxy Club for us. We played again before Christmas, and then The Clash played there on the 1st of January, '77. Gen X played the night before. So we rode out Acme Attractions and then we rode out Andrew Czezowski as well. Then Jonh Ingham and Stewart Joseph came along.

Was it you who had the book?

No, Billy had the book. We were round his house, and we'd always thought that Chelsea was a naff name, and I was looking through the bookcase and saw the book. So there it was. We'd gone through thousands of names, but it was perfect.

You must have been under a lot of pressure when Gen X started, going public so fast?

There was a lot of pressure, but we were so lucky – we'd found Derwood, we had all the songs written already, and we were reviewed, with photos, on the first gig. We didn't come up with the painted T-shirts until a bit later. I used to do paintings on my T-shirts. Billy, who wasn't as good as me at art, used to do coloured Mondrian squares. That became the Gen X look.

It was very competitive, with all these bands and managers getting started at once.

The guys were Malcolm and Bernie, John Krivine and Steph. Steph still owns BOY. And Andrew Czezowski, who ran the Roxy, which was good for a while, but it exploded into media so quickly that it became nonsense with UK Subs. In the early days, The Heartbreakers and Siouxsie and us, some really great groups.

There was all that stuff about orange juice, and being political . . .

That was rather amusing, cos The Clash were overtly political because of Bernie's influence. He always wanted it to be heavy left-wing, anarchy, and Billy and I were just not like that, we were nice middle-class boys, and our parents didn't like rock'n'roll at all, they wanted us to have proper jobs. It was nothing to do with smashing the system. We could never be that, and the *NME* turned on us really quickly. Tony Parsons became very hardcore left-wing.

We did an interview with the *NME*, and the myth of the orange juice came from Billy and I asking for orange juice when the guy asked us what we wanted to drink. The fact was, Billy, myself, Derwood and John Towe had all been to the Hammersmith clap clinic; all four of us had VD, and we'd all had the injections that very morning. So we couldn't drink for two weeks.

283

Did you try to be political for a bit? I seem to remember a political press release.

Stewart and Jonh Ingham had this sort of 1984 idea, tried to make it like mission control. We didn't really care, we wanted to be like The Rolling Stones. Billy really liked The Beatles. We probably said loads of dopey things, everybody does when they're just starting.

Did you have a hard time with the press?

Yeah. After the orange juice thing, but as the group became bigger and clearly more rock'n'roll, the press began to get hostile.

Wasn't success a big problem for punk groups, who thought in terms of being cult groups?

Yes. Excess and drugs, all the things that punk was supposed to be about, and as they became bigger, they all wanted to be The Rolling Stones and not the MC5. One minute it was down Ladbroke Grove, the next minute it was driving through Los Angeles. You can't help it, it's such great fun, you just can't help it.

There were a lot of songs about London in punk.

It was very much like The Who. We all did go on the tube, even when we were making the first album. I'd moved out of Mick's gran's into my gran's, back in Fulham Palace Road, and it was all like The Who and The Kinks.

When did you get the sense that punk was actually over?

I think when the Sex Pistols broke up, it was over for me. While they were touring America, it was still punk. By then, Generation X was a rock'n'roll group, and The Clash were The Rolling Stones.

Did you get much violence?

Yes, we had terrible trouble. Everybody wanted to beat up Billy Idol, just because he was so good-looking. We played at Derby Assembly Rooms, and there were all these Hell's Angels in the audience, and one walked up on to the stage, punched Billy in the face just once, and Billy just flew across the stage like a ping pong ball and landed in the drum kit, and the guy brushed himself down and walked off,

284

and no-one did a thing.

I just stood there, paralysed, and we continued playing, and Billy got up, dusted himself down and continued singing, like nothing had happened. I was rigid with fear.

Didn't Derwood get hit by a bottle?

At Leicester University, someone threw a whiskey bottle at Derwood; it hit him in the face, and he had to go to hospital. I remember when we played the Lyceum, we walked on stage and it was like Agincourt, with bottle and spit. We were being supported by the UK Subs. It was hideous. They thought it was about spitting.

Rat Scabies started the whole fucking thing with spitting, at one of those early Damned gigs, he thought it was really brilliant, spitting at the audience, and the media picked up on it, that became what punk was about. But the Sex Pistols were never about spitting. Rat Scabies, single-handedly, was responsible for the most moronic element of punk. I always thought he was an arsehole, and still do.

Viv Albertine

Leading punk stylist and guitarist of The Slits. Witnessed the Sex Pistols' third show at Chelsea Art College and joined the floating pool of musicians around Sid Vicious in the bedroom group The Flowers of Romance – a name given them by John Lydon. Helped to define the new female radicalism. Interviewed in London's Camden Town, where she showed me letters and lyrics by her friend Sid Vicious.

I was brought up in North London, went to comprehensive school in Muswell Hill, then Hornsey School of Art, now Middlesex Poly. I drew from an early age. I went to Hornsey at seventeen.

What was that like?

I was all excited by it because I'd heard about the sit-ins in the sixties and everything. We had a very good art department, but when I got there they'd all clamped up, got rid of all the aggravating factors and tutors, and it was the same old story. I was very young when the sixties thing was going on, I just caught the very glamorous end of it. I think it affected everyone my age very much. Everyone our age and up to ten years older, I suppose.

Because there was a sense of possibility?

Yeah, the optimism was very appealing to a child, let alone to a young adult; the optimism of it, the colours, the softness, the excitement, the affection, free love and everything. Hippies all smiling at each other, the interest in the arts, the caring; all sorts of things that appeal to a child, a sense of fairness. I think that sense of fairness came out in punk as well, they all wanted things to be fair, no unbalanced stuff – whether you were devaluing the swastika, or questioning why you made love, or why you held hands or whatever it was, it was very strict, and fair. I think it was a leftover from the hippy thing.

286

How did you get involved in what became punk?

I went to Chelsea School of Art where I did textile design, which was where I met Jane Ashley, actually, and Mick was on the fine art course, but I had another friend there called Rory Johnston, who was something to do with the music business. He worked with Malcolm for a long time. It was him who told me to apply to that college, he was there as well. He'd heard of the Sex Pistols cos he knew Malcolm and so I went to the gig at Chelsea School of Art.

I completely caught the atmosphere, immediately, it didn't need any explaining; it was a matter of attitude, and fuck everything else, I can't remember the music or anything. It was just something I understood, and that was it. Yeah. It was like a soulmate, or a kindred spirit, and that was it really.

Can you remember what the audience was like?

It was about half full. Rory introduced me to Malcolm, he was very charming, polite, not snobby or anything. That's all I really remember. Mick wouldn't go, I remember that. He'd heard of them, they were Cutie Jones and the Sex Pistols then, I think. He wouldn't go because he was getting a group together and they were considered rivals, which they always were. So I told him about it the next day, said it was great.

Once that had happened, did it give you an impetus?

Things slowly started to change. I got closer to Mick, as a mate, he'd come round to the squat in Shepherd's Bush, and slowly the way I dressed and he dressed started to change. We probably went to the shop then, I was picking up on it and it was growing. Mick went through quite a few groups, I suppose it was the early Clash; I can't remember who was in it though, it went through so many auditions and singers, through a year and a half.

Did you see any other Sex Pistols concerts?

I went to almost every one from that point. The St Martins one, I think I got there and it was finished. I saw the 100 Club ones later on. There was a period when I was learning to play guitar, when I sometimes wouldn't go to their gigs, thinking I must get on with my

287

own thing, there was this very strong rivalry thing, which was really weird. I don't know why you couldn't take the evening off.

I think there was an intense pressure for people to do things, to get something out.

The Clash used to have meetings around our squat all the time, which was really annoying: Bernie, you know, you'd be banished from your own kitchen.

Political meetings?

Exactly. On and on.

Did you see the Sex Pistols getting better, or were they just the same?

The first time I saw them I don't even remember what the noise was like – the thing is you get to know the songs so you don't know if they're getting better. It never mattered to me anyway, I was no great musical critic at the time, I'd never learned to play an instrument, it didn't bother me. I'd been to see bands like the Edgar Broughton Band who couldn't play; it was nothing new to me, a band who sounded a mess. I'd been going to gigs from quite young.

Was going there a social event as much as anything else?

Oh yeah, you'd see people you knew, check out what they were wearing.

What sort of clothes did you start wearing then?

Leather. Black and pink, high heels, practically everything from SEX in fact. It had to be very strict. I remember Sid teaching me about the size and shape of collars. I remember having a pink mohair jumper which I gave to Jane Ashley, and Sid said that was the most horrible thing I'd ever done, to give her such a jumper. Then I had to buy a pair of Doc Martens, cos going out with Sid you'd get into such trouble, I needed a pair of shoes you could run in.

When did you first meet him?

In a pub, in Portobello Road, I can't remember the name. He was quite polite, I'd heard a lot about him, a friend of John's. They looked like bookends, the pair of them, both with spiky hair. I was expecting spiky hair, and when I met him he'd shaved his head, looked hideous. I can't remember how we got friendly, I think I just rang him up, I was very bold in those days, I would just ring somebody up and say, 'Come over', or 'I'm coming over', or 'Do you want to be in our group?'

I think it was before he played with the Banshees. I always felt very uncomfortable with him – he was so strict, and so idealistic, and so clever, which people don't seem to realise. Do people realise that Sid was really bright? He was so sharp.

What was his strictness about? The way you looked?

Everything. It was down to the way you looked, the way you spoke, the things you were hung up about. If he could find something you were embarrassed about yourself, or fucked up about, or didn't have worked out, he'd home in on it, and you'd be in pain from his verbal haranguing.

What was he hung up about?

He had this fantastic disguise of a sort of loping, playful, get-wise Jamaican expression, and if you ever did confront him with something that he was embarrassed about, he would just be barefaced, and admit it, and you'd lost your power. He was very clever, and the reason he went scooting downhill, he was so idealistic, and he really couldn't stand the world and its pettiness.

I don't want to make him out as something brilliant, cos he was a pain in the arse in many ways, but he was the type of person, which lots of junkies are, who are so idealistic that they just can't handle life as it is.

He used to wear this massive swastika on his back, I think he was probably the first to do so, and first of all he did it like Lenny Bruce would use the word nigger to devalue it, to bring it into a context where it's not important; you know, it would be worn by young kids, to say it's not important, it doesn't matter any more.

Once a taxi driver stopped, and when he saw Sid's jacket he wouldn't take us, and Sid said, 'He's an idiot, he should have taken us, the long way round, ripped us off for anything he could get out of us.'

He seems also to have been a real stylist; more than any of them, he seemed obsessed with clothes, and the way you looked.

He was, but funnily enough, he didn't have much sexuality about him. He was like a toy almost. We'd go to the shop and Vivienne would put a pair of trousers on him, and you remember he wore those pegs with thousands of safety pins in them, and he went in there one day and Vivienne said, 'They're terrible, you can't wear them any more', and he'd go, 'Oh, all right then.' If you did suggest something, he would take it up, but he had such a lively mind that it was rare that someone would get there before him.

He couldn't be bothered with principles. He taught me something really interesting, and I always thought that one should have certain principles. He taught me that in different situations, you should always be ready to change your ideas. As quickly as the situation changed, you have to reconstruct your whole mind, and that's how Sid lived, and that's why he would do the things he did. He thought it was really unhealthy to hang on.

That's a very intense way to live.

I can't tell you how hard it was to be around somebody like that.

When did that start to go?

Probably when he joined the Pistols. Just before.

Can you tell me about the Flowers of Romance thing, what that was all about?

There was me, Palmolive, a girl called Sarah. We were rehearsing in Jo Faull's squat. That was probably how I got to know Sid, he wanted to be in a group or something, and I said to come down, he was going to be the singer. John thought up the name, The Flowers of Romance, and it was the hottest summer, '76, we spent it all indoors in this bloody squat, every day. We did have discipline.

It was a bedroom band. We couldn't keep time, Sid went from being a singer to also playing saxophone. I wrote my first riff which was quite good, which turned into 'So Tough'. Even when people came in who could play, it still didn't get going for some reason. It was a bunch of interesting-looking people, and we'd get interviewed

290

when we'd never done anything and could hardly play. We'd go into pubs in Notting Hill and Soho, and people would come up and interview us, Jonh Ingham and others.

It was a great name.

It was absolutely perfect – you're the flowers, and what's romance – it's lies. These children are The Flowers of Romance.

Did you write any material, were there any songs?

It was so hard, cos I could hardly play. Sid picked it up like that [snaps fingers]. One night I went to bed in Shepherd's Bush, and Sid stayed up with a Ramones album and a bass guitar, or a guitar, and when I got up in the morning, he could play. He was so quick. That's why he had to look thick, he had to slow himself down.

Funnily enough, that comes over in the early pictures. I've been looking very hard at early pictures, and that comes across.

I've got a letter from him here, which he wrote from Ashford, but you can tell from his writing that he's not a thicko.

[Looking at material.] This is all fascinating. Did Sid write 'Belsen Was a Gas'?

Yes, I don't know if it's in here, but there's some lyrics in there. This is his wallet that he used to carry around, I don't know how the fuck I've got it. This is Sid attempting to write lyrics, it's really embarrassing: anyway, he wrote a version of it.

This is something that I've got to get to grips with. Everybody said it's so disgusting and everything, but it's a horrifying song. It's really frightening . . .

But not in some namby-pamby, isn't-it-naughty, isn't-it-wrong, but accentuating the vileness of it, rather than saying, oh it's wrong in a social-worker type of way. But people were simplistic about Sid wearing massive swastikas, and Siouxsie with her whips and everything. I think we were slightly naive about how it would be taken, but we didn't give a shit anyway, if they didn't understand. I couldn't talk to my mother for ages.

She couldn't cope with it?

It wasn't that at all, she wanted to know about it, I just didn't want to communicate it. It was really weird. It was too convoluted and complex, and too much needed to be explained, to talk to someone about it. Within a year and a half or so, it was all right.

I got really pissed off with Sid when he wore one of the T-shirts with the Cambridge Rapist mask on it, do you remember that one? I'd tried to tell Sid about how frightening it was for women on the streets, and how hard it was to laugh at it. How Jewish people must have felt about the swastikas really, but being removed from that I could understand that one.

He said, 'You should just scrawl across it, "Defend Thine Honour", and it makes it a different thing.' Just wearing the Rapist mask is one thing, although I couldn't quite see the point of wearing it, but then to scrawl across it, 'Defend Thine Honour', it's suddenly active instead of passive, and I thought that was so clever of him to turn it round.

So did the band just drift apart?

When Sid said he didn't want me in it any more, it wasn't that I didn't fit in, but I wasn't giving enough to it, I couldn't really play, I felt a bit intimidated by him still, even though I'd hung out with him, practically living with him for almost a year, just as mates, hanging out together, so I was a bit upset by that for about a week, but there was so much going on in life, and then The Slits started to happen.

I think he got asked to be in the Pistols, and I remember him asking me whether I thought he should do it or not. It was like, if he did that, he would be giving up something of himself. He knew that, but we all reckoned they were just the best, so it was just too much to turn down, really.

One of the interesting things, just from the point of social history, is that people could live in squats then. Young people could live in the centre of London.

Yeah, that's true isn't it, we all did. I used to leave my squat in Shepherd's Bush with not a penny in my pocket. I used to get on to the tube and at the other end say, 'I've left my purse at home', go to the Speakeasy or the Roxy, blag your way in through the door, get bought drinks all night, then share a taxi or get the night bus home. I'd literally leave with not a penny in my pocket.

That's very tough, survival . . .

Not really, it was just ingenuity, you knew you could do it. You had that sort of energy then. Getting on and off the tube was the hardest thing, you'd end up going home or sharing space for the night with someone you didn't want to. I don't mean sexually, just not being able to get home. There was a terrible fear of boredom, actually, an absolute horror of it which I don't think I've ever shaken.

In what way?

Well rather than spend a night in, you'd do that, for a start. Or you'd go out every day in that hottest summer and practise, just for the sake of not being on your own, you had to fill up your time with worthwhile things. I've never shaken that, and it's quite a problem, in a way.

Did you keep on going to Sex Pistols concerts?

Yeah.

Did you feel that it was changing at any point?

It became more and more popular. At the beginning of the 100 Club gigs there was hardly anyone there, and I can't remember how many weeks they did, six or ten, but by the end it was packed, cos in the meanwhile the Grundy interview had happened. It went from being an underground thing to an overground thing, through the media, and lots of people came down. That was a big change. Until then it was twenty or thirty people, the Bromley lot, and a few others who'd meet at Louise's, that lesbian club.

Did you go to Louise's? What was that like?

It was a tiny little place on the ground floor. You'd just check what other people were wearing, which wasn't just fashion, it always said something. You might have your hair cut in the most hideous way, but it was an interesting thing for a woman to have done, or Siouxsie wearing something with her tits hanging out, but it was acceptable, for the sake of how daring they were being, or what statement they were making. It was like wearing your thoughts, and your attitudes to life.

I think one of the things that I liked about early punk was that it was, not a word that was fashionable at the time, androgynous.

Yeah. The way we used to dress was garnered from Frederick's of Hollywood, or fetish magazines, but then you'd wear Doc Martens with it or have such a look on your face that if some creepy little man dared to turn around and say anything to this fantasy figure in rubber stockings, a negligee with all kinds of fancy condoms hanging around the edge like a fringe, high-heeled pink leather boots, it was, 'Fuck off, you wanker!' The contradiction in that image must have been absolutely flooring to a man, I should think.

What sort of reactions did you get?

Everything from absolute, open-mouthed amazement, to actual physical violence. Ari got stabbed in the bum outside Screen on the Green. We were attacked lots of times, and we had to fight, but it was such an ambiguous, contradictory image, the way we walked, so much of how you present yourself affects how you're taken. Fuck what you're wearing, if you walk like a queen, or like a panther, or like a docker, how you present yourself is still read. It was a very confusing image.

If a bunch of girls giggled, I would give them hell, or if an old lady turned around . . . I remember once in John Lewis, these two old ladies were staring at me and making comments, and I turned around to them and said, 'Look, your hair is purple, how can you possibly be pointing and laughing at me?' They just clammed up. But I said it very aggressively, I was very aggressive at the time. These two old dears with purple and blue hair couldn't see that they were as strange as I was.

Why were you so aggressive at the time?

Because it took a lot of courage to be out on the street and constantly be inviting attention. I had withdrawal symptoms afterwards – it was a real strain, and you need some sort of energetic push to get you through it.

Can you tell me how The Slits got started, cos they'd already begun, hadn't they?

I think through Caroline Coon they got in touch with me cos they wanted a bass player, and I didn't want to be a bass player, I was a guitarist, so I said no. Anyway, I thought they were naff from what I'd heard, with black paint all over their faces, and very childish and silly.

They'd just started off in Ari's basement or something?

Yes. I saw them play at Harlesden, which I think was their first gig, and I was just knocked out. Ari was so sexy, she really turned me on. Palmolive was great, and Tess on bass. Occasionally in life, something seems so right that even though all the odds are against you, you just go for it, and I just kept ringing them up, cos I thought, I've got to be in that band. I was a fan, then the next thing, they said, 'Come down and play with us.'

Did Kate Korus [original guitarist] get the boot?

Yeah, I don't know if I was so forceful or it seemed so right, I just felt completely drawn towards them.

When you started playing with The Slits, what sort of guitar were you using?

I had a Gibson Les Paul Junior. Sunburst, which I hated, I had it sprayed black with little bits of glitter in it. Knocked down the price by about a hundred pounds, doing that. I bought my speaker off Steve Jones.

I remember that guitar drone was everywhere that year, and it's the only time I've heard it on record [The Slits' *Bootleg Retrospective*].

Keith and me used to work a lot on sounds. We used to talk about guitars and guitar sounds all the time. We had this thing called guitar depression. He used to say, 'I'm so depressed', and we used to talk and talk about what had been happening that day, and he'd say,

295

'You've got guitar depression, Viv', cos he was guitar-mad, he'd been playing since he was quite young.

It was being depressed from learning to play an instrument, how you try to feed your personality through it, and this sound wasn't quite trebly, so it was like a buzz-saw crossed with a wasp. It was just a matter of whacking all the treble up and distorting it, really. Again, that was another thing you had to be strict about, your guitar sound. There was no sign of a twelve-bar in anything you did, except the Pistols.

It took a long time for Keith's talent to come out. I had it with Flowers of Romance, and he had it with The Clash, where if you're not amongst the right sort of people, your artistic ability doesn't come through, and you can go through these guitar depressions, or artistic depressions, where you start doubting your own ability or whatever; but given the right circumstances, it does come out.

So how did you construct songs, in the end?

What would happen was, a few scraps of words, I'd walk around with a book, everywhere, writing down conversations and things. You've got to write it down the minute you hear it, that's one thing I taught myself to do. So that was the first thing, scraps of words and things, and then it would be a matter of sitting in your room for hours and hours, faffing about until you came up with a riff, put it together with another riff, play it to the rest of The Slits, they'd add a bit on, take a bit off, and that's how the songs were written. Then it had to be memorised. We cassette-taped all our rehearsals, arguments and everything. They're hysterical.

Was that LP on Y records [*Bootleg Retrospective*] compiled from those rehearsal tapes?

Yeah. I can't remember where from.

The exciting thing about it was, if you take it on its own merits, it was people trying to find a way to communicate, and there was a lot of that in punk, you had the process of articulation in public view.

Exactly, we always said we'd rehearse in public. We went out on tour before we could play.

296

That was really exciting.

Yeah, but don't forget, we're not insensitive souls, and it was very stressful, again. To be out there. My first gig was at the Edinburgh Playhouse, thousands of people, the first time I'd ever walked on a stage, and I couldn't play, you know? I had a lot of bottle, but you need a fucking lot of bottle to do that. Although it's funny to watch, it's actually painful to feel, you're not acting out these things, you actually mean it.

What were the personalities of The Slits like?

Let me see, Palmolive was fiery, Spanish, definitely had Spanish eyes, those sexy alive eyes that are always focused, never sort of fading out like British eyes glaze over. Intense woman, fairly religious, deep down. Sensual, undisciplined.

Tessa: Irish, Catholic, quiet, Tessa's the hardest one. She was such a private person. Honestly, people who had known her for years didn't know her. I don't think she's so private now. She just held it all together, yes, as we all did.

We used to have massive arguments about people getting drunk or stoned before we went on, because we couldn't play before, let alone if we went on stoned. That was one of the main things for the first few years. It took years for each person to become that responsible, before Tessa and Palmolive learned that they mustn't let the rest of us down. By going on pissed, or whatever.

What about Ari?

Well, she was fourteen when the band first started. Absolutely sexy, with that Lolita type of sexuality, which she also quickly became aware of and became a parody of it, which was also funny. She had, not exactly no pride, but no shame. You've heard she would piss on stage? Can you imagine a young woman, with all the pressures on women to be pretty and acceptable and this, that and the other, hoick down her knickers and piss on stage?

She didn't care what she looked like, what she smelt like. There was really something to learn from that. I could never be as free as she was. I don't know where she got that freedom from, I think it may have been trying to annoy her mother really, cos her mother

297

[Nora Forster] was groovy, she was good-looking, she was a model.

How did Ari and Nora get on together?

They fought, all the time. It was hard in those days, cos we used to live round Ari and Nora's place. There was constant screaming between the two of them, and they probably understood it, but for other people living there, it was hard.

Was she going out with John then, or was that before?

No, she wasn't, that was quite a lot later. She went out with Steve for quite a long time.

And she had gone out with Chris Spedding.

Yeah, she was living with him. But I think that was over by the time we met Ari, and she was fourteen then. They'd split up. So that was Ari, the sexuality, absolutely without shame, which was probably out of wanting to annoy Nora, it was actually very interesting, and brave of her. She wasn't stupid, she soon sussed out that it wasn't particularly attractive in some ways, although it was in other ways. It was challenging.

To me one of the most extraordinary things was Palmolive's drumming.

The energy there was fantastic. Did you know she couldn't keep time? After a few years, the group couldn't go on with that constant worry on stage that the fucking thing wasn't going to be held together.

But the actual blocks of sound, did she do that all herself?

In a way it was worked on by all of us, but she did it herself. Only she had that energy and passion, and she looked so great playing drums; but we all worked on each other's guitar, bass, everything, singing. You can hear on the rehearsal tapes. Fucking painful, but we were very strict with each other: 'No, that sounds hippy-ish', 'No, that sounds like some old 10CC riff'. Everyone would have things to say about each other's parts.

The song I really liked was 'What a Boring Life' – that idea of boredom was really important, all the way through punk.

298

You'd do things to alleviate the boredom that if you sat and thought about them would be quite frightening, to fill your life up with something interesting, or something challenging – which is kind of like what the situationists did as well, wasn't it? You'd make a phone call to someone you didn't know well and ask them round, or go out to a situation, in the middle of the night. Things you just don't do any more, it's all gone so straight and dead, no-one's spontaneous.

The first interesting thing about The Slits was that it was an all-women group, and yet you didn't specifically address that problem.

It was enough, our attitude, the way we looked, anything was enough without being specific about it, and we knew that. Any more would have gone into social-worker stuff, so that's where it stopped.

What sort of reaction did you get?

You know on the White Riot tour, it was us that caused the mayhem. Every morning, the coach driver had to be bribed to let The Slits on to the coach. Everywhere we went, we had to almost be strapped to our seats, every hotel we had to be smuggled in. It was a combination of us being who we were, not being nice little girls, which if we'd been men, it would have been, Oh, aren't they great, you know, like the Stones or whatever, or the Pistols. Because we were women there was this constant sexuality.

The coach driver had to be bribed, because we made such a noise on the coach, but because his sexuality was disturbed by this contradictory image of these women with wild, matted hair, probably quite pretty. Ari's sexuality, only fourteen, a skirt that didn't hide her bum. He must have found it so threatening and so exciting at the same time.

You wouldn't talk to the press either, would you?

We did talk, but we wouldn't play the game. If they sat down and said, 'Right, how old are you, where do you come from?', we'd say, 'Fuck off, if you can't think of any better questions than that, don't bother us. We don't spend hours writing our songs, making sure that they don't say a lot of horseshit, for you to come along and trot out the same questions.' We felt that we'd made our job interesting, it's up to them to make their job interesting too.

You would get people like Jane Suck or whoever, who would conduct an interview as if it was an event, and you'd get others who'd trot out the same old questions, and we just wouldn't let them get away with it. At the same time, the blokes in the record companies are not the sort you would associate with, fucked-up blokes, totally naff human beings, and there you are trying to deal with them.

Is that why it took you so long to get a contract?

No, we got offered contracts quite early, and we didn't want them. We didn't want to make a record that was just a load of bish-bash. When we made an LP, we wanted it to be something that would last, that we would be fairly pleased with, quite intricate. The live stuff was quite live, but it wasn't time to record, and when it was time, we didn't have much of a problem at all.

What were the other people on the White Riot tour like?

Subway Sect: they were a great band, very Velvet Underground. Vic was witty, deadpan, definitely talented. Very intense little group, and again, very strict about their music and what they said, and how they looked. Not to move and not to pose and not to wear their guitars low. They were one of the first bands who wouldn't have that macho low guitar. They were quite intellectual.

What were The Clash like then?

Well, I was going out with Mick at that time, it was right in the middle of our massive affair. So every night there would be rows and screaming and crying, as I remember. They were good blokes, a good laugh, got on great with them.

Did Mick change?

From putting the band together he had a fantastic self-deprecatory sense of humour, which he still has, but it was better then. He would laugh a lot more than he does now. I can't say he changed that much. The situation just exaggerated, at one point he was mad about rock-'n'roll, trying to get a band together, the next time, he was in the band and mad about rock'n'roll. It was always going to be his life, above everything.

You were very briefly in *Jubilee*, weren't you?

That's another thing we were strict about, we had our bit with *Jubilee*, we were supposed to do three or four more scenes, and we suddenly thought no, this isn't right for our image, and we don't want to be associated with it, and we went round and told Derek that we felt that it wasn't right for us. I don't know where these notions came from.

Everybody was very much against *Jubilee*, I remember.

Yes. It's okay, watching it now, but at the time, everyone was so nit-picking about everything.

It's partly because he was part of a previous generation, I think.

I think because one doesn't have a lot of control of oneself on film, you never know what's going to get cut in or out. That's a bit frightening, that it's out of your control, and you had to be in control of everything otherwise it started to get misinterpreted.

Were you ever going to work with Siouxsie?

Yeah. Very briefly, in the Flowers of Romance time, me and Sid were going to get together with them. It's good that people who were young and supposedly undisciplined, we were all beavering away like mad, writing things.

Did you ever see much of John Lydon? What was your impression of him?

It's always hard between man and woman, or boy and girl, cos there's always a sexual thing. I found him attractive, so that would cloud things a bit. He was like the height of the strictness, really. Him and Sid. He was very judgmental, and yet he would tell lies all the time. It was very mentally debilitating, a cross between lies and blatant, brutal truth. Certain characters that are frightened of themselves, they tell the truth and then cover it over with a lie, they don't want you to know who they really are, I suppose.

John has definitely got a strong female side. You can see that with his body, and his closeness with his mother and all sorts of things; he's got a very strong female side which may be as frightening in a

301

very male environment. But he's always had a bunch of Finsbury Park, real lads around him, ex-prison types.

Do you think there was a puritanism in punk, about sex? Where do you think that came from?

I don't really know where it came from, but it was definitely there. Sid would call it squelching, and he wasn't into it, he didn't have sex often, for a very long time. And when he did have it, he went overboard, with Nancy. I don't know if they were putting it down because it was something they couldn't confront – too complicated or too grown-up. It's so hyped, as well, sexuality, you've got to be careful of it. The thing is not to get drawn into the crap, and to find yourself.

Did you feel that the androgyny, or the lack of machismo or whatever, changed during '77?

Yeah, it did become more macho as people's rock'n'roll tendencies started to sneak back out again. But there were those who stuck to questioning it. The whole thing was about looking at things with a fresh eye, and sexuality was one of those things that had to be looked at. And that meant stepping back. But there were those who really didn't give a damn about questioning things, and just rock'n'rolled away.

I think of The Police as being the turning point in the commercialisation, and the Boomtown Rats. They were nothing bands, no-one would have looked at them twice. I never got disillusioned with the strictness of punk, actually, because I've always been that sort of person, a questioning, strict, puritanical sort of person. So it was right up my street. I hated people like The Police, who weren't strict.

What about The Stranglers?

Oh god. That's what I couldn't stand, people who came in on the bandwagon who had none of the interesting side to them.

Did you stay in touch with Sid after he took up with Nancy?

Yeah, Nancy used to stay around my place quite a lot, and I used to stay at her place as well sometimes, when Sid was away. I couldn't believe how Sid changed, from this sharp and incisive mind, which he did used to hide under this thicko exterior, but he was really sharp.

Someone like that has to hide it, otherwise it's just too painful for them. To this little whimpering boy. It was just the drugs that did it, he'd just given up, really.

Did you think that part of the deterioration had to do with having this really simplistic public image?

People say that you do start to believe what you act. I just think he gave up on everything. He couldn't be bothered with life. It wasn't at all surprising that he died at the age he did, and the way he did. It was completely predictable. I'm not saying I predicted it, but I wasn't at all surprised.

Even when you first knew him?

Yeah, it could have been. I'm sure he said a thousand times, 'I'm going to die young', and people say it, but with Sid, it wasn't a shock at all.

He went right into it, didn't he?

He let go of everything and went right into it. It's almost like insanity when there's a point when you can hang on to a straw, and hold on, but he let himself go. There was also that never being frightened to try anything, to change his mind. If the opportunity to do something came up, he'd do it. It didn't matter if he did it well or badly, he just did it.

What did you think of Nancy, did you like her? Did you respect her?

No, I didn't like her, and I didn't respect her, but I didn't mind her, which is different. She wasn't someone I would have chosen for a friend, I certainly didn't respect her opinions or her attitude, but I didn't mind her being around. She was so easy to focus on because she was such a screaming pain in the neck, and it was so easy to blame her for Sid's downfall.

Everyone liked Sid, you couldn't help but like him, he was really loveable, and it was convenient to have this object to blame everything on, which was completely wrong. It was his choice, it was part of him, having a woman like that – this intrusive alter-ego of Sid's.

But as a person she was so annoying. Anyone with any sense would have hated her, she was a whiner and a whinger. Once Malcolm did something she didn't like, and she was going, 'One day I'm going to cut out my heart and put it in a jar and send it to Malcolm.' She'd talk like that all the time, really intense and bitter, as if the whole world was down on her – which it was, cos she was so annoying.

She wasn't anything, she wasn't intelligent. I mean, lots of people weren't nice, John wasn't nice, but he had other redeeming factors, and she didn't. She had no redeeming features at all.

Do you take the line that they really loved each other, that they had a real relationship?

Definitely. Relationships are all about people filling each other's gaps, aren't they, and that's what they did. They just had more extreme gaps. He would have affairs and so would she, and they didn't mind about it. She would actually boast that she had given him a sexual vibe, which she had, in a way. He didn't have that vibe, he wasn't like a man until he met Nancy, he was like a teddy bear.

In The Slits you changed from that punk thrash to playing reggae . . .

Well, reggae was the most important thing happening, from about '77. So you couldn't help but be influenced by it. We definitely didn't like the ugliness of the punk sounds, cos the more you learn about music, the more you learn what you like and what you don't like. Also Ari was mad about reggae, which had a lot to do with the influence. We used to fight about how much of the influence should be allowed to creep in.

Dub, I think, was one of the most amazing things that happened to music. Dub is fantastic, the space, the dropping out instead of putting in. That minimalism, yes, and dub was a more beautiful version of that; whereas punk did it in an aggressive, metallic way, dub reggae did it in an ethereal, sensitive way.

Glitterbest were going to manage The Slits at one point weren't they?

I've got tapes of phone calls between us and Glitterbest, and Malcolm not being there. We'd have meetings with him in the funniest places in London. He'd say, 'I'll meet you at the little gazebo in Soho Square, three o'clock', or Ward's Irish bar, and we'd talk, but it never came to anything, he was too busy. That was just before the Pistols went to America.

I seem to remember a story about a plan to fly you out to Mexico, and make a film with you there.

There was often talk about making a film together, but it never came off.

Can you remember what that film was going to be?

It kept changing. I remember once he was going to make Ari into some sort of sexual thing, and I said, 'No way, over my dead body', and he said, 'Well we'll have that conflict in the film then', you know?

You were talking about a close-knit network, when did that start to fall apart?

I suppose when everyone started going on tour and becoming a working band, really. The Pistols were always playing around London, and we were always rehearsing in London, and Mick and them were getting the group together – it didn't last very long, hanging around the clubs. As soon as everyone went on tour, everyone became a musician just like any jazz musician or whatever. You don't see your mates any more, and suddenly you're in the career of it all, and it's a bloody bore, you know?

Jah Wobble

Jah Wobble – born John Wardle – met John Lydon at Kingsway College in 1974. He was one of the group, all called John, who haunted the King's Road in general and the SEX shop in particular in the mid-seventies. Had a fearsome reputation during 1976 and 1977, thanks to a couple of well-publicised fights. Turned to playing fundamental bass and became a founder member of Public Image Limited. A long-reformed character; very thoughtful and perceptive.

So where were you brought up, John?

Stepney, East London, I was born there. I had quite an interesting life, in a low-key sort of way, from out of that background. I went to the London Nautical School. I wanted to go to sea. I had a little bit of a seafaring tradition in the family. I'd go down to the docks – there again, the butt end of the docks, it was when they were closing, it seemed like the butt end of everything.

I went to a heavy-duty Catholic primary school in Stepney. Tatty brown textbooks showing the thriving docks of the early fifties, and black people cutting sugar cane in the Empire, weird stuff like you sponsored a black child in Africa, you chipped in a couple of bob every week, and you moved your child up these stairs to heaven. It became a thing where we'd cheat, you'd pay your money and move your child three steps up. When you got your child into heaven you got a certificate.

I may be wrong, but the whole generation that was around that punk thing were all the eternal misfits. It was manna from heaven. I felt very gawky, didn't know how to approach women or anything. Then the punk thing came along, and suddenly it was hip to be tall white, pale and skinny and gawky.

That's what was nice about pop music, and still is – the possibility that you can reinvent yourself.

For me, with my family, it was get a job or piss off. The future was, go east, young man, to Dagenham, and have 2.4 kids. Everyone moves out of the East, right from the fifties. It was Labour who kept that going right through the sixties. So if you're in Stepney or Poplar, you go east. If you're from south, you go to Bromley. For their days out they go to Brighton, for ours we'd go to Southend. A huge expanse of mud.

I was incredibly lucky because I've got a lot of friends out of that working-class thing, which isn't as rigid as it used to be. You're given aspirations of doing things, and it's got worse. I was able to break free of that, I was bloody lucky. I faked it; even when I got into Public Image, I'd be Jah Wobble the Hipster, when I still had the emotional response of an insecure fifteen-year-old out of Stepney.

So you went to the Nautical School?

I got expelled at fifteen. You had a lot of working-class there, and I suppose all boys' schools have their rituals, and I was able to do more or less what I wanted. I was a bit of a Bilko character. Swing things my way. I'd get my name marked down in the register and I'd be away for weeks at a time. They knew, and they were happy for me not to be around. I got more and more anarchic and pushed it too far. They said if they found me on the premises again, the police would be called.

It must have been very frustrating to be bright in that culture?

That's exactly right, and I did get bitter about that. I found I had a flair for music, but there is a prejudice against that. I'm not embittered, that's just the way it is. At the worst extreme, if you're black there will be a prejudice against you.

So, were you into music at all when you were younger?

Yeah, for some reason I got into black music, into reggae, and me and my mate Ronnie used to go to the soul clubs and the all-nighters, shebeens, and that heavy reggae beat always fascinated me. Lee Perry was going, King Tubby. I was quite into that. It was a bloody good era for the stuff I was into, real social-commentary stuff at that time. Blackbyrds, Jimmy Castor Bunch, Ohio Players.

I liked the odd rock band. I liked The Who, and Hawkwind as well, I'm ashamed to say. *In Search of Space* was my favourite. Certain things would just affect me. I used to go and see them, I even liked that corny slide-show they used to do. It was very simple but it was very fucking moving, you know.

I went to a college of further education, and that's where I met John and then Sid. That's exactly what I was looking for, when I was about sixteen. I was already an angry young man and all that. It was that horrible Roundhouse scene then. It was only when I met them that I started going down there. The real butt end of the sixties. Totally desperate. Then it was all the denims and the afghans, a real sad apology for a scene.

Can you remember the bands?

Keith Christmas, real horrible fucking acts, you know. I would despise all that. The first band I got into was Rod Stewart and The Faces. They were quite a good raunchy rock band, as raunchy rock bands go. And reggae, they called it bluebeat then. That's what I liked. Also if you were that age there was one or two of these places you could go to, you had to really look for entertainment, which is a character-building exercise.

So, after you got kicked out you went to Kingsway?

All I knew then was I desperately didn't want to work. Images of being enclosed by council flats, feeling very claustrophobic and dissatisfied with life. I went there and it was horrible. I didn't like hippies, I was more in the skinhead tradition, but there was a real lame atmosphere.

Then I met John and I thought, grab on to this geezer. He had a lot of charisma. I'd always felt I was an oddball, and John seemed like another oddball. He was about three years older than me, but he'd had meningitis or something and he'd missed three years of school. I thought he had a bit of individuality.

What were you both wearing then?

Nothing very special, John looked in the Roxy Music sort of line, and me rather a thug. Nothing too elegant, I'm sure. That *Great Gatsby* thing I thought was pretty cool at the time, grey pinstripe suits. Then I met Sid. I found that the rule of thumb for appearance at that time was that if somebody dressed good, they had personality. Now if someone dresses trendily, it's a sign of no personality. That's a big difference.

Anyway, Sid was going around one or two of the trendy stores and I knew one or two others. Out Ilford way was a big trendy area for some reason. Really into clothes and stuff. John came along one day with dyed, shaved hair, and he was saying almost that he'd found his new way of life. It all seemed to happen on one day. He was excited about something.

He'd had his hair long?

Yeah, it was sort of Rod Stewart-ish. A black tux and baggies, a little bit of the Camden Market look.

And those tank tops with the sort of art deco designs on them . . .

Ah, now you've embarrassed me; I used to have them and the shirts, and I must have looked a complete cunt. And those motifs of Clark Gable on the shirts. I must have looked a cunt, really . . .

So why had John shaved his head?

He'd just had it cropped. Sid was at Hackney College and he was coming down to Kingsway then so I was knocking about with them and it really satisfied one part of me, cos it was everything I always wanted at school, pals like that. Everyone seemed a bit dimmer than me, which may sound a bit arrogant, but . . .

Did you go to where Sid lived with his mother?

I went up there a couple of times. There were a couple of funny things that stick in my mind. I took speed for the first time, the sulphate, up at his house. And Sid once leant against the wall drunk, and the wall had just been wallpapered, and there was a huge grease-mark that had soaked off his body on to the wall, like chip fat that was there for ever.

How had the grease got on to him?

He was just a greasy unwashed sort of person! I think it was Sid who first went down and met McLaren, I think he introduced John to all of them. That's what I recall. I'd go down the King's Road but I wasn't terribly interested in it. It didn't excite me too much. I'd go down there a couple of times and we'd really fuck about, we'd be really obnoxious and totally out of order.

What sort of things would you do?

We'd go into a ladies' shoe shop and demand to try on stuff, and dresses, and we'd act very camp. All that really appealed to me. And I loved Sid cos he liked to upset people, piss people off. Really take the piss out of people.

Was Sid the instigator rather than John?

John would be very conscious of image. I think he's the kind of fella that would want effect C, and to get to C I have to go from A to B. He's got an assumed logic. John Gray was quite a quiet person, but everybody in that group was sarcastic. Sid had found out where Bryan Ferry lived, and he wanted to go round there with a bottle of Martini and demand to be let in. John would have had too much pride to want to be seen trying to get in. Even though he desperately wanted to.

Sid wouldn't worry about that, he'd just steam in. I'd be on the periphery of it all, cos I had all the other things in my life, but to me it was all just a big laugh. When the penny dropped with me, you should stick in with this, son, this could be a way out, I stuck in with it, I used the thing. So when the Sex Pistols thing started, I was up for starting something myself, and that was about it.

Had any of you ever thought about being in a band?

Absolutely not. It was astounding, because I'd always had those fantasies. When that possibility started to occur, that was when the penny dropped. The funny thing is that I can't remember having any feelings of insecurity about whether I could do it or not. It was a lot of energy. I remember sitting with John and speeding, and I heard The Last Poets for the first time, and one time we were saying, 'Yeah, we could all go on stage, me you and Gray, on congas', which is an absurd thought now, but at the time, the end of '75 . . .

***This Is Madness*? Is that what you were all listening to?**

Yeah. And the reggae and the soul. Sid was a really big Roxy and

David Bowie fan, and I never liked David Bowie too much. I thought *Young Americans* was pretty good. I've never been a big Roxy Music fan, though there was one or two tracks I loved.

Presumably also you were finding out about drugs and drink as well?

Yeah. Drink, to my cost. I had rather a bad problem, quite quickly, years later. I loved to drink. It's a part of that process of reinventing yourself. Speed, yes – I never liked dope.

What was John listening to at that point?

Alex Harvey Band, was one of his things. I remember going with John and a mate to see Alex Harvey at Croydon. They were excellent, that's when he used to come through a wall. The other things were obscure things like Stockhausen that I'd got out of the library. Electronic music. Another thing, I used to listen to a lot of short wave radio. That noise affected me, it was noises with me, the noise of a really heavy bass.

When did you see the Pistols for the first time?

I remember going to the Chelsea College of Art . . .

What was so good about the Pistols in those early days?

Well, John had all that charisma, he carried all that on the stage, I just thought they were a good, raucous band, and that Steve Jones was a good rock guitarist, he was like skipping on a few years, and Paul Cook was a good drummer in that rock idiom. Right from the first time I saw John, he had something quite special. I hate to sound like one of those cunts who goes on about Jim Morrison, but he had a certain charisma.

For some reason the London Irish have produced a lot of very talented people, and it happens that a lot of my best friends have been of London Irish stock. Maybe a certain magic, a down-to-earthness. A bit passionate, also, that Celtic thing.

I know why I'm an oddball quite well, my family was brought up bloody hard, and they didn't want that for me, so me and my sister were educated as best they could, I was introduced to reading at a very early age.

But you start to read books and you get sensitive, and you have to cover that up, else you'll get accused of being a nancy if you show any sort of sensitivity. So I know why I'm an oddball. The music industry is full of oddballs, because it's a dumping ground for us.

It's the only place in this country where you can do it. If you think about it, there are very few places in this country where you can move across class.

Absolutely. Loads of times I've lost my temper when people say, 'Oh, that's rubbish', cos you'll always get some parcel like some self-made East End businessman who likes to think he's the exception to the rule, and they don't understand. It's so true, you can't move across class boundaries.

Didn't you get violent on a few occasions?

Yeah. Anger has always been a big problem with me. As long as I can remember. There was one down at the 100 Club with Nick Kent that was just a joke, believe me. That was not one of those occasions. I was sitting there with Sid, and I didn't know who Nick Kent was. I've talked to Nick a few times and he seems like a nice chap. He was with some geezer who demanded that we step aside, they couldn't see the band or something.

Maybe this didn't happen, but this is the way I remember it. I said 'Fuck off', which was pretty standard. Sid chained him. Sid wasn't a rucker, he just lashed him with a chain and then I had a go, but we were just mucking about really. What I didn't know then was if you set yourself up as a hard man, someone will come looking for you who's harder than you are, which I didn't fancy.

Sid took it much too far. We used to fuck about like that, winding people up then just running away. Sid would joke that way, but he took all that a bit too far. I was sort of a slippery character at that time. It was a middle-class scene, and they didn't like it when working classes come down and got involved . . .

. . . which you could play on, because they didn't know much about . . .

It gave me mileage for years, and I've found that I've had to tone myself down over the years, I've wondered, why did so-and-so react

312

to me like that? Don't you realise that they find you very intimidating. There's many people who feel that way about the class system but can't articulate it, and it comes across as having a chip on the shoulder. It was very much an art-school trendy scene. I was set up as a bit of a growler, but I'm nothing compared to what I know.

Sid was strange. We used to go to see the psychiatrist, for a laugh. He went to see some psychiatrist-cum-counsellor, and I said, 'It sounds like a laugh', and Sid said, 'I'll ask him if you can come', so we went up there a few times and we wound this geezer up. We told him life was just so boring, we might as well just kill ourselves, and he tried to talk us out of it. But Sid decided to be a heroin addict, it all seemed quite premeditated.

It was a conscious decision?

Yeah, it was strange, he wanted to be one, he became one and he became a fucking nuisance.

Were you there on that occasion at John's flat at Gunter Grove where someone had a go at Sid with an axe?

Sid had these feelings of rejection, and he came up the house one night, and it all got a bit ugly. It shouldn't have come to that but it did. That was a crazy scene. It was ugly and depressing; when it got to all these coke dealers and hairdressers hanging about, I got out. I think he hit his head on one of those mud scrapers, there was a scuffle.

Did you go on the boat trip?

Yeah, that was a laugh. I think I started the row, as it happens. All I remember is we'd come off, and Vivienne Westwood and McLaren yelling 'Fascists!' at the police, and all the duckers and divers like myself who'd been at it hammer and nails on the boat just slipped away, and they all got nicked.

I was just standing having a drink and some geezer barged me. I said, 'Watch where you're fucking going; and he said something back and pushed me again, so I chinned him. I wanted to put him in the water. And it was all off, it was a good fight. McLaren come up to me and said, 'Let's hijack the boat.' I said, 'Fuck off, that's piracy, that is, you silly cunt. You do it, Malcolm, you're the manager.'

313

What did you think of Malcolm?

Very bright, a brilliant conceptualist, obviously he's got a darker side. I've never had any dealings with him.

Do you thing he did a good job for the band?

The way I see it, and maybe the way John would see it, I don't know, it's a long time since I've seen him, but John has never had to go out to work, and that's down to McLaren indirectly. Like me, I got in PiL and I was very happy to fly round the world. I was on the dole at the time, and then you start to think, hang about, this isn't straight, the dole situation, they were on my toes. What you perceive as your wants and needs change.

I suppose he did the business for them. John felt bitter cos he found it hard to get dough out of him, it was always money, and I remember one nasty night, we went up the West End and this whole coachload of geezers saw us, it was Jubilee time, and it got very nasty. It was lynching time. John and me and John Gray and four or five others ended up in some restaurant, barricaded in, it was nasty.

I think John felt that with Malcolm setting up all this publicity, he wasn't on the fucking streets, he was in limos and taxis. It was bitter. I'm still like that today, if I know somebody who's really got the needle with somebody else, I've always been a bit above it all, but I just think, it's not my fucking problem. I'd go round to Chelsea Cloisters and he wouldn't come out. I can understand that paranoia a bit more now.

This manufactured intensity all the time, it isn't necessary. There's always people who'll come along and feed that sickness. I used to think it was a bit like Colonel Kurtz at the end of *Apocalypse Now*.

What was the story with the Speakeasy with Bob Harris?

We'd go down to the Speakeasy and there were all these old rock types who'd had their nose put out of joint, it was a bit like we did by the Blitz scene, ooh, it's not like the old days. They'd get a bit paranoid and comments would be passed, then glasses would be passed if you know what I mean. Really pathetic, people who were old enough to know better, really.

Harris felt really threatened by this, cos I think deep in their hearts they felt they weren't very valid, these people.

It was a bit like going down the King's Road again, wasn't it, annoying the shop assistants?

That's it, yeah, the same kind of stuff. I think back on it and we would and should have got bashed, but they'd look at you and think, ah, they're just kids. If I went out and did the same things now, I'd be killed. But then people didn't know how to take what came to be known as punk rock, and they used to be quite frightened. Whereas now, it's just a label. I used to go round with a leather jacket saying 'Pervert' on the back, I don't think I was even seventeen. You could not get away with it now, it's too dangerous.

I didn't like the swastikas . . .

I remember people trying to justify it and that was worse than wearing it. It does not wash. I would never wear one. I'm very much against fascism.

Were you planning PiL before the Pistols split up?

No, I wasn't seeing a great deal of John, all through that time. He had all his satellites around him, and he'd get bored, and he'd want me on the firm for a couple of days. I'm into all the star-sign stuff to some extent, and John's an Aquarius, ain't he? It's part of them, they like to have people around, they like a lot of bullshit as well. So many of us want the world in our image, I know two or three others just the same, and when that turns to the shadow side, it's ugly and very negative.

What did you think of the Jubilee and all that stuff?

Well, I'm very anti-royalist anyway. I hate those pop stars bowing at charity dos to royalty. I'm not into that. That's one good thing about the Pistols, and there'd be such a mob of us, it was safety in numbers. Fuck the Queen.

Were there street parties in Stepney?

Yeah, the night of the Jubilee we went down to some cemetery in Hackney, and we emerged from this cemetery, drunk, drugged and dressed punk, in the middle of this street party. It was madness. It got kind of crazy, not at all nice. It was the same with the Royal Wedding a few years on.

315

One last thing about the Sex Pistols period: when you saw them in Penzance, did it feel different from how it had felt?

Yeah, John was already having rucks at the 100 Club, walking off and refusing to come on again and stuff, so you had the antennae out, you could feel monkey business. At the 100 Club, it would send a shiver up your back, and that had gone.

From what I've seen, people like McLaren aren't really into music, people with that kind of mentality will often put spanners in the works and be negative. People try and do that nowadays, people involved in that scene who will be bright, bordering on cruel and nasty. It was a sick scene, there was an unhealthy vibe with a lot of the personalities. Maybe I saw it that way because I was an insecure kid, but I trust my intuition and my antennae were up then.

I remember thinking it was ugly. You know that Dennis Potter play where the grown-ups are playing kids [*Blue Remembered Hills*], it was like that. And when you put emotional cripples together, you get something very powerful. It can be good or bad, and it can be directed either way. It had to burn out, it was the same energy of a four-year-old asserting itself on the world, when it throws a tantrum. It wasn't going to go anywhere else.

It's interesting you should say that; the first time I saw The Clash and heard them play 'White Riot', that waa-waa-waa sounded to me like a baby crying. Poly Styrene talked about that when I spoke to her recently.

Well, she's Buddhist – I don't think I ever would be, but a lot of Buddhism is just bloody common sense. I wouldn't knock it, I think it's a wonderful solution. But I remember her being a strange girl who talked of hallucinating. Whenever people talk that way I tend to think, is this a fucking sham? I've seen a lot of people act weirder than they were to impress people, but I remember thinking, she's for real.

Did she hang around Gunter Grove much?

Yeah, I think she freaked John out.

So how did PiL get started?

I'd gone back home, I'd been staying in this squat and everyone else had left, I'd gone back and stayed over Christmas, and February came up, and John phoned. I was on the dole, and all I was doing was reading the papers about the band splitting up, and the next day John called and said, 'Come round, I want you to be in my band, with Keith.' I don't remember feeling much about it; I thought, 'Yeah, it'll be all right.'

Paul Simonon from The Clash was round there, and we just started the band up. I'd just done a bit of plonking on the bass up till then. I'd had offers to be in bands before, but I thought, a bit arrogant, unless I could be in something really good, with good people, I don't want to do it.

Had John moved into Fulham by that time?

He must have got the place from Christmas to the February.

What was the scene like at Gunter Grove?

It got quite poxy at times, people had quite a tenuous grasp on reality, and we'd make up these problems, it got really hippy. Group therapy going on, with some people doing heroin, some doing speed, some doing both. We'd be up for three days on end, talking paranoia, conspiracy theories and shit. The phone's bugged, and the people across the road, and everyone secretly knowing it's a lot of bullshit, but just getting off on the whole trip . . .

John said when I asked him about it, 'I just had to disappear for two years, I had to do that.' It wasn't very nice, but he had to go into that bunker. Who used to be around?

John Gray, Dave Crowe. Somebody would bring someone round for a night and they'd be there for two weeks. I used to crash there whenever I wanted, and I knew the minicab office at the end of the road quite well. It was three floors, a couple of big rooms, usually full of people. A lot of youth was on the firm. I don't like all that, I just thought, this is supposed to be working. Recording, like. I liked studios, and there was a lot of energy there going untapped.

What sort of deal was signed with Virgin?

In my view, we could have had better, if we'd held out a bit. I think it was for eight LPs. You get your recording advance, it's just like the old companies, it still goes on now. It wasn't too clever, and there was grief from the start. I knew the scene, that co-operative vibe is fucking bullshit. If there's dough about, skulduggery comes into play to some extent with these things.

There was much excitement at Virgin when we'd done the first single, it was just what they wanted. It was funny, cos the rest of the stuff that we did wasn't.

Was the idea of the album cover to present yourselves as a corporation, like a company?

Yeah. Dennis Morris was in the forefront of getting that together. He didn't receive enough credit for that. John thought up the name, Public Image, and then make like a company, doing battle with other companies – we'd just signed to Virgin, you know. I was powerless over that side of things. And I was only nineteen or twenty. Then Dennis had the idea for the *Time* magazine spread.

It was creativity, and good ideas, but you could say that the game was already up, as for punk ideals and all that. It was all over. PiL will go down in the annals of history as quite an important little band, I think.

But it wasn't punk, was it, it was post-punk?

Most definitely. I wanted to do something which was true power, not choppy rhythm guitars out of time, loud. I wanted something with true power. When you're thinking about music you're thinking about something supposed to have a lasting effect. That bass will be reverberating for years.

I'd been into the reggae side of things, the real bottomy bass, your 30 Hertz sort of stuff, and that seemed to be a natural way to play bass, rather than going plink, plink, just playing the root note on the guitar and thickening out the lower end of the guitar chords, particularly in the punk time. I actually wanted to play bass figures and patterns so the music would be heavy, it would have a real physical effect.

318

That first single was great, and it started with your bass.

It was the first proper bass line I had. And we had a good drummer, Jim Walker, on the firm, a very powerful drummer. Jim was one of those typical fellas who's come up through the rock thing, rehearsing, doing support and all that, which I'd never done, and he cracks it in a big band, and it's all bullshit, there's nothing happening. He was there for the first handful of gigs, but then we didn't do anything for a long while, cos the others had stage fright. I'm an arrogant fucker so I never had that.

All that stuff about PiL 'experimenting with the line-up' and all that . . . people want to see you get up on stage and do it, that's what it's all about, and that's when I started having bad needle with them. When its predictably unpredictable, it gets boring. If it's marvellously unpredictable, yeah, I love anarchy. But if you know the band is going to throw a tantrum sometime in the next five minutes, it gets boring, and you start to feel embarrassed.

What was it like onstage?

Keith walked backwards and forwards. John would be doing various things. He'd lie down on the floor sometimes. I sense he really didn't like performing, he didn't want to do it. That's when I started to get the hump with them. I remember saying to John, 'If you didn't want to come here, why are we here?' It was a lot of bollocks about experimenting with audience reaction; John just didn't want to be on stage. But that was the scam. We did some good shows, though.

Can you remember the first gigs you did, at the Rainbow?

I remember being out of my nut, turning up at the first one, a lot of fucking about and all that, getting a terrific bass rig up for it. Going to John's after, then on somewhere else. It was Christmas Day and Boxing Day, and the second show I'd been speeding from the night before and continued drinking and speeding through the day, nothing to eat and all that, and turned up about ten minutes before we were due to go on stage.

I remember they wouldn't let me in, them horrible bouncers up there. I was waiting outside, and everyone's panicking, and I couldn't get in. Eventually somebody come along who recognised me from the day before, so luckily I got in. I had the old armchair, we sent it all up a bit, second-generation punks all over the place going, 'Don't sell out, maan', you know? Neanderthal, double-thick. John would make them go mad, wind them up.

The first gig I did, I think it was Brussels, the crowd was going mad. We'd just stopped after a number, and there was all these armchairs around, and we all sat down, talking and drinking and laughing, as if we were having a social evening at home; and we'd start playing again and stop, and this geezer kept gobbing right at me, and I went up and kicked him in the face, and somebody was going, 'You should not have done this.' It was like war sometimes.

I saw the first Rainbow show and I remember it being very introverted.

We were just nervous. They weren't very good shows, we barely had the material.

You mentioned you remembered the night Thatcher was elected?

Yeah, we were down at the Townhouse, we must have been doing the *Metal Box* sessions. Being a little bit of a sharp cookie, I remember saying, 'Bad news, you know.' I remember being angry that night, because nobody seemed to give a fuck. They were very apolitical, and I was angry.

CHAPTER FIVE

The Suburbs

Photoshoot for *Anarchy in the UK* fanzine, autumn 1976 (Ray Stevenson)
L–r: Debbi Wilson, Siouxsie Sioux, Steve Severin, Linda Ashby, Sharon, Simon Barker
(back); Sue Catwoman (front)

The Sex Pistols' first fans came from the suburbs, because that's where they played many of their early shows. Although the band played a few high-profile dates in London, Malcolm McLaren realised that the best place for the group to develop was away from the media glare. So he booked them into colleges around the capital: that's when they didn't simply gatecrash gigs.

Although the group were all from inner London, they picked up their most rabid fans from the outer suburbs and beyond. Among them were the close-knit group that later became known as the Bromley Contingent, the teenage stylists who became a central part of the Sex Pistols' impact as they spread from the music press to the nationals. Several played a part in the Grundy incident.

This chapter includes conversations not only with key members of the Bromley Contingent, but with critical peers like Croydon native, Captain Sensible. Also featured are musicians like Vic Godard, Marco Pirroni and Steve Walsh.

The glamour of the inner city is often best envisioned by outsiders looking in.

Shanne Hasler

Very early Sex Pistols fan who saw one of the group's first out-of-town dates in 1975. Struck up a friendship with Johnny Rotten, who wrote about her – with characteristic cruelty – in 'Satellite'. Later formed The Nipple Erectors with Shane MacGowan. Interviewed at her then home, right by Gospel Oak railway station, London; slightly obdurate and hesitant.

I was brought up in Hertfordshire, in a place called Ware. I went to St Martins and did fashion for a term, but I hated that. I went to Middlesex Poly for two terms then got thrown out, cos I was into the music. Probably I was the hippest person there, purely by accident. Very anti-establishment, I hated the world, ripped my clothes, scalped myself, pierced my ears. I made myself look hideous to shock the tutors.

When did you first see the Sex Pistols?

I was on Foundation Course at St Albans, in my second year, and it was around Halloween in 1975. A band just turned up and played, we didn't know who they were. We hardly even bothered watching them, but we were dancing because they were so terrible. We thought they were a piss-take of a sixties group. They were very slow, very amateurish. A youth club group. Apparently one of them was crying afterwards because it was so bad.

It was peculiar, cos they had the same hairstyle as I had. I was going through this thing, chopping my hair off and dying it. I used to get old grannies' corsets and things from charity shops. That was how I got talking to them. John Lydon came up to me cos he couldn't believe I dressed like that. He asked if I'd ever been to a shop called SEX, and I couldn't believe there was a shop called SEX, and he said there was a girl there called Jordan, who dressed like me. He said I'd have to go down there and meet her.

323

Did you do that?

I went down there with a friend. We got taken out to lunch by Malcolm McLaren. He took me round the shop and explained how all the clothes were made. There was a lot of rubber, very unusual clothes.

Why were you dressing that way yourself?

I had a terrible childhood, I think it was a reaction. I don't know. I came from a middle-class background, and it was the hypocrisy of that, cos I was illegitimate. I hated that thing of everybody trying to be nice and well-mannered, and behind the scenes, people weren't really. I didn't want to be part of it.

Did the other people at art college think you were weird?

I think they thought I was a scream. I had a great time there. I remember one time doing my hair with green food colouring, and walking down St Albans High Street, and being shouted at. People still wore flares and had long hair at that time. I just wanted to be noticed, but I was very shy at the same time.

When did you see the band next?

McLaren gave me his number, and when I phoned him he said Vivienne was giving a talk at the ICA, which I went to. Johnny Rotten was there. I think that was the next time I saw him. He was very nice, and took me back to Finsbury Park and put me on a train back home. Really well-mannered. Nothing like the image. After that, I went to several gigs. There was one at Central, one at Welwyn Garden City, twice more at St Albans.

Were they starting to get better?

At Welwyn Garden City I turned up and I'm not sure if they'd already played or if they hadn't bothered, cos there was nobody there. Bernie Rhodes got me in free. It was the same at Central; six people, maybe more, around the outside, and me and a friend of mine. They did a really good set, it was exciting. I thought Glen gave the band a much better feel than Sid Vicious. They just used to take the piss, annoy people cos they were so apathetic.

At the Central, Lydon chucked the microphone at me, trying to get me to join in. Nobody did that sort of thing. Looking back on it, I think he must have taken a lot of speed or something. I was quite naive, I thought he was just mad. He was very aggressive and then by turns very childlike.

Anyway, they played at High Wycombe and the place was packed with people sitting cross-legged on the floor, students with long hair and joss sticks, shouting abuse at them. It was great. I remember he just lay down on the stage, and some bloke leapt out and started thumping him, and there was a great big punch-up. We got pushed around, and eventually they left the stage.

Did you spend much time with the group?

I knew John the best, cos he had spoken to me in the first place. It was just peculiar that I happened to have that look. It was very much about being individual. I thought he was interesting, but I thought the others had an IQ of about 2.

Did you go back to John's place in Finsbury Park much?

Yeah, when I moved to London I lived in Highbury, so I'd go shopping to Sainsbury's and I'd drop in.

I heard that John wrote 'Satellite' about you. Is that true?

That's what I heard from Sophie Richmond. Glen said that I was Johnny Rotten's girlfriend and he wrote 'Satellite' about me. Sophie typed out the words to 'Satellite' and I was really insulted! The nearest thing we ever did to going out was walking around St Albans hand in hand after they played there. I was wearing bin liners . . . !

He must have written 'Satellite' when he first met you, they played it from very early on.

I used to speak to him on the phone and he mentions that in the song. Maybe I should have written one back. But what's the point?

Did you see the Sex Pistols again after those few times?

They played twice more at St Albans. The third time there was nobody there, there was a remedial art course and a girl had died, and they had a wake, and nobody turned up to the gig. The fourth time they were supposed to play, I turned up at the 100 Club and McLaren was really offhand, he didn't want to know me any more. He was very friendly at first. St Albans? No, not gonna do that, waste of time. And The Damned did their first gig, so I just booked them. They were really pleased, they got eighty quid, a fortune.

What were The Damned like on their first gig?

Hilarious, I really liked them. That vampire thing, then there was Ray Burns who became Captain Sensible, in a white suit and white square shades, he just stood there, didn't move the whole time. I thought they were hilarious. I definitely went for the humour. The Clash didn't have any humour at all. I'd seen them all in the audience at the Pistols gigs, and I'd seen The 101ers, which I thought were a bunch of old teds at the time. It seemed funny to see them in all this gear, being a punk group.

After the Paradiso, did you go to the 100 Club, the Nashville . . . ?

Yeah, the whole lot. I hated it, cos I felt it was my discovery, and there used to be me and whoever I took along, and usually John's friends. John Gray and that bloke Wobble. When everyone else got into it, I don't know who they were supposed to be abusing. Before, it was the students, and general apathy. But then there was the fight at the Nashville which was started by Vivienne Westwood for publicity. That was shocking, at the time.

Did John change?

Yes, he became more and more unapproachable. I went into The Cambridge once and they were sitting in there, I had to meet somebody and I just said, 'Hello.' The next time I bumped into John, he shouted abuse at me, 'Who do you think you are, not coming over and talking to us.' They were sitting there like big stars, and that puts me off. I don't want to know people when they get like that. I didn't want to be seen to be sucking up to them.

I didn't know what was going to happen. I thought at the time he was on the same wavelength as me, you think you can change the world. Open things up a bit . . . it did open things up, a lot.

What was the 100 Club Festival like?

Well, I was standing in front of the girl who got blinded. I was hardly aware of it at the time.

Did Sid throw the glass?

Yeah, he did. At the Paradiso, that bloke Wobble was there and he was throwing glasses. I don't know what that was about, really. I thought they were wankers, basically.

Did you go and see any of the other punk groups when they started?

Yeah, I was curious. In '77 I grew my hair, went natural. It seems funny really. It caught on in the papers, and there were people changing on the train going to the gigs . . . it was a load of sheep, imitating. I started playing myself, cos I thought, anyone can do that. That attitude was good. That was something removed from the Sex Pistols. I started playing bass, cos it had four strings. 1977.

So you got fed up with the scene and started trying to do something yourself?

Yeah, it got predictable, after Grundy. I met this Italian bloke at the 100 Club called Claudio, who called himself Chaotic Bass, and his friend Ray Pissed. They used to wear school uniforms and ties and he had a toothbrush and toothpaste in his pocket and he used to jump up and down brushing his teeth. It was humorous. We tried to do a group called The Launderettes, cos it was just a racket. It was all very childlike in a way. It was a very creative time.

Captain Sensible

Ray Burns, bassist, guitarist and living presence of The Damned. One of the small pool of musicians moving towards punk in 1975. Interviewed in Brighton, on the South Coast of England, where he was living at the time – this was after his huge number one hit, 'Happy Talk'. The Captain was sparky and combative, feeling – rightly – that the contribution of his band had been downplayed at the expense of his one-time rivals.

I was born in Balham, then moved to Croydon, Thornton Heath. I went to Stanley Technical School, in South Norwood. They taught me how to hammer red-hot lumps of metal, on an anvil, and how to make patterns in sand and pour molten metal. Really strange stuff. I got into A levels, doing Geography and Art. I got chucked out cos I wouldn't do Maths. I was a typewriter mechanic, toilet cleaner, gardener, loads of stuff. I worked for British Rail for a while.

Were you interested in music then?

Yeah. We only started playing cos music was so boring in the seventies, it was dross. Bay City Rollers and Brotherhood of Man. So we bought our instruments and we were crap.

How did you meet the others?

We were working at the Fairfield Hall. I was a toilet cleaner, Rat Scabies was a cleaner. He got sacked before I did. He only lasted about three weeks.

Did you see any groups there?

Yeah, we saw loads. On Sunday evenings I was an usher, and Marc Bolan came down, and there were all these manic T.Rex fans. It was the policy at the Fairfield Hall not to let anyone get up and have a good time. But I got involved in this rush to the front, swept along with the crowd. I was in with all these sweaty female bodies and looked up at Marc Bolan and thought, that's the job for me. At that point I decided to make an effort, and get practising.

How did you come together as The Damned?

Rat went off to an audition and came back the next day with his hair cropped, and Brian James was obviously giving him a big pep talk, this is a new thing, played him MC5 and stuff, and he said they were looking for a second guitar player, so I went along. I think Tony James was the bass player and they gave him the elbow cos he was too interested in his clothes, so I got the job as a bass player, and they chopped all my hair off as well.

That was London SS, then when Chrissie Hynde joined it changed to Mike Hunt's Honourable Discharge. It was her idea.

Was that anything to do with Malcolm?

Yeah, that was Malcolm's. He put us in rehearsal for two days, then came down with Helen [Wellington-Lloyd] and Rotten and all these people, and they sat there watching us, laughing, and told us to fuck off. No commercial possibilities.

What was Chrissie like then?

She was very entertaining, much more so than she is now. She had a brilliant voice, but she didn't want to sing, she just wanted to be a good guitar player. On the way back from wherever we'd played, she would sing in the tube station at the top of her voice, cos she liked the echo. She'd sing the songs she would do later as singles, like 'It's a Thin Line Between Love and Hate'.

So what happened after Malcolm told you to fuck off?

Brian James drifted out and then came back, and we started playing ourselves. We used to take all the gear on top of the bus to rehearsals, next to Malcolm's place, a church hall in Bell Street. Vanian used to get the organ going. Brian and Rat had met him at the Nashville. They thought he looked good.

Where did you play your first gig?

329

I think it was Norwich, the University. It was organised by a girl called Shanne Hasler, who I was going out with at the time.

Why did you call yourselves The Damned?

That was Brian's idea, I've no idea why, but it turned out to be quite true; we didn't come out of it with much, and everything that could go wrong did.

Didn't you play with the Sex Pistols at the 100 Club?

We did some gigs with them, yeah. All I can remember from that was Rotten shouting down the microphone, Malcolm, get me a drink! And that stupid cow Siouxsie standing down the front in her £200 bondage suit, in amongst all these urchins in clothes that didn't cost anything. I thought that was gross. She came up to me once, and she was always dressed in expensive gear, and she said, 'Captain, you're not a real punk and The Damned never will be.' And she walked off. Silly cow.

Was it the urchin thing that you liked about it?

Well I was a hippy type, I used to go to all the festivals, Glastonbury and everything, used to live in squats ever since I left my mum and dad's place, so I could identify with that sort of wacky lifestyle. I was like the hippies, really, with teeth. It was easy for us. We used to squat in Kilburn. Later, I used to live in a squat in Acton with Sid Vicious and Sue Catwoman.

We used to sleep together in the same bed, farting contests all night long. This was long before Nancy came along. I was always getting him out of fights, usually with roadies. Most of them had long hair and Black Sabbath T-shirts. He'd go up and say, 'You're living in the past, you tosser, why don't you cut your hair?' And he'd break a bottle or something, and say, 'I'll cut your hair for you', and of course they'd just punch him in the mouth, and Sid would go down, he was no great shakes as a fighter at all.

Was there much camaraderie between punk groups in the early days?

Very little. Officially, when we talked to the press or anything, it was all slagging, but I used to get on quite well with Strummer and Rotten.

But the Pistols and The Clash never got on at all. Strummer and Jones went round to Rotten's house because he'd slagged them off in one of the papers. They tried to explain themselves, and Rotten just said, 'Fuck off, who's interested, I'll say what I want.' Apparently Mick was crying.

But we got on with most people, cos we were just a hopeless bunch of slobs, we didn't threaten anyone. We used to hang out at Hennekey's in Portobello Road. Tony James and Mick Jones and those people would wear what I would call the rock'n'roll gypsy look, high heels with studs and handkerchiefs everywhere.

Did you just learn the bass there and then?

Anyone who can play a guitar can play bass.

What sort of a racket were you trying to make?

We just did it, I never thought about it once.

Going back to what Siouxsie said, did you feel a bit outside of the hip elite in London?

Yeah, maybe a bit. There was a certain snobbery to it, but out of town it was fine, we didn't have any airs and graces, we were very approachable. We'd always be drinking with the people coming to see us.

How did you get your name?

We used to go up to Lawrence Corner for cheap clothes, and I got this shirt with epaulettes on it, and we were going off to the punk festival in France [Mont de Marsan, August 1976], and I was totally drunk, and pretending to be the pilot, and shouting, 'It's all right, it's all right, everything's under control, it's on auto-pilot at the moment', and because I had short hair I suppose I could have passed for the pilot, and people were getting upset. And someone said, 'Oh it's fucking Captain Sensible.'

You were the only punk group at that Punk Festival.

Yeah. Rat fell off the drum kit, he was so drunk, and because it was such a rickety stage, he fell twenty foot down on to the floor, bit the dust. We were making so much noise we didn't realise he'd gone down, and at the end of the song, we looked and said, 'Where's Scabies?' This little head appeared over the side of the stage. 'Sorry about that, guys.' I don't remember much about it.

Did you take a lot of speed?

Sacks of it. As much as I could possibly get.

It sounds like you and Rat were nearly out of control, most of the time.

Totally, I'm amazed we actually came out the other side of it. We were always shinning along ledges, four or five floors up, to get into someone else's room, to piss in their bed. The worst one we ever did, we'd seen this flag on top of a hotel, a collage of all the flags of Europe, and I thought, I want that, it would be great as a backdrop. There were two buildings together, with quite a big gap between them, ten storeys up, and we jumped across, got the flag . . . should have died, several times.

What was the story of being thrown off the Anarchy tour?

That was one of the saddest things, I've always been upset about that. Jake Riviera [Stiff Records label boss] didn't trust us, and he put us in a different hotel; we were in Mrs Bun's B&B, and they were in flash hotels. When they were in Derby, our representative, Rick Rogers, was at the meeting with Bernie and these people, and the councillors wanted to see the show. He said, 'Okay', and the rest of them said 'No, we won't.' Which is quite right, that's what I would have said.

Then he said, if the Pistols won't play, then The Damned will. I wouldn't have played, it would have split the ranks. I'm really upset about that, and so is Rick. He realises that was wrong. But I was fuming, we were locked up in this hotel and didn't know what was going on. Of course after the Bill Grundy thing, they didn't need us, they were news after that. We came out of it looking like a bunch of tossers – which we were, but not in that sense.

Everything happened really quickly then, from first gig to first record. Did that seem natural?

I thought it would be a five-minute thing. That's why we called ourselves by wacky names, so we could keep signing at the DHSS; that's why there was Johnny Rotten and Rat Scabies and Captain Sensible. I didn't know I'd be thirty-five years old and still called Captain Sensible. I thought it was a five-minute joke.

What was it like, playing before you had a record out?

Dangerous. In London you'd have people who were into it, mostly people from other bands. People who thought it was interesting would stay around, but one time we cleared an entire audience at the Nag's Head in High Wycombe, we were left playing to the bar staff. I had a thing about beards, no-one with a beard was allowed in. 'I'm not playing till that fucking geezer with the beard fucks off.' And of course he took all his mates with him.

But it was dangerous out of town, we'd constantly get into punch-ups with people who wanted to kill the punks. It was different at the time. They'd smash the windows in the van, slash the tyres, and they'd be waiting with bricks and bottles, all that stuff. And we'd have to take the mike stands to bits and just lay into them, it was outrageous.

In Leighton Buzzard we got chased by this rampaging mob. We ended up in the woods, round the back of this leisure centre, and I sneaked back and hid in these swimming baths, and I saw Vanian and Rat being chased off into the woods by all these blokes with bottles. I think anything that's different annoys people. We had plenty to say and we said it. And a lot of people still liked Yes and groups like that, when we were totally alien to that.

You did the first album very quickly.

Yeah, that was fun. We did that purely on cider and speed. Nick Lowe was mixing it with lolly sticks attached to the pre-fade buttons, and he was pushing four faders with these lolly sticks. I thought that was really clever.

Were you aware of what was going on in the outside world then?

No, there are a few lost years there, I don't remember much about anything. I was doing everything except heroin. Loads of acid, that's why the albums got weirder.

What happened with the second album?

I wanted to work with someone from the Floyd. I suppose it was Syd [Barrett], really – I loved the first two albums, *Piper at the Gates of Dawn, A Saucerful of Secrets*. We ended up with the drummer [Nick Mason]. We had Lol Coxhill on it, which was the only saving grace of that album. I won't have it in the house, it's total shit.

If I ever go around someone's house I instantly smash it and give them a tenner, and say, 'Sorry about that, go buy yourself a decent record.' It was thrown together in a week, appalling.

Punk unity had gone, so you were going your own way.

Us and The Stranglers were always shunned from the punk group. I admired them, cos they didn't give a shit. I don't believe in rehashing the old things just to make money, you've got to be true to yourself.

Weren't you the first English punk band to go to the States?

Yeah. They never understood. I remember a radio interview where they were playing some tracks, and the interviewer said, 'I can't really listen to this, my favourite punk groups are Elvis Costello and Blondie', something like that. The audiences didn't like us, and they used to throw ice cubes at us, which was pretty mild compared to what we were used to. We thought, what a bunch of wimps.

How many dates did you do?

About ten. We did CBGB's and Max's Kansas City. They liked us in Max's. But they didn't understand the humour. Brian's amp kept breaking down, so we'd tell 'my dog's got no nose' jokes; they'd get five songs of thrash, then a few jokes.

The blitz-guitar stuff stopped when Brian left, I started writing the songs, and I was into sixties pop. We played *Nuggets*, and The Left Banke, and Floyd in the van.

Why did Brian leave?

Partly it was the Girlfriend Syndrome; he was with this girl Erica [Echenberg] who used to tell me off about my excesses of the night before, and I'd say to Brian, 'If you've got some grievances, why don't you tell me, I don't want to hear it from your girlfriend.' Also

334

Brian wasn't coming up with the goods, song-wise. After the second album was so appalling, I lost all respect for him. I thought, I can write better stuff than this.

Why did Stiff get rid of you?

Because the second album was a turkey. Basically, they thought we'd run our course, and if I was them I would have done the same.

When do you think punk stopped?

I don't think there was such a thing as punk, it was an attitude that existed before punk, and it still exists now. It was a way of me existing without the state infringing on me; as little as possible, anyway.

Did it make an impression when the Sex Pistols split up?

Well, the only band that impressed me were Crass, and that was years later. We actually sat down and talked about things. People say The Damned were a rebellious group, and I think we were, but I didn't know what I was rebelling against. I hated school, they were drumming stuff into me that I didn't believe. When we debated things with Crass, they made a lot of sense. That was when I started thinking more politically. I did a record for them, which I'm very proud of; I think it's the best thing I ever did.

Siouxsie Sioux

*Frontwoman of Siouxsie and the Banshees, and major face of the
punk era. Along with Steve Severin, Simon Barker, Simone and
Berlin, she was among the group of striking Sex Pistols fans who
became known as the Bromley Contingent. Along with Jordan, The
Slits and Poly Styrene, she presented a radical new femininity that
completely changed what was possible in popular culture.*

I always gravitated towards the city, I hated suburbia. Some people
stuck to their local town, like Bromley. You could hang out there
and feel pretty grown-up, but I hated it. I thought it was small and
narrow-minded.

There was this trendy wine bar called Pips or something, and I got
Berlin to wear this dog collar, and I walked in with Berlin following
me, and people's jaws just hit the tables. Later on if I'd have done
that I'd probably have been assaulted. But I walked in and ordered a
bowl of water for him. It was hilarious, I got the bowl of water for
my dog as well! People were scared!

Did you always live in the same place in Chislehurst?

Yeah, I suppose so.

What were your interests?

Edgar Allan Poe, and having an older brother and sister there was
always music there, R'n'B, Tamla Motown, The Rolling Stones and
The Beatles. But stories, gruesome stories. Old books of my father's,
Aztec mutilation rites, done in matchstick diagrams, someone's
entrails being ripped out. I was always outside a lot, too. I hated the
street we lived in, bordering on middle-class. More puritanical than
proper middle-class in a way, almost spiteful.

What did your dad do?

He was a laboratory technician, he used to work up at St Albans in a mental asylum. He used to tell me stories about autopsies and things. He died when I was about fourteen. Up until then I was up on medical things, zoology and things.

Did his dying affect you a lot?

I suppose it must have done. I felt guilty that I didn't grieve. It must have been ten years later I wished I could have known him.

What did you do in adolescence, go and see groups?

Not really, I didn't hang out with people. The time I started going out to concerts, I'd go to Biba's, I'd started getting interested in clothes and things. The Rainbow Room. I used to think what a gorgeous building it was. I was besotted with the Art Deco, Art Nouveau. That was my escape from humdrum.

Did you buy Biba's clothes?

Only from their bargain bins. The rest was jumble sales really. I think Bowie and Roxy had a big part in that. Whoever latched on to them were that way inclined. The whole thing, not just the music. It aroused something that was quite dormant, that was causing frustration. I suppose I was more of a Bowie fan, there was that much more material. They used to play a lot of their music at Biba's. I was attracted to the music they played there.

There was a whole thirties revival thing going on then as well. I think the wedge haircut came from *Cabaret*, it was an important film.

Actually that was very much part of the gay scene. My sister was a go-go dancer, that's another one of my routes for getting out, I used to go with my sister on her dates, to The Gilded Cage, The Trafalgar, and I loved it, bright lights, total unreality. She used to sew sequins on her bikini, and add chains and stones; she'd made costumes when she was younger, with all the feathers and all that. I used to go with her, and occasionally some of the pubs would be half gay, half straight elements to them.

What sort of music did they play in those places?

337

It was Disco Tex and the Sex-O-Lettes, Bowie and Roxy, Barry White was huge.

When did you leave school?

In '73. I hung around at home for a bit, and my mum was trying to get me to go to secretarial college, and I did go to one for a few months. You can imagine, shorthand typing, god. I never stayed long enough to do any exams or anything. I thought I might be a model or something. I'd go round to the agencies, and already I was into heavy make-up, bright colours. They said I was too skinny and too made-up. They wanted busty and natural models.

But I would have hated that anyway. So I worked in pubs and clubs in the West End, the Valbonne, that was one of the places where my sister worked, they had a heart-shaped pool there. It was great hours, eleven to half-three. In the night it was rich Arabs and everything, but during the day it was businessmen – just the local punters. I'd bring my record collection and dance to it on the floor by myself. Bowie, Brass Construction, *Hard Work* by John Handy.

Who did you meet first, Steve Severin or Simon Barker?

Simon I think. I met them through a girl I was at school with. I bumped into one of them on a train. That was when I started going to Vidal Sassoon's to get my hair done, different tints. But I saw them again at the Roxy Music concert. That would be '74, where they had the big video screen. They didn't hang out in London, they just hung out in various bars in Bromley. I led them astray, up to the West End.

When did you first find out about the Sex Pistols?

I'd been to the shop before I knew about the group. I'd bought some fishnet tights with gold and black tassels on them. They'd had a fashion spread, really nice drainpipe trousers, pink satin with black lace over the top, and the Gene Vincent shirts. I found the shop independently of knowing about the group. I remember Vivienne, she looked gorgeous. I was really attracted. She had blonde hair with purple pink lips. She looked great.

Simon and Steve told me about the Pistols, they'd been to see them at Bromley Art College, I think, and they'd been to see them at the El

Paradiso in Soho. The first time I saw them was some college again, it might have been Beckenham. There was just a few students wandering about, and everyone kept their distance. It wasn't aggressive or anything, it was just an end-of-term thing.

They just played their music. Rotten didn't like it, but he didn't really glare at anyone the way he did later. Glen was the loudest. I thought he was trying too hard. He used to do backing vocals and I know he got asked not to do them. He'd do them in tune. He was the one who'd be decked out in the SEX gear, and it would look squeaky-clean on him. It was at the 100 Club that all the insulting the audience started. It became much more of an event.

Do you remember the party at Berlin's?

Yeah, there was a huge row with the neighbours. The Fetish Olympics, it was called. Everyone was extremely outrageous, a lot of people weren't ready for it. Ooh dear, what have we walked into? Horrendous neighbours, it was almost a punch-up. I answered the door. 'You slut!' 'Don't you call me a slut!' 'I'll call the police, I'll tell your parents on you.' The garden was overrun with people either cavorting or throwing up over the fences. It was quite mad.

The band were there as well, weren't they?

Yeah. Again, a very funny cross-section of people. A few that I'd known just through the clubs, who didn't have a clue who the Pistols were. Some of Steve and Simon's friends who led a Jekyll and Hyde existence, who were very shocked. I wore my fishnet tights with all the gold tassels with nothing else on but this apron with a naked lady with tassels on her boobs. Really tacky, and the bondage stilettos as well.

I remember noticing the people who didn't make an effort, who just turned up in their jeans or whatever, but some people dressed as Hitler or whatever, vinyl. Quite a few suspender belts. The invites said, come dressed as your fantasy, or something.

What had you done with your hair at that point?

It went through so many changes. It was very very short, with coloured bits at the front, then it grew but I kept it quite short. I had longish bits around the sides and I'd just sweep them round, and I'd had flame colours going around like a halo. Then black and red. The original Catwoman hairstyle, pretty short then up at the side with a red streak. I was still having my hair done free then.

I got it bleached and I remember hating the bits at the side, getting home and just cutting them off, the very very short, hacked blonde hair. Blonde is something all brunettes think they want to be; I was blonde for a couple of months and decided I looked better with dark hair, and dyed it black.

We've got to talk about the swastika at some point . . .

It was always very much an anti-mums-and-dads thing. We hated older people. Not across the board, but generally the suburban thing, always harping on about Hitler, and 'We showed him', and that smug pride; and it was a way of saying, 'Well I think Hitler was very good, actually.' A way of watching someone like that go completely red-faced. We made our own swastikas.

So was it just something that had to come up in English society?

Maybe. I think everyone who used that image, there was that film, The Damned, and everyone who saw it thought it looked great. There was nothing coming out about what went on in concentration camps – and probably we would have been the first people to be persecuted if that was to happen again, but it was a way of getting back at the older generation that we hated.

When did you become aware that there was something more? Did you get into arguments about it?

No, I became aware when skinheads latched on to it, and took it quite seriously, and it was used politically, and started talking about race, and I thought, whaat? Hang about, you know. I'm completely the opposite in my views on race. I liked the look of it, the colours, red, white and black, that's why. Then it became an issue, and I thought, fuck off. No way.

When you saw the Pistols at the 100 Club, which was the best one? Can you remember a particularly good one?

They played Bang's, it was called the Sundown. I seem to remember really enjoying that one, cos it was different, a bigger stage and you could see Rotten move for the first time, whereas the 100 Club was very cramped. Bang's was one of the places on the scene, although we didn't think of it as a scene then, you'd see people that you'd seen at gigs. And Louise's of course. But the Sundown was more like going to a concert. It was in the summer. People were always jumping into that fountain at Tottenham Court Road.

When did you first start attracting attention as the Bromley Contingent? When was that phrase coined?

That was Caroline Coon, when we went to Paris. A lot of people have got away with dismissing it and making it what it wasn't, just by coining that phrase. I didn't like being called the Bromley Contingent. It was the beginning of the labels really.

It was nicer when it confused people. It was a club for misfits, almost. Anyone that didn't conform. There was male gays, female gays, bisexuals, non-sexuals, everything. No-one was criticised for their sexual preferences. The only thing that was looked down on was being plain boring, that reminded them of suburbia.

How did your performance at the 100 Club come about?

There was a vacant space for a group, and it was being discussed at Louise's. Perhaps someone had pulled out. Malcolm was saying, 'We need another band', and I volunteered. 'We've got a band.' And we hadn't, we spent the night trying to find a band. It was the next day rehearsing with Sid Vicious on drums. Billy Idol said yes at the time and either couldn't be contacted or was too embarrassed to say no. Obviously he wasn't interested. Marco Pirroni we knew, he was a friend of Sue Catwoman's, and Sid, and me and Steven.

Had you known Sid already?

We'd seen him around at the gigs, and knew him vaguely but not well. He was such a nice boy, a real sweetie. I think he just believed all the hype about being violent, and ended up being someone that no-one knew, really. It was a real shame. It was when he got involved with that horrible woman, Nancy, that it all went to pot.

When did you first call yourself Siouxsie?

I invented it that night when we came back with the title for the group. *The Cry of the Banshee* had been on a couple of nights before, and we just thought 'banshee' was a great word. The film wasn't much good – Patrick Mower grovelling in mud a lot of the time. The name just stuck.

What was the gig like? Sid played minimally, didn't he?

He was very much a fan of Moe Tucker. Boom, splat. I liked it. I think it captured the spirit of how to do things, it was a shambles, but something much more memorable than doing half a dozen songs they'd rehearsed. It was like 'Sister Ray' or something. Listening back to the tape I could hear 'Smoke on the Water', just in wafts, but it all fitted.

It was taking the piss out of all the things we hated. Whether Marco put it in for whatever reason, and me wailing over the top of it, not singing the lyrics but singing 'Knocking on Heaven's Door' to 'Smoke on the Water' and 'The Lord's Prayer', and Steve trying to find how to turn his bass on, or something. And Sid with this bulldozer rhythm, relentless banging.

How did you stop?

We expected to be stopped by outside forces. We didn't envisage being able to get away with it, really. One of the songs was 'She Loves You', and also 'Young Love' by the Bay City Rollers. What song do you really hate? What would you like to throw in as a shock tactic? What can we mutilate and destroy? It was all our least favourite things. We were that age when we were questioning everything. It probably stopped when Sid did one drum roll and stopped.

So you became minor celebrities . . .

Infamy was what it was. I remember coming off the stage and it was really brilliant. It was the first thing I felt I'd really achieved. I was scared, going on, but it was addictive. I couldn't believe it. People were saying, 'You ought to get a group together.' It had just been something to fill that gap for one night, but I didn't bank on getting hooked on it.

Bill Grundy was after that. I was blonde then, with one eye and a star, I was very pert and very cheeky, very Larry Grayson. This horrible old man trying to chat me up, and I was going, 'Well, really! Whooo!' Rather than, fuck off, you dirty old man. 'Get you!'

What were the band like when they went in to the Grundy interview?

I've got a feeling that Malcolm was geeing them up, maybe stirring it a bit. The group were trying to act nonchalant, but probably a bit nervous as well. I vaguely remember Malcolm sowing the seeds, getting them pissed off.

Did you feel that it was snowballing by the time of Grundy?

I just thought, blimey, everyone seems to want to know what's going on. How do you prepare yourself for that sort of attention? It could have remained as our own private youth club, or whatever, but all of a sudden, seeing yourself in a newspaper, and the wrong comments that are there, the wrong title that you're given. 'They like to drink brown ale and throw up' – no we don't!

You remember Eater? The time of the Anarchy tour, they were doing some college dates around Ealing and Finchley, and we went to one of those, and we were looking in horror, they were wearing these light bulbs in their ears. They had the make-up but it was really badly done, and they looked like brickies. Already it was getting spoiled, being put down to a fashion.

About the time of the second Screen on the Green I thought it was finished, and when Sid joined it became very stylised, and Rotten's sneer; I just thought, they don't mean it. The audience weren't the same bunch of stupid hippies any more, and there was this, you can't be a fan of ours now cos you've got a band of your own, kind of attitude.

When did the Banshees get good?

There were always bits when we were good, when our guitarist Peter Fenton wasn't too erratically self-conscious. We sacked him on stage. He just went into a guitar solo, this horrible Led Zeppelin thing. We just steamed into him, unplugged his guitar.

Why weren't you signed for so long?

343

We were a product of free enterprise, we weren't musicians. The Pistols were very much part of rock'n'roll, they weren't breaking down any aural barriers at all, it was rehashing what had gone before, and it was what they put into that that made it theirs. Without Rotten, they would probably have just been a pub band, in all honesty. Talking about breaking down walls and actually doing it are different things.

On our naivety, we made this noise that was ours, part design and part untutored hands, not hearing ourselves for a long time, and starting out with something like 'The Lord's Prayer' – that was our set, or three quarters of it. When we started, we had about half a dozen songs. 'Carcass' was one of them, 'Helter Skelter', 'Psychic Badge', 'Captain Scarlet', 'Make Up to Break Up'.

You were well advised – was Nils a good manager at that point?

At that point he was the right manager. He had picked up a lot from Malcolm, obviously. The exciting thing was, everyone was a novice. Nils was a novice and he did bugger things up financially in ways that we found out since, but in all, he was the right person for us then. He wanted to be in the group, he wanted to play guitar. He was that excited when he saw us at the 100 Club. We needed someone that was excited by it.

When you'd got quite skilled at what you wanted to do, you made a very interesting sound, you all bounced off each other . . .

That was when we played The Vortex. There was a quote from Glen, 'I don't know what it is, but it isn't rock'n'roll'; it would be funny to look at all those old reviews, they don't know what they're talking about. A lot of people forget that the Pistols were hated by a lot of the music press, and The Clash were the ones that they plumped for. They seemed like teacher's pets to me, the goody-goodies.

I thought it was nonsense, spouting all this politics, I thought it was parrot-fashion. I wasn't interested in politics, but I didn't think they were either, they were just muppets. It was a cheap trick to gain some street credibility. And they've all eaten their words since. That was another thing, you had to mention the kid on the street.

Did that come in with The Clash or with Sham?

344

Both. Clash started it and Sham turned it into kid-in-the-pub-on-the-street. It's amazing the sort of people that it attracted. There was that awful group, The Vibrators, too.

Instead of the ambiguity, everybody started becoming very straight again.

Yeah, but a lot of boys started looking like me, we attracted that ambiguous sexuality. The Pistols lost all of that, The Clash never had it.

You picked up the hardcore audience as well, from the Pistols.

About the time of the *Sounds* front cover, and we played the Music Machine. Marc Bolan was still around. He was at the gig, and he had to be nudged when we did '20th Century Boy'. He didn't recognise it.

What happened when you got arrested at the Rainbow?

We supported The Heartbreakers. 999 played as well. We were waiting for a cab outside, and this meat wagon turned up and they just started pushing their drummer, Pablo, around, and I went over, said, 'Leave him alone, we're just waiting for our transport', and they started getting quite nasty, and I went for them, went for this policeman's balls and got dragged, kicking and screaming into the meat wagon, and everyone else was going, fucking hell.

Kenny Morris got pulled in as well. I spent the night in Holloway and in the local nick in Islington, and they were threatening to strip-search me, and making very lewd comments about what I was wearing. That was the first time in a long time that I'd felt sexually threatened. I'd got clear of all that cos I scared people.

They're very big on humiliation really. I was aware of that, and I was laughing at them, and then it got even worse. They couldn't cope with that. Being rather camp, and insinuating that they were that way inclined, closet cases. 'What do you get off on, wearing uniforms? Watch where you're putting your truncheon, dear.' One was going, 'If you don't shut her up, I'll bang her head against the wall.' So I had to go to Holloway, cos I couldn't stay in the same prison that they were in.

I was the only girl arrested. They confiscated my shoes and made me walk across the police car park in the rain with no shoes on. Petty things, you know. Spent the night in prison, went to court in the morning, was found guilty without being tried. Wasn't allowed a phone call. Sort of thing that happens every day.

When you were eventually signed to Polydor, did you find that situation easy to work with?

It was always a matter of going into Polydor with clenched fists behind your back. If anyone said anything you didn't like, you wouldn't stand for it. A lot of it was holding out for what we wanted, and a lot of people weren't interested, it was a bit of both. I was very proud.

Did you get a reasonable advance?

It was reasonable, but it wasn't the sort of figures that other people got. I was aware that we didn't concede that much either, we got points that went up, year by year.

Virgin signed a lot of groups that meant they had eight albums to do in four years, something outrageous. They got a lot of money up front, but they were young people, and they probably spent the money immediately. Then they had to make eight albums, and on what? They didn't sell enough records to get royalties. They didn't see the royalties for a long time.

But when did you feel that that whole period was over?

When the Pistols came to do their album, I wasn't interested in hearing it. We had live tapes, that didn't transcribe to record. I really liked the Buzzcocks for a while, The Ramones and Talking Heads really kept the momentum up, that interest. I never saw it as a movement.

Was that dominatrix thing something that you were conscious of, that you wanted to express?

It wasn't self-conscious, it was just what was going on, really. It was what suited me, and it was definitely anti-tabloid, typical girl. The Slits were very different, they weren't glamorous, they were very earthy. And the boys in the band hated the male who would read the *Sun* as well. *We* hated that kind of thing, the lowest common denominator.

346

Berlin

Bromley Contingent member and teenage outrage. Host of the infamous Baby Bondage Party attended by all the Sex Pistols and their entourage of that time. Interviewed at his then home in London's West Hampstead, Berlin is witty, indiscreet and highly aware of his moment in history.

I was born in Greenwich and lived in Catford, and eventually moved to Bromley when I was nineteen. I had a stepfather and I bunked off school when I was thirteen, cos I was being bullied for being a poof, and I went to college to try and do Drama and English and Art, but at the same time I had a nervous breakdown, so it didn't really go anywhere.

I saw this girl called Max on the bus. She looked like Little Nell, and I followed her to the top floor of this department store, into this restaurant, and she met this coloured girl who was wearing pyjamas and a plastic mac. This was autumn '75, and I thought, I must talk to these people. I was wearing an army coat and red wedgy hair, and they looked so exotic, and I got talking to them, and the end of this conversation, this girl Max says, 'I'm going to see my boyfriend's boyfriend now, and I thought this was fab.'

Anyway I started this flirtation with this black girl called Simone who lived in Beckenham, and I lived in Bromley, and we'd meet for tea. She then introduced me to her boyfriend called Simon Barker, and I began a friendship with these two, cos he was like a Bowie clone, and she was like Ava Cherry. Blonde hair. The next person I met was Simon's best friend Steve Bailey – Severin. This is where it gets slightly interesting. It was the four of us going around together. I was about fifteen.

Were you a Bowie boy as well?

347

No, I was much more of a Liza Minnelli clone. I was going up Camp Tree, basically! So Steve was seeing this girl called Pat, and Simon was seeing this girl called Jill, really naff suburban girls. They decided to throw this party called the Nuremberg Rally, you had to come as some fascistic whatever. I decided I'd go in drag – make-up, pencil skirt, the whole trip – and walked up this suburban back alley in Bromley towards this party.

Simone was wearing black plastic trousers, she had blonde hair and this black plastic thing across her tits with cut-outs so her nipples stuck out, and Steve was wearing black jeans and a black boxer top. And this girl was coming, called Siouxsie, and while all this was going on, who was getting off with who? It was very suburban. At one o'clock the doorbell goes, and in comes Siouxsie with like monk's hair with these blonde flicky bits, gold lamé dress with swastikas on her cheekbones.

She was the campest thing, a Betty Boop character, that was her whole trip. She had this girl with her called Myra, with a Cleopatra bob and a feather boa. Well, she immediately took to me, being in drag. I was always being mistaken for a lesbian, and she was thought to be my girlfriend. The party all ended rather bizarrely, everybody got really drunk, nothing really much happened, there were all these flirtations going round.

Was *Cabaret* a big influence?

Yeah, it was. Joel Grey, a man with loads of make-up on, it was a very strong image. That Nazi image, the black boots and everything, that was how my dress developed. I'd wear nothing but a white shirt, black tie, cropped black hair, black tights, this fabulous pair of black boots up to here, imitation leather, and a black jumper.

What was the point of the swastika? Just to annoy people?

No, there was this thing, because I was so enamoured by Christopher Isherwood, all of that *Cabaret* bit, and the paintings, Otto Dix . . . You know when you make a big change in your head about who and what you are, you change all the way through. So I started calling myself Berlin, Steve started calling himself Steve Spunker, and Siouxsie used to call herself Candy-Sue – before she got the Siouxsie.

But there was something much more serious about it as well.

I think it was naive. Siouxsie was seventeen, eighteen, very young. What do you know of all that? Also the element of dare, you won't tell me what to do. I think it was all to do with sexuality, finding your adolescent self, and all that. Image and drag and camp and make-up. It was always associated with the gay scene, all of it.

When did you go and see the Sex Pistols?

The first time I saw them was their first gig at the 100 Club. After I started to go out with Severin, and we'd go round his house and listen to The Velvet Underground, Lou Reed. In a way, Siouxsie mirrored herself on all these pop stars, Nico and Patti Smith, and he mirrored himself on John Cale, Lou Reed, and I was their little plaything, it was a kind of *ménage a trois* situation to begin with. They went out together for a long time.

The Pistols were incredible. I can remember in detail, walking down the steps of the 100 Club, and just noise, basically. I can remember who was there, there was Paul Getty, Vivienne, Malcolm, Helen, Siouxsie, Steve, Debbi, Tracie, Sharon, all these people who were the Bromley Contingent. I remember Johnny crouching on the stage, wearing a red jumper with a white collar, safety pins, jeans, orange hair, and screaming.

I said to Steve, 'Where is this energy coming from?' It was a totally different thing, aggressive, violent, and at that point it didn't incite the audience as much. People were just standing there.

Where do you think that energy did come from?

Sulphate. I think that got them going. I had a party for them soon after, and there was sulphate everywhere. I can't remember meeting them. They were very aloof. Paul was the nicest one, he was like a puppy dog. He was lovely. Steve Jones was the macho bastard. Glen I didn't like at all, he was arrogant, naff, a bore. Johnny was totally aloof, out of his head. Mostly sulphate and beer.

I had the party about May or June '76. 8 Plaistow Grove, two doors down from David Bowie's old address, number 4. It was on a Saturday and it was called Berlin's Bondage Baby Party. You had to come as your kink. So there was Siouxsie, who was dressed in a

349

plastic apron and tights, that was all. No knickers, nothing. And she had a leather whip. I'm sure if you go down to 8 Plaistow Grove you can still see the whip marks on the ceiling.

Simon had invited them after the 100 Club, and the Pistols turned up, all of them. It was a complete and utter riot. I can just remember my bedroom, and walking in there, all the bedclothes were on the floor, all the books, the records. All the clothes. The curtains were wide open, so all the neighbours were getting the full benefit of Marilyn Monroe singing 'I Wanna Be Loved By You', and Johnny lining up sulphate on the grooves of a record.

He was wearing a black rubber T-shirt, those fifties trousers with the glitter bits in them, the glasses. Pale, skinny. Masses of sulphate. He was charming, I was introduced to him, and he was very nice. Very charismatic.

How much do you think he got from Malcolm?

I think he was quite original. He's very intelligent. If it had been Paul or Steve in that position, it would have been more Malcolm, but Johnny was stronger than that. I never had very much to do with Malcolm at all. I felt he was a nasty piece of work. He wouldn't really focus on people. Vivienne was bad enough, spouting all these ideas about Russia and communism, all that stuff. She was impossible to talk to, it was all monologue.

No, I think Johnny was pretty original. He was young, and open, but obviously the most intelligent out of all that lot anyway. His vibe was like that, he wasn't macho, like the other three were. Even Sid was quite blokey. He was very different. A little bit androgynous. Asexual.

What was Bromley like then?

Really suburban. Oppressive, there is no place for young people to go, no youth centres. We decided, there was this one wine bar where you weren't hassled too much, so one day me and Siouxsie went in there, and I'd put on a dog collar, and a lead, and went down on all fours, and I was barking and cocking a leg, and we went into this wine bar, and she goes, 'A bowl for my dog and a vodka and orange.' And they brought it, too, and everyone was laughing and jeering, it was the most outrageous thing ever.

350

Didn't you get beaten up?

Never in Bromley. In London I did, when I moved up to Chelsea. Oakley Street. I can't tell you the parallels between those days and *Goodbye to Berlin*.

Which clubs did you go to?

There was this place called Chaugerama's. It was where the Roxy was before it became the Roxy. A dingy dive where the worst transvestites in the world went, and all these businessmen. Chaugerama's, Sombrero's, and then Louise's were the ones that most people went to. There was Masquerade that became the Showcase, in Westbourne Grove. There was Rob's I went to once or twice, that was Bryan Ferry's hang-out, very chic.

Siouxsie introduced everybody to Louise's. Six of us went out one night to this very exclusive, very heavy lesbian club in Poland Street. We pressed on the doorbell looking like god knows what, a cartoon probably. Madame Louise at the door, 'Hello, darlinks, okay?' And her faggy American boyfriend going, 'Hi!' Three quid to get in. Three quid was like ten quid now.

We went in, and it was very quiet. Red tablecloths, mirrors everywhere. They played soul and Doris Day and campy stuff. Lush disco. And of course, Diana Ross's 'Love Hangover' was a very pertinent song, we used to practise that campy dance in Siouxsie's place. So there was us six weirdos and four or five very very resentful, middle-aged, middle-class dykes. Me and Siouxsie looking so bizarre on this empty dance floor.

That's how it started. We started going there, the six of us, and then we met Linda, who was the DJ's girlfriend, and she liked us because we were outrageous and peculiar. She started to invite us back afterwards to her suite in St James's. She had an apartment, you'd walk through reception and through the coffee lounge and you'd come out into a courtyard, and round there you'd find this entrance, and up on the third floor she had this really plush place.

How did she get that?

Through kinking, she had a basement flat in Earls Court that she shared with another prostitute, and they were doing kinks, some

351

well-known people, very weird. She'd work twelve-hour shifts and earn three hundred quid. Which was a lot in those days, and so she had this other place for her and her girlfriend Caroline. That was where those sofa shots were taken in the *Anarchy in the UK* magazine. That was much later, though.

Who else was on the game?

Tracie O'Keefe, my friend Sharon, Debbi was for a while. They all did it together. Debbi and Tracie ended up being great buddies. I did it for a bit, it was quite fun. I went with them. I met this woman called Dominique, who was part of that scene and fell in love with Tracie, and we used to go out and do all these crazy things. The band used to go to the prostitutes in Shepherds Market. Steve and Paul, being really laddy.

It strikes me that a lot of that punk scene was quite like Warhol.

Everybody loved The Velvet Underground, and Nico. Siouxsie and Steve were big fans, Simon, we all were.

Did you ever see Sid Vicious?

Yes, I did a television thing with him, that London Weekend show with Janet Street Porter. It was such a giggle. It was to do with Keith of Smile, and hair colour, and being punky and changing your hair colour. They sent cabs, and Simon and Siouxsie and Debbi and Simone and me and Sid all went. It was the first time I'd ever been on television; it was like you'd imagine it to be, queeny directors going yes, lovey. This was . . .

Pre-Grundy?

Oh yes. We all waltzed into this studio and we were made to sit in these white boxes. All I remember is Sid having this black jacket and punky hair, and a used tampon clipped on to this thing, and spitting, all the time. He wouldn't stop doing it. He had cigarette burns on his hands; you could see them from the audience. Speed paranoia. Real burns, like you'd have to do it for a minute, or something. Bad burns.

So what happened to it all?

Caroline Coon ruined it, funnily enough. She opened it right out by putting it in *Melody Maker*. This is Johnny Rotten, this is the Sex Pistols, oh wow. Before then it was fine, you could go and drink in Louise's till three o'clock any night of the week. You might find five lesbians and Johnny down there, it was really great, really original, new. I was only sixteen or seventeen.

We had this fabulous place and then you'd get this really straight couple from Edgware or Ealing; and of course Madame Louise, charging three quid a time, if she had a hundred and fifty people down there she's rolling in it. The drinks were £2 a time. She wouldn't turn people away from her door. It went disgusting.

There used to be summit meetings upstairs with Malcolm and Vivienne, when Siouxsie was forming her band, to get management. Nils and everybody would be hanging around there. Everything was heightened by drugs, drinking your face off and taking dexedrine, blues, sulphate. This big fat man used to come down from the black clubs, trying to sell you Mandrax and downers. I can't take speed at all, it makes me sick.

Who used to stay at Linda's?

Everybody. It was like, after Louise's, she had two big bedrooms and a front room which had two couches, so most of us who didn't have the money to get a cab and couldn't be fucked to get a night bus, most of us lived in the suburbs, so we'd go round to St James's and kip on her couch. Nancy, Sid, Adam, Johnny was always there, not so much Glen Matlock, he was so macho and straight and boring, he wasn't a regular face like Johnny and Adam and Jordan.

What happened afterwards, when it became popular?

I drifted more into the gay scene, away from the punk scene, because it had become ugly and quite violent. It was never violent at the 100 Club, and I went four or five times. It was aggressive and heavy but it wasn't violent. When I went to the Roxy I had to leave after a while, there were glasses in people's faces, really bad.

Marco Pirroni

*Original SEX habitué, later guitarist for The Models, Rema Rema
and, most famously, the version of Adam and the Ants that had the
huge hits – most of which he co-wrote. Interviewed at his home in
Mayfair, London, then full of SEX and Seditionaries clothes. Very
dry, with a wicked, sardonic sense of humour.*

Had you lived in Harrow all your life?

No, we moved there when I was about ten, we used to live in Camden
Town, Kentish Town. Harrow was dull, pretty awful, completely
straight. It was just a suburb, except that it had a lot of greasers and
teds and skinheads for some reason. I was never a skinhead, I was
too young, they were dying out when I was getting into clothes. I did-
n't hang around in Harrow. I went to school and college in Harrow.

When did you start going down to the shop?

It must have been late '74. I can remember the first thing I bought, a
pair of pink lurex socks. I wanted to buy a pair of brothel creepers,
and they had these horrible ones in black and grey suede. The shop
was called Let It Rock, there was a sofa in there. The first big thing I
bought was a blue-and-white-flecked box jacket with black collar,
which got nicked. Johnny Rotten wore it a lot. I look at the Caroline
Coon book and see most of my clothes.

**Were these things originals that Malcolm had got, or had he had
them made up?**

Mostly he had them made up, but there must have been some original things. I know the shoes must have been old lasts that he'd had
made up. If you want to talk about Malcolm and clothes, you should
see a guy called Sid Green, used to make them. I went to see Sid a
couple of years later to get some suits made. He said Malcolm used

354

to come in with these strange fabrics. They were original fabrics. Malcolm had a pattern book.

How had you found out about the shop?

I'd been to Roxy Music concerts and I'd seen people wearing leopard-skin and snakeskin brothel-creepers, so I knew there was somewhere that was doing things like that. It was the year that *That'll Be the Day* came out, and I'd read that Malcolm McLaren had made all these clothes for the film, and I heard that he had a shop, so I went down there figuring he must have all this stuff, and he didn't.

Every time you went in there, he'd have one item in there that didn't fit you, and he wasn't getting any more in. It was always like that. Vivienne and Malcolm were serving in there, and a tall coloured guy, and a skinny blonde guy that may or may not have been Michael Collins, I can't remember. Jordan wasn't there yet. I went in on a Tuesday afternoon and the first person I saw was Vivienne.

Did you ever work in the shop?

No, I used to hang about there a lot. Most afternoons actually. Then I realised they must be getting really sick of me. I used to just sit there. I bought all the obvious things in the shop, but there's things I never bought that I wished I had, that I didn't like then. I thought they were just boring. Plain black jodhpur boots . . .

Did you ever get any trouble from wearing the clothes?

No, I'm pretty big, so. Everyone else I knew had lots of trouble, but I never did. I was just lucky, no-one was ever sure what I was – some kind of gay Hell's Angel glam ted, you know.

Had you started going to college when you started hanging around the shop?

Yeah. I was studying art. I went to the art school, but they threw me out after a year.

When did you first see the Pistols?

April '76 at the 100 Club. I'd tried to see them a couple of times at the Paradiso, but it was cancelled, or I'd got there too late, but the

355

100 Club was the first time. They were supported by the Suburban Studs, who were dressed up like the guy from *Clockwork Orange*, and they had cardboard cut-outs of the Bay City Rollers on stage. Even then I didn't understand why. I went by myself cos no-one else wanted to go. Everyone else I knew was really straight.

What was your impression when you saw them?

Well, you couldn't hear anything, I never heard any of their songs till I saw them at Notre Dame Hall. The thing that impressed me most was that Johnny Rotten sang with his hands in his pockets. He was like, really bored. That was what stuck in my mind. They didn't get me thinking in a different way, I was already thinking that way, but I wasn't sure, it just confirmed my suspicions. It also made me think, I could play better than that geezer.

How had you heard about them?

Through the shop. Malcolm said, 'Oh I'm managing this band called the Sex Pistols', and for some reason, the scene at that time was Crackers and The Lacey Lady where everyone went, it was a soul-funk scene. Nothing to do with rock. I thought it must be a funk band, I associated it with Sex Machine. I couldn't envisage anyone doing rock at that time.

But I went, cos it was Malcolm's group. I thought they'd probably look good. When the punk scene first came along it seemed slightly intellectual, slightly arty, and the soul scene wasn't, it was booze, and having a dance. What I couldn't understand was there were all these guys who looked so weird, yet they were so straight. Bricklayers. I couldn't understand why that was.

How did the soul boys dress?

In a softer punk way, there wasn't much leather. There was a lot of peg trousers and winkle-pickers, stripy shirts; it was more Acme Attractions than SEX. There were very few people wearing SEX clothes. Lots of see-through T-shirts. Not many of the porno T-shirts or anything like that. People wearing safety pins arranged neatly. Plastic sandals, cropped hair with razor partings. Lots of earrings. That sort of look.

Did you go to Acme?

Yeah, a lot. I didn't like their clothes as much. They had more originals. I went to Acme first when it was upstairs, before they moved to the basement. I liked their stuff, but it wasn't as exciting and glamorous. Dusty old jeans and jackets. I don't think I've got anything from Acme now, though I cherish my SEX clothes.

Can you remember what sort of music they played in The Lacey Lady?

James Brown, 'Peeping Tom' [actually 'Tom the Peeper'] by Act One. It was before disco, it was funk. There was no rock at all. It was the only thing I knew about, an arty little scene. The other thing that must have been going on then was the Andrew Logan set. They were much older. There was nothing, and yet thousands of these bizarre-looking kids were going to Brighton, and they were completely ignored. The King's Road on a Saturday afternoon was packed. Not a word.

When you saw the Pistols, did you find you met other people quickly through it.

Yes, in those days if you saw someone walking down the street dressed in a similar way to you, you'd say something, you'd see them at a Pistols gig. It wasn't a great surprise to see these people there, I'd seen them before.

Who was there?

At the first gig I went to, Sid, Siouxsie and Steve, Jordan and Vivienne, those were the only people I knew by name.

What was the impulse behind doing the Banshees at the 100 Club Punk Festival?

I just got asked to do it. Literally the night before. Billy Idol was going to play guitar, but he wanted to do his songs, and then he pulled out cos Sid just wanted to make a noise and Steve couldn't play. I didn't really know Siouxsie and Steve. So we had an abortive rehearsal at The Clash's place on the Monday, where we realised there was no point in trying to learn any songs. So we did a Velvet Underground feedback thing for hours and hours.

What did it sound like?

Horrible. Sid was doing Moe Tucker, I was doing 'Sister Ray', I don't know what Steve was doing. I did have a tape of it, I've had several tapes of it, but I keep losing it. I kept reading in interviews Siouxsie saying we should have done it all night till we got thrown off, but I remember me and Sid looking at each other and we were fed up, so we just stopped.

What was your impression of Sid then?

I found him immensely funny, actually. A complete piss-taker. Very witty. He creased me up, this really dry humour. 'Let's listen to accordion records for three hours', stuff like that.

What did you do after the Banshees? Did you want to form a group?

Yeah. I was going to join Sid's group, The Flowers of Romance. I had been introduced to Sid by Jordan in the shop, and he said his band needed a bass player, so I said, 'I'll play bass.' I couldn't play bass, but I thought I could learn. We had a rehearsal set up, but the night afterwards was the glass-throwing incident where he got locked up, so that got forgotten about. I drifted into a band with a couple of friends at college, and that was The Models.

What did you think when punk started to gather steam? Did you think it was going to be very successful?

Yeah, I did. I couldn't imagine how it would end up, but then I couldn't imagine it staying as it was. I knew it was going to get bigger and bigger, I knew that eventually I would get disenchanted with it. I didn't envisage things like 'new wave' happening, when people like Elvis Costello came along. It was like the pub-rockers' revenge. I never thought about how I would look back on it ten years later, I just got on with it.

How did you feel as more people came along?

After Bill Grundy, that was the end of it for me, really. From something intellectual and almost artistic from a lot of arty people in weird clothes, suddenly there were these fools with dog collars on and 'punk' written on their shirt with biro. Like Sham 69. I saw their first gig at the Roxy, they were supporting Generation X. There were about four people there, and Jimmy Pursey was leaping about like an idiot.

I've never forgiven Jimmy Pursey for making it into a terrible excuse to be stupid. He came along and was telling me what punk was all about. I went down to The Vortex and they were on. 'This one's about all you cunts who think punk's all about getting clothes from the King's Road and Kensington Market and Oxford Street.' I remember my friend saying, 'Oh, what good shops are there down Oxford Street?' I dunno . . .

Did you like the fact that there was an arty side to punk?

Yeah, I did. A very elite side. That was the interesting thing to me. It was like that Velvet Underground scene, the Warhol set. Film-makers and poets and artists and god knows what. There wasn't many musicians. Everyone wanted to play bass, as I remember, I think they thought because it had four strings it must be easy. It's true, everyone played bass.

It was like the Factory, with Malcolm as the Warhol figure. There were cliques. That's why I hated it when people like The Damned, who were what we used to call monkey-boot punk . . . When people started wearing Doctor Martens, that was the degeneration of it all. It became an excuse to be stupid.

The shock value was great. I loved it. I remember wearing lime green Levi's, fluorescent green socks and fluorescent green winkle-pickers that I'd got from SEX, and gold glasses, and I went into Harrods. It was amazing, but it was more fun for me, cos I could retaliate. No-one ever picked on me, so I could pick on them first.

And you saw the Pistols after that?

Yeah, the last time I saw them was the Screen on the Green gig, and by that time Sid was playing bass, and he was hopeless, it was horrible; and Rotten, or Lydon, used to have a real presence, a command over the audience, and the audience didn't care, they were just chucking cans at him, and at Sid. Sid didn't know what to do. They commanded no respect. Punk audiences had been taught not to respect performers, that No Heroes stuff.

I thought The Clash were better musically, but I felt that the Pistols were more important. I liked being a Pistols fan, wearing clothes from SEX, being involved with Malcolm and Vivienne and Jordan. There was another faction, an unhip faction, which were The Damned fans. Guys with green plastic sunglasses. Big lapels with lots of badges on. Ties round their necks. And they always had to write 'punk' on themselves, to let people know.

That was the difference. People coming into it later were like that. If I wanted to be a mod, I'd go down to Johnson's and buy a suit and one of those little hats and a tie and the white socks, but I wouldn't really be a mod.

What did you think of the Seditionaries clothes?

I really liked them. I had everything. By Christmas, Malcolm and Vivienne and Jordan and Michael were all dressing completely in black, and I thought, that's what the new collection is going to be, and it was. Around the turning point from SEX to Seditionaries, I bought an Anarchy shirt, and I didn't know what to wear it with. It didn't look right with pegs and winkle-pickers. It wasn't fifties, it wasn't rock'n'roll.

Did you grow apart from Malcolm and the shop, or did you stay involved during '77/'78?

I was involved, but I didn't really buy anything. There was a stereotyped punk look: Destroy T-shirt, leather jacket, jeans or bondage trousers and brothel creepers, and spiky hair, blond or black. That was the standard look throughout '77. I'd got disillusioned cos it had turned stupid. People calling you punk out of car windows, about twenty times a day.

I remember being attacked by teds on the King's Road. Started pushing me about, and I was terrified, but I started pushing them back. I was good at giving people dirty looks, which was useful. I was down the King's Road with Steve Strange one afternoon, making a phone call, and suddenly this huge ted came along, and he was handing out leaflets to the big fight down at Margate.

He said, 'You coming down for the fight?' 'No.' 'Well look, there's a fight down at Margate, so-and-so beach, punks versus teds, come down, it'll be good.' He talked to us for about ten minutes, and we were going, how come you can be really friendly to us now, but want to kick the shit out of us down there. He couldn't really justify it. But he was dead nice. Ended up having tea with him.

Did you have trouble in Harrow with the teds?

Yeah. I never actually got jumped, just jeered at. In fact I met one of them in New York years later. I was at a club, and this bloke comes up and says, ''ere, you from 'arrow?' 'Yeah.' 'Well, I'm one of the teds who used to shout "cunt" at you, and "poof", as you used to walk to the station.' 'Oh yeah?' Those were the days.

Vic Godard

Singer and writer for Subway Sect, the most fascinating and hermetic of all first-wave punk groups. Saw the Sex Pistols in February 1976; it changed his life. Interviewed at his home in Mortlake in West London, where I had previously visited him in July 1978 to do a long Sounds *article. Time seemed to have stood still in the intervening ten years.*

Were you brought up around here, in Mortlake?

Yes. I went to secondary school just down the road in Sheen. Then I got to the age where you have to get a job, panicked, and went to Ealing Technical – to get out of getting a job. I hated it, it was horrible. Spent a couple of years there. I'd chosen the wrong thing to study. I was doing a thing that sounded good, European Studies, but in reality it had a hell of a lot in it that I wasn't into at all, like economics, statistics.

If I'd've looked around, there were degree courses that I would have been interested in, but it was such a quick decision, I did it on the very last day that I could possibly apply for college, and that one would do. I was starting a group at the time, and all I wanted was a way of getting out of having a job. A panic decision.

I didn't like music at all for about ten years. I liked it when I was very young, then I went right off it about 1966, and I didn't get back into it until about '75. I used to like The Kinks when I was really young. It wasn't that I didn't like what there was, I just didn't know about it. I drifted off into an area where music wasn't important, like football and stuff like that.

When did you go to Ealing?

I was still there when the Punk Festival was going on. I must have gone there in '75, and when the White Riot tour came along, I was officially still at college then, but I'd virtually run off without telling anyone, and when the tour was nearly over I asked if I could go back, but they wouldn't let me. They said if I'd have given them a bit more warning, they would have let me.

How did you get involved in forming groups?

I got involved with a guitarist who was at the same school as me, but he only came when we were in the sixth form. Rob Simmons. He was really into rhythm and blues, Dr Feelgood, he had all the records by the early sixties people, Stones, Yardbirds, he was into Chuck Berry, Jimmy Reed was the real hero – and I started getting into all that as well. We started playing their songs at a youth club at the end of the road, they let us practise in there. He was the best then, the rest of us would bash tambourines and things.

Were you aware of punk starting to happen by this stage?

It wasn't happening then, really. We saw the Sex Pistols virtually by accident, we were just walking past the Marquee one night and heard this noise coming out. We went in there and saw Jordan on the stage and Johnny Rotten in the audience, throwing chairs about. We thought that was really good. They were brilliant, absolutely fantastic.

Did that change your ideas about what you could be doing?

Completely. We'd been doing rhythm and blues stuff, and this blew that right out the window. We loved their image, but we weren't that mad on the actual music. We liked parts of it. I'm not sure if their music changed after that, or whether we liked the fact that it was so unprofessional.

When you first saw them, was it very raw?

Very, there were loads of mistakes. We never liked heavy guitars, but the reason we liked them was it sounded so shambolic that it didn't sound good enough to be professional. When they got tight, and more what you might call a rock band, we went off them a bit.

Did you go back to see them?

Yeah, we saw them every time they played in London. The Nashville concerts were brilliant. Fantastic. But every time they played they got a bit better. Glen Matlock added a lot to them, with his backing vocals and his bass lines. I went off them after that.

363

I still don't like 'Anarchy in the UK' – that was a real disappointment. When it came out I thought it was awful. It didn't have any edge, it sounded really puny, an attempt to sound loud that didn't come off.

I liked 'God Save the Queen'. I remember the first time they did that on stage. It was some college in Hendon, and he was reading the words off a sheet of paper. It was pretty shambolic, they'd obviously only just worked the song out. It was a riff with John singing over it.

Our favourite was 'Did You No Wrong'. They used to do that one first, and then as an encore. Our second favourite was 'Don't Give Me No Lip'. Each time there would be some change. Sometimes the guitar sound would be fantastic, and other nights it would be useless.

Funny thing though, there's not that many concerts that are fantastic, and quite a lot of theirs were, in those days. When I went to see Dr Feelgood in small pubs, the first times I saw them, they were brilliant, electrifying on stage. There was so much excitement packed into a small place.

You had Dr Feelgood, but they were getting a bit bigger, and you had the smaller R'n'B groups like The Michigan Flyers and the Count Bishops. They were all right, it was quite good for a night out, but going to see the Sex Pistols was a really exciting thing, you'd look forward to it all week. Up till then, all those groups used to be in the audience and get up out of the audience. The Sex Pistols never seemed to do that.

They kept themselves to themselves?

Yeah. I don't know what it was about them.

Actually there is a period that I've missed out. When we were going to see the R'n'B groups must have been about two years before the Sex Pistols. That was when we started listening to the New York Dolls. Going to that shop in Paddington, Bizarre, to get the latest Modern Lovers record. The big thing was waiting for the Television single to come out, 'Little Johnny Jewel'. Rushing out to get it and bringing it home. I had this idea of what sort of music Television were going to be like, after reading so much about it.

Did the single fulfil it?

364

No, it was completely different to what I imagined. I couldn't believe it, I must have played it non-stop all day. I thought it was the best record that had ever been made. Everything about it was so revolutionary. If you'd have told me what that record was going to be like, that it would have a five-minute guitar solo, I would have gone, whaat?

But when I learned guitar, that was the first thing I learned to play. Note for note. Like Debussy's piano music was different, so this was different to other rock music.

Did you like The Ramones and Patti Smith?

I loved The Ramones. That was a bit surprising, it was more mundane music, it wasn't earth-shattering, but it was good to listen to.

What did you call yourselves, to start with?

We didn't have a name.

You learned guitar, started writing music . . .

When I learned guitar, I'd already heard Television, and although I liked the image of the Sex Pistols, they weren't as interesting to me as Television. I wasn't into the same old rock chords – I wanted to play a music that was too difficult for what we could actually do, so what we came out with was a mish-mash which sounded like the Sex Pistols without the heaviness. We liked The Modern Lovers, and we had the *Nuggets* records, anything like that was fantastic.

With the Sex Pistols, it was the image, more than anything else. The way they didn't say thank you to the audience all the time. Which is quite funny, cos now one of my big heroes is Tony Bennett, and that's all he ever says. He comes on and says, 'Thank you, you're wonderful, I love you.'

What were the first songs that you wrote?

The first song I wrote was 'Don't Split It'. Three chords, the simplest thing. 'Nobody's Scared'. Some of the songs I wrote then, I don't even remember the titles of them. A lot of them, bits of them, turned up in other songs later on.

Where did the ideas for 'Nobody's Scared' come from?

365

I was at college, so that's where that's from. European Studies. I wrote it one day when I was bored in the college library. What I was trying to do was change the way rock songs were written. To take out all the useless words and to pare it down, take out all the Americanisms.

I didn't mind what went into the song, as long as the language was different to what had normally been associated with a rock song; all the 'yeah's and the 'baby's. That's what I was interested in, from the point of view of lyrics. That's what I liked about Television. I liked the way you could listen to something, and every different person who listened to it would get a different story from it.

Were you influenced by The Velvet Underground too, at that stage?

Yeah, that was all the twangy guitar stuff. Their music was too difficult for us, apart from the easier songs. Some of them had augmented chords and things in them.

You wore very plain clothes. You'd turn up in white shirts . . .

We used to dye everything grey in those days. In a big bath. We just liked the colour. We did go through a period of liking black and white for a while, then later on we started wearing brightly coloured T-shirts, like a tennis shirt with three buttons, but bright red with hoops going around it.

When was your first gig?

That was the Punk Festival at the 100 Club.

How was Malcolm McLaren involved?

He paid for our rehearsal time when we first started, and got us to play at the Punk Festival, supervised the rehearsals, and he reckoned we were good enough to do it. He just wanted as many groups as he could. When he first came to see us, he thought we were so awful that there was no way we could do it. So he booked us in Manos in Chelsea, eight in the morning until seven at night, all week, and paid for it. And we were on there the following week.

We only had to do about five songs, over and over again. 'Nobody's Scared', 'Don't Split It', I can't remember the other two, I don't think we ever did them again. 'Out of Touch' was possibly one of them.

Where did the name come from, the Subway Sect?

I don't know about the Subway, but the Sect came from . . . we desperately didn't want a name with 'The' and something with an s on the end. That was the thing to avoid, and there weren't that many ways around it. We liked the idea of a Sect.

You *were* a sect as well, in a funny kind of way. Very purist.

A lot of it came from the guitarist, Rob Simmons. He had such definite ideas about everything, and you couldn't make him do things that were far from what he wanted. He might not get you to do exactly what he wanted, but you wouldn't be able to go too far the other way. Rob came up with these ideas that were so outrageous that none of the rest of the group would do it. He wanted to have our shoes glued to the stage, before we went on, so we'd go on in our socks and get into the shoes, so we couldn't move.

There was a big argument between him and the bass player, Paul, was that Rob wouldn't let anyone go on stage with their guitar lower down than about that [points to upper chest], and Paul said he just couldn't play the bass up there. So when Rob wasn't looking, he'd let the strap down a notch, and Rob would notice and say, 'You've got to put your guitar at least one notch higher than that, or I won't go on.' He'd like a song one minute, and then go right off it.

One gig we did in Manchester we got an encore, and we didn't know what to do. The drummer really liked to do 'Don't Split It', cos he got to do a drum roll at the beginning, and Rob said, 'If we do that, I'm not playing.' What happened was, we all went on, the drummer did the drum roll, Rob didn't come in, I didn't come in, and Paul played about one note and stopped; then Paul and the drummer got up and walked off and left us on our own, so we got up and walked off too. That was it, that was the encore.

Where did you get that scratchy guitar style from?

That was down to Rob really. We never used ordinary guitars. Fender Mustangs have that sort of sound anyway. That was why we bought them. There's no way you'd ever play Gibson Les Paul or a Strat. We seemed to be doing the same thing as the Buzzcocks, only they were doing it in Manchester. They were into all that.

367

Obviously we'd both been listening to the same things, whereas the Sex Pistols were listening to different things.

Steve Jones had obviously learned to play from listening to The Rolling Stones and the New York Dolls. We really liked the Dolls, but what we wanted to sound like was the Velvets or the Seeds. Nothing remotely heavy. The Sex Pistols were heavy, to us, but we forgave them that. It was when their singles came out, they were like Slade singles, but it didn't matter. A Slade single is heavy, but because it's commercial and well produced, it's all right.

How did you get involved with Bernie Rhodes?

That was through Malcolm. What happened was, after that week, we obviously wanted somewhere to practise permanently, and he persuaded Bernie to let us practise at Camden, at The Clash's place. So we first went down there on a Sunday morning and had to get Bernie out of bed to let us in. We couldn't believe it when we saw him, this bloke in a stupid leather jacket with chains on the back. He let us practise there that day and he never kicked us out.

Did he effectively become your manager, or was it by default more than anything else?

No, he asked us if we wanted him to manage us, at the Punk Festival.

What was it like rehearsing there with The Clash? How did you get on with them?

Alright. We didn't keep the same hours as them. They used to practise late at night, and we used to practise in the daytime. If they ever were in there in the daytime, we just used to hang around until they'd finished. At that time, they did a hell of a lot of songs that didn't have anything to do with politics, and what they did was change them all to make them a bit more political.

The songs they did before they went political were much better than the ones they did afterwards: 'How Can I Understand the Flies', that was my favourite song, and 'I've Got a Crush on You'. They were like a proper sixties punk band. An American *Nuggets*-type group. But when they started that political crap, I went right off them. There wasn't any need for it, really.

368

The same thing happened to the Sex Pistols cos their songs weren't like that at first either. You don't need to have a song about politics, really. We used to have songs like 'USA', we changed that when they started doing 'Bored with the USA', we changed it to Eastern Europe. It was more of an image thing for us. We looked as if we came from there, anyway. All the grey stuff.

What was 'USA' about? I talked to you about it then and you didn't like America at all, did you?

No, I still don't. It was everything to do with Americans. The fact that we have anything to do with them really gets up my nose.

So what went wrong with The Clash, did they just take everything too seriously?

Mick Jones became too violent. I only ever liked The Clash right at the very beginning, when he was a bit unsure of himself. He was playing the same stuff, but if you're playing that sort of stuff, it doesn't sound too bad if it's far in the background – but as soon as you turn it up, that's it. A lot of it might have to do with the actual sound of the guitar – the sound you get from a Les Paul through a particular amp, an Ampeg or something like that.

That was the main reason we didn't like The Clash, or the Sex Pistols later on. I thought they were the end of rock'n'roll, but as it turned out, they weren't. The Clash reinforced that.

When did it become obvious that the Sex Pistols weren't the end of rock'n'roll?

It must have been when they first had a record out. They weren't so bad though, it was all the rest of the stuff that was going on, the other people that forced the situation. They couldn't stand against it, they were already in it. It doesn't have anything to do with music, really.

What was it like going on the White Riot tour?

Brilliant. If someone didn't go to boarding school, and felt they were missing out on not going to boarding school, like me, it was like having that all again, that you could throw things all over the place, get the fire extinguishers out . . .

What were the audiences like?

They would have clapped anything. Anyone could have done anything and they would have gone mad. They liked us best when everything went wrong, when the amps didn't work, and things like that.

The bill was The Slits, The Prefects, The Jam, you and The Clash ...

Not always, that was only the big towns. There was about six dates on the tour in the big towns, and those were the ones all these other groups came up for. The Buzzcocks were all right. The Jam were terrible. The Slits and The Prefects were really close with us.

You didn't talk to the audience much did you?

The worst was this gig we did in France, there were all these bikers there. Punk hadn't taken off in England really, so you can imagine what all these rural Frenchmen made of it. They didn't like The Clash much anyway, but you can imagine what sort of a reaction we got. It was a disaster; every single one of us was out of tune, and not just a little bit. Miles out of tune. The bass was so far out of tune it wasn't worth even trying to sing in tune with the guitar.

We didn't give a damn, we were just laughing our heads off. I remember Mick Jones thought it could ruin The Clash's set, and he was so worried he kept running on to the stage trying to fiddle about with Paul's bass, trying to get it in tune. These bikers were going mad, really getting violent. Booing the whole time.

So what happened next? You recorded the John Peel session, and the single? The single didn't come out for a long time, did it? Almost a year.

Every record we ever made took over a year to come out. Bernie. I don't know why, he just had a thing against putting records out.

Was he trying to make you mysterious?

To this day I can't work out what he was trying to do. It couldn't have been mystery, cos if he wanted us to be mysterious, he wouldn't have had us work so much. He didn't let us bring out records, but he kept making us play live, all the time. As soon as one tour finished, we were on another one. And none of it was to any end, because when a record came out, it was always when I didn't have a group to go on tour anyway. When we were on a tour, we never had a record out.

What did you do after the White Riot tour?

We did our first tour on our own. The Prefects came to see us but they didn't play. That was just us in the back of a Transit van. A driver and us four. The driver was also the roadie. Baker. I really liked him, he was one of the original five that started up round here. He's living in New York now, he's got his own taxi firm or something.

The next big one would have been with the Buzzcocks. We did two tours with the Buzzcocks. Both were enjoyable, I got on so well with them and we really liked each other's music a lot. I still like the Buzzcocks' music now; out of all the punk groups, they were my favourites. On tour with The Clash, after the first two nights when they went on stage I wanted to get as far away as possible, they made me cringe, but with the Buzzcocks, I'd watch them every night, and never get fed up with them.

What did you find embarrassing about The Clash?

Little things, that stupid bloody 'Police and Thieves', with Mick Jones going 'ooooh-yer'! Even if I managed to watch the rest, when they did that song I had to go out.

Did you like Joe?

Yeah, I really liked him. If Mick hadn't been in the group, I probably would have liked them.

How was Subway Sect changing, while you had the original group?

I was learning to play guitar, so when we started playing on stage that made a big difference to the music. We had a lot more scope. Also we were reliant before on the chords that Rob could play, which was limited. What he did was good, but it was limited. That was probably the best time, when I started playing guitar. The first time I played guitar on stage was at the Gibus [Club in Paris], for seven days on our own, then after that we did The Lou's tour.

That was a great tour, cos again, it was the same sort of music as

371

us. The Lou's were a lot more rock'n'roll than us, but they had the same sounding guitars. Not as scratchy as us, but not heavy. They liked all the same books as us, even. I was getting into Baudelaire at the time. That's what the blonde girl in The Lou's used to like. I always liked French literature.

But we split up. Bernie wasn't prepared to wait for Paul and Rob to learn their instruments, and I wasn't really, either. They just weren't getting any better. You wouldn't have minded if they were really trying, but they weren't even practising, at all. They were at a standstill, and they weren't good enough. If we'd've kept them in the group, we would have been doing the same music for ever.

Had the original energy fizzled out?

No, everything apart from the music was great. We were getting on well, and Rob had some really good ideas, but if he could have done something else, it wouldn't have mattered. I tried to get him to do lyrics, but he felt he couldn't do that. I think he was just lazy. It was a shame though, cos you always knew that Paul just wasn't a musician. He got by for a period of time, but I had hoped that once he got the basics, he would then start learning properly, but he didn't.

So you wanted to say things and do things, and you weren't able to.

Yes, and the only way I could find out about it was if I learned the guitar myself. That was what forced the issue, the fact that I'd started learning the guitar and within a couple of months could play better than Rob, and I wondered, why isn't he getting any better?

Some of your contemporaries became very successful. Were you just not ambitious in the same way? Or were you hampered by management?

Yes to both. I was never that ambitious anyway. If I hadn't got married I might have gone on and tried to be a success in music, but once I got married, that was it for me. I just like listening to music now. I wasn't successful cos I wasn't that single-minded. When we were playing somewhere, and there was something I'd rather be doing, I just wouldn't turn up. Which was unheard of. The Clash would never not turn up to a gig.

Steve Walsh

Member of Sid Vicious' band The Flowers of Romance, and early punk face; did a key early interview with The Clash for punk fanzine Sniffin' Glue, issue 4. Later moved to Manchester and formed Manicured Noise, a rigorous post-punk group. Articulate, spiky, quite caustic – no rose-tinted glasses at all.

It was funny to see all these old records on the jukebox in SEX; I didn't know them but somehow it felt right, they'd rediscovered all the right things, they were obscure, underground, and raw-sounding. All around you were hearing that slick production, disco production, or that LA production, which was like a blanket thrown over the whole of life. Especially in the suburbs.

Wall-to-wall brushed denim, guys wearing brushed denim flares, nightmarish clothes, nightmarish feather haircuts, and this was the background to all this. People wanted to change. That whole way of looking in the seventies was out of order. I don't know what they were thinking about. It's all very camp and everything, it's quite a laugh now, but I can't believe that people actually wore them.

What did you think of the Punk Festival?

That was odd. I don't know what I made of Siouxsie but I liked Subway Sect, they made a definite impression, they looked suitably down-at-heel. I didn't like anything too dressed up. It was obscure. It seemed right, very rough and real, what it was about nowadays. Seeing things as they were. Something lucid about it. I remember quite liking Siouxsie, but they looked quite posey.

What did you think of Sid at this time?

I'd never got to know him. I'd seen him around. At one time he had greased-back hair and a gold jacket, and then in pink trousers at the punkfest. That was when the glass-throwing incident was supposed to have happened. I'd see him wearing these ripped red pegs and spiky hair.

The first time I met him was at the ICA when The Clash played. The Flowers of Romance were looking for a bass player, and said they'd have me as a second guitar and look for a bass, but I didn't want to play bass. That's how I got into the band with him and Viv. I used to go up to Davis Road to this squat, with old grannies living downstairs, and we'd rehearse till about five in the morning, taking speed.

What were Sid and Viv like?

They were really nice. I knew from the beginning that Sid was a lot more intelligent than he let on. He was actually a very sweet guy, in a lot of ways. Sure he had a nasty streak, but he had a lot of problems, a funny upbringing. I don't know about sexually, I always thought of him as totally androgynous. He never struck me as gay. Me and him and Viv used to sleep in the same bed together.

What was Viv Albertine like?

She was all right, she was funny. I was always very shy with girls, and she was a lot older and more sophisticated than most of them. Most of those punk girls were really straight, but dressed up in these weird clothes and too much make-up. Siouxsie was weird. I didn't really get to talk to her much. She was like a cat, or something. Severin's a funny fellow as well. Inscrutable.

Things must have gathered steam. I moved into this place in Davis Road, and through the autumn we started rehearsing more, although we never got it together at all, we never found a drummer who'd play without a hi-hat. Sometimes we rehearsed at The Clash's place. Viv and Sid were quite matey with The Clash. I must have been hanging around, taking more and more speed in this place in Shepherd's Bush, playing the same riff for hours and hours . . .

Did you see any of the concerts in the autumn?

I went to Notre Dame Hall, with John Maybury. But things are a bit foggy around that period. I wonder why.

374

Did you see that concert at the Royal College of Art?

Yeah, I was involved in a little fracas there. There were all these northern art students, industrial design students or shit like that, and they must have thought, eee, poonk rock! Chucking these glasses. I remember seeing one hit Strummer's head and he just carried on playing, he had a head like a brick. Something out of a cartoon.

Then after the concert finished, we'd gone over and had words with these people, and I'd been speeding, which is probably what gave me the idea to get into this stupid fight. Then Vicious steamed in, but the really impressive one was Strummer, cos he got straight off the stage after he'd put his guitar down and made a bee-line for this trouble, and the crowd parted as he went for it, and just dived in like some intrepid *Boy's Own* hero, laying into this horrible art student wearing one of these Harry Fenton leather coats.

I remember getting on the back of one of these, pounding him on the head, but rather half-heartedly, I didn't really want to hurt the guy, and Campbell pulled me off. He hauled me off backstage. Luckily I knew him. About sixteen stone of the cunt. He'd broken someone's arm the night before. My friend Kenny Morris, who I'd never associate with violence, he got a few kicks in, with his winkle-pickers. Someone must have got some good wounds from that.

Didn't you do some writing about then as well?

I just did that thing with The Clash. I knew more people than Mark Perry. So I went down and did that *Sniffin' Glue* interview – the seminal one where all those things were said.

Were they nice to you?

Yeah, I liked them. I liked Strummer, I saw a Tom Waits poster on the wall, and I'd seen him at Ronnie Scott's – I was into the beatnik thing as well. He was into Kerouac and Burroughs. Punk wasn't the be-all and end-all. It was the absorbing thing, you'd throw out all your old records.

Were you aware of Malcolm and Sophie and Jamie at that point?

They were shadowy figures. I'd met Malcolm at Louise's, drunk some more champagne with him. He said he'd been to Camberwell,

375

'amongst many others'. I thought I should get to know this guy, but there was something forbidding about him; he seemed big-time and I didn't feel I had anything to offer him. But he's always interested me. Vicious would always have bad words for him.

Sid used to work there on Saturdays, and he was afraid of Vivienne. They used to give him about five quid for working there on a Saturday. She used to put on that Animals record, 'It's My Life', and dance about the shop in bondage trousers. Vivienne was disturbing. She looked great then, this wacky older woman with the white hair. She used to call me Jimmy, even though I told her my name was Steve. There was something weird about her.

They were older, and they were doing this, looking like that. They were obviously . . . lifers, you know? In it for good.

Did you like being part of an elite?

Yeah, it was much more fun being part of an elite. That Christmas of '76 was a definite point in history for me. It was spent in a really slovenly fashion. Viv Albertine had got this amazing flat by then in a studio in a mews off the Fulham Road. We were hanging around there. I'd got really pissed the night before and I slept on the floor and then went round to Caroline Coon.

I arrived quite early, Sid was there and the TV was on and records playing. It was looking all set to be a really horrible day, like a traditional English Christmas in slightly different clothes. But then The Heartbreakers arrived. That was the first time we'd seen them. That roadie Keith came staggering out, mandied out of his head.

I remember there being quite a lot of hostility between the two camps.

Everyone wanted to see what Thunders looked like, whether he looked how he did before, which was like one of those shrunken voodoo head things. Thunders and Jerry Nolan walked in and they were a disappointment. Thunders looked like some vaguely gone-to-seed Italian New Yorker. They staggered in out of this taxi and sat down on the sofa and Thunders says, 'Hey, are you Sid Vicious?' Any advantage they had was blown.

Was Sid already getting an attitude?

He always had the attitude. He was never like that with me, or with certain other people, but he would use his appearance to test people.

What about that psychotic side?

There was, yeah. But it was like a lot of psychotic people, I could never decide whether it was pathological or whether he was just a big baby. We slept in the same bed once after he'd been drunk on Special Brew, and he pissed in it. He wasn't a typical hard-man, and he never pretended to be, either. If the chance came for some serious violence he'd weasel out of it. Stab him in the back was his idea. There was nothing macho attached to it with him.

There was a kind of worthlessness with him.

So what happened with that party? I remember Roadent being there, being really nasty to everybody.

Yeah, he was a bit of a Nazi. I remember him upstairs at the RCA gig saying he was going to form the British National Socialist Youth Party, I didn't know if he was serious or what. He was always around. After dinner, Steve Jones showed up with all those cronies that he used to have. He was doing this Rod Stewart impersonation with a standard lamp with the lamp knocked off, there was this live socket within inches of him.

Someone had their fur coat nicked by Steve Jones's friends and a knife was thrown and everybody fled, as they were wont to do. There was a big myth built up about punks being hard nuts. They were the first to run when there was any violence. People never perceived the irony of it. It wasn't macho violence, it was more subtle than that. It was subtle, psychic violence.

Genesis P-Orridge really wound me up at the ICA. We just saw this synth stuff and thought, what a load of wank. Suddenly there was Genesis and this other long-haired hippy rolling about on the floor, wearing Doctor Martens and booting each other. Everyone pulled back and watched. I just thought, what are they doing? And later in an interview he said, 'All the big tough punks pulled away, didn't want to get involved.' Of course, it wasn't their fight.

There was a difference in what the violence was about. When I was about seventeen I'd read about Schwarzkogler and Nitsch and all

377

that, so I knew about rolling around in offal, it was no big deal that someone would do that. It wasn't special. What was more interesting was that people were doing it in a different way. There was a bit of intellectual poison seeping in, but they had it wrong, I thought.

What happened to Flowers of Romance?

I don't know, it all went really funny. I think everyone had been kicked out of the group by the time Sid joined the Pistols. Viv Albertine had been kicked out, she had started behaving like a real arsehole at one point, self-pitying, hanging around with Johnny Thunders. Sid and me conspired to kick her out of the group, then I was on my way out. We had some talk, and I didn't feel it was going to happen. I didn't really care about the group.

Sid was hanging out with Keith Levene, they were doing drugs together by then. Drugs in a group of people causes these little alliances, you are in this week and out next week. Especially with speed. I'd been in for a while but I started falling out of things. I didn't have the stamina or the interest in keeping up with all that. I left but I still stayed friendly with them. The group fell apart. A lot of the equipment was nicked, guitars and amps just went missing.

Did you have any songs?

We only had one song, 'Belsen Was a Gas'. There was nothing right-on about the music in The Flowers of Romance. Sid wrote that riff, definitely. That was the only song I remember that group doing. I think it was just an excuse for hanging about. Being in a band – or being seen to be in a band – was quite important. There was a lot going on, we used to go out every night. We'd go to Louise's. I'd been there a lot before, on funny nights of the week. You'd end up there on a Wednesday night after the Roxy.

Did you see people turning themselves into commodities?

That probably happened later. Most of the people around you didn't feel there was too much that was bogus about them. People were forming their identities, and some were attractive and you'd want to know them, and others . . . well, you didn't want to know them. Down at the 100 Club I'd pogoed down the front, but after that,

378

when new people came along that I didn't know, I felt more distant and aloof.

I went to the Screen on the Green the second time. I'd taken whiskey and valium and speed and got really out of it, and went down there. Sid was playing with them by that time, but I thought they weren't as good. Matlock was better, even though his attitude was wrong. He was a valuable foil for their raucousness. I never liked them that much as a group anyway.

Did you ever get to know the Pistols?

No, there was always an aura of cool around them. Even when I got to know Vicious I was always very wary of speaking to Rotten. I had the impression he didn't like me. There was a heavy, frosty kind of atmosphere that hung around them.

What happened after The Flowers of Romance broke up? Had you finished art school by then?

No. What with all the drug-taking and the spending of money, I'd met some really unsavoury people, and one of these came after me, and I had to scoot back home. I shaved all my hair off and decided that was the end of my punk phase. I'd had a shitty time with a lot of the people, the drugs had got nasty. Things were falling apart, the Pistols were getting more popular, out of the reach of the original people, and the gigs weren't places to go to any more, there was no sense of intimacy or belonging.

There was no centre. It had become dispersed. They were becoming much of a muchness, and for me there was only ever the Sex Pistols who had that pure idea. It seems stupid now, but that's how I looked at it. Groups like Eater and The Damned, I hated it all. Once there was only one place to be, and now there's lots of places and I don't want to be there, so I just didn't go after that.

Was there a sense of let-down, that the promise had disappeared?

I don't think I ever hoped it would become anything. Maybe a lot of people naively hoped it would become something, but there was no idealism in punk, it was a negative, cynical reaction. Almost a gesture of futility, a demonstration of the futility of youth culture and

379

rebellion and all these other silly attitudes that history has handed down to us. The futility of pop music, and of ever changing anything. After a while the music became unlistenable.

Groups like 999, so horrible. The Boomtown Rats. I saw Sham 69 at The Vortex, and there were all these skinheads swinging off the stage. I'd always liked skinheads as a style, from the first time around, but these new guys were fucking awful. Brutes. That was violence but not what I wanted to know about. I was being snobby, I felt that the herd had got hold of something that the herd should not have got hold of. I thought that punk was intrinsically elitist.

I began to think that if it got unleashed on a broad basis, it would become more of a nightmare. It was all very well for art students and arty people to fuck around with notions of violence, but if it got outside it would be appalling. And sure enough, it did get on to a mass level and it did become appalling. Mindless violence was just a feature. But who can blame them, people *en masse* are not going to perceive the subtleties.

Debbi Wilson

Bromley Contingent member. Heavily photographed and quoted in Jonh Ingham's October 1976 'Welcome to the (?) Rock Special' article in Sounds. *Worked in SEX and Seditionaries. Interviewed in London's Maida Vale, around the time that she worked on Alex Cox's* Love Kills *as a researcher and production assistant. Her perceptive memories are tinged by a slight disconnection.*

When I was about nine, we moved out to Edgware, which was suburbs, semi-detached houses, really horrible. We were on a council estate. I went to a school which was mixed between middle-of-the-road Jewish and working-class. It was surrounded by these really big houses, but most people who went to the school were really poor, so it was an odd place to live. The mixture of suburbia is like all the dregs of the city centre shoved out to these little houses.

Were you just living with your mum then?

No, my mum and dad. Then they divorced when I was about twelve, and I was living with my dad. In fact I left home not long after, when I was about fourteen of fifteen. I didn't want to live there, I hated the school I was at, I hated where I lived, I never got on with anyone there. Some people see their old school friends; I've never seen any of them.

Was there nothing to do there?

Nothing. But then you're quite near to London, on the Northern line, so I used to go out, 'up to town' as they used to call it. But I don't remember going out around there at all. It was really rough, and this naff attitude.

So were you interested in pop music at all when you were growing up? Or did you just ignore it?

I wasn't interested in the charts, but I remember being more interested in music than anything else, the idea of bands. Marc Bolan was quite hip, and then I liked Bowie, and quite liked Iggy Pop, cos I felt they were on the fringe. Our generation was Bay City Rollers and Mott the Hoople, you'd go to the local youth club and dance to those records. I remember a lot of soul music and early sixties music, which my mother and father always played.

So when did you leave home?

I started going out a lot, not going to school, and stopped going home half the time, and sort of floated back now and then. I stayed in Chelsea quite a lot, cos Tracie O'Keefe lived there.

How did you get to know her?

I got to know Simon and them, from the Bromley Contingent. The Sex Pistols were just starting. They'd played a few gigs, and we used to hang out at Crackers. There was a lot of Bowie influence around at the time, everyone who dressed up trendy liked David Bowie or jazz, there was nothing different. At Global Village it was soul, it was dreadful really, I don't think anyone listened to the music, just posed.

Tracie was hanging around that lot but not all that much, she really did come all the way from Bromley. Then she went to live with Berlin in another house in Chelsea with another girl called Blanche, and a little gay guy called John. It was in Chelsea, Cheyne Walk, and across the road Bob Marley's band used to live.

Was it a squat?

No, it was a rented room at the top of a house. It was just outrageous there cos there was Blanche in a big room with John, and Berlin and Tracie. I used to go and stay there a lot, and we'd sit on the balcony and we'd be screeching across the road at the Bob Marley band, howling. It was so camp, and that I suppose was the first really we got into the mixed gay thing, and everywhere we went was pretty gay, the Sombrero and places like that.

I was about fifteen, so I was pretty naive. I met Linda Ashby, and it was all interconnected. That part of my life gets really confusing, about where was I? I know we started going to Louise's, but I think the Pistols' involvement in the gay scene came mainly from the Bromley Contingent. Siouxsie was very influenced by gays and stuff, and there's Berlin and Philip Sallon.

But it was confusing to me then cos girls would really fancy me, and because I was young I thought maybe it would be the craze to just go with girls. I didn't know about my sexuality then cos I hadn't had any experience with men. I didn't know whether I was meant to be gay or not. I was going through an odd period in my life. I didn't know any different.

What were you dressing in at the time?

Ridiculous stuff, I remember having a pair of pink Bermuda shorts and these open floppy pink sandals. For the Screen on the Green gig I made my own T-shirt with zips at the side, and great big enormous dungarees, and had my hair cut short and dyed blue, and wore plastic sandals. I was still finding my way about clothes. I don't think anyone really knows their way with clothes at fifteen. We created the style by not being educated about dress.

How were you making money then?

I wasn't really making any money, they were all making money from prostitution and stuff, but I wasn't doing that at the time. Berlin was on the game, John, Blanche, Tracie, and Linda of course was on the heavy stuff, whipping sessions . . . but she was quite professional about it. It was all Park Lane, it was the campest, most outrageous place in the world. All these outrageous queens going around in punk gear and black leather going ooooooh!

What sort of people did they get?

Oh all sorts, cos Berlin was so pretty and John was so young that even straight men would think, I've gotta go for this just to see what it's like! It got to a stage where prostitution wasn't that terrible a thing to do, it became quite a part of the new London. None of it was serious, it was completely mental. It was never a case of making money; everyone would make lots of money, go down the Sombrero and spend the whole lot in an evening.

383

People think that the early days of punk were all banging along at Sex Pistols gigs, but the early days for me were camping it up down Park Lane with a gang of trannies, and looning about. When me and Tracie hung out, we were going off down Park Lane, getting hold of some Arab and not doing anything apart from ripping him off of a whole heap of money.

Tracie was from Bromley?

Her background was middle class, middle of the road. Her dad had done fairly well as a chartered accountant or something like that. She just was wild. I wasn't particularly wild at school, but I got wilder as I started going to more nightclubs and stuff, but I think the life made you wilder. We had this thing that no-one else was doing, prostitution, and hanging out in London, going down the Speakeasy and stuff, and then we'd go touring, across the country.

When did you first see the Sex Pistols?

I can't remember, everyone says you must remember your first gig, but I can't. It was something like . . . I saw them at a hall first some-where, then at the El Paradise club, definitely. I just thought they were the most brilliant thing I'd ever seen in my life. I don't think I was old enough to judge, but I just knew I had to know this group of blokes. There weren't many punks around at that time.

When did you start working at 430 King's Road?

I started the first day that Seditionaries opened. I worked the last two weeks of SEX, packing the old stuff up. Malcolm had got really fond of me by this time, I think he had a crush on me, but I didn't have a clue. I knew, but I was silly and young and flattered. I remember him saying he'd really like me to work in the new shop. So I said yes. That was when I stopped being friends with Siouxsie, cos I don't think she liked me for getting that job.

How did you get on with the other people in the Bromley Contingent, the other bands?

At first I got on with them really well, we were just like a big gang really. The gigs just consisted of the same people really and all of them I really liked, except for when me and Tracie headed off more towards the Pistols, cos we went on every tour, and we were the real steadfast fans; I think we became the most fannish of all. I couldn't really see Siouxsie running up to Birmingham on a hitch-hiking tour.

We went to France, actually, to that gig [at the Châlet du Lac, Paris, 3 September 1976].

What was that like?

Brilliant. We all piled into this van on the way to Paris. It was very uncomfortable, eight of us all piled in. Siouxsie had a topless bra on and we got out and there were just thousands of people outside the gates, and we had to try and get through this club with Siouxsie with nothing covering her tits.

What sort of reactions did they get, and did you get?

Well we were looked at, we were pretty mad, I was the short blonde spiky one and there was Siouxsie, the tall dark titless wonder, and there was Steve and Simon and Berlin, and they wanted to know who the hell we were, and there was a lot of aggravation, we were nearly knifed. Then John came out in one of those first bondage suits, it was a fantastic sight, and just stood there. Everyone just stood there in shock.

What happened on the gigs that they played around England?

The early gigs were pretty minor, there weren't that many people there. The most fantastic tour was the Anarchy one because by that time they'd got famous cos of the Grundy thing. By that time news had got round that these people were coming to town, so that's when it really got . . .

You were on the bus weren't you? What was that like?

It was really mad. It was very druggy, everyone was trying to stay awake all the time cos of the long journeys. We all had to go to Cleethorpes for the night, then we had to travel for nine hours to get to Poole the next day, so we had this nightmarish coach journey, and John was in a foul mood, and I was just enjoying myself. We got to Poole and the hotel was like a three-storey house, and we all clambered upstairs, three bands.

We went to our rooms and John said, 'I'm not going to stay here', and I said, 'Well you're gonna have to, this is where we've got.' He said, 'It's got nylon sheets on the bed.' 'But John.' 'I'm going on strike.' So I said, 'Come into my room.' So me Tracie, Nils and him all clambered in this room with two single beds, and he got on the floor with one of these nylon sheets over him and said, 'I'm not doing anything until we get out of here, I'm staying here.'

So we all did the same, and eventually Malcolm came in faffing around, oh dear oh dear, and he called the record company and got the Holiday Inn which was like six storeys, this enormous Holiday Inn overlooking the harbour, and we took over two floors of it. It just shows that when they wanted to get the money, they got it. That was Malcolm trying to save the bucks, the first hotel, and then realising he wasn't going to get away with it. And John acting like a real superstar by that time.

Who was the one out of the band you knew best?

I definitely knew John best. I think we got on the best, I liked the things he said. The others were really nice but they were much simpler. John was horrible all the time, and I found that fascinating. I was in awe of him. I think he had the most to say, but he washed himself out eventually.

He knew Malcolm better than everyone. He could see that Malcolm would've liked to have been up there and been Johnny Rotten if he could have been, but he was just Malcolm the manager. John knew that, so he had the one thing over him. I'm Johnny Rotten, you're Malcolm McLaren. I'm really famous, I'm the star. He played on that all the time.

Did he become more aggressive?

When I first ever met him he was really skinny, young, really sweet-looking, and quite naive in a funny sort of way, then he got more older looking, and confident and quite bossy, and quite nasty. It was fear, I think, fear of fame. You'd go places and people would recognise him, and he was quite frightened.

For all of us, one day we were walking around, then suddenly it was Johnny Rotten this, that and the other, kill him, you know, murder him. He was quite young, and I don't think he coped as well as he'd like to. He kept changing all the time, right up until the last time I saw him. He was very unaware, sexually, of himself. I don't think he'd really had much experience with women.

John was lovely to me, probably one of the best friends you could ever want. He was never horrible to me once, through the whole time. Maybe it was because I was young, and also because Malcolm liked me a lot, and he wanted me because Malcolm wanted me. There was that competition thing. There was that thing where Malcolm would ring up and say, 'Is Debbi there?', and he'd say, 'No, she's with me.'

I suppose I was quite tough really, and I was mucking around, and instead of being a groupie I was more like a friend of the band, so I wasn't just some girl hanging around the band, I was in some way contributing towards it, because I was working with Malcolm. On the Anarchy tour I paid my way by selling *Anarchy* magazines the whole time, I made fortunes.

We were in the magazine, so I would sell the magazine and say, 'Well that's me.' I wasn't just some groupie, I was working to publicise the band on the tour.

You lived with John for a while, didn't you?

Yeah, we went to live in King's Cross, and I stayed there for a long time. That was when I was working at Seditionaries, and before he bought his house in Gunter Grove, we all lived in a house together. That was paid for, and he moved in about eleven blokes, which was Wobble, Steve English, Anthony English, Paul Young, people like that, John Gray.

What were they all like?

Well, John Gray was his old friend from school, motorbike mechanic. Very nice. John did surround himself with nice people in a way, some of his oldest friends. John Gray was very quiet, record-collecting type, a piss-taker. They were all piss-takers, Wobble and everyone. They were all John's mates, he had to feel that he had his mates around him. They would riot and go mad, and John would go to sleep.

He must have gone really nuts, cos he was the figurehead of all that publicity.

He did, yeah. He got really angry about the band, he'd say, 'Oh, Steve's a wanker', and 'Paul's a wanker', cos I think he always wanted higher things for the band, you know? He'd get really annoyed about everything. So he'd come back and have all his supporters so he could shout at them and tell them, and he had his family who were really close to him. There was always all that support there.

But I think he was very frightened. Somehow John spent the early years totally surrounded by people, and then he lost everyone. I don't know why, cos I think he was a nice person really. I think he got confused about who really liked him, and who used him. Certainly I never felt that I used him, and I actually did genuinely like him, and I got incredibly upset when I realised that John thought I was one of the users.

Weren't some of his friends pretty violent though?

Well, they were, they were quite violent boys. Paul Young was mental, very working-class, they were all from his estate . . .

Which estate did he come from?

Six Acres.

How did you think he got on with his parents?

I think his mum adored him. He's very different from all the rest of the boys. I think John changed an awful lot when his mum died. He had a strange sense of doom about him. From all the fame, as it patterned out, John was becoming more weird. He got into more weird subjects. He was very influenced by lots of people, which I think shows how young he was then. He was very intelligent. I think he was very influenced by Linda Ashby, and he was quite into religious things.

What was it like working at Seditionaries?

I was there for a couple of years, full-time. It was good. When I first worked there it was really quiet, we used to open from eight until nine at night, it was me, Jordan and Michael. All I can say was it was very busy and a lot of hard work and a lot of fun, I really enjoyed it.

What was Vivienne like?

She wasn't around all the time, she left the shop for us to run, and she was off making things. She wasn't anarchistic, she really wasn't. She was pretty much, you've got to be here on time, do your work, she was a hard worker. There was no getting away with anything, with her. It was a very upmarket shop where people were terrified to walk in, we'd have people hovering outside the door for hours deciding whether they actually wanted to come in. Then we'd have customers, we could almost convince people they looked wonderful in anything. I actually got into the job quite a lot, and got into the styling side of it, and really did want people to look good, so I was quite honest about whether people looked a pile of crap in bondage suits or not.

Did you have any trouble with teddy boys?

Yeah, we did. We had a period at the beginning where it was lovely and peaceful, and we'd have people like Derek Jarman in, and everyone was toffee-nosed and it was the height of fashion; then we had these working-class lads in saying have you got a T-shirt for five pounds? It was so weird cos we were dressing people off the street, and we were dressing international designers. Then the teddy boy season started, and it was horrific, terrifying.

We hated the shop down the road, which was BOY, there was a war going on, they were ripping off everything we had in our shop, but they used to ring us up and say, 'Teddy boys on the go, quick', and we'd all scamper and put up bits of wood. And we did actually have a terrible time, they smashed in the windows at least four or five times. That was Chelsea football supporters as well, we really were hated up there. It got terrifying, we used to hide in the cupboards.

Did they come in?

Oh yeah, quite often they'd come in and we wouldn't see them and we'd suddenly see three football supporters and a couple of teds. We got to be really good with the teds, cos some of the older teds used to come in when it was Let It Rock, so they knew Vivienne and everything, and we got quite diplomatic with them. Look, you know, we're just doing our own thing . . . but it got quite heavy sometimes, and I'm really surprised that I never got my head kicked in.

389

Did they trash the shop, inside?

There was more violence out in the street than there was actually in our shop. I'm surprised how we managed to get away with it so much, and I think it had a lot to do with it once being Let It Rock. We had three framed T-shirts, one with Gene Vincent, and that was the one thing that they used to think, well if they're still putting up Let It Rock things, they must be all right. Also they knew Michael from the old days.

What did Vivienne do?

Vivienne's attitude was, the word 'seditionaries' means to seduce people into revolt, and her ideal was that you should make people revolt. She actually got off on it because people were rebelling against something they didn't want. She hated them, she thought they were repulsive and loathsome, but she liked the violence. Her attitude was, 'Don't be so ridiculous, stand up for yourself', and we'd say, 'Viv, there's a six-foot-two girl out there waiting to beat the shit out of me', but Vivienne was saying, 'Now don't you worry.'

There was a lot of that going on, Vivienne's political views, which were really hard to cope with, because they were not real. It was like, 'Anarchy, this is good, people are wearing our clothes, do you not realise they're going out there and they're fighting, they're showing the world what they've got', and me and Michael were in the broom cupboard, going, 'Yeah, but we're really scared!' Vivienne was a tough old bird, she really was.

What did you think of the band after the Grundy thing?

I still thought they were great, but I was really upset about Glen leaving. I missed Glen, because he made the band. There was the sex-maniac guitarist, and there was John the wild and outrageous person, then there was Glen who was meek and mild, and there was Paul. John stood out so much it made the band really unusual, but when Sid came along, it turned it into mayhem and madness. I quite missed Glen's peacefulness, though I don't suppose John would agree with that.

Why did he leave?

I think John wanted him out. It's funny, John really liked Sid cos he was his friend, but he didn't like him that much afterwards. John will say how much he loved Sid, now, but . . .

Where were you living when you were working at Seditionaries?

I hovered around at John's, then I had a place with Blanche somewhere in Chelsea. One of the back streets in Chelsea, one room, two beds. I stayed there for quite a long time. Life wasn't very organised. I used to rush off to work, and open up, and I'd been up all night, and when you're young you can handle it; even if you've been up all night, you look fine. Also I was taking drugs and stuff, keeping me going a lot of the time.

Were you on the boat trip? What do you remember about that?

I remember me and Tracie going on that, and it was really, really exciting. My memory of it is vague, but I remember it being a bit of a hoot, everyone pissed, then the band came on and I was standing near Wobble, and Wobble started throwing things out the window and he hit some journalist, and that was when all the violence started. I think it was 90 per cent caused by Wobble, actually.

Were you picked up by the police?

Yeah. In fact it was all Glitterbest, eleven of us. I think we were the people putting up the most resistance, probably. I remember Tracie being picked up and me jumping on someone's back and hitting this policeman, leaping on his back cos Tracie got caught, and I got dragged off to the cells. Then Malcolm put up money for us all . . .

Did the police give you a bad time?

They didn't really, they chucked me in a cell – I think they probably gave us all a pretty bad time, we were all pissed and laying all over the floor, it was pretty hectic. There was Jamie and me and Sophie and Boogie and Vivienne, I think . . . We were laying out on the floor, drunk, and they were throwing us into cells and screaming at us, and it got in the papers the next day.

What happened to Tracie? What did she die of?

Cancer. Leukaemia. I wasn't working at the shop at the time. I'd been kicked out of the shop, because John had left the band and I stuck up for him. So I lost contact completely, then one day I went up to The Water Rat in Chelsea, sitting outside, and I said to someone, 'How's Tracie?', and they said she was quite ill in hospital, she's got a cyst or something.

I tried to contact Vivienne to find out what was wrong and she wouldn't tell me. She said I wasn't allowed to go and see her, no way was I to go anywhere near her, so I didn't go to see her, and I went off for ages, and eventually I got a phone call from Johnny, actually, saying that she'd died. It was very quick, very sudden.

Was she very young?

About seventeen, eighteen. A pretty sudden death.

What was she like?

She was mad, but she was nice. She got into heroin in the end, when she was dying, which I thought was a bad thing. So it was like the last straw, people can only go so far, and some were getting more and more into drugs, and more and more down. It became a morbid time, people were popping off left, right and centre, it was like the aftermath; we'd had the fun, and suddenly John had left the band, the Pistols didn't know if they were coming or going.

Tracie took that very very hard, when the Pistols broke up, and I think partly the reason she got into heroin was that she got very upset. I went off with some mad guy who I had a bad time with for two years, and John got more withdrawn and into himself. Everyone around that scene was slowly falling apart really, cos when you've been in a close-knit thing and suddenly you're all just pushed away into your own direction, there's a sort of aftermath.

It was like the death of something.

Why do you think the band broke up?

John got really pissed off. Malcolm had had it with John, and John had had it with Malcolm and the band. Sid was very chaotic on the tour and everything, and John rang a couple of times from America saying he'd just had enough of it all. But I was surprised when they split up, I thought they wouldn't, I thought it wouldn't end. You know? – this isn't really happening, I'm sure it's just a row and it'll all be okay soon. But in fact it wasn't okay.

Did Malcolm and John get on well at the start?

I don't think they ever did really hate each other, it was a power thing. If you've got two powerful people, you're always going to have that clash of personalities. I think John all the time tantalised Malcolm, and Malcolm just drove John to tantalising him. It was a really odd friction between them. Their relationship was quite childish. Also, when you think of the way Malcolm has taken from people, and the way he's dropped people, he isn't very trustworthy.

We were all getting older, and we weren't any longer these kids who could be manipulated, we were all getting personalities of our own. It's really easy to dominate kids, but when you start getting older, he couldn't really handle that. I think that's when Malcolm started pulling out, when John started asking for real things, and all of us, in the shop . . . he must have started thinking, let's get down to some younger people, and he did.

What did you think of Glitterbest?

I got on with Jamie and Sophie quite well. When I lived in the Borough, Elephant and Castle, with Wobble, we moved into this really weird flat together; I used to pop round and see Jamie and Sophie a lot. I liked them out of all the Glitterbest people, I preferred them to Boogie. I think Jamie was brilliant actually, and he was a real support to Malcolm – which again, Malcolm used.

There were these children playing and then there was the grown-ups all around. But we were all Malcolm's workers really, it was a big organisation, me in the shop, Tracie in the shop, Jamie doing the graphics, Sophie doing the typing, Boogie doing whatever he was doing, Vivienne running round selling Anarchy T-shirts, and the Pistols selling records. It was a small organisation that got big.

And what do you think Malcolm wanted out of it?

He wanted fame and fortune, and what better way to get fame and fortune than to sell anarchy, really? I don't think, politically, he had one real feeling in his body about what he preached, when I think about it now. I think it was all to do with fame. But then again, one could say he was a great dictator. Certainly I was one of the children who got led into it.

CHAPTER SIX

The Team: Glitterbest

Steve Jones, Johnny Rotten, Glen Matlock, Paul Cook, Malcolm McLaren and Nils
Stevenson, spring 1976 (Ray Stevenson)

Glitterbest was the company set up in 1976 by Malcolm McLaren to incorporate the Sex Pistols' management team. Although McLaren and his lawyer, Stephen Fisher, were the only shareholders, many other people joined the payroll as the organisation around the Sex Pistols expanded – particularly after the group signed to EMI Records in October 1976.

Among the first recruits, in early 1976, were two brothers from North London, Nils and Ray Stevenson. They were joined in late summer by Sophie Richmond and Jamie Reid, fresh from activist politics. Also involved at various points were John Tiberi, Dave Goodman, Simon Barker, Barbara Harwood and, in the later days of The Great Rock'n'Roll Swindle, Sue Steward and June Miles-Kingston.

While the actual musicians in the Sex Pistols made the music, played the shows and bore the brunt of public disapproval, many of the people in and around Glitterbest provided the support that helped to make the group resonate so powerfully. This assistance was qualified by the management style that McLaren had learnt from the situationist movement: scission and expulsion.

Nils Stevenson

Sex Pistols' co-manager and key punk figure, pictured in many early shots of the group and their fans. Managed the Banshees from 1977 until 1982. Well-placed to see the group's interpersonal relationships, as well as their slow rise to fame during 1976. Very sharp, charming and amusing; a King's Road hustler and a true London boy.

I was brought up in Dalston, near the Balls Pond Road, until I was about eleven, when we moved to Finchley, which was horrendous, but Dalston was great. My first memories were in the late fifties when my brother Ray would have these parties around the house and we'd have all these rockers coming over, the coolest looking people I've ever seen. That stuck with me.

There was this area called the Waste, where there was a market on Saturdays and you'd see all the rockers hanging around the coffee bars. And of course it wasn't like that in Finchley – I felt very out of place there, cos my accent was wrong, and I ended up going to a private school so I was always a fish out of water.

When I was sixteen I went to art school in Barnet, doing an environmental design course, then decided I just wanted to get away and do something, cos I didn't have any knowledge of the outside world, I'd just gone from one institution to another. So I went off and I ended up working for Richard Buckle, ballet critic at the *Sunday Times*.

That was great fun, just had to dress up in this mad purple Edwardian suit and high-heeled shoes and open the door for Frederick Ashton and Rudolf Nureyev, and pretend to be his boy. The only person I wasn't allowed to meet was John Gielgud. Whenever he came round I had to be in a different room cos they thought he'd just jump on me!

I was just having fun, eating all this brilliant food, getting drunk all the time. There were two of us worked for this guy Buckle, Ian and

397

myself, and when Stravinsky died there was lots of tears around the flat, and Dickie went to the funeral in Venice, and when he came back there was this memorial service at a church in Covent Garden, and there's this picture of me and Ian in this incredible costume, laying a big wreath. So I've always liked dressing up . . .

There was an exhibition in this church in the piazza at Covent Garden. Buckle had seen the Warhol exhibition and loved Warhol, so he decided to do prints of himself and people he liked standing in front of Andy Warhol paintings. I got to be one of the people standing in front of the Warhols, and I was brought in to look after this exhibition that was going on in the church. That led on to the gala at the Coliseum called *The Greatest Show on Earth*.

That was just outrageous; it was to save a painting by Titian, *The Death of Actium*, for the nation. It had all the people I talked of before, Nureyev and Fontaine, Wayne Sleep. He got out all the original backdrops for the pieces, Picasso and Cocteau backdrops, but after that, there was nothing else to do. Buckle was getting very ill by then, and shortly after that he retired to the country, all his friends were dying, and I had to go and find something else to do.

I spent some time in France, then came back here and did some dreadful jobs, then about '75 I met Malcolm, I was going out with June Bolan . . .

Were you involved with music at all then?

I'd always been a big fan, although I was always more interested in what people were wearing than what they were playing – like the Hush Puppies that Mick Jagger was wearing, and where he bought them. At twelve or thirteen if I bought a record it was always an EP, because it was cheaper than an album and it had a picture of them on the front. People that looked groovy.

Did you start going out then?

I used to go from Finchley down to Dalston. I used to buy mod clothes down there at Joseph's and have it altered, and truck around with these funny haircuts, the Steve Marriott type of thing. I used to be a dead ringer for Steve Marriott. Then the mod thing went and Ray got into the hippy thing, and I got to know his friends, and I started hanging out with an arts group called the Exploding Galaxy. They lived in Balls Pond Road, and at weekends they used to smash up pianos and have be-ins and stuff like that.

How did you meet June?

I knew Marc. I always adored Marc, cos of Ray, really. Ray used to take pictures of Bolan and Bowie, he was very tight with them both, and when I was a kid I used to do these hippy paintings of Bolan and give them to him, so I got to know him and June then. Then I met June at a party in '74 or '75, and I gave her my address and she just shot over in the Ferrari one day when I was living in Barnes. We were together for nearly two years.

She was the first really intelligent woman I'd met, she was so well read and everything. I was twenty and she was thirty at the time. I always had a love of cars as well, that helped. She had this fantastic Ferrari Daytona, brilliant car, so it was nice trucking around in that. The funniest quote I read was when Marc and June split up, he told one of the papers, it's really great not being with June any more, cos I don't have to buy a new car every week.

What was the King's Road scene like then, pre-punk?

It was fun. It was all the older rock'n'roll types, centred round The Roebuck. And further down, at the Potter. After I split up with June I opened a shop with Lloyd Johnson in Beaufort Market. Doing sixties stuff. He already had Johnson's in Kensington Market. He lived up the road from me in Barnes, and he'd look after me when I was broke, he was very benevolent like that.

So we opened this shop that was an absolute disaster. I'd got to know Malcolm a little bit by then cos he used to come to June for advice. He was thinking about this band the Sex Pistols which he'd heard rehearsing at that point. June had passed herself off as being very knowledgeable about the music business, and so he'd approach her in The Roebuck and ask her for business advice mostly.

I think it was to impress as much as to get any advice, actually, cos then, those kind of people just thought of him as a freak from that mad shop. He didn't command a great deal of respect, he was always being busted and things, so the two topics of conversation were him asking June a bit of advice, and me asking him what was going on with the court cases.

Were you aware of the kids hanging around there or not?

Alan Jones was one of my best buddies, and I used to hang out at the Portobello Hotel when he worked there, cos I could get some free drinks and something to eat. Alan used to take me into the shop before I knew Malcolm, cos he bought all that stuff, as you know. Every single thing they ever produced. But there weren't many kids hanging about there until after the Pistols really.

When they were doing the ted stuff there was Jones and Cook and people like that, but they weren't the real hardcore types that went in there later. When they had just turned to the pervy gear, you had old men going in there to buy their pervy stuff, and the odd freak like Alan. But people like Alan were very rare. He was the only one I knew of at that time that used to wear that stuff in the street.

So you got to know Malcolm . . .

I got to know Vivienne first, I used to hang around with her a lot, I used to really fancy her. But nothing ever came of it, cos then I got to know Malcolm as well. They'd both come over to Barnes and drink this hundred-year-old Scotch that I used to get access to. They'd often bring Chrissie as well, the four of us used to go out to Andrew Logan's parties and places like that, and eventually Malcolm asked me to come and work with him on the Sex Pistols.

Had they played by that stage?

When he asked me to do that, I saw them at the Marquee, and it was so great, I thought it was the best thing I'd ever seen, and after that it was me bugging him. Originally he asked me to co-manage them, this has always been a bone of contention, but once I saw them play I decided I definitely wanted to do it, and I don't really remember what arrangement we made . . .

What were they like when you saw them at the Marquee?

Completely mad. It was a bit like Iggy when he played at King's Cross, it was fantastic, so exciting. The band were all over the place, not playing very well, and Rotten saying, 'I've always wanted to watch this group play', and just walked off stage with this long microphone lead, and sits in the audience, and sings along when he wants to, and throws Jordan across the floor, throws chairs about, and I knew I just had to be involved.

Why did you turn them down before?

I'd met Steve and Paul in the pub. They were being very nice to me and I just thought, why are they being so nice? They were being nice cos they just were nice, and I wasn't used to it in the King's Road, people were all star-fuckers one way or another. These two cockney boys being pleasant made me feel odd. They didn't look anything, they weren't wearing the groovy clothes or anything, they just looked like a couple of football hooligans.

So I thought I wanted to see the group first. I didn't see Rotten at all until I went to the Marquee. The next one they did was Andrew Logan's party, and then after that I was working for them.

They'd done some art schools and places like that, but the Marquee was their first proper venue.

I think they smashed up some of Eddie and the Hot Rods' equipment that night...

An artistic statement...

Quite right, they were a bunch of crap. They were banned immediately from the Marquee as a result of that, which was probably just as well.

So what did you do?

I just did anything that wasn't being done. I spent a lot of time just driving them about. We went on ridiculous journeys up North. Malcolm would give us just enough money to get there, then you had to fend for yourself, so Steve would steal chocolate bars to eat. You really had to make sure you got your money, and people didn't want to pay, after seeing the group, cos they were used to these R'n'B groups, cos that was the way they were being sold.

These places like Barnsley or Hull. Lots of frightening times, playing these really straight places in Hull, in front of these fishermen.

They'd fight, and I used to surprise myself, cos I'm totally non-aggressive, but your adrenalin would be so whacked up, I'd be up on stage sometimes, pushing punters off, kicking people and stuff.

We had to call the police in at Barnsley, this awful place out in the sticks, there was no buildings about or anything, just this pub in the middle of nowhere. But the place filled up and things got a bit hairy, so I made the landlord call the police so we could be escorted out. That was one, and in Hull things got very nasty, we had to high-tail it out of there.

Why was that? Would Rotten bait the crowd?

Yeah, he'd get quite lippy, put them down and things like that, but it wasn't too bad. It was just the look of the group and their lack of professionalism used to incense these people. They wanted a hippy group with long hair, they could accept that, but these kids really pissed them off.

How did you work out the money situation?

You'd try to get it up front, but if you couldn't, you'd play it by ear. If it looked like it was going to be all right, if you were in a more sophisticated or cosmopolitan kind of place – like Liverpool – you could be sure of getting the money afterwards, but if you were in some dodgy place like Hull or Scarborough, you'd get the money up front. You knew you'd always get paid all right at Eric's, it was a younger, hipper crowd, but there was a lot of pubs on that tour and they were the really dodgy ones.

Did you ever get left without any money to get home?

Many times we'd have to put what money we had in our pockets together to get home. We never actually got stuck. We'd have the cheapest, cheapest vans. We had one to go to Scarborough that wouldn't go up hills, so we had to look at the Ordnance Survey map. I remember Glen worked it out, this ridiculous route, all the way around everywhere, hundreds of bloody miles, but it was flat, so we could actually get to the venue.

You'd tell Malcolm about all these problems when you got home, and he'd be very apologetic, but the same thing would happen again the next week. You knew you had to fend for yourselves. He was doing his shop; you know, if the group happened, well, fine, but it was all advertising for the shop, the main priority was always the shop. He wanted to quit the group many times, as did Rotten.

Why was that?

Malcolm was all right initially in that period, because he could just get rid of the group then and not lose money, he'd probably break even. After that, when the hustle was on for record companies, the pressure was getting to him and he'd often talk about quitting, cos I don't think, at times, he understood what was going on. You gotta remember that he went into it wanting the Bay City Rollers, and it was typical of Malcolm that it was his inadequacies that made things happen.

Did he actually say that, that he wanted the Bay City Rollers?

Yeah, of course. He was a big fan of Tam Paton. He'd met him at The Portobello and he was always terribly in awe of powerful people. He loved the idea of Larry Parnes, the Svengali manipulator, but he ended up with these mad kids, these hooligans.

What were they like at that stage, when you started working with them?

Rotten was very shy and unsure of himself. Steve was still the wide boy, Steve and Paul would always be out together. Glen was the out-cast, no-one ever wanted to share a room with him or anything. They didn't really get on with him, I don't know why; still, there's always one like that in a group. They have to pick one, as the scapegoat, fine, and their life could carry on. I think they thought he was a bit middle-class in his attitudes as well, and they didn't like that. Very class-conscious.

Rotten would generally want the company of everybody but would be too insecure and would put on this weird front all the time and wander off by himself, kind of watching people to see if they had noticed him doing it. Terribly shy. I always used to share a room with John, Steve and Paul would share a room, so what Glen would do, I haven't a clue!

403

Did John know what he had got himself into, or was he just along for the ride?

I think he was just along for the ride originally. His friend John Gray was the musicologist, he'd always be pumping Rotten full of ideas, playing him Herbie Hancock records, *Crossings* and all that stuff, geeing him up. I think it impressed Gray that Rotten was in this group. But I don't think John thought of it as a career. Perhaps Steve and Paul did.

What were they like in the van? Who used to sit up front?

I think Rotten always insisted on going in the comfy seat! 'I'm the star, fuck off.' It was probably Steve and John in the front with me . . .

Did they used to bicker?

Oh yeah. Ridiculous arguments going on. You can imagine how petty John can be about anything, depending on his mood. It could be quite uncomfortable with all four of them together. It was all superficial, as soon as they'd be on their own, everyone would be sweet as a nut. Never anything important until about six months after I'd been with them and then things started to get really strained. John was being quite serious about splitting.

Were they on a wage?

Not until they signed with EMI. Most of them were on the dole so they were getting some money.

No wonder Steve was thin . . .

He wasn't on the dole or anything. He couldn't get any money, so he was really hustling about. We'd try and have as much money as we possibly could when we went out on the road. You'd come back with five or ten quid and Malcolm would keep it or whatever, but it wouldn't be a great deal of money.

Do you remember the fight at the Nashville?

Yeah. That was just nonsense, wasn't it? Vivienne got up to dance or something and someone sat in her seat. No, she sat in someone else's seat. It was ludicrous. I couldn't believe seeing Malcolm wade in. I was shocked! Glen hit someone over the head with his bass, I remember seeing Steve dive in. I think John was thrashing about with the mike stand. Ray took a picture of it. It was just lunacy. But they were really good gigs, the Nashville ones. That's when things really started coming together.

What was people's reaction to them at that stage?

It was funny, some people used to shout out, 'David Bowie!' We couldn't understand it, as if that was the nearest thing people could think of. People would stop in the street and look at John.

Were they taking any drugs at all then?

No. Only speed. It wasn't there a lot, but if there was anything about, it was speed. John was doing it mostly. I think Sid used to get it for him, Sid was a speed freak.

When did they start gaining confidence? When did they start getting good?

Around the time of the Nashville. They weren't playing very sophisticated music, were they? It was just a matter of keeping in time with each other. Steve started practising hard at home in Denmark Street. Glen could play, as you know, and Paul could keep time very well. Steve getting a bit more dexterous, and Rotten learning some discipline – because before then he'd just go, 'Fuck it', in the middle of a song and stop singing.

At the 100 Club once, they'd just done a couple of songs and John was just fed up with it, and he started to leave, he got off the stage and walked up the stairs. And Malcolm saw and shouted, in front of everybody – mind you there weren't many people there, I think that was part of the reason John was fed up, cos everybody there had seen them before – Malcolm shouted, 'You get back on that stage or you're over.' Really furious, and John did; got straight back on the stage and did the whole set, and even I think a couple of encores.

Were you aware of Steve and Siouxsie and Simon and all those people?

I wasn't aware of them until they started inviting the group to parties. I remember being very taken with Siouxsie as soon as I saw her.

I thought, yeah, a little star. We got invited to some parties – real sexy parties where everyone ended up fucking each other on the floor. It was really good fun. I think it was Berlin's place, out towards Bromley. Then another time, Billy Idol had a party. They always ended up as these orgies, it was great really.

What was the first Screen on the Green gig like?

It was great. The most memorable thing about it was Steve always threw up before he went on stage, always, without fail, cos he was so nervous. So he opened one of Roger Austin's filing cabinets. But the funny thing was, the next time, he remembered where he'd done it the last time and did exactly the same thing again. He could be quite piggy sometimes.

That was when I first became aware of Siouxsie I suppose, cos she was dancing on stage with Debbi and Tracie, and you saw this nice balance, a female Rotten kind of thing, only much more sexy in a conventional kind of way.

It was quite packed, and with the films as well, the Kenneth Anger movies, it was a marvellous event, but very hippy in a way. Malcolm and I both arranged it, the whole thing, we had carte blanche to do what we wanted, and both being from that arty scene, one way or another, you came up with a very 1967 type of event really.

It was a big thing at the time that punks hated hippies, but now it seems there are a lot of similarities . . .

The people in control were a lot of old hippies, weren't they? There were some very bright people, and the hippy things that you remember were the things that were done by the bright hippies. The thick hippies didn't register because they didn't fucking do anything. But all the artistic, intellectual people who picked up on it and could be of help were old hippies that had cut their hair.

What about the Paris trip? You were over there for what, three or four days?

It was so refreshing, that trip, playing this fantastic place that was absolutely packed. It was a riot to get in, and the punters had no idea what the group was actually like, and they were absolutely devastated, really pissed off, when the group played, but it was marvellous to get out, and everyone got very close again, the whole group was very close for the whole trip.

Billy Idol drove his van over, didn't he, and the Bromley people slept in the van. It was fucking great. But the group kept Siouxsie and all those people at arms length, it had got a bit elitist in that way; already, by Paris, the group had got a bit full of themselves and they were keeping the crazy fans at arm's length. I think perhaps Steve and Paul were embarrassed by the way Siouxsie looked. John would open up to them a lot more.

They must have felt a bit weird about the way they were being packaged, at some point?

I wasn't really aware of that. They got pissed off when they had to start paying for their clothes, but that was all petty stuff. When things were going well and they saw results, it was fine.

What was Malcolm doing to manage them? Getting gigs, looking for contracts . . . ?

Yeah. He was such a workaholic, when he did put his mind to doing Pistols business, he was 100 per cent doing it. He was working out of Helen's flat in Bell Street for quite a while, cos he'd split with Vivienne for some reason. Dryden Chambers was later, that was around the time they signed to EMI.

Did you ever see them write numbers, or compose?

I saw Steve work out his bits a lot, but I don't think I ever saw John doing it. Rehearsing was such a racket, and getting a new song together was such a pain that when they were doing it I'd generally go out.

Did you go to the recording sessions with Dave Goodman?

Goodman made them do take after take, and it would never be right, and there was no dropping in, it was always do it again, do it again. Completely pissed off.

What was the live sound actually like?

One remembers it coming together and being pretty good, but that's back then. It would probably sound crap now. You saw them develop from not being able to play, to being pretty tight, so after three or four months . . .

Do you remember the Punk Festival?

The Pistols were up in Scotland at the time, doing a gig, The Clash were on that night. It was the time when things started happening, you got exciting people coming to the gigs. The band were excited at that time to get a review in *NME*, I remember Steve running out on Wednesday to get the music papers to see if there were any reviews.

Where was John living at the time?

He was in Finsbury Park, at his mum's, then he finally got a flat in Hampstead with Sid. It was a real dive, horrible. Sid was always at the gigs, but that's all. You'd see him at the shop sometimes. He was nice, a nice kid that was doing too much speed. John used to tell me that Sid was very bright, and not to be deceived, I used to give him a lot more credit than some people did. He became the caricature punk, though, didn't he?

I was wondering where John's anger came from.

It was his Catholic upbringing, he was a textbook-case fucked-up Catholic. He had every Catholic neurosis in the book. He was terrified of sex. Absolutely terrified.

How did Nora come on to the scene?

She was Chris Spedding's girlfriend, and we used to go to Chris's place in Wimbledon, and there was this really sixties-looking groupie type wandering around, she really had that vibe, like Anita Pallenberg. Then she started coming to gigs and Steve got hold of her, and she was so rich and good-looking, Steve spent a lot of nights with her, for whatever reason.

Did the group eventually sign a management contract with Malcolm?

Yeah, I split shortly after that, cos I was so furious. I looked for my name, and my name wasn't on it. This was just before EMI, and I told them not to sign it, basically. Malcolm had it drawn up when he realised there was a deal in the offing. I remember reading the contract at Denmark Street and saying to the band, 'Don't sign it', because I could see how heavily in favour it was of Malcolm.

I can't remember the ins and outs, but there were some other things in it that weren't kosher at all, so I was pissed off because I wasn't on there, and I thought I was getting a percentage of the management. I'd always been led to believe that I'd get some points out of it, and I still had some loyalty to the group, and Rotten was saying, 'It's all right, if you don't get a part of it, I'm leaving', and all this, which was all nonsense.

Then they signed with EMI, and Malcolm was going, 'Come on, boy, get in the picture, get in the picture', and I wouldn't get in the picture, I was so furious, and I just fucked off, everyone went down to Louise's and I threw a moody all night, and left shortly after that.

Do you remember that Notre Dame gig, the first one?

Yeah, Glen stuck his bass through the only legitimate piece of equipment. I was egging him on, actually. On the side of the stage. I just thought it was marvellous to see Glen going mad, it was brilliant. He was playing up to the role, I think. He stuck his bass right through this amp, and he looked really happy for about a minute then he sort of went 'Oh fuck', when he realised what he'd done. It was the first time he'd really let go in an angry way.

Steve was always such a wanton character, and what's so special about him is he does exactly what he wants to do, the second he wants to do it. It's quite remarkable to be able to do that, but to see Glen letting go like that was absolutely marvellous.

Do you know where John was getting the lyrics from?

I never thought about where the lyrics were coming from at all. It's remarkable that John would have come up with those lyrics on his own, but I don't remember Malcolm sitting down with John ever, and telling him how to write a song. In retrospect, I think he's a lot brighter than I gave him credit for at the time.

That's what was wrong with the Pistols in a way, they were too bloody good, for their purpose. They became the style of the time

409

because they were so good. Instead of demystifying it and showing that anyone could do it, they proved that anyone couldn't do it, because they were so good.

I see Lydon very much as the X factor that Malcolm didn't bargain for.

Right after they signed I think things were all right, because they had a huge foe in the shape of the media and the record company and they got strength from each other. Malcolm was very much in charge then because there were so many problems that they needed Malcolm to sort out. So things were probably all right. Then there was an ego-battering between Malcolm and John.

Do you remember the Grundy incident?

I was down at the Roxy rehearsal room down in Harlesden, they were meant to be rehearsing there before they went out on the tour. It's funny to think that Malcolm would have it all planned out, they'd have this sound stage, PA and everything, and they were meant to rehearse, but they got the Grundy show at the last minute, and they were whisked off there in a limo. I didn't even know about it until late that night, when the shit had hit the fan.

Was Malcolm shitting himself?

He was terrified. We were still full of the ethic of upsetting things and being bad boys, confrontation, demystification, all the situationist crap, and I found it remarkable that Malcolm was so upset about it.

Did they do much rehearsing at the Harlesden stage?

No, the tour started pretty soon after that, and it was madness, they just couldn't play anywhere, it was ridiculous. Me and Mickey Foote were setting up this PA, pulling the bins out of the truck and setting them up, knowing that we weren't going to play. Sure enough we'd be told, 'Sorry boys, it's off', and we'd pack it all up and back to the bloody hotel, nothing to eat or anything and off the next day, it was miserable.

Why nothing to eat?

No-one ever thought about getting the roadies anything to eat, it was a mess.

The group used to just sit around, giggle a lot; and they were travelling in style for the first time, they had one of those big buses, so they were all right about it. We were getting tons of press, so you felt something was happening. That's when Malcolm was doing very well. He stuck to his guns when the civic authorities insisted that the group play, and Bernie really wanted them to do it. Cos The Clash weren't getting any publicity out of the tour, the Pistols were.

What was the relationship between the bands like on the tour?

On the tour it was all right. It was always all right with The Heart-breakers, but with The Clash it was like, the foe. On the tour it was all right, but in London the two groups wouldn't hang out together or anything like that.

What were the actual gigs like?

When they did actually get to play, they were bloody good. There was a party atmosphere and a lot of tension was released when they got to play.

How did the band react to all the publicity? Did they get paranoid at all?

I think that's when they felt they were really right. Everyone felt that it was right and important, what we were doing, cos we'd come out of that little Soho, Andrew Logan thing, playing the 100 Club and having a few fans, and suddenly they had this huge spotlight on them. They thought it was great.

When did it go sour then, cos it seems to have gone sour some time over the next six months.

I'd gone by then. When Sid came in, things started going very wrong, and knowing Malcolm, I think he'd probably got a bit bored. He never was all that closely involved. He'd backed off quite a while before that, really, I think it was all getting very big and they weren't really ready for it. Which was probably just as well.

I shouldn't think Sid was, anyway.

No, he certainly wasn't.

So you left after the Anarchy tour?

Yeah, before Sid joined.

Is the story true that Malcolm offered you two or three hundred quid for the year's work?

Yeah. Three hundred pounds.

Did you take it, or did you tell him to fuck off?

Fuck, I took it, I was broke! Jesus! Definitely. He would have been quite happy if I'd told him to fuck off, he could have kept his three hundred pounds.

Ray Stevenson

The Sex Pistols' first official photographer. His stylised pictures filled the music press in 1976 and early 1977, before his expulsion from Glitterbest, and served as an excellent introduction to the group. He self-published the first Sex Pistols photo book, No Future, *in 1978. Interviewed at his then flat near the Thames in Bankside, London.*

I grew up in Dalston until I was fourteen, then the family moved out to Finchley, which I hated. As a music fan, I heard Buffy Sainte-Marie was on the radio one day, and something clicked, I said I was a photographer and blagged my way into her reception. That felt really easy, and I went on from there with folk stuff, until I saw Hendrix. That changed me a bit.

I got a couple of things published, Sandy Denny was the first. But I was only sixteen or seventeen. I took a picture of Sandy Denny and gave it to her, and somebody else would say, take it to *Melody Maker*. Karl Dallas was the music writer of the time, he started saying to bring stuff in. It wasn't a living. I had a job at the BBC starting about '74. I hardly did any photos, it was all darkroom.

Nils was working at Beaufort Market, I think he was doing American stuff. He had the hots for Vivienne, and she was going on about the Sex Pistols and he got interested from there, and the stall thing just died anyway. I'd had my fill of music. I hadn't been to a gig for so long, and Nils had free tickets for this show, and he wanted photos, so it was a bit of help I could do. I think I first met Malcolm when I took the St Albans pictures to Bell Street.

What were they like at St Albans?

I'm sure I would have thought they were terrible. It was different altogether. There was a sudden point when I realised how good they were. It was probably the 100 Club, that telepathy, tension thing, where Rotten would be slagging off the audience, and Steve and Paul would be doing something, and they would just go into a number at the perfect moment. Rotten's control. I was seeing them very much as amateurs, and to imagine this bozo kid from Finsbury Park, with no schooling, no history of music at all, was phenomenal.

Did he have that at St Albans?

I don't think there was enough audience there to work with. I suspect he was a bit arty, and there was a fair element of Malcolm in it, so it would be coming out of an art angle rather than an excitement angle.

Did you realise that the pictures were going to be used on hand-outs and stuff like that?

Malcolm liked the St Albans stuff, which I didn't think was that special, but there was an element of me working for free, which obviously made me quite interesting. I remember him ordering some photos for use on handbills, but I didn't know how they were going to be used until I actually saw them. I think he paid for prints. After my expulsion from Glitterbest, I totted up everything I ever got from Malcolm and it came to £96 in two years.

What was John like?

He was great in a room with two other people in it. Make it three, and he started being Johnny Rotten – 'Why are you so ugly?', and charming little comments like that. I think the persona was always there, in its embryonic state. He was excessively ugly, as you can see in the St Albans pictures, he obviously had no luck with girls, so the defence mechanism was to be either funny or aggressive, and that's the one he opted for. Tempered with humour. Acid comments. I don't think I ever heard him tell a joke.

Was Malcolm very much in the background in the early days?

Certainly in the background of the band's image, but he worked really hard. Regardless of what time he went to bed, he was in the office at 9.30, ten o'clock, through till six. He was very impressive in that way. He was really hustling, but then he had to, cos he didn't really know what he was doing.

414

What was the idea of the photo shoot, when you took a day around Soho?

We'd done some live stuff, but music papers go through phases of wanting lots of live stuff, then glamour, shirts off, pictures of pretty boys, all that. Then they want particular themes, so the wandering round London was what the music papers wanted at the time. It was a walk around London with some kids, having a good time.

What were the Spedding sessions like?

It was the band's first time in the studio, a learning process for them. Spedding didn't inspire me with a great deal of confidence. They went in for demo tapes, and that was what came out, decent sound on everything, and no playing about.

Did you enjoy the 100 Club Punk Festival?

Yeah, a lot. I was taking photos all the way through, but it felt like a breakthrough, a consolidation of the movement, if you like. It was a fairly insular group of about twenty or thirty people, for whom no other music existed.

What was the reaction of the audience on the Paris trip?

They didn't like it. There were a couple of people who seemed to understand it, some word-of-mouth thing, explaining the aesthetic, but basically there were forty-year-olds in tuxedos and stuff, who would probably have gone to the Hippodrome or something. This was the era of John Travolta, and they were very surprised. I don't think the club really knew what they were getting.

In Paris I was complaining, because the Pistols had a particular hard loudness in their PA, Fender stacks. And Glen said, 'You should do what I do, wear earplugs!' I didn't realise he'd been wearing earplugs through all of these gigs, for months. He took me to this chemist, and he even knew the French for earplugs, and he saved my evening.

What did Malcolm buy Steve for his birthday in Paris?

A woman. Isn't that obvious?

When we got back after the Anarchy tour, Malcolm dropped us all off at Denmark Street, and he gave everybody a fiver each and we went to some pizza joint. Steve ordered the food and disappeared. We thought he'd gone to the bog or something, then he came back, ate his food and then asked for money to pay for his food. He'd just slipped out and spent ten minutes with some hooker. The man was insatiable.

Can you tell me about the session you did for the *Anarchy in the UK* fanzine, of all the Bromley Contingent?

That was at Linda's place, she had a suite at the St James' Hotel. I turned up there and I'd hardly met any of these people at that point. She told me to set up in the kitchen, which was awful, so I set up in the living room, took a couple of snaps and went back to the kitchen, which had by then been covered in graffiti. So we moved back into there, it looked just right.

Malcolm organised the session, although he wasn't there, he just called up various people and told them to turn up and get their picture taken. I don't think the *Anarchy* magazine had been thought of at that point. One of the purposes of the Pistols was to act as clothes horses for Malcolm's clothes, and people still weren't seeing them, so the idea was to get them photographed and published.

The problem with that session was that if the band had been there, we could have got the pictures into *Sounds* and *NME*. But there was just a bunch of fans. Hence the *Anarchy in the UK* magazine.

What did you think needed to be done when you photographed the Pistols?

I don't think I was creating anything for them, their look was down to them and Malcolm. My job was to show newspaper readers what they were doing, as much in focus as possible. There was teaching them to be photographed, as well. I used to try to show them the contact sheets, so that next time they could mentally refer to the contact sheets and remember what didn't look right.

Were they good subjects?

Yes and no. They were good because they did things, but then there was the pose that they didn't want to be photographed, they saw being photographed as part of the ageing rock star machinery which had to be rejected, at the same time as wanting to be photographed.

What was the band like before Grundy?

I don't think they were very different, except that Steve had the biggest change. He was always the joker, but he didn't get over the shock for some time. He never really got back into his old form. He would probably have taken it seriously if he could have understood. He was illiterate, so all the newspaper stuff he had to either have read to him, or else got the feel of it from other people, their attitude to what was going on. He had to watch himself, because being jokey, naughty, it could be in the papers the next day.

He had to put a lid on it?

Not consciously, but it came as a shock that being himself could stir up all this trouble. I think Malcolm must have given him a telling off after the Grundy show, before he realised what the consequences were, and how they could be used.

He was the main instigator on the Grundy show?

The only one. It's very strange, how with that and all the subsequent publicity, it was always Steve – the spitting and the sick and whatever – it was always Steve, with this boring name, Steve Jones. But Johnny Rotten makes better copy, so Rotten got credited with most of it.

What was the atmosphere on the Anarchy tour like?

Rather like school holidays, with guitars instead of bucket and spade. Whoopee, we're all going to Derby, Leeds, etcetera. Leaving London, there was a feeling that we were escaping from all that pressure, not realising that it was waiting for us up there as well. EMI were being funny, so it was away from the EMI situation. It may have started Glen on his road to alcohol appreciation. It did with me, cos all we could do was check into motels, and drink.

What was the atmosphere like when they were recording at Wessex?

I don't think they knew enough about it to find it difficult. They didn't know what to do, and there was no-one there to tell them anything. Dave Goodman didn't really know, and somebody said it was like chucking mud at a wall. I made some suggestion about solving a problem over Steve's guitar sound, and Malcolm said,

417

'He's just a photographer, shut up.' But I still knew more about it than Goodman.

Did you ever get any money out of it at all?

The same as Nils. He was co-manager through all of this, and as soon as Malcolm got the EMI money, it was, 'Well, Nils, you can be a roadie now.' Nils says, and I tend to agree with him, that he held the band together. Malcolm was doing the stuff in the office, which was good and necessary, but Nils was getting them fed, and patching up the arguments between John and Glen, and between John and Malcolm.

What was John and Malcolm's relationship?

There must have been a love of one kind or another for it to have turned into the kind of hate that continues now.

Why did you stop working with the Pistols?

Because I was still just about the only punk photographer. *Time Out* asked me to do some pictures of BOY clothes, and I asked Vivienne for suitable models, and she went crazy. *Time Out* are the enemy, BOY are the enemy, and therefore I was the enemy as well. And pretty much threw me out of the shop. Nobody told me, I didn't know what their feelings were about these people.

A couple of days later, Malcolm and I had agreed that I was going to get the exclusive on the Screen on the Green gig. Then I got a call from Malcolm on the day, saying, 'We don't want you there.' I asked why, and he said, 'It's none of your business.'

Have you spoken to them since?

I said hello to Vivienne once. She said hello first. In fact she and Malcolm turned up at the pub with Nils and Cookie. She said hello, Malcolm said nothing, and I didn't want to be there, so I left. Then Nils started working for Malcolm again, and I went up to the office and we all went for something to eat. I went along, and he was so entertaining, I really enjoyed the evening.

What happened for you through '77?

418

I took pictures of all the punk bands, and by then Nils was managing Siouxsie, so there was some involvement there, though not as great as with the Pistols.

Were you surprised that it fanned out so strongly?

I'd been through it before with the hippy thing, and there must have been a point where I made the comparison, which was the same in reverse, the uniform of nonconformity.

When did you put out the first Sex Pistols book, '78?

Yeah, that was after I'd got the boot from Malcolm, and the band was still going, so it was the obvious thing to do. I had loads of problems with printers and designers – you can't do your own book unless you're an NGA member, all that.

Did Malcolm try to stop you?

I finally did it all myself and printed 2,000 copies on my own, and I think I gave a copy to Steve, knowing it would get back to Malcolm. I wasn't hiding anything. The cover was bright yellow, with the Pistols' logo on it. I got a writ, saying they were going to injunct the book, on the grounds that the distinctive yellow colour was owned by Glitterbest! The Pistols logo they probably had a case for, assuming that they actually paid Jamie for it anyway.

So I was obliged to go to a lawyer myself and it was great. He took each paragraph . . . 'Glitterbest representing the popular group known as the Sex Pistols', for which the defence was, there is no popular group called the Sex Pistols. Cos there wasn't at that time. The colour yellow was easy. That cost me £350 and I never heard from Glitterbest at all after that, until Stephen Fisher tried to sue me again over the sentence about him in the book, on the court case.

Dave Goodman

Sex Pistols' first regular live sound-man, and producer of many
seminal studio performances, including their July 1976, October
1976 and January 1977 sessions. Interviewed at his house near
Crystal Palace, South London. An unreconstructed hippy, good-
natured, full of rollicking – if sometimes tall – tales.

How did you get involved in the first place?

Me and a mate, Kim Thraves, had a PA hire company called Sound
Force. I'd spent about eight years in a pro band, backing all these
American artists who'd come over. Drifters, Ben E King, Flirtations.
In off periods we'd bang out this semi-psychedelic stuff, Steely Dan
meets the Average White Band. Brass section and Hammond organ.
We put an album out on DJM in early 76.

Albion phoned up one night, and the van was still loaded up, to do
a gig at the Nashville – fifteen quid, just a young band, their first gig
or something, they're called the Sex Pistols. They were support band
to The 101ers, and they were using our PA as well, a typical Albion
con. They turned up late, didn't do a soundcheck, but they were nice
enough guys, except for John, who was a bit stand-offish.

Malcolm had taken the band out to see Eddie and the Hot Rods
and the Count Bishops and everyone before they started gigging, and
he'd wind them up the whole time. He'd talk about the beer-gutted
apathetic old farts out front, they need fucking shaking up, don't
they? Their version of 'Substitute' was so bad it was good, and their
attitude was, if you don't like it, you can fuck off. God knows how
they got away with it. It was great, that attitude.

People had got used to tame bands, playing really tight, and when
they came along, it was electric. I really thought they were the hottest
band in the world, at the time. I went up to Malcolm, asked if they
had any more gigs, and he said, 'You're the first person who's offered

us any help.' We did another one there, where it was their own gig, all Malcolm's art-school people came along in their Roxy Music gear. Then we moved over to the 100 Club.

What did Joe Strummer think of it?

That first night at the Nashville was when Strummer went crazy for the Pistols, kicked our monitors in, and left The 101ers a few days later to get The Clash together. We had to go down and kidnap Mickey Foote from the squat and hold him to ransom to get the speakers replaced.

Did you go around with them in the van?

Yeah, we'd hire the van and pick them up, on a little float, it was all done hand-to-mouth. Had to make sure you got paid. We had some good times up North. It was good that Malcolm got them up there. The gigs were varied.

Did they improvise at all on stage?

They'd jam a bit when they got on stage, making sure everything was working, and it turned into something they called Flowers of Romance, after Sid's first band. They'd be stoned, we turned them on to dope. They would have got into it anyway, but we had the supply.

How did the band get on?

I think Glen felt that they didn't live up to his expectations, musically, and didn't see what they did have. Glen would have taken to heart things that John said in rehearsal. Kim and me used to talk to John a lot, boosting his confidence.

Where did John get the ideas for his lyrics?

He used to do a lot of acid. He might have got a lot of things from Malcolm.

How did Malcolm and John get on?

Something happened between them that we don't know about. Malcolm and John were very close at one point, likewise Malcolm and Sid, but he didn't want to be John's father figure. Malcolm reckoned

421

it was the Catholicism, that you thought if you did something wrong, you could be forgiven for it. But to me, it was paranoid shit.

What were the Denmark Street demos in July done for?

They needed some good tapes. I heard the Spedding tapes just after they came out of the studio, and they didn't happen. They sounded like rough mixes, guitars not loud enough. I said I could do better with my 4-track, so they said, 'Do it then.' We recorded all the first stuff in Denmark Street, over two weeks. They'd play live, maybe four or five takes of each song, then overdubs. I think we overdid it with the guitar overdubs, but they worked.

Is it the remix or the original on [Sex Pistols bootleg album] *SPUNK*?

Good question. I think they were the originals on *SPUNK*.

What was the Chelmsford Prison gig like?

It was the day Paul quit his job, so we had a big piss-up. Jonh Ingham came along, Malcolm didn't. We had some Thai grass before we went in there, and they let us in.

It's a top-security prison, and we were talking to this bloke who was coming up for parole. Hawkwind was the last band they'd had, passed acid out, played for ten hours. They let the guys in, Ingham had to stay backstage in the dressing room. The warders telling us, 'Don't talk to anyone', people were passing us letters.

This bloke Thor came in, six foot eight, muscles like you wouldn't believe, goes right to the front and sits down with his right-hand man. The band's really late coming on, they're getting wound up, and John comes on and yells, 'Fucking wankers! The Queen sends her regards.' The guards couldn't believe it. John changed the words of every song so it was directed at them. Very clever.

After the first song, he goes, 'If you don't like it, you can fucking go home. Stand up and dance. Where's the rules, let's have a riot.' After the second number all the black guys got up, wanted to be taken back to the cells. Then Thor stripped off, threw all his clothes on stage. No-one else would, and the guards said, if you hit him over the head, you'd just break your truncheon. The guard said afterwards, they'll be happy for a few weeks. They didn't get their riot.

Had they got better by the time you recorded them again in October?

The single version of 'Anarchy' was done in October, at Lansdowne. They were booked into the Deep Purple studio in Kingsway, by Polydor, but that never happened. They got sued by Lansdowne cos they'd written slogans and stuff all over the walls, so we went up to Wessex. We did the 'Anarchy' that was on *The Great Rock'n'Roll Swindle*, 'No Fun', 'Substitute', 'No Lip', 'Stepping Stone', 'Whatcha Gonna Do about It', 'Did You No Wrong'.

It sounds like a lot of care went into those records.

Oh yeah, a lot of sweat. We were all into it.

EMI didn't want 'Anarchy' anyway, they wanted a pop song, 'I'm So Pretty', as they called it. Glen was going along with that, but 'Anarchy' was the strongest and that was what it was going to be. We got money to do the single, and we did the whole set. I was called into EMI, and Mike Thorne had gone in there with Glen and done their own mix of my thing behind my back. They played me this acetate they had of his mix, and I just freaked.

They didn't do any recording with Mike Thorne?

Yeah, they took them into EMI's 8-track. They did about five or six tracks with Thorne. It was so-so. Next thing I heard, they had Chris Thomas to produce. It was a kick in the teeth when Chris Thomas was picked as the producer, but I can see how it happened.

Why were you brought in again in January '77 to do those tracks?

Don't really know. Malcolm said the band were dejected after being sacked from EMI, so he booked them into Gooseberry for a week with me and went to Paris.

Did you continue to do the live sound through '77?

I did the Anarchy tour, then that was it. I started The Label in November '76, and wanted John to be a partner. It was going to be called Rotten Records. He had to ask Malcolm whether he could, and Malcolm said no. The first bootleg, the Burton gig, was on Rotten Records. John got me to record the gig, and took away the tape. I never put out any bootlegs, it must have been him.

423

What were the Paradiso gigs like?

That was with The Heartbreakers supporting. I think that was when Glen walked off stage, refused to do an encore. That was about the end of the band with Glen.

***SPUNK* we're going to find out about, aren't we? I'm sure it was Malcolm.**

I'm sure he probably did the first five thousand or something, and everyone else copied it, cos thousands were sold in the States, and so many people you meet have got it.

Who owns those tapes?

They owe me money from the stuff I did that was released on Virgin; I only ever got the first quarter while Malcolm was still involved, and since then, I've been getting statements from the receivers, but they're not in a position to pay me cos my contract was with Glitterbest. Chris Thomas is in the same situation, and he took the receivers and Glitterbest to court and lost the case, so unless the court instructs the receivers to pay, we don't get paid. Yet Virgin are selling the records and taking their money at source. What Malcolm tried to set up for me, when he wanted to sell out, was that I had my contract with Virgin, so I would get paid no matter what situation the band were in. I'm not in a great situation. The tapes I've got are what I recorded on my own equipment and was only paid minimal expenses, so in my opinion, they're mine – but as far as the actual recordings, I acknowledge the artist's royalty, and the publishing is separate anyway.

EMI would own the first lot of proper recordings?

The thing with EMI, the contract I had with them was only for 'Anarchy' and 'No Fun'. All the other stuff, they didn't know they paid for that anyway, and that was somehow licensed to Virgin, so EMI still didn't claim that. There's alternative versions and rough mixes I've still got, which are the only copies – 'Silly Thing' and 'Here We Go Again'.

I suppose that Glitterbest would own the later ones, in theory. The ones you did after they were sacked from EMI . . .

424

Yeah, they paid the studio bill. Malcolm said to me, 'Work those tapes.' He couldn't, he thought it was below him.

So now you've basically settled out of court . . .

We haven't spoken. Me and John haven't spoken.

He turned against me, became totally paranoid, accused me of working on Malcolm's side. This was when Public Image were rehearsing in secret. Virgin weren't allowed anywhere near them. I had a passion to help John with whatever he was going to do, I had dreams of the music he could come up with. I wanted to get him into instruments, keyboards. I took him the tape of 'Johnny B. Goode' and 'Substitute' and stuff, and Wobble and the band were there, he was out getting pissed.

I heard them jamming, some great sounds Keith was coming up with. They used to jam for hours. None of that ever got recorded. Simon Draper asked me what the stuff was like, and I didn't know they hadn't been signed. I said, 'They're a bit untogether, but, you know . . . ', and the next thing, John comes looking for me, saying I was trying to stop them getting signed. He's never spoken to me since. I wrote him a cheque and he cashed it.

Sophie Richmond

Malcolm McLaren's secretary, in fact the mainstay of Glitterbest right until the company's dissolution in 1979, discharging her duties with a sense of responsibility rare in this story. Politicised, rigorous and thoughtful. Her contemporary diary formed the narrative spine of Fred and Judy Vermorel's Sex Pistols *– the first ever book published about the group.*

I lived abroad most of my childhood, in the Middle East.

Was your father a diplomat?

Yeah, and I came back to boarding school when I was eleven. They got out of the Foreign Office when I was fifteen – that was in the mid-sixties. I did my A levels in Newcastle on Tyne, and went to Warwick University, in 1969, the year after Paris. I did History, which was a compromise, I really wanted to do Arabic. After University I moved to London, at the end of 1972, met Jamie, moved to Croydon. The first time I met him was at Sheffield at some conference, he was flogging *Suburban Presses* or something like that.

Just to go back, were you interested in politics through 1968?

Che Guevara first, I think. I remember cutting out the photos of his body from the newspapers. 1968 was very exciting, and the Vietnam stuff as well. There was so much of it happening, and feminism as well, the first women's conference was in 1970 at Oxford.

Did you join any organisations, or was it just being involved in groups?

I didn't actually join any. There was an occupation at Warwick in my first year, and we all went along to that. The great question was academic freedom – E.P. Thompson, a very good speaker. You just get swept along, and you don't know very much, an awful lot of people know a lot more . . . finding out what Marxism was all about, socialism and this, that and the other.

I met Jamie again just through political people really. He was running a printing press, and I was interested in printing presses. I think I moved in with Jamie in '73, the press had just moved down from Crystal Palace to Croydon. I learned to print, then quite soon after, I suppose a year later, Jeremy and Liz went of to Hastings, so it was just Jamie and me really.

You'd have been printing the actual magazine, *Suburban Press*?

No they had all been done, they were Jamie and Jeremy together. We did *You Can't Tell a Book by Looking at Its Cover*, which I haven't looked at for a long time, and all the general stuff, disabled magazines, and the Nixon book, *World Revolution*, the theoretical magazine, *Fish Out Of Water*, which as far as I remember was a sort of *Suburban Guerilla* thing.

Yes, after the miners strike of '74 we did a lot for that, that was great, miners coming down to talk to anarchists in squats and stuff, unbelievable it now seems. And the three-day week, all the lights going out. Thinking, what the hell are we going to do, really. We were thinking of selling the place and moving to Scotland at the end of '75.

How had the initial contact between you both and the Sex Pistols been made?

I think Malcolm phoned or dropped in – I've got a feeling we didn't have a telephone then – and said, 'You must come and see this band', and one time he came by and needed to get Chrissie Hynde and people together for a rehearsal, with half The Damned. We had seen Malcolm when the shop was being turned into SEX, from Too Fast to Live. Jamie and Malcolm had been in touch sporadically.

How did they get on?

It was rather mysterious to me, I couldn't see who was doing what to whom, and why! There was clearly a vibrant relationship. Quite soon I came to see Jamie as quite subordinate, but that was wrong. I

427

thought that Jamie was hanging on to Malcolm's coat-tails and I was hanging on to Jamie's, but I don't think that's entirely accurate. I think Malcolm needed Jamie, he needed people and was gathering them. It was quite a strange group of people.

What did you think of the shop when you went?

As a feminist I hated clothes – I hated buying them, wearing them, everything to do with them. But I was very impressed. I started liking the clothes, but I still couldn't get on with them. I found it all very strange, and felt rather outside of all that scene. I liked Jordan and Michael, I liked knowing people who were into that kind of thing; you can admire people for being very together on any level.

When did you first see the band?

Spring of '76, the Nashville gigs, one with Ted Carroll doing the records in between. The Sex Pistols were supporting The 101ers as they were then. That was the second one, I think. They were very exciting. I wasn't terribly critical in those days; they made a nice, exciting noise, and after you'd seen them a couple of times, you could hear the songs. It all seemed nice and fresh and dirty, a good thing in terms of what else was happening.

So Malcolm started to gather all these people around him . . . he'd obviously decided . . . he'd gone to see you and basically the three of you were in touch after that?

Yeah, pretty much, and Jamie specifically stayed in London to remain in touch, cos the idea was that we were going to move to Scotland and do something or other. I worked on a press up in Aberdeen for a while. I got a job there just for the summer. Jamie went to live with his brother Bruce and Marion, and I was in Scotland until September. It was that very hot summer.

Do you think that made a difference in any way?

Mmmm! I think the Brits are very responsive to the weather, emotionally, and like the hot summer of the French Revolution, if you get a long spell of weather like that, and everybody's on the streets and you can't believe it's going on, and you don't have to wear any clothes and do any washing and so on – I think it made a lot of difference. It's such an extraordinary event, a summer like that.

As soon as you got halfway down Scotland, you noticed. Aberdeen seemed really lush, and then after that everything was brown. It seemed as if everything was getting out of control on a larger scale, and that was encouraging.

Did you see the band again at all before you went to work for them or did you just get into it?

Jamie was seeing them right through the summer, they were playing quite a lot. There was one Hartlepool or Middlesbrough gig that we met at, and they were going round the country with Nils, then I came down for the Screen on the Green early in September, just before I moved back.

And did it feel like something that was quite powerful? Becoming more powerful? Or was it not something that you saw in that way?

What I liked was feeling a part of a lot of people that I didn't know very well, but again, as one did in the political period, you had something in common, which was something that had been dying away, and so there was a resurgence of that. There was a feeling that you weren't on your own. That was what I liked.

There was just a feeling of diffuse intimacy going on, that you could talk about anything and not feel out on a limb; you knew you were in something that wasn't in the least bit explicable, but was very enjoyable, and you just wanted more of it. To see where it went.

How important was the band in that?

I hardly knew the band at that time, and what I liked about them was that their songs seemed to be about reality, as opposed to what was going on in the charts, and that it was partly about fun, but there was the odd bit of social comment.

Do you know where they got that from? Did they sit around and discuss things? When you were there full-time from the middle of September, was there discussion going on between the band and the people around them?

429

By the time I was working in the office, all the songs that were ever performed had been written, practically. Jamie told me of sitting in a pub one night in the summer when I wasn't there, and doing 'Anarchy in the UK' with John. I think he put in a lot, politically, at that stage, I'm not sure what Malcolm was thinking. And John was certainly very receptive to that. Malcolm was less explicit, politically, than Jamie was.

So when you joined, had Malcolm signed a managerial contract with the band? Or did he ever?

Yes, there was a contract, certainly. It was probably signed about the time – this is a guess – about October or November. After they signed to EMI, Stephen Fisher must have said, sort this out.

So you would have joined at a point where the record companies were interested, and Malcolm felt the need, instead of doing it out of Helen's flat, to get an office. Was that the Dryden Chambers one?

Yeah, we got that I suppose in October.

A lot of the actual events are covered in your diary anyway . . .

If I was Malcolm, I would have fired me.

Was it such a bad emotional experience, being in England at that time? Do you think it was just you, or was it just what Britain was like at that time?

I think it was me as well, because there was this curious thing going. I had a very good friend called Elaine, from university, a gay woman who shared our flat at Lant Street [in Borough] for a while, and her kind of gay-politics ultra-feminism and the Sex Pistols did not mix terribly well, so there was a lot of argument. I get very depressed when people I like conflict, and I was finding it difficult to keep my relationships as I wanted them to be, and also be involved in all that – and things were very difficult with Jamie.

Was he drinking a lot?

Yeah, we all were! The stress, the social activity, and also Jamie and I didn't have a proper place to live, we just had a room in a flat that was horrible. It was twenty-four hours a day, no stepping back to think, or weekends. There was always something that had to be done, or talked about, or people to meet. So basically we were drinking a lot.

What was Elaine's critique of the Sex Pistols?

At that time she was friends with The Derelicts, do you remember them? Sue and her sister Barbara. And I got to know The Derelicts, and Sue and Barbara split up and Sue went into Prag VEC. The critiques, well, male rock'n'roll kind of things, and there was endless churning over the Nazi stuff. At that time Jamie and I were living with this American woman, Pat, who's Jewish, so there were a lot of arguments about that.

Where did the Nazi thing come from?

That was a joke, yeah. I saw it as a joke, like everyone at the end of the sixties taking over all the British war stuff, *Oh What A Lovely War*, and I saw it as another move on that front. But then when it came to people buying T-shirts with swastikas on, and so on, everybody got very alarmed. All my old hippy lefty friends. I was completely ambivalent about it.

I think you can say that it was politically very naive.

The mid-seventies were very much the time of National Front and International Socialist confrontations, so yeah, one didn't want to be encouraging those thugs. Malcolm always said of that T-shirt – Destroy, with the upside-down cross – that he was making a more general point about leaders, which was a bit too subtle for the average National Fronter, or even the average punk. I think it was a bit of a pipe dream, in that sense.

Did you ever discuss politics with Malcolm at all?

No, he's not that interested in politics. He likes to be mysteriously subversive rather than explicitly anything, and I think that's a good position. He's an opportunist as well, and you can't lay down a line if you're that sort of person.

So you got the office set up in Dryden Chambers. What did you do?

431

Answering the phone mostly, and calling that bloke Dave Crowe in Birmingham about gigs a lot. After they'd signed to EMI there was setting up the tour that never happened, which was endless, getting publicity done.

It was fitting yourself into an industry that was felt to be inherently hostile, and of course I knew absolutely nothing about how it worked, and practically everything about running a band, getting gigs and all that side of it. It all seemed to pull up questions of principle all the time, it was a great strain.

What were the band like then?

Steve and Paul I found very reassuring lads, you know? Nice. John was the one who was the most serious and intelligent, and the most interesting to talk to. I think he likes women in a way that Steve and Paul don't, traditional male attitudes. He really likes female company. I think already he was a little bit edgy about Malcolm, and I was in between, mediating, that was my role. It was awkward.

What would that edginess have been caused by?

I suppose there was a matter of who was in charge. They were very close, they used to go off for meals together in '76, and long chats, and that ceased at some stage. Mutual suspicion.

Did you have any observations about how the whole punk thing developed?

From September '76 one of the things I liked was that there were an awful lot of women about, and that stopped very quickly. You would go down to the Roxy or wherever, and it would be like a heavy metal gig, 90 per cent men. There were still women bands, and there were women in bands, but I did feel that women weren't in it in the same way. To start with there was Jordan and Siouxsie and Viv, powerful people putting things in, and that stopped.

When you were in the office, particularly after Grundy, did you feel under siege from the outside world?

I got a call from EMI saying the Sex Pistols had sworn on TV, this is it. I just laughed, it was ridiculous. The press weren't around a lot, they were at the A&M time, but not then. There were phone calls but Malcolm always arranged things if he was talking to anyone outside the office, cos it was really chaotic.

I get the impression that Malcolm was initially very taken aback by the Grundy thing. Is that correct?

He certainly didn't know how to cope with it. None of us did, cos it seemed such a ludicrous thing for everybody to get upset about: swearing on TV. Compared with daily life around the Sex Pistols; one hears an awful lot of swearing. It seemed so Victorian, and the size of the backlash was absolutely stunning, you know?

Why do you think that was?

I'm still bewildered by it, but it's obviously to do with conventions about what goes on telly, how much of real life was allowed on the telly; and it was a violent breach of those conventions.

So what happened, did the phone calls start as soon as it had stopped?

No, I got this one from the bloke at EMI, sounding seriously worried, cos he was obviously aware of the grossness of it in terms of TV convention. That was immediately after the broadcast, and then nothing until the following day when we saw the newspapers.

What was everybody's attitude to that?

I think Malcolm may have been going, oh shit, but everybody else was quite exhilarated by it, getting all that attention, it was great. It was a kind of takeover, like an occupation. I think he seemed on top of the situation, the next day. He could always think of something to say, that's what impressed me about him, during the various crises say something that worked.

During the Anarchy tour when all the dates were cancelled, what was the point of carrying on as though they weren't cancelled? Was that to embarrass EMI, or was it just a blind faith?

It was a blind keeping-going; if we cancelled this, then we'd disappear, in a sense. So to go on around the country creating a flurry registered that we were still there.

Did you see any of the dates on the Anarchy tour, or were you stuck in the office?

I went to Manchester and Plymouth. Manchester was fantastic, Plymouth was kind of drecky – everybody pissed in the hotel, being wild.

There seemed to be a drastic change in the band, was it the Grundy thing, and all the attention?

It was a combination of the signing for real money, and the Grundy incident, which was the thing that precipitated Glen leaving, really; and once Glen had left, there were practically no more songs, and that was a problem.

Why was that?

They didn't rehearse, they couldn't bear to be in the same room together half the time; it was a real effort in the spring of '77 to get them to go to Denmark Street, try to write new songs. Glen could write tunes and they couldn't. They could produce words and chords, but they couldn't write tunes, like 'Submission', so they were finished as a creative unit once he'd gone.

Who else was working in the office then? Simon Barker?

Simon was for a bit, he must have been running errands, so there would always be someone at the phone. Boogie seemed to get attached around the time that Glen was leaving. He played an interesting role in all that. He was basically trying to keep Glen in. I thought the band should decide.

Who did decide in the end? Glen decided to leave?

This is a construction, not a memory: John proposed Sid, and Malcolm said okay. The other two didn't like Sid. And although it was John who got him into the band to replace Glen, as soon as Nancy was on the picture they were no longer friends.

What did you think of Nancy yourself?

It's difficult, because I've read her mother's book since, so that's kind of superimposed on my memory – but at the time I hated her cos she was such a terrible problem, and I wished she would just go away.

434

But my feelings alternated – on occasion you would see them together and you would just think, babes in the wood. They could be really sweet together.

If it was true, when did the Nancy kidnapping incident occur?

Yes, it was perfectly true. August or September '77. Sent Sid off to the dentist, and we'd just got his Maida Vale flat, and the idea was to put Nancy on a plane back to America. It was completely mad and I don't know why I landed myself in it. What it resulted in was me and Nancy standing in the street arguing for three hours, and then I called the office and said, 'I can't do this', and Malcolm and Boogie came down, and had no better success than I did.

I had her in my car actually. We didn't get as far as Heathrow. We just had this endless argument, about Sid and Malcolm and things.

There seems to have been a long time when nothing happened, between the SPOTS tour and the second Anarchy tour. What was going on, mucking about with the album and the film?

Album, film, putting the singles out, making promo videos for Virgin; but also everybody got so paranoid, Johnny didn't like to leave his flat. It's extraordinary reading the diaries how much physical violence there was, and how many court cases there were to go to. I was quite shocked to read – Steve attacked here, Paul attacked there, John, Jamie, the stuff in the King's Road going on.

Again, it's like transgressing a barrier that you don't know is there, and this one was about the Royal Family, and no-one imagined that in Britain in 1977 anyone would give a shit about insulting the Queen.

What did you feel about the people in the group from the summer on? Were they changing, becoming more rock star-ish?

John was very difficult to deal with. I couldn't grasp the extent of his paranoia about being on the streets, and I didn't have any idea how vulnerable he was feeling, and one of the things that nobody took much account of was that these were four kids who were pretty young and didn't have a lot of experience, and suddenly they shot to fame, and how were they coping with it? It's the kind of thing that middle-class people can spend three years with an analyst for, you know.

435

Paul and Steve were quite realistic, and once they got their flats they were happy, they were easy, and they wanted to go on, would co-operate with the film and so on. Sid was just impossible, and John made everything as difficult as he could. Partly to get attention, he always had me running around, something Malcolm hated. I'd go off and deliver his wages for him and Malcolm would say, 'Make him come to the office.' I saw that pretty much as him wanting attention from Malcolm.

What wages were they on?

Probably fifty quid a week by then. Possibly forty. Twenty-five quid to start with, and I think there were two rises, one to forty, and then fifty quid a week by the time Russ Meyer was around. John and Steve and Paul were very much up for the film at that point, but John very quickly turned against it, he thought it was too Monkees, or Beatles. I can see his point.

Was Malcolm spending all the money on the film?

Not in '77, but by the time the band broke up, all the money went on the film, quickly, at once.

So the money that you got through '77 – obviously you got more money as the records were selling – what was the money going on? Just keeping the band and the office and the whole operation afloat?

Yeah, we bought their flats, obviously, and clothes, and there were always special expenditures, taxi accounts and instruments and gear. It went very quickly.

Did you see any of the SPOTS tour?

I went up to Wolverhampton. That was the only one, it was great. They played very well, and enthusiastic crowd, lots of money at the end of it, then back down the motorway to London. Rock'n'roll.

You didn't see them at Brunel? What was that like?

Jesus that was a terrible gig. Was that with The Ramones? There were Ramones about. I can't remember much of the gig. I remember the hall smelt of smelly feet, cos it was the gym.

Did you go to the States?

Yeah. Not for the first couple, I got there for Baton Rouge, then Dallas, that was a nice one, then San Francisco.

What was good about the Dallas concert?

Well, Sid was quite out of it, but they did play well and it was packed with lots of interested people. It was quite wild, and Dallas was a place that appealed to me anyway.

Did you travel on the bus, or with Malcolm?

On the bus from Baton Rouge up to Dallas, then I took the plane to San Francisco. I didn't take the bus, it was too male, god! Sid and John and all the crew, you know? And the Warner Brothers guys. I do remember Noel Monk. Sid was ill, John was pissed off, and Steve and Paul were relatively quiet, their usual selves.

Everything about that tour sounds horrible.

Well the nicest bit that I remember was the bus journey between Baton Rouge and Dallas, and it was snowing . . . driving across America, great articulated lorries turned over by the side of the road, stopping to buy little souvenirs, little keyrings with guns, and so forth.

You saw the last concert?

Yeah, it was very good. They played brilliantly, it was very powerful, and a huge place, everybody reacted very well, though obviously the problems with Sid, you know, drove everyone to despair. It did seem funny to me, at the time, that they should come to the heart of hippy-land and be defeated, in a sense.

What was going on through '78?

Putting together the film. After getting Russ Meyer over, there was a succession of lesser lights. Finding them hotels, typing film scripts, endless stuff of that nature. There wasn't much shooting done that I recall. There was Sid in Paris, that great venture.

When was Sid in Paris?

That must have been after they had come back from Brazil. It was quite long days, I remember. I didn't want to be near Sid, he was getting worse and worse. You could spend hours talking to him about everything he needed to do to get himself together and he'd say yes, yes, yes, and it was a complete waste of time.

Was he completely taken up by the idea of being a Sex Pistol, did he become the character?

Yeah, I think he did. But it was obviously a fantasy that he was living in, and completely out of it on drugs from the time he met Nancy.

When was all that stuff in the Rainbow shot?

I'd forgotten about all this. That was . . . oh yes, Julien Temple takes over. Once we had got through our fourth director and we'd all disappeared, and taken loads of money, that would have been autumn of '78, with Tenpole Tudor and Irene Handl; and Jeremy Thomas of course, organising a great deal of that.

When you left Glitterbest, what went to the receivers? Was there stuff that was removed?

The accounts, principally, and contracts.

And all the Matrixbest [production company] stuff as well?

Yeah.

Shooting schedules?

As far as I can remember I never received anything like a shooting schedule. There must have been stuff, but I can't remember any pieces of paper – just money, thousands of pounds.

So the film was put together in a really grab-bag manner?

Yes, on what money we had. I do remember one day telling Malcolm that there was no money in our account – that would have been August '78 – and he spent two days hustling round with Stephen Fisher, and got hold of more from Virgin.

What was the relationship with the shop by then?

Hardly any. Viv came by the office very occasionally, but it seemed to me that Malcolm tried to keep the two things separate. Unlike at the beginning, when Viv was very much involved in the clothes, and being at gigs. She's quite political, more political than Malcolm. We kind of missed each other. I liked her.

Presumably in the autumn of '78 you started having really bad Sid problems, and starting to cut the movie and stuff?

And the impossibility of getting him to do anything, and Steve and Paul coming in to do a few final scenes. The script changed throughout the shooting, according to what could be done. And trying to put that *Swindle* album together – where was the material going to come from?

And also the court case was starting to lurk very seriously in the background?

Malcolm was spending all his time with Julien on the film.

Why did it go to court? Did Malcolm not think that it would go to court?

I think you would have to ask Stephen Fisher about that. Malcolm just wanted the film finished, and that was the thing which kept us going in that direction. It could have all collapsed at that stage, which the receivers would have come in to pick up.

So in a sense, he knew that the thing was approaching, and he was desperately trying to finish the movie?

He knew that it was approaching, yeah, but preferred to work on the movie rather than deal with it.

Then Sid died just before the case?

It was pretty horrific. Malcolm went over to New York. I had been on holiday in North Yemen when Nancy was killed, I came back, and Sid was I suppose already in jail, and Malcolm got the lawyers. He did a lot at that stage, got involved with Sid's mother, went to New York and stuff, and in fact there were plans for Sid, once he got out of jail, but I can't remember what they were.

439

You went right on to the end with Glitterbest, did it have a very bad effect on you?

I got an awful lot out of it, but it was very horrible towards the end, just watching this bloody film over and over again with various accountants and receivers, who were charming City types. The man who came to the office was a more Dickensian figure, in his thirties, and he kept saying things like, 'I really regret that I got into accountancy', and 'It's all so boring', clearly envying us; and it was interesting to me to learn about accountancy.

He was the one bright spot at that time. But it was dreadful being in the office with nothing to do – Malcolm never being there, Malcolm and Jamie off fighting with Virgin the whole time, and no band to speak of. I came out of it thinking, what do I do next?

When did you leave Glitterbest?

It must have been June '79.

The court case was in March. Was there a lot of animosity? I seem to remember Jamie saying that Malcolm had been quite unkind to you both, that he regarded you as a turncoat.

Yeah, there was. I felt that my responsibility at that stage was to get everything neat and tidy so that the band could proceed with their lives, and I didn't see any other way of doing it. Now that it was all in the hands of the courts.

Jamie Reid

Sex Pistols' graphic designer and integral part of the Glitterbest
management team. His designs for the Sex Pistols have become inter-
nationally famous as exemplars of the punk style and iconic images
from a key moment in British social history. With Sophie Richmond,
the politicised heart of Glitterbest. For a fuller interview and account
of each artwork, see Up They Rise: The Incomplete Works of Jamie
Reid, *by Jamie Reid and Jon Savage (London: Faber and Faber, 1987).*

How long did it take for you to develop a style which you were
happy with, as far as the Pistols were concerned?

Obviously with that Aberdeen poster, which sticks out like a sore
thumb, it's nothing like the stuff I did later. The answer was staring
me in the face because I'd already done it. A lot of the images came
from stuff done in the early seventies. Again, that was to do with
what was at hand at Suburban Press. Xerox and cheap printing, rips
and blackmail lettering.

Did you ever discuss with Malcolm and the band what should be in
the images?

I kept very quiet, cos everyone wanted to be the star in that situation.
Initially I had arguments with Malcolm, who originally wanted them
to milk that Bay City Rollers phenomenon, and that wasn't on, when
you had the likes of the band themselves.

Malcolm and Vivienne were not happy with making the band so
overtly political straight from the start, from the Anarchy flag, even
up to 'God Save the Queen'. But I just used to keep quiet and get
them in to the fucking printers. I used to talk to John a lot, probably
more than Malcolm. Malcolm and I knew each other's heads, so we
didn't have to blag a lot. We'd criticise. I used to talk to John about
Suburban Press, about situationism.

441

The Sex Pistols seemed the perfect vehicle to communicate ideas that had been formulated, and to get them across very direct, to people who weren't getting the message from left-wing politics. They were totally untouched.

How did the group respond to that?

It was a merry-go-round. It was just assumed that it was right. There was surprisingly little talk about the words that John had written, what the tunes of the band were, what my graphics were, what angles Malcolm was taking. We didn't ask why were we sacked by EMI, what we should do with the Anarchy flag, or why John put a line in a song. It was just right for the time, and it was very exciting, very enjoyable.

When did it become a deliberate thing to keep the band off the graphics?

Pictures of the band? I didn't see the need. What's the point, when you're on the front page of the *Sun* and the *Mirror* anyway? And they were ugly – not really. I wanted the graphics to articulate what the song was about, and what the attitude of the whole band was.

Did they mind not having their mug all over the place?

I think Steve did, a bit.

Did you feel something coming up during 1976?

There was such an obvious hole to be filled. But we had to do a lot of it off our own backs, we had to create it. I think that is ultimately why the Pistols went too far out on a limb. We were alone more than people think. They'll hate this up in Manchester and Liverpool, but it was very much what we were doing in London at that time, around Louise's. Associates of Malcolm, and it spun out from there.

Going back to the EMI sacking, I don't think it was the outrageousness or the Grundy interview that upset them. It was the fact that Malcolm publicly exposed deals. As you know, you can get a banner headline in the dailies saying, 'Pistols sacked again for £75,000' – it's peanuts. They didn't like having that made public, the ins and outs of their business.

442

That's what freaked the high-ups at EMI. They were investing money in that brain scanner at the time with the Thorn link-up, and people putting big money in didn't like that association with the Sex Pistols. To a company like EMI, pop music is just a trivial little thing, but they didn't like the associations.

Up to the point of actually getting product out, and perhaps two or three months afterwards, was when we were most powerful, because people didn't know about Malcolm's background and my background and Sid's background.

They didn't know which direction we were coming from. In the same week we would be accused, quite seriously, of being National Front, and in the next breath you were mad communists and anarchists. It's pertinent to English politics. They like to label you really fast.

Throughout the punk period you had the emergence of Rock Against Racism and this, that and the other, which at the time we felt was a very bad thing. You could see the journalists taking over, becoming establishment. RAR happened, but it ends up with something as sickening as Band Aid, which reeks to me of all the pomposity of early colonialism and imperialism.

We've talked about the cynicism and nihilism that has come after punk; do you feel partly responsible for that?

It has a lot to do with the way it was interpreted. There was a lot more fun to the Pistols than most people would believe.

When did you feel that the Sex Pistols lost momentum?

The week we got arrested, Jubilee week, I thought really as a pop format there wasn't much further the idea could be taken. It should have been the end of the band.

443

John Tiberi

A.k.a. 'Boogie', Sex Pistols' road manager and assistant from early
1977. Formerly with Joe Strummer and The 101ers. His photographs
of Sex Pistols during the Sid period are classics. Very striking and
conspiratorial. His recollections – taped at his studio in London's
Maida Vale (the interior set for the Sid Vicious 'Something Else'
video, now demolished) – are vivid and full of intrigue.

I didn't do much of the traditional stuff in the sixties, I didn't go to
clubs much, but I was interested. I had a scooter in '64, played tru-
ant, went off to museums and things. I started to travel a bit in '66,
'67, and I didn't get back into school. My first job was in a library,
which became full-time, then I answered an ad and ended up as a
photographer. From sweeping the floor, up. It was in Soho, and I
really liked that. I carried on from one studio to another.

What was Soho like then?

There was a lot of activity, a very busy place. The sweat shops were
the surprising things, machines rattling away. It changed after dark.
The red lights went on. I liked the mixture of races. Jewish, Italians,
Greeks, Maltese, Pakistanis.

How did you meet Malcolm?

Malcolm was staging the band at the 100 Club, he was getting the
A&R men down there, puffing them up. He had Ingham and Coon
pushing them, and this was the time that John had a fight with Glen,
and ran off. That was when I met them. I thought the singer running
off was great. I went up to Malcolm, and he told me to fuck off.

I think he knew who I was; I was with The 101ers and he wanted
to get on the bill at the Nashville. They were getting a bit of press,
but I had the wrong end of the stick. I thought it could be good for

us. It was the wrong thing to do. The first press they had was with Eddie and the Hot Rods, which said basically, don't go and see this group. It was like a breath of fresh air. The thing at the Nashville went ahead through the agents, I didn't see Malcolm about that.

Did the group make much of an impact then?

I think they did it twice, and the first time was the one where they had the fight. It wasn't very good for The 101ers.

I got involved with The 101ers as a roadie, really. I had big aspirations for them, but they were a very loose bunch of people. I called myself their manager. There was another guy called Mickey Foote, with whom I shared that title. Their charm was their simplicity, and that was their undoing. Joe had some ambition, but he hid it; in that era, and being a squatter, you're not supposed to have that ambition.

Did you get involved with The Clash when The 101ers split up?

Bernie had ideas about starting a group, and he walked into the dressing room after a gig. He'd got Mick and Paul, and he needed a front man, and started feeding Joe the high-level sales crap, and it worked. This was after the Nashville gig. I went along with Joe. I got disillusioned when I met Mick Jones, decided it was too thin. It was a very shallow concept. They seemed like a band like the one Joe already had, mixed up about their motivations.

In many ways I found the same with the Pistols. But there was something more coming out of it. Joe went through a personality change, went into a sort of Bernie phase. A Camden Town version of the Pistols, with Jackson Pollock thrown in there.

I had a lot of loyalty, and when I went to see Malcolm, I found a place for that feeling, wanting to join up. It was after Grundy, it was a lot to do with that. Grabbing the situation. He had dexterity and savvy, he was a bit of a magician. I went to see him in this office in Dryden Chambers, and I must have had some picture in my mind. I knew Bernie, and I thought Malcolm was going to be just like that.

I went up to Caerphilly on the Anarchy tour. I didn't see all the stuff outside, I arrived when the gig was in progress. There was about twenty-five people in the place.

Had the group changed?

445

Not really. John was an excellent performer. Not the same as Strummer, but the same focus. He was the spokesman of the whole energy. More like Gene Vincent, traditional four-piece group. The Stones or The Who.

When did you actually actually join up?

I think Nils had had a showdown with Malcolm that very week. But the main thing that was going on was Glen. They were out of EMI; I seem to remember all the masters coming back to the office in the first week, so the full weight of this firing hadn't occurred. Glen was given his papers.

I liked Glen. There were two factions. I liked Steve, but I liked Glen for opposite reasons. I had taken a liking to Sid from one evening at the place he lived with Viv Albertine. They had their group, but he was very shy, but also threatening, which was strange. I had to take them down to the supermarket and show them how to shoplift. Sid was impressed. They didn't know how to set up a squat, all the practical skills The 101ers had.

I supported the idea of Sid being in the group, although I didn't know any of the nuts and bolts behind Glen being thrown out. He seemed to have different values to the rest of them. Malcolm didn't give any defence for Glen, and I took that lead. Thinking now about how it affected the group's songwriting abilities, it seems strange that Malcolm was unaware of that.

Malcolm probably wasn't all that interested in the music, was he?

Perhaps he didn't weigh that up. There was an agreement written up. It now seems Malcolm must have imagined it would be okay without Glen, and that it would be all right to get this other guy in the group. Sid was a drummer, wasn't he? It was kids, fighting with each other, it was good stuff. They had enough songs for an album, and if they needed more, perhaps they could get Glen back into the group as a songwriter. But that didn't happen. Glen got proud.

Who was in the office at that time?

Just Malcolm and Sophie. Jamie was Sophie's boyfriend, just an odd bloke really, and Simon Barker came in to do the mail. I didn't really work there. The first thing I had to do was go off and buy a car with Glen, after he was paid off. A Sunbeam Alpine, which was very non-punk, it was light blue.

Malcolm wanted to organise a tour. He'd set up some dates in Europe, cos they couldn't play in England and he wanted to keep the group in practice. They were under his feet, in the way. The dates were in Holland, and the promoter was the guy downstairs, Miles Copeland. I talked practicalities with him, and we were in business.

It didn't make sense to me, getting rid of Glen, but everybody said they didn't like him, and that was it. The obvious thing was class. The next thing was the Screen on the Green, the second one.

How was the film *Sex Pistols Number 1* put together?

Julien wasn't around then. He came in first for the Screen on the Green. I met him in the Roxy. I had to get hold of footage, I was getting Sid out of hospital. They didn't need very much looking after. Sid's rehearsing. Malcolm's visiting companies. Perhaps Malcolm had started thinking about *Who Killed Bambi?*

Anyway, Malcolm asked me to get hold of these bits of footage from the Anarchy tour, to make a showreel. I don't know where he got the idea of selling the band as a visual act. I was very motivated by the Angry Brigade, I thought that was fantastic.

Was it original stuff, or was some of it re-filmed?

It was all re-filmed. It was very early days in video technology. The only place we could get the Grundy programme was from a guy who had recorded it. It was a promoter who did all the country and western gigs, and Sophie had rung him up to get him to record it. He was a competitor to Copeland. A different market. It was Philips format.

But Julien did the re-filming, he shot the video image on to film and edited it into chronological order at the film school, overnight, and showed a cutting copy the following night. It was very stirring stuff, propaganda-oriented.

What happened in Berlin?

A mountain got created out of a molehill at the Speakeasy. The guy's injuries amounted to a black eye. It was just so clichéd, after Sid's other trouble at the 100 Club, with the beer glass. But it put the kibosh on the whole A&M thing. All Malcolm's plans were scuppered.

This time round it wasn't funny. This is the time of that interview that ended up in *The Rock'n'Roll Swindle*, with the cheque. A lot of it was heartfelt: what the fuck are you doing, you're supposed to be making hit records, and these people keep giving me money. He was beginning to act desperate. The calendar wasn't on our side, for the Queen thing. July was the big day.

The group were just a pain in the neck, really. Rotten was becoming a pain, Sid was becoming more so. Basically they wanted to play. It was felt that the group should be out of the way, occupied. Jamie took them to Jersey, I can't imagine why. It was a disaster; the police followed them, they got word from the airline, Jamie was freaked out.

I think it was a stroke of genius, packing them off to Berlin. Rotten was a precocious little shit, really. Trying to think of what this little shit wanted to do. We stayed at this place that was like the Connaught of Berlin [The Hotel Kempinsky]. There was nothing much to do, except to entertain the bastards. Got in touch with the record company, who were a bunch of boring German bastards. Yes, we have the record. I think it was EMI, actually.

We hired a VW and bombed around Berlin, around the wall, in fact, all around these towers. Sid was a real tosser for not having a passport. If he had, we would have gone over. But I couldn't imagine leaving him behind. It was fun, though.

The band loved it, they didn't have a stage to play on, but they had fun. Getting into fights with film crews. It had got out of balance, as far as John and Sid was concerned, the whole thing was getting very top-heavy. It was removed, but it did connect with Malcolm pushing in rehearsals to write some new songs.

The only one really interested in it was John. He found East German TV in the hotel room, he was knocked out by that. He was a grammar school boy, another Glen, really, but a bit of a closet case. He came from a rough family, but he was the softie. The youngest, the thinker. He didn't have a very honest relationship with the others in the group, he was acting a role.

John and Sid were very close when they were at college together, but later John found him a bit embarrassing. I know when they were finding places to live – in John's case to leave home and in Sid's case he didn't have anywhere at all, and they were staying in places together – there was friction about Sid's drugs, but also about something else, which I'm not sure about, that built up between them.

Steve and Paul had each other, and they had their own mates. They didn't hang about at John's flat.

After Berlin, Virgin must have been next.

Branson talked about getting behind the concept, if you like, and I saw Branson as a daring person. I had more contact with that early-seventies scene than any of the others. I only thought it was a good idea to do one single, Malcolm was trying to do that, but they wouldn't have it. They wanted to take advantage of the situation to get a long-term contract.

So many people really tried to stop 'God Save the Queen'.

I remember a Capital Radio phone-in request show that got a special dispensation from the IBA to play the record, and then take comments. It was rather trite. And I think Virgin was a mistake. They had them worked out wrong. It seems a short-sighted way of looking at the group to see them having to meet deadlines.

The whole thing of the Jubilee, it was a chance to take a crack at the power of the media. It was a semi-political, agit-prop statement, trying to get the name on buses, and they wouldn't have it. How can we sneak it in? No safety pin, either, thinking that people who knew, would know.

They hadn't had a real hit at that stage.

That's true, but that was the bait. The first company to get them and hold them. Why not just keep going?

The group must have wanted a hit.

Oh, the group wanted to be a pop group. They had no reason to be snooty about Glen, they had all the same ideas.

I played a part in what happened, but I don't think anybody directed what happened. Malcolm did take the driving seat, and did the job, but if that thing had come out three months earlier, as it was going to with A&M, it would have been a very powerful statement, and it might never have come out with EMI.

We're forgetting the great groundswell that was happening in the music industry, saying fuck Number 1, anti-chart. The chart with no Number 1. The chart that said, it isn't important any more. It's grandiose to talk about how it affected the media. What was important was how it affected the music business.

What happened with the boat trip?

Branson did pay for a lot of things there, and he wanted to pay for more. I don't know whose idea it was, but it was a good one. I'd imagine it was the Virgin press department. This is where Branson came in, the media buccaneer. Virgin had a sort of over-educated view of it all – I always cite the *Never Mind the Bollocks* case – misconstruing the whole point of it. It must have cost them five grand, and they won the fucking case. With Rotten there. Did he turn up? Having Johnny Rotten coming out winning the court case is not the image this group wanted. The press didn't report it that much.

I remember the 'Pretty Vacant' video for *Top of the Pops*, the idea was to catch Rotten's ego. We didn't have to do that recording. Virgin paid for it. I can't understand why I took the group to that TV studio in the first place. I suppose we gave in, didn't we?

What was Sweden like?

In terms of playing, the group took full advantage of it, they were really good. Better than America. It had been a long time. It was quite a simple tour, in a van. There was a private airplane at one point. We went up to the very top, a very strange gig. It was summer, so it wasn't that cold, but it was bizarre.

The gig in that town was in a bar, there was no nightclub. Just a saloon. Sid was away for a very long time from the table and Paul volunteered to go look for him, and he was gone for a bit, so when I got in there, there was Paul getting this guy from behind, who had Sid held by the padlock, the chain, up the wall, going white in the toilets. He was a big guy. It was the only time Sid was threatened.

All the gigs were strange. There was this fanatical teddy-boy element in Stockholm. They broke up the gig, and the police put the group in a van, blue lights flashing, and driven through town to the hotel. The hotel had to barricade the doors, cos these guys were coming in through the gardens, bashing at plate-glass doors, it was crazy. Steve went out. He had a black leather jacket, and he pretended to be one of them. He had to go out and find some chicks.

I liked all that, it was like The Beatles in *Help!* There were places where there was no stage. Those photographs Dennis Morris took, with some punk going mad and John six inches from his face with a microphone. It was totally different from the 100 Club. At that point they hadn't played anything bigger than a three- to four-hundred-seater cinema. The Swedish gig that was filmed was the biggest gig they had ever done, in a college. After two weeks they were tired but happy.

John had the words for that song, 'Holidays', but he didn't actually write it until the soundchecks for that tour, it was the only time they put together any of those songs. 'Bodies' was put together in the studio, more so than any other song. But as far as I remember, they were both written during those soundchecks.

What happened on the SPOTS tour – was that mad?

I suppose it was. Did we have two secret tours? Or one tour in two halves? There wasn't a good one, there was just a mad one. There was another European trip as well, to Holland. That was in Sid's drug era.

It was a bit stupid sending him to Holland if you wanted to get him away from drugs.

In Amsterdam I took Sid to get laid, early one morning. Woke up with an erection. I don't know how he got up the nerve to ask me, or how it happened. It seems to be a preoccupation with taking the initiative! But it was quite cute, a very nice girl. There was a time when someone tried to rip him off as well. I had to save him.

What did you think about the *Never Mind the Bollocks* court case?

From the Queen thing to the American tour they weren't getting into the national papers. The court case wasn't what we wanted. What do you do, win a court case to make the word 'Bollocks' legal, and retire? The Pistols were not in the press in the way they should have been, because there was nowhere for them to play.

451

One idea was for them to play on common land, over which there are no byelaws. The idea came from funfairs, and we went out to see some circus acts. Yeah, you can get a tent here, another thing there. We decided to go with the fairground idea, and that was all coming up for the next summer.

What was important about this American tour? I can't remember what was in the air. The most important thing, still, was the film, and Warner Brothers. A number of really silly things had happened with the album, between Virgin and Warner Brothers, and Warners were coming up with the rest of the dosh for the film, so the group has got to get there. It was lucky.

Malcolm didn't want to go to America, for all his inhibitions about the critical gaze of all those envious people. It was talked about long before, and we knew we were going, and the basic guidelines of the Southern states were hammered in from the beginning. It was a wonderful idea, and Malcolm came back with stuff saying, they're dead against it!

We had local support groups: a Cajun group in Baton Rouge, a heavy metal group in Dallas. It all worked when we actually did it, but they couldn't understand the idea: the latest English signing by Warner Brothers should do a couple of major venues, some press, get a reaction, then come back and clean up. What are they doing all this for? They wanted factory towns – Detroit, Cleveland, Pittsburgh – they thought that was the style.

Where did the problem with the visas arise?

In England. [The American Embassy in] Grosvenor Square asked for information, and I had to go around trying to get people to remember when they'd been busted, which in Paul's case was a very lengthy process. The question was, do we tell them, or do we let them find out? We told them.

We had to put these things on the form, somebody minor had a look at it, passed it up to somebody else who put two and two together and it was stopped. But it didn't reach the ambassador. Fisher started provoking higher levels on an appeal, when there was no appeal process, and Warners had to step in, from over there. They started to lobby Congress.

Basically, Warners had to put up a surety, something like a million dollars, that the group was not going to fuck about. That was what crippled the tour. Also there was a time limit – they had four days after the tour to get out of the country.

Presumably the surety was the reason Warners got so heavy with the security?

Very. Shit, they were scared. They took over the minute we got there. We got off the plane. We did the immigration thing like normal people, then this little ferret bloke, Noel Monk comes along, and all the luggage come straight through on a trolley. Warner Brothers started to talk. Then in the lobby, NBC tour manager coming back to the States, on this bus. This is the bus to the car park! TV, the lot. Anyway.

The first night, in their room with Rory Johnston [Glitterbest US representative], I was saying, 'This is going to fall apart, they don't understand any of it', and Rory said, 'Don't worry, I'll speak to them.' Malcolm fell in line. It pissed me off, cos the performance suffered. It's pumping up all the stuff we didn't need, luxuries.

At the beginning, the Warners road crew were sycophantic rather than heavy?

Sycophantic with the pop stars and heavy with me. The group could look after itself as a group, but Warners weren't going to look after the individual parts of what they were making. And there I was, looking after Sid. To begin with, we were being put into the wrong kind of hotels, being given the wrong kind of service. Soundchecks were something I had nothing to do with. In England I had total control over that job, but it was taken away.

There were two camps developing, between Malcolm and John, but that didn't come up until later. It was another tour to be done, another album, what's the point in arguing? We were all practical about it, Malcolm included. He suddenly developed a strong sense of pride, seemingly out of nowhere. But then it was the first time any of us had been to America, and I wanted to enjoy it, I didn't want all these problems.

The tour was straight into Atlanta, first gig, cos we were late. That first night Sid disappeared, went AWOL to get a feel for America,

453

maan! Sid found these fans, straight out of Ziggy Stardust. Glitter make-up. That night he went missing in Atlanta, he just showed up again in the morning. Maybe that was the night he turned up with a massive gash in his arm, cos he couldn't get a spike. The alcohol wasn't working. It was cold turkey.

These kids were good at dressing up, but they couldn't get him anything. Sid had a spike relationship, which is quite a separate thing. People have been known to get off shooting up water. He had these massive Quaaludes, horse tablets, but they weren't hitting the spot he wanted. You could say, why weren't you looking after him, Boogie, but there you go.

Whilst I was arranging visas, he and Nancy had been at it for four days solid. Sid went home and had his private life, and it wasn't a case of me looking after him, shaking his willy and putting it away afterwards. Nancy provided a connection to turn Sid into a full-blown addict, almost overnight. That was while they weren't playing, which was between Sweden and the SPOTS, after the European tour.

Wasn't Sid going to be thrown out of the group that autumn?

Yes. I don't know why we didn't just get her busted, it would have been easy enough. I don't know why we decided to bundle her into a car and take her to the airport. This was after Sweden. Who knew that Sid was getting strung out? Sophie probably, but we were all overstretched. I had a few clues. Holland went okay. He wasn't strung out when they went to Amsterdam.

Did the American tour go from bad to worse very quickly?

The essential problem was the lack of central control of the situation with these people wanting to take over, and Sid. I was ignorant of all the power-politics that Malcolm had laid at Warners. Thinking back, he was freaked out by what this thing had turned into, a monster. He's trying to get the film money, he's hoping that they're going to like what they've got, and he's hoping they won't arrest him when he steps into the country.

The whole thing is suddenly underpinned by this surety bond, which wasn't planned. When he did arrive, he didn't have any great command of the situation. Neither did I. We were looking a little bit silly. Nevertheless the band was playing gigs, and it was a bit of fun.

Was the FBI around?

In Tulsa. There probably was in Atlanta, somewhere. There were a lot of people there, coming to have a look. TV stations, Marshals from other states. There was Tom Forcade, and that guy Lech Kowalski. They were fun. We thought they were FBI. They were following us. I talked to Forcade when I picked up some footage from him. He was a nice guy. Blew his brains out, didn't he?

At San Antonio were weren't allowed to go and stand in front of the Alamo, that was definitely going to lose us a million dollars. It was debilitating. The gigs went on, and Sid was getting control of his stuff, and smoothed out. I think he went on the bus with Rotten. Nobody from head office was around in those intermediary dates. We were all taking the bus, and Malcolm was taking planes, always. With Rory, probably. Then the bus went on with John and Sid, and Steve and Paul and I went in the plane. It was a long haul, a two-day haul on the bus. Rotten was demonstrating quite a strong tendency to isolate himself, but that wasn't particularly unusual. Malcolm was too, but then Malcolm didn't go on tours.

There was no hint then that they were going to split up. So why did they?

In San Francisco, arrivals got a bit staggered. I think John and Sid did not turn up the day before, they turned up the same day in the afternoon. We'd been there for two days, at a hotel in SF. We moved in, and Steve and Paul were doing the soundcheck, and that's when they turned up. I can't remember if they had booked into another hotel then. I don't think they had. But after the gig, John did.

This was the biggest gig they'd ever done, and Bob Regehr, Mr Warner Brothers, turned up. He's in the hotel, talking about the gig with Malcolm, rock'n'roll rapport, and I'm not really involved, but essentially, the issue of where Rotten is, is not part of anything. Nobody's paying any attention.

The beginning of it comes from John, directly. John said, 'I don't want to stay with the rest of them.' This is what I'm told by Noel. As far as I remember, he gave me the address. I'm getting mixed signals, they don't really want me to know – this is a management matter, or something. I don't think Malcolm was letting on if he had noticed. Regehr was just swanning the whole thing.

By the next day, he was talking about the record company interfering with 'his artist', which is off beam in the other direction. Anyway, they started acting up on each other. John came over to the hotel, in a room, and Malcolm went in and came out again, and that was about it. Steve and Paul were in another room, and Sid . . .

The night after the gig, that same night was the one that Sid OD'd. I had to drive back to the hotel. One of the kids he'd found phoned me up, because they knew what hotel it was, because they were groupies. They said, 'You better come and find us.' An easy address: the corner of Haight & Ashbury! Talk about irony. It was a squat, and he was going blue on a mattress on the floor.

I picked him up and walked him around, and he was very lifeless. Those fucking kids . . . it wasn't their fault, and they were pissed off. They were brats, they didn't live there, it was just a shooting gallery for rich kids. They got this alternative doctor-type person, a very powerful kind of guy, and we drove him up to Marin County to this doctor's place, and gave him acupuncture. This was in the morning; when I got back to the hotel, Rotten had arrived back.

Sid was asleep. I had to go back there, and Sid was waking up, looking like he'd never even been in the Sex Pistols. Suddenly the whole weight of the thing has hit him. The next day we all went out separate ways. Steve and Paul flew to Los Angeles. I went with Sophie to Los Angeles to wait for my connecting flight, for my ticket, with Sid. I think John went to New York.

We went to a doctor who prescribed some methadone pills, then we got the plane to New York. A red-eye, probably, and Sid flaked out, he must have had something else too, he just didn't wake up. We were in first class, too. We took him in an ambulance to a hospital and they plugged him in, and he'll be okay. It was a drug-induced coma, which was a pretty big deal, I suppose. It wasn't an OD. Then it snowed, everything was snowed in, even the roads.

Tell me about the 'My Way' sequence, in Paris.

Julien has stuck to the story he made up on the spur of the moment, which is that he basically shot the whole scene. Malcolm has written a long letter to the receiver, which says that Julien fucked up a good idea, so Julien is defending his case, and he's exaggerated, as all film directors do. We were all prepared to work as a team. But the media would much rather go with the idea of one person, exaggerating their own worth.

Sid was the Sex Pistols, because he was their number one fan, and that was the greatest thing about having him in the group. Once he was in the group it was, oo-er, never thought it would be like this, where's the chicks? Sid was getting quite demoralised, cos the dream was broken. Not only the dream of being a pop star, but this thing, with which he was in love, as a fan, as a guy at the 100 Club, that's his PR. Rather than the group dying, the audience dies.

After the split, I'm the only guy who can look after Sid, and that aspect comes into Paris. Malcolm hasn't got any money to make this film, Warners aren't signing any more cheques. Sid was all we had left of the Pistols at that point, and I didn't want to go. I didn't get on with Julien. I like the guy, but I don't like the way he thinks he has to work. They phoned me up and asked me to come, and Malcolm is very difficult to say no to.

The first meeting is in the bar at the hotel, talking about the footage they've already got, which is fuck all. It was a dodgy time, he'd run out of steam. We were talking about 'Belsen Was a Gas', as a single. They weren't too keen on that, Fabrice and the other guy from Barclay Records. We've got a nice catalogue! Johnny Halliday . . . and that was how 'My Way' came up. Malcolm liked it cos it got the French going. Who's going to tell Sid?

Sid isn't so sure, but we worked it around him. The development of the scene was worked out between Julien and myself and Sid, and Malcolm. But when it came to the actual shooting of it, Sid worked it out himself. We did a rehearsal, and it was great, and we said, 'Okay, can you just . . . ', and he did it again, exactly the same. He knew exactly. He had great intuition about cameras. He understood perfectly.

The track was recorded with Sid and some session men. Steve put guitar on afterwards. For 'C'mon Everybody', I had to put Eddie Cochrane in one ear, and he sang along perfectly. But no-one thought it was going to work. That was the background to it. They were done really cheaply at dodgy studios. No studios would deal with them. They didn't want him around.

When did you leave Glitterbest?

The following year. Before the court case. I have no doubt that Branson financed Rotten's court case. I'm sure that's why they were in Jamaica.

What were you doing in Jamaica?

I had several pieces of blank paper, which Malcolm had signed to make false promises to Rotten, which I didn't consider worthwhile doing. It wouldn't have given the film that incentive they needed to raise the dough. I spoke to Branson and Rotten on that trip. Rotten was taking the piss. Arrogant. Branson was just having a difficult time. I shot some film of Big Youth.

Did you try and shoot John?

He wouldn't let us, and I didn't expect him to say yes.

From the beginning, Malcolm had put the advances and the artists' royalties into the movie, and there was nothing wrong with doing that. It could be construed that he was playing around with other people's money, but it was all to make the group more money. He was doing it with their permission and knowledge. It was taking advantage of opportunities that could not be missed, filming things that had to be filmed when it happened, to record the group's career. It was more than a wonderful defence.

The company were putting the skids on the group's money, and their involvement in the group's product vis-à-vis the film – that was more likely to be construed as interference in the group's career than anything Malcolm had done, and that is what Branson did. He told Steve and Paul, he's spent your money on his film, and I can't afford to pay you unless you come in with me. So that's what they did. John didn't like the film anyway.

CHAPTER SEVEN
The Propagandists

L–r: Malcolm McLaren, Steve Severin, Nils Stevenson, Caroline Coon
and Jonh Ingham, Louise's, October 1976 (Bob Gruen)

Despite punk's apparent hatred of the media in general, it was highly mediated from the very start. Because it was so novel and confrontational, it had to be explained and humanised for any kind of wider audience. After Neil Spencer's February 1976 NME *review, the principal music-press writers to cover punk were Caroline Coon (*Melody Maker*) and Jonh Ingham (*Sounds*).*

Their vivid, partisan, sociological reports helped British punk to develop to the stage that it attracted music industry and wider media attention. During that period, the weekly music press was read by hundreds of thousands of fans without attracting the attention of Fleet Street or the mainstream media in general, an under-the-radar version of the teenage news.

From summer 1976, another arena opened up for punk writing: the fanzine. Self-produced rock magazines had been around since the late sixties, but Mark Perry's Sniffin' Glue *took advantage of the new Xerox technology to create the blueprint for the hundreds of fanzines that would follow; A4-size, photocopied, with amateur graphics, they were eye-witness reports from within.*

Neil Spencer

Wrote the February 1976 NME *review, 'Don't Look Over Your Shoulder, but the Sex Pistols Are Coming', that announced the group as something radical; the final quote was, 'we're not into music, we're into chaos'. At the time, the* NME – *the* New Musical Express – *was the brand-leader among the four music weeklies – the others being* Sounds, Melody Maker *and* Record Mirror. *Neil Spencer was the features editor during this turbulent period.*

Tell me about how you got started at the *NME*.

I knew Tony Tyler. When I came to London I got a job on *Beat Instrumental* and *International Recording Studio*, with Sean O'Mahoney, who used to do the *Beatles Book* and The Rolling Stones *Book*. I left – I'd foolishly decided I'd had enough of rock journalism and wanted to become a teacher. Tony eventually graduated to *NME*, I'd stayed in touch with him. I started to write, cos they didn't have a decent soul writer.

Then Nick Logan found out I had production skills, because I'd been involved with magazines for ages and ages, and I started working part-time at *NME*, one day a week. This was 1973. Then a job came up, and Nick offered me the features editor's job, much to everyone's surprise, including mine, and I said yes, straight away, and that was me fucked, for the next twenty years.

Were you a London boy?

No, Northampton, East Midlands. The armpit of the English Midlands.

What was happening on the *NME* when you joined?

There were people who were into Mott the Hoople, Steve Harley, Roxy Music, Sparks. I'd sort of thrown all rock'n'roll music out the window in 1970, when the cowboys came along. I woke up one

Saturday morning, I remember it very clearly, and I thought, I've been had. I was much better off before acid, I'm a mod really, I should go back to my Rufus Thomas records – and I got into reggae, I got into the skinhead thing, belatedly. I was never a skinhead, but I liked their music, and their clothes.

There was a lot of very racist attitudes around, even being a white working-class lefty who was into black music. The taunt usually was, Neil wants to be black. People would take the piss, no-one knew what the fuck I was on about.

So the dominant thing was slightly tarted-up white rock?

It was split between art-house rock, which was the Ian Macdonald, Tony Tyler, Charlie Murray, Nick Kent axis, and real rock'n'roll – Jethro Tull, Greenslade, all those dull chaps. It was also a period of great nostalgia for fifties rock'n'roll. Everybody was putting out *Pinups* retrospectives. The John Lennon LP. Bryan Ferry, *These Foolish Things*.

Big nostalgia, not just for the fifties. It shaded into kitsch and camp with Elton John, and all that glitter. People like Nick Kent would come into work with make-up on. And there was the head-banging, Marquee school of rock, that was also very strong. Tony Stewart, Steve Clarke, James Johnson, Julie Welch.

Had the process of rock journalists becoming stars started?

Yeah, it was promoted. Very heavily. By Nick Logan, and Ian Macdonald. I think Ian had far more to do with the *NME* than he was given credit for. He was the ideological dynamo behind the whole thing. He was a very bright, intellectual, intense man – very dynamic, to the point where he would fly right over the top about everything. He would hold a new belief very intensely and would argue passionately for it. He didn't have his feet on the ground.

I was a sort of intermediary, cos there were people on one hand who had leaden feet, who had this sort of male collective attitude towards rock'n'roll, which I thought was boring and stupid. I was funky, I liked dancing, I still do, and a problem I always had with the hippy movement was that they couldn't dance. They used to hold it in contempt. But I had one foot in that camp, cos those people tended to be a bit more proletarian.

462

Then there were the educated, middle-class rock ideologists, who tended to be the stars. The ones who wanted to dress like Keith Richards. Kent and Murray and dear old Pete Erskine, and one or two others. Ian and Tony. People who would take a lot of drugs, get into Roxy Music, and so forth. Because I was in neither camp, I could relate to everyone and no-one.

How was Nick editing the paper in all this? Was he laissez faire, or was he hands-on?

He was both. He always had trouble delegating, and still does. He and Ian were the visually accomplished people, they knew how to make the paper look good. One of Nick's great virtues as an editor was that he would give people their head. He's a natural stylist, and a bit of a mod, so he brought a lot of things to the paper.

What was the style of the paper then? Was it influenced by *Creem*?

Creem, American *Rolling Stone*, *Crawdaddy*: those were the big influences. Also a lot of leftover attitude from the underground press, which Charlie, Ian, Nick and much more tangentially myself had all been involved with. Ian I think was involved with *Frendz*, briefly. There was also *Street Life*, a bit later. *Street Life* was a great magazine, it was the first magazine that could possibly threaten the *NME*.

I think that the radical break that happened with punk obscured things like *Street Life*.

I was very political, and I was passionate about black music, but in terms of white rock'n'roll, I used to like Dr Feelgood, Ian Dury, people like that. That was a good night out. I wouldn't hang around the Speakeasy. I'd go and see pub bands with my friends. I didn't have any hard ideological position, and they all did, so when punk came along it was very hard for them to react to it.

It didn't conform to the way they looked, the way they saw things. They felt threatened. I couldn't believe the reaction when it came along. It was so unbelievably reactionary. There was this big thing about musicianship, for example. They can't play! That was the first thing, when I went down to see the Pistols. So fucking what? People were shouting that, at the Pistols. 'You can't play!'

Can you remember any ground-breaking pieces, prior to punk, in the paper?

Nick Kent and Charlie Murray in New York. It was all very American, let's not forget, completely fixated on the USA. They wrote pieces about the new CBGB's bands, Richard Hell and Talking Heads. Obviously Nick Kent had a big New York Dolls fixation. Nick was almost in the Sex Pistols, on one level. He should, in a way, have been in a punk band. Maybe ultimately he was too fixated on The Rolling Stones, but he had a lot of punk attitudes.

Tell me the circumstances of that February review.

Tony Tyler and Kate Phillips had met the Pistols at some event or other, and Malcolm had invited Tony down to see them at the Marquee. They were supporting Eddie and the Hot Rods. Tony called me up, invited me down with him. We arrived at the Marquee, and the guy at the door said, you better get in there quick, there's a riot going on.

We walked into the Marquee, and a chair sailed through the air, across the room in front of me, before I saw anything else. There were only about twenty or thirty people in there. And there they were, playing away. Complete brats. Instantly, it was a very powerful memory.

Were they already focused?

I thought so, yeah. Very English. I remember mentioning that they should get into The Kinks, in the review.

In a way, punk did come out of pub rock. The Pistols didn't, but a lot of the people who made punk rock possible, like Ian Dury, came out of pub rock, which was more a continuation of sixties rock-'n'roll, in terms of R'n'B roots, and people like Dr Feelgood, writing very directly about their experiences. It had that honesty to it. Which was fucking great, really refreshing.

And quite working-class, as well.

Of course, that was the other thing. I think that was one of the things that appealed to me about punk. A certain sort of validation of ordinary people.

Did they remind you of mods at all?

A little bit. They had those big fluffy mohair sweaters. I remembered those from when I was a kid. That was a rocker fashion to which I aspired when I was about ten. When it got going, it was very mod – exclusive, looking down your nose at everyone else. Do a lot of speed, have your own clubs, your own dress code. Also very accessible, and very English. And very art-school. Things may come and things may go, but the art school dance goes on for ever.

I wrote the review, Tony wrote the headline: 'Don't Look Over Your Shoulder, but the Sex Pistols Are Coming'.

Did you talk to them after the concert?

Yeah. We had quite a long chat, but I didn't tape it. 'We are into chaos.' They all said that. I think Malcolm had told them to say that. 'We're not into music, we're into chaos.' I didn't find them hostile or difficult, or any of those things that they were meant to be. I actually thought they were quite nice guys, you know. Paul especially was very easy. Steve Jones I never liked, and still don't like. I thought he was a wanker.

The others, they were a bit odd, spunky, you know, but I don't know why people found the punk scene so difficult. I never did understand that, the hostility from the rock writers. These people who ten years earlier had been considered teenage rebels, why they had so much trouble with people who were basically just like them, ten years on. I thought that was pathetic, a real example of how yesterday's revolutionaries become today's reactionaries.

One thing that put me off punk was the violence. Which was a problem. There was always violence at the early gigs. I think it was a way of shaking the hippies, it was like what you do to your parents, really. They don't want you to wear something, so you wear it. The hippies were into peace and love, which was a great ideal, but it degenerated into a sort of gloopy, soggy passivity. I was into peace and love, but I was also a big reggae fan.

Peace and love were big with reggae, at least it was then. But they had a much more militant attitude. Jamaica is a desperately poor third-world country. Most reggae singers came from unbelievably poverty-stricken backgrounds. There's no way they're going to be

465

anything but rough and tough. I suppose I saw in reggae a chance to reconcile hippy ideals and roots militancy. Great music, of course, the true continuation of all the sixties soul which I loved.

What do you think was the connection between reggae and punk?

It was strong, because anybody who had ears, like John Lydon, was listening to reggae. That was the cutting edge of music, as has been subsequently proved. All the innovations in music in the eighties originated in reggae music. Twelve-inch singles, disco mixes, dub. Dub most of all. Different rhythms. That was where it was at. And certainly, once punk was up and running, reggae became a sort of natural partnership.

Don Letts had a lot to do with it, cos he played all that stuff down at the Roxy. I remembered Don from doing an interview with Bob Marley where he came in and sold Bob some weed. He was wearing a pair of bondage strides, with zips all over, and Bob was going, 'What kind of pants you call dem, bwoy?' 'These are punk pants, mon, militant.' I've got all this on tape, Don Letts telling Bob Marley about punk music.

Bob had just been done for dope, and he was saying, 'I should have had a pair of them pants, they would have had to unzip every pocket.'

It was very funny, coming the other way, cos I used to go down to the reggae gigs, and there would always be the same six white guys and six white girls down there. Suddenly these punks started showing up at these reggae clubs and gigs, and the culture clash was wonderful. They'd come along with these really vulgar red, gold and green badges, and they had this really funny Dr Martens skank that everybody did. And all out of their boxes on speed and weed.

The black people were well bemused, man. Because the black scene then was much more isolated than it is now. To see this influx of young people, who had no racist attitudes, who were in great support of the music, and who of course brought with them lots of attractive young women, was quite welcome.

It didn't work much the other way, you didn't see many black people at punk gigs, did you?

Well, the music wasn't there, you know. What the Caribbean community in this country values in music was not to be found in punk

466

rock. Except for the rebellion, the dislike of the way things were, and the hostility toward The System, with a capital 'S'.

Did you see the Sex Pistols as galvanising the whole thing?

Of course. Them and The Clash. I saw them at the Nashville, I saw them at Brunel University, much later on. That funny party of Andrew Logan's where John was rolling on the floor with Jordan, down by the Docklands, Wapping.

How did they change?

Barely. They played tighter. I thought they were quite a good band, apart from anything else. The Clash got better as well. I thought The Clash were absolutely dreadful when I first saw them, but I still liked it. I always liked the Clash clothes. They came up to King's Reach Tower once, with their splashed paint shoes.

So, what happened at the *NME* during punk?

Oh god, a complete split. The paper was absolutely split down the middle.

It took quite a while for the coverage to get going, didn't it? At *Sounds* there was Jonh Ingham . . .

That was my fault, in a way. I didn't get the feature in early enough. Nick asked me if they were worth a feature yet, and I said, not really. They aren't quite ready. So yeah, we were a bit late. There was Tony Parsons, Julie Burchill, myself and Nick Logan who were the people who liked punk rock. And Nick Kent.

Everybody else was basically hostile, even Charles Shaar Murray. People didn't see the music in there, and they couldn't handle the attitude. Whereas I thought with the music, some of it was okay, and I liked the lyrics, but I really liked the attitude. That was the thing. Come and see the Sex Pistols, go home and shave off your moustache.

What about Tony and Julie?

Tony Tyler hired them. Nick was not on the scene much at the time. He was recovering from a nervous breakdown. He didn't want anything to do with the machinations, he was looking for a way out of the *NME*. He wanted to go out in a blaze of glory. He came back and did six months of great issues. It was left to Tony. Tony's final list was full of so many people who subsequently went on to work for us, it was uncanny. Andrew Gill and Paul Morley were both on that list.

Did he frame the 'hip young gunslingers' advertisement?

Charlie wrote that. [The result was the appointment of Tony Parsons and Julie Burchill.]

Did they have an immediate impact on the paper?

It was pretty quick. It only took a month or so. There was a couple of naff pieces by Tony. Fleetwood Mac, stuff like that. But they got into it really quickly. Saw through all the bullshit I was talking about earlier very quickly as well, which made them disliked, of course. But I liked them.

I was very much the liaison person during this time. I was number two on the paper by then, and I was Mister Diplomacy. I was the one who had to take Tony out of the room when he hit Monty Smith, for example. There was also Max Bell, Mick Farren, they were very anti-punk rock. So I was the middle-man. Good times though.

When did they start going out together?

Julie said she was a lesbian when she arrived. But she went out with Max Bell for quite a long time. She had a fling or two with a couple of other people, and then got together with Tony.

When did you take over the paper?

1978. It was post-punk by then. Punk ended for me sometime during '77; it was that gig at Finsbury Park, where they had The Clash, The Jam, the Buzzcocks, The Slits and Subway Sect, and I reviewed that. There was a bit of a riot there, so everyone got their riot, and I just thought it was fucking pointless. This isn't any fun. It wasn't where I was at. By then it was obvious that the good bands were going to go on and become Good Bands in the usual sense.

But the idea that it was radical and progressive and that it was going to change things, that was always an illusion that I didn't share with the punks. Having been a hippy. It took us about three years to

468

realise that we weren't going to change the world. It took the punks about eighteen months. I never thought it could or would. But it did change the world, in some ways.

It certainly changed the music industry, for the better. No doubt about that. It established independent labels, which was a good thing. It broke down that Yankee dominance. It helped reggae. It helped bring recognition to all sorts of people, like Ian Dury, who wouldn't otherwise have got an audience. They'd been going for a while, and couldn't get anyone to listen, cos they didn't wear cowboy boots and sing about Alabama.

How did the writing at the *NME* change with punk? Was it more ideological?

Yes, but with a wider agenda. You have to remember that punk wasn't the only thing that was going on then. There was important politics going on, with the rise of the National Front, and a lot about nuclear power, that sort of thing. There were the first beginnings of what in 1981 was a very strong CND movement. So CND turned a corner, and also some of the hippy ethos was maturing into ecology. Greenpeace was just getting going.

We ran a lot of that stuff in the *NME* at the time. We were trying to push back the boundaries on all fronts. We were doing stuff about comics, literature, film – all the stuff that was left over from the underground press. That was why we did it, and I pushed that side of it very strongly, to see what we could get away with.

So what happened after punk?

I thought it was all rather good. I didn't subscribe to the view that punk was great and then it was all awful again. Punk always said, we've got to destroy in order to create. That was fair enough, and it destroyed a lot of illusions. Illusions that hippies had about themselves, the music business had about itself, music journalists had about themselves.

But they forgot the second part, the creation, because they didn't actually follow through and create very much, with the exception, I would say, of people like The Clash.

What did you think when Thatcher got elected?

469

God help us. I was extremely conscious of it. I think we did see it coming. We'd lived through Ted Heath, who now looks like a pussy-cat, but at the time it wasn't a lot of fun. It was a very reactionary and retrogressive regime, and it was obvious from the outset that she would be a lot worse than him.

I think Jim Callaghan was a fucking disaster. The only Prime Minister we'd ever had who was not elected, and he represented all the worst aspects of Labourism at the time, and none of the good ones. He was more Wilsonian than Wilson, without any of Wilson's vision and rhetoric and understanding of working-class people. Coming from Liverpool he had that instinctive rapport, which Callaghan never had.

One of the worst things was that one of the principal dynamics in British society at that time was racism. It was very powerful, very institutionalised in the police force, and young black people had a real, justified grievance. There was loads of fucking nonsense going on then. And white people in general did not know or talk to black people. They weren't interested in their culture, and they were oblivious to the depth and strength of those feelings.

I'd seen Thatcher on television talking about 'alien culture', and I'd seen Oswald Mosley on television, which became the subject of that song Costello wrote, 'Less Than Zero'. The signs were there to see. Enoch Powell was still a force. So I knew we were in for a rough ride, but I don't think any of us foresaw the ruthlessness with which she would dispatch the Tory aristocracy, and the fact that she did get on top of the British establishment.

No-one saw her ability to do that. I certainly didn't. But I knew we were going to have a hard time. She was Thatcher the milk-snatcher. That was where she was at. She took away from us that which was rightfully ours. Take away from kids their little bottle of milk at playtime. This was an emblem of the welfare state, and she carried on doing exactly that.

Caroline Coon

Writer and activist whose Melody Maker *reviews and features – including 'Rock Revolution' (July 1976); reports about the Mont de Marsan and 100 Club festivals; and the first ever music press interview with The Clash (November 1976) – did much to promote the Sex Pistols and punk. In 1977 she published a collection of these pieces:* 1988: The New Wave Punk Rock Explosion. *Passionate and combative, interviewed at her home in Ladbroke Grove, in London's Notting Hill.*

It was November or December 1975. A lover of mine had barricaded me out of my flat, and I thought, fuck this, and went to stay at the Portobello Hotel. Alan Jones was working behind the counter and he said he was going to a Sex Pistols concert that night. I'd heard about them in Malcolm's shop. Alan was wearing one of the slitted T-shirts. It was more like a party, none of the press were there at all.

I went into one of the *Melody Maker* editorial meetings, and said 'I've just heard this fabulous band', and they said 'No, forget it.' But I'd been looking for it.

How had you joined *Melody Maker*?

At the beginning of the seventies I'd backed off Release [the drugs charity she had co-founded with Rufus Harris] and gone to university. We had tried so hard to effect some change, and when Richard Neville was finally sent to prison, we were numbered people. They had brought in the Emergency Act for Ireland, which they were then using against people who organised demonstrations in England, and being one of those people, I was so fucking exhausted. I joined the *MM* sometime after that.

At the end of '67 I was so angry with the authorities for not paying any attention to the idealism inherent in the psychedelic movement, and in one of the last meetings at the Home Office I said, 'Look, you guys, if you have refused to pay any attention to this passive way of presenting what the youth of today need, then beware, cos the next generation of kids are going to come on to the streets with knives, and they won't be half as fucking polite as we are.'

I knew that because they had crushed the hippy movement, the next generation would come up with something far more aggressive. I didn't realise that the aggression would be so negative. I'd seen our idealism matched with aggression. I didn't expect to see our idealism denigrated and matched with aggressive negativity. I felt very split about it, but it was very interesting to look, as a journalist, at what was being said.

When I went to interview those boys, it wasn't my place to argue with them, I was there to ask questions and listen. At one point when they were slagging off hippies, I suddenly understood that they had grown up reading about hippies in the tabloid press, and what they were doing was spouting the shock and the filth of the hippies, the disgusting drop-outs. So I said, 'The gutter press did to hippies exactly what they're going to do to you.'

Punk was an art movement that became commercial. It's a natural thing to happen. The original music of the hippy era was Soft Machine, Arthur Brown – wonderful stuff, but not particularly commercial.

The great disappointment of the era was that Jagger, instead of spawning a really asexual movement, spawned a horrible kind of machoism. I thought with Jagger, with his lipstick and long hair, at last we were going to get real equality, real androgyny, but he was yet again a fucking macho pig. Horrendous. That was what spawned the women's movement.

Stokely Carmichael gave a talk at the Roundhouse, and women identified very much with the Black Power movement, as an oppressed group. A woman put up her hand and asked where women fitted into the black struggle, and Stokely Carmichael said, 'Horizontal'.

That movement was all about men being as permissive as they liked, as long as the women sat at home putting flowery patches on the jeans. So the women said, if we can't join the revolution with you, we'll have to have our own.

Did you see a similar androgyny in the early days of punk?

There was a dichotomy between the managers, being pornographically sexist, and the bands, who were overriding that. So although Malcolm and Bernie were trying to pull the bands into bondage and little boys and all that stuff, the bands ran with the ball in a different direction. You have to look at the managers – their colour, class, sex, where they came from. The artists using the managerial system, but not really behaving the way the managers wanted.

Although Malcolm and Bernie wanted it to be really sado-masochistic, the bands satirised it, and that was very useful to women, to take the piss out of that ridiculous bondage stuff. It was disappointing that the old-fashioned views of Malcolm and Bernie contaminated the new approach of the artists. When you first met those bands they weren't anti-women at all, but there was a denigration of women came in very quickly. For the women journalists it was murder.

Do you think that there was a sense of punk's own impotence built into it when it started?

No, I think it was planted into those kids, the residue of the impotence that certain people felt at the end of the hippy thing. The politics being fed to those bands was that old-fashioned anarchy. There was a time when that was useful as a reaction against Victorian state control, but anarchy in 1976 was useless.

That was the undoing of the punk movement; they chose a philosophy that was uncreative, destructive, and annihilated themselves. I went rushing to Release and said, 'Look up the law on offensive weapons, cos I think the government is going to use the fact that punks are wearing razors to annihilate the punk movement.' But very quickly, it was obvious that they weren't going to be any problem to the government at all.

Were these ambivalences about punk in your mind at the time?

I was writing only about bands I could enthuse about. I reported that things were happening, and what I personally felt about it was irrelevant. They were exciting and fun, there was so much good humour in it, and furthermore, every so often one has the privilege to see young artists create on the spot.

I was fascinated by the dilemma of an artist who has an idea, and not yet quite the technique with which to express that idea. That was superb. To see them struggling to get the songs across. That got a white-hot fire going on stage.

What do you think those ideas were?

Anger at being the flowers in your dustbin. I disagree with the fashionable idea that the English are incapable of confronting the present. They were writing about the society they knew about: the tower blocks, the dole queues, the schisms in society about race and sex. As usual, they were in the vanguard; artists see what is happening before most other people. Joe Strummer wrote 'White Riot', and two years later the streets were in flames.

Who do you think were the really valid punk bands?

To begin with there were the three bands – the Sex Pistols, who to me were the pop band, The Clash, who were the rock'n'roll band, and the vaudeville of The Damned. They were authentically punk. Then you had Eddie and the Hot Rods, who sounded punk, but said punk is dead, we're nothing to do with it. The Stranglers were interesting because they wanted to join in the party. They were a different generation, but intelligent enough to want to be part of it.

Then of course The Slits, Siouxsie and the Banshees. The Slits were superb, but unfortunately they were victims of English philistinism, in the sense that they thought it was good not to be educated. Ari was the typical rock'n'roll brat, and they didn't have the tools with which to take their art one step further. I adore Viv Albertine, but she was a victim of the denigration of the post-sixties education system, where you didn't have to be articulate. They didn't want to be called musicians. Technique is irrelevant. But you can't paint unless you know how to use a fucking paintbrush, you can't write a book unless you understand how to put words together. That was the tragedy, and as wonderful as The Slits were, their philistinism, their not wanting to get to grips with the tools of their art, made it difficult for them to take it any further. They were also victims of music-press chauvinism.

When did you first go into SEX, and what sort of a presence did it have then?

474

I went into Let It Rock. There was nowhere else in London you could go for clothes which suited the times. Right from the first time she opened. I could never speak to Viv Westwood, she didn't like me very much. I went in there very humbly, saw the clothes and backed out again. I was never on the scene through the whole punk era, I only went out as much as was necessary for the job. I would stand against the wall and watch.

So how did the Pistols develop during the first few times you saw them?

They were having such fun. They were divinely happy and active and partying. Steve told me he wanted to play guitar like Jimi Hendrix. Chris Spedding gave them a confidence they hadn't had, and he said he heard what he thought were the most expressive guitar lines he'd heard in two decades of working in rock'n'roll, and he produced their first demo tape.

Did it strike you that John and Steve formed two centres for the band?

They were different personalities, like Strummer and Jones, really. Paul had the most stable family background. Steve was a typically abused child. But Steve was the musician in the Pistols. John was a pure artist. Like a young Rimbaud . . . he was thoughtful, happy, angry, beautiful. I don't think Johnny ever realised how beautiful he was. They were so insecure, socially. And Sid was hanging around then, and he was just stunning.

Was Sid as stunning as the band?

He was one of the most glamorous beauties of youth, but he was a very disturbed boy. He was great friends with Paul Simonon, he was attracted to that crowd, but then he wanted to be involved in a more definite way.

You know we got arrested at the 100 Club? When the police did their Gestapo raid, and grabbed hold of Sid . . . I really don't think he threw the glass. The thing with the London punks was that the aggression was theatre. A mock-satire on aggression. The whole scene was very un-violent. But as soon as it got more known about, the punks came along from Manchester, and they thought it was really

475

violent. You were getting the kids from out of town who didn't really know how to behave. They had to react to the spitting by being violent, not realising that Johnny's spitting was really terribly funny, that it was theatre.

So I don't think it was Sid, cos he was part of the scene. When they carted Sid off, I went into Release mode, running out behind the police, asking where they were taking him. Why are you arresting this guy? So they threw me in the police car as well. He was beaten up in the police station, to the extent that he couldn't have his picture taken. I wasn't beaten up, so I had my picture taken.

I took him to Offenbach's, then I took him to Fortnum & Mason's for tea, which was very funny. Fortnum's is a place where you can go no matter what you're wearing, but for the first time I'd walked into Fortnum's and the manageress reeled back in horror and said, 'Sir, would you take off your jacket?' This shredded leather, and when he took off the leather he had this incredibly filthy, shredded T-shirt underneath.

What about the incident where Sid had a go at Nick Kent, just before the bottle incident?

Well, that wasn't anything to do with punk. Sid was kind of corrupted by Malcolm's encouraging him to be the side of him that should have been calmed down a bit. A more caring manager would have wanted the artist in the boy, but he was encouraged to be Malcolm's vicious little toy. Sid got very violent, and we eventually couldn't invite him to our parties.

Did you think that the speed around . . .

At the beginning there wasn't!

Where did it come from? And when?

I might be very naive, not being a druggy person, I'm blank on it, but as far as I could see there was hash, but there was no drugs, and that was the nice thing about the punk scene in those early days; compared to the hippy thing, there wasn't. I thought maybe the education about drugs in the sixties had come through, and kids didn't want that any more.

476

The first time I saw Sid he was definitely tanked up . . .

Okay, but he was definitely turned on by the older generation. Jonh would know more than me, but I think he would say that in the early days there was no drugs there. Hash, booze.

Did you go to Louise's a lot?

On the job, two or three times, but I was working hard, I'd go and do the interviews, going back home and writing. I didn't hang out.

For me, meeting Jonh Ingham was wonderful. For the first few months we were competitors, but you couldn't publish it, and when we realised we couldn't publish stuff, we weren't in competition any more; but we would unite to get the story across, so we used to go to gigs a lot more together. I had the sociological overview, and Jonh was the writer. I was learning to write at that point. I was interested in the trauma of childhood, and how this new generation were dealing with that. What fascinated me was, a generation earlier, kids could not live at home, and what was so incredible about these kids was that they were living at home. They were deprived of love, lots of them were badly abused, but they could go home every night.

What was John Lydon like in that respect?

You have to look at his Catholicism. He was wracked with Catholic guilt, which is a classic dilemma in art. Look at John as the Catholic artist, and his whole ambivalence about permissiveness was clashing with his working-class, Catholic upbringing. He had a very warm extended family that adored him.

It was partly a rage of intelligence, wasn't it?

He was frustrated like any working-class child who is very bright; nothing in school captivated him, he was at a seedy school, and all those kids found refuge in art schools. If there's an interesting hiatus in rock'n'roll now, it's that anybody who was creative during that twenty-year period went into art school.

What was Glen like?

A middle-class child, very straight. He was the Monkee, wanted to write pop songs. He couldn't stand Malcolm's violent theatre, and he

477

got out cos he wanted to write pop. He was horrified by the theatre, the chaos, and the tragedy for the Pistols was that they lost their tunesmith. He was writing the melody lines, lovely tunes. He was a nice guy, and he didn't fit in.

We should talk about the swastika . . .

That was a fashion thing. It came in before the first punk rock festival. About three months before that it had become a fashion item with Malcolm and Bernie. I'm terribly suspicious of Jews being anti-Semitic. Jonh and I were horrified. I think people tried to defuse the horror of the swastika by using it, but that's not how it was worn. It was a side effect of Malcolm's New York Dolls thing, and yet again the kids overrode it.

You see Malcolm as being amoral?

Utterly. In the back of the SEX shop, he was catering for a whole lot of outlawed sexual behaviour. The rubber came to the front of the shop, but I think he had a whole connection with rubber parties and all that . . . fine, what adults do to each other, but when he goes tampering with adolescents and children . . . and when Jews get excited about dead bodies and use the trauma of their past as a sexual turn-on, that's very suspect, and that was going on.

Don't you attribute anything positive to Malcolm?

I'm taking an objective view, and I think anything that is destructive is evil, and I do blame Malcolm very much for some of the deaths that happened. Malcolm could have handled Sid in a much more caring way.

Maybe it got to the point that Sid couldn't be helped any more, but part of Sid's relationship to Nancy was about those people's misogynist view of Nancy. If those men had said Nancy is wonderful, she's not a slag, Sid might not have been so drawn to her. He was very protective of Nancy.

He loved women, he wanted to be cared for. It was their destructive, anti-feminist, macho attitude to women which drew Sid, because Sid was going to do anything that Malcolm said he shouldn't do. He could have had a much broader relationship with women had

478

they not been personae non grata. There were a lot of women around Malcolm so long as they were secretaries and office girls . . .

Nancy was wonderful! This whole rock'n'roll thing about groupies. The reason we women journalists were so denigrated was that the male journalists were so jealous of our access; those guys wanted to be groupies. They were groupies but they couldn't fuck the band. Any virile women around were immediately slags, whores.

Jonh Ingham

Sounds *writer who published the first feature on the Sex Pistols in April 1976. With Caroline Coon, he chronicled the movement as it unfurled throughout 1976, when he left* Sounds *to manage Generation X. As one of the first contributors to Greg Shaw's* Who Put the Bomp *fanzine, Ingham was schooled in rock fandom, and his detailed, obsessive articles did much to spread the word and the mood.*

When did you first come to England?

End of March, 1972, from Los Angeles. Born in Australia, British parents. First moved to Vancouver, when I was ten, for a year, went back to Australia, moved for good in 1964, when I'd just turned 17, to Canada again. My mother had this big thing that she wanted to move to America, and of course there were big quota problems then, so her thing was, you get to Canada, and you can get into America from there.

I went to Cal Arts, the film school. I can't remember when I wasn't completely obsessed with movies. At Cal Arts, they had a general courses section. Robert Christgau was a teacher, he had a class on popular culture, and I took his class. The first week, he handed out fifteen copies of the same album, and said, 'Okay, everyone is going to write a record review for the next class.' He came back and said, 'Well, you've got some potential, if you want to keep doing it.'

Can you remember what the album was?

Yeah, it was a Guess Who album.

So you said it was a bucket of shit?

Yeah, more or less. The class was really interesting, and that's how I met Greil Marcus, he worked with me very much as a mentor, he got me published in *Creem*.

In America, the rock critics were taken seriously, and took themselves seriously, as opposed to England, at that time.

Oh yes, Christgau treats it very intellectually – a critic in the true sense of the word. He made me look at the thinking process of criticism in a very intellectual way, which definitely helped.

I came to England to go to the London Film School. That lasted one term. There was no equipment, it was this dreary old warehouse, and I was doing quite well with writing, I got involved with *Rolling Stone*, and so after the summer I never went back to school, it just seemed like a waste of money.

Who else were you writing for? English *Creem*, and *Let It Rock*?

Yeah, I ended up being the editor of that for a while. I was freelancing for *NME*, I did a couple of things for *Oui*, *Rolling Stone*, both here and America, *Creem* and things like *Fusion* and *Phonograph*.

I arrived at exactly the moment that Bowie took off. Bowie was someone that really fascinated me. All the cool people were saying how cool he was. The Flamin' Groovies were supporting him, and I was friendly with them, so I'd keep seeing him all the time. The London Poly gig was great. The ceiling is like eight feet high, the sweat is pouring down the walls, and he had all the moves, down on the knees, giving the guitar head. It was like a gig in a cafeteria.

Did you feel there was a propensity with English kids to be very stylish . . .

Oh yeah. It was the height of the platform shoes and all that stuff, which I found fascinating, and it still amazes me to this day. It was kind of shocking at that point. English people will do almost anything, there is no look too outlandish. In America, if you did some of the stuff you saw every day walking around town, those parents would kill their children! It would be a major crisis in the family.

I'd seen Alice Cooper in America a few times, as he was coming up, and that was so completely outlandish and wonderful. It was great. Then I saw him at Wembley, with Roxy supporting. I wrote a review of it. There was this thing in LA at the time, this debate about 'decadence', and you would see all these people on a Friday night, they would put on all this weird nonsense, you got the feeling that

481

they had put on this mask, and they would put on their suit and tie and go to work the next day. The phrase that I remember to this day was that in England, the only difference between Friday night and Monday morning is forty-eight hours. I thought that summed it up.

When you're reading this stuff from afar, as I was for about twenty years, from the beginning of Beatlemania, you look at it with a very finely-tuned eye. Even though I was in places like Australia and Canada, it was constantly being drummed into me, almost in a subliminal way, how English I was. Strange presents from my grandmother who had gone down to Carnaby Street and bought me something mod, you know.

What do you think were the harbingers of punk, between say 1972 and 1975?

Roxy Music were fabulous. I was well into that one, all the way. Same with Bowie, I'm sure for all the same reasons everyone else was into it. But there was a sense of boredom about the whole thing. With Roxy and Bowie, you didn't have the feeling of a movement. There was no explosion like there had been in '64, '65, '66. There was frustration, more than boredom.

At the time of the Iggy concert at the Scala, I don't think the word punk was even being used about the sixties groups. At what point did they start calling stuff like the Chocolate Watch Band . . .

Around the time *Nuggets* came out.

I think Lenny Kaye set it, there. Before that, they were garage bands. The Iggy concert was important in that it's extremely well remembered by those who were there. The myth that's grown up around it has influenced a lot of stuff. It was a midnight concert at the King's Cross cinema, and the reason we were all dragged to it was to see the Flamin' Groovies doing their first English concert, and then there was the Stooges.

If you were into all this stuff, going to finally see this thing was a big moment. Iggy had about a thirty- or forty-foot lead on his mike. He could go anywhere in the audience, which he proceeded to do.

First of all, he was all in silver; silver hair, silver jeans that barely covered his hips, and these winkle-picker shoes which I think were also silver. He's pictured on the back of *Raw Power*. That was weird enough. And James Williamson's got this rouge and lipstick on, whatever. Little high-heel shoes and stacks of Marshalls behind him.

The second Iggy went out into the audience, he would just grab people, and I got extremely nervous. You could feel immense fear, from everybody. The last thing you wanted was to have this maniac attack you. The sense was very strong that this man will do literally anything. He wasn't going to keep it within the bounds of sanity. Fuck entertainment, within the bounds of reasonableness!

There were a lot of technical problems, the mike cut out, and came back, and he started to sing, and it cut out again, and he went, 'Oh fuck', and threw the mike down, and it bounced back up about two feet off the ground, in about four different pieces. Iggy stands there and starts singing 'The Shadow of Your Smile'.

That was when I was really impressed, more than anything else. Up to that point it could have been someone who was just completely out of control, but he was very clearly in control. He had the best bored look I've ever seen, and in a way he was just singing to himself, but he was singing to everybody, and people started to shut up.

I was very into the Flamin' Groovies as well. They were brilliant. They were like the ultimate anglophile American rock band, I think they understood the essence of it very well. Other stuff . . . Roxy, obviously. I liked their sense of theatre. And it was fun, there was a great sense of humour about Roxy. They weren't serious at all. The Stones were still doing some good stuff around then, but look at the paucity of it. Nothing else comes immediately to mind.

I was writing about a lot of the classic rock figures of the time. What was I writing about? If I didn't like something, I didn't write about it, that was a rule. The idea of slagging something off because you didn't like it was anathema. One thing that Christgau drilled into me: knowing why you like something is easy, understanding why you *don't* like something is much harder. Is it just you, or is there an objective reason for that?

I always wrote from enthusiasm. This is probably another reason that I thought propaganda was more important. In Greil's words, I had the gift of persona. I was always very conscious of trying to write a verbal movie. Coming out of film school, I wanted people to see the whole thing. I would exaggerate for effect, quite a lot, and I would give people the benefit of the doubt.

Queen were interesting, when they came along. I always loved Sweet, much to the disgust of everyone around me, I thought they were great. I was ribbed constantly about that. It was pop, and I was totally into pop.

Dr Feelgood?

They were very good live, I never really got into their records. And there came a point . . . obviously you can't be twenty-two and doing loads of speed forever, which was clearly what it was all based on. There again, by the time they were famous, I was well off them.

I got married when I was twenty-one, and here I was doing the whole suburban thing. Trying to support the wife, and doing what I thought was the thing you did, even though it was completely detached from all of it. Going broke, I got myself a job as a publicist at EMI, and a year later, Island Records called up and said, 'Come on over here', and being young and snotty and knowing more than Chris Blackwell, I was out of there in about six months.

That's when I started writing for *Sounds*. I went back to *NME*, and by then Neil Spencer was in. The reason I went to *Sounds*, this was the summer of 1975, I was hacking. I got about six stories out of one interview with Sadistic Mika Band, that's the sort of level I was working at. There was a staff revolution, the first major staff revolution at *Sounds*, Penny Valentine and all those people all left. I knew there was an in there, so I went up and joined.

By 1975, were you aware of the SEX shop, and Malcolm?

Oh yeah, but I never went down there. When it was Let It Rock, I went and bought some lurex socks. It was the teddy-boy time, it was interesting, but I was never much of a one for nostalgia, and I perceived it as a nostalgia thing. But what I did find interesting, in quite a detached way, was when I went past and it had become Too Fast to Live, Too Young to Die. I found it quite fascinating that a person would change the name of their shop.

There was different clothing, you could see there was a movement forward from the teddy-boy stuff. Let It Rock was drapes and crepes and lurex socks. Jordan was there, even then. She sold me my socks! By Too Fast to Live, they'd covered the window so you couldn't see in. They had leather vests with chains and studs, and the naked-girl playing cards attached to them. It was halfway between teddy boy and SEX. It was quite bizarre.

When it became SEX, it was great, there was pink plastic wrapped around these leathers. It was great that you couldn't see in, and there was these six weird models with the straps around them. You had no idea what was in there. I knew Chrissie Hynde almost as soon as she showed up. She was working there, and I'd see her at gigs, and she had the rubber mini-skirts, and the T-shirts with the lines of nonsense that didn't mean anything.

Thinking back it seems strange to be fascinated with all this stuff without ever feeling the need to go in there. Partly because I never felt that I would want to wear it.

Malcolm later said, 'You had to have the shop. You had the band wearing the strange clothes, and you needed the shop as a place for the kids to go and buy the clothes.' And Bernie's problem was that he didn't have the shop. At that point, it's not about the band or the music, it's creating a lifestyle. The reason the Small Faces happened was there was the fashion that supported it, and with punk there wasn't that, they had to create it.

That was Malcolm's genius, he understood all that very clearly. You couldn't just have a band wearing strange clothes, in that respect they're just a costume. To create the broad base, you needed the outlet to sell the clothes the band was wearing.

Did you meet Malcolm before you met the band?

Well, here I am sitting out in Ealing, writing these stories for *Sounds*. Twenty-four, going on twenty-five, and being increasingly bored with music. The sense that something has got to explode just from the sheer boredom. There's two stories: you interview the band, and you're on the road with the band. How many times can you write that thing? Especially for a weekly.

There was no future, except that I knew I was getting very sick of writing about rock'n'roll. I was able to peg people at quite an early stage in their career and be fairly accurate. I thought, let's start looking for the unknown groups, and start being a pontificator. Point some fingers. I never told anybody this, I was just doing it. The only one that comes to mind was I saw Doctors of Madness.

One day I opened the *NME* and there was this review, 'Sex Pistols' – and just the name alone, my god, that is just brilliant. From that point, the band was just incredible in my mind. I think Neil Spencer wrote the review. Immediately I was a fan, I wanted to see this band. I was loading so much imagery into this name. It was like the first hearing of The Who. The Who? It was a name that just hit you like a sledgehammer.

The Sex Pistols was the first time in years that that kind of thing had happened. It was a dangerous name, it had that word, SEX, in it. It was aggressive. The fact that they were young, they were clearly uncontrollable, from the review, it all sounded very intriguing, and this fit into my plan about finding new groups. But I didn't have a clue about how to go about finding them.

It stayed in my mind, and I must have read that review about five times, across a period of time. I couldn't understand why I was fixating on this, but it was coalescing all these frustrations, and it kept coming back to the name, how strong that was, as an image. It told you who the band were. The Clash also, to some extent. Ten years later, it's just a name, like The Who. The Clash didn't sound right. But the Sex Pistols did sound right.

Anyway, I came out of one of the weekly editorial meetings, and there was a message for Vivien Goldman from Malcolm McLaren, he wanted to talk to her about the Sex Pistols, and I leapt. I went, 'Vivien, you're not going to like this band. Let me call him back.' And she wouldn't have liked it. I never did ask Malcolm why he had called her rather than me. He was calling who he thought would be the best person, with all the papers.

So I called him back, and he'd been calling about a gig at El Paradise, so that's where I went and saw them. So I did this review, and first of all I had to see Malcolm, did an interview with Malcolm, and then I got to see the band. That was the sequence of how I actually got to them. I saw them play, then talked to Malcolm, maybe a week later, then maybe a week after that, I talked to the band. It was March. They'd been together three months.

486

It was a strip club, the size of a good-size living room. There's rows of seats, and a stage up there that couldn't have been more than ten feet wide and maybe six feet deep, with a mirror behind it. The early Pistols crowd were there. Jordan and Viv Albertine. Caroline was there. The Arrows pop group were there. A strange assortment of people. And Ray Stevenson walked in and started setting up umbrella strobes. I started getting really cynical at that point, I'm thinking what is this shit?

And they came on, and John's wearing this ripped red sweater, and his hair and his Ben Franklin glasses, and I liked him, immediately. They looked funny. There was some stuff between the songs where John was trying to be Johnny Rotten, was very funny to me. It was like a comic book. It wasn't the madman we all saw nine months later at all. He was saying, 'You'd better like what I'm doing cos otherwise I'm just wasting my time' – and that had me grinning from ear to ear.

All the songs kind of sounded the same, but they were clearly different. The thing about them all sounding the same was just from people who didn't listen. While a lot of the songs were similar, some really worked as pop songs, and others were like, well, it'll be over in two minutes. That was apparent while it was happening, it wasn't something you thought about afterwards.

But at that point I decided I was going to write about this band, I like this. You couldn't analyse or intellectualise about it. I had the sense that something was going on here, that this was something to follow. And it wasn't called punk. Malcolm actually hated the word punk, he liked 'new wave'. He insisted that we should call it new wave. It was only when people like The Jam showed up, and they were being called new wave that he said, 'No, we're not new wave, we're punk!'

How many people were at that Paradise gig?

Oh, fifty to a hundred, but it was a full room. It was a small room, one of those shop fronts down Soho. Sticky floors, dim lighting, a kind of bar set up on a table with some bottles. It was like a private party, in a way. I was talking to Caroline, I'd met her through mutual friends, this was maybe the third time I'd met her. She'd

487

been following them, she used to go to SEX all the time, and she was getting peeved that she was going to get pipped.

So when you wrote about the band, what was Malcolm like?

Yeah, I wrote this review, and the editor of *Sounds*, Alan Lewis, asked me what they were like, and I started talking, they were very interesting, and Alan says, 'I want a feature.' And I'm like, 'Wait a minute, they're only three months old.' But Alan wanted a feature. I was going over what I'd said to him, wondering, why is he jumping at this? But I called Malcolm, said, 'I want an interview', and he told me to meet him in a restaurant – coffee bar – on the King's Road.

It was the middle of the week, at about 11 a.m. I walk in, and there's only Malcolm there. I say, 'Where's the band?' He says, 'I just want to talk to you first.' And he did the whole rap, from top to bottom. And listening to this was like hearing all this stuff I'd been thinking about for two years. And what was galling was that he was not only saying what I'd been thinking, but here was someone who had actually gone out and acted on it.

I admired him immensely. He knew exactly how to package all that. What's popular now? Do the opposite. People are wearing flared trousers? Wear straight legs. Long hair? Cut it short. People are taking drugs? The Sex Pistols don't take drugs. This is an interesting point, when we get into drugs. When they get into drugs, they are corrupted by us older folk.

So I talked with Malcolm for an hour, hour and a half at least. It was so articulate, and it was all the stuff I'd been thinking. He was really intelligent, that was the part that really impressed me. He's got this flesh nylon turtle-neck T-shirt on, a leather jacket, and these drainpipe SEX trousers, and I kept looking at that shirt, thinking how sweaty and uncomfortable, and I was really impressed that someone would want to dress like that!

So I went back, and Alan asked me about it, and I said, 'This guy is brilliant.' I'd made an arrangement with Malcolm to meet the Pistols. He wanted to meet in Denmark Street. Malcolm tells me to meet him at twelve-thirty, I went up there at exactly twelve-thirty, and he's standing there with Nils, and Malcolm says, 'Where have you been, you're late, they've gone already. They came at twelve, waited twenty minutes, and they've gone.' Yeah, right.

So we made another appointment. Let's meet at seven-thirty. Again, it's outside, in Denmark Street, so I show up at seven-twenty. He's standing there, and Paul and Steve and Glen are there, and Malcolm's going, 'You're late again.' I say, 'No, I'm early.' He says, 'We were just about to leave.' And I say, 'You know, fuck off. You're winding me up.' And he laughs, and I've passed a test.

At this point, I had a beard. I'd had a moustache and I really hated shaving, and I'd decided that I'd let it grow until my 25th birthday and then shave it all off. So I had about six weeks of growth, way past designer stubble. We go to that awful pub down at the corner of Cambridge Circus there. John's down there with a couple of girls. So we're walking down there, I'm talking with Paul and Steve and Glen, we're talking about bands.

All this is in that first interview, almost exactly as it happened. Through this, I'm getting on very well with Steve, which is odd, cos in many ways we're completely opposite. Paul's a nice guy, he's very normal, and we're having a nice time, and the interview starts, and Malcolm is sitting there, and he'll answer questions that are directed at them, if he thinks it will serve his cause better. I can't remember everything we said, but it's all on paper.

And all the time, John's sitting there, very politely bored. And they're talking about him like he's not there. I get the story about how they call him Rotten because of his teeth. And I'd got from the first interview with Malcolm the story about the jukebox, and the wire coat-hanger for the microphone, and they're talking about John, and how he doesn't like rock, and so on. And John's sitting there, and he's quite intimidating, but I'm not going to be intimidated.

And they're telling me why he's doing it, but finally I turn to him and look him in the eye and say, 'Okay, I've heard it from everyone else – why are you doing it?' And it's like a snap edit, one frame he's normal, and the next frame, the kilowatts are on. There's no transition at all. 'Because I hate shit' – and he rants on and on, I hate this and I hate that, glaring at me. I look at Malcolm and he's got a nervous look on his face. You know, don't look at me, it's not me, it's him.

I just cracked up laughing. This boy was incredible, you know, he really amused me. He's going, 'I hate hippies.' I'm finding myself defending myself to this kid, going, 'I'm not a hippy, I've never been a hippy, I just haven't shaved.' From the first sentence, I was absolutely sold. So I handed in this story. I can't remember if Alan said he was going to put it on the cover or not, but he liked it.

One of Malcolm's comments to me was, 'I don't think until I open my mouth, and then I've got to follow up on what my mouth is saying.' He's thinking as he talks. When I'd met him in Denmark Street, this was about three days after he'd been thrown down the stairs by John Curd. That incident made him realise one of the planks in his platform was to go outside the music business totally, to form your own alternative to what was going on in the business.

Malcolm wasn't Machiavelli at this point, at all. He saw himself as a manager, in the traditional sense of the role. He was the fifth Sex Pistol, in that sense. He was doing a lot of controlling, in the sense of the manipulation of money, all those things, but they hadn't worked out the roles. He didn't control, in the sense that he manipulated the process later on.

The Nashville was the next gig they played. I was standing at the back, and they were playing. It was with The 101ers, and it was mostly a 101ers crowd. Here we were with Malcolm trying to get his band into situations where they were so completely one hundred and eighty degrees from anything else around. They were so alienated from what was going on at that point that it was beyond confrontational to put them into these situations.

One of the things was, you can't get in to see the Sex Pistols for free. You have to pay, because then you're going to see them. You're not going to have a pint and see some band on a stage, playing. That was impressive, and quite interesting thinking, and opposite to what other people were doing, you get your band in front of an audience. What he was doing was creating an audience that was specifically for the band. And the shop, and the clothes. Even at that early point, it was about the clothes.

There's a tendency now to see it all as intellectual processes, but there were very long instinctual developments. Vivienne said to me that summer that SEX clothing grew out of the fact that Malcolm would be out, and that she'd show him things, and he'd go, 'This is great, but I don't like the pocket' – and he'd just rip it off. And sometimes it wouldn't come completely away, it would just be hanging down. And she thought, why not incorporate that into the clothing?

Anyway, that night there were about twenty Sex Pistols fans and maybe three hundred 101ers fans. The 101ers were big at that time. I couldn't understand it, I thought they were boring. There were always these pop prophets coming along, and Joe Strummer was this week's flavour. So I'm watching the Pistols playing, from the back, and they're not being very good, it was kind of disappointing after everything up to that point.

Suddenly Vivienne is slapping this girl's face. I'm at the back, the stage is down there, and she's in the front row, off to the side, and going, whack! whack! whack! Slapping this girl. And this guy comes barrelling over and grabs Vivienne. Whether Malcolm has watched the whole thing, I don't know. The next thing this guy is ten feet away across the stage, with Malcolm about a foot behind him, fists flying out. The classic photograph. And John, with this look of glee, dives off the stage and starts throwing a few punches as well. Steve came forward and started pulling them away, apart from each other. Steve tried to break it up. Then of course it was complete mêlée. They went on to finish. Vivienne said afterwards to Caroline that she was bored and decided to liven things up. She just slapped this girl for no reason at all. It was extremely electrifying, I'll say that.

Can you remember what song they were playing?

No, I didn't know the songs at that point at all. I was aware of 'I'm Not Your Stepping Stone' (which I didn't recognise as a Monkees song). I knew 'No Feelings', I knew 'Vacant'. I knew 'Submission', which was completely different. Up until they recorded it, it was just another rave like the others.

They finished the set, and about ten people went like [half-hearted applause], and there was a group of fans around John at that point. I found myself staring at him, and feeling intimidated, and again I went, this is absurd. So I went over and said, 'Hello', and he has this great big grin on his face, and said, 'Hello.' And I'd passed the test. I remember feeling that distinctly.

Then The 101ers came on, and the first song was 'Too Much Monkey Business'. Which Joe said later was a deliberate choice. He

491

said that was the night he realised that The 101ers and everything about them was completely passé. That was the night that he killed the group, in his head. That was the point also where I said to myself, there is no point in writing about this analytically. The point is to encourage this, because we need it.

We're going to appeal to some kid about nineteen, reading *Sounds* in the suburbs, who is as bored with the fucking situation as I am. And is looking to get excited. Telling him about three chords in the key of E, all that shit, is not going to get him excited. Telling him about this madman who's going to leap offstage and punch people who his manager is doing his best to demolish while he's playing, that's interesting.

But, what is the point of taking that intellectual approach to music when clearly, this group is going to be appealing to fifteen-year-olds, and no fifteen-year-old wants to read about that. They want to get excited by all the cool shit, the clothes, the noise. I mean, a person who is going to be turned on by intellectual analysis, in my mind, is not going to go for the Sex Pistols. I saw it as propaganda, far more than analysis.

Was Malcolm seeing it as a movement even then?

I felt that he was doing what I did, and he acted on it, because that was his personality. He could see what was coming in off the street. I wasn't off the street, I was living in Ealing, for god's sake. The idea of relating to kids on the street never even occurred to me. I think it was very different for him; he saw kids, strange, weird kids who didn't relate to anything.

The thing that impressed me through that first nine months was how intelligent the whole thing was. I remember that disco out in East London where The Clash played [The Lacey Lady], and bin-liners had just showed up a couple of weeks earlier, and Mick Jones and I were just falling about, talking about how it was so fucking stupid, but what a great idea, you know. At that point it was just another alternative, it wasn't the uniform or anything.

Mick was saying about the whole movement, how intelligent it was, but at the same time there was this real undertone of stupidity. That was part of what was so appealing about it. He said, 'Probably when it gets popular, it's going to get really stupid.' There's prophetic words.

At the time I never really thought about the effect that people were getting from the writing I was doing. But it was the only place that it was being treated positively. Caroline was able to get some stuff in there over the summer. The fact that it was being done in an intelligent way meant that it was appealing to intelligent people.

The Nashville gig was April, and then you started going to see the band a lot?

There was the 100 Club gig a few weeks after that, every Tuesday through May, June. They were supporting, and they were just playing, it was very fresh and new, and nine tenths of the audience would probably be for the headlining band. At that stage we're talking about fifty people. A hundred would be a good gig. I must have known Sid by this point. I was most friendly with Glen and Paul, and Steve to a slightly lesser level. You could talk to John, but you couldn't call yourself a friend.

Did you start to get to know the fans?

Well, if you're talking about fifty or a hundred people and you keep seeing each other in the same place, you're going to get to know each other. The point where I realised something was going on, there was a review I did, there was a headlining band that was so abysmal . . . someone in the band wore a fez. It was early summer, and Paul Cook said, 'You've got to review this band, they're so bad. You've got to warn people away from them.'

So I did that, and I put a bit at the end about the Sex Pistols, and the improvements or whatever. Within about two or three weeks after that – and this is about a two- or three-month period, and I've written about them three times – and a secretary from EMI asked me, how are your band the Sex Pistols doing, and I'm like, they're not my band! But it occurred to me that this was the third or fourth person who had said this to me. And I decided, there's something really going on here, and I'm going right in it.

At this point I didn't know about The Clash, I didn't know there was such a person as Bernie Rhodes, and in a sense I was on the edge of it, despite being in the middle of it. Mick wasn't at those Pistols gigs, nor Joe, nor Paul. Never saw any of that stuff. But they knew Malcolm.

The strength of *Sounds* was their attitude of, if it moves, give it two pages. What was the *NME*'s attitude?

They weren't doing anything. In the middle of all this, Farren wrote that Titanic feature. I'm like, wait a minute, you're a year too late on that story. This is absurd. The thing that really pissed me off was that they were patently and consciously ignoring it, at that point. Clearly they'd seen the Pistols, I was ranting and raving away, and Nick Kent knew these people. I just accepted that it was a conscious decision on their part, and it seemed to me that they had become part of the obsolete group. It annoys me that in the revisionist history that's been written they've been given the credit for it all: 'Mick Farren wrote the Titanic piece and after that it all exploded'. Bullshit.

It was a great summer, that had a lot to do with how everyone had great spirits about the whole thing. The next event was the Lyceum. What was really strange was that it seemed such an amazingly unimportant gig. They're third or fourth on the bill to The Pretty Things at the Lyceum; I mean, come on. And they were so absolutely petrified before, backstage. Steve couldn't talk, he couldn't utter a word, he had the look of death on his face.

To them, it was extremely important. It was the first time they'd played in a big space. John was really nervous. I found that strange. It hadn't occurred to me that for them, they wanted to win people over. Perhaps they were scared by the sheer physical size of the joint. That was the night that John stubbed out cigarettes on the back of his hand while he was singing. I remember talking about that in the review. It frightened me.

By that point we were rolling joints, and I think Louise's was in full swing by then, so the 'we don't take drugs' was just publicity by then. He had the most manic look in his eye when he did it. It was back to the Iggy thing in a way; you couldn't predict this person.

Whatever gig I saw between the Lyceum and Manchester, there was a quantum leap in ability from previously. Up until this point, they were getting better at it, but it was still the same kind of noise. They were getting better at being the same thing. But suddenly there was this major step up in musical ability. Glen was phenomenal, the bass playing was tremendous. Paul was right on the beat. In one night, suddenly they were all just there.

494

Suddenly you knew that this was a really great band. The next time, their second show in Manchester, was about two weeks later, it was a next step up again. It was light years ahead of what we'd just seen. It was amazing. That was the first night they did 'Anarchy', and that was just monstrous. It was so cool, and there was no warning. The first we knew about it was when they were on stage.

That was also the first Buzzcocks gig. I didn't talk to Howard very much, I talked to Pete Shelley. And it was another punk group, and they weren't from London, so it was clear that it was spreading. It was great fun, and the feeling that there was another band, the sense that the movement was growing. And Malcolm was a great theorist through all this stuff. There was no us and them thing going on, everyone was in it together.

He was doing some great pontificating. Opening his mouth and seeing what it says, dispensing advice here, there and everywhere, encouraging everybody. That was the thing, he was encouraging anything that moved, that looked interesting. Later on, anything that came up that challenged the Pistols' supremacy, that he couldn't control, then immediately he didn't like them any more.

Punk had got quite Stalinist by that stage.

Malcolm made the Pistols invisible. The kids are there, and you can't have the Pistols. I guess it worked, but it was a dumb thing to do, making the band Olympian. There were much better ways to have done it.

It took him about two days to deal with that whole Grundy thing, before he got control. I think he was completely freaked out. Wouldn't you have been? That was the ruination of the whole thing. It was right on the eve of that first tour. We could get into Malcolm's ideas. To begin with, he wanted to do a package tour, where every band did fifteen minutes and they all used the same equipment. Three bands would use one set of gear, two bands would use another and the Pistols would have their own.

If that had been allowed to go on its merry way, without Bill Grundy, it would have grown very slowly across all of 1977, like a snowball. It probably would have ended up being a lot more intelligent. But in one day, the entire country became punk. And that's the death of it. Anyone who's smart is going to stay away from it.

Did you go to the Mont de Marsan punk festival?

Yeah. I think I wrote about it. I saw The Damned's first gig. That was bizarre; they never rehearsed, they didn't like the idea of rehearsing. They were all playing at this white-light speed, and just by chance things would mesh and then fall apart, and mesh again, and because it was so intensely fast, you had this phasing up and down, it was really odd. It was funny. It was great.

What did you think about the swastika?

The summer of 1976, Dingwalls, with the Flamin' Groovies. Jordan was in her brown-shirt outfit with the swastika, which really bothered me a lot. I really wondered about that. The party line never washed with me at all, it was such bullshit. Once the image has been born, it's so easy to be born again, you know. The first time is like a major breakthrough, but after that, it doesn't go away. I was always really scathing about that whole swastika nonsense.

Did that set up a distancing element, with something you were already very enthusiastic about? And did you regard it as integral to the whole package? Or was it just something somebody did that you thought was bullshit?

Mostly the latter. It definitely had a major effect on the place, in a very negative sense. John made me introduce him to Ian Dury, who was wearing razor blade earrings. They'd been going at each other. Ian had these earrings, he had a skin crop, they were such spiritual brothers, and Ian had been into that trip for a while. Ian and John are really going at each other, with this sarcastic, snide, vaguely polite back and forth.

John turned to me and said, 'Why don't you introduce me to this guy?' And so I did, and once they'd met, all holds were off. I wish I could remember what was said. They were having a grand time, slagging each other. It was barbed, but it was in good humour.

It sounds like John had worked out what he wanted to be, and he was growing into his role.

Absolutely. He had a very articulate idea of who he was, and he was very professional about what he was doing. He took his job seriously.

496

What he worked on was sharpening who he was, and making it larger for the public. Knowing he was good, he wanted to be the best that he could possibly be. He wanted to be the best around. All the band did, but he didn't see it in a musical role, at all.

Steve wanted to be a good guitarist, Glen wanted to be a good songwriter. John isn't thinking about music at all. He hated rock'n'roll, he was a reggae man, and he liked The Doors. He saw it completely outside its musical context. It was the death of rock'n'roll. It was about making a big fucking racket and annoying a lot of people.

How much do you think drugs had to do with it? The chemical theory of pop is pretty important.

Oh, absolutely, it fuelled the entire course of twentieth-century popular music. But drugs in what sense?

Well, by the end of 1976, speed was pretty ubiquitous. When did the drugs start to come in, and why was it speed? As opposed to dope, or acid?

Acid, I'm sure, was perceived by them as a hippy drug. Dope too. Speed had all those wonderful advantages of being very cheap, you don't take very much of it and it lasts an extremely long time, and it's great to have that feeling of energy. It came in during the late spring, early summer. By the time of the Mont De Marsan festival, there was speed going on at a pretty furious level.

I'm sure that when Malcolm was doing that No Drugs thing, they probably weren't taking a lot of drugs. They got into it because of people like me, older people around them, who weren't going to give up their drug habits for the sake of Malcolm's party line. And if you break out the drugs, they're not going to say no. That wouldn't be punk. It felt great, speeding through the night.

Do you remember going to Louise's?

I was never into discos, and I think with the kids at Louise's it was the same thing; they'd done it all, and this was the next new thing. It was basically a lesbian club. It was like the club house, you'd go down there on a Friday or Saturday night, and you'd see the same hundred people, and it was slowly getting bigger.

Another thing was, we never, ever said where it was. That was a conscious decision by Caroline and myself; write about it, but don't say the street. Being snobbish and elitist. We didn't want the sightseers in there. One of those great hot summer nights, everyone in there was on acid. Nils wasn't, but all of the Pistols were. They were very funny.

It struck me that there were people in that early crowd, the Bromley thing, and there were two guys who were clearly gay, but they weren't defensive, they weren't at all concerned what anyone thought. This was like the next crest after all that gay consciousness-raising in the early seventies.

The next thing is the 100 Club Punk Festival.

Ah yes. What were we going to call it? The rock critics' need to categorise. I remember during the afternoon, when people were first putting their gear down there, Brian Watts was going, 'There's going to be hundreds of people here tonight, this place is going to be jammed.' 'You're out of your mind.' 'Really? It's been going for two days now.' And sure enough, we came back for soundcheck, and there's two hundred people outside.

I remember the first time seeing a punk I didn't know on the street. I thought it was really cool; someone I don't know.

What were the actual performances at the event like?

The Siouxsie thing was all one long medley. I think they stopped once in fifteen or twenty minutes. When she started doing 'Goldfinger', it was bizarre. What a revelation, that you could do an oldie in punk. By then, party lines were starting to be drawn, what was and what wasn't allowed. And doing an oldie like that just seemed so strange. They were great, Sid just kept going.

They kept droning on, because Sid wouldn't stop. They'd had one rehearsal, he'd never played drums before. It was kind of childlike, very monotonous, four-four, but at least he kept a beat, as far as I remember. Finally she just went over and took the drumsticks away from him. They did 'The Lord's Prayer' as well, which was kind of interesting. I think it was the first time on stage for all of them.

The Clash were interesting. Did Simonon break a string that night? There's a photo of Joe tuning Paul's bass. At one point he turned a

498

radio on, and it was either tuned to police radio, or it was something on the BBC maybe, but there were these voices going back and forth . . . it was very strange.

The Pistols were just absolutely phenomenal. That was one of their great peaks, the place was going berserk. From the time of the Lyceum onwards, they would be completely different every two or three weeks. One night Steve would just do nothing but feedback and noise, and two weeks later he would just play notes, with no noise at all. Around the 100 Club, he was putting it all together, so you'd get these sheets of noise with really clean playing in between.

You could see all this building really fast, as they got it more together. John was getting much better in terms of projection, and also they now had an audience, so he didn't need to be defensive all the time. The Screen on the Green was another landmark one. He had a capped tooth, and he knocked it out with the microphone, during the first or second song, and he was in intense pain, and he went completely over the top.

'Anarchy in the UK' wasn't analytical or intellectual in the least. It's something I could never get about the Bernard/Clash thing. I could never believe that Strummer was actually serious about that stuff. He was definitely smart, but to me, with his background and education, it was like, come on Joe, you know better than to believe Bernard, this is a load of rubbish, and yet he would espouse it completely.

When did the politics start coming in?

Later in the year. A lot of those party lines were drawn by the journalists writing about it. Up to that point, they weren't very articulate about what they were saying. Certainly in that political sense. I found the stuff much more sociological before then. Mick saying he'd never lived below the sixth floor. Those things made a lot more sense to me, because it was a lot more about human beings, rather than these political lines.

What were Subway Sect like at the 100 Club?

Great. I always liked them a lot, and that was one of their best performances, actually. They were all in these grey school pullovers. slacks and stuff. It was more like punk jazz, in a way. It wasn't all like three chords, all thrashing away. Everyone had a completely different approach to how they wanted to do it. None of that stuff ever made it on to record.

Did you do the Chelmsford prison pamphlet?

I reviewed it. The thing was, you weren't allowed to get up out of your seat. The number one guy was in there for murder, and he was huge, and he sat front row, centre, and everybody else took their cues from him. So if he didn't like you, you were ready to be mincemeat. So for the first ten minutes he was giving John all this lip, in between songs, and John just kept giving it right back to him, and the guy thought it was really funny. So then it was cool.

And they had maybe one band a month, so any entertainment is good, you know. Someone threw a shirt up on the stage, and John was swinging it, and dropped it right in front of him, and just stood there and leered at the guy. The guy had to get up out of his chair to get the shirt, and he was really nervous about it. Suddenly this guy who was clearly in there for drugs, long hair and all that, a total hippy, burst out of his seat and started raving, and the guards didn't do anything, so the whole place got verging on wild.

Where did John get all this chutzpah from?

I think just confidence from playing a lot. They were a working band. They were off across the country playing three nights a week, living in the back of a van, doing the rock'n'roll bit. They worked their arses off.

We were all doing speed at a fair rate, at that time. Mick Jones says he doesn't remember recording the first album because he was on so much speed. He did say that only about a year later; and from my own case, when I came back about two years later, I was walking up the street and saw The Vortex, and I'd completely forgotten it existed. There are huge blanks in my memory from doing that stuff, speeding my brains out.

The White Riot tour at the Rainbow, standing in the lobby during the interval between the acts, and all you could hear, you remember those cellophane beer mugs, was the grinding of those plastic glasses under people's heels, and that to me became the sound of speed. Three thousand people grinding their heels on plastic.

The big article you did after the 100 Club – 'Welcome to the (?) Rock Special' – established the fans as part of the whole thing. There are quite a lot of definitive statements in that . . .

I can't remember whether that was my doing or Alan Lewis' doing. The problem was, there were only about eight bands. I'd just read Nik Cohn's piece in *New York* magazine about the original guy that became *Saturday Night Fever,* and the thing that really impressed me about it was how he'd created a piece of fiction out of investigative journalism. I was up against the same problem: how do you tell the same story, over and over again?

At this time, the *New Journalism* book had come out, by Tom Wolfe, and that really focused my thinking about writing. It was clearly written as a textbook. He was talking about the rules, and how to break the rules, and what were the rules of 'new journalism'. I always felt that the 'I' in new journalism was just narcissism; that wasn't the point of journalism, to write about yourself.

But that's why the piece starts with Siouxsie, walking through the streets. I should have kept it up, maintained that through the whole thing. I did three interviews with Sid, and he was saying the most horrendously violent stuff. I just recoiled from it, instinctively. Also it could have jeopardised his court case. But there was all the stuff about squelching, and 'I don't like sex' . . .

The other thing about Sid is that he had an incredible sense of humour, and he would try these things on, just to see what your response would be, in the form of a joke. No-one ever got that. The sneer thing. This was in the days before, I think, a lot of the drugs. Caroline took him to, I think, a Christmas party at *Vogue,* and she said the women were just all over him, instantly. They were fascinated by him.

Do you think he started to play up to that violent image?

It's hard to say. The thing was, when he got busted, Caroline was right in there, too. I was standing about four feet away from him, some band had just started playing, and these six cops walk in, single file, and just surround him, and just pick him up and start carrying him out. They never said a word. It was The Damned. I knew he didn't like them.

I saw him walking by, sneering, and he came over to the bar, where I was standing, and said something. There was a break, and Dave Vanian saying some girl's just been hit in the face with a glass. So they called an ambulance, and the police come automatically when an ambulance is called. A cop came in, had a look around, and then they hovered on the steps for about five minutes, and then this whole frog-march thing.

And of course everyone just stood there, stunned, for about five seconds. Then one of The Clash, it was either Joe or Paul, started up the steps, at which point about fifteen other people . . . Caroline was right at the head of all this, I'm about twenty feet back and I can hear her going, 'What's going on, excuse me, officer' – being really polite, and all this is going on at a fast walk, any faster and they'd be running.

And just when we get to the pavement, there's an old guy, in his forties, the main police officer, and she goes, 'Look, what the fuck is going on here?' And he goes, 'Right, her too.' And she gets piled into the car with them. At this point we're still going out together, and so I'm wondering what to do. Right, where's she going, let's get her out. She heard them doing over Sid, cos they were separated just by a partition. When it went to court, I stood his bond.

She was organising by this time. She knew what to do and where to go, what lawyers to get, and I agreed to put up my house to cover his bail, and we were away. I didn't see him between when they arraigned him and set the date, and the real court case. He had to come back from that Swedish tour, so I hadn't seen him for almost six months. And suddenly Nancy is there, and I'm like, Jesus, who is this. She was such bad news, it was so clear, right away.

In this case, he was eternally grateful that I'd put his bail up for him. And after the court case, I got his whole opinion of how I'd been in the dock. I was the first witness. It was this lady barrister, and she was so over the top, going at me, basically saying, 'You're a liar', because I didn't say what the police had said. They'd said they'd talked to him, that they asked him to come with them.

Did he get off?

Yeah, of course. There were about three people, and after that, Caroline was there, and there was no defence by the time I was finished, there was no evidence, and they'd wrongfully arrested him. But that was the only time I ever saw Nancy, and it was the last time I saw him.

Were you aware of the Notting Hill Carnival?

Oh yeah, every year. I missed the riot. The weather by that point had become oppressive, and I think that was a contributory factor to the riot. There was a drought that year, it was like eighty degrees. There was intense heat for months.

What happened through September, October?

There were new bands by that point, it wasn't just the Sex Pistols and The Damned. One night when Keith Levene was doing The Quick Spurts, he was talking to me at the Roxy, which had just opened, saying The Clash aren't new, they are the classic rock'n'roll form – which was true. Doing four-bar breaks instead of eight, and playing faster, but with the breakdowns and everything, it was a rock'n'roll band. There was this intense thing that everything had to be new and different.

When do you think that stopped?

Only when it became institutionalised, in 1978 or so. At that point, talking about the politics, The Clash as romanticised by Tony Parsons, struck me as so much sixties-style revolution talk. It always struck me as stupid, even then. There's no way you're gonna tear down America, gimme a break. Hearing it again, these guys had even less of a handle on actually changing anything than they did in the sixties, you know.

But Malcolm was really into this alternative, in terms of the rock-'n'roll thing, there was a real socialistic approach to it that worked. He seemed very genuine about it, and he seemed to have the where-withal to make it happen. What I liked was that it was equal parts show business and politics. The idea of the first package tour, which was what the first Anarchy tour was meant to be.

He wanted a stable of bands . . .

Yeah, the Brian Epstein, Larry Parnes mentality was clearly at work. Then the minute the Pistols thing broke, and he saw that you could go to record companies and get large amounts of cash, he abandoned all that. He always knew you had to get with a regular record company, there was never any talk of alternative record companies. He did want to be commercially successful. He thought the Stones were a good primer for the route he had to take.

Then suddenly, here he was, just going for the money, and claiming that this was what he intended all along. But this is the guy who never thinks until he opens his mouth. It wasn't a plan at all. That's when the revisionism started. It was great situationist politics: make up the ten rules of rock'n'roll out of the events that happened. Then make it seem that that's what you intended all along.

What did you think about the record deals?

The thing about record companies at that time, when there was basically two bands and about five other people, Malcolm and Caroline and Vivienne and I used to see each other quite a bit. We drove up to Manchester together, spent four or five hours in the car. Everyone was quite serious about making it happen. It was clear that this was the only thing that was going to break through all the sloth, and there was a lot of tactical talking going on.

I don't think it was ever talked about that they would not go for a major record label. There were no alternatives back then. It was, how do we get them on to a major label? He went and saw people with the Chris Spedding demos, then in the summer they got the real demos together, spent a week in the Denmark Street flat with a 4-track, and took those basic tracks into an 8-track studio, did the vocals there, and mixed it.

That's when they first worked with Dave Goodman, and they had good sound, for a change. That was another big change, when they could hear themselves, and they sounded great up front. He talked to two labels with that demo. I think he talked to Mickey Most.

Did he talk to Polydor?

Later on in the summer, with the 8-tracks. But that was Chris Parry, and the Pistols were just too extreme for him. He liked them, personally, but they were too extreme for the company. They went for The Clash with a vengeance, they really wanted them. I took the tape of the Clash demo out of the studio, stole it, the Guy Stevens one. We were doing a Generation X thing there, and we looked at the shelves and there was the tape, and I just grabbed it.

It was all quite assiduous, he was talking to these people, working them, and the intelligent record companies were coming to them. At the time of the big 'Rock Special' story, I started getting people calling me at *Sounds*. Dan Loggins would like to talk to you and find out about this punk thing. I said, 'Tell him for seventy-five pounds an hour I'll be happy to talk to him.' And the message came back that that was why he had an A&R department, he didn't need to pay someone. 'Yeah, that's why you called, wasn't it?'

When the Grundy interview happened, Miles Copeland showed up, immediately. He was the first of that established rock'n'roll scene who showed up. At that time, it was really cool that someone like Miles Copeland was showing up. It was all okay until Grundy happened, then everybody freaked. You weren't going to get close to it. People got much more conservative about their choices. You had to sign bands, but you had to find the ones that were acceptable.

It's interesting that Branson and Copeland showed up.

At that point, Richard was seen as very perceptive and cool. He was actively trying to sign bands up, when a lot of people weren't. But at the same time he was practising sixties-style record politics, screwing the bands with his contracts.

You mentioned a Sid story . . .

One night when I was in hospital, The Clash walk in, with Bernard, which took me totally by surprise. I never thought of myself as a friend to these people. After the operation I was sitting there in the hospital and Sid came walking in. I was stunned by it. It was so hard to figure the guy out, because of the way you perceived him, publicly, and then who the person really was. This was three days before Grundy, and all the people on the ward were like, who is this person? Two minutes after he left, another friend walks in wearing twinset and pearls. Two ends of the spectrum.

What was the operation?

Collapsed lung. I think it was the result of six months of taking speed. The thing at *Sounds* was, when I could do all the work, they just loaded more on to me. And being the artist, living your art, typing into the night. The collapsed lung coincided with me going, I just can't do this any longer. I'm so bored writing it, even the punk stuff. Had to stop.

Did you go to the Notre Dame show in November?

Yeah. It was very stylish, very posed. Everyone being quite defensive about their coolness, while projecting like crazy. It was very silvery, very bright. That was another Malcolm thing, white lights, which I always liked. Everyone's getting more flamboyant with the clothing, but John's in a white shirt with a skinny black tie and trousers. There was no uniform, no rules. They'd been out of town for a while, they hadn't played in London for a couple of months.

I remember people gobbing on the director . . .

Yeah, it was Rat Scabies got that one going, I think. The man who invented spitting. It's funny how you can put a time and place to it, so specifically.

You were in hospital during the Grundy thing?

Yeah. I missed the show, but I saw the apologies afterwards, on the TV. And the next morning they were in all the papers. There was a little thing on the front page of the *Guardian*, and looking around the ward, I realised that every front page had them. Explanations of punk.

Caroline's opinion was that it was a slow night for news. They were sending people around checking the presses, and when they saw that one paper was doing it, they would do it too, and so it builds across the night. Manufactured news. It's quite amazing that Grundy promoted it – the fact that you could swear on TV and promote it, rather than say no.

Do you think the Grundy incident defined what punk became?

Oh yeah. I think that's the thing that ruined it completely, in the sense that in one day, the entire country knew about it. If it had gone on, with the Anarchy tour, it would have built across the next year, as a slow, amorphous thing. It would have been much more positive, it wouldn't have been as stupid. It would have kept a lot more of its art-school image.

I think parallels with the swinging sixties era are appropriate. There were multiple layers within this movement. I think the same thing would have happened. The idea that bin-liners was your uniform was just so stupid. The lowest common denominator was thrown out as what punk was.

Did you go on the Anarchy tour?

I saw the second last show, Plymouth, and they were quite depressed by then. It was the depths of winter, and they were feeling like they were under siege for the entire tour. I'd been out of hospital a week and a half, I was barely on my feet by this point. I remember The Clash. Joe was rolling around the stage getting tangled up in this red cable, and got up with this mad look on his face, the red cable twisted around him, it was a great image.

I don't think the Pistols were very good. I think Glen was probably on the way out by then. It was very depressing, they were being cancelled all over, and the band wanted to play. They aged a lot, in that year, under the pressure. Look at the photos, it's quite clear.

What happened after the tour? Caroline's Christmas party?

That was just after the tour. We caught the bus back up, and it was the day the pop papers came out, and there was a lot of anti-punk, anti-Pistols stuff. Debbi was on the bus, and Tracie and Sue Catwoman, and there was a real feeling of depression on the bus. Then there was the party, and that was so strange. I was in no condition to control any of that, at all. It was very intense. And it was quite pleasant until The Heartbreakers showed up.

The idea was to give a Christmas dinner, because it had been so depressing on the tour, and a lot of those people had no homes to go to, or their home life was shitty. So Caroline was going to cook a turkey dinner, the whole bit. And I was amazed at people like Sue Catwoman, because after a while you accepted the mask as who they were – and all of a sudden they'd be thanking you, and being very

507

sincere about responding to the invitation. It threw me off balance to find they were real people behind it all.

The Clash were there, some of the Pistols. I don't think John showed up. Judy Nylon and Chrissie Hynde came together, dressed all in leather, and they were both being very strange that day. Sensible was there. Mick Rock was there, and Sheila. But when The Heartbreakers showed up, that sound guy, Keith Paul, was bouncing off the walls, he couldn't stand up, and they were all completely fucked up.

They started making calls to America on my phone, and I called him on it from the other side of the room, I was so completely pissed off by this point. It was all out of control, and I was annoyed with myself that I was in no position to handle it. So I flipped, I said, 'Hey, fuckhead – stop.'

There was a fucking contest going on, Steve and Paul seeing how many girls they could fuck. Paul would appear and say, 'Three!', and twenty minutes later Steve would come downstairs and go, 'Four!' At some point I went up to my room, and I'd locked the door, and the door was shut, but half the door jamb was sitting on the floor. Obviously it had been kicked in by Steve or Paul so they could fuck some girls in there.

I didn't know at the time, but it got back to me later that someone had shat in the towels in the downstairs bathroom, and folded them back up. I think it was Sid or Roadent. There was a lot of stuff going on in that bathroom, and Sid was in there a lot.

And there was the French guy who had his coat stolen, and he was going around accusing people, then he pulled out this switchblade and threw it into the door. I just found this hysterically funny, it had reached pure theatre at that point – I could have cared less what happened next. Everyone dived for cover, except Mick Rock, who stood there and started talking to him, really slowly in bad French. That brought him down a bit.

Did the Pistols change after the Grundy incident?

I didn't know anything about Glen getting fired, but it was always the other three, and then him. He came from a different background. I went to the Screen on the Green show where Sid played with them, and it was just like this Ramones thump. They'd become irrelevant, in a way.

What happened next? You started managing Generation X...

Well there was a point when I was in hospital where I was thinking, this is the end of being a journalist, I'm not interested in that any more. What am I going to do? It seemed incredibly stupid to have helped create this situation and then not take advantage of it. I didn't want to be a manager, so I thought I'd start a record label. Stewart Joseph and I were talking one night, and he said he wanted to manage a band. I said, 'You're crazy, let's start a label.'

One of the lawyers we talked to said the only way we'd make money as a little record label is if we manage the artists on the label, so we ended up back in management – and it was, why have a record label when you can do what Malcolm did?

When did you go to LA?

Christmas of 1978. By that stage it was clear I couldn't work with Tony James or Billy Idol, they were so obstinate. You couldn't persuade them of anything, certainly it wasn't in my ability. I was still worn out from the collapsed lung, and all the work with Gen X. So I went just to hang out, and I was out there for a month. It was seventy degrees, it was sunny and beautiful. I came back to London and it was twenty-eight degrees, and it was summing up what I hated about London, and I had money, so I left. I didn't think about it, I just did it.

What did you think of the LA punk scene?

It was all right. There were some good bands around. People like The Screamers were great. I liked The Weirdos. The thing was, these people never wanted to succeed, it didn't matter to them. Most punk bands in Britain were after success. Over there, they didn't give a shit. It was just indulgent nonsense. England's size helps a lot, in that sense. In LA, they were literally a drop in the ocean, and nothing had any real effect.

Mark Perry

Mark P, British punk Everykid and founder of Sniffin' Glue, *the first British punk fanzine and originator of the fanzine style: A4, rushed typing, homemade graphics, reporting from the front line. Closed* SG *in 1977, after twelve issues, and formed the band Alternative TV. Remains true to the punk ideals that he did so much to disseminate in 1976 and 1977.*

The first record I ever bought was the *Yesterday* EP by The Beatles. I listened to Zappa and 'serious music' while the kids at school listened to chart stuff. The first gig I went to was The Beach Boys in '71 or '72. Shortly after *Surf's Up*. The second was Amon Düül, except that they were busted for drugs at customs, and never turned up.

Danny Baker was working at Musicland [record shop in South Molton Street, London]; he had the best records, the best taste. At Danny's I first heard Todd Rundgren, Stevie Wonder. I think there's a bit of Danny's past he'd like to forget around that point. He was getting a lot of records for nothing, let's just leave it at that.

When did you start working at the bank?

1974. That was about the easiest job to be had at the time. Graham Parker was good at that time, Dr Feelgood, Count Bishops, Roogalator. I still think he should have been another Elvis Costello. That would be the start of it, really.

Sniffin' Glue was being planned before I ever saw the Pistols, based on the first Ramones album, July '76. People say that in August '76 there were suddenly all these new bands where there was nothing before, which is crap. It was a continuation of what was going on in America for years. The early punk bands were R'n'B-based, coupled with the political scene of the time.

What did you particularly like about the Ramones album?

510

I remember liking that the songs were so short. That was important. The lyrics about daft things were impressive. And they looked great on the cover, which is always important. When they played the Roundhouse they were supporting the Flamin' Groovies, who I couldn't stand at the time. I was blinkered. They both played at Dingwalls a few days later, and I got chucked out for glass-throwing during the Ramones set, so I missed the Groovies.

How did *Sniffin' Glue* actually start?

The fanzine *Bam Balam* was in about its fourth issue, but it didn't have any new stuff in it until later. That stuff should be compiled and brought out again. That was the inspiration for it really, it showed that you could do a magazine and you didn't have to be glossy. Also Rock On used to carry some country and rock'n'roll fanzines.

So I asked Phil in Rock On if he'd sell a fanzine if I did what was happening with the new American punk bands, and he said. 'Yeah, great.' So once I'd sold the first copies, I got the run off my girl-friend's photostat at work, she ran off the first twenty or fifty for me. As soon as they saw it, they paid for some more to be done. All that about *Glue* being the first fanzine is crap, though. You had *Bam Balam*; *Hot Wacks* was before me.

Did you think about what you were doing, or did you just do it, straight out?

When other fanzines started to come out, like *Ripped & Torn*, and Shane [MacGowan]'s one-off, *Bondage*, they were really unprofessional, and if I'd just done it on the spur of the moment, I'd probably have done something like that. I think *Sniffin' Glue* was well laid out. It was the first time I'd ever done anything like that. I approached it like a project in school.

Did you call it after the Ramones song?

Yeah, and Lenny Bruce, who I just got into at the time. I had the *Essential Lenny Bruce* compilation, I think on UA, with the glue-sniffing joke on it.

Did it get a lot of attention straight away?

It didn't take very long, cos they were bowled over by it at Rock On. The first to react were Eddie and the Hot Rods, they loved it, and they invited me to a gig, and so before the second issue I went down to Hastings with them. That was great for me, I was on cloud nine, I was with one of my favourite bands. Also in that van I met Caroline Coon and Jonh Ingham. I still had long hair then.

Had you wanted to get into the music press?

Previously I remember wondering how reviews were written, whether you could just send them in. There's this really daft letter I once wrote, and *NME* once used it as a Blackmail Corner. It said, 'Emerson, Lake and Palmer, the World's Ninth Wonder!' It was my review of an Emerson, Lake and Palmer gig, and *Record Mirror* printed it. I was chuffed about that.

But I was into the whole thing – the music, the papers, the books, the T-shirts, everything. It never entered my mind to see *Glue* as a stepping stone to that, unlike a lot of other people at the time. My idea then was to get a group together, really. I think I had a guitar at home . . .

When did you first see the Sex Pistols?

August, at the 100 Club. They were brilliant. I remember I was wearing this beautiful satin jacket, and it got ripped to shreds. I was in heaven, this was it, I'm really into it. Johnny Rotten kicked me in the shoulder, I was in the front row. The sound was rather hollow, amateurish, but it was exciting. And the sneering, and the audience put-downs and the gobbing. We were pogoing and smashing into each other.

When I first met Sid Vicious I hated him, I really did. The second time I saw them I went as the *Sniffin' Glue* editor. I was in a relationship with Caroline then for a couple of months. 'How are you Sid?', says Caroline, 'this is Mark, who does this fanzine. Show him your fanzine, Mark.' That kind of scene, and Sid sort of goes, 'What the fuck's this', and screws it up, and chucks it away.

By the third or fourth issue you'd developed an idea that went beyond the magazine, that anyone could do it.

People never believed me at the time, but I really didn't care about the magazine. It was the ideas that were important. That piece in about number five, where I was saying go out and start your own fanzines, was brilliant. It was a stroke of genius, and I meant every word of it. I did have an ego, but it wasn't the *Glue*, I wanted to form a band.

By that time, I wanted to go out and do it. I had things to say, and I couldn't stand the thought of being a journalist, sitting down and actually writing. It was a means to an end. Most of the things in the *Glue* were just written straight down, no looking at it later, which is why you get all the crossings out.

But as early as issue 3, you'd started talking about punk as a generation, not just a bunch of bands.

I did realise the importance of what it encompassed, and I also had that enormous ego that was necessary to actually get on in punk. Johnny Rotten had it, Strummer had it, Rat Scabies had it. I thought, if I say this in the *Glue*, it's going to happen. I knew that, and that was what fuelled me, knowing that it was being taken seriously.

Did Steve Mick come in with you on the first one?

I think he drifted in during the second or third. He was my best friend at school, and he was a freak. Not a hippy, but a freak. He was a very powerful person. Used to go round with a woman's fake fur on. If you look that strange, people stay away from you. We fell out badly.

We used to think about what to have in the *Glue* for twenty-eight days of the month. Then the last two days, we'd just do it. We used to lock ourselves away. No-one else was allowed in. Not girlfriends. But he had this girlfriend who used to go with him everywhere. I'd say I was in complete control, he did stuff for me; like the Subway Sect article, he'd do it. I did it and he helped.

What did you think when you started getting written up?

I started thinking it was a great scam. These people are idiots, but we're getting away with it. I started being invited to explain punk to people. Did a few TV things. It wasn't until later I thought I'd influenced anything. The funny thing is, I've never really liked punk

513

fanzines very much. My sort of fanzine is still the *Bam Balam* sort of thing. Discography, information, looking back on things.

You thought there needed to be a change then?

Definitely. None of those fanzines wrote as well about punk as Caroline and Jonh, or, later on, Paul Morley. That thing about being morally superior to the music press goes out of the window, because pop is part of capitalism, it's the modern world; you might as well ride it, just get a kick out of it.

What did you think about the Pistols signing to EMI?

I knew that was part of the scam, really. I didn't really take the Pistols very seriously. I knew the scam was going to be important, cos I wrote a piece for *Time Out*, reprinted in the *Glue*, saying, this is political. What is happening is political, and if people hear what this band is saying, blah blah blah.

Early punk was very elitist . . .

very much so . . .

. . . but it had the populist rhetoric, about tower blocks and so forth. Did you perceive that?

I think it came out in a few things. The first thing we wrote about the Pistols, we did slag off the audience a lot. Poseurs, they were just like fashion people. We said that 'Anarchy in the UK' was just to sell Malcolm's Anarchy shirts, and all that.

I also remember going to interview The Clash up at their warehouse. Steve Walsh did the interview but I was there, and they were really over the top. Complete prats. Paul had a gun, I don't know if it was real. Trying to be heavy. And they had a go at me for liking Eddie and the Hot Rods. Those guys wear flares, all this.

To me that was bollocks. Mick Jones spent three years before punk learning how to be a rock'n'roll star. He wasn't a hooligan. In that sense the early New York bands were a lot more honest.

Did you ever believe in punk as being a working-class movement?

I think I did, but I must have been blind to what was going on, really.

I was spending most of my time at clubs in London, not in Deptford. If I lost touch at any time it was during that punk period. All it was was music biz. We were deluding ourselves that we could ever reach working-class people. If a few of us had got our heads together, we might have got something through at least. We were deluding ourselves that we were writing for the kids.

In early punk there was more of a class mix . . .

I remember being very conscious of it. When Danny Baker came into it, he had a better way of putting the revolutionary ideas than me. Danny was great at restating the Deptford stance.

By the time of *Sniffin' Glue* twelve, Alex Ferguson and I had got Alternative TV together and we were doing the circuit. We did Falkirk, on a tour in Scotland, but we were another band in the scene. The punk thing only lasted about six or seven months, not even a year that there was a punk scene. I think of the Roxy; when the Roxy went out of Andy Czezowski's hands, you can forget it. The Vortex was never the Roxy, it was brutal, horrible.

Why did *Glue* fold? Did Danny not want to do any more?

I don't think so. I let him get on with it, but I might have given the hint to Danny that I didn't want it to continue. Before that, it could have died easily. After a while I didn't have anything to say any more. The fanzine explosion had happened, all was left was to review bands, which wasn't the point, you could do that in *Sounds* or *NME*. I didn't care about it. I was fed up with packaging the anger, selling the magazine.

How did you get involved with Miles Copeland?

I met a guy called Nick Jones, and he said, 'My boss would like to talk to you', and they took me out to dinner and offered me the A&R job. I think I wasted that opportunity, cos Jake Riviera and Roger Armstrong were both thinking like that. Miles did a lot, and because of his background, he took a lot of shit. But after The Police, he never thought any more about labels. He signed the Cortinas up to fucking CBS after one single.

Did you like The Jam?

Couldn't stand them. Even when they put out records. I liked 'A Bomb', 'Tube Station' and Strange Town', but they were shit when they started. So contrived. I saw late '77 being dominated by Wire and The Fall, Siouxsie.

Me and Danny signed up Sham [69] for Step Forward [Perry's label, backed by Copeland]. No-one else wanted to know because they were the real kids from the terrace and they were scary – people didn't want to know this shit. I was into Sham 100 per cent. In a way, Jimmy [Pursey] was refreshing, cos we were getting torn away from what I thought it was about, and Jimmy was the bit that was missing. They were going to take it down in the gutter again.

And then Jimmy turned out to be a frustrated artist as well, a mixed-up kid, he wasn't the hard nut.

Weren't they also the hard nuts who'd given you a bad time at school?

I admit now I was playing at being a hard nut, and in that role I could get away with it. But to Jimmy Sham, I was some toffee-nosed record-company man. I enjoyed the scam, but I remember Jimmy refusing to go on one night, because all those kids were there, and we were saying, 'But Jimmy, they're The Kids', and he said, 'Yeah . . . but they're horrible.' It ended very badly.

When did Alternative TV really start?

Genesis P-Orridge influenced me a lot. I went to dinner at Sheila Rock's house, and Gen was there. He knew about the *Glue*, and we exchanged numbers, and he let us use his space for rehearsal, about March, and we started playing live in about May '77. Just like a normal band from then on. We were stating influences like Can and Zappa, trying to bring in something a bit different. Alex was very into the Velvets. I hadn't heard much of them up until then.

I knew we had to extend the songs. It all went wrong though. Our first single was two punk songs, which was a let-down. We had a bad time in Scotland supporting Chelsea. The audience just wanted to pogo, go wild, and we were saying, 'Don't you realise you're in jobs that are eating your brains out?' And they're going, 'Liven it up a bit, faster!'

Towards the end of '77 we chucked Alex out, cos we weren't enjoying playing live. Had a terrible scene in Manchester. Marc

Bolan had just died, and we tried to do 'Get It On' as a tribute, and the crowd was trying to kill us . . .

Did you get flak for writing about Step Forward bands in *SG*?

Yeah, a bit. Deservedly so. They were all in the late *Glues*, when I was bored. We shouldn't have been writing about them. Mind you, we were taking ads by then. I wanted ATV to be like the *Glue*, I wanted to say things that weren't being said, cause a bit of a stir. What spoiled punk was the obsession that it had to be rock'n'roll. To me, the best punk band by '78 was Throbbing Gristle, the only band who knew what the fuck was going on.

When did you do the Here & Now tour?

That was the summer of '78. Punk by then was a joke, a stance to sell records, just another section of the rock business. Miles Copeland wanted us to tour America, and I really didn't want to do it, and then this hippy came up to me one day from Here & Now, 'Do you want to do a free tour of Britain?' Why didn't I think of that before?

And it was great. We played the universities, Warwick, Canterbury, Stonehenge. Stonehenge was awful, there wasn't anybody there. People listened to us on that tour. After that, we found it really hard to get back into it. We couldn't play, cos there was just two of us, and then we did the Greenwich Theatre, which was a riot – we ended up chucking a piano off stage, trashing the lights, the police got called.

Were you aware of what was happening in the country then?

Not really, I was just interested in the band. I thought of myself as an artist by then, and I felt that whatever music did, the rest of the world would carry on regardless.

Was that because you were disappointed by what had happened to punk?

Oh yeah, I was disappointed. Looking back, I was a right drip then. Made some good music, but I was a drip. Just into my art.

CHAPTER EIGHT

The North-West

Handbill for The Electric Circus, Manchester, Sep–Oct 1977

After London, Manchester had the most passionate and well-developed punk scene during 1976 and 1977. This was brought into being by two seminal Sex Pistols shows at the Lesser Free Trade Hall (on the site of the Peterloo massacre of 1819) in June and July 1976, that galvanised a few score local musicians, writers and ne'er-do-wells.

Vital in creating these links were two young musicians, Howard Devoto and Pete Shelley, who – attracted by Neil Spencer's NME *review – saw the Sex Pistols in February 1976 and returned to Manchester to spread the news. They were assisted by a small but devoted coterie of local fans and Tony Wilson, whose* So It Goes *was the only TV show to feature punk during 1976 and 1977.*

The city's principal punk club was The Electric Circus in Collyhurst, one of the very few venues to host the Sex Pistols during their notorious December 1976 Anarchy tour. When it closed in October 1977, the city's talent came out to play: Buzzcocks, Magazine, The Fall, John Cooper Clarke, The Drones and Warsaw – the group who would become Joy Division.

Howard Devoto

Howard Trafford, co-founder, writer and singer of Buzzcocks. Co-promoter of the Sex Pistols' two Lesser Free Trade Hall shows. Left Buzzcocks in early 1977 to form Magazine – who debuted at the last night of The Electric Circus. Interviewed in London, in a break from his then job in a photo agency; simultaneously self-deprecating and fiercely proud.

I was born in Scunthorpe and was there until I was two. I then lived in Nuneaton until I was ten, then Leeds, more or less till I went to college in Bolton in 1972. I first went there to study psychology, and I gave that up and started on a humanities course, history and philosophy. It was very much a case of not knowing what the hell to do. It was a last-minute thing.

I got in at Bolton so I went there, and when they started the humanities course in '74, that was more what I wanted to do, inasmuch as I wanted to be at college. I was living in Bolton until September '75 when I moved to Lower Broughton Road. The house was owned by one of the philosophy lecturers, and shortly after that, things began.

I listened to music from when I was nine or ten. The Shadows. I saw Gerry and the Pacemakers and Cilla. My father took me to that. He was an accountant, and wasn't interested in the slightest. I didn't enjoy it very much, but I did like listening to the records. I wasn't particularly into The Beatles, I listened to the Stones, they were probably my second thing. After the Stones it was Dylan.

Around 1970 I read an article on the Stooges, with photographs of Iggy walking on people's hands, and I thought, I've got to hear some of this. I bought the first Stooges album, and I can't say I liked it very much, but when Bowie got involved with Iggy that rekindled my interest. I got *Raw Power* when it first came out, then *Funhouse*. I think I just liked 'I Wanna Be Your Dog', 'No Fun'.

Iggy had never played, I'd never seen him, and I was having the experience of going to see college bands and hating them, and feeling, maybe I'll do something, with no serious ambition to do anything with it. I would never have conceived that I would end up doing what I've ended up doing. In my mind it didn't get much beyond performing at college, but being confrontational, it was going to have some sort of impact on people.

Listening to the Stooges records, it sounded easy to do, to me. His personality and the music attached to some unfortunate trait I had. I wished to annoy, to be exhibitionist, to be self-destructive, all those things.

So you put the ad up on the college notice-board?

Honestly I can't remember what it said, but I'm sure it mentioned 'Sister Ray' on it. I probably did mention the Stooges, maybe I didn't.

I met a drummer, an engineer, and Peter [McNeish] and I did go and rehearse a bit with him, we weren't doing any of our own songs then. There was something off Eno's album, 'The True Wheel'. We tried some Stooges things. I really liked 'Your Pretty Face Is Going to Hell'. I wanted to sing that. Plus some less distinguished things, early Rolling Stones, but that came to nothing, we never played.

Peter lived in Lower Broughton Road for a while, several doors down. The ad was up in autumn '75. We stayed in touch and were reading *NME* in the bar together, when we saw Neil Spencer's 'Don't Look Over Your Shoulder' article. The fact that they played a Stooges song and said, 'We're not into music, we're into chaos' – ooh, that's interesting. And off we went down to London.

That was in the Neil Spencer review.

I remember one of the reasons we went down was I could borrow a car that weekend, and we thought, let's go down and see if they're playing. Richard [Boon] was at Reading University, and we called in and picked him up, and I called Neil Spencer at the *NME* from Reading, who told me they were managed by this bloke called Malcolm who's got a sex shop on the King's Road, and he didn't know whether they were playing or not. So we drove in from Reading and along the King's Road thinking we were looking for a dildo emporium, and we found the shop with 'SEX' on it. As I remember, Jordan was there, and she said Malcolm would be back shortly, so we came back later and Malcolm was there, and we saw them twice that weekend. High Wycombe and Welwyn Garden City, both college gigs.

I think at Welwyn, Screaming Lord Sutch was the main attraction, and I remember John smashing their microphone down and stalking off the stage. I think he said he was going to be sick, and went and threw up in the toilets. When he came back there was some argy-bargy over whether they could borrow Screaming Lord Sutch's gold microphone. He was certainly being very abusive and moody.

[Devoto wrote down the set-list. It reads: 'Did You No Wrong', '(Don't Give Me) No Lip', 'Understanding', 'Looking for a Kiss', 'Seventeen', 'Whatcha Gonna Do about It', 'Submission', 'Stepping Stone', 'Pretty Vacant', 'No Fun', 'Substitute'.]

I remember his shoes, and his ratty red sweater. We thought they were fantastic. We really did. It was: we will go and do something like this in Manchester.

Did you talk to the band when you saw them at High Wycombe?

Yes, I remember going up nervously, saying 'Are you Johnny?' . . . they were fine. I'm sure they were flattered at people coming all the way from Manchester to see them. We certainly didn't look like their kind of people. We had no look, no dress sense at all.

I said to Malcolm, 'Do you want to come and play at my college if I can get you in there?', and he said, 'Yes.' This was probably just before we left. He said, 'If you can set it up, we'll do it.' So I must have tried to persuade the Students' Union to put them on, but they wouldn't go for it. They'd never heard of them. There was very little in the press.

So I started looking round for a venue, and someone told me about this little hall above the Free Trade Hall, and I phoned them up, got it for £25 or something, and meanwhile, like on this ticket, we were planning to play ourselves – 4th of June 1976. But we hadn't got it together. We played at this textile students' social evening. That was me, Peter, Garth and some other drummer that we'd never played with. I don't think we played any of our own songs.

We'd got the look together by then, somewhat. I remember wearing some long pink boots and striped jeans. They turned us off after three numbers. We played 'The True Wheel'. There might have been a couple of Peter's songs, like 'No Reply', 'Get On My Own'.

I can't remember how we met John Maher. We met Steve Diggle at the first Lesser Free Trade Hall. Malcolm was on the pavement outside the Free Trade Hall, hustling kids in, and Steve was wandering about trying to meet someone, he wasn't coming to see the Sex Pistols, he was going to a pub, and Malcolm told him, 'Oh your friend's inside', so Steve paid his money and saw the Sex Pistols, and somehow we ran into him.

We got about a hundred people, which wasn't bad at all. I remember the band being very pleased.

The first one was the 4th of June, the second one was 20th of July, and we got ourselves together. We'd heard about this band Slaughter & the Dogs. We'd never seen them play, but they were making themselves sound like they were vaguely appropriate. We played eight or ten songs and opened the show. It sold out. And the music press came up to it.

Were you nervous?

I don't remember having enough time to be nervous, in a way. I'd organised it, there was all that other stuff going on, Malcolm bitching about the PA, this, that and the other. Suddenly we were on in five minutes. I'm sure I was nervous. I never got that nervous anyway, in a way that was perceptible to me.

Was that the one where you yanked out Peter's guitar strings?

Yes.

Was that planned or spontaneous?

I think there was a planned element in it. Exactly how it was going to happen I don't know, but we had talked about doing something like that.

Did you talk to Peter about the ideas you were trying to put across with the group, in the early days?

524

I can't remember planning that much. Certainly what we did was fairly strongly based on what we'd seen with the Pistols. We were following some sort of brief, but you can hear it in *Spiral Scratch*, affecting a London accent. I did have my own words, and Peter had written songs before that.

Looking back, certain things surprise me. There was an affected aggression, but you're bound to be like that when you start out. 'I'll give you a subterranean profile'. I think these were insults that I'd written earlier, as well. Not everything that went into those early songs was written in that period. Partly diary, partly ideas for songs if they ever happened, poems. I know some of the lines went back earlier than that.

Where did you get the name Devoto?

A distant relation of mine who I last heard was a bus driver in Cambridge. His name spun across my ears one day and caught my attention. I hadn't thought about names, until one day Peter introduced me to someone as Howard Devoto. Pretentiousness is interesting. At least you're making an effort. Your ambition has to outstrip your ability at some point.

Your third gig was the Screen on the Green?

Our second one was the one at The Ranch, where I'm wearing the New Hormones T-shirt. 12th August. The Ranch was attached to Foo Foo's, the club run by Foo Foo Lamar, the local Danny La Rue, and this was a small disco that played Lou Reed and David Bowie stuff on a Friday and Saturday night. We got stopped at that. One of Foo Foo's heavies came through from the main club and told us to stop, cos he couldn't perform in the other room.

When did Richard become your manager?

I think he came up to Manchester after finishing at Reading, that summer. I knew him from the same school at Leeds.

When did Linder turn up?

I met Linder at the first gig we played. We went to some all-night drinking club afterwards. The Screen on the Green was the third or fourth. I remember it being all right, the stage was rather high. There was a feeling like that we were outsiders, The Clash and the Pistols were Londoners. There was a bit of that. I don't remember there being a particularly great response to us.

It was amazingly heady. My life changed at the point I saw the Sex Pistols, I immediately got caught up in making things happen. I was in contact with Malcolm on a weekly or fortnightly basis, making sure he paid for the hall in case they never even turned up. Suddenly there was a direction, something I passionately wanted to be involved in. When we saw them, there wasn't any hint of what was to come, at all.

We did our first gig, it was in the music papers the following week, but because we're in Manchester we're not in, and cos there's no-one else doing anything, it's all happening in London really. It wasn't as if there was hundreds of people phoning up, promoters offering gigs or anything; nothing happened.

So you had to create something in Manchester?

Yes, there was The Ranch, and then the Holdsworth Hall thing, in the centre of Manchester. We didn't know about hiring PAs and all that.

Why do you think it all happened so quickly? Did it connect with what people wanted?

Yes, because it was so interesting, that in some way I was trying to do something akin to it four or five months before I heard about the Sex Pistols. Something that would have been based more on the Stooges than a dreamed-up notion of what they were about, so just the fact that I had tuned into something, and other people were tuning in and making things happen, leads me to believe that there was something in the spirit and meaning of it that connected with a lot of people.

I think Tony Wilson would say the same. I suppose there was Malcolm and Vivienne there ready with a look, as well. It had all the ingredients.

What did you do about your own look?

I remember buying those blue jeans and having them taken in.

Richard spattered a shirt . . .

526

Yeah, that was a bit later. We bought a bit of stuff from SEX, the T-shirts that were two squares. I had the New Hormones one and one with I Love You You Big Dummy on it. We did some of that.

Where did the name New Hormones come from?

That was from something I'd written quite a long time ago, about wanting them. What I need is some new hormones.

What happened in the autumn?

I remember playing with Buzzcocks about ten times. I don't think I ever wrote anything, I used to do the listings for the local gigs. We played with Chelsea on 10th November. Gene October and Billy Idol on guitar. I remember not liking them. There was the Holdsworth Hall, then we came down to do the 100 Club for two nights, which was the second London gig, and we played this pub in Stalybridge on the way down.

We were on last at the 100 Club Punk Festival, I remember a lot of people going. I think we were offered the choice, did we want to go on second or last out of four, so we chose to go on last, but everybody else there knew more about the timing of things, like when the audience goes home. The Vibrators played, who we thought were appalling. But my memory, again, is of feeling a bit outside of it. But that's partly me.

Was *Spiral Scratch* recorded very quickly?

Yes. The first song we did was 'Breakdown' – we did that three times, by the third one they were probably just getting the sound right – and then we did the others, one after the other. I sang the vocals live, and we did one overdub on a couple of them. Probably about three hours. Now, it seems very fast to me. Mickey Mouse-ish. We went back and mixed it for a couple of hours.

Was the idea for 'Boredom' from your notebooks?

Some of it was. I wrote a song about boredom, but I think that was of the moment. It's surprising how quickly you can pick up and make things right. How little can be picked up and made to feel appropriate. Quite obviously there was a feeling that certain things were right, and certain things weren't right at all.

Boredom hadn't really been done until then.

I can't think of anyone beyond the Stooges really. 'It's got real content', I remember Malcolm saying to me at the Screen on the Green. Real content.

'I'm Living in a Movie' – is that how you actually felt, or was it something you used to describe?

I think everybody feels that some time or other. The curious thing is why it can often be a pleasant experience. Why would I want to describe something if I never felt it? A song is something I walk into while singing it, and singing as an activity becomes its own world. I don't know what that is.

Why did you decide to put it out yourselves?

Being in Manchester, there are no record labels up there. Again, it's the ambition thing. How ambitious is one? I don't think we had much idea of the way things were swelling. A lot of people in our situation would have realised, hey, there's something happening here. We just didn't have that sort of wherewithal at that time.

But we had some other sort of wherewithal, which made us borrow money from Pete's dad, book a recording studio and have records made. Before it there was only Stiff. I called Dave Robinson in a vague attempt to find out something about things, and him being vaguely encouraging.

Had they created a precedent?

I suppose so, but it wouldn't have meant that much to us. It was stuff you would read about in the music papers – most of which is happening elsewhere.

Why did you leave the Buzzcocks?

Partly to finish college, partly with making the record I felt that was enough, whatever we'd done had crystallised into a relatively immortal form. It's hard to say. That record did an awful lot for the Buzzers, which we never anticipated. We had 1,000 pressed, and wondered if we would ever, ever shift them. It sold in two weeks. Mainly through Rough Trade and Virgin in Manchester, John Webster was manager.

They were really supportive. We ended up pressing something like 15,000, of the first lot. I can remember Malcolm McLaren saying, 'It's really odd seeing a record from somewhere else in the shops.'

We kept in touch through '77 occasionally. There was a point after Glen had left, and he came up with some other guy, and an idea which I suppose eventually became the Rich Kids.

So you decided to stay in music?

Yeah, all the time I was helping the Buzzers out. I went to a lot of the gigs. The Rainbow thing with The Clash and The Jam. Was that the White Riot tour? And I got involved with the record company negotiations with UA. I couldn't stay away.

What did you feel about what was happening to the Buzzcocks over that period?

Peter was a very good songwriter. I was amazed. I never loved everything they did, but some things were quite wonderful.

When did you start putting Magazine together?

I met John McGeoch in April or May '77, through Malcolm Garrett, who was sharing a flat with me at the time. I don't think we played anything together. Peter had played me the 'Shot by Both Sides' riff, and 'The Light Pours out of Me' he'd done a little bit with, and it's possible John and I played a couple of those things.

It wasn't until the summer of '77 that I stuck up a notice in Virgin Records, and met Martin Jackson and Barry, and Paul Dickenson, who were probably the first in each of their respective disciplines that I met. John was away in London with his parents, and when he came back in September we started rehearsing together.

You must have done a demo really fast, cos you'd done one when I came to see you in October '77.

Yeah, certainly within a couple of months, early August or September.

When did you sign to Virgin?

I think it was late October. The only two record companies I remember talking to were UA and Virgin.

Did you get a big advance?

No, but we got a contract that was pretty strong on artistic control. They were all talking inconceivable figures. We just wanted some money to buy some equipment, basic things. We negotiated quite hard with them. Apparently Simon Draper said on a radio programme once that I was the first artist he had met who wanted to know about everything. It was a reasonable deal. It rapidly became inadequate, when we got a manager, and we had to pay a manager.

What did you think of what was happening in Manchester then?

We still felt part of it. Certainly those nights at The Electric Circus I remember being a vital social scene. There were lots of bands coming up. Joy Division were just beginning. Artistically I never liked that much of what other people were doing. I kind of liked The Fall, I saw them at an arts centre, playing in the basement. In '77 the big event was Iggy playing Manchester.

Magazine happened very quickly, again. You got press quickly.

We signed to Virgin just after that Rafters gig, 28th of October, but we could have signed to them without having played. Carol Wilson had been at the last night at The Electric Circus, and she was with Virgin Music, and that's how word had got back. We asked Virgin not to announce it, we recorded 'Shot by Both Sides' and 'My Mind Ain't So Open', and it came out the third week of '78. We were getting bits of press. There was your piece. Paul [Morley] did a piece for *NME*.

Then the single came out, we did that tour, we were still punk enough to say there wouldn't be any guest-list at the 100 Club. I remember arriving at the club and seeing Simon Draper in the queue to buy a ticket! I don't think it was treacherous, I really think it happened, there was no guest-list. We did that tour – Sandpipers, Rafters, Eric's, Nashville, Barbarella's. That would have been the first tour I'd ever done.

What was that like?

Christ knows. It was practically the totality of all the gigs I'd played in my life, in one week. For the first time we had a manager, Andrew Graham Stewart. He was involved with Tangerine Dream, and

530

Simon Draper introduced us to him, so things were taken care of reasonably. At that time I didn't feel right unless I slept just before going on stage, which is a really hard thing to organise on the road. But I had to sleep for an hour or two, which looking back on it now is weird, to me.

'Shot by Both Sides' was a hit, wasn't it?

In the real, real charts it got to the lower 30s. We went on *Top of the Pops*, the only time I've been on.

Was that fun?

No, it wasn't fun at all. I think I was quite bad on it, cos I was determined not to look like I was having a good time, and we lip-sync'd, and we actually re-recorded for it, which you're supposed to do, at least in those days. Made a more deadpan vocal of it, cos the single had quite a contorted vocal on it. We don't want to go over the top, do we?

There was no way I could lip-sync to that vocal. It just didn't work, it certainly didn't do anything for the single. There was a lot of hubbub at the time, covers. I remember being accused of manipulating the media, which I had no idea how to do.

Were you aware of what was going on politically?

Not particularly. I was rigorously apolitical. That's where the title 'Shot by Both Sides' came from, a socialist friend saying, 'You're going to get shot by both sides.'

Were you aware of Mrs Thatcher being elected?

Not particularly. *Secondhand Daylight* was just coming out. What happened later in '79 was that we toured the States for the first time, and that changed things for me an awful lot. My father died while I was on tour in the States. Dylan produced his first religious album, the Iran hostages were taken, the Russians moved into Afghanistan. By the end of '79 I was almost on talking terms with an apocalyptic vision of the world. I don't really call that political.

Pete Shelley

Peter McNeish, Buzzcocks' co-founder, writer, guitarist and front man from early 1977. Co-promoter of the Sex Pistols' Lesser Free Trade Hall shows. Interviewed at his then home in North London; witty, precise and mischievous – much like his best songs, which remain some of the most enduring of the whole period.

I was brought up in Leigh, Lancashire – about thirteen miles west of Manchester, about twenty-two miles east of Liverpool – during the swinging sixties.

When you were at school did you go and see any groups?

No, the first group I ever went to see was at the local cricket club in about 1969, they put on an all-night ball in a marquee, and amongst the groups there was Juicy Lucy, they had Stack Waddy, and top of the bill were Marmalade, who'd just had their hit with 'Ob-La-Di, Ob-La-Da'. That was the first time I saw live music. The first group I went to see was T.Rex, on the Hot Love tour, May 1971.

Did that make a big impact?

Yeah, it did. I had a front-row seat and it was just as the T.Rex thing was taking off. 'Hot Love' had just been released, so it was really exciting. It was on a Sunday – I remember because the local rugby league team had just won the Rugby League Challenge Cup in '71, and so as I went off to Manchester, they were arriving back in triumph, to huge crowds at Leigh Town Hall.

Leigh was mining and cotton. All the women used to work in the cotton factories, all the men used to work in the pits. Leigh, Atherton and Tyldesley are the three towns that were supposed to have the largest number of pubs per head in Britain. It's true. It's where Georgie Fame comes from, the big star from Leigh.

You went to see the Bickershaw Festival?

Yeah, that was in '72. We didn't get a ticket, like half the people there we sneaked in, and like all festivals it was a big mud-bath. It was an exciting new thing, people going around trying to fill you with drugs. We never bought any cos we didn't have any money. It was an alternative culture, still very hippyish. Beefheart was on, Family, The Kinks, Hawkwind were on the first night. Donovan, the Flamin' Groovies, the Grateful Dead.

So were you looking for something alternative at that time, something a little bit different?

Well, as well as T.Rex I was also into The Beatles. The first single I got was 'Hey Jude', and the first album was *Sergeant Pepper*. Along with John Lennon also came Yoko Ono at that time, so I was really into the Yoko Ono solo albums. I loved the noise she was getting. I think 'Why' is a great track, I still play it. And in some ways it was a precursor of punk; it was fast, the guitars were all over the place.

After that, I started putting a band of my own together, I'd been writing songs since '71, just as I was doing my O Levels. I really started getting into music again about May '73, just as I was finishing my A levels. During '73 I had plenty of time free, cos I'd done my A levels and it was the summer; I didn't start college till October, so I had plenty of time to listen to music.

I managed to con my parents into getting a stereo cassette recorder so I could tape things – I had a thing with the local record shop where I could buy a record, take it back the same day and they'd just knock 50p off. So I managed to tape all the albums that I wanted.

So did you start playing then?

I started playing guitar in January 1970, and round about '72 was when I first got an electric. In '73 I started doing some experimental tapes but I was also writing songs, like 'Telephone Operator', and 'Raison d'etre' was written in about '73/'74. 'Love You More' was written in '75, 'Homosapien' was written in '74, 'Paradise' in '73, 'Sixteen Again' in '73/'74. Some days I'd write two or three songs.

Was it difficult to get a group together at that point?

One of the hardest things was to find a drummer. There were no drummers. Well there was one, but he used to play in about three or four bands and he wasn't really interested in music. It was always hard to find people to play with.

There used to be stories of an agent who lived in Wigan who could get you gigs. It was like, always distant. It was more showbiz than pop – all pop music was showbiz then. There were people who were the stars, the rest of it was imaginary showbiz, and London was where everything happened.

Who were the local bands then? Were Sad Café going then?

They probably were, yeah. Gentle Giant came from round there as well. It was all progressive rock. I was in a band at school that did mainly covers, I played rhythm guitar. I was in there mainly because I could work out the chords from listening to the records.

So what happened first – you went to Bolton, didn't you?

Bolton Institute of Technology. One rung under a polytechnic. It always tried to get polytechnic status but never quite managed it. I was doing electronics.

Was that practical or theoretical?

Mostly theory, there was some practical. Communications, instrumentation, physics and maths, and also computers; that was where I first got my hands on a computer, a PDP-8 with 4k of memory! It occupied a room all on its own, which had to be cooled. It would overheat. There were four teleprinters run off that, so I think you were lucky if it had 1k.

I knew Howard cos I'd started a college electronic music society, cos it was easy to form societies, I found out. We used to invade the music room once a week and play stuff. Howard was doing a video project and wanted some electronic music, so he first approached me. I'd seen him around the college; we had mutual friends but we didn't actually know each other.

The next thing was, there was an advert on the college notice-board. I'd been in the bar and there was nobody to talk to so I was reading the notice-board, and this notice said, 'Wanted, people to form a group to do a version of "Sister Ray"'. I knew all the Velvet Underground albums back to front. So I gave him a ring, because there was nothing much happening. Me and Howard struck up a friendship and spent more time together, writing.

He was living in Manchester then?

Yeah, in Salford. The house was owned by an Australian philosophy lecturer. Howard was doing humanities, he was in his second year. Then one day we met up in the coffee bar and he'd got a copy of *NME*, and have you seen this, about a band called the Sex Pistols, who'd played at the Marquee, who played Stooges numbers – cos we were working our way through *Raw Power*.

It was a Thursday when Howard got the *NME*. I had an NUS meeting in London on the Saturday. Howard was thinking of going down and meeting Richard Boon in Reading, he was doing fine arts there. Anyway, he was going to borrow this car, and then we split the petrol money, and I claimed the train fare, and we ended up down at Richard's and he'd seen the thing in the *NME* as well.

So we went to find out if this band was playing anywhere. We phoned up *NME*, spoke to someone there, and they didn't know, but they told us they had this manager, Malcolm McLaren, who has this clothes shop on the King's Road, so we drove into London and found SEX.

What was the shop like then?

There was still a lot of the Let It Rock stuff in there, winkle-pickers and drape coats, as well as some of the T-shirts. When we got back to Manchester, me and Howard started making some T-shirts out of this awful, cheap nylon. I had those fabric crayons, so we were drawing and ironing on the colours, doing it like that, just pillow-case designs.

The square cut . . .

Also I was with Howard when he got his first pair of straight trousers. I remember going into Manchester and he found some trousers he wanted and asked if they had any narrower. They said, 'Oh no, there's not much call for them.' It was all flares in those days. But he had them altered, so they were drainpipes.

535

What happened when he walked around the first time with those on? Was he stared at?

We'd started going more and more – I'd started henna-ing my hair, and I think Howard did as well, so we were on the way to being stand-out-ish. We saw the Sex Pistols at High Wycombe, and the day after they were playing at Welwyn Garden City, and so we went to that one as well.

What were those gigs like?

They were good. First of all we were struck that they were no better than we were, so it gave us a bit more to hold on to. People thought you have to work for years in order to get into the industry.

What was the audience reaction like?

They were college gigs, those two, so heads of the bills were Mr Big and Screaming Lord Sutch, so it was still in that yawning gap, going for a night out drinking Newcastle Brown. At one of the gigs they had a brick put through their van window, so there was antagonism at that early stage. It was a rough noise, it wasn't refined, pruned. On the second one John had flu, he had to keep going off to puke up, and come back on. It was a bit chaotic.

Did you talk to them?

I spoke to John before he went on stage on the first one.

Were they nice to you?

Yeah, they've always been nice people. Since the press got hold of it, they brought in more of the hooligan element, the football terraces. It was never like that before.

Were they surprised that you'd come to see them from Manchester?

I can't remember them being surprised. Howard was doing the pub rock column in the *New Manchester Review*, so he was chatting to Malcolm, getting his number, and they kept in contact cos Malcolm was interested in getting the boys out of London, up North. I think the next time I saw them was in Manchester.

Also we were saying yeah, we should get it together, cos after we'd

536

seen them the first time, me and Howard were sleeping in the living room and as we were going off to sleep Howard was quizzing me, like if we got our band started, what was my commitment. Would I stick with it, was it a hobby or was I into living the life, and I said, 'Yeah, I'm into living the life.' It was also from that copy of *Time Out* that we got, that we got the name Buzzcocks.

Was that a review of *Rock Follies*?

Yeah, it was a preview of *Rock Follies*; it said something like, 'Get a buzz, cock.' So we became the Buzzcocks.

So how did you find Steve Diggle?

That goes on to when the Sex Pistols were actually coming up to play. We were supposed to play with them, but the guy who we only knew over the phone, who was the drummer, when he found out we were going to have a gig in two weeks, as it was, bottled out. We had my friend Garth standing by to play bass, he was the only bass player that we knew, and he bottled out as well, so we got this band, The Mandala Band, to play with the Pistols.

We were organising the thing, we put an ad in the *New Manchester Review* for a drummer and bass player, and on the Friday afternoon we arrived at the Lesser Free Trade Hall, and Howard said to me, within earshot of Malcolm, that someone had called him, a bass guitarist, and they were going to phone back. So as the doors were getting ready to open, I was in the box office, taking the money.

Malcolm was going out in the street saying to people, 'Come on in, there's a great band on from London, you know, they're going to be famous. Roll up, roll up.' There was this guy standing on the steps, saying he was waiting for somebody, so Malcolm said, 'Oh, are you a bass guitarist?' He said, 'Yeah . . .' and Malcolm said, 'Oh, they're in here . . .' and he brought him inside to the box office and said to me, 'Here's your bass guitarist.' And there was the bemused Steve Diggle, with collar-length hair.

So I said, 'I'll be through here in a few minutes, go up to the bar and see Howard.' Anyway, a few minutes later Malcolm brought in another one, and it seems that Steve had answered a different ad in the *Manchester Evening News* about six months before, so it was a

537

real farce. I said, 'Now you're here, come and see this group.' And he liked it. So we said, 'We've got a band, not too dissimilar', and we made arrangements.

Then there was this girl advertising in *Melody Maker*, saying she wanted to play with musicians. Howard showed me the ad, and I said, 'Great, she could be a drummer, like Moe Tucker!' But it turned out she'd only just got a kit and she didn't really fancy doing gigs. She'd had a visit from this other drummer, who turned out to be John Maher, and he'd left an address, and Howard went round to see him, and saw the sixteen-year-old Mr Maher. So we were happy, we had all we needed.

When we met Steve Diggle that was June the 4th. We organized a repeat performance with the Sex Pistols cos it had gone really well, it had come out in profit, it was only £32 to hire the hall. For the second one we did posters – 'with support, the Buzzcocks'. The good thing about that gig was that Malcolm was using it as a publicity exercise, and put on a coach for journalists to come up from London.

So it was your first gig and you got reviewed?

Yeah. We had our first review by Jonh Ingham. I even got a name-check, so I bought three copies of it, you know, instant stardom. There was no turning back then. It was actually the doing things, and people either liking it or not liking it. Or entering into the mystique of being written about.

What did you play that time, 'I Can't Control Myself' and all that?

Yeah we did that. I don't think we had 'Breakdown', we had 'Time's Up'. We smashed my guitar up. If the truth be known, it was stage-managed. I'd bought the Audition guitar especially to smash it up. Howard and I ended up wrestling with the guitar and pulling the strings off it and smashing it up. It was great being able to get lots of noise and feedback.

There was already some bitching, wasn't there, between you and Slaughter & the Dogs?

They were a bit more football-terrace, arrogant, so we kept our distance. They were into Mick Ronson and the New York Dolls, which

Morrissey liked, he was the New York Dolls fan club secretary.

So what happened after that gig? Did you start playing others?

We played that gig, which was July the 20th, then the next gig we played was a thing at The Ranch, sometime about August. We went to see Frank [Foo Foo] Lamar at his sauna, we were trying to get somewhere to play, so we went to see him. He was there with his towel on, we finally convinced him.

You didn't have to do anything?

No no, there was no chance of that! He was quite notorious for that. But he said we could put something on. We did eleven or twelve dates with Howard.

You must have done the Screen on the Green after that?

Yeah. That was the first Clash outing as well. It really freaked out John Maher. He thought most of the people there looked like extras from *Doctor Who*. But in the audience there was Siouxsie Sioux, Steve Severin. In between they were showing Kenneth Anger films.

All the gigs we did were fun; even the bad ones had a funny side to them. Then we did a gig with Eater, they came up and we did one with them at the hall in Deansgate. There weren't all that many places, but then The Electric Circus, who'd been putting on Gentle Giant and all the progressive groups that were going around, they started putting on things, and Chelsea came up to play, with Billy Idol on guitar, and we played there.

Were there many people there?

Not really. There was quite an entourage come up from London but there weren't all that many. Richard Boon reckons that was the first time he met Ian Curtis. Curtis had been to that French punk gig, and he came over to Richard to ask if it was going to be the kind of music that they'd played down there. That was Eddie and the Hot Rods and The Damned.

Howard was doing a pub rock column?

Ah yes, this was really disastrous. The main place for pub rock was the Commercial Hall Tavern, Stalybridge, and Howard got us a gig there. We played two sets, cos one of the first things we decided was that we wouldn't do any pub gigs, that was the main circuit. You'd just end up having to play covers all the time. It was quite a phenomenon, and you became addicted to the easy money and stuff.

Not only was it hard for you to be original and escape from that, you also had to go without the money, and that, psychologically keeps you trapped. In the first six months of the Buzzcocks, all we did was write songs, we actually had material. Howard had reams and reams of poetry that he wanted to put into a new form, and I'd just pick up a guitar and write melodies.

Anyway, you played Stalybridge?

Yeah, all these bikers and their girlfriends came along, and they sat there with their helmets on the table beside them and they didn't like us at all.

What were the other groups like at the Screen on the Green? Did you watch them or were you backstage?

There was no backstage there, we were all out front. It was great. I spent most of my time pogoing up and down the aisles with Linder. They were playing songs that by then I knew, so it was just like seeing my favourite group.

Linder had met us after the second Pistols gig, we went for a drink, and shortly after that Howard and Linder started going with each other. We started using her artwork. That was another thing that was different about it, it wasn't just a band doing music, we were a band doing music who knew other people who did other things, and those things were incorporated, like Malcolm Garrett. It wasn't just the music, it was a focus.

So you played about ten gigs – what was the last one you played with Howard?

The last one was on the Anarchy tour; 10th December, Electric Circus.

Oh of course, the Stockport Tapes [first demo session], when did you do those?

That was at Revolution Studios in Bramhall Road. It was just a little 4-track. In September, the day after the Eater concert, we went down to London to do the Punk Festival.

What was that like?

Well, I remember seeing The Damned signing their record contract, during the nebulous time waiting for the soundchecks to happen. The Vibrators played, they had these windows painted on the drum skin and curtains over the bass drum so that every time he hit the drum the curtains would flap about. I think we were the last thing on, we were on the second day. At the end there were a few people left. We played basically the stuff on the Stockport Tapes.

Basically, Howard was doing the words at this stage and you were doing the melodies?

I remember the day we wrote 'Boredom', he was working a night-shift at the tie factory, and he came back and during the night he'd written these words, and I looked at these words and while he was upstairs before he went to bed, I worked out a couple of notes and wrote 'Boredom'. Stuff like 'Orgasm Addict', I wrote the first verse and the chorus and he wrote the rest of it. Sometimes with the early stuff we'd work together; he'd write something, and I'd write a verse and chorus or whatever.

Songs like 'Boredom' and 'Orgasm Addict' and 'Oh Shit' were quite different things for pop groups to write about then, weren't they?

Yeah, that was part of the brief of the emerging punk thing, it was about being the outsider – and it was like Dostoyevsky.

Was that something that attracted you at the time, that the attitude to sex was different?

Yeah, but in some ways it spilled over from the Bowie, androgynous part of it. It was a whole different attitude about sex. It was quite exciting, but I don't know. It was about as far from monogamy as you could get, and then again it wasn't screwing everything in sight. Sex was something that you did with people, the same as having a drink. It was escape from the boy meets girl, gets married, settles down.

541

'Orgasm Addict' is very witty. Was that about anybody, or just about the whole situation of people who get sex-obsessed?

It wasn't about anyone in particular. During that time, a lot of the places . . . like The Ranch was a gay bar really, and gay bars were the places you could go and be outlandish with your dress and not get beaten up, you could almost get into cross-dressing, without it being a big hassle. People were bohemian, while everybody was trying to conform. That was what the reaction was among the general public. The Sex Pistols were never really outrageous. You see that Bill Grundy thing, there was nothing to justify the reaction that it caused, it was really quite tame.

They didn't give a shit, which was what disturbed everybody. But that bohemian attitude is very important; it's something that nobody ever brings out. That's what attracted me to it from the beginning.

Also, when people were singing about anarchy, and Tony Wilson and the others going into the whole thing about the situationists, it was like an art movement. People were throwing in all these ideas. It wasn't only the freedom to make the music you wanted; there was that, but it was also that there were other people with other ideas.

Can you remember when the Sex Pistols were on *So It Goes*? Were you in the studio that day?

We almost had a fight in the hospitality room there. There was a band called Gentlemen, and I got into an argument with the guitarist. He was going, 'You can't play your instruments', and I was going, 'Well, so what?' He was getting really irate cos he'd been learning his craft for years, and all these people coming along and not playing the game – not only playing badly, but making money out of playing badly, and using that as part of the selling point. One of the Pistols' roadies had to step in and separate us.

What was the actual recording like?

They only played the one number. The audience was bemused, I think, cos it was just the normal rent-a-crowd. It was an entertaining show, it wasn't really for people coming on making rude noises and throwing microphones about. Nils and John were wrestling.

Did you see the Grundy thing on Granada?

We didn't get it up in Manchester, we got the shock-horror news the following day. We knew all the people involved, so it was just really funny. It was really weird. It made it exciting and newsworthy, cos if you can get people annoyed then you must be doing something; be it right or wrong, you're having an effect.

Did the newspapers get on to you?

Not as I remember. There was more of an arena, a set-up. The Sex Pistols were the main attraction, and everyone else were supporting acts. When Caroline Coon did her first article, she had Yachts as a punk band, the Hot Rods – it was a mixture of old music that had been around that wasn't progressive rock.

During the Anarchy tour they played The Electric Circus for the first time – what was that like?

There again, it was an event, it focused everything that was going on in Manchester around The Electric Circus, then the Circus saw that there was an audience for that kind of thing, and put more bands on. It went from twice a week to eventually five times a week. I just kept bumping into loads of people that I knew from college. It was like one of those killer parties that you go to every now and then.

Did you start living a punk lifestyle around then, did you spend all your time going out?

It was about then that I started going to The Ranch two or three times a week. Everybody used to drink Carlsberg Special, out of the bottle, with a straw. It was definitely an underage clientele there, most people were about seventeen.

What did they play there?

They played any punk record that came out, there weren't all that many at that time. Loads of Bowie. It was very '73, they played Gary Glitter and stuff like that.

At that point were you aware of yourself as gay, or not?

543

I've always had a mixture, it was a very bisexual time, really. A lot of girls went to The Ranch, it wasn't how you would imagine a gay club to be – it was almost like a youth club with alcohol. One of the reasons they shut it down was there was so many underage people in there.

You decided to make a record . . .

Spiral Scratch was a bit of a gamble, we had to borrow the money. Five hundred quid – my dad got a couple of hundred from the Friendly Society, and some friends of Richard's and Howard's put money in, and we had this artefact. We didn't think anything else would happen, it was fun doing it.

It was a memento. It was early days, there was no record company interest or anything like that. We had a thousand done, and we checked each and every one of them for scratches and stuff. We rejected about twenty-five.

The day they arrived we bought two bottles of Spanish red wine and drank a toast to it, and the toast was that we'd sell half of them, so we'd get the money back. With a few phone calls to Rough Trade, in four days, we got all of them off our hands.

Why did Howard leave?

The main reason was that he started the band when he was in his second year at college. By Christmas 1976 he was in his third year, and he'd been told by his tutors that he'd have to muscle down and work or he'd have no chance of getting his degree, and because we'd only done a few dates and we weren't rich out of it, and he didn't want us to stop and not do anything till he'd done his finals – so he left sometime in February '77.

There were no gigs coming up then anyway?

We recorded *Spiral Scratch* just after Christmas at Indigo. We knew Martin Hannett. Anyway there was some scam where he could get records pressed and you wouldn't have to pay for them, or something, so he became the producer.

Obviously the versions are much better than they are on the Stockport Tapes. How did you work out for that solo in 'Boredom'?

We were just playing it one day, and I just played the two notes. And we all fell about laughing, so we kept it in. In some ways – because I'd been in these sub-heavy metal bands before – really punk evolved from sub-heavy metal played badly. That's what it was, fast riffs and singing over the top. It wasn't like the Jan Akkerman thing, where you put in as many notes as you can. So in writing the songs, like where the key changes in 'Boredom', it was like throwing in a chord and see if it sticks, you know? Trying to get things to happen in a way that it wasn't happening before.

'Boredom' was quite a current word at the time, wasn't it?

Yeah. No Fun.

Was The Ranch the only place that punks went?

The Ranch and The Electric Circus. Rafters started about June or July '77. Then a bit later there was the Factory, as it was. That took over from the Circus. In some ways punk was classless, but at the same time it was easy for it to be called elitist. Elitism was a good thing, but it was a theory, it wasn't anti-intellectual.

So what was the attitude when you went around dressed in drain-pipes and plastic?

It was just anything, I knew this girl whose dad was a rag-and-bone man, so I used to go around and get first pick out of all the rags which would come in. During '76 I had my ear pierced, and after that I put a safety pin through it, and people used to say, 'Ooh, doesn't it hurt having a safety pin through your ear', and I had a razor blade on the safety pin and that would cause lots of fascination.

But you never got any hostility?

No, the only hostility we got was once leaving The Ranch in August '77 we were walking through Piccadilly Gardens, and someone asked us for a light, then we walked on, and the next thing I knew I was knocked down. But then there was a lot of the gang thing with the punks and the teds, echoing the mods and rockers. It started becoming a teen youth identification thing, rather than the interesting art experiment it seemed in the early days.

When did you first notice that happening?

The Grundy thing got it out into the open, about being rebellious, and it became more violent, and then at gigs all the gobbing started. At first the gobbing was people who didn't like the bands.

When did you first see that? The Anarchy tour?

I suppose it was happening then, but from the White Riot tour onwards you used to come off stage and chip it off your hair afterwards; you got used to it. It was bad when it used to land on the strings and deaden the strings when you were playing. You'd have to wipe it and carry on. But people used to do it as a genuine sign of approval, because they'd read that at these gigs the audience spit at the bands, and the bands spit back at the audience.

When did fanzines start in Manchester?

The first one was *Shy Talk* by Steve Shy. I did *Plaything*, two of them.

What was the idea of those tiny little magazines?

The whole revolutionary spirit, being able to get out ideas that are suppressed. Almost like leafleting. The leaflets said, this is not all there is, there's something else. A Pandora's box. William Burroughs things.

With the one-page magazine there was a further acceleration, it was like a condensed fanzine.

I started doing mine because my brother had hired a photocopying machine. There was a teen magazine called *Oh Boy*, which was full of these churned-out groups of young boys in their underwear. They ended up stopping it, it was going over the top. To photocopy that and get it out for the shock value of that. The first one I did, which I liked the best, was the one with lots of short bits in, joined up with dots. On the second one, I went into a bit of a polemic.

Did you play a lot in the North, from early '77 onwards?

We put some dates in around the White Riot tour. We played in Warrington, then we played the Band on the Wall for the first time with John Cooper Clarke . . . it was a very early one, the first time he'd played with a punk group. We took him to London when we did

546

The Vortex. That was how we got our break in the first place. If Malcolm hadn't called us up and said, 'Do you want to play Screen on the Green?', we would have been entirely a Manchester thing, but by going down there, that got more of an interest in the whole package.

Things were building up. There's always this thing with the way the public perceives a group. A group that is written about gets known about, but the joke was, all of us were nobodies. We wouldn't have stood a cat in hell's chance of getting public attention through anything but what we were doing. They lumped it all together and called it punk.

If Malcolm had taken a tape of the Sex Pistols to all the record companies, there would have been no chance, for any of us, but once it became a media event, it was interesting. That's why you can't talk about punk without including the people who were writing about it.

The White Riot tour was important, that was the first proper road show. The Anarchy tour hadn't managed to do that, its notoriety went ahead of it like a leper's bell. But with the White Riot tour, The Clash had CBS behind them. They played everywhere. The Clash, Subway Sect, The Slits and us. It was great, everyone got on with each other. The Prefects played a few of the gigs. There was something there, and it was all outside the established music business.

Originally we were put in to replace The Jam. The Jam played Edinburgh, but they were being snotty. Because they started up at the same time and they called themselves 'new wave', and they wanted to do their own tour, they didn't want to be on this White Riot tour.

The crowds were very excitable, it was like good-natured vandalism, enthusiasm. It wasn't like later, when you had invasions of skins, causing fights, National Front people. There was a gig we did in Bradford when somebody got stabbed.

We must have played the Rainbow in June, I remember meeting Andrew Lauder then. There was a lot of people sniffing around then. Virgin had started their spree of buying anyone with short hair, then there was a call from Maurice Oberstein, on the day we actually signed to UA, asking us to sign to CBS

It was a three-album deal, and then two. We managed to get in all the nice little things about artistic control. That was the important thing. We signed in August and went into the studio in September, to do 'Orgasm Addict', and 'Whatever Happened To . . . ?'; also 'What Do I Get?', but we didn't use that.

You brought your own ideas into the music industry, in terms of packaging as well as the subject-matter of your songs. How did you get Malcolm Garrett?

He was at college with Linder, and so the first thing was a collaboration between them. We met Kevin Cummins the same way. He was sometimes more important than the bands; he and Paul Morley were almost a double-act.

How did you work with Richard? Did you discuss a lot of things?

Yeah, things came together on a day-to-day basis. Each single was a new thing, and things happened quickly.

What was the idea behind 'Whatever Happened To . . . ?'?

I'd had the idea for the song for ages, and I mentioned it to Richard, and he came up with the words. He also came up with the words for 'Just Lust'.

It's strange how managers could be creative then.

They didn't start off as managers, their input was creative, and when you hit the music industry, that's when it starts getting odd, because people who've been doing particular things aren't going to see themselves wearing different hats. Once we were in the music industry, people had become more diversified, there was nothing really to pull people together again.

Richard Boon

Buzzcocks manager, artist and writer. Co-founder of New Hormones Records, which released Buzzcocks' first, ground-breaking EP. A great believer in punk autonomy and a great supporter of local acts during that period. Interviewed in London; patient, precise and on occasion combative.

In 1975 I was doing fine art at Reading University, and getting very bored. Yes, there was a history of art component, but it was 75 per cent practical. One was encouraged to find one's own area of interest and pursue it. I was very interested in black-and-white paintings, and I began to work on making a series of very simple marks from a fixed position – pretty minimalist – and I had worked myself into a cul-de-sac, and basically stopped painting.

How did you meet Howard, did you go to college with him?

I'd known Howard from school days at Leeds Grammar School. I'd met Peter once before at a party in Bolton, when I'd gone to visit Howard, who was studying there. Peter was really interested in whether I could get his group to play in Reading, something I didn't do.

Were you at all interested in what was going on in popular culture at that time?

I have always been a casualty of popular culture!

So in 1975, what was happening, or not happening, as far as you were concerned?

I listened to a lot of Detroit punk, and the New York Dolls. MC5, Stooges, New York Dolls. I was still vaguely interested in what moves David Bowie was making, and was increasingly disillusioned with nostalgia for Bob Dylan and The Beatles.

549

Some people say that through the last six months of 1975 they could feel that something was going to happen. Did you perceive that something was going to happen?

Oh yes, I think I did. Someone on the course who was doing film, we used to speculate about how great it would be if there were a group who couldn't play. Because everything was bland, soft disco and hard rock everywhere, and there was no sense of any new development, which I think gives rise to frustration.

Do you think the Sex Pistols were created by that frustration, or do you just think they filled the gap?

Some of both – they were definitely a creation, but they were also an idea whose time had come.

When did you first see them, can you remember?

It was in February 1976. Neil Spencer had written a crucial review, and my friend Howard phoned up saying, 'Did you read this? Wow! I just called the *NME* and it seems they're playing this weekend, and I'm coming down with a friend, can you put us up?' And I was so glad someone had organised something like that for me so Howard and Peter and I went down to see them on the Friday evening, and it was just great.

Was it instant recognition?

Yes, I think it was, Johnny was particularly impressive. It was a horrible students' union college thing, with a terrible DJ who really wanted to be Mike Read, and there were all these louts who couldn't relate to the Sex Pistols at all, they were very disappointed. They were sitting along the front of the stage with their backs to the stage, signalling to their mates, and Johnny crept along the front of the stage and tousled their hair. One of their mates from the back came running and picked Johnny up and threw him on the floor, and started piling in – this was during 'No Fun'. Johnny kept on singing, and crawled out from this mêlée and crept back on stage and the number ended. It also ended the show – the DJ came on and said, 'Oh, yer, well, boys and girls, in the *NME* they say, "We're not into music, we're into chaos", and I think we know what they mean, har har.'

So of course we got chatting, and back in Reading, Howard and Peter were saying, 'Yes, yes, we can do it.' They'd been planning to form a group to do something for a while.

What were the group like when you talked to them?

Johnny was very twitchy, and charismatic and off in a corner – not hostile, but totally wired. The lads were quite friendly, they were also interested that two people had travelled hundreds of miles just to see them. It must have been one of the first times it had happened, so a link was established, and sometime after that I booked them to play at the art department in Reading in May.

And did they play?

They certainly did – supported by Harry Kipper of The Kipper Kids. They were ex-Reading fine art graduates.

And again, was it the same reaction?

They went down pretty well with the fine art department! Hardly anyone came to see them, but those that did really liked them.

Was the result of seeing them that you wanted to do something yourself, did you start putting something together?

Yes, I really wanted to spread the virus. I booked them in at Reading, that was the only thing I did directly, and I was in regular contact with Peter and Howard who were by now shaping up the group, and Howard was arranging to get the Pistols to play in Manchester, and trying to get the group together in time. The first they weren't ready, but when the Pistols came back to Manchester a month later they were. I went up to Manchester and found somewhere to live, and when my course finished I moved up there.

Did you see that the group were improving rapidly at that stage?

Steve was throwing more rock guitar shapes on stage, and Johnny was getting wittier and more ironic. He was very disparaging about the material they were delivering to the audience, and was constantly surprised that the audience found them at all interesting. He always called them his little chickadees.

It was quite complicated stuff really, the early Sex Pistols, wasn't it? I mean, the mass market does not readily take to irony.

No. I think it was due to the people surrounding the Sex Pistols encouraging a particular kind of context. But Johnny was a compelling performer, and seemed too to be operating with a sense of performance, which was quite rare. It came with the spectacle of the performer being up here and you being down there.

Did you see any performance art in the Sex Pistols?

A little, yes. I think one thing that Bowie did, apart from generate a nation of casualties, was to bring that kind of intelligence to play on a rock stage. So it was theatre, in more of a Brecht or Artaud way than having props and giant robots and Alice Cooper tack – which was also theatre, in a very musical way. Roxy offered a more showbiz approach.

The rhetoric about the Sex Pistols at the time was that they were a radical break with everything that had gone before, and what now appears, although they *were* a radical break, is that there is a continuum with various things that had been going on in seventies rock.

I think the break was that they were young and that they set out to foster and incite a younger age-group than people like Roxy Music were addressing. In a way, Roxy addressed the teenyboppers almost by default. But they were aiming to have fun with the Richard Williams, Serious Culture age-group. Malcolm had a whole series of tape loops which he would unfurl at the drop of a hat: 'Young Kids! Short Hair!'

What did you think of that event at the second Manchester concert?

I was very surprised by how many people were there, all kinds of people seemed to have come out of the woodwork. As I walked in, there was a crowd of lads in the balcony doing some kind of football chant, shouting, 'Giovanni Dadamo doesn't know anything about punk!', over and over again. I think by then the Pistols were getting tighter, less sloppy, and in some ways, by the time of the Anarchy tour they'd become boring. It was more polished.

What people tend to forget is that during that summer they were off in the van with Nils and the PA playing for sixty quid almost anywhere, and they played all over the country in these poky little clubs, probably with almost no audience, and maybe two people who were like, galvanised as a result. They were helped by Jonh Ingham and Caroline Coon specifically propagandising.

How do you think they had that power, was it just that they were powerful performers, and that they were an idea whose time had come, or was it that there were quite a lot of ideas going in to them?

Yes, there were a lot of ideas going into them, many of which were implicit, and several of which were explicit. So explicit, in fact, that they were written on the shirts they were wearing.

What were some of the implicit ideas then, that they were taking stuff from – of the then contemporary art world, as well as pop?

Oh, the New York loft scene particularly, and some of the difficult Italian and German performance art things – and some of the British performance art things, which were still in a very primitive state but had a lot of currency among the art school crowd.

Do you think they would have picked up on even The Kipper Kids?

Perhaps even them, because there was a floating community of people who were those people and it's not insignificant that they played for the Logan thing. I mean at Reading there were quite a lot of people who were involved with Roxy Music and the Moodies.

Remember The Moodies? An all-girl cabaret group with Polly Eltes, and Anne Bean of the Bow Gamelan Ensemble, she was two years ahead of me at Reading. All of those people moved to London, and along with people from London colleges became part of the context of what was happening specifically in London.

How London were they when they started?

They were a mod band, they did covers – Small Faces covers – they liked to be flash, look sharp, carry a bit of Sex and Threat. And pilled up.

And because it was ten years on from mod ideas.

Well there were quite a lot of ideas around mod as well. Not that I remember, but the groups that became the psychedelic groups began as mod R'n'B bands.

When the Buzzcocks played, were you managing them at that stage?

No, just a friend.

And that was the gig where Peter kept on playing while Howard ripped all the strings out. What were they actually like then?

They were very fast. They did a Ramones song and they were two seconds faster than The Ramones! I can't remember which one it was. They were a blur of guitar and a blur of words. They were cheap and nasty, but I guess they were uncomfortable. They just wanted to get off stage as quickly as possible. 'We've put ourselves in this situation!'

I think people obviously picked up from The Ramones – music for people with short attention-spans. They were a postmodern, highly stylised event, and I really liked an interview in *Punk* where they said they had a five-year plan. After the first album they knew what the second album was going to be, and had several ideas – none of which came to fruition.

Was that concert a base for people getting started in Manchester, do you think? Did it all happen because of those two concerts?

Yes, I think so. I mean, it brought people out of the woodwork who thought they were just alone in their rooms, interested in all this, and people began to meet, particularly after the second one. People were saying to each other, 'Didn't I see you last month?', and a pocket-size community was forming as a result.

You obviously stayed in Manchester. Did you get involved with the Buzzcocks fairly quickly afterwards, on a professional level?

Well, my degree of professionalism is probably questionable anyway, but I used to answer the phone, book that rehearsal studio, hire that van, and there was nowhere to play. In Manchester and I think in London too there was a developing sense that you had to make your own entertainment, and a degree of mutual support, so as the people that became the Buzzcocks had arranged for the Pistols to play in Manchester, we got to play with the Pistols in London as well.

The Screen on the Green. What was that like?

554

Lots of fun. Peter Shelley entertained the queue by flitting in and out of the van playing 'Roadrunner' over and over again – one mustn't forget the early Jonathan Richman. An incredible number of people seemed to be in The Clash, but there were an awful lot of old ideas being put around – a Kenneth Anger film. I wasn't very happy with Siouxsie's swastika, and still am not. That was a bit of self-indulgence.

There was also a sense of people competing for copyright on presenting those ideas. At the Screen on the Green, The Clash went out into the alleyway to get dressed, so that no-one could see that they were wearing plastic ties and slogans and paint-spatter. There was that urge to secure their turf.

Was Paul Morley's magazine *Out There* [published summer 1976] significant in Manchester?

Yes, when a magazine is published it establishes a currency of ideas, that become communicated, passed around.

What did you think about *Sniffin' Glue*?

Sniffin' Glue was lots of fun. It was very important for marketing that idea: here's a chord shape, here's another, that's all.

They didn't do that, everybody's got that wrong. It was a magazine called *Sideburns*.

But the idea of do-it-yourself. Surplus technology. Fast technology. Ease of access. And against that whole thing where the rock media concentrated on technical proficiency, the Yes-solos syndrome. It was quite important for someone to be saying that you don't need lots of equipment and lots of skill – or any skill! – just intent, and ideas.

There still wasn't much media interest, was there, apart from the rock press. Did you see it going anywhere or did you just carry on from day to day?

There was a sense of time running out, because people were organising their own events, you never knew whether this would be the last one, there was a definite tension about it. But from the Screen on the Green onwards, there was a real sense of campaign, that something more coherent had to emerge. There was the publication of Malcolm

555

and Jamie's *Anarchy in the UK* mag. That seemed to be a tactical device to get some information out to people.

During the autumn did you come down to London much or were you too involved with the Buzzcocks up in Manchester?

I was still trying to find places to play, and trying to make events, so we approached The Electric Circus, a heavy metal disco in a derelict cinema, which had been an early-seventies hard rock venue, basically to create and support the little audience that there was in Manchester, and there was a gig with Eater and there was one with Chelsea.

With Billy Idol?

Yes, and Steve and Siouxsie came up, Debbi and a couple of other people. Ian Curtis turned up. I was on the door, and he'd been to the Mont de Marsan festival in France, and he thought it was great that all this was happening because he'd been in his bedroom thinking no-one else was interested – as had most of the people who were actually there.

What was your audience, about fifty?

About fifty and gradually growing as people brought their friends.

In what way was the identity of what was going on in Manchester different to what was going on in London?

Well, it was a backwater, and the things that would happen were still major rock gigs in the Free Trade Hall and the Apollo, and there was little else – apart from scarce access to any records and the weekly consumer papers. But there was a group of people in Manchester with a community interest that was very different to anything in London. People found that they had friends with a common interest, and would just socialise outside these sporadic, key events. People began to hang out together.

In the autumn you were busy with the Buzzcocks, you did some tapes?

Yes, that was in September, to get the songs down on tape, just to hear them really, and we gradually became approached more seriously, we went to Liverpool, and moved around Manchester, not going very far.

Did you go to the 100 Club festival?

Well it was Chris Spedding, who was just awful, The Vibrators and The Damned. Us lot were tagged on the beginning of what was a really sleazy, boring rock'n'roll pub rock bill. I think people didn't really know what to make of them. The London response to Howard was perplexing. He performed with difficulty, personal difficulty, I think it was a real existential dilemma for him. He had a curious microphone technique.

What did you think of the supposed violence? Did you see it as being pursued as theatrical, or as real?

Well, with the Pistols there was just a threat, the violence was something for the yellow papers. I thought of it as being completely incidental, very localised and small-scale.

Did you go to the recording of *So It Goes*?

No, I didn't go to that, but that was important locally. It did have Jordan throwing a chair around. You can just see Howard and Peter in the background. The performance was a little styled for television but it was fairly accurate. It was very quick-witted of Wilson to book them, although Howard had been pestering him for months and months.

What did you think of the Sex Pistols signing to EMI? Did you think anything about it, or did you see it as being inevitable?

I think it was very entertaining, but yes, it was probably inevitable, because Malcolm was increasingly desperate to front a show. It had to happen.

At the time of Grundy, did you think time had run out?

I thought it was very funny, and it just seemed to be total media hysteria, which of course always changes everything.

Did you notice a change in Manchester?

Yes, audiences began to form, picking up very much on the dustbin-liner and bad make-up angle.

They did two dates on the Anarchy tour?

557

Yes, when the Anarchy tour played Manchester there was already a distance between the characters who were in the early audience and the larger audience that was now there. I thought the Sex Pistols were really sloppy, and The Clash were really vibrant.

The Sex Pistols were under mounting pressure, and the whole tour was fraught with media-induced problems. I'm not saying I wasn't as interested. They were still good, but Steve Jones was a rock star, acting in a very old-fashioned manner, and with John the playfulness had gone. Some of the sharpness was still there, he was still engaging, but something had happened, life was being made very hard for them. Life became heavy.

The Clash were really coming up then, weren't they?

Yes, they played Manchester twice, came back having had several dates on the tour blown out, and I found the difference between The Clash performances was remarkable, they were glowing, tight. Joe Strummer was Eddie Cochran!

When did you record the *Spiral Scratch* EP? Late December, was it?

Yes. The Anarchy tour had happened, and the EMI thing had happened. That winter, something that was striving to give birth to itself was beginning to retreat, and there was a feeling that if there was nothing else, there should be a record – and it might have been instructive to do one's own.

The Buzzcocks phenomenon was desperately unskilled, with no industry experience at all and no resources. No-one was really sure that this was going to become a career base, it just seemed worth documenting the activity, perhaps as the end result, perhaps the only result. There was also a feeling amongst the group and myself that this could illustrate part of the do-it-yourself, Xerox-cultural polemic that had been generated.

You were saying you did black and white paintings. Did you like the fact that punk was very black and white?

Yes. And red. I liked that. Colour Xerox machines in those days were few and far between. But there were only one or two commercially operating. So we raised some money and recorded it very quickly.

Who took the picture?

I took the picture on the steps of some statue in Manchester Piccadilly, with a polaroid, which was a joke. A very Walter Benjamin, art-in-the-age-of-mechanical-reproduction sort of joke. Because any kind of material has to go through the same stages of printed reproduction; but it was also a joke on the fact that it was done, it was instant replay.

There was a great thing – the first Anarchy date in Manchester, Peter and Johnny and Strummer had all just gone blond, and were stood at the bar talking about hair dyes, it was just wonderful!

Why was that happening, was that all to do with self-re-invention?

Yes, people were changing themselves and re-inventing themselves, or changing the invention. I'm sure it was all lifted from people like Jackie Curtis and Candy Darling and Ingrid Superstar, and that whole personality presentation that was very mutable.

There's a very interesting line from Larry Parnes to Andy Warhol. You had these extraordinary pop names that Larry Parnes gave to his artists, like Johnny Gentle and Billy Fury, all those pre-pop art ideas. Malcolm also had a big Larry Parnes fetish, that whole Jewish manager trip.

And the package shows. The Anarchy tour was a very Parnesy thing. Larry Parnes is incredibly significant.

What did you think of the Buzzcocks' songs?

I thought they were very intelligent and very funny, lyrically facetious, and that's why the period of the Buzzcocks with Howard was difficult for people to digest, because there was a lot of confusion about the ideas that were going in, some of which co-operated and some of which conflicted. They were very catchy, in a Ramones sort of way, but very full.

Did you notice how the humour in punk was completely lost?

Completely, yes. 'Boredom' was satire, it was taking the piss out of the whole scene. A lot of Howard's writing was parodying the apparent parameters of the scene. It was deceptive.

559

It would be interesting to trace the changing use of the word 'boredom'. It was all over the place. I found it again recently in a situationist pamphlet. Were you aware of the situationists at that point?

Yes, I had my battered copy of *Leaving the 20th Century*, Vaneigem and Debord. That was just my own interest. I'd probably blame the *International Times*. They used to lift quite a lot of situationist material, particularly the comic strips.

Did you see much of that going into the Sex Pistols?

Yes, it was pretty obvious. At least, if one had been exposed to the material it was. It was engaging to see it. Jamie's graphics were definitely rooted there.

Do you think that gave them an edge? Was it playful or political?

Both. If every act is political, having fun is political too. There was obviously a lot of sharp, ageing hippies knocking about, or people who had been exposed to the ageing hippy culture.

It was interesting, the commodification of anarchy was quite fascinating, and there was a fairly oblique attempt to make that propaganda move, so that maybe people would go out and get their Woodcock Penguin *Anarchy* out of the library, or steal it from WH Smith.

Do you think that was one of the things that propelled the Sex Pistols into being the social force, rather than simply pop music?

Yes, very much so.

What did you think in '77 when Glen left and Sid came in?

I felt that in the latter half of '76 there was a degree of alienation with Glen anyway.

So that sense of it being a small community had disappeared and it was now more localised?

Yes, absolutely. It was still important to maintain some kind of link, but local interest became more paramount, and because of recent activity the Buzzcocks were becoming a viable working group.

Howard particularly was uncertain about all those uncertainties that had focused – and left. And as a consequence of the record proving popular, the phone began to ring: 'Come and play here!'

I think Howard left because he was uncertain, and the rest of the group wanted to continue. When we started to play outside Manchester we met people in Liverpool and Birmingham. We played at Annabel's, a horrible toilet – but Peter responded by bringing his songs to the fore. He'd been writing songs for years.

They never played London until the Harlesden Coliseum in February 1977. It was a very important gig for Buzzcocks. The record had been out and become notorious, and it was our first London date since that had happened. They had to establish their territory, and take it with a little bit of stagecraft. They played at the Roxy wearing pinstripe suits and green carnations! Peter had been reading *The Green Carnation* when he saw the Sex Pistols.

What was going on in Manchester had a different quality to what was going on in London.

Yes, local activity was seen to be important, although still itself open to the same sort of mutations that had happened in London, and in the media. The group that became The Drones had been Rockslide, a Bay City Rollers-type act – punk rock overnight. They were operating on the media definitions, these were the shapes to throw, and they threw them, and it was tacky, basically, and pretty thoughtless.

But there were also groups like The Fall beginning; and the group that was to become Joy Division were struggling – also tacky and captivated, or colonised by the media interpretations of punk; and The Worst, but they had a real sense of humour. It became deliberate policy as Buzzcocks developed and eventually signed, to take local groups down to London as supports, and keep passing that Olympic torch on.

What did you think of the pop media by that stage?

Well Jon, you were a fascinating writer in those days!

Yeah, yeah, yeah. But it was changing a lot, wasn't it?

The papers were taking on new writers, including Paul Morley and

Jane Suck. The papers were falling over themselves trying to come to terms with the new market. But there was a lot of confusion, and editorial policy was very tentative. People were very worried about making policy decisions that might lose a whole section of the readership.

Fanzines were already parodies of themselves. I have a feeling that I did the first newspaper cut-out background. I did a little book of Howard and Peter's lyrics, which went out to a few people – just put a piece of A4 hardboard on a newspaper and cut it out, and stuck the lyrics on it. *The Secret Public* was an interesting intervention; it was still operating on a DIY-access level, but it was instructive in a different way.

When did life start to become normal again, after all this?

Late '77, early '78. As 1978 progressed, the routine was established, the industry treadmill, apart from the independent-label development, which did something different.

It brought a different level to the structure.

Rough Trade was very significant in the way it was committed to supporting independent endeavour, and established a network for disseminating that information. They expanded the mail order, they established links with sympathetic retailers round the country, and began an exchange of that recorded information which became the distribution network that we all know as The Cartel.

But within that there was a climate where almost anything could sell, there was a bandwagon effect where if you could sell five thousand copies of anything, you would do that, without necessarily having any information to put across, or any ideas. But it did begin the regional bases of activity that were very important.

So when the Sex Pistols actually broke up, they were almost irrelevant, weren't they?

Yeah, they'd definitely had their day.

What did you think of the whole A&M, Jubilee business?

It was pretty ridiculous, an over-reaction, but it obviously showed that they'd tapped a nerve. I think the SPOTS tour was quite interesting because they were going out to re-affirm the regional audience and climate that it subsequently engendered. The Jubilee thing was a delightful strategy, it was great to see that record at number one.

Did you see the band ever again?

I saw them on the SPOTS tour, the Lafayette [a club in Wolverhampton]. It was pretty horrible, there were about forty beefy guys across the front of the stage, and an awful lot of stupid fighting, very unnecessary sloppiness. Things were out of hand, and disturbingly amoral.

Where had that come from?

I think the media played a significant part in generating that, but I think circumstances made it harder to have a focus and direction. I think their tactical plan had become a bootstrap operation, from day to day, and became increasingly incoherent; something that seemed like a good idea one day was inappropriate the next. It was probably that time they didn't play for quite long periods.

I think 'Holidays in the Sun' is a wonderful record, one of their best in fact. I remember it playing at the last night at The Electric Circus.

'Holidays in the Sun' was a very different kind of record. They'd had trouble with material for a while. I remember when we went to see The Clash at the Rainbow, Sophie Richmond was talking to Howard, saying the Pistols were having trouble with lyrics, and he wouldn't be interested in helping out, would he? That was curious.

At the Rainbow the seats got destroyed just like with Bill Haley, and Joe made increasingly democratic moves like taking off his T-shirt and throwing it into the crowd, and putting on a T-shirt that someone in the audience threw back at him. Joe Public.

There was that working-class thing as well, wasn't there . . .

. . . which particularly Sham were playing with. I think the working-class thing was something that the media interfered with particularly and played on that lowest-common-denominator thinking that the gutter press like to impose on the working class. The working class

563

are not 'Hersham Boys' – some of them may be, but it's very dangerous for those kind of role models to become re-established.

The threat posed by earlier, more sophisticated punk was that intelligent young working-class people would THROW OFF THE SHACKLES OF OPPRESSION! and STEP INTO HISTORY! Even in a dumb way, all that possibility was closed by the response to the Grundy thing.

I see the Grundy thing as being absolutely key in the whole way of the thing.

'I Kicked in My TV Set, Says Angry Father of Four', and 'Must We Fling This Filth at Our Pop Kids?'. The filth and the fury. Yes, I'm sure it was absolutely crucial. If it hadn't happened I think it might have just withered away. It's too hypothetical.

Do you remember a concert that Buzzcocks gave in Stoke, with The Slits and The Prefects? In March '78. I remember Rob Lloyd completely winding up the audience.

The Prefects were doing songs like 'VD' in thirty seconds, punk thrash. Yes, he really wound up the audience. He was desperate for some kind of identity. Full of resentment and frustration. I also remember on the same tour at Cambridge Corn Exchange, seeing someone being carted out with their head pouring blood, it was horribly violent. People thought they should live up to the idea of a good time being going out and beating each other up.

Tony Wilson

Manchester's prime booster, music impresario, television personality, co-founder of prime independent label Factory Records. Was almost the only person in the UK to showcase punk on television in 1976 and 1977, thanks to his show So It Goes, *which also showed the first Sex Pistols TV performance. Interviewed in Manchester, ebullient and sure of his own myth.*

I start with having gone through that period in '73/'74 when I was quite bored by music, and then Christmas '75, a man called Dennis Brown who I'd been at university with put me on to Patti Smith, *Horses*. About the second or third of January '76 I bought it, and what a great album.

In February 1976 it was announced that Tony Wilson would be expanding his *What's On* music show to a network rock show in the summer, and I got two letters within a couple of weeks. The first from a kid called Stephen Morrissey, containing a battered copy of a New York Dolls album, and I have to say I didn't know who the fuck these people were. He said, 'Why can't we have more music like this, Mister Wilson, and please can you do something about it when you get your new show.'

We went on preparing *So It Goes* to be a quick-moving, groovy, fast TV show, that didn't have too much respect for the music because the music was pretty shitty. Then I got a letter and a cassette from a guy called Howard Trafford, and he said, 'This is a really wonderful group just started up in London, they're coming to Manchester on June 4th, Lesser Free Trade Hall', and that of course was the Sex Pistols. So I began a conversation with Howard.

Did the name Sex Pistols attract you?

The name was strong. It wasn't until I sat in that concert hall with

565

about thirty-seven people, between thirty and forty people that first night, that I realized what was going on. The second time, six weeks later, when the Buzzcocks did their first gig and Slaughter & the Dogs were on the bill, there were about a thousand people, but the first night, I didn't know what the fuck was going on, until they played 'Stepping Stone'. As soon as they did that, it was clear that they were deeply and remarkably and fabulously exciting.

I went back to Granada and said we absolutely must put them on the show, and the researcher, Malcolm Clark, was asked to check them out with me, and we went to Walthamstow Assembly Hall, and that again was a completely non-attended gig, maybe eighty people, of whom forty were a large, single-line semicircle, just out of gobbing range. And then we put them on the show.

The other thing that happened was in the middle of May, Martin Hannett had called me to say I must come and see this group Slaughter & the Dogs at The Shed, in Stockport. I dropped acid and went to The Shed. You know now that any music critic worth his salt will tell you that the British love dressing up as women; that was Slaughter & the Dogs, wearing their Bowie dresses.

Wasn't there a band called Gentlemen on with the Pistols on that edition of *So It Goes*?

And the Bowles Brothers, yes. We decided to make a virtue out of our last show, with three unsigned bands. The Sex Pistols behaved pretty badly. They had a row with Clive James. They had drunk quite a bit. I was doing my intro to them, talking about the last four weeks, and you hear John go: 'GET OFF YOUR ARSE! WOODSTOCK COMING TO GET YOO-OUW!!!'

Was what went out edited down?

Yes. They were meant to do three and a half minutes, they agreed that and rehearsed it, and there was five minutes left, and they just kept playing for seven minutes and kicked their equipment apart. Two days later the director edited it down to three and a half minutes. He did a good job, but someone threw away the original take, which was a shame.

Did they record another number?

No, that was it.

What did Granada think about it?

Shock horror, the audience was dumbfounded. As they came off stage there was complete silence except for the footsteps of the producer, Chris Pye coming down the stairs from the box to try and hit somebody. Everybody was wound up. The next day I was in trouble at Granada, there was bad feeling.

One of the services in Manchester was that every Thursday night you had *What's On*. So I was doing that for a local programme, it was my job in the culture. I backed off for a couple of months, I was so depressed by the response to *So It Goes*. People didn't like it cos it was too fast, it was irreverent, it wasn't *The Old Grey Whistle Test*, which was dull and dead and became fashionable because we were the opposite, which people hated.

The Electric Circus had opened, I think for heavy metal, and suddenly they saw this new thing happening, and did one night a week of punk. At the same time The Ranch opened; I never went to The Ranch, but suddenly you've got places and a community culture.

I resigned at Granada over the Anarchy tour. Roger Eagle rang me from Liverpool. I'd had a documentary I was making on the Pistols cancelled by Granada on the morning I was to start shooting it, cos my producer Linda MacDougal had read Ronald Butt attacking them [in the *Daily Mail*], and called Granada and said, 'Don't give Wilson his crew.' This was after Grundy.

The next day, Roger Eagle rang me to say the police had been down to Eric's and said, 'If you put this group on, you will not get your licence next time it comes up.' So I prepared for the *What's On* show that week, 'What's Not On Is the Sex Pistols', and I then got a memo from Linda MacDougal saying, 'There will be no mention of the Sex Pistols in this programme', and I walked out. Already you see, it's a community.

Something obviously quite illogical happened over the Sex Pistols that autumn . . . what happened?

Authority. For some reason, as soon as a name like the Pistols comes up, it becomes an obsession with the establishment culture because

567

it's not in their control. Simple as that. In Manchester then, there was a community, like San Francisco in 1967. A small city is just the right size for these kind of things.

Did you follow the whole thing through '77?

In '77 it seemed very political, but by the time Factory started, we all thought we were nurseries for the majors, and you did the first single and then sell them on. It was par for the course for us to sign Orchestral Manoeuvres in the Dark. The political sensation of '77 when you were doing it yourself had vanished by early '78. Tosh Ryan [of Rabid Records] sold out to EMI with Jilted John, and CBS with John Cooper Clarke.

JCC was very important, cos like any scene it had many aspects to it, and he was the poet. We had the designers, Garrett and later Saville, Linder, and there was Morrissey too. He was the intellectual in the corner of the playground, never get a fuck in his life, and I thought he would be the writer of our generation, which of course he did, but he became a pop star as well.

Now you get to January '78, there's all these indie labels around, but I'd got stopped doing *So It Goes*, and Alan Erasmus was managing a group called Fast Breeder. Eight months later he gets sacked as manager, and there's Alan sitting there with Dave Rowbotham and Chris Joyce. Same day my accountant is saying to me, you don't make any fucking money at Granada, do you?

That conversation on 24th January combined with the news that Alan had been fucked over, I went round and said, 'I'll join you to manage these two, we'll form a group around them.' Alan's suggestion was to add Vini Reilly, and that was the origins of it. We never found the right singer, but the rhythm section of the Durutti Column ultimately became the rhythm section of Simply Red.

The Stiff/Chiswick Test [April 1978; a talent night organised by Stiff Records and Chiswick Records] was the great night in Manchester, that was the fulcrum moment. That was the night Joy Division came up to me. All the groups that had started in the wake of the Buzzcocks, and that night at Rafters twelve groups played. Eleven of them were boring, the twelfth was fantastic, played two numbers and had the plugs pulled. I was accosted by this guy in a raincoat who

568

said, 'You're a fucking cunt, why haven't you had us on the telly?' And I said, 'The reason I haven't had you on the telly yet is everybody has a turn and your turn is next, Mister Warsaw.' I put them on about six weeks later, doing 'Shadowplay'. That was Ian Curtis.

That night, though, I saw eleven interesting bands with nothing to say, and one with a lot to say. A lot of the groups around that night had been around since '75. They hadn't begun in the middle of that culture like Warsaw. That saw the coming of Joy Division.

By the time the Durutti Column were ready to play, Rafters is no longer a hip place, and we wanted a new venue, and we sorted out the Russell Club. I met Peter Saville at a bad Patti Smith concert in '78. Instead of it being a group doing one night for our club, again, there was a group of people who knew each other, like the Tiller Boys, Madame over in Liverpool – Margox [Margi Clarke].

One of the great achievements of Manchester was that when Suicide supported The Clash the following year, they were bottled and canned and fucked over at every gig in the country, including London, except when they played the Factory, when fifteen hundred people went berserk, loved it. We were that advanced. There was a subculture there, The Residents and Suicide seemed to go together with a certain bunch of people.

There was the whole thing coming out of Sheffield and Leeds that we were aware of, Human League and Cabaret Voltaire, who were good friends. So we began these nights, we stopped for three weeks and came back and began the Factory. We were looking for a name, and Alan saw a sign saying 'Factory Clearance', and said, 'Right, we'll call it the Factory.' Nothing to do with Warhol at all.

That summer went, and the club was fine, the Durutti Column was fine, and we began to think about how to get a record out. Roger Eagle said he was going to restart Eric's Records – they put out one record the previous year, Big In Japan – and would I be their A&R man. The night before, I went over to Liverpool, I was on acid, and I looked at this South-East Asian copy of Santana's *Abraxas* – they used to do album sleeves in thin paper, with plastic over it.

The next day I'm driving to Liverpool thinking, we could do a sleeve like that – it could be two seven-inch singles, no-one's done that since *Magical Mystery Tour*. And Roger and Pete Fulwell go,

'Okay, we'll do a twelve-inch single, one group on each side', and I'm saying, 'Let's do four groups', began to describe what was to become the Factory sampler.

When was the decision made to do the Joy Division album on Factory?

It was made by Rob Gretton, I had no vision of it. I had got around to the point of view that you merely take your artist on to the major label. Bob Last had done it with Fast Records; at the time it seemed like a good idea, looking back it seemed like a terrible mistake. Sure enough, we sold Orchestral Manoeuvres, Joy Division were getting really hot, and Andrew Lauder came in on behalf of Martin Rushent, they were going to put [Rushent's label] Genetic on Radar [Records] on Warner Brothers. Great, wonderful.

In the Band on the Wall one night, sometime early '79, Gretton says, 'What about doing the first album with you and then going to Warner Brothers?' My first reaction was, 'No fucking way. What'll it cost?' 'Six grand.' We sketched out the deal on a napkin, or whatever. What I didn't know was that Gretton was thinking, this Factory stuff works. If it does work, this is so much more fun than signing to a major; if it doesn't work, we can sign to a major then.

We did *Unknown Pleasures*, pressed ten thousand, sold five thousand off the back of the truck, the other five thousand came home to Palatine Road. As soon as you'd got going, suddenly the mood changed, and by the end of '79 there's Rough Trade, and that political identity you felt about being an independent label had arrived – but it wasn't until maybe six months after *Unknown Pleasures*. By the time you got to *Closer*, it was all there.

Linder

Fine artist, then working in montage, examples of which were used on Buzzcocks' handbills and the sleeve for their second 45, 'Orgasm Addict'. Produced The Secret Public – *an all-montage fanzine – with Jon Savage in early 1978. Interviewed on a sunny day in Fletcher Moss, a beautiful park between Didsbury and the River Mersey.*

I was brought up in Liverpool, lived there till I was nine, in Wavertree and then Huyton. Extremely normal, so normal it was horrible. My dad was a bricklayer, and my mum used to work in a biscuit factory. I longed for the exotic things in life from an early age and never got them. Shoes. Still have the same problem.

Then you moved to Billinge?

Yeah, it was like *Brookside*, overspill from Liverpool, and they hated the scousers. At school I was the novelty, cos I was from Liverpool, the foreigner. The education must have been better, cos I was immediately top of the class in Billinge.

Were you interested in music?

Yes, I was interested in everything I couldn't have. I got interested in classical music then, cos we never had any in the house, so I'd get these old 78s from my aunties and dress up in old scarves and dance around the living room. Not so much pop music, cos everybody liked it.

You went to art school?

Yes, in Manchester, in '72. I was the year above Malcolm [Garrett] and Peter [Saville].

Wasn't that a shock for your parents, for you to go there?

Yes it was. I was the first in the family, the big event. Especially doing

571

art. I went from Upholland Grammar School. That was a one-year foundation course, then the degree; it just became a degree as I did it, before that it was just a diploma. Graphic design and illustration. I was lucky, my tutor was a woman who had crossed over from fine art into graphics, and she was wonderful, she let me do everything I wanted.

Did you meet Malcolm and Peter there?

Yes. I did my foundation and first-year graphics, and then went off to London in the summer holidays, met Howard, came back dressed in PVC and my life had changed; and then I got to know Malcolm and Peter. I went to the Sex Pistols, Buzzcocks, Slaughter & the Dogs concert. The first time ever. The girl I was with fell in love with Howard Devoto and said, 'Please can we stay and talk to the singer.' So we stayed, but then the singer took more to me!

Why did you go to the concert?

I was sitting in Manchester's Southern Cemetery sketching one day, walked out, and this van was parked outside with a poster tacked on, saying, 'Malcolm McLaren presents the Sex Pistols' – and the names, McLaren sounded all tartan, and tartan and sex and pistols and guns, so I suggested to this friend that we go. Then in the afternoon I was tidying up my room, and I kept finding safety pins, and I was pinning them on my clothes . . .

What was the scene like at art school just before then?

It was all Roxy Music, quiffs and gels. I remember when punk came along, suddenly all the nice shirts that had been worn were being painted and crayoned on. The same shirts I'd seen earlier. And the tuxedos being ripped up.

What did you think of the bands when you saw them that first time?

I remember going into the Lesser Free Trade Hall, and I think it was Johnny Rotten who took my money, and I saw Vivienne and Malcolm, and I just knew that something strange was going to happen. I just knew it. These people looked so separate and apart and so different.

Were they threatening, or just different?

Not threatening at all, just fascinating – me longing as usual for something different. Exotic, and these strange leather trousers and mohair jumpers. It was just so strange . . .

What were the Pistols like?

Johnny was wearing this big mohair jumper that seemed to be growing all the time, the fluff getting longer, and arms growing out, like an octopus. It was a shimmery night. All this energy and light.

So your life was changed. In what way?

It was quite immediate. I started talking that night to Howard and Peter, and I think I met them again the next day. I wanted to do some graphics, anything to get interest, but from then on we were all together.

Did it change your graphic style?

Yes it did. I was getting really tired of drawing, and I began to do bits of collage, quite naturally. I remember going off to London and taking lots of photographs and coming back with them, and what could I do with them? I started to loosen up a lot and use collage, then I got bored with that and went from collage to montage, using scalpels, glass cutting; no drawing, I'd had enough of that.

What was the Screen on the Green like?

That was an adventure, we hired the van and all went down in that. Borrowed a camera for the night. I remember being in the bar with Vivienne and somebody else. They came up and said, 'Who are you a fan of?' At the time I thought, what a daft thing to say, and I said, 'I'm a fan of me.' How dare you presume, you know?

I remember Vivienne standing at one side, jumping up and down and screaming, I thought she was wonderful. Wasn't The Clash on that night? They had these badges like smashed mirrors, and I thought it was a strange thing to wear. I didn't really approve of the Tommy badges. It was a bit off-putting, it didn't tally with my idea of what was happening. I thought, no.

What were you wearing then?

Gel on the hair, pots of eyeliner, red lips. It was tight and black. I remember Pete not knowing what to wear, so he wore two pairs of my footless tights. I think a cleaning woman's pink smock. And his hair was bleached blond. He was wonderful that night, so full of energy. I took pictures of Siouxsie and the girl who died, Tracie. And Simon Barker.

I remember asking a boy I didn't know to come outside, so I could take his picture, he had this chain through his nose. Then the next week the same boy was on the cover of the *News of the World*. It really began to happen then, shock horror, this boy has his nose pierced and wears leather . . . he was from Wales.

I think I saw virtually everything then. It all tended to blur into one. I met Morrissey at one of the very early Electric Circus gigs. It must have been at Johnny Thunders.

People used to go to The Electric Circus and The Ranch. Which was first?

It was The Ranch for quite a long time. The police came down one night and did a really brutal search and closed it down. Underage gay boys who were so bored, they'd tried every permutation of sex by the age of fourteen. I think they wanted cuddling more than anything else.

Did you ever have any trouble cos of the way you looked?

Oh yes. I went off and spent every penny I had on clothes, PVC and bondage trousers, and Manchester just hadn't seen it, so walking down the street was like a travelling circus really. Not pleasant at all. People were rude and really offensive. Strange to think of it now.

Were things happening very quickly?

Whoosh! Things were moving, there was this delicious rushing feeling, it was a very exciting time. I can't put an exact date on it, but I think it stopped quite quickly. I remember this really intense period, but perhaps it wasn't even a year long. It got watered down. As soon as the papers got hold of it. I was writing about it for my thesis, in my final year. By the end of it there were articles in *Woman's Own* – 'A Guide to Punk'. I thought, it's time to stop.

When did you start getting your work out?

574

The Rafters handbill with Buzzcocks and Manicured Noise would have been one of the first things, although I did a very early Buzzcocks poster, but it was awful. I've hidden it away. Then having to change my name. I must have left college, cos I was on Social Security, and the DHSS were getting on to people who were in groups. Richard, Howard and I found the house in Lower Broughton Road, and it seemed quite neat.

It must have been quite intense.

The phone was always ringing and The Worst would come around. I remember the teddy-boy scare as well, in the really early days. On the bus, there were these two teddy boys in front of me and they got off at the same bus stop as me, and they were going down the tunnel following me, and I thought, this is it. My death. They followed me up the path and I went in the house and they knocked, and they were actually really sweet. They wanted to arrange some concerts to prove that punks and teds could get on together.

When did you leave college? Did you leave before you qualified?

No, I did the whole thing. I remember having my bondage trousers as part of the degree show.

Presumably you didn't think of having a career in graphic design, you were just involved in a group of people and that was what you could do.

Yes, Richard did the *Spiral Scratch* cover, but I was involved. Then there was 'Orgasm Addict', and they asked me to do it. I asked Malcolm about it, and I was quite happy to give it all to Malcolm really, I wasn't bothered about being a designer as such.

Did you ever see the Sex Pistols again after The Electric Circus?

No, I probably didn't, did I? Everyone else went off to see the SPOTS tour, but I didn't for some reason.

Can you remember what you thought of the Roxy Club?

I remember lots of reggae being played. I think I saw X-Ray Spex, the Buzzcocks . . . and there were all these mirrors around, people would be dancing around, just looking in the mirrors. Looking at them-selves. Taking speed. Dark, lots of string vests, nipples – yes, lots of nipples at the Roxy, it wasn't quite done in Manchester. And huge queues, huge queues to get in. Star-spotting, there's so-and-so, and pretending not to notice . . .

You did *The Secret Public* . . . did you get any reaction out of that?

Yes, a lot. People presumed when they saw my work that it was a male artist, and they were shocked when they found it was a male and female doing it. I got quite a strong reaction.

Did you feel that people were starting to steal your work?

Yes, I remember a few things around. I used a lot of bodies without heads, for quite deliberate reasons, but some people did it cos I sup-pose they thought it was easy. I did a few of the sleeves for Magazine; with 'Shot by Both Sides', Howard had distinct ideas about what he wanted, and I went to Malcolm for some advice about type, I wanted something classical.

Had punk disappeared by then?

Yes, there were still people spitting and stuff like that, but people still expected it from Howard. Then Buzzcocks were getting rather distant, cos they were signed and getting successful, and I lost touch with them quite a bit.

What happened next?

I'd got fed up with montage, and I'd made some masks and things, and then I thought, why not sing? It seemed like an easy thing at the time. So I must have begun writing, and started Ludus around then. Tony wanted Ludus and A Certain Ratio to start off Factory, we were sup-posed to be the first singles to come out. But because of the Buzzcocks family I felt more loyalty towards Richard and New Hormones.

So really you switched from designing to performing?

Yes, I stopped drawing. I remember the montages being very sterile, then getting more into textures, then not getting anything out of them, seeing montage everywhere.

576

Were your concerns still the same?

It was almost the same thing: what is female, who am I, and what am I supposed to be? Obviously I couldn't get very far away from that anyway. It was fun, playing with words instead of images. Digging deep and finding a voice and playing with the voice. It was really enjoyable, and I wasn't concerned with being successful. It was really stupid in a way, just doing it for the pleasure of it.

What happened to all the crying babies in punk? Did they turn into crying men?

No, cos men don't cry. You're not allowed to. They all started getting too well-fed, and stopped crying.

Can you remember what the colours were from that period, or was it just black?

Red. Black, white and red.

CHAPTER NINE

1977/1: The Roxy

Poly Styrene outside Beaufort Market, World's End, early 1977 (Falcon Stuart)

After the Grundy incident in early December 1976 it became very hard for punk groups to play live; at least two thirds of the dates on the Sex Pistols' Anarchy tour were cancelled due to council bans. Live music was the lifeblood of rock music then, and it looked as though punk would be suppressed just as it was coming to prominence.

For about five months, the Roxy Club in London's Covent Garden became punk's engine room. Run by Andy Czezowski and a cast of characters, it was located on Neal Street, in a former rent-boy bar called Chaugerama's. There was a small area upstairs, but the main action happened in the basement, which contained a stage, mirrored walls, and enough room for about two hundred people.

Launched by two Heartbreakers shows in December 1976, the Roxy showcased dozens of new groups from all over the country – and, thanks to DJ Don Letts, popularised reggae and dub among the punk audience. Its place in punk history was cemented by the Top 20 album, Live at the Roxy WC2 (recorded between January and April 1977). After Czezowski was ousted in April 1977 it continued to feature punk groups, but by the autumn, the action was elsewhere.

Andy Czezowski and Susan Carrington

Manager of the Roxy. Had previously been McLaren's accountant and, briefly, the manager of The Damned. Interviewed in the offices of the Fridge, the successful nightclub in Brixton that he ran with his partner Susan Carrington. I'd interviewed them both for a Sounds *Roxy piece in summer 1977, and we carried on where we'd left off.*

Andy Czezowski: It happened by accident. People think they have control of their lives, but I don't think they have. I was basically out of work, and I had a common-sense approach to facts and figures, ever since I left school, it was pretty obvious stuff. I found myself one of the few unemployed people in 1974 – only two hundred thousand of us at the time.

Susan had bumped into a nice Jewish boy called John Krivine. I met him once or twice during that time, but had no reason ever to meet him again, but bumped into him and Steph at a party, through mutual distant friends. He was also running a Saturday-morning stall up at Notting Hill, under the arches, doing fifties retro stuff – but nobody else was, at the time.

Susan Carrington: They had those wonderful overcoats, that was then taken up by those people in Covent Garden. Flip. I actually worked for John Krivine, on the stall, for the first few months. In Antiquarius.

AC: I got involved just by hanging around, through Susan. They couldn't do their books, they didn't know what they were doing. They were very untogether people. They still are, probably. But they had to pay their VAT, and I said I'd do it, cos I had nothing else to do. They had gone into the basement at Acme by then.

SC: Donovan Letts came in at this point. I'd stopped working for John, and Don had been working in a Levi's shop up the road.

AC: He was a Michael Jackson character at the time, all fluffy hair.

SC: He transformed his image quite drastically, over a few weeks.

581

Jeanette Lee came on the scene, and they ran the basement at Anti-quarius. It became a meeting-place for the fifties skirts, stilettos.

They had a scooter in the middle of it all . . .

AC: I think it was a Lambretta. They went scouring for stuff. Steph was an old ex-mod, still scouring old shops and warehouses for any old junk he could find. He would buy whole boxes of stuff and drag it down to the shop.

SC: Did you know the person who does Contemporary Wardrobe? Roger Burton? They actually used to work together, and somebody called Jack English. They used to buy up old warehouses, this type of shirt that I'm wearing. They collected stuff and sold it on.

Tell me about Vivienne.

SC: Vivienne Westwood changed my point of view. I first met her in about 1974.

AC: She and Donovan were either having it off, or just about to have it off, there was some connection there. When he went to work for BOY, she got pretty pissed off, and she called him . . . what was it, something terrible – I can't remember now. Anyway, she split up with him, and this was when she was still moderately friendly with John Krivine, and she was in trouble, financially, she had the tiny shop and the books weren't getting done.

SC: Malcolm was in America with the Dolls . . .

AC: He couldn't have done it anyway. It was all piling up on her, and they got chatting, and they said Andrew does ours, and so she rang me. We lived in Streatham, she lived in Clapham, so I popped over and had a chat with her, and just as I was arriving, Chrissie Hynde arrived from the States, to stay with her. That's where I first met Chrissie Hynde.

So I said, 'Fine, give me all your junk.' I just systematised it all, came to a total, and said to the taxman, here's your cheque, now get off her back, sort of thing. That's all it was.

Were they making a lot of money at that time?

AC: There was a lot of money going through, but because her whole viewpoint was non-business, she just wanted to do things, create things, instigate things, so there was no point saying she made x per cent profit this year. None of that came into it, that wasn't the purpose of it, she just wanted to exist in her own way. They weren't short of cash, cos everything was done on a cash basis.

There wasn't any structure there, she lived on what she needed to live on, which was nothing but jasmine tea, funnily enough.

It wasn't SEX then, was it?

AC: No, this was Too Fast to Live, Too Young to Die. I was involved in the tail end of that, and then about two weeks later, she said, 'Come down and see the shop.' And it was SEX.

SC: She came to our house, and at that time I was wearing jumble-sale stuff, had henna'd hair, and you know how people used to collect royal stuff? Edward VII mugs and all that? She came in and said, why have you got all those things on your wall? Why are you wearing old clothes, and not your own? She really made me think. Funnily enough, she was wearing second-hand army surplus stuff. Lawrence Corner stuff, in black. She was very thin . . .

AC: Hair all over the place. Purple eye make-up. Very interesting. She said, 'You must come and see Malcolm's new band.' Malcolm at this point wasn't anything special, a nice Jewish boy from North London, running up a bit of schmutter, and on the fringes of the rock business. A thirty-year-old teenager, basically. She was very aggressive . . .

SC: I thought she was wonderful. I was her biggest fan.

What did you think about the shop? Did you like the clothes and the band?

SC: I loved it.

AC: How old was I? About twenty-six, and by the time I'd got a job when I was about nineteen or twenty . . .

SC: You've never had a job!

AC: . . . you know, working, and you'd buy a record at the weekend, and you slowly detach yourself from being a youngster, working and earning – and being sucked back into that was great. This is what I've always liked, but you'd forgotten that you actually enjoyed it. And they happened to be the ones. It could have been anyone. I always feel things happen more by chance. Malcolm was considerably older than us.

Where were you brought up?

SC: Elephant and Castle. I went to the worst school in the world. Andrew was brought up in Brixton, went to school at Kennington Boys' School.

What did you do after you left school?

SC: I went to teacher training, cos I didn't want to work, and no-one wanted to take me at university, so I had some silly jobs . . .

What about you, Andy?

AC: Well, I failed all my exams, cos the teachers really weren't up to teaching me. My whole approach to life was much more positive than England could provide. And my parents always believed that any job in an office is going to be better than any job which is manual. So I was chucked into an office. It didn't make any difference to me, a job was a job. It provided me with some cash, it was a hundred yards from home, and it was enough. I got sacked from there, it wasn't living up to my high standards . . .
SC: He wanted to take over the company, at sixteen . . .
AC: . . . and I was going around the clubs, checking out bands. Including the Ram Jam, the Locarno, all those sorts of places. Which was where we met, of course.

What was the club scene like in about 1974?

AC: I don't know, we stopped going to clubs when we bought our house, when I was about twenty-one.

When did you see the Sex Pistols?

AC: At St Martins, their first date ever. The second one was two or three days later, Central. They wanted to do the other one as a warm-up, cos they'd never played in public before. That was a proper date, whereas St Martins was just in the common room . . .

Did you like them?

AC: They weren't that good. They had this date to support someone else at the Central, and they upset everyone, because it was racket upon racket . . .

584

SC: That was probably what I liked, that it upset everybody . . .

AC: Yeah, the students reacted for a change, not their usual student approach. There were half a dozen people hanging around, which was Jordan, Vivienne, Malcolm, Susan, me. I can't remember anybody else.

After you saw the band, what happened then? Did you get more involved?

AC: I was still seeing Vivienne, doing her books, and I'd go to the shop, buy a pair of trousers. This was late 1975. John and Steph decided they wanted to open a shop in Notting Hill Gate, at the top end.

SC: It was called Acme Attractions . . .

AC: It was supposed to be a wholesale place. The idea was to paint it all grey, put some steel up on the windows. It looked really good, it was one of the best shops around at the time. It was completely opposite to what was going on, people were still selling kaftans and all the rest of it. Tom Waits had his picture taken outside of it, cos he thought it looked wacky.

Where was it?

AC: Right at the top of Portobello Road, past the Westway, about ten shops past, on the corner.

SC: What you're building up to is how you met Rat Scabies . . .

AC: I'd met Rat Scabies and Captain Sensible at one of the Pistols gigs. They were sort of auditioned for the Pistols, but didn't make the audition. I ran into them in Portobello Road and they weren't doing anything, and I was painting the shop, a couple of days' work and so I gave them a brush and told them to get on with it.

And they said they were starting up a band, and why don't you come and see us? 'Sure, why not.' They came back about a month later, and they'd put the band together. 'We're going to be called The Damned, isn't that great?' 'Yeah . . . sounds all right.' And it went on like that. I've got a feeling that the first date was outside London, actually. They didn't have any space to rehearse or anything like that.

At the time I was driving this red fifties Consul around, and John had this warehouse down in SE7 or SE10, somewhere like that, and I had the keys to that, so I said, 'Why not go and rehearse there?' So we went along to the warehouse, made a huge racket and then went home again.

Had you fallen out with Vivienne?

AC: No. All she said was, she swore me to secrecy about what she was doing. And since I wasn't a conniving, scheming shit, and I wasn't going to open a shop, it was of no interest to me, so that wasn't a problem. So, the two things went on in parallel. So there was no breakdown of communications, but there came a point where she needed someone better than me – at which point I introduced her to a friend who was a pukka accountant.

Did they get many actual fetishists in SEX, or was it mainly kids?

AC: I think they did. I remember a time when a Daimler drove up, with a big fat white guy with rings on, with either one girl or two. He came in, and either he knew her or was connected as a supplier. I mean, she supplied him with stuff for fashion shots. So there was an element of that, but not a lot. See, I was never one to hang around. I'd go in, chat for half an hour, take the paperwork away.

So what happened with The Damned?

AC: They had their first gig at some art college outside London, which ended up with the usual punch-up at the end, because they were total rubbish, as far as the students were concerned. They were all energy, not one of them would calm down, they were all on speed. It was a hectic rush of noise, basically.
SC: It was heavy metal, really, dressed in ripped clothes . . .
AC: There were about three punks at the front, and everybody else was pinned to the back wall. That was fun. I think we got paid. There was an argument, of course, they said they didn't want to pay for this rubbish . . .
SC: Rat Scabies was particularly obnoxious for no apparent reason.
AC: They played the Nashville. The Pistols played there . . .
SC: Malcolm went up a notch in my estimation, cos he saved Vivienne from being punched in the Nashville.
AC: Well, Vivienne was a very aggressive girl, and I think someone close to her had said something, either about the way she was dressed, or about the band. Anyway, The Damned did a date or two there, I can't remember. There was a lot of press about it . . .
SC: It was Caroline Coon and Jonh Ingham, and it was blown up

586

into this great romantic notion, they loved every minute of it . . . and it was good.

AC: It wasn't good, Susan, it was exciting.

What was the French trip like?

AC: Oh, well there was this crazy French coke dealer . . . and I don't know if it was true, but I heard he was set up by this shady Moroccan-French dope dealer to put on this festival. I wasn't really that interested either way. There wasn't any punk outfits at the time, it was strictly the Pistols and The Damned . . .

SC: there was Nick Lowe . . .

AC: . . . and Roogalator, sort of pub rock bands. The Pink Fairies. Anyway, they hired this coach. It was organised by that record shop by Euston Station. Bizarre. French hippies, basically. They said, not to me but through Rat Scabies, 'Okay, you can do the date', and there would be hotels at the other end, and five pounds a day, and maybe a hundred quid when it was done.

So we all jumped on the coach, with Caroline Coon, Jonh Ingham, somebody else and maybe five bands. We were the only ones who were punks, and the rest of them had read about punk. We cornered the back end of the coach, and there was myself, in T-shirt, safety pins and tight plastic jeans, and the others nearly as appropriate. I was probably the more dressed up in that respect. I'd bought stuff from Vivienne.

Of course, Caroline and Ingham found us more exciting than the old farts at the other end of the coach, which was the Roogalators, and Nick Lowe and all the rest of it. We had to stop off at Lyon, because it was a fairly long trip, and by then we definitely had to split up, cos there was different lifestyles going on here. I was never into drugs. They were all speeding, they went through pounds of the stuff. Dave Vanian didn't, he pretended. He played the game.

We were booked into hotels and they wouldn't, couldn't sleep. They were climbing on parapets, six floors up, waking up Nick Lowe and the Pink Fairies and everyone, wondering what was going on. Saying, 'Get up, let's have a party', and it's six in the morning. The concierge woke up, kicked them out. Fortunately I got myself locked away in another room and said, 'Nothing to do with us', you know.

587

Lunchtime the next day, they're getting a bit tired. They sleep for a couple of hours, have another handful of speed, more beer, pissing in the road, and off they go again. We arrived down there maybe six or seven in the evening, booked into a very nice hotel. Didn't have any money, so at this point we're hassling for cash – where's the promoter, we could do with a fiver. I fortunately kept myself a couple of quid so I could buy a steak dinner. So we left them.

The next day was the festival, and once again they hadn't slept all night, more speed, running around the hotel, climbing out of windows, concierge going bananas. He had to call the police about two in the morning, by which time I was asleep. They were just about to arrest them all, and they woke me up, saying, 'You've got to get these boys under control.' I said, 'I don't work for them any more.'

Then Jake, or the promoter, stepped in and sorted it all out. I just wasn't interested. So, they get to sleep at eight or nine in the morning, but they're supposed to be on stage at twelve. 'Come on, you're on stage.' 'Nooo! We're not going on first! There's nobody there! We'll go on if we can do another set later on.' The promoter says, 'Okay, on you go.'

Anyway, they go on, do this barnstorming set to about fifty people and a chicken. And they were getting high from doing their set, and creating mayhem and being a genuine punk band, coming off stage wanting to do another set, but there about twenty more bands to come on. And for the rest of the day I'm getting earache – 'When are we going on?'

By this time, the festival is a disaster. It was a bullring, and I would think it would have held about three to five thousand people, and there was less than a thousand people scattered about. The promoter had had enough and taken a fix of heroin. I managed to squeeze something like fifty quid out of him. Everyone got back on the coach. The coach and the hotels were paid by them.

And then the daggers start coming out, amongst all the bands, not just us. And it was more speed, more of everything. 'We don't want you for a manager, you're a wanker!' And Jake comes over, and it's, 'Don't do your washing in public! If you've got something to discuss with your manager, do it outside the coach.' 'Why don't you be our manager?' 'Alright then, I'll be your manager.'

I'm just sitting, looking out of the window. I've had enough of this crap. So from about two hundred miles out of Mont de Marsan, Jake is the manager. Then they start accusing me of spending all the money. They'd spent it all on booze, and that was the end of it. The whole thing was foul. The only good thing was that I got to speak to the manager of Roogalator, Robin Scott, who went to art school with Malcolm.

When we got back to London, Malcolm was setting up the September 100 Club festival. Perhaps that was organised before they went to France. They had about three or four dates on the trot. I went to see all of them. He didn't like The Damned at all, in some ways they upstaged the Pistols. I think Jake dropped them, and Ron Woods took over. Maybe Jake was never actually their manager.

They played the gigs that were already lined up for them, which included the 100 Club. Ron Woods saw the whole punk explosion going on, and came back, by which time the club was booked. Ron took them on. That lasted a month or two. I can't remember the one after that, but that's when Jake stepped in. Meanwhile I'm going on, still doing stuff for John Krivine and Vivienne.

Suddenly Steph decides he wants to manage a band. And this band was called Chelsea. Gene October, Billy Idol, Tony James, and the drummer John Towe. That lasted about two days, and they came up to my room, cos I was working in their office. 'You manage The Damned, don't you?' 'Well, not any more.' 'We're looking for a manager.' 'OK, fine, but you've got to get rid of the singer.' They had a gig at the Nashville, and at that point I said the singer had to go.

Why?

SC: Gene looked a bit bored. And when you've got Billy Idol with his sparkling eyes . . .
AC: . . . and they said, yeah, they were thinking about it anyway . . . I said, 'Why don't you put Billy up on vocals?' 'I can't really sing.' 'Well, you can sing as good as him, and you look better, and you can't play guitar that well, so you might as well get another guitarist in.' We auditioned, and we got Derwood, who was basically a heavy metal guitarist, lots of thrash stuff.

This was coming up to December, and I was trying to get gigs, but the punk thing had exploded and no-one wanted to know. The Pistols had done, or nearly done their tour. Nothing but mayhem every-where in the papers. I hadn't quite got rid of Gene October by then, and he said, 'I've got a friend who's got a club in Covent Garden', which was called Chaugerama's.

What was it like inside?

SC: Dirty, dark, dingy, small . . . red lights, leatherette . . .

AC: We changed it, we repainted it. The guy who ran it, 'the one-armed bandit' we called him, was a German-Swiss guy. René Albert. They were the leaseholders, and they were about to lose their licence over incidents in the past, before us. Noise nuisance, other factors. It was a dodgy little hole, basically. It was a local rent-boy hang-out. Because he was a barrister, he kept getting extensions and delays and all those games, and I came along and offered them money, which was better than what they were earning.

SC: We booked it for two nights in December. He had nothing to lose, if someone was going to pay him to hire it, fifty pounds . . .

AC: We provided all the staff, and even the drink. There was no drink in the place, so we bought some cans of beer. Hired a PA system and put them on. The first was Generation X. I'd got rid of Gene by then. He introduced us to these people and I just dropped him. So, Generation X was Billy Idol. The handbills were printed up, the night was successful, they got their money.

In order to get the premises, I had to put a deposit down. Ralph Jedraszczyk and Barry Jones had built themselves a little studio, just a 2-track and a microphone, and I asked them to lend me some money for the deposit. They weren't rich by any means, but they had this guitar, and I said if they hocked the guitar they could come in as partners. We managed to make enough money to get the guitar out of hock, it was back in again for the second show.

By then the Pistols' Anarchy tour had finished, and Johnny Thunders was in town – and he had no bookings and needed cash, for obvious reasons. We met him and Malcolm in that pub in Wardour Street, up from the Marquee, and I said, 'Malcolm, why don't you do a date?' But at that stage Malcolm was pushing the line that the Pistols were banned by the GLC and the world over, which wasn't true, and he wasn't prepared to let me put on the Pistols as a show.

Why was that?

AC: Oh, just his own cunning. On top of that, someone else doing something and getting credibility for it. If I managed to put the Pistols on, he would have felt he had lost his grip. But he said I could have Thunders, and I thought, great, I had a date before the next Generation X one, so why not put on The Heartbreakers. Fine. I put hand-outs on the street, the place was full. Great. They did a good set.

Then we had Generation X again, and then it was New Year. I spoke to The Clash, and January 1st was the launch of the permanent nights at the Roxy. I think it was a Saturday, cos Friday was the only night the place had done any business; they used to have a lot of East End thugs in there, and René Albert wasn't prepared to let me have a Friday, cos it was the only night that was full.

After that we had to get a regular deal with him – we hired it for £300 a week. We didn't make any, cos it all went to him. At that stage The Damned owed me money, about £200, but Jake wanted the gig, so I said, 'Well, if you do one night for free, I'll take that cash cos they owe it to me, and I'll book you in every Monday for a month, and you can have 50 per cent of the door money'. And it was a stormer, one of the biggest nights we had.

SC: . . . tore down the ceiling.

Who did that?

AC: Everybody. I think Johnny Thunders started it, and they [The Damned] saw it and got into it. After that it was any outfit we could find – the Buzzcocks, The Stranglers . . . Fridays and Saturdays were the best. During the week was the usual hard problem that they are everywhere – but we didn't know anything at the time, so The Jam had about four people, on a Thursday, and yet Saturday would be full, just because it was a Saturday.

Do you know when Chaugerama's started?

AC: I don't know for sure; it would have been 1972 or 1973.
SC: It wasn't gay until later.
AC: I think it was one of the first gay clubs. It wasn't what you think it was, it develops into that if you don't control it.

591

What were the other gay clubs at the time?

SC: We used to go to a lovely one called Mandy's, in Henrietta Street. They did a promotion with Richard Strange, which was called Hell.
AC: We only had a licence until 1 a.m. Most of the kids didn't mind that, and then the rock people went on to the Speakeasy. We went to Mandy's, which was a mature gay club, very small, and we got to know the owner, and three or four of us would pop in there to unwind. They thought we were colourful young people . . .

What sort of music did they play?

AC: Disco, and David Bowie, which was quite wild, for them . . .

Did you go to the gay clubs in Chelsea?

SC: His and Hers, which is the Sombrero. And Bangs, used to love Bangs. We had a little fashion corner. And we went to Rod's, which became Country Cousins . . .

It's interesting, because everyone thought punk was macho, and there was a big gay thing.

AC: A huge gay thing. We were colour for it all, with our leather and studs. Gay guys were more fashion-conscious, and they would have known about Vivienne and her crazy shop, and thought it was wonderful, colourful and different. They didn't see us as a threat. But if we'd gone anywhere else, we'd have been barred immediately. The gay community accepted another oddity within its ranks.

I blame Thunders for bringing smack into it . . .

SC: He was their hero. They wanted to be rock'n'roll guitarists. It wasn't just Thunders, they wanted it . . .
AC: I caught hepatitis from Sid Vicious, by sharing his needle. It was late '77, after the club was closed. We went to see Barry, and Keith Levene was there, and Sid was there. This was while all the business about sacking Sid was going on – if he doesn't clean up his act, etcetera.
SC: Sid said, as soon as we arrived, 'You won't tell Malcolm I'm here, will you?'
AC: It was only speed, not heroin. Injected speed, and that's where I

got it from. The only time I'd ever taken speed in my life.

Did other managers start coming to the Roxy?

AC: I had Miles Copeland coming down to pick my brains, he thought I knew what I was doing, which I suppose I did, more than anyone else who was around . . .
SC: He had people like Curved Air, he was completely out of it . . .
AC: In February or March he came down, sniffing around. His brother was in Curved Air, but they weren't really performing. He had his own agency, and his brother had an agency in New York, and via them he brought over Cherry Vanilla and Wayne County. Thunders was already here.

I remember meeting these three gay managers from New York in The Ship that February: Peter Crowley, Max McCarre, and Leee Black Childers.

AC: Leee Childers eventually had it off with Gene October.

He showed me a picture of Gene October in a gay magazine . . .

AC: Miles thought he could come in and take over the scene. He came to me cap in hand; he'd paid for the air fares for all the New York groups to fly over to play the Global Village. They'd pulled out, cos they'd heard it was a punk thing, and the only place was me. He said, 'Can you guarantee me three hundred a night?' 'You're joking, I've never paid more than about forty pounds to anyone, including The Stranglers and The Clash.' To make three hundred, you would need the Roxy to be full, and more . . .
SC: The Roxy only held 150 people, officially. For The Damned we had four hundred in there.
AC: We did some sort of deal, cos he was already committed anyway. We put on the American week. And I could have Cherry Vanilla if I booked The Police. That was the deal. They had the same drummer. I don't think Sting was involved with them at the time.

I think he was.

AC: It was pre-blond. The reason they went blond was they got a job to be in an advert, and they had to be blond for that. They got rid of the Polish guitarist, and carried on. I put Cherry on, who was pretty crazy, everybody went wild at that, and Wayne County of course brought the house down, and I think The Adverts supported Wayne County, I'm not sure. And we had Thunders, and the full house just about made three hundred quid, so they got their cash.

Who did the handbills?

SC: Barry Jones. He thought it was selling out to publicity . . .
AC: He was embarrassed about doing it, he felt bad about it cos he wanted to be a musician.

We were robbed, the night of The Stranglers, they took The Stranglers' tour money and all our money. They were probably in league with the police, although I can't be sure. We were locked in this cupboard, it took us an hour to get out and call the police. We gave them perfect descriptions and nothing happened.

What was the last night?

SC: Siouxsie was the last. We were physically pushed out, by Réne Albert . . .
AC: There was no lease, we paid them cash at the end of each week, the whole thing was ropey. What happened was a chap came out of prison for manslaughter – he was one of the hoodlums who used to come to the club before we had it – and René Albert showed him round. The place was packed full of kids who were buying lager, and he must have thought, I'll have some of this.

I think René Albert tried to flog it to him, I'm certain he did. He knew Jock McDonald, and he was young and had spiky hair, so he thought he'd get Jock to run the club. So this guy did some kind of deal and we were ousted, and from that point it went downhill and they lost their licence, and René Albert did a runner, cos he'd taken this crook's money.

You were booted out?

AC: He wouldn't let me or Susan in on the last night. By that time the scene had expanded, the Marquee was beginning to book people. But they managed to get the Boomtown Rats in, and Gary Numan, who was punk for about a week. One or two others, and then it died off.

On the last night I was hanging around in the street wondering what the fuck's going on here, and Adam [Ant] comes up to me and says, 'I think you're really great, why don't you be my manager?' I had nothing else to do, so I said, 'Alright then', and that was that. That lasted seven days.

I don't think you were made to manage bands, Andy.

AC: I can't put up with children, that's for sure.

But before I left, Mike Thorne came along and said, 'I'll sign you up for a record if you'll let me do the production.' I said, 'Sure, why not, go ahead.' He gave us some money and that was it.

Have you got tapes?

AC: Oh, we've got the master tapes for the whole lot. The 24-tracks are still in store, at EMI. I've got 24-track masters of all the performers and more, including Siouxsie and the Banshees and The Slits.

SC: Siouxsie wouldn't be on the record, she thought it was selling out.

AC: We've got recordings from the toilets, conversations on the meaning of punk. That was quite good. A nice middle-class boy from North London trying to pick up this South London girl, describing what punk was all about. That wasn't used.

So, what happened next?

AC: Well, someone came down to have a look, and we told him we were being kicked out, and he had a place in Hanway Street, and I went to look at it, but it was too small, it was tiny. He said he'd got a mate who had a place in Wardour Street, which turned out to be Crackers, which was a normal disco, which was vile, but it was immediate, I could have it the next week. So I created a name, The Vortex. It was going to be The Void.

The first night was going to be Snatch, Adam and the Ants, and The Slits, I think. So that was a good bill, got it promoted, turned up on the night it was all supposed to happen. The same guy there, said, 'Who are you?' 'I'm the guy who's putting the show together.' He says, 'You're not any more. Out!' They effectively took over. They kept the bill, the bands didn't know any different. They were all signed to appear, they said, 'Where's Andy?' 'He's not here tonight.'

It turned out that the three guys were mercenaries, who did a bit of heavy stuff for people. I found that out and I didn't want to tackle these big, ex-Scots Guards mercenaries. And this is what happened at The Vortex, these guys were knocking the kids around. They liked a bit of action. Those particular guys went on to kidnap Ronnie Biggs in Brazil, we saw them on television. So we felt, next time, we own our own place. Twice in a month was too much.

Poly Styrene

Co-founder, writer and singer for X-Ray Spex; ran a clothing stall in Beaufort Market on the King's Road before forming the group. X-Ray Spex played a few times at the Roxy, and were featured on the Live at the Roxy *album. Interviewed in London, Poly was both ebullient – with an infectious laugh – and rueful about a period in her life that was both exciting and troubled.*

I was born in Bromley, and grew up originally by the Tower of London, and then Stockwell. I went to Manor School, in Stockwell. I left school at fifteen. In those days, you were allowed to. I got a job straight away in the fashion industry. Obviously they liked young people because they had a feel for the latest trends, so I ended up doing most of the buying, at a very young age. It was a Jewish company in Poland Street, who had several shops all over the country. I can't remember the name.

Were you very into fashion?

I was a fashion-conscious kid, yes. It was about the time of Mr Freedom and Biba, so I suppose I was wearing that stuff. Long, Biba-type clothes, satin blouses. Oxford bags and massive platform shoes. And 1920s hats. Very romantic. And I loved pop. That was the culture that I grew up with. I was born in 1957, so I was ten in 1967.

My family sort of split up, they couldn't get on very well. My father's family was in Saudi Arabia, my mother was typically English, so there was a clash of cultures, really, Middle East and West. I stayed with my mother. It was okay; I don't think it's particularly ideal, living with one parent, but it's better than living with two parents who are quarrelling.

Were you the only child?

No, I had a brother.

So it was quite tough on your mother?

Yes. She was steady, she had lots of steady jobs and things. She was from quite a good middle-class family, had a good education; worked in magistrates' courts, and she could manage to keep us. Very capable.

It must have been you that rebelled. When did that happen?

When I was about twelve years old. The first way I rebelled was by becoming a vegetarian, which was quite tough at the time, cos your parents are educated to think you need to eat meat to be healthy. Eventually I convinced my mother, and she became a vegetarian as well. We had a dog, who would sit under the table, and I would siphon off all my meat to the dog.

Did you go to festivals?

Yes, when I was about sixteen there were all these free festivals, like Windsor. We used to travel around, I became a complete drop-out at about sixteen. I used to travel around like a mendicant, with no possessions, bathing in streams and rivers, eating at free-food kitchens at the festivals. I did that for a whole summer. It was a fantastic adventure, but now I look back on it and I'm sort of horrified. I'm amazed that I'm still alive.

You might have been a bit too young to do that, really.

Yes, I think I was ahead of my time. But it worked out, because I met all these Hare Krishna people, they were also travelling around the festivals, chanting these mantras. And there were people who were definitely looking for something, beyond their immediate situation. It was mind-expanding, in a sense. When you do travel around the countryside, you realise that nature and things are controlled by higher forces.

So, you had quit your job by then?

Yes, I thought it was a rip-off. I could have got promotion and all the rest of it; my boss loved me, he mentioned moving up in the company. He used to see my far-out clothes, and he wanted me to go and buy them, cut them up and make cheap copies of them for the mass market. So I threw it all in and became a hippy for a year. I saw lots of groups and fringe theatre.

Who did you see that you liked?

I never really saw anybody that I was crazy about. In fact, what I got was that I didn't want to be a hippy, actually! I was younger than them, I was only a kid. The cleanest thing I saw was the Hare Krishnas. The hippy scene had got very dirty. I just wanted to be clean-cut, and get something together, I didn't want the drugs and the sex life, which is what the hippy scene used to be, without much of an aim in life.

When were you involved with Falcon Stuart?

I met Falcon when I was about fifteen, at a theatre called Oval House, by the Oval cricket ground. Then I met him again when I came back to London, and I told him I had some ideas for a band, and we got involved . . .

Didn't you have one single as Mari Elliott?

Yes, one single, which was a sort of acting thing, really. GTO Records, if I remember.

That wasn't really you, was it?

Well, it was me, in a sense, but it wasn't supposed to be about me. It was influenced by my street-theatre thing, acting out the part of somebody, really. It was sort of a joke. It was called 'Silly Billy'.

So when did you first see the Sex Pistols?

On my eighteenth birthday, in Hastings, on the pier. I remember them distinctly, they stood out from all the hippy bands I'd seen before. I'd seen this tacky Day-Glo sign with 'SEX PISTOLS' all over it, and I thought, gosh, I wonder what that's about, it looks pretty. I knew it couldn't be something from Soho, it was just too clever.

I thought it sounded very Freudian. Guns are associated that way, aren't they? At least, that is what some people say. And it is, in fact, male egos, trying to dominate. It went back to fertility rites and the

599

maypole dances, it was symbolic of that. Young girls dancing around a maypole . . .

So when you went in, what was it like? What were they like?

They were incredibly young and fresh, that is what I remember, and they couldn't play their instruments very well. The sound was terrible, but they had a certain charm, because of their youth and naiveté.

And enthusiasm?

Yes. Energy.

What effect did that have on you? Did it make you want to get involved with whatever was going on?

It gave me something. The idea that you don't have to be like one of those big established rock acts with a big name, and platform boots, long hair, on speed. Or cocaine. I didn't want to take speed anyway. I guess you could – I mean, I'm sure they did, didn't they?

That was in the summer. Were you aware of things like punks on the street, or anything?

No, there weren't any punks.

So how did you get involved?

It's a question of peer pressure, isn't it? You go out and meet people, see people of your own age doing things, and after that you get all sorts of things together to compete with your peers, identification with a particular generation.

At that time, you had to get something out, get something done, very quickly. Did you go and see any other punk groups?

I think I saw The Clash. I went with you, actually, to that. We went to all sorts of places. The Roxy, I can't remember them all now. It was Fulham Town Hall, seeing The Clash.

What did you think of them?

There again, it was energy and enthusiasm, basically – the way they were writing about, this immediate, contemporary sound and surroundings. As opposed to, you know, large rock, pop sex, drugs songs, and Eric Clapton. They were writing about more immediate things in society. They weren't superstar heroes, they were writing things that the average person would probably relate to, I think. It was definitely a change of consciousness.

What sort of consciousness do you think it was?

Complaining, basically. It was a frustration with material society. That is what they were criticising, but they didn't really have an alternative. It was very negative, an analytical look at the environment they grew up in. They were stripping it down, piece by piece. It wasn't painting the world to be a very beautiful place, it was ugly. I liked it for that, it was a good shake-up. On that level, it was fantastic.

What did you think of the anger?

Well, anger is usually just frustration, you can't have something that you want. There's a different kind of anger. Anger and violence I don't like, but you can be aggressive. The aggression to get that message across, I thought that was quite good. Aggression can be used in a positive way.

Did you feel that there was a point at which that was very creative and positive, and after that point it became very negative?

I agree with that, entirely. Even in the way it was created, after a point if definitely became too negative. It's a question of philosophy, isn't it? Once you have taken it all away, you are left with a sort of void. You have to have something positive, and there wasn't. There was a big gap, and I think they slipped back into what was there before, more or less. It's unfortunate.

It's interesting that you think it was positive, because most people don't think that. I remember that energy as being very liberating.

Yes, it was. I like to see things, and go out. Some of the statements being made at the time were true. But people don't want their nice little world to be shaken up. They were refreshing, anyway. They may not have been perfectly performed, but they were refreshing.

Why do you think it didn't go anywhere?

It was a lack of vision. It was kind of passionate, but there wasn't any real vision. I don't think the business even wanted it to. The people who were the so-called leaders of that generation didn't really have a positive solution, and for the business . . . they were just a commodity that sold. They wouldn't want anything too serious.

Unfortunately it just came on like another form of entertainment, which is okay, but it's nice if you can entertain with a message. But I don't think anything particularly positive evolved out of it. I think it opened a lot of people's minds to change, and it certainly got rid of that hippy thing. But that was only a small section of the population, wasn't it?

When did you start the stall at Beaufort Market?

I can't remember exactly. I must have been eighteen or nineteen. I just started it, from very little. I didn't need hardly anything to do it, I started selling as soon as I opened, and I had lots of friends making things up on sale or return, and it sort of took off. It was working by itself.

You had some Mary Quant plastic shoes.

Yes, I had some leftovers from the sixties. I used to go to shops and buy up old stock, things like that. Anything that was a bit different. It was funny, because some of the old things I used to buy, modern manufacturers actually started making the things in large quantities. I used to have designers like David Bloom come around and buy a lot of my stuff and copy it. I expected that, because I'd already worked in the fashion trade before.

I just wanted to do something that was fun. I wasn't planning to make a big business out of it.

I remember a lot of Day-Glo, plastic flowers, things like that.

Yes, it was great – take a cheap plastic bag and stick a lot of plastic flowers and things that nobody would really bother to buy, but all of a sudden they became very trendy, and people wanted them. Some things were vile, but so vile they were cute. It was meant to be an extreme version of tack.

How long did you do the stall?

602

I did it until the music started taking off. It was a great wardrobe for the music as well. We would walk into the shop, put something on, have my photograph taken and be in the newspaper the next day, and it was all just fun, fun, fun. It wasn't calculated, it was very juvenile, wasn't it, really? It was younger than teenage, it was pre-puberty stuff basically, don't you think? I think that was good.

I think the punks were trying to see things as they were. It's a sign of intelligence, to question everything. If you just accepted everything that was told to you, I would say that you weren't very intelligent.

How did you put the band together?

I just advertised in *Melody Maker*. 'Young punx who want to stick together', or something like that. Punx, spelt with an x. And they just sort of appeared.

Had you already written songs by this time?

I wrote them before. I think I was writing every day. Every week, we had a new song to rehearse.

What were you trying to say with them? They were very much about consumerism, turning yourself into a product . . .

I saw what the other bands were doing, and I didn't really want to talk about that. It wasn't my thing. I was more interested in consumerism, plastic, artificial living. That is what I felt strongly about. I had done that natural living, in the country, travelling around, living in harmony with nature. I felt that a lot of things were unnecessary. At that time there was so much junk around, and I mean garbage.

The idea was to throw it back in people's faces? I remember you first came out in exaggeratedly tacky clothes . . .

Oh, yes, that was the idea, just sending it all up. Screaming about it, saying look, this is what you have done to me, turned me into a zombie. I am your product. This is what you have created, do you like her? My favourite lines were, 'Freddy tried to strangle me, with my plastic popper beads, but I hit him back, with my pet rat . . . ' It was a plastic rat, in those days, I took it on stage.

Did you write the songs in Beaufort Market, around that time?

Yes, around then I was selling plastic popper beads. It was all a big fantasy, really, it was just funny, but in a certain kind of way it had a message.

What was 'Identity' about?

Well, it was about looking for an identity. I thought that people were suffering because they were looking for something to identify with, and they couldn't find it. You have got a body, and it may be a black body or a white body, or a German body, and everybody is trying to identify with some particular ethnic group, or particular sex, or even a generation.

You don't have any real identity, other than these bodies, and then seeing this frustration and anger, because you have this class identity – working-class, rich person, intellectual . . . everybody is identifying with a particular body, but the body is a temporary thing, obviously it is going to die, it is not eternal.

So, this is false identification. I felt that the punks didn't know what to identify with. Some were identifying with their dogs, dressing with a dog lead on . . .

And 'Oh Bondage! Up Yours!'?

It was about the bondage of the material life, actually, being in bondage. It was a call for liberation. I am not going to be bound by the laws of consumerism, or bound by my own senses. You're tied to these activities for someone else's profit.

So, you had three or four singles, and they were successful – at least, a couple of them were – and the LP. What then? Did it become routine?

It felt like that at the time, yes. I wanted to really expand the material, advance a bit with the material, but the audiences weren't really ready for it. Things happen so slowly, your audience is ten years behind what you are into. Or they were ten years away from what we wanted to do. They were into the thrash, and I was already a year over that, I wanted to progress to something else.

I remember the LP came out after the band split . . .

Yes, it came out a year later. And to go and tour with it for another year, that same old thing. I suppose maybe I was a little impatient, and with maturity and foresight I probably would have seen that it might have been worth it to pace it a bit more slowly. It moved fast. I liked it fast, but once it got rolling I wanted to keep it going fast, on to newer things. But things don't work like that, you have got everybody there, it's like a machine . . .

One of the things I liked about X-Ray Spex was the way you wrote about London, going down the tube . . .

I wanted to write about everyday experiences: 'Warrior in Woolworths' I was trying to write so that it would be historical as well, you know? Some songs are timeless, they don't mention dates or places, they are just a question of emotion. That's why people can do cover versions all the time. I was trying to do more like a diary of 1977.

Did you used to go round to visit John Lydon at his house in Gunter Grove?

Yes, I used to visit him sometimes. I shaved my head on his balcony once, and clogged up his razor.

What was it like round there?

Dark. Macabre, you know. He was pretty nocturnal, never had any light coming in. And he had his mother's tombstone for his headboard. And coloured people round there, smoking ganja, and lots of little horror pictures on the wall, and he would talk about ghosts and things, and there were upside-down crucifixes on the wall. Just generally trying to be a spooky character. But I think he's a bit of an actor, really.

Do you think some of that rubbed off on him?

Yes, he's probably haunted now.

I mean, do you think he was playing for a certain kind of negativity?

He was playing with it, yes, trying to live it. I don't know why. He was drawn to that darker aspect of things.

Did that upset you?

605

Not really. I suppose I thought he was more than he was, you know? Basically he is quite a nice person underneath it all. One thing I liked about John was that he was vegetarian, so in that sense he was actually more compassionate than people that look respectable, that are eating raw steaks in expensive restaurants.

How did you stop being involved in the music business? Did you have some sort of breakdown?

Actually, what happened was that I saw a UFO. I had a bit of a shock, like a breakdown to a certain extent, which is quite common after you've seen one of those things. I was on tour in Doncaster, and staying in this hotel after the gig, and it must have been about two or three in the morning, and I couldn't sleep.

I looked out of the hotel window and there was this sort of energy, a bright, luminous pink, and it had a disc shape. But it was so fast, like faster than the speed of light, and it was on a subtle platform, the effects of it hit me – I was inside the window, but the radiation actually hit my body. I was suffering afterwards, my body kept going hot and cold, it hit me in my solar plexus. I told everyone, and they just thought I was going crazy, they didn't believe that I saw it.

I had to go to hospital, and I had to get analysed by so many psychiatrists. I don't know why. I mean, UFOs are quite common. I've spoken to the leading UFO expert in the country, and they said yes, I definitely saw what I saw. He said people see them, they get some kind of heightened perception, and I definitely experienced that after I saw it.

They gave me tons of tranquillisers and tried to make me forget that I saw it. They told me I didn't actually see it, and if I still thought I did, I was sick. They used to send me to occupational therapy, and had me paint what I saw. And I would paint it, and they admitted that I saw it, in a sense, and in another sense, they said that I didn't see it. It was horrible, to be put into that situation.

Seeing them is a kind of heightened perception itself ...

Yes, that's the Jungian theory. It's like certain people can see auras, and you can't say they're not seeing them, because they can see them, though not everyone can. Some people are more psychic than others.

If you're going to be a performer, even what you did in the punk period, you're going to have a bit of that, aren't you?

Basically, yes. It's a subtle energy you're working with, isn't it. Music, sound. There are lots of mystical people involved in music, working on and creating different moods, the whole thing. In ancient times, they had these arts. The arts are mystical – unless it's commercial sort of art, which is pretty gross.

At one point, John Lydon was an extraordinary talent, wasn't he? Where do you think he got it from?

I think he was a yogi or something in a previous life, definitely powerful and mystical. He could have been empowered. I've been told by a guru that some of these people, like Jimi Hendrix for example, are empowered, they come up from the lower planetary systems, and they are empowered to attract a certain kind of people. They take them and they don't live very long, and they take their followers down to the lower regions with them.

John survived.

Yes, John is still around. I don't think he is a bad person.

He did have a sort of symbolic death, though, didn't he, when he changed his name.

Yes, actually he did. And Sid definitely did, he was like that. People say that Sid was very intelligent. I never noticed it when I talked to him, but he may have been. I saw him at a particularly rough time; he was with Nancy, and he had completely gone off on heroin.

Where did you meet him?

At John's, playing around with a great big knife.

It didn't look like much fun around there.

No, it was a hellish planet.

Were they nice to you, or not?

Well, I was different to them, I had a different energy. I used to get on quite well with John, but Sid was kind of crazy. He was just gone.

607

So what happened after the UFO? Did you stop making music?

I didn't know why I saw this thing, it was like an omen to me. I wanted to take a break and rethink everything I was doing. So that led me to a psychology course, but I didn't agree with what I was learning there, which was atheistic, in the form of science. Then I got involved with mysticism, and then back to yoga. Then I started making music again, in what I considered a more positive way.

It took a long time to get over it?

I had relapses afterwards. It was a shock to the system, sometimes it was like it was happening all over again, the whole thing. Some people don't recover.

Don Letts

Roxy DJ and film-maker, whose Punk Rock Movie *captured the rawness of the music and performance on Super 8. It remains the best record of punk as it happened. Also part of the punk inner circle, friendly with both The Clash and Johnny Rotten. Formerly an assistant at Acme Attractions on the King's Road. Interviewed in Ladbroke Grove, his stamping ground.*

I was brought up in London, primarily Brixton. Spent all of my life in South London, a regular primary school, then grammar school, Archbishop Tennyson's. At that time I was the only black man there, which was strange. From that point on I was completely immersed in white culture, specifically rock'n'roll: Led Zeppelin, Captain Beefheart, The Nice, hard rock stuff. I'm grateful about that, cos it broadened my horizons.

My dad was a bus driver originally, then a chauffeur, and my mother was a dressmaker. My dad had a sound system when he first came over here, but I was too young to remember that. When he was in Jamaica he used to show open-air films, so he was a projectionist and into sound, so it's funny that I'm like a manifestation of what he started.

I left school when I discovered rock'n'roll. It took me, there's no other way to put it. They all said I was crazy, my parents freaked out, but to this day I've never regretted it. No-one has ever asked me what I achieved at school. I thought about it; suppose your mum died the night before you had to do an exam, and you messed up your exam, and you're judged for the rest of your life on that one day's performance. Unfair.

I ended up getting a Saturday job on the King's Road. I met John Krivine, who had a shop in Brixton selling jukeboxes and twentieth-century antiques, Acme Attractions, and he decided to go into clothes, opened a stall in Antiquarius, and asked me to work there.

609

That was '75ish. Bernie Rhodes had a stall there about the same time, selling bits and pieces – old reggae records and the odd shirt, which I think he designed. It was quite an interesting stall.

I take it that Antiquarius wasn't so antiquey then?

Oh no, it was totally antiquey, we were an oddity in there. Then as Acme Attractions grew more successful we moved downstairs to the basement, and that's where Acme really came to fame. I used to play reggae very loud on the jukebox upstairs and they hated it. They were really glad when I moved downstairs, but I played the music even louder then, and still annoyed them.

When did you first start hearing reggae?

When I was a kid, my father played it at home. It was our natural music. Byron Lee & the Dragonaires, and King Stitch, the Skatalites. It was rock steady and blue beat. Prince Buster . . .

By the time Acme was going, what reggae was happening?

Keith Hudson; Skin, Flesh & Bones – the dub stuff had started. The DJs Big Youth, Fred Locks, Dillinger, Trinity, people like that. It was all happening. At school I got lost in rock'n'roll, but after I got back into reggae. I found it an appropriate soundtrack for day-to-day listening. It was the loudness of the music that attracted people downstairs to Acme Attractions more than anything else.

I had it done up like a sort of third-world living room, I'd sit around posing in my dark glasses and let people serve themselves. The shop was a collection of the subcultures of the last thirty years. I must bring Jeanette into it, cos she really was instrumental in getting me into punk. This little girl came along and I took a fancy to her and gave her a line, and asked her to work with me.

As this was happening, SEX was happening down the road, and there was a little bit of competition, because I almost worked for Malcolm before I worked for John. He was in America doing the Dolls, and I got friendly with Vivienne and waiting for him to come back so I could work at SEX, but I ended up having to work for John because I needed money, whereupon Vivienne didn't like me any more, cos I was working for the competition.

Anyway, me and Jeanette opened the basement, and while we were doing that, punk rock happened. I must admit I nearly missed the whole boat, out of jealousy, because punk was happening and we got wind of it, and she started checking it out. I was going, 'Yecch, what is this nonsense!' She took me to a Pistols gig at a place in Kilburn that isn't there any more. That's where I first saw the Pistols.

What did Acme Attractions sell?

Very similar to what Malcolm was selling in Too Fast to Live, Too Young to Die: winkle-pickers, very loud peg trousers, drape jackets, twentieth-century antiques, tin cars, jukeboxes. Like I say, anything from the subculture of the last thirty years. At first it was all old stuff, then we started having to make up new things. Which was when we became really successful, because you'd be able to adapt things – have a drape jacket in a modern fabric.

People would travel from all over the country to come to the shop, it was quite a scene. People would come down on Saturdays just to find out what was going on. It was like a club. I had a bartering system; if people didn't have the money to buy something I'd give it to them for what they had, or if I really liked the person I'd just give it to them.

The rock stars started to come down, that's where I got to know Patti Smith. Various people passed through. That's when I first got to know John and Sid. Sid especially, he came down a lot. Of the people who came in, 30 per cent came in to see Jeanette. It cannot be denied.

Was there much sniffiness between your lot and the Seditionaries lot?

Not between the staff. I got on with Jordan and Michael very well. But Vivienne blanked me out, and that was the end of it. Before that we used to hang out, we used to go to shows together. I found them very exciting people. I liked their creativity, their constant search for ideas.

What did you think of the whole King's Road ambience, coming from South London?

Even when I was around Brixton, I tried to be a little different myself, dress different from the other kids. I'd come home with my black patent trousers, and the other kids, my Jamaican friends, they

611

thought I'd gone mad, they thought I was such an idiot. But it made me feel stronger to think there were other people like me out there. For a black man to do what I was doing then was kind of brave, now I look back on it.

So the first punk gig you saw was the Pistols?

I couldn't understand a word they were saying, but there was an energy, and you knew that something was going on, and it was going to get bigger. I remember feeling that I wanted to be involved myself. That's what was great about it. If you had the brains for it, you could be a fan, or you could realise, he's just a regular guy like me, I want to do something. And that's what I did when I picked up the Super 8 camera.

When punk rock started happening, the then accountant for Acme Attractions, Andy Czezowski, decided to get involved by opening the Roxy, and he asked me to DJ. Which I was dubious about, because I wasn't a DJ, but I thought fuck it, I'll have a go. And at that point there were practically no punk records. I used to play The 101ers, the Pistols, and apart from that, nothing but reggae.

I used to live in Forest Hill with four other Rastas, and they heard I'd got the job at the Roxy and they laughed at me; Rasta working with punks, he must be mad. A couple of weeks later Andrew says he needs more staff, so I said, 'You wanna have a go, guys?' 'All right.' Ended up with me, Leo Williams, JR, Tony and another character called Big Joe, all big black guys from Brixton, working the Roxy. We built up a really good thing with the punters there.

There was never any trouble at the Roxy, ever. Our bouncer, Joe, he never had to hit anybody. You might have to wipe the spit off your trousers occasionally, but . . .

How long did you continue with Acme Attractions?

Until John Krivine decided to revamp and become BOY. We moved upstairs on to the King's Road, and I couldn't stand it. Basically I saw that as the epitome of selling out. Catering to what the punters wanted, which was Destroy T-shirts and bondage trousers. That, and the intimacy had gone. A lot of shady things went on in that basement, a lot of wheeling and dealing. BOY was a box with a window on to the street, and you couldn't do anything, it was like being an animal in the cage.

Were you there the day it got raided [for the window installation by Peter Christopherson, which simulated burnt fragments of a boy's body]?

Yeah, I was the one who got charged for that crime. They charged me with indecent exhibition, under a law that was passed during the Napoleonic Wars to prevent people exhibiting their war wounds to get money. And so now I've got an indecent exhibition record. Which makes me sound like a pervert, doesn't it?

Can you remember when BOY opened?

About the time of the death of punk rock, I should think.

Once you started at the Roxy, what was your typical evening? What time did you arrive?

If I remember, it was about 7.30. I think the club was open until about 1 a.m. I just sat there and played the records I liked; I never played requests, I couldn't understand why anyone would want to hear the same record twice. In the end, people wanted me to just play reggae, and not bother with the punk rock. There wasn't that many good tunes in punk, you could play all the best ones in about twenty minutes.

Did you see the bands there?

Of course, yeah. I remember how the bands from up North were always a lot more together musically. They'd done more graft. But they looked stupid. I guess that's a typical North–South thing, where the northerners work harder and the people from the South go for the image. I used to feel sorry for the northern bands for that. I remember most of them were awful.

The only people who really came home to me were the Pistols, who never played down there, The Clash, Siouxsie and the Banshees, The Slits, Subway Sect, Buzzcocks. The Heartbreakers were fairly impressive the first couple of times you saw them, but once you realised that was all they ever did, that wore off.

There was a degeneration factor involved there too. Did they bring heroin down straight away?

613

I think it's a bit naive to blame it all on them, there was already quite a bit of speed around. If anything, they just compounded the idea by making it appear cool for a while. I personally didn't know anybody that did it. There was a bit of it going on, but it wasn't any big deal as far as I could see.

You managed to film Keith Levene shooting up didn't you? I was amazed that he let you film that.

I might not even have been holding the camera then. A friend of mine was holding it. It made me too ill to see people inject.

Who was that guy who slashed his stomach?

If I remember rightly he was a postman or something, it was a typical example of somebody getting hold of the wrong end of the stick. I filmed it because that aspect of it was relevant. It did exist.

Was that aspect something that came up during your tenure at the Roxy? Surely the Roxy was very different at the end of that time ...

Don't forget I left with Andy, so when all the people who read the magazines and thought that punk was putting in a safety pin and cutting yourself up were coming down, I'd left.

But didn't the place change just in those four months?

Yes, definitely there was a demise after the first two or three months, in the last month it did fizzle out, basically because the best groups were starting to make it big and we were getting the dregs down there. When the Roxy closed down the next place was The Vortex, and that was indicative of what came up.

You didn't have anything to do with The Vortex did you?

I think they tried to get me to DJ one night, and I went in and they said I was playing too loud, so I thought fuck this and I left, just walked out.

Wire

Graham Lewis and Bruce Gilbert of Wire, interviewed together. Wire played several of their early shows at the Roxy, and sounded great on the Live at the Roxy *album. From outer London, Wire were sarcastic, conceptual and rocking all at once; a combination that resulted in incomprehension at the time, but which has rendered them one of the most enduring groups of the period.*

Bruce Gilbert: Tape loops and noise was my main interest just prior to Wire starting. Making tape loops, performing with them. The idea of getting something going that was happening on its own.

Did either of you see the Sex Pistols during that period?

Graham Lewis: I saw them twice, at the Nashville and the Screen on the Green. The Nashville was really funny. Someone took me. People were expecting pub rock, and they got this group that was playing really funny versions of Small Faces songs that I had in my collection. The singer kept asking people questions, and they weren't used to that. The person who took me was embarrassed.

Was that the night they had the fight?

GL: No, but it was hilarious, a great clash of culture. It was confrontation: 'You won't like this, you wouldn't remember it anyway, because it's by the Small Faces, and you've got no culture.'
BG: The second time we played was at the Nashville, and George Gill, who was in the group then, used to break a lot of strings, and by the end of the first number had broken most of them. He had a friend who had lent him a guitar, and George hit it once and decided it wasn't in tune and stuck it between this bloke's legs, and the audience looked, and he said, 'What the fuck are you looking at, just get back to your fucking beer.' That's what was going on, it was perfectly natural.

Did you ever see them, Bruce?

BG: I did, at the 100 Club. It was very strong and very rude. I remember going to see The Ramones at Dingwalls the first time they came over. There was a kerfuffle at the door, it was obviously McLaren, and he was trying to get his mates, his group in, and they were so dangerous-looking, these boys.

It didn't look contrived, but they looked like Dickensian urchins, they had shoes on but no socks, and the three of them looked like they couldn't have got that way without being alcoholics, or out of it, but they were young boys, and they were perfect. It was a bit like the first photographs of The Rolling Stones, with mothers saying, they must have fleas.

What were The Ramones like?

GL: I couldn't believe it. It was glorious. They came on stage and it was semi-lit, and they just stood there for what seemed like an age. Joey Ramone said, 'Woman, shut your mouth.' And it all started, and it didn't fucking stop, this delirium of noise, you walked in and out of it, a physical environment of noise.

When did you start putting Wire together?

GL: I think it was about October '76 . . .
BG: It wasn't called Wire at first, it was called Overload, and it played once, at the art school, I was a technician there. The others were students. I seem to remember rehearsals on summer days, and it came a point where it broke up, and then Colin and George pursued it and asked me to come back and be involved in it. We needed a drummer and a bass player.
GL: I met Bruce through Angela Conway, and you asked me if I'd like to go to Watford to engage with these two other characters, both equally obnoxious and aggressive – that was George and Colin Newman. I said I played bass, which was a lie. I came along to this room and made a noise for a while, then I went home. I got a phone call in the week from Bruce, saying would I like to repeat the experience, and I said 'Yeah, fine.'

It occurred a few more times, without a drummer. Three rhythm guitars and a bass. Rob Gotobed had been the singer in a group called The Snakes, and decided that he wanted to play drums. He couldn't play but he was keen, and he looked right, somehow, so we started from there. Rob came up with this idea that maybe we should play in time, and in tune, and at that time we were playing mostly George Gill's songs.

The first time we played was in the bar at St Martins, and they pulled the plugs after about fifteen minutes. It must have been towards the end of the year. The second time was the Nashville, supporting The Derelicts. The Derelicts were very right-on. We played the Roxy, supporting The Boys, and at the end of it Andy Czezowski said, 'Come back when you can play', which we thought was quite a compliment.

BG: We got somewhere regular to rehearse, in the basement of a squat, and then George broke his ankle and was unable to come, and we carried on without him, and without the squealing guitar solos it suddenly became more coherent.

GL: We were putting things together all the time. Colin stopped playing guitar, and the sound got more compact – one articulated noise rather than the sheet of noise it had been. Rehearsing three maybe four days a weeks, twelve hours a day. The place was in Stockwell, you'd come out of it a mustard colour, it was like a large ashtray. We were putting together about two songs a day. We came up with simple arrangements.

That was when we met Dave Fudger from *Sounds*, who offered to find the cash for us to make a record. George did come back and play once, in a plaster cast, again at the Roxy. At the end of it, it was very apparent that the space had gone for what he was trying to do, so he went.

What did you find yourselves writing about?

BG: A mixture of things, in the sense that we weren't inhibited, we could write songs about what was going on in England, we weren't trying to write songs about America. There were songs about media and perception – radio and TV, information. At that time I was listening to a lot of radio, as I still do, and I was struck by the quality and distortion of information.

Did you edit down a lot?

BG: For live sets, we'd play whatever we had, but when George wasn't in any more, we threw everything out that he had even partial ownership of. The best thing he and Colin wrote was 'Mary is a Dyke', which should have been recorded. A great loss.

When did you get your manager?

GL: We had Andy Czezowski on a month's trial, and he didn't pass. Mick Collins was an old college friend of Bruce's, who had some experience in the trade.

BG: Mick felt he could get back in touch with his artistic roots in some way, that the creative life could go anywhere, and wasn't confined to rock'n'roll, or preconceived notions of what you could do in the rock'n'roll business. It was an ideal choice.

GL: I think Andy thought he could bring a Svengali touch to what we were doing, but the more we got excited with how it was developing, it was less and less pop as far as he was concerned.

I remember him kidnapping Colin and attempting to get him into a pair of pink leather trousers, which freaked Colin out. He was saying, 'Well, aren't the rest of them going to have pink leather trousers?' I think that's when there was a definite parting of the ways.

How did you get on to the *Live at the Roxy* album?

BG: Andy Czezowski said there was something going on, and we accepted it because we were going to get paid £35 to play two nights, and we just wanted to play. We arrived, and this long-haired, Scott Walker, knitted-jacketed character in pixie boots came up and said, 'I'm the producer, and would you like to use the tuner', and we said 'Look, we've got enough problems, mate. Bugger off.' He turned out to be Mike Thorne.

GL: It was a good idea to mike up the toilets and everything. It was a very good concept, to record the whole club.

BG: It wasn't until a bit later that Andy said, 'They're interested in putting you on the record.' I can't remember which was which night, but they used '12XU' from one night and 'Lowdown' from the other. They were very chaotic evenings, about five groups on each night. There wasn't a lot of time to think about it.

I remember the Buzzcocks being very nervous but looking very composed in comparison to how I'd remembered them from the 100 Club, and in comparison to everybody else. It was obvious that they'd been working on what they were doing, they'd been editing, which was why we felt sympathy with what they were doing. It was that quality of being self-contained.

The chances to play were so few and far between, the rest of the time you just did it because you wanted to do it, really. So many of those bands were just jumping on the bandwagon, really.

Was '12XU' about anyone in particular?

GL: It was a collage. It came from three different directions. We used to start songs off with 'One, Two Fuck You', and then we decided we'd censor ourselves, rather than being censored, which is where the X came from. Then the androgyny of the sexuality of the song developed further, so you didn't know whether it was a woman and a man, a man and a man or a woman and a woman. Also it was very mundane: smoking cigarettes, magazines, advertising.

BG: 'Got you in a cottage' was ambiguous, as well . . .

GL: They didn't understand that in America, they thought it was rural.

BG: That was more about the heavyweight characters who were around, rent-boys . . .

One of the things I liked about _Pink Flag_ was the twenty-two tracks. Was that a definite idea, to do something very concentrated?

BG: That's what it was. People said they were very short, and it was curious.

GL: Was it one song or was it two songs?

BG: When the text ran out, it stopped. We hadn't thought of them being any length. That's how long they were, and when they stopped, another one started. It meant that you could get twenty-two of them into forty-three minutes.

It seemed to be accelerating . . .

GL: Compressed . . .

BG: One of the closest things I ever read, I can't remember who wrote it, was someone was comparing, in a very optimistic way, what

619

was happening, with the Futurists. That approach. Creative, rather than stylistic. That was a satisfying way of looking at it.

GL: Being in it, you never get the experience of what it's like from the outside. You're concentrating on what you're doing, and it lasts however long it lasts.

There was a song periodising the year 1977. What was that?

GL: 'It's So Obvious' . . . "'77, nearly heaven. I can't wait for '78'.

The year itself was fetishised.

BG: By the end of the year, that feeling had gone . . .
GL: The sun shone a lot as well. '76 was the drought, but '77 was good too.

Did you feel that the feeling of there being something you could plug into had started to disappear?

GL: I think we were more confident about what we were doing, but we weren't part of the social scene, which had cracks and factions and star systems, the inevitable things. We were getting on with what we were doing, in terms of music. 'Practice Makes Perfect' appeared, and that set off a whole new direction in which to work. There were lots of careers being built.
BG: Orthodoxy had arrived. Record companies were still searching for their 'new wave' group, and the way of packaging it became formalised, and the people who were encouraged by what was happening were actually doing things, but the openness had gone. It was a matter of getting the outfits right, and the photographs. Some very bright people were still going for it . . .
GL: And the political pose too had become formalised. A lot of worthiness.
BG: The axis was still there, but it was getting narrower.

How did you feel about the reception you got for *Pink Flag*? Were you disappointed with the way it was written about?

GL: Gloom and doom. Jane Suck wrote a review about us playing at the Marquee, which was very positive, but the sub-editor had added the headline, 'Grey, something and mesmerising' and after that, people's imaginations just closed up. That was it, they didn't feel they needed to even reach for a dictionary after that.

BG: It's looking at things in two completely different ways, one through the eyes of what was written in the press, and what was our reality.

GL: The songs weren't jolly, or good-time.

BG: A lot of the absurdity went right over people's heads.

GL: Colin was writing a lot of the music then, and it was a deconstruction, a piss-take of rock'n'roll music anyway. The structures were rock'n'roll, but taken apart and put back together again in different ways. This is how they go, but not quite. They swerve.

After the album came out, did you start touring in your own right?

BG: Yes, because of the activation of this so-called 'movement', places to play opened up all over the country, circuits appeared.

GL: There'd be a venue in every town, and the disciples would be there. Of something which had occurred a year previously.

Was it funny, sweet, sad?

GL: A mixture of all of those things. Very naive in lots of cases.

BG: It was a once-a-week thing, and they all got dressed up and expected to have a riot.

GL: Some said, it's terrible, I'm a punk and I get beaten up. The most bizarre one I ever saw was in '78 when I met Claude Bessy, I was going to a club in Los Angeles, and seeing people that I knew in London – not those people, but people who looked exactly the same. For instance Sue, Andy's wife. It was well-observed. Here we have three Billy Idols, a couple of Sids – he wasn't that big then.

Replicants.

GL: Exactly the same as the *Rocky Horror Show* or something like that; or previous to that, there was always a Bryan Ferry, or an Elvis, Status Quo, Lynyrd Skynyrds.

Didn't you have a riot when you played Newcastle?

GL: That was at the Guildhall. There were about five groups on. Skinheads in Newcastle at that time weren't sixteen-year-old boys, they were guys in their late twenties, working in the shipyards, wearing steel-toecap boots, and they're serious about their violence. During the second group, this psychopath got up and placed the drummer's teeth down his throat. It was Friday or Saturday night with a full hall, and the beer ran out half an hour before we went on.

That wasn't good. We played, went off, and there was an encore. We came back on, and I saw one of those frozen moments – I saw this bloke walk through the crowd, choose someone, indiscriminately, hit this bloke, and the whole place went up, a hundred and fifty people just beating the shit out of each other. We stopped, there was nothing to play to any more. It was over, they closed the place after that.

BG: A delightful bloke at the front with a coat hanger wrapped very tightly around his head . . .

GL: . . . next to the two blokes with LP covers with eye-holes cut out, looking like the Ku Klux Klan.

BG: Extremism, mutilation.

There was a lot of science fiction in punk, if only that it was trying to get to grips with the future in some way. Did you ever notice that?

GL: I think there was a lot of desire to be in the future, rather than in the place people were.

BG: The model for that was *Clockwork Orange*.

GL: I think there was a hangover from the Roxy Music thing, the glamour taken further. Very Dan Dare.

So by '78, the connections that you'd had were gone.

BG: Even before that it had all got a bit sad, in terms of one's own optimism about what could happen. We were committed to the project, not only as a group, but we had a contract to fulfil, and all that.

GL: 'I Am the Fly' was about that recognition that it had finished. Some of the imagery in it was about these previously anarchic characters who had become the shop-window fodder for very large corporations. That was the start of the song.

TV Smith

Singer and co-founder of The Adverts – Roxy regulars, featured on the live album. One of the most passionate believers in the punk ethos and the possibilities of the period, which he captured so well in his allusive lyrics. The Adverts had one of the most fondly remembered punk hits, 'Gary Gilmore's Eyes', but quickly lost their way. Interviewed at his house in Stamford Brook, West London.

I was born in Hornchurch, and lived there until I was about twelve, then transported to Devon, where I met Gaye, and we came back to London cos we knew that was where we had to be to have a band. Gaye lived in Plymouth and I lived in a village called North Taunton. We met at art college in Torquay. It was actually a polytechnic with an art department.

I did A levels but I got turned down by all the universities, and that left second choice which was a foundation course in art, and as soon as I started that, I started getting bands together. I'd been writing songs already, it was a logical thing to do.

Had you been to see a lot of groups when you were younger?

Yeah, and it was always a special occasion to see a group then, in Devon. You'd travel thirty miles or so, to Exeter or Plymouth, you couldn't just waltz down to the local pub and check out the bands. It was something special. I saw whoever came down. The first live acts I saw were Ralph McTell, the Heavy Metal Kids. Cockney Rebel came down to the West Country quite a lot. If a band bothered to come, we'd go and see them; most bands didn't come any further west than Bristol.

In Devon, were you writing some of the songs that you used when you became The Adverts?

Some of them. I was looking through the lyrics today, and there's a sudden change to better songwriting at the time The Adverts happened. It was very sudden, cos some of the songs I'd been writing a couple of months before were just embarrassing really. Something clicked, and it started to work. It's difficult to say what was me coming out of adolescence and what was the atmosphere of the time, but there are a lot of references to the new wave, so I must have been very affected by what was happening.

What did you think that atmosphere was?

I'd picked up an *NME* and seen what must have been one of the first Sex Pistols reviews and how Rotten had been throwing chairs around, and I thought, shit, he's got there before me. That was exactly what we wanted. The only thing that came near it was Iggy's *Raw Power*. That kind of feel. Something that wasn't to do with authority, that got to what we were feeling. If music doesn't correspond to what people are really feeling, it's nothing.

Had you been affected by *Raw Power*?

Yeah, I'd get up in the morning to that, every morning.

Did anybody else down there like it?

Yeah, Gaye liked it. I can't remember anyone else.

Had you thought of playing music like that?

Not really, the songwriting in the band I had at the time wasn't like that at all. It was called Sleaze. That's the Cockney Rebel, Sparks thing that was going on at the time. We saw the Pistols at the 100 Club, and the Notre Dame Hall. It was nice to see something happening, and when the Roxy opened, that gave us our first gig.

Where were you living at that time?

Hammersmith.

And how did you get in touch with Mike Dempsey?

He came down to the Roxy. And gushed. Probably not the first, the second. One of the first two, Jake Riviera came down and wanted to sign the band to Stiff. It was so easy to get a record deal, that we didn't really notice it.

Why was that?

There were a few smart people around who saw that there was something happening, that was going to be exploitable very shortly, and the smarter labels like Stiff would come and see what was happening before the big boys heard about it.

We were together by the end of '76, September or October. We didn't get a drummer for a long time, it was us and Howard Pickup rehearsing together, on our own for quite a few months, and in desperation settled on Laurie Driver. It worked out very well for the band, although at the time we all hated each other.

Laurie was from a different social background altogether, he was a real London boy. But it created the kind of clash of personalities within the group that made it work, on edge.

Where did Howard Pickup come from?

We put an advert in the music press. We had no idea that it would work, but we gave it a try.

Were you aware of lots of other punk groups coming along, and the need to get something out quickly?

We didn't know there was a movement starting at the time, it was every band for itself. Other groups were such a small proportion of the bands around that it wasn't obvious that something was happening. There was an urgency because we wanted to do it, and even if no-one else was going to do it, we were.

It was the first taste of the outside world for me, really, cos after doing a year's foundation course, and art college, I had no clue. What I enjoyed doing was music, but there didn't seem the way to do that, so I spent a year discovering drugs and getting into trouble.

Were you struck by the Grundy thing, when punk went public?

At the time I just thought it was a bit of fun. But seeing it again, it all seemed very knowing – Grundy going, let's have it, I'm in the entertainment business too, let's entertain. He certainly stimulated it, and it

625

was what everyone wanted. We wanted it cos we wanted a lot of dirty, snot-nosed bands about, undermining the establishment, and the *Sun* readers wanted it because it was a great opportunity, good copy.

Were you excited by the Sex Pistols when you saw them?

Yeah, and it was very encouraging to know that someone was going out and doing it, who couldn't play or sing very well, but it still worked. There weren't many bands around like that, and it wasn't obvious that you could actually get away with it. We weren't going to be the next Roxy Music.

What was your first gig like? Jumping off the precipice?

Absolutely, yeah, all of the gigs in the first six months were like that, then we started to feel more comfortable with it, and people were saying it was great, and from that point on, that was probably the rocky road down. It wasn't a group that you could plan. We didn't know if it would work or not, but we thought we'd try.

What were you trying to present?

Two things: the lyrics, I worked very hard on them, and also thrashing out the demons, as soon as you hit the stage. All that contorting around isn't really anything to do with the words, but then people are very disparate things in themselves.

What were the demons that you were trying to exorcise?

It's personal, again. The demons of living with yourself. That takes in everything around you, the political atmosphere, social atmosphere, struggling with your own personality, and that's what comes out. We wrote 'One Chord Wonders' in Hammersmith, and it literally took twenty minutes. It must have been the quickest song I've ever written. Twenty months is more like par for the course.

I love that line, 'When we're halfway through our favourite song, I look up and the audience has gone' – did you ever feel like that when you were performing?

Everyone who leaves while you're playing weighs very heavily on you when you're fairly un-self-confident anyway.

Was 'Bored Teenagers' an early one?

Quite early, yes. I think you can see that a lot of these are very personal. A lot of punk bands seemed very responsive to the politics of the time, but I don't think I was the only one who was writing about personal problems.

Were you very alienated?

I think so, but isn't every teenager? The TV and everything would like the teenager to feel that he's part of the big wide world, all buying the same things and listening to the same records, but it isn't really like that. Thank god it was out in the open then. It isn't the solution, but it's a start.

Were you reading a lot at that time?

Yeah, I've always read a lot. I was reading all sorts, everything from cheap horror novels to . . .

Science fiction?

Yeah, J. G. Ballard – 'Drowning Man' was ripping off the atmosphere from a couple of J. G. Ballard books. I used *Crash* for something as well. . .

So you got a lot of interest very quickly. What sort of deal did Stiff offer you for that single?

It was a one-off deal, there was virtually no money involved. There might have been a small advance on the publishing. But it didn't matter at the time, it was worth it. We quickly found out about the cynical attitude of the record business, even with a company like Stiff. Although they were doing it in a mocking way. It was still a big shock to see the record cover, and there was a big picture of Gaye's face.

Somehow we'd expected there would be a piece of artwork or something, and it suddenly hit home – we've got a good-looking girl in the group, and that's what's going to happen. We hadn't realised that before. It cheapened it for all of us, that people would find a gimmick in what we'd hoped would avoid all gimmicks.

627

What did Gaye think about it all?

I don't think she cared either way. It was boring for her to have to present herself as this figure, she didn't want it. It seems inevitable now that it would happen, but looking back, nothing surprises me about the record business. It wasn't quite so idealistic, even at the beginning, as we fondly remember it.

You were idealistic, and that's what mattered.

Obviously, otherwise it wouldn't have jarred to find those around you weren't living up to those ideals.

Did that get worse, that problem about Gaye, or was it just a running problem all the way through?

Once we came to terms with it, it was no longer a problem. We just carried on doing our thing, and felt that okay, Gaye was a draw, and would bring people into our Advertian world; a lot of people were on the same level, and when people liked a song, they understood it, all the kind of shit that gets in between disappears.

Did you get good reactions to those songs, early on?

Very Pavlovian – as soon as we had a record on the radio or something on TV, everyone loved it. Gigs always have a very ritualistic response, I think. The instant reaction was that there were tons of people jumping up and down, having a good time, which is a nice thing to be able to do for someone.

You must have been quite an early draw, cos the hit, 'Gary Gilmore's Eyes', was your second single, wasn't it?

But I think the live Roxy album came out first, with 'Bored Teenagers', so that was another step on the way.

From the songs you were writing, you seemed to care very much about what was happening to punk and new wave. Were you trying to write songs almost like bulletins on that?

Yes. 'Safety in Numbers' was the ultimate in that way. It was becoming apparent what was certain to happen, and I couldn't resist writing about it. We released that one straight after 'Gary Gilmore's

628

Eyes', probably the stupidest thing we ever did. Mike Dempsey was very unhappy about us choosing that single; the music press said we were biting the hand that feeds us. That's what happened. You're not supposed to be critical about the people in your clique.

When did it become apparent to you that the energy of the whole thing was dissipating?

There was a change from the middle period of the Roxy, up to then. There was a very good atmosphere, anyone could come down and they didn't have to look like a punk; do what they wanted, enjoy the bands or not, but enjoy themselves. Then The Vortex opened, and there was this feeling that the violence was always just under the surface, and you should like this and you shouldn't like that. It was very unpleasant.

Why do you think that was? Do you think it was drugs?

This kind of movement has a way of happening. It's difficult to explain. It's nature, things degenerate. This was a fast-moving movement, and it went through its whole cycle very fast. It reminds me of the way the hippy peace-and-love turned suddenly into hard drugs.

Were you surprised when 'Gary Gilmore's Eyes' was a hit?

No, it seemed to go right from the very first moment. I never had the expectation, it was the first proper record we'd done with a big company, and we wondered what had happened – oh, it's a hit. That's how it goes, and it was desperate disillusionment after that. In popularity terms, that was the high point. Suddenly everyone liked us, we were on television.

The only trouble was, it then froze; that was what people wanted from us. We'd only just started, and a band that should have developed into something extraordinary was hampered by public expectation, and with all the internal problems and tensions within the band, and this tension from outside that we hadn't asked for, the fuse was certainly lit for the big bang that ended it.

When did that happen?

I suppose from the point that 'Safety in Numbers' wasn't going to top 'Gary Gilmore's Eyes'. Suddenly we were likely to be one-hit wonders.

It's a terrible feeling to think that the public perceived the band as having peaked, when you'd just started. We certainly paid with a rapid descent.

What happened next? The album?

They came out about the same time. The failure of 'Safety in Numbers' was partly masked by the fact that the album had a short but well-received period of success. I loved it when Jane Suck was talking about how us recording an album was like crossing the Red Sea, it just had to be the title.

It was a miracle that we could finish a song at a gig, let alone record an album. It wasn't for want of rehearsal, that was just the way we were. No amount of preening by the record company could change it. I think everyone knew that Gaye had a big speed problem, and the fact that Laurie was jealous of the attention that she got. He got hepatitis, and he went through a little heroin phase; they hated each other.

Howard put himself up as a wise elder of the band, but under the surface he was seething. He'd been schizophrenic, he'd tried to kill himself over the love of some woman. We had to pull out of a few dates, and say he'd had food poisoning. Gaye had metamorphosed into a completely different person. This strange drug-sodden, dealing with fame, and trying to continue writing in any kind of logical way. No-one outside our immediate circle understood what was going on. It makes it extraordinary that we managed.

What did you think of that period, '76/'77/'78, how does it seem to you now?

At the time, it seemed that things could get better, from things that were happening, and the youth you were mixing with. It doesn't seem logical that it should turn out like this. Maybe it is just natural human selfishness.

Pauline Murray

Co-founder, singer and writer in Penetration, one of the first and best
punk groups from outside of London. They played the Roxy in April
1977, a couple of months before they recorded their first demo tape
– a burst of pure punk clarity. Interviewed in my then flat in Maida
Vale, London; Pauline is a true believer, retaining the passion and the
idealism of the period.

I was born in a very small pit-village called Waterhouses, at a time
[1958] when a lot of the pits were closing. It was called a 'Category
D' village, and they pulled it all down. When I was ten we moved to
Ferryhill. It's south of Durham. Waterhouses was about seven miles
west of Durham. The first place I lived was a very naive place. Ferryhill was more corrupt. Kids stealing from shops, which I'd never
come across. Not a very nice place really.

But I lived there, went to school there, met Peter there, Peter Lloyd.
He was older than me, really into music, so from the age of twelve or
thirteen I was going to see bands in Newcastle, London, everywhere.
I think the first gig I went to see out of the area was Lou Reed at the
Crystal Palace Bowl, when he had the black eyes. We saw the New
York Dolls at York University, the time they did Biba's. They were
great but the crowd detested them.

You'd go to the City Hall, which was the big gig and there'd be
groups like T.Rex and Roxy Music. Earlier than that, Mott the
Hoople, Hawkwind, anything that was on. I saw loads of bands. You
could watch things as they came along, track it all through. Cockney
Rebel, and then nothing for a long time, then we started to go and see
Doctors of Madness, which were really awful.

There was a real change. We'd see bands like Eddie and the Hot
Rods or The Winkies, pub rock type things. Doctors of Madness
were a big record company band, and then we saw the Sex Pistols

631

play on the same bill as Doctors of Madness in Middlesbrough. They wiped a lot of bands out. It sounds a cliché but I saw it happen. They lost all their confidence, those bands, when the Pistols came along.

What did you do first? Did you see the Sex Pistols or did you go to the shop?

We went to London every so often and we'd read some review of the Pistols at the Nashville, looking really good. We'd go down the King's Road and I saw this person sitting there and I said, 'That's Johnny Rotten', and we got off the bus and followed him. We were real provincial fans, and he went in this shop. We'd seen the shop before when it was a rock'n'roll shop with a leather jacket in the window, but we hadn't been in there.

So we followed him in there and Jordan was in there with Malcolm. Peter had a word with Malcolm and asked if they were playing anywhere, and the next thing, Peter got a call from Malcolm asking was there any gigs in our area that they could possibly do, and at that time there were none. Then in May we found they were playing in Northallerton, which is nowheresville, and it was literally like a row of garages, and the end one was a nightclub.

The people in there were like your regular crowd. No stairs, just a few tables around, small PA columns. They came on and it was like nothing we'd seen before, it was so funny. The reaction of the people was amazing. They were totally manic, mad. It was different to what we'd seen, we'd seen bands roll up with all the trucks and tour buses. This was a totally different level. We spoke to them after that gig. There were a few more actual fans by then.

I don't know whether those gigs were before or after the Screen on the Green, but we went down to that one. I remember Graham Parker was on at The Hope and Anchor just before it, there were two things going on and the Pistols were playing. It started at midnight, and there were all these taxis rolling up. The Slits were there, and the Buzzcocks with Howard Devoto, The Clash with Keith Levene and Simonon, who both looked the same. It was great.

Why and how did you form the band?

It was after seeing the Pistols. I'd never attempted to be in a band or anything like that. We met Gary Chaplin, we lived in the same place, and he was always trying to get a band together. We were eighteen at the time. He organised practices two nights a week. The first gigs we did with the proper line-up, one was supporting Slaughter & the Dogs at the Rock Garden, and the other was at our old school, which must have been the autumn of '76.

Then in April '77 our first London gig was at the Roxy; Peter had rung up Andy and asked him to put us on. We did the gig and there were The Slits and The Clash and the Pistols in the audience; at that time it was a happening place, everybody went there, so we played our gig there, and things went on from that.

Why did you call yourselves Penetration?

At the time there was a fanzine called *Penetration*, which wasn't particularly good, and there was the Iggy Pop song. We couldn't think of a name, so it was Penetration. At Screen on the Green it was quite hip to have *Metallic KO*, I remember seeing Severin hovering about with a copy under his arm.

When did you record those demos?

It must have been '77, June or sometime. We had a manager at the time who was the manager of a record shop called Listen Ear in Newcastle. We were lucky, because we were the only band up there of the kind, and we used to support every band that came up, and so we were seen around a lot. Gary took a tape to Virgin Records, the shop, which was really bad quality – we'd done it with a cassette player in a youth club – and they sent it on to Virgin.

They couldn't make out what the hell it was, so they put us in a demo studio, so we came down to Maida Vale, a place called Virtual Earth. We did the demos for Virgin. We did about nine songs. I think it was an 8-track, but we did it all in a day. We went back and Virgin said they weren't that interested but they would do a single.

What sort of advance did they give you?

We didn't get anything. For 'Don't Dictate' they put us in this studio in Brighton that they had for nothing – they were trying it out, we didn't get any money at all. So we recorded that, and after that they weren't really interested again. Then we just carried on, doing gigs. We were playing anywhere.

What was the second single? It had 'Never Never' on the B-side . . .

'Firing Squad'. They weren't even going to do that. By that time we'd picked up a London management company, Quarry, who managed Status Quo and everything, so Peter had said we ought to sign with them, and they paid for us to record it, and then John, our manager went back to Virgin, and they put that out. Again, no advance and no further interest.

Had you signed publishing?

Just for those tracks, with Virgin. I think we probably had advances, but I don't think we saw any. We were so naive, not interested in money at all. Not business-minded, just keen to do what we were doing. We were getting gigs. Then Gary left the band and we replaced him with a fan who knew all his parts. We did a Buzzcocks tour with Neil Floyd, which did us a lot of good. We did so much in a short space of time.

Then Virgin said, 'If you want to do an album you're going to have to add another musician', so we drafted in this person who was quite unsuitable, but we just didn't care about anything. We just worked him in and carried on. The first gig he did was at the Marquee, we were headlining. It was really packed, it was the night when Virgin were going to decide whether to sign us or not.

It was so hot the drummer left the stage in the middle of the set, and at the end of it the drummer and the guitarist were fighting in the dressing room when Virgin came in to tell us we had our deal. We went ahead with that and we were hanging about Virgin a lot then, and this is when we came across people like Sid. Sid would come into Virgin and terrorise the staff, and we'd sit in the video room watching Devo videos, and he'd be spitting at them.

Then he teamed up with Nancy and we did The Vortex with The Heartbreakers, and we gave Sid a lift home in our van. He was completely mad by then.

Do you think he was just living up to the image?

634

I think it was the drugs. Nancy goaded him along, she was as wild as him. Plus he was a bit bored, he had nothing to do.

Can you tell me about some of the songs?

I hadn't written any stuff before so it was very pure, like you had your eyes open for the first time and you were looking around. 'Duty Free Technology' was inspired by a short story I read called *The Machine Stops*, by E. M. Forster. People living underground, completely dependent. It was to do with how we depend on technology. I don't know where most of the lyrics came from, I just wrote them down.

But it was all a result of seeing the Sex Pistols?

Definitely.

So what was it about the Pistols that gave you that clarity of vision?

It was like seeing reality. You'd seen so much bullshit and believed it all, you don't know that record companies hyped the bands. It was such a real thing. Also what they were saying, you don't have to have all those restrictions, you can look at anything. It was personal expression, you weren't tainted by a scene or anything. You were there on your own, your own music.

Was there a scene in Newcastle?

No. There was nothing going on. We came from Ferryhill, which was the sticks, it was odd that anything could come out of that place. But Newcastle was the city and there was nowhere to play. The last time anything happened in Newcastle was in the sixties, with the Club A-Go-Go and all that. It was all dead by then. Our manager put on a gig with The Adverts and Warsaw, who were then going to be Joy Division. It was good, like punk rock was starting to happen, but it was a one-off.

Did you travel much to Manchester?

Yeah, we used to go to Manchester and Liverpool, to Eric's. We met people like The Fall and the Buzzcocks. It was starting to link up by then.

Who was there in Liverpool?

Not Liverpool bands. There was Big in Japan, who were more art school, but Eric's was a really good club, it had a great atmosphere there. In Manchester we played The Electric Circus. We played there with Buzzcocks and The Jam. I didn't like The Jam at all, they were cynical biz types. They had massive flight cases and all this gear, everyone else was poverty-stricken.

Had Patti Smith and The Ramones made an impact on you?

Yeah, I'd heard *Horses*, which had a massive impact on me, purely from the way she sang, the way she looked. She was a big influence. I didn't understand a lot of it until much later. She was a lot older, and it all sounded strange, you didn't know what the lyrics of things like 'Redondo Beach' were about. It was something you could learn from. I remember hearing Blondie's first album, The Ramones, Patti Smith, Television. It sounded really different.

Did you get an advance towards the album?

We got an advance, but we were signed up to this real rockist management company, and they took the advances and we were on a wage. The money all went through them. We did gigs as well, so we were doing all right.

Were you pleased with that first LP?

Yeah, it was a real buzz to record it. We did it at just the right time. We recorded backing tracks at a cheap studio just off Oxford Street, then we went to places like the Manor and the Townhouse to finish it. At the end, listening to it I felt quite emotional, I couldn't believe it sounded like that.

So what went wrong?

It started to go wrong when we went to America. The first album was well received. It was the culmination of the couple of years before, but we went to America to promote it and that was the end. We were there for five weeks. By this time we were incredibly tired, we'd done a lot of gigs, and the two guitarists in the band weren't there from the beginning, it had lost its centre.

CHAPTER TEN

1977/2: The Jubilee

Jolt, Jubilee issue, number 2, June 1977 (Lucy Toothpaste)

The zenith of British punk was reached in June 1977, when the Sex Pistols released the 'God Save the Queen' single right on time to coincide with the Queen's Silver Jubilee. When the world's media came to the UK to cover the royal celebrations, they had the perfect anti-story: a foul-mouthed pop group who dared to point out the reality of England in the late seventies.

Although they had already been the object of a tabloid scandal seven months previously, the Sex Pistols became public enemies number one after the success of 'God Save the Queen' and the well-publicised fracas surrounding the Jubilee holiday boat trip down the Thames. Several of the group and those around them were attacked in the following weeks.

The events of June 1977 marked the moment when punk became an international media event. It also broke the Sex Pistols, four young musicians who simply wanted to enjoy their success. From that time on it was virtually impossible to see them in the UK, and they recorded almost nothing after that summer. But their anti-Jubilee protest cemented their place in history and turned punk into a national archetype.

Al Clark

Sex Pistols' press officer from the Jubilee onwards; former Time Out *journalist and long-standing Virgin staffer whose urbane patience did much to protect the group in their most controversial period. Also well-placed to observe the political games played out between Richard Branson and Malcolm McLaren. Interviewed in London just before he emigrated to Australia.*

I started working at Virgin Records on the 3rd of June 1974. The Virgin offices were at Vernon Yard [off London's Portobello Road]. The label was exactly a year old, and *Hergest Ridge*, [Mike] Oldfield's second LP, was about to come out. Only eight LPs had been released in the first year. Henry Cow had only made one of them by that stage. I loved arguing with Chris Cutler. It was a different world. There was a lot of debate, and arm-wrestling, and discussion, that you don't get in muso land.

It's curious that Henry Cow, with their politics, should have been involved with Richard Branson.

At that time Richard was associated more with radicalism. There's no question that he created a climate around Virgin which was consistent with the aspirations of Henry Cow. They would have had trouble finding a record company more theoretically in sync with their outlook. The shops had that air of people being able to put on a pair of headphones and stay there all day.

We signed Supercharge in '75. I remember reading an interview with Simon Draper just before I joined, where he said he'd like to sign a band like Slade, which I found striking. But already they realised that the kind of groups they had were too confined, leaning towards the musicianly and the cosmic. Simon wanted a rowdy, crowd-pleasing band.

639

Supercharge were funny and noisy and clearly thought everybody on Virgin apart from them were wallies. They were the beginning of the turn. By the end of '76, after three years [of Virgin's existence], the records were doing okay but rarely more than that, and with this deadlock, there was punk. This company found itself in a universe it was going to have to adjust to.

Was the change a collective decision?

It was collective in that we met regularly, and it was a very opinionated company. As it turned out, a whole lot of options to renew came up at around the same time. One memorable night at Richard's house in Denbigh Terrace, it was clear that if the company didn't change gear, it would just trickle along. We discussed all the people we would have to commit to for some time longer, or decide that it wasn't happening. It was a very turbulent evening, involving a lot of bridge-burning.

It wasn't so much that it was 1977 and we weren't trendy enough, it was more the absence of vitality in the company. The reggae series, whilst they had the vitality, also had a restricted audience, ten thousand at most. Nobody was dissatisfied with what there was, but we had limited resources, and we couldn't afford the time to spend on people who weren't going to build things.

People at Virgin were going out to clubs far more. There was a sense that something was going on, and if we didn't know what it was, then we didn't deserve to be a record company. There was another element that said we were the kind of record company we were, and that we should just plod along, and stick to what we were known for.

I thought we should do both: to continue with the people we were interested in, and replace the ones we weren't interested in with people we'd go out and find, rather than people who'd turn up in Vernon Yard with their Afghan coat and the artwork for their concept album under their arm. I was very suspicious of punk, though. Partly because I was hearing it too much and not seeing it too much.

I remember talking to A&R men at the time, and hearing them fearful and insecure for the first time in their professional lives. They had got accustomed to a world that was easy for them. They dreaded the notion of it ever becoming difficult. Life was very easy in the mid-seventies. Parties were on a large scale, cars were abundant and flashy. Big salaries, drugs, anything you wanted.

It was as if the lazy aristocracy was having to contend with a peasant's revolt on its own doorstep. They were having to go out on missions into a rather dangerous universe, and often at such gigs you would see A&R men standing together at the back, as if holding on to a life raft, and what was going on at the front alarmed them.

There was the threat of physical violence, music that they wouldn't choose to listen to at home, and they were nervous about being ridiculed. The notion of being out of touch, of not being at the heart of things, had a really traumatic effect. It's easy now to see that a year later it got assimilated, but those early months engendered a lot of fear and insecurity.

All of these A&R men and others had been accustomed to a lot of misbehaviour in their lives, but it followed a pattern. The bills got paid. Essentially, they were acts of destruction and abuse perpetrated by people who ultimately understood the code, who knew that you had to apologise in the morning, and that the record company were mates. Everything was understood. Good old so-and-so wrecked another hotel room last night.

What was menacing about the punk groups was their capacity for rage and for destruction wasn't in that mould. It was more to do with the record company being the enemy. This creates immediate discomfort. Some of it was fake, of course, it was shown to be ritual rage, but the effect of such deep-rooted rudeness is hard to overestimate.

I think Sid came down to the Reading Festival in '76, on a bus. He got drunk and behaved abominably. When the coach stopped in a traffic jam he got out, and with cars passing by, he had one of the longest pisses I've ever seen anybody take, by the side of the road. It was almost celebratory, he was looking around him, enjoying his audience. The English have a way of going collectively quiet when someone is misbehaving in a way they can't join in.

I was very intrigued about where it was going to go. This was the first time I'd wondered whether the world was going to stay the same. I was torn between my curiosity in something that was going on that was having an effect on a largely moribund industry, and on the other hand, not really liking what I heard very much. I was accustomed to eloquence in such a position.

The kind of upheaval that people like Henry Cow would describe was a politically based one, to do with theory and argument and structure. If you're accustomed to resolving your life in terms of ideas, you find it peculiar when it's coming in a tidal wave, and debate, if it can be called that, is conducted in a series of shouts and gestures and declarations.

My only concern was there was such a blanket dismissiveness towards anyone who had existed before, other than Iggy Pop, the Velvets, the usual litany of acceptable heroes. Everybody was being cleared out, which of course is the essence of all good revolutionary thinking in the heat of its initiation. You're supposed to demolish the old order. But I thought that to display the same hostility to Randy Newman as to Emerson, Lake and Palmer was short-sighted. But it wasn't reasoned argument.

By the time I was in the heart of it in the summer of '77, Malcolm – who clearly saw himself as the orchestrator of punk – had changed the rules, in his dadaist way. He was already declaring that what it was really about was ripping people off and upsetting people. Initially you felt that there was more to it. I think he said it well before the *Swindle*. Because he managed and was as famous as the group around whom it all revolved, he viewed the whole thing as his toy, and he decided what it was.

His interviews of the time alternated between a marvellously self-righteous rage at significant times, such as when he got arrested after the boat trip, full of barricade-storming rhetoric; and a rather capricious, greedy, totally materialistic attitude towards exploitation, which was all the more remarkable for being so brazen.

What was the first punk band you saw?

X-Ray Spex. I can't remember where. They were extraordinary. I went with a fan, which helped. I thought Poly was stunning. I thought 'Oh Bondage! Up Yours!' is one of the records by which it will all be judged.

Didn't Virgin talk to Malcolm in '76?

There was a discussion before EMI, then it all started again immediately after A&M. I think within weeks of that, 'God Save the Queen' was on the release schedule. It was by no means a unanimous decision that the Pistols should be signed to Virgin. There was a lot of opposition from people who felt it was more trouble than it was worth. On the other hand, Virgin had been founded on its sparky defiance of the rules, had lost that, and signing the Sex Pistols was a good way to revive that spirit in the company, albeit in rather different circumstances.

Did the people in Virgin start changing their image?

I think the people who were changing their image had already done it, and the people who weren't going to were clearly not going to be bullied. I think there was an element in the decision to take them on, that we could handle it where the others couldn't.

It's easy to see why Malcolm and Richard fell out. They were so similar, and in Richard, Malcolm met his match. He didn't like that very much. Once the group was signed, Richard threw himself into it. He couldn't be viewed as the enemy any more. Virgin did a lot to support and defend the Sex Pistols during the rest of that year, through court cases, all that extraordinary press, John and Paul getting beaten up. The general climate of hostility and outrage towards the band.

They may have behaved worse before they signed to Virgin, but the reaction to them was far more dramatic after they signed. It got into the Jubilee stuff, people's sense of patriotism was offended. For a few weeks the band seemed to me to be sitting targets for absolutely anybody with a grievance. I've never known so much national hatred focused on a pop group. It was the apex of eight months' worth of history that for the majority of people started with the Grundy appearance, and then the Jubilee happened.

They had conveyed the image of being hard, indestructible; they became targets for the same sort of people who walked up to Robert Mitchum in bars in the fifties and wanted to try it on. They got treated as if they had no feelings, that their doctrine was being voiced back at them. And of course they didn't want to be treated as animals.

You must have been plunged into it, from a press point of view?

My life changed. My personal life changed as well. I was going home to a semi in Ealing where I would read goodnight stories to my children after a hard day telling Fleet Street no, Sid did not attack this man in the street, and having to comment on the latest allegation about their purportedly appalling behaviour. It was pretty weird. I got a death threat, plus the usual element of menace about the family.

During a two-month period when the group were under attack, Malcolm didn't want to talk to anyone, and they used to call me up. I found myself spending at least twelve hours a day being the mouthpiece for a band that at that stage I barely knew. I'd met them all, we'd chatted in the office. And since I was defending the group, I became the enemy to those people who thought the group should be ritually burnt or otherwise wiped off the face of the earth. It was that virulent.

What were they like when you first met them?

Quieter than I'd imagined. Fatigue was beginning to set in. The gulf between John and the rest of the band was in evidence. I think he found the rock'n'roll laddishness, by his standards, of Steve and Paul, tiresome. Even his friend Sid was becoming a liability, and he was fed up with having a junkie in the band. They did some filming at the Marquee one morning, and John just sat there smoking, on his own, and Steve and Paul chatted, and Sid hadn't turned up.

It was clearly destined to burn brightly and briefly. It's very tiring to be that much at the heart of things, and waiting for you to do the next thing. Particularly as they didn't choose seclusion. It wasn't like one of those tours that you can absorb yourself in, between flights and Holiday Inns. They didn't know what they were going to do next, cos Malcolm was improvising from day to day. Would a tour be a sell-out? Would they do individual dates and pretend they'd been banned everywhere else?

They were banned by the GLC, weren't they?

I think so, yes. A lot of the banning was hype. Steve and Paul, on the surface of things, were the most stable, and in a way they suffered the most. I think they wanted to be in a band that performed, and what they'd turned into by that summer wasn't a proper group at all. Even

644

when they did those dates in the autumn and winter, they were more like missions, excursions into enemy territory.

What do you think they had become by that summer?

The stunt aspects were close to Malcolm. He had to feel that he was engineering it, but there was also a lot of fear, because of how they were viewed. There was unease within the group. It wouldn't have taken a lot of predicting that they would break up in America.

Did they change much over the summer with all that pressure, as people?

I think the first rush of aggressive enthusiasm was over, apart from Sid, who was too out of it to notice; they felt very vulnerable. They had engendered a collective hatred beyond what they'd anticipated. The world, certainly the music business, was longing for a way to humanise them; the interview that John did with Tommy Vance, where he played Tim Buckley and Peter Hammill records, was used that way. He has taste after all!

Were you much aware of the level of vituperation between Glitterbest and Virgin at that time?

Oh yes. It was a curious kind of warfare in which you're also collaborators with each other. Like two armies that spend half the day shooting at each other, and the other half having cups of tea. It was irritating to Malcolm that Virgin had first accommodated the group so quickly, then they felt had alienated their affections, by being more powerful, more practically helpful to the group and probably by that stage more charming as well.

Did you observe much tension between the band and Glitterbest, particularly Malcolm?

I felt that John and Malcolm were falling out. John was fed up with being a puppet, and he had enough pride and spirit to feel that if it was going to work, it had to be according to the way he viewed things. Malcolm in turn wasn't going to give all that up. Malcolm still wanted to channel the group emotions towards another great moment.

In the early autumn of '77, the distance increased over *Who Killed Bambi?*, which John wasn't at all keen to do. Malcolm was very keen on it. John made his displeasure very clear to Russ Meyer, who wasn't accustomed to that kind of rudeness. Meyer is a tough, Good Old Boy, but once again, he wasn't used to all this from this little shit.

There are many reasons why Meyer left. There's the story about how he got one of his friends to shoot the deer and the crew walked off in disgust, and they were left stranded in the middle of the countryside. About him and John falling out. And then there's the great story Malcolm came out with, whose veracity I've never been able to settle one way or the other, about Princess Grace being on the board of 20th Century Fox. That was a cracker.

It must have been quite unusual in your experience, to have a group which was managed so strongly.

Malcolm McLaren literally ran the show, and I'd never met a manager like that before. He clearly had absolutely no time for creative artists, he thought *he* was the creative artist. I think that's one of the reasons that he and John fell out, I think John was just getting a bit creative, John wanted to exist as a person, and Malcolm thought he was being the real precious little prat, and that he should just enjoy being a Sex Pistol.

He was almost too intelligent, in a way?

Yes, and too questioning, and fed up with the feeling that he was being manipulated, and that he had no contribution to deciding how much, or how little . . .

Was there an extent to which, from your point of view dealing with the press . . . you had the big splurge around 'Queen' . . . was there any sense of anti-climax after that, by the time you got around to 'Holidays in the Sun' or *Bollocks*, you had this slightly ritualised situation . . .

It was slightly ritualised, but the fact that they were doing these guerrilla, one-off shows meant that there was still a lot of excitement surrounding them, there was a real curiosity about where these by then viewed as forbidden warriors would turn up, and what was going to happen when they did turn up – were people going to . . . was there going to be a bloodbath?

Did you go to see any of the SPOTS tour?

No, I didn't go to any of the guerrilla dates. I set out for Brunel University and the traffic was so heavy I decided to give up. I couldn't bear the idea of getting there, running the gauntlet, and then finding that it was all over.

Why were those dates set up in universities? Did they think that no-one else would have them?

I guess they were the kinds of places that co-operated easily with Malcolm's schemes, taking bookings at very short notice, hyping up the event without naming the group . . . yeah, I think a Student Union social sec would be far more in sync with an adventure of this kind than a local promoter. But they did non-university stuff as well, they did somewhere out in Norfolk. But the whole notion of how banned they were was pretty suspect.

McLaren had this great thing about wanting to reach the kids, the fourteen-year-olds, and then playing in university student unions. Doesn't add up to me . . .

I always found that 'kids' stuff a bit condescending, not as much so as when pomp rock bands used to talk about them, but almost. I think the group was interested in its audience, but I always find that 'kids' stance a bit certainly on the borders of bogus! But the thing about Malcolm, he legitimised all his paradoxes by acknowledging them, he could argue a case for them. But how can you think this and this? Oh, easily!

What did the other Virgin acts think? What did Steve Hillage, say, think when he came in and saw the Pistols lounging about? And what did they think?

Well, they didn't come in often enough for there to be much inter-facing with other Virgin bands. I think like all the previous generation of heroes they were a bit worried about whether they were going to last or not. It must have been quite intimidating for

647

people who thought that popular music was a place where you built a career and you went on, you grew up in it, and suddenly it looked as if it was all going. What do I do now?

Of course, they needn't have worried, although for some it did change – Emerson, Lake and Palmer for example, couldn't get away with it any more. And Yes only managed it through re-forming with Trevor Horn as their producer.

What was the feeling about the Biggs single, was it felt to be rather a bad idea?

The one Glitterbest contradiction that I found a bit tricky, for all Malcolm's barrow-boy persuasiveness, was the one that used swastikas so much, and the Nazi references. They would always say they were trying to demystify it, and bring it out into the open. Essentially it had rather a nasty aftertaste, and having that guy dress up as Martin Bormann, and Sid with his Nazi T-shirt, he walked through the Jewish quarter of Paris with it on, a situationist act . . .

I wonder how many times Sid just did acts of stroppiness, and then Malcolm thought he was being 'situationist'. But no, I didn't like the Biggs single. I liked 'My Way' a lot, but that was the side that I played. Now there was an icon that needed demolishing – possibly the most narcissistic song of all time – so I suppose the play element took over, from then on it was pure play; what could we do next to get up people's noses, now there isn't a group?

I remember ringing up Biggs once. I called him up to ask him if he would do a few interviews on the phone to promote the single, and he said, 'Well, I don't want to do anything until I'm paid some money', and I said, 'Well, what money?' He said, 'I did this deal with Malcolm and he hasn't paid me yet.' 'Oh I see, well, we can't pay you, legally or even technically, cos we're a company and we can't send money to a man called Ronald Biggs in Brazil.'

And he said, 'Well, do you think I'm due some then?' I said, 'I expect you are, you're entitled to some royalties unless you've signed everything over to Malcolm.' 'Where did the record get to?', he asked me. 'I think it got to about number four.' 'I understand that if you get into the Top 5 you get a house and a car' – which was such a gloriously late-fifties pop star's mother and father talking – and I said,

'No, you don't, you just get some money.' And he said, 'Look, why don't you bring the money over to Rio in a suitcase, and when you get here you'll have the best time of your life.' This sounded promising. Anyway, the whole thing was in the hands of the receiver by then, and so Ron just got whatever Malcolm gave him on the spot, and nothing more.

It doesn't surprise me.

I liked it, I know the concept got bigger after the group split up, cos Malcolm was running the concept, but everything was much more powerful for having a group in existence. I know Malcolm thought that was rather old-fashioned. 'This isn't an ordinary band that plays gigs and stuff . . . '

They were when they started . . .

Yeah I know. But you can't keep up the fabrication for long, even if you do release records called *Flogging a Dead Horse*.

Did Sid change?

He lost his vitality. He was no less violent, but it had a very round-shouldered and whiney and pathetic quality to it, there was no vigour, no fizz. I just felt he was so disconnected from the world, so uninterested in the world, apart from the aspect of it that was to do with junk. Maybe that happens with everyone, I don't know. I think it was a combination of junk and too much myth-making, too many stories to have to live up to, too much baggage.

It was very marked, and yet occasionally you would feel the ingenuousness, his intrinsic desire to be approved of – not liked, but approved of – but then it became more, borrowing fivers, going round London in a taxi, to score . . .

Did he used to borrow a lot from people in Virgin?

He did until they cottoned on. I think one afternoon he showed up and borrowed a fiver from just about everybody in the building. While the taxi purred outside.

Do you think Sid really had a talent and could have – if everything hadn't happened – had a solo career? He had two big hits, didn't he?

His talent was iconoclastic, it wasn't orthodox, and if Malcolm had an orthodox career in mind, it's indulging in sentimental wishful thinking. I thought Sid's main talent was getting up people's noses, and his second talent was a sense of the absurd; how much of it was engendered by him and how much by Malcolm I don't know. For example, if it was Sid's idea to do 'My Way', then that was brilliant. He may have had talent, but he didn't have any judgement.

I suppose it depends whether he would have allowed himself to evolve. People who try and stay the way they are perceived very rapidly become anachronistic bores, and that's what Sid would have become. I couldn't really perceive in the way he spoke about things, and about himself, a real curiosity about art or life. Perhaps by then he was just far too interested in junk to be interested in anything else.

Was it still a shock to you when all that happened, happened?

A bit, yeah. Yes, I was surprised. Retrospectively, I needn't have been. It was a very strange, over-heated affair, which combined with such phenomenal drug-use and such tempers. It felt to me that Nancy didn't like life very much. She liked Sid, certainly, and the idea of being holed up in a rather grim hotel with each other, and each other's habits, and each other's volatility . . . you know, it must have been pretty pressure-cooker-like.

What was Malcolm's attitude? Was he very upset about Sid?

Yes, he was very protective towards Sid. I think Sid was his favorite. Sid was more like a Sex Pistol than any of the others. John, towards the end, must have been such a pain in the arse for Malcolm because he was failing in his duty to respond, as a Sex Pistol.

So Malcolm really was emotionally involved?

Well, I'm sure, because Malcolm thinks exploitatively, that exploitation was a factor, but I think he cared for Sid, and he wanted to get him off, and I think he spent quite a lot of money, definitely. You see Malcolm could go very swiftly and fluently from rabble-rouser, in a sort of streety way, to smooth-talking, American-boardroom eloquent.

650

And he got out of prison and his mother gave him the junk, didn't she?

Yes.

What did you think of the court situation, where the thing was effectively put into the hands of the receiver? Was that to stop it becoming an unholy mess?

It was felt that Malcolm's affairs were in a state of such disarray that they had no choice. There was something rather poignant about the Sex Pistols' supervisor being the receiver. No man can be less anarchic than Russell Hawkes of Spicer and Pegler. And it became rather weird, when the film of *Swindle* came out, and we are its distributors, to find myself talking to Mr Hawkes once or twice a day, to check out a legal point.

How did they see it all?

It was just a job to them. A rather peculiar one.

What was John like after the band break-up? Did he come in much?

No. He became a bit pallier with Richard after the Jamaican outing. He shut himself up in his house in Gunter Grove and I hardly saw him at all during that period. I felt he was living a rather unhealthy life. He looked as if he was going the classic burnt-out rock star's route, the shutting yourself up factor, the getting up very late and having weird parties, watching television drinking beer, smoking dope – and then there was Wobble, and all those people who used to be round at the house.

I thought that was a very unpleasant bunch generally, and I subsequently got to like Wobble, but it was evident from the start that he had a great potential for danger, and it felt a bit like the rock star with his bunch of heavy cronies, and I wasn't at all attracted to that scene. I'd hear reports from people who'd go round there and just get insulted, and they'd leave, and they'd wonder why they'd bothered.

That's a dead period for me. I was basically uninterested in having anything to do with anyone who clearly wasn't interested in the world, living in this weird limbo, and the situation got worse and worse until he went to live in America; and even there, there was a lot of beer-drinking, he put on a lot of weight. I think he lost what he

had, and he hadn't yet found something to replace it, which of course
he did subsequently. The first Public Image album had come out, and
it's a pretty good record.

**The final thing I wanted to ask you was about the knock-on
effect on Virgin. Wasn't there a stage where you had signed and
successfully marketed the Pistols, that you started signing punk
bands willy-nilly?**

We had already signed XTC, I think we may have already signed a
deal for 'Bondage' with X-Ray Spex. Obviously after we signed the
Pistols, people started coming to us.

All those groups, Jesus . . .

Ha ha, naff punk bands! Well, I saw them all, Jon!

Didn't you get fed up with it all?

A bit, but there were usually two or three songs in each group's reper-
toire that I liked, so I used to make those make my evening.

It did become one of the premier labels for punk, didn't it?

Yes.

**Would you say that the Sex Pistols did, in fact, successfully revitalise
the company?**

Yes, briefly – though they may have not existed as a group for long
after joining us, i.e. seven months – but they just gave it a jolt. After
them the company was not going to be the same. Not because the
people had changed very much, but because their attitude towards
their work had. They just didn't want what had gone before any
more. There was such a lot of vitality around anyway, in contrast
with the extremely moribund first half of the seventies.

**Why do you think people still find them interesting? Because of the
myth, or because of the vitality?**

Because nothing has happened since to eclipse them as people who
have an effect, however temporary, on the culture of the country.

Dennis Morris

Sex Pistols' principal photographer from spring 1977 onwards, responsible for many memorable images of the group in 1977, including the 'God Save the Queen' video shoot and the boat trip; was also involved in the early days of Public Image Ltd, particularly the cover of the first album. Interviewed at his then studio in London's Mayfair, just off the Edgware Road.

I was brought up in Dalston in the East End. I belonged to a choir and we wore Eton suits, with the collars and everything. They were patronised by Donald Paterson of Paterson Products, one of the inventors of top photographic equipment, so they had a photography class. The choir was almost like a boarding school, but it wasn't. You went there for singing lessons.

Didn't you have the piss taken out of you?

That explains how I dealt with going down the street wearing something bizarre – I had that when I was a kid. It's no problem for me now, cos when I was a kid I'd be done up in this collar and dinner suit. But that's how I got into photography. At school I used to do pictures for local community centres and stuff; when I was eleven I had a picture on the front page of the *Daily Mirror*.

All my pocket money used to go on photography books, I'd read things on the old masters, and one day I was down in Hyde Park at a huge demonstration and I took pictures, ran down to Fleet Street with it, and they developed the film and had a picture of one of the PLO leaders who flew in secretly. I didn't know that, but they bought it off me, paid me twenty-five quid, and it was syndicated, and I thought great, a lot of money for one shot.

How I got into the music scene was I'd just read about Bob Marley and the Wailers coming to England, so I rang up Island, went to see them, and they said to go down to the Speakeasy, and I went down there with my pass, and they looked at me and they knew I was too young, but because I was black they probably thought I was connected with Bob or something. I took loads of pictures.

Peter Tosh didn't like me for some reason, but Bob and Family Man really liked me, and Bob said, 'Come on the road', so I bunked off school for two weeks and went on the road with them. I was fifteen, and disappeared for two weeks, took loads of pictures. I went to Island, who bought a load of pictures off me. I didn't hear anything more until two years later this album called *Catch a Fire* came out, and pictures of Marley on the front page of the *NME*.

I was just leaving school, and the biggest thing you need for working in photography is published work. So I had that, and it started from there. But that first time I covered them as a reportage photographer, so I covered everything, not just on stage but soundchecks, playing football in the dressing room, and that's how I photographed the Pistols and everybody else.

After Bob Marley you were doing more reggae stuff?

Yeah, I was doing reggae stuff, but there was no outlet. I was always bubbling under, with my love of music, but luckily I had a bit of a start, so when the Pistols came along in '77, John was reading magazines and seeing my pictures, and when they signed to Virgin, I was lurking about on the scene, he said, 'I want that guy who takes all the reggae shots.' That's how it started. The Marquee, the boat, Sweden – basically, I was with them all the time through that period.

Can you remember what those set-ups were like to shoot?

For me it was easy, because John liked me to work on things, cos I knew reggae music, he loved reggae music, so we used to sit and talk, and became great friends. Also, McLaren thought it was a good wind-up for a punk band to have a black kid working with them. It was perfect. Because of the way McLaren worked, anybody who worked with him had to have initiative in some sense.

You'd arrive at the Marquee, or the boat trip, and there's no PA, only monitors, so everyone had to use their initiative. So for me as the photographer, it's, where's the lighting? No lighting. But because

I'd studied reportage photography it was perfect, you never wanted proper lights or anything, it was always available light, it was no problem for me. The more haphazard, the better.

The Marquee ones seem very posed and stylised.

That was when I had proper lighting. It was a video shoot, and a secret gig. It was straight, white light. Four stands, but the first time they'd had proper lights.

What sort of state were the band in when you started working with them?

Sid had just joined them. He was getting the buzz of it, and he'd just won the girl he'd always wanted, which was Nancy. He was now a rock'n'roll star, so she wanted him. He'd been chasing her for months and then suddenly he had money and he could maintain a habit. That's how he got caught up into it.

John was really upset cos he liked Sid, and John being the person he is, he's possessive about friendships, and he felt a bit uptight about Nancy moving in on his mate. Steve and Paul were just, you know, where's the girls? Just getting on with it, they couldn't believe their luck. John figured he was on to something and he could make something of himself.

When you took that picture of them doing 'Pretty Vacant', did you stay there for long while they were recording it?

I was always there when they were recording, yeah. The way they approached the studio was the way any so-called great rock'n'roll band would approach recording. While John was doing his vocals, the others would be fucking around, trying to put him off, maybe, but in putting him off, getting a certain edge, a certain humour to it, a sneer which even when Steve was playing guitar, there was an attitude to it.

I guess the studio must have been one of the only safe places that they had at that point.

Not really. We went out for a drink at this pub nearby and some guy recognised John and came over, and started something, and Sid put a glass in his face. Straight away, run. They were never safe.

What do you remember of the boat trip?

It's quite a blur for me. I remember it being fun. I was taking loads of pictures, everyone was having a good time, and the point I remember was when we actually docked, and then everybody had to make up their own minds about what to do. I think the situation was manipulated to get press out of it. Up to that point it was quite a good trip, but something had to be done to make it more than just going up and down the river.

And just before the boat went in to dock, suddenly these launches were there, I suppose McLaren had this ace up his sleeve. He always had a fail-safe, it wouldn't have been enough for the boat to go up and down the river. He did something to create that whole thing. In those situations, John never retaliated and he always got away with it. Sid always got done, and John was always the diplomat, he saw what he could do. Sid was a bull in a china shop.

Did you see it getting heavy for them during that summer?

Not really. I think it was heavier for the audience. The heaviness for the band came from Joe Public, not from the audience, which was in awe of them. You'd always get a few bottles thrown on stage, but they'd miss. They'd always be aimed at John, they'd miss, and John would make this person seem an absolute wally, and no-one would throw any more bottles on stage.

But Joe Public on the street, that's where the danger was. Any move we made, we did it quickly and quietly and get there, and that's it. But McLaren always put them in that situation. There was supposed to be transport, and where was McLaren? No-one had any money.

Can you remember what the Swedish tour was like?

That was brilliant. That was another situation where we turned up in this hotel, there was at least two rooms short. Boogie and Roadent didn't have rooms. Nor did Jamie. And there was no facilities for Roadent. That was how he got his name, cos he always ate what was left. And whatever floor was left, that's where he'd sleep.

The first place was this club, the stage was like this high, and there was a rope as a security barrier, and all these Swedish kids who had been into Status Quo or something just went berserk. I suppose cos

656

they were into heavy metal, the whole thing was like heavy metal to them, but being that close it made them go completely berserk.

But it was easy for the group. The only problem was the usual spillage on the stage, people knocking over equipment. But it was never ever the right set-up. Bad mikes, bad PAs . . . but it was good for them to unwind.

It sounds like the Sid Vicious band was at its peak then.

Yeah, cos he'd had the opportunity to learn, and to fit in. That tour went well, then they came back and did the secret tour, and all the disasters started. It was decline for Sid in some ways. He was getting really out of it. I was sharing a room with John, and he was beginning to think of other things, and you could always hear Sid smashing up his room, and the screams of girls in Steve and Paul's rooms . . .

Why did Sid smash up his rooms?

He missed Nancy, he wanted to bring her on tour and John said absolutely no way. She came to the Brunel gig, cos John conceded. Sid missed her, he was a very lonely character and he fell for the whole rock'n'roll trip. After people screaming at you, wanting to get at you, and you're dumped in this square room, with just about enough of everything to keep you going.

That's the other thing, if you had a bit of this to smoke, or a bit of speed, it's just enough to get you on the edge, so he used to wreck his room. Then in the morning, McLaren would just turn up with this wad of notes, and he knew the cost of the hotel rooms, and the guy would look at the wad and go, 'Yeah, all right.' It was over, and McLaren would leave it up to him about whether to ring up the papers and say, 'They Wrecked My Hotel!' One thing he always avoided was police public prosecution.

Sid looks kind of lost in a lot of those pictures, like a little kid.

He was never the bad boy, he was like Michael Jackson playing bad. He was a very lonely person, and I felt the crowd destroyed him. It's the sort of paranoia that pop stars get into, they can't face being on stage any more and they end up destroying themselves through drugs.

657

What about the gigs on the SPOTS tour? There was Nottingham, Coventry, Doncaster . . .

That was just before they went to America, and basically nowhere was big enough and nowhere had a big enough PA. It was soul-destroying. More so for John, I think. Steve always had a laugh, Paul being the drummer was a bit in the background, but for John, cos he never had proper microphones, his voice would go after about the second number. It was hurtful for him, and cos he wasn't a trained singer, it hurt him.

He was beginning to make plans. He was really into the space of reggae music, he wasn't really into the thrash. For me, and for them, I think we realised that punk only existed in London. That was maybe five hundred people up and down the King's Road, but you went outside, there were these kids with long hair and Status Quo jackets and god knows what else, and they only did what they heard, or read they were supposed to do in the papers – spit, throw bottles, aiming to hit people.

In London, people threw them to miss, like Russians throwing their vodka glasses, but out of London they were serious. The violence in London came from the audience, a gang thing. Never audience to stage.

What about the final tour around Penzance and all those places, did you go on those?

Yeah. Brunel was the disaster. That was the one Virgin used as their showcase. Branson himself was there, Simon Draper, just about everybody. The PA was about 1K, and the hall holds about two thousand people. When they arrived there was big friction between John and Sid. At that point John was on his own. You'll see from the pictures that by then the Public Image thing had started to creep in, the white jacket, the tie. The Ferry thing, with the riding boots and the leathers.

They walked on stage and there was nothing, John couldn't hear himself, no-one could hear him. It was utter disaster, and that was when they realised that the merchandising was going on. After the soundcheck we left the hall to get some Kentucky, and there were these guys with everything: Pistols badges, T-shirts, everything. John and everybody walked up and just turned the whole thing over, you know? Who's getting the money?

When they came back the whole thing just erupted, a lot of violence from the audience. Towards the band. That was when Sid went into that mode. It was the first time he cut himself. He did it in Penzance, the last one before Brunel. He broke down in Penzance. He went back to the hotel and he couldn't eat anything. It was drugs, but it wasn't just that.

The audience was real close, and expecting a lot. He broke down from that, he was sick all the time, throughout the day. It was at that point that he had his first joint, he never used to smoke before. He threw up straight after it. But it got to him then. It was the worst gig they ever did, as far as I'm concerned. It was one number then literally about twenty minutes before the next one, one of those.

Wobble turned up at Penzance as well, didn't he? Wasn't that the first time he'd appeared for a while?

Yeah, and that was when everybody realised something was going down, cos John was being really friendly towards him. It was the beginning of the end, and the start of something new. After Brunel they went to America, and I didn't want to go. When John came back he asked me if I wanted to continue and I said, 'Yeah, of course.' That was when PiL started.

Can you remember anything about their mood when they were going to the States? Were they looking forward to it?

I don't think John was. I think unlike the others, John knew rock-'n'roll, he'd studied it. America had always been the killer of bands, one way or the other, unless you've got something happening out there to go and tour America. John knew it wasn't going to happen, and whatever, he wanted to come out shining.

Did you go with John to Jamaica?

Yeah, it was me who took him out there. When he came back from the States he was talking about wanting to go off somewhere, and I suggested Jamaica, and John talked to Branson about it, and Branson asked me to go with him. It was to get John's head together again, basically. A series of things happened out there. Devo were happening and Branson was just getting into reggae music, and John and I became advisers to Branson about reggae.

Did you sign anybody?

Yeah, we signed loads! U-Roy, whoever had the best smoke really! Branson had this briefcase full of money and he'd be saying, 'What do you think, guys?', and we'd be going, 'Yeah, sign him!' We stayed out for about a month.

Wasn't somebody from Glitterbest out there trying to take pictures?

Yeah, Boogie turned up, hiding behind bushes, everywhere we went; we'd see trees rustling across the way, and this lens poking out. We threw him in the pool one day with his camera.

PiL took a long time to put together. What was the idea behind it?

We had a series of meetings. Originally I was going to be the bass player. Anyway there was this audition, and all these people, and when it came to the bass, me and Wobble had this big fight, throwing chairs around, and in the end I said, 'Sod it, you be the bass player.' Levene was on the scene, he'd played with The Clash and he wheedled his way in as the guitarist, then John said he'd found this Canadian guy who was a bit weird, and he was the drummer, and basically John spoke about the name, Public Image Ltd.

At this point I'd started to put concepts together, and that's when my involvement came in. I was closer to John in his confidence, and I suggested to make it like a pill. It was for Europe, I'd break everything down to initials and it was like aspirin. Then on the sleeve, he said, 'Why don't we go to the opposite, I'm fed up with all this punk thing. Let's wear sharp suits.'

There was this black guy called Kenny in the King's Road, he did these zoot suits, so he was getting into all that. So I said, 'Why not make it glamorous.' Hence that sleeve. John was *L'uomo Vogue*, Wobble was *Time*, Keith was *Mad*, and the drummer Jim was *Him*, the gay magazine. Basically using the logos, and photographing them in a way that would fit. That whole concept spawned everything like Spandau Ballet that came after.

Derek Jarman

Writer and director of Jubilee, *shot on location in London during 1977 and early 1978. Artist and independent film-maker, of the previous generation to punk, who took the first film of the Sex Pistols in February 1976. On its release,* Jubilee *was met with poor reviews – including a vicious rant from Vivienne Westwood – but time has revealed its strengths. It remains one of the only visual records of London during high punk.*

I was more a part of the sixties generation with Hockney and Procktor and that gang. It was coincidental that I got involved with Andrew Logan. I was at college with Andrew's brother Peter, I shared a studio with him. In '69 Andrew came to London and eventually moved into my studio at Butler's Wharf. '74 he moved in there. The cross references were reinforced by that.

In what respects was that 'Them' generation different?

They weren't as successful. In a way they were victims of The Look, whereas the sixties generation created *a* look. By that time, dyeing one's hair blond was pretty second-hand, after David Hockney had done it. One had missed out on the sixties in some ways, although I was slightly older and had revolved around it. If you want me to be very rude, I never thought they were anything other than fun people to be with.

So when did you notice something moving on from that, was it Jordan?

I first saw Jordan outside Victoria station in '74 or '75. I didn't know who she was, she was just a very startling image, more than anything I'd ever seen. She was wearing white patent high heels and a very short mini-skirt with a plastic, almost see-through front, and a T-shirt, and a beehivish hairstyle. Very blonde. I think it was Egyptian make-up at the time, and she looked stunning.

When we did *Sebastiane* in the autumn of '75 she was down there, and she didn't make the differentiation between generations that the musicians or Malcolm or Vivienne did. Malcolm was Fagin, always the con man of the first order. He would be out with the people, and then denouncing them for fun in the press, and no-one really cared. I don't think anyone felt it was personal, they realised it was part of the ploy.

But the genesis of *Jubilee* was originally a Super 8 film with Jordan. It was to do with Jordan and whatever she wanted to make, but it grew in the course of early '77, and it was Jordan who brought in the punk element, because we wanted musicians involved. I had started collecting fanzines and things, people had started selling them down at the corner of the King's Road in the market there, and it got amalgamated with writing the script. Jordan specifically brought in Adam Ant, who she was working with.

What could be seen as a rift between two generations didn't occur with Jordan. I don't think she felt it. There was a continuity. The interesting thing was, Johnny would be very rude to me when I went out, or Vivienne would make a T-shirt, but it was almost a compliment. It was differentiation in the marketplace.

Did you ever see the Sex Pistols play?

Only once, at Andrew Logan's studio. I remember Jordan coming to ask me to bring my camera up, cos the band was playing. I didn't know who they were at that stage, I don't think any of us did. I went up and they were on the stage Andrew had constructed for *Sebastiane*, so it had all the marble up, and all the remains of the set. Obviously I can't remember what they were singing because it was all completely new, and it was a high-energy racket.

There were about ten or fifteen people there, and Jordan and Vivienne in the front row were egging them on and gobbing at them and pretending to have battles with them, and Johnny turning his back and singing mostly to the wall, rather than to us. I remember having to be careful with the camera even with that small number of people there, cos it was all over the place. Jordan was rushing around wrestling with people. It all happened late one afternoon.

As far as I was concerned, Jordan was the original. Without Jordan the shop wouldn't have worked. She was the original Sex Pistol. Everyone else came in and saw Jordan dressed up, and the attitude, and it took off from there. She was the Godfather, the Godmother if you like. And yet she was the one out of all of them who never capitalised on her situation, really, she fulfilled the whole philosophy, of damn-you, and she let it die at the moment in her life when it was dead.

My connection with it all was very peripheral, but once *Jubilee* started it became less so, because it created a focus for about four or five weeks. Jordan actually helped and collaborated a lot with it, not just with bringing people along. I'd seen Adam [Ant] on the street, and I mentioned I'd seen this lad with 'FUCK' written on his back, which I thought was written on with eyeliner, but Jordan told me she'd actually carved it in with a razorblade. So he came along, and gradually one person introduced another.

The Banshees came along, and we did videos of all of these bands, and I don't know where they all went. We filmed The Slits, the Banshees, Adam, Chelsea and Wayne County. I knew Gene [October] already, cos he'd been around the gay clubs for years, and he transformed, he'd always wanted to do something, and he felt he could fit in here. I don't think the others would think of him as an originator, they thought of him as a bandwagon-jumper.

Everyone was summed up in *Jubilee*; the moguls really were still in control and it was never really going to upset anyone, and people who thought it would were under an illusion. The other problem about such a revolution is that it's very difficult to carry it through with such negativity. In order to carry out a revolution, people have to agree about something. There wasn't that spine there, so it was an art movement, relating to other art movements of the century, finding its sources in dada and things like that.

You obviously seemed to be saying that punk was all about England. You made a film about England. Why did you think that?

I just liked the energy of the whole thing, and whether it was misdirected wasn't worrying me. It was suddenly being critical about things that everyone was being critical about. When Johnny got up and sang 'God Save the Queen', that conversation could go on at any bourgeois dinner party, let's face it. The same sentiment, but here was someone

663

singing it, up front. It was funny to see those people scandalised.

That was where I parted company with a lot of my friends who thought they were completely mad and tasteless and ridiculous. I just felt that a lot of those people actually think the same way as these punks, underneath, but are not voicing it in any way. Obviously there has been some sort of protest running through my whole life, against my bourgeois background, against the way homosexuals are treated, and so forth, and seeing people protesting about these things, one felt . . . kinship.

On the other hand, I could see that some of the things they said they were doing, they certainly weren't. I mean, the destruction of a record company is very minor. Had they even managed to physically destroy EMI, it wouldn't have made any difference to the world whatsoever, because EMI is of no consequence compared with the KGB or the CIA. It was a storm in a teacup. On the other hand, they were the nearest enemy to hand. I don't know how they would have dealt with the KGB . . .

You have to have that ridiculous sense of possibility, otherwise nobody does anything.

It livened everything up every day, apart from anything else. There were mad stories in the press every day, and it was fun to see that. The boat trip down the Thames, things like this. It was the last time that youth seemed to get it right; wherever they were going to end up, it seemed that everyone should at some point in their life go through this disenchantment with what is received.

Did you feel that it was specifically English?

Oh yes, all those Union Jacks and things. It was worrying in that sense, because dada leads to Weimar, and that sort of anarchy, which leads to the repression – and I put this into *Jubilee*, because I thought it was rather unfocused. It was a lot of understandable and very correct disgust with everything around, but it isn't focused, and in its own funny way, it did end in repression, with Margaret Thatcher's England.

Jubilee told that parable, and at the time it was complete fantasy, based on supposition, and in time it came true. Indeed, everyone had signed up, particularly the next generation like Adam, who became an old-fashioned pop star. They all signed up in one way or another, so Adam's role in that film becomes quite poignant in an odd sort of way . . .

That laugh he gives on the rooftop . . .

That was Adam's reaction to my very pedantic and perhaps rather ridiculous writing. He was genuinely laughing at the thing, a truism about the concrete towers and things. But afterwards, I think people did become more aware of the trap in the concrete tower blocks then; but later it became a central issue, they started to blow them up. Odd things come true from *Jubilee*, like the church becoming the night-club, which was the Limelight.

So it was a prophetic time, a time of heightened sensibilities?

I think *Jubilee* set out to be prophetic in its own way, to take that course, which was at odds with Vivienne and her side of punk, who were being very down to earth about everyday things, whereas I was intellectualising and moving it into another area. After all, I didn't have the sexual or economic problems of being eighteen or nineteen.

Would those sexual and economic problems have been different from any other time?

No, they're the same problems but they change their form, and either it tries to collaborate in order to get itself out of the situation, as it seems to be doing now, or goes into revolt, and punk was the last time they did. The alternatives sweep backwards and forwards in a strange way – the next generation went out of their way to join Mrs Thatcher's economics.

Did you see English archetypes in punk?

There was a lot of pantomime, with Jordan, which has been a very important element in English art.

What about Dickens?

I think the Dickens was slightly invented, by Malcolm, for the *Rock-'n'roll Swindle*. That recycling of the past had already begun in the sixties with the Aubrey Beardsley stuff. There was nothing new, doing pirates, but one interesting area was the concentration on polymorphous perversity, the sexuality of the clothes. I don't think that had happened before. You could buy those things in sex shops but people didn't wear them on the streets.

You think that's what caused the reaction, that it touched a raw nerve in England?

Yes, I think that's where the raw nerve was. Sex really gets the English going, and you couple it with people in bondage gear, singing about the royal family, and you've got it, haven't you? The royal family is a great symbol of bondage, because they are completely trapped. You cannot think of any individuals who are more in bondage to the past. All those straps and chains are symbolic, and it's all very interesting.

A lot of the lyrics in punk are trying to get to the unconscious . . .

Oh yes, if art is important, then punk is important. I see punk as art, as simply as that. It was socially engaged, and very naive sometimes, but deliberately so. I can't believe that the people who wrote the fanzines weren't deliberately misspelling – they were intelligent people who were doing this. It was like Edward Lear, in a sense. I saw a continuity in it, and it was very exciting. But I wasn't eighteen, so I didn't go out to punk venues; I would have been completely out of place in them.

Do you think the England of the time was decaying?

Yes, obviously decaying. The whole Docklands region was derelict. It's hard to remember how you really felt when these people were just the boy you saw walking down the street, like Adam. I thought he had a good face, so we put him in as a sort of hero figure. A lot of the people became household names, for a little while. Anyone looking at *Jubilee* now would probably think I got the Famous Adam Ant, and the Famous Toyah – so oddly enough, *Jubilee* now has a cast.

Barbara Harwood

Sex Pistols' driver for the SPOTS tour and Glitterbest associate during 1978 and '79; she worked with Jamie Reid on the book history of the Sex Pistols that the company was hoping to publish with the Great Rock'n'Roll Swindle film. When I interviewed her in her then home in Kilburn, North London, she was working as a homeopathic therapist, an occupation which coloured her memories.

I suppose when I was in my teens I knew that things weren't how I wanted them – socially, generally, the whole culture – but I didn't have much idea of how I wanted it. So I wanted to break out of that, and there was an energy that was breaking away, being rebellious against that. That was the initial thing, the innovative impulse, away from the status quo.

I had a lot of internal conflict, the hippy thing was breaking away from that, but it didn't have much energy. It had vision and ideals, but there seemed to be no reality in it. It was very intangible, cloud-cuckoo-land. There was a whole lot of stuff that was denied and shut down. It was all twee. There was a denial of the more instinctual, darker side of people. The only time it was around during the hippy thing was with the Yippies and the Black Power.

Darker isn't pejorative, it refers to the more instinctual sides of ourselves. In psychology, and astrology, the dark indicates the shadow self. People were focusing on the light and bright and loving side, and there was a whole part of me that wasn't being expressed in that, and by the time the hippies became fashionable, by about 1968, and it went into the general culture at large, everybody was wearing their hair long, and you had people who were weekend hippies; by that time I'd lost interest in it.

That's when I started getting into esoteric things, magick and meditation and things like that, started working on myself. Then I went

667

off to the country for a break, had kids there, and did the country thing – sawing logs and drawing water from the well, having no electricity – but coming back to London in 1974, and in 1975 I was trying to find somewhere to live. That's when I was living in the King's Road.

Did you ever go to the shop?

Yes, but not a lot. At that stage it was daunting. That was when it was SEX, it had those big pink plastic letters, and the window, you couldn't see in, they had the rubber wear in the window. I used to go past almost daily, I only lived two streets away. I knew something interesting was happening, but I was on the outskirts, it was voyeuristic at that stage. Then I guess in 1976 I really started to go out a lot, and feel more involved.

Were you working at the time?

No, I wasn't. I was living on social security. It didn't cost anything to go out; wherever we went, we were on the door, so we'd go down to the Roxy and Andy Czezowski would just let us in, and if we went to Louise's we just went in. There were always a lot of people around.

What would you have been wearing at that point?

When I was first around I had very long hair, I could sit on it. I used to back-comb it right out, so it was like a bush, and it was dyed red. Then I decided to cut it. Cutting it was really amazing, it was symbolic. I gathered it all up on the top of my head and hacked away at it. It was all over the place. Then a friend of mine called Derek cut it, and I had it black and short. A couple of people cracked that I looked like Keith Richards.

So you were more interested in the scene, the whole lifestyle.

Yeah. It was a mix, I guess. I was around with The Heartbreakers a lot, but the music was an excuse to have a lot of energy moving around, having a good time. The social occasion of it, people getting together. I spent quite a bit of time with them. The gig and the music was a small part of it. Wherever you'd been, you'd end up going back to somebody's place.

668

There was Leee Black Childers and Gail Higgins in Islington, I was round there most nights at some point. They were great. We used to have hair-dying sessions, everybody used to get round a table and we used to do each other's hair. Gail has loads of photos. She used to take her camera everywhere.

So you were enjoying the social aspect?

That's how it was to begin with. It was wild, we had a lot of fun. There was a strong closeness between people, we were living in each other's pockets at that time, and the other thing was that there weren't a lot of people with transport, and I had my van. I used to drive people around a lot. When Siouxsie was getting her band together, she'd say, we're doing a rehearsal at such a place, can you collect our speakers and take them over there for us.

It was fun to do things like that. That became part of the way I interacted with people. I'd take them to gigs. I'd take people from one party to another, one club to the next. It was an old Austin Cambridge van. The night of the boat trip, The Ramones had a party down the King's Road, and I got pulled. I had a van full of people coming away from Country Cousins. I had The Heartbreakers and Paul Simonon and they wanted to breathalyse me.

As I was being breathalysed, I heard the van doors open at the back, and I could hear people creeping out of the back of the van and walking off down the road. A mass escape, in case the police decided to get curious. I got back in the van and it was only half occupied. I'd lost half a dozen people. I failed the breath test but they let me go. It was the night of the Jubilee, so . . . that was a shock.

After that I got the Mercedes van. Sometimes people would hire me a van, like when I did the tour with the Pistols, the SPOTS tour, we hired a van, and Roadent drove the equipment van and I drove the van for the band.

How did you get involved with that?

A couple of ways. I got friendly with Sid at Louise's. I'd met him originally at the Speakeasy, at one of The Heartbreakers gigs, then when I was down at Louise's he came over and talked to me. We spent some time together. It got so that we would always stop and speak, check out how things were, and we got really friendly. Also I was going out with Roadent, who was roadying for The Clash.

I was living in a big house in Alperton, on the way out to Harrow from London, so all the kids who lived out that way, like Marco and The Models, instead of going home, they used to stop at my place. Then Steve Strange moved in with me, and people would drop in who lived that side of town. Sometimes if we didn't have transport we used to hitch along the Westway.

Hitching with Steve was amazing. He was great. He used to flirt with the guys who picked us up. If we went out together, we'd sometimes go and cruise up and down outside of The Coleherne. He used to pretend I was his sister. He had such a great line of chat, people used to go out of their way to take us home. We used to have a real good time, being naughty.

There was something childlike about a lot of it?

Yes, wickedness, naughtiness, things you were never allowed to do when you're a kid. Things that one doesn't normally do.

There was a spate where Sebastian Conran would come around almost every day on his motorbike and we'd go into town to gigs and stuff, and because Joe Strummer was living with Sebastian, Joe would come too. Roadent used to come out, and being really friendly with Sid, I hung out with Roadent a lot. When the band came back from Sweden and the S.P.O.T.S tour came up, Roadent left The Clash and went to roadie for the Pistols, and I went with him.

I took the band around with Boogie in one of those twelve-seaters, and Roadent took the lorry for the equipment. No longer everything crammed into a small space, and they went one day ahead.

What was that tour like?

It was strange, out of London. Up till then, everything for me had been mostly in London, and suddenly it was off to these corners of Britain. There wasn't much to do. There was just us, instead of us and all our friends, with places to go and things to do. I was trying to concentrate on the job, while this riot went on in the back, people coming up to pour packets of crisps and peanuts over me. Coca-Cola. In the front, I drove and Sid or Boogie sat up front next to me, with Paul and John and everybody in the back. We'd arrive at the place, plug in and away we'd go. It was quite riotous.

The audiences were starved of anything, and all hell broke out when the band came on. Roadent and I trying to keep control, keeping an eye on Sid, turning his volume down if he was too out of tune. Stuff like that. I used to get down behind his speaker and give him encouragement. 'Come on Sid, get it together!'

Sid and I got arrested in York. That was quite funny. We were doing a gig in Scarborough, and Sid used to get cravings for sweets. He always wanted to eat in the middle of the night. So we'd go out to the van and go looking for something to eat, and the night in Scarborough, we'd all been up in John's room, Dennis Morris had joined us by then, and Sid wanted something to eat. Boogie and Sid and myself went out around the town. Boogie was driving.

We found a shop with some pies, but we started edging out of the town, and it was, 'Let's go out on the moors.' There were shops getting their newspapers in the early morning and we decided to drive to York across the moors, and suddenly on the outskirts of York we were pulled by the Old Bill, and they took us in for questioning, the three of us, and of course we had some drugs in the van, so Sid and I had to eat them all.

We looked strange, not at all what you'd expect to find driving across the moors at that time. When they got us in there, they put us in different cells for questioning. We were there for hours. I used to live in York, so I told them all about my school!

Suddenly this big policeman came in and said, 'You know we've got one of the Sex Pistols here, don't you?' So then they started pumping us about which Sex Pistol it was they had, and I wouldn't tell them.

But finally they decided to let us go, and we met up downstairs and drove back to Scarborough, and the first thing Sid wants is ice cream. So we got some ice cream and went back to the hotel. That's when I got into an argument with Roadent, cos he got jealous about the fact that Sid and I had been having a scene. That got a bit edgy around Scarborough. It got a bit tense.

Had Sid changed?

He got tougher, like the image. Malcolm used to say that Sid was a natural talent. He had that childlike rebelliousness, but he was really soft underneath, a real sweetheart. But there was this sex and drugs and rock'n'roll image, and I didn't know which was in charge with him sometimes.

When we were in Plymouth I got a sense that the image was in charge of him, when he got quite upset in the hotel, in a real mess, and he wanted me to go away with him for a bit, and for me to help him get himself together. He was asking me about homeopathy, why I was doing what I was doing, why I was with the band. Why I didn't take him away and sort him out. I was rather flippant about it, thinking that that wasn't what the band needed. The band needed Sid as he was.

It was quite a weird conflict, knowing that he needed his image, the whole persona that he had, and that the band depended on it, and here he was suggesting that he wanted to get himself together. It was all so momentary, standing looking over the sea. I didn't take him very seriously, and anyway, I couldn't possibly afford what he was asking me to do, it was more than I could give him. I had kids back in London, I couldn't do that. So he got on with the show.

When we got back to London I dropped Sid off at home, and there was a gig down at Dingwalls. Sid and I went down there and Nancy showed up. Sid got into a fight with Joe Strummer and had a cut over his eye; I had to take him to the Royal Infirmary to get stitched up. I suppose I was operative in getting him and Nancy back together again. I took Nancy with us to the hospital, and Nancy asked him to come with her and Sid said, 'No, I want to stay with Barbara', and I said, 'No, I think you should go with Nancy.'

Had you had enough?

I don't know what it was. Anyway, they got back together again. At Christmas Eve, Malcolm rang me and asked me to help organise the Christmas party at Huddersfield. So I went down to Virgin, just after their Christmas party, and we loaded on the big Christmas tree from their entrance hall, filled up my van with flags and banners, and I drove up to Huddersfield with it and decorated the hall. It was a benefit for the firemen up there.

So there were two gigs. There was one in the afternoon for all the firemen's kids, then one at night. It was a really good party. Everybody was kids that afternoon. It was being young and naughty and taking it to the streets. Things you'd never be allowed to do, and being very tough and aggressive with it. It was all the things I'd wanted to do, after all the anger and upset that I'd never expressed when I was a kid. I felt like a strong person, for possibly the first time I felt in charge of my own life.

I was driving The Slits around all this time, too. That was great, being around an all-girl band. There was the four of them, and me and Nora. Six women, aged between fourteen and however old Nora was. That was schoolgirl stuff. It used to get quite bitchy. Viv Albertine and I had this really stupid confrontation, over something like I got the room with the bath, and they were the band.

How did all this stuff interact with the outside world?

I don't know how much I saw the outside world. My circuit was quite small. I was very much relating to others in that group. A lot of it was the sensationalism, the impact we were having, that was the key thing for me. Then there was the letters, from nutters in the newspaper. Watching Malcolm and Jamie organise and manipulate a piece of media coverage. It was inspiring.

Did they work well together?

Yeah, they did. But watching the way they dealt with the outside world, what they targeted, their political intention . . . that was the next phase, after the naughtiness, the riotous element, then I got more of how the world was responding. Before, it had been sensation; now it became more targeted. Once I got around Glitterbest, and saw the amount of organisation and intention around Malcolm's part, and Jamie's part . . . That was just before the band split up.

Late '77 I started being round the office a lot, cos Malcolm and The Slits were thinking about working together, so I started being in the office. I'd been doing things with The Slits and they were negotiating with Malcolm for him to become their manager, so I was in the office a lot, seeing what was going on. I got friendly with Sophie and Jamie.

Was it Sid's death that gave you the impetus to get back into homeopathy, or had you already had that?

No, that gave me the impetus to stay with it, Sid had triggered it off. I prescribed people, here and there, I'd been dabbling about with it, but I had never dreamed of practising. I had been interested in it from a philosophical point of view, but I did know enough to prescribe remedies on occasion, so a day came when I decided to do it.

I can't remember what decided me. I imagine Jamie must have had some influence in the decision, I would have talked to him about it. Sid had had something to do with it. So 19th September 1978 I started doing the classes. At that time, Jamie and I were working in Dryden Chambers. There had been the Ronnie Biggs single, and the film was going on.

Did you ever see any shooting scripts?

Julien and Malcolm would be together a lot, we'd all go out and eat, and they'd go on about what they were going to do next day and next week. They'd talk over who was going to be involved, all that sort of stuff. Then there was the phone call saying that Nancy was dead, then Sid was in jail, and everything had to stop.

Malcolm flew to the States, and then Malcolm and Richard spent a lot of time together trying to get him out on bail, and I was going to go to New York and be there when Sid came out, and I was getting everything organized, and the same day I got back to the office and Sid's mum rang to say that she was sitting in Sid's room, and he was dead, and what should she do?

The call came into the office. That was on the Friday afternoon, I think. We went and got drunk, Malcolm and Jamie and I went to the French pub and got maudlin, blaming ourselves. I blamed myself. Each of us blaming ourselves and telling each other we weren't to blame. Oh, it's not your fault. What could we have done that would have made any difference, stuff like that.

The next morning I went to college, and it was really sinking in, all the newspapers were full of it. Placards on the street about Sid being dead. I walked into college and I'd been crying all night, in a terrible state. I cried all weekend, and I decided that I was going to stay with the course. Over that weekend, all my conversations with Sid came back.

You have conversations with people and at the time they don't necessarily sink in, but something happens like that, and it all came back, the night that Sid and I talked about it in Plymouth. If I'd got the homeopathy together before, when Sid asked me for help, I would have been useful to him. There were times when we were on tour that he wasn't out of my sight for a minute over twenty-four, forty-eight hours. That was the only way I could envisage being of any help. Like a mother or something.

But if I'd been practising homeopathy, I could have had a constructive way of helping him access his own resources. One of the reasons Sid's quite important for me in my life still is in my resolve to help people use their own resources, to accept being in charge of their lives, and to have a system of healing where the focus and intention of the support was to do yourself out of a job. Any good healer, the main motivation is to make yourself useless in the end.

Is there any one particular remedy that you associate with that period?

From a homeopathic point of view there was a lot of syphilitic miasm. That has a lot to do with self-destruction on one hand, but also it has to do with a self-destructive creativity. For example, self-destruction comes in many forms, but if you're fanatical and obsessive and highly creative, you often tend to be self-destructive. Your creative drives and bents don't leave room for themselves. You see that with Van Gogh lopping his ears off.

On the other hand, there's this real charge, a lot of the classic stuff that's associated with punk, the self-mutilation, the wearing of black, the physiology, the thin, pale people, the angular people. One thinks of John and his teeth, rotten teeth, syphilitic manifestation as well. A lot of the world's major geniuses have been syphilitic miasm.

CHAPTER ELEVEN

Sid Vicious

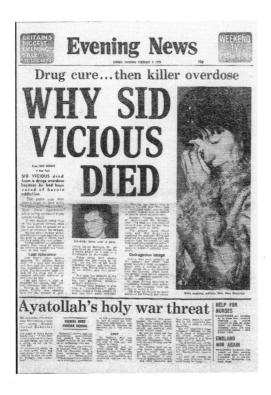

London's *Evening News*, 3 February 1979

The first stage of the Sex Pistols saga ended in February 1979 with John Lydon's court case against Glitterbest, and Sid Vicious' death in New York.

After John Lydon left in January 1978, the Sex Pistols were a group in name alone, and the circumstances surrounding the three remaining musicians and their management company became increasingly chaotic. While Malcolm McLaren attempted to finish The Great Rock'n'Roll Swindle, *Steve Jones and Paul Cook continued recording new material and overdubbing old Sex Pistols tracks for the soundtrack album. Sid Vicious left the UK in August 1978, settling into a twilight Manhattan existence with Nancy Spungen that was dominated by drugs: heroin and methadone in particular.*

After Nancy Spungen died in still unexplained circumstances at the Chelsea Hotel in October 1978, Sid Vicious was in and out of custody. When he was released on bail in February 1979, his mother, Anne Beverley, organised a party for him. She also arranged for dealers to come by with a batch of heroin for her son: it was so strong that it killed him.

Joe Stevens

Legendary photographer, friend of John Lydon, witness to the Sex Pistols' break-up and Sid Vicious' last days in New York. American, moved to London in the early seventies, where he took photos for the underground press and the NME *under the name of Captain Snaps; took many excellent early shots of the Sex Pistols in 1976. Moved back to New York in early 1977. Interviewed in a car weaving through New York's Lower East Side, before we settled in a cafe.*

By the time you left, what did you think of the way the Pistols were going?

They did that Anarchy tour, and I decided to stay off it. I hadn't done anything for the *NME* for a while. Pennie Smith did it, and then Chalkie Davies, and both of them became pals with The Clash. Chalkie took his best pictures of The Clash, so it helped their careers a lot. And I got to move to the States. They had to stay in their own fucking country and do it.

I was never a rock photographer in the States, I was a political photographer, covering street warfare. Now I had a chance to come back to America – they had to take me, I didn't have to use any pseudonyms, and I brought the whole file system with me, the two filing cabinets. I didn't see any point in running punk into the ground. If I was in America, it would come this way. And it sure did.

What was the American attitude to Sex Pistols? They must have been very puzzled.

You know, when there's another 'British invasion' happening? Initially, no-one really knows what it is. At that time, there weren't any videos, so it went on forever, people wondering what the hell it was. I ran into some people in 1980 who thought the Sex Pistols were some kind of vibrator.

679

So your next contact with the band was going on the American tour?

Yeah. The *NME* called me and said, 'The Pistols are touring, how would you like to go on it?' They gave me $167 to do an eleven-day tour, and all the flights. I missed the first one. This sounds like my deposition for the Rotten case. I missed the first gig, which was Atlanta.

If the Pistols had fulfilled all their engagements in America, their first gig would have been in Philadelphia. That didn't happen. Jimmy Carter's administration were having trouble deciding whether they should be given visas. They were given a two-week visa to do eleven dates. That is rare. Luckily, they were aligned with Warner Brothers, and Warners, being all gangsters, pulled some strings.

So, I met them in Memphis, found the hotel. The gig that night involved Sid getting a lot of trouble with his security. He was brought over to detox, and to do gigs, and we saw the man, Sid Vicious, walking around, cold turkey, in the lobby. The rest of us are having a nice gin and tonic, and sandwiches . . .

What sort of a state was the band in? Had they changed?

Yeah, they weren't speaking to each other. Cook and Jones hung out together, they'd go bowling. Rotten would have nothing to do with McLaren. Sophie showed up for that gig. The first thing she said to me, she described them as 'this fucking poxy band'. I began rooming with McLaren. They all had twin rooms, and his other bed was going unused.

What I did next was go to the British press – the *Sun*, the *Mirror*, the *Evening Standard* – and I said, 'How would you like a daily briefing, from the inside?', because McLaren didn't want the British press to know where the gig was. He told Warners, don't give them anything. That was the idea, to wind them up. They're used to this, we've been doing it in England, it's like a circus. They'll find the gig, they'll buy their own tickets. No comp tickets for the press.

I was an exception, cos I was in the inner circle. So I'd give press briefings in the lobbies of the hotels. 'This is what happened last night: Sid almost fell out of the window, Rotten is spitting up this big green stuff, McLaren's got a bad cold, Sophie's threatening to go back to London', blah blah. 'McLaren was on the phone to the lawyers for six hours last night, keeping me awake, anything else you

680

want to know?' They'd say, 'Yeah, where's the fucking gig tonight, you cunt?' And I'd whisper, 'It's in a bowling alley', wherever . . . the gigs were not announced to the press. The kids would find them, and sell it out.

What were the gigs like?

Well, one of them was the second best rock'n'roll show I'd ever seen in my life. San Antonio. It had everything. It had violence, great music, the band was storming, even with Sid screwing up. Rotten was on top form, his voice had cleared out. Annie Leibovitz, who was doing a cover story for *Rolling Stone* – Charles Young was doing the whole tour – she had everything stolen from her bag at that gig, including all the shots from the night before. Lenses . . .

I thought I was being fondled by some girl behind me. Turned out it wasn't a girl at all, it was a little guy, stealing my lenses. I couldn't move, you know? I'm sure you've seen the photographs. Beer cans flying. At the end of the gig, the beer cans on the stage were about three feet deep. Unbelievable gig. That was the one where Sid clunked a kid over the head with a guitar, then went after him again. The security guys finally grabbed him . . .

Why? Was the kid taunting him?

Yeah. But these weren't punks. We didn't see any punks, the entire tour. Maybe a hundred, the entire tour. These were rednecks and hippies. Just about to get rid of the flared trousers and get a haircut. All that stuff was seconds away. All the Pistols needed to do was leave town and let these kids have a chance to get to a barber's shop.

What about the other gigs?

Tulsa, Oklahoma, in the snow. We walked from the hotel because the cars wouldn't work in the snowstorm. The band, everyone went to this lonely fucking country music hall, pictures on the wall of all these country stars. People outside giving out these flyers . . .

'Repent of your sins'?

Yeah. That was a good gig, but San Antonio was really great. There were two in Texas. I think the other was Dallas. In Dallas there were

681

these real punk girls from San Francisco, Haight-Ashbury. Six of them had jammed themselves into a VW, driven all the way to Dallas to see the Sex Pistols, and they wanted to meet Sid. They found Sid after the gig. The thing was, they'd do a gig, go backstage, throw their guitars down, and then they'd go out and have a beer with the audience. They always did that. Until the end.

Did they seem disparate to you, or did they still put on a show as a band?

Well, I never saw Sid play with the Pistols in England, but yes, Sid had his pocket of the stage. He would steal the limelight from Rotten. Sid had his little area where he would cavort, throw things around, knock over amplifiers, and Rotten would have his area.

What was the last show like, in San Francisco?

One thing that was pretty accurate in the movie, they were stiff, they were boring, they were unhappy and unhealthy, all of them had terrible colds. I was sort of running the whole show. McLaren was half dead from sniffles, a really bad head-cold. They had to bring in an acupuncturist to relieve the congestion for Steve Jones, I have pictures of him lying there with wires in his face. And it worked.

They were a typical British punk rock band on tour, they were all unhealthy, including the manager. I was the guy who called Ronnie Biggs in Rio, spoke to him – if we were going to go down there, where would we stay – and he offered to call Philips, which was their label down there, and get them to call me back, and put them up in a hotel. And if they put you in the right hotel, you could play there, there's a lobby and a club. He cooked all of that up and we were gone.

So Malcolm, Sophie and Boogie were the Glitterbest team. What happened with the travel arrangements? Didn't Steve and Paul go their own way? And Sid and John on the bus most of the time?

There was a problem. In order to keep Sid off smack, they certainly couldn't put him on a plane. Also to keep him away from drug dealers they had Warner Brothers security, Noel Monk [later to be manager of Van Halen], who thought the Pistols were shit. They were carrying guns. To protect Sid from himself.

682

You couldn't take guns on a plane, so the logistics were, there would be a coach for travelling between, say, Tulsa and San Antonio, when you could actually do it and arrive on time, and on the coach you would have these chaps with guns – and that would take care of that problem.

They actually roughed Sid around, they didn't take any shit from him at all. It didn't matter to them, they were getting paid to take care of him. If he tried to get out of his bunk, they'd push him back in. It started getting rough; they'd catch him stealing things, going through people's luggage, they'd beat him up, but not badly enough that he couldn't work.

What was Lydon like in all that?

Just being in a state of misery. His first time in America, on a coach with these gun-toting hippies, and Sid.

Who by this stage he wasn't getting along with at all, because of the junk.

No. I set foot on that coach only when it was outside the gig, I was never out in the desert on that coach. Bob Gruen didn't have the money for a flight, on one leg of the tour, and he was on the coach, sleeping in a bunk. He wakes up and sees Sid removing his boots, and Sid holds a knife to his throat and says, 'I'm keeping these, right, Bobby?' And Bob goes, 'Yup, you're keeping them.' Of course later, when Sid was asleep, he tried to steal them back, but it didn't work. Sid died with Bobby Gruen's boots on.

The other touring party flew. Me, McLaren, Sophie, the British press, the *Rolling Stone* crew – and they were great cos they had credit cards. McLaren I don't think to this day has a credit card. He doesn't think that way. He's not a bread-head, not really.

Wasn't there a journalist from *Punk* magazine, too?

John Holmstrom, Roberta Bayley and Legs McNeil. But not for all the gigs.

What was Tom Forcade doing on the tour?

He was quite the visionary, Mr Forcade. He thought it would be great to have a punk rock movie, a feature about the Sex Pistols, so he went to Warner Brothers. You know that stuff in *DOA* with Bob Regehr, the Warner Brothers executive on the phone? That's all documented, it's real stuff, he's slagging off the Pistols, and he doesn't know that Lech Kowalski's cameras are shooting for a Sex Pistols movie. He isn't connected to punk rock.

So when the Forcade people actually put their cards on the table and said, 'We want to make a movie with the Sex Pistols', Warner Brothers thought amongst themselves, decided it was not a bad idea, but with Sid all fucked-up on smack, this was the wrong tour. Let's do it next time, when Sid is all nice and healthy. So they did nothing but bust the chops of the Kowalski film crew, including breaking their lenses.

So I never had a chance to chat with any of that film crew at all. I'd see them in the hallway, sneaking around, and they got some good kamikaze movie-making done. They paid to get into the hall, they'd buy tickets from kids, and Forcade was coming up with all the money. If they needed to buy rolls of film, they went to him. He didn't come to the gigs, he'd stay in a hotel and run the whole machine from there. We didn't know about this until later.

The Sex Pistols had broken up, we're back in my apartment, a big blizzard is covering New York, and Forcade lived round the corner, gets my number. The *New York Post* printed this article, picked up from the *Sun-Sentinel*: 'The Sex Pistols broke up in San Francisco the other night. Sid Vicious OD'd and he's in a hospital in Queens. Malcolm McLaren doesn't want to speak to the press. Warner Brothers in New York wants nothing to do with the whole case. Johnny Rotten is staying in the apartment of his friend Joe Stevens in New York.'

So all of a sudden, my apartment becomes real popular with the press. I was doing press briefings on the steps. So now Rotten is out of a job, two days early, fired from the Pistols . . .

Let's go through the events, through the split . . .

They had to do eleven gigs in two weeks in the States. The next gig booked was in Stockholm. It would have given them about five days to rest up after flying back from San Francisco. McLaren gets this brainstorm, why don't we go to Rio and see Ronnie Biggs? I was the only one in the touring party who had ever been to Rio, so that qualified me for a ticket. So when they went to Bob Regehr, they got eight first-class round-trip tickets. I still have my ticket, San Francisco to Rio, Rio to New York.

One of the riders in Rotten's contract was that Warners had to get them into the country to do their shows, and get them out to their chosen destination. Their tickets said Rio, Stockholm, London, and they were back where they'd started out, end of contractual obligations. So I'm on the phone, cooking up McLaren's business. Meanwhile, Rotten is not staying at the hotel, nor is Sid. They wouldn't let Sid in, anyway, so they didn't even try. Warners said they'd put him in another hotel, they were staying in San José.

Rotten wasn't told anything about Rio. He rings McLaren's room and he gets me. McLaren is snoring. He had an idea he was being kept in the dark, about everything, and I broke the news to him. I said, the plan is, you do Winterland, then the next day we all take a 6 or 7 a.m. flight to Rio, stop off at Mexico City and do some gigs down there, hang out with Ronnie Biggs, the Great Train Robber. He said, 'Whaat? They expect me to sit in a first-class compartment with Sid Vicious, to go and fuck around with this guy who beat someone almost to death with a club?'

So that was the end of that. He didn't want to co-operate with that movie, *Who Killed Bambi?*, he had nothing to do with that film. It was just more icing on the cake, he was fed up. McLaren didn't want to be a manager any more, it was too many hassles. He didn't want to worry about it, he was losing interest. He should have done something, he couldn't take it the full step, but I'm glad he did what he did.

This conversation was before the gig at Winterland?

Yeah. We had a couple of days prior, cos some of them had to drive in from Texas. Sid meanwhile had found the little girls, and they're turning him on to some San Francisco smack. The Warner Brothers people know it's the last gig, they're starting to give Sid some leeway. Sid was well out of it. That was the only gig he did on smack.

So John wants to know about the gig, what time is it, why are we working for this hippy promoter Bill Graham, who would be the support act? In the end it was The Avengers. They were okay, but they were not what I wanted – something faster, something crazier,

685

give them something to look at. As it turned out, The Avengers were on. They were actually Bill Graham's choice.

So Rotten says, 'What's going on?', and I tell him the plan. 'I'm not going', he says. 'I like sushi and I'm not staying in a nice Japanese hotel like the rest of you cunts.' He didn't know where Sid was, there were three hotels. We were in the Miyako, Rotten was in a flea-bag, and Sid was in another one. Actually, I think they let Sid go to Haight-Ashbury and watched over him with those girls.

So I said to John, 'Why don't I talk to McLaren, I think it's a tragedy, I don't think this has to happen. Maybe rather than getting you guys all pissed off, we should cancel this Rio business. But I'm not the manager here, it's not my business.' So I tell McLaren that Rotten wants nothing to do with Rio, nothing to do with Ronnie Biggs. He doesn't think there'll be enough time to do everything and get back to London. McLaren says, 'Well, fuck that cunt.'

They do the gig, it's a disaster, There's a party backstage afterwards, Rotten picks up a girl, brings her back to the San José motel. We've got another day before Rio. Rotten calls again from San José, gets me again. I tell him I have tickets for him and me, a 7 a.m. flight, and that Warner Brothers security were going to come and get him, and pick up Sid, and we'd all meet at San Francisco airport.

It seemed like it was going to happen because Rotten's complaining wasn't having any effect on everyone's plans. The next morning, me and Steve and Sophie and Paul get into a taxi for the airport. We never saw Rotten, McLaren, Boogie or Sid. We saw the flight take off, and we drove back. I've got pictures of Steve and Paul, sleeping in the back. At that point we knew something nasty was about to happen.

Lydon had taken a taxi from the San José hotel. Initially he'd refused to leave his hotel room, wouldn't go to the airport. When he found out where we were staying, he gets into a taxi and shows up on his own at the Miyako. This is the emergence of Johnny Rotten as a man. He's about to be fired from the band, and he's doing things on his own. He's years away from getting his own cheque book, but this is the first time I'd seen him actually take charge.

So, he shows up. McLaren is still crashed out upstairs. McLaren used to spend about two hours a day awake. If there was a gig or something, then he'd go right back to bed again. Which was very weird. Rotten walks into the restaurant, and there's Steve and Cook and me. We're having Japanese food and drinking lots of beers. We'd gone up to Steve's room, smoking joints. What could we do? He didn't show up.

We were sure it wasn't going to be Rotten's fault, it was going to be Sid's fault. They could find Sid dead or something. We hadn't heard yet. The three have a talk. Steve's saying John was stupid, that they should have gone to Rio. Cook was sort of agreeing. So I say, 'Why don't we go up and see McLaren, catch the magic two hours before he goes back to sleep again.' And we went upstairs, and that was the break-up.

They were all in the room together?

Yeah, me too. I lay down on my own bed, everyone scattered about, we ordered some beers. They sensed that the manager wanted nothing to do with it. Cook and Jones were very pro-McLaren, but they saw there was no way to get McLaren going on this any more, he wanted nothing to do with the band, and Steve just said, 'Well, that's it, I'm pissing off.' And that was that.

Was Lydon arguing with Malcolm?

No, I was. I wanted to take them over. I said, 'When Robert Stigwood decided he didn't want to manage the Bee Gees, the Bee Gees went on.' Everyone looked at me and said, 'What are you talking about, the Bee Gees? This is the fucking Sex Pistols! This is a big break-up!' I said, 'Managers are a dime a dozen, you know', and I was wrong.

What did John say to Malcolm?

He said, 'You're a miserable stupid cunt, you've been stitching me up ever since you met me. With the police, with people beating me up, robbing me, calling my house in the middle of the night, annoying me, telling lies about me to the press. And now you want me to sit on a plane with Sid Vicious for hours, you stupid cunt. To talk to some idiot who coshed somebody on a train.'

McLaren said, 'You're turning into another fucking Rod Stewart, we don't need you, go and find some cocaine.' It was bitter. And there's me walking around saying, 'I'll book the guys into Madison

687

Square Garden, two dollars a head, two nights. I know the rental is seventy thousand dollars, I can get it from the mob.' They're looking at me – cos at that point they didn't really know what Madison Square Garden was. And I could have done it.

McLaren's looking at me. At the Garden, in the big room, that's twenty thousand capacity. He says, 'They just did their biggest ever gig; it was 4,700. How are you going to fill twenty thousand?' I said, after this tour, no problem. Fights on the airplane, guns on the bus . . .

How long were they in the room, having this discussion?

Thirty minutes. Then everyone dispersed to the bar, and it was misery for the rest of the evening. Standing on their own, getting pissed. It was awful. That was the worst night of the tour. I was being Henry Kissinger, trying to get them back together. They were my favourite band. They kept me going as a rock'n'roll photographer. I would have stopped.

Where was Sid at this stage?

Haight-Ashbury, bombed out of his head on smack. The next day, Cook and Jones and McLaren went to LA to talk to Regehr and bring back the tickets. Sophie was meant to take Sid back to London. That failed. He OD'd on the plane, turned green and they had to drop him off at Jamaica Hospital, Queens.

Had he taken the smack before he got on the plane?

Yeah. A couple of extra things in case they searched him, he didn't want to have it on him. I don't know exactly what he'd taken, but I think it was smack, and pills.

So, Rotten and I were iglooing around in New York City, while he was in Jamaica Hospital, and I asked for Roberta Bayley. She liked Sid. They only way to visit was like three or four days later, when he was over it. She took care of Sid while he was out there, brought him copies of *Punk* magazine. Rotten was broke, he had about thirty dollars in his pocket.

So everyone split up? Cook and Jones and McLaren and Boogie went down to Rio . . .

After a couple of weeks, I think. They used their tickets from LA.

Rotten was staying at my house, Forcade is round the corner, he calls me. I'm screening calls for the guy, he's just lost the best job he ever had. He's still a young man, he's never been to New York, he's freezing. My apartment's heat's been cut off. We don't have any money cos this lab is suing me. They didn't leave him with any money.

Forcade says, 'I can take care of that right away, I can come around with a shoe-box full of greenbacks; all he has to do is sign a release for whatever we want to use in the movie.' His part of whatever, licensing his appearance. I said, 'I don't know, I'll have to talk to him about it. What kind of money are we talking about?'

He said, 'Well, this is what I want.' He stated what he wanted, and said, 'That is worth fifteen thousand dollars, I'll bring it over.' So I tell John, and John says, 'No fucking way.' He said, 'I don't need that money now, I'll need it at another point.' He was so smart. I wasn't pushing him on, but switch it around, I would have gone for it. The movie came out anyway.

Anyway, we got in the car, and on the radio we hear, 'From Jamaica Queens Hospital, we have an interview with Sid Vicious!' We go up to Spanish Harlem, I have this punk girlfriend, the bass player from The Erasers, pick her up, and we're driving around with Rotten in the back, smoking drugs and drinking beer, listening to Sid doing interviews from the hospital. Amazing. They had yet to play New York.

How long did he stay?

He was snowed in, they couldn't get flights out, so, five days. I said, John, you're a Warner Brothers recording artist. Do you mind if I call my connections at Warner Brothers, they could put us on to bigger people, and then they can send some idiot down with some money. You can pay me back what you owe me, I can cook, we'll have some money for pot.

So I did it, and they stonewalled him, they wouldn't have anything to do with Rotten at all. They didn't know which one they wanted. Which punk, which little dirt-bag.

What was John thinking of doing?

Get back to England, get a band of black guys and do reggae stuff.

What happened to Sid, did you see him that time?

I didn't go out there, no. They stuck him on a plane. I don't know who did that, it must have been someone from Glitterbest. Maybe Sophie stayed. But Roberta said no-one was visiting.

What happened next, Sid playing in New York?

Sid and Nancy came to New York, to play with Mick Jones at Max's. Awful. A whole bunch of them were extremely drowsy. They were out of tune, Jerry Nolan could hardly hit the drums. They'd done a whole big bag, I think, upstairs.

And of course Nancy was alienating all the press. All the press that were actually in bands, like Lenny Kaye, all the people who weren't press who were big shots – all of a sudden, this little broad is giving them shit at the top of the staircase. She's running the door that night. It was like trying to get into the White House.

I'm not sure of the chronology, cos I wasn't hanging out with them, but the first time I'd seen Sid Vicious in New York City was on stage at Max's, and it was the first time I'd seen Nancy.

McLaren came to New York – this is before anybody died – RCA London had paid for him to come over, and the plan was to go meet the board of directors at RCA Victor New York and tell them how much you'd like to run RCA Victor London. So he flew over, calls me as soon as he checks in, says, 'I don't like hotels, I like motels. I like your flat.' I'm going, 'Who is this?' I think he'd stayed there once. So I said, 'Check out, come and stay on my couch.'

We go to breakfast, and I ask him what he's doing, tell him his clients are staying in the Chelsea. 'I don't want anything to do with Sid,' he says, 'is he still with that awful woman?' I said, 'Yeah, we should go up and visit, he is your client.' He goes, 'Fuck those people.' That was his attitude before Sid killed anyone. McLaren devoted himself to it, as soon as that happened.

So, he comes to the flat, and the next day he gets all decked out in his red plaid suit, with straps holding the knees together, fixes his hair real nice, real pretty. Cash from Chaos T-shirt on, goes up to RCA Victor, looking for the job. Doesn't get it. He comes back downtown, I said to him, 'What happened?' Well, they asked what he would do with RCA Victor in London. He said he wanted to get all the Elvis Presley shit out, that's paying the rent. Said he wasn't sure about that cunt Dolly Parton, with those big knockers. We'll get rid of her. They're looking at each other, going, next. He started flapping his arms around, doing strange things, and they got him out of the room. He got a free ticket out of it, but he goes back to London.

Next time I speak to him, I'm sleeping, I've been out clubbing, and it's noon. He calls me from London, and says, 'What are you doing sleeping? You should be up at the Chelsea, Sid's got himself into a bit of bother.' I said, 'How do you know that?' 'Someone called me from New York, tipped me off.' He said, 'Call me as soon as you find out what's going on, tell me what police station he's in.' 'Police station? What did he do?' 'I don't want to talk about it over the phone, he's got himself into a bit of trouble.'

So I went there. Nancy was still in the bag. They were talking to Sid in another room. They took him to a downtown police station, I never did find out. As soon as I had the chance, I called McLaren in London, who was prepared to fly out that very moment. He alerted Ma Vicious, she showed up about twenty-four hours after he did.

The legal people who handled Sex Pistols business in America, Pryor, Cashman, Sherman & Flynn, they were entertainment lawyers, they didn't know shit about criminal law. They had the case, and they sent some guy down to the courts, and McLaren and I show up in court for the bail hearing. This entertainment lawyer got Sid out on fifty thousand dollars' bail, after he's been accused of killing an American citizen.

Did you get Sid's story about what actually happened?

Yeah. Nancy is dead, Sid's been inside, he's been released. He goes in again for trying to bottle Patti Smith's brother in Hurrah's. He'd been saying something to some girl, and Todd Smith got involved. So he's back inside again. McLaren comes over again. They let him out, but the court is starting to get really picky about Sid, as to what is he really on about? Does he want to go back to England in his lifetime? Or in a box? What is his fucking story?

They put him with his mom, he's got to get his passport, got to go for urine tests, when you go for methadone. So, he's got to watch what he takes. He's staying in this flea-bag hotel, Seville Hotel,

691

uptown. So he's there, McLaren is crashed out on my couch. Sid hates staying with his mom. I'd taken pictures of him standing with his mom, and he looks real uncomfortable.

I get a call in the middle of the night, Ma Vicious. 'Joe, is Malcolm there? You got to wake him up. You've got to get over here right away, Sid's done something to himself.' So I wake up McLaren, we go flying uptown, we get to the hotel room and there's Ma Vicious, doing circles. There's Sid on one of the twin beds, in the corner, near the window, and he's opened up one of his arms, but he's done it the wrong way. He's done it with a throw-away razor.

Nancy bled to death out of negligence. She hadn't been murdered, the incision was only half an inch. That's a little-known fact. The prosecution was going to have a hard time convicting him of first-degree murder, when it was revealed that the wound was a half-inch incision, below the navel. If you want to kill somebody, you'll have to cut them up. This was not a real murder.

So there he was on the bed, and I'd been out the day before on an assignment, with my micro cassette recorder and camera, doing something. It was still in the bag, and I took it out of the trunk of the car. I didn't take any pictures of Sid at that time, he was close to death, mom doing the spins. Malcolm goes over to the bed and says, 'What have you done this for? We were going to get you out of jail, you stupid cunt.' We're both thinking he's on his deathbed.

Sid is saying to Malcolm, 'You've got to get me something to finish me off. Get me some Quaaludes. So Malcolm says to Sid, 'I'll get you some Quaaludes, don't worry' – and what he's really doing is going up to the payphone and calling an ambulance, Ma Vicious hadn't done that yet. He calls Bellevue Hospital, quite close to where the Seville was, leaving me on the second bed, my bag between my legs, and I lean over and say, 'Why the fuck you wanna do that? McLaren is busting his chops, the record company is coming up with all the money to get you out of jail' – cos I thought I was talking to the soon-to-be-late Sid Vicious.

Did you put your tape on?

Yeah! He just said, 'I want to be with my Nancy, I want to be left alone. I don't want to talk to any more New York City policemen. I don't want to be with my mum', he says. 'I'd rather be in the hospital ward on Rikers Island than be with my mum. I hate that cunt.'

Did he have a bad time in jail?

No, there was a guy who took care of him. We got some copies of the Sex Pistols *Punk* issue to him, and he showed them around, and the people read about his murder case and they thought he was a hard nut, and they left him alone. He was a pussy.

I asked him what happened with him and Nancy. He said, 'You know how The Dead Boys poke each other with the knives through the leather jackets? The kids in London do it. Nancy slapped me in the fucking nose after I'd just been punched out by the bell hop, looking for drugs.' He was loaded on Dilaudid. When you're on Dilaudid, you don't like to be touched – a big problem, like your skin is paranoid.

He said, 'She smacked me in the nose just where I'd been punched by that guy, and I took the knife out and said, "Do that again, I'm going to take your fucking head off", and she stuck her belly right in front of my knife.' So it was a combination of him pushing, her pushing. 'She didn't know, I didn't know that we'd done anything really bad. She crashed out on one bed, I crashed out on the other, I woke up first and decided to go get a bit of methadone. Took a forty-five minute taxi drive.' He was guilty by negligence.

So while he was out on the taxi ride, she was bleeding to death?

Yeah, while he was out, she got out of the bed, filled up the entire room with blood, crawling around. The way we guess, she sees herself in the mirror and collapses. That's guesswork, but it might have happened. The last thing she saw, according to the DA's office, she was face up, she was looking at the pipes under the sink. When I saw her body in the bag, she was still in the same position. The murder guys said that to me. They said, 'Why, you wanna take a picture?' They must have this bad idea about photographers.

What else did he say?

He said he stuck her, but Sid and I both knew what she meant to him. She cashed his cheques. They just cashed a thirteen-hundred-dollar

693

cheque they got from Virgin. They were feeding them money to keep them out of London, I guess. The reason they had the fight was she couldn't score drugs. If you were alone in America, and I was your source, taking care of a lot of your problems, and you hated my guts, I bet you still wouldn't kill me.

They didn't hate each other though, they just liked fighting.

Right. They were partners in misery, and they did have these pacts going, according to The Dead Boys, they were always talking about killing each other, cos life was pretty miserable. They couldn't shit. It was like those kids who would draw designs on their arms with razors, it wasn't any more malicious, and Sid didn't need to put out of commission the person who was keeping him afloat. This man never had a cheque book in his life, no bank account, didn't know what the fuck was going on.

They cashed the cheque, she was so obnoxious that she scared away the drug dealer who had just left the room . . .

Who was the dealer?

Rockets Redglare, the actor. He was pretty obnoxious himself, but he didn't get along with Nancy, so even with all that fucking money she still couldn't score. So when he returned to the room, he said, 'What did you get?' 'Oh, I never want to see that fat cunt again.' 'Never mind that, what did you buy?' Then they had the fight, and that's what caused her death, that argument.

What happened with the bell hop?

While they were waiting for Rockets, Sid decided to go down to all the junkies' rooms, he was banging on doors and somebody complained, and the bell hop decided to kick ass. Sid got belligerent, and the guy whacked Sid in the nose, and he stood there crying.

Have you still got the tape?

Yeah, but I promised Sid I wouldn't play it to anyone. I played it to Malcolm, then put it to rest. McLaren was running around trying to get this kid out of jail, and he was a killer – well, not much of a killer. But we didn't know what to do with him when he was out, we didn't know what to do with him when he was with his fuckin' mother. We talked about having meetings with Allen Ginsberg and the writers' organisation, PEN. Ginsberg released this great quote, saying that Sid Vicious would not be able to get a fair trial because of the nature of his art and persona. How do you think you'd do in a court of law on a murder charge with the name Sid Vicious? That name alone is going to get him a jail sentence. We all concurred on that. Then they all Om'd – pictures of McLaren sitting around with all these Om'ing hippies, fuckin' hysterical.

What happened to Sid after that?

He was back in Rikers again, because of the Todd Smith thing. I think he was in there over the Christmas holidays, they clean him up beautifully – vitamins, sleep, he no longer has scabs on his arms, he puts on a bit of weight. I hadn't visited him on this one; he's bottling people, come on! Why do I concern myself with this?

I hear that he's being released on bail the next day. I had introduced him to a girl called Michelle Robinson, and he walks into Max's and it's, 'Hey Joe, buy me an Amaretto and cream', a favourite junkie drink, sweet, so I went for that, and he starts hitting on this girl that I'm with. I warned her, 'He might give you a fuck, but he might kill you.' 'Oh no, he's a sweetheart.' I knew he'd probably go right to her house when he got bail. He did.

I didn't know what Ma Vicious was preparing; I wasn't part of that crowd, didn't want to be. She knew he was getting out, she got his favourite meal together, spaghetti bolognese, and she figures he's going to want to score, so she calls up the dealer, a British guy living in New York, I'd rather not say who. So Nolan and all these guys are there, and they're eating spaghetti bolognese, Sidney's looking great, and the smack arrives.

The dealer says there's a problem with the smack, it's 100 per cent. Five weeks before it was unheard of, but something happened to the smack scene during that time, and it was 100 per cent pure. Sid says, 'Get outta here', but the dealer says, 'Please, just take a little bit', and Sid takes a little bit, but just before he adds water to it, he adds a little bit more. He turns blue, lost respiration, what they describe as bouncing against walls, having trouble breathing, but survives, doesn't die.

The party disperses, Ma Vicious on the couch, Sid and Michelle in her bed in the back room. In the middle of the night he gets up, apparently goes to ma's purse, grabs the smack, shoots up a load, goes back to bed and dies. She wakes up, she's got to get him to a methadone clinic at 9 a.m. – he has an appointment, you can't go cruising into a meth clinic at any time. She tries to wake him, and he's stone dead. They call the police.

At this point, I'm leaving my house downtown. Walking past a café like this and they have FM radio on, and I hear, 'Sid Vicious found dead in girlfriend's Greenwich Village apartment. Stay tuned for more details', so I go down there. I assume that since they're announcing on the radio, they've already removed the body. When I arrived, there's a cop outside. I go up the steps and he says, 'Get outta here', but Michelle sees me and she gets me in.

I didn't take any photographs but I taped some stuff. I thought he would be gone. Ma Vicious is freaking out, Michelle was taking time out from freaking out, then getting back into it again. I said to Michelle, 'You know, Hendrix died, and all those people and the story starts to change after a while, so why don't we set the facts down now, and who knows, the truth might just stick.'

So we go into the bathroom and she tells me the story about the party and everything, and I go back into the living room and I tell the same thing to Ma Vicious – be straight with me, I won't fuck you. Keep it straight. She says, 'Let's go in the back room where it's quiet.' In the back room there's a little table lamp, the bed all rumpled, and I still think Mr V is gone, and she tells me how she got her son his final smack. 'I thought he was gonna buy some anyway, I thought I'd make it easy for him.'

At this point I don't have much room on the bed so I push something away, and it's Sid's foot, they just put a sheet over him. And there she is, telling me how she bought the smack. That was in the *Express*. Nobody seemed to mind, as long as they got the stories down.

Was Malcolm upset when Sid died?

Yeah, I think he liked him. Sid was a funny kid, and I think they had their battles, but he liked him, and that was why the rift with Rotten was so obvious. Rotten used to make a point of not being terribly humorous at all around McLaren. Sid had a sense of humour that penetrated with McLaren.

But John knew he was a sweet pussy, and that he stitched him up into a name and a lifestyle that wasn't going to help him grow up and get out of his miseries. He was always trying to come up to the hype, and Rotten knew that he'd stitched him up with that, and I think he felt some guilt, although he never confessed that to me.

The interesting thing about McLaren, there was so much drugs and sickness and death around that group, so many horror shows. McLaren is a two coffees, a beer and a pack of Marlboro guy, that's it. The whole thing wore off with them, sitting in hotels and hanging out with a whole bunch of degenerates, but it never affected Rotten. He'd take whatever you had, but if it was in the family of heroin, forget it. He was never into that.

The court case was a straight fight between McLaren and Lydon, wasn't it?

Originally it was Glitterbest against Lydon, which involved Ma Vicious, Cook and Jones and Stephen Fisher, the lawyer from Glitterbest, and McLaren, against little Johnny.

By the second trial, Cook and Jones and Ma Vicious had moved over to Rotten's side.

Cook and Jones did a switch during the first trial . . .

At the very end. McLaren acted irresponsibly in putting Mr Johnny Rotten out of business. Signed them up at an early age, that he should have been acting as a guardian and was acting as a scoundrel, he was impatient and petulant, and he had no time for what he had started. That's what I said in my piece, and I stick to that.

It wasn't about where the money had gone?

No, no-one knew about that yet.

That first court case was a real mess-up.

But it freed two movies that would never have been released, *The Great Rock'n'Roll Swindle* and *DOA*. They needed permission to go with them, and Rotten refused to sign. As soon as the official receiver was put in charge . . . What did he know? He was a fuckin' civil servant, he'd sell anything to pay the bills, to keep the shop open. He sold rights all over the place. He became the Sex Pistols' manager, in essence, and saw no reason that *DOA* should not come out, he saw a lot of money in it.

What did you think about the second court case?

It was brief. That was McLaren giving up. He had his movie career going and he had to show up in London for this dreadful court case he had no chance of winning. He surrendered.

Where did John get the money from to fight the case?

Warner Brothers America. When I was staying with him in London between cases, he had an account at Barclays, and Bob Regehr, Assistant VP of Warners, had sent him fifteen thousand dollars to buy the flat at Gunter Grove. And at another point, monies for the case.

Did he get any from Branson?

Someone told me that it would have been a cool move for Branson to finance the case on Lydon's behalf, but I don't know if he actually did or not.

Who financed the second case?

I think it was all the same money, but I noticed something. I was flown over twice for depositions, and Public Image were in operation then, and they picked me up at the airport, put me up, fed me for a month, wouldn't let me go home. They paid all my bills. I said, 'I'm missing work in New York', they said, 'We'll pay you.' They gave me £500, and that happened twice. The third time, I submitted the same bill for loss of earnings, and I'm still waiting for it, so something had happened.

John went through a very introverted phase after the Pistols . . .

Yeah, he turned into a couch potato. He's basically lazy anyway, he'd rather watch TV, drink beer, smoke pot.

Why do you think they all still hate each other?

I was talking to an old girlfriend from the sixties. We lived together, but we can't remember what drew us together in the first place. I guess it's hard for Rotten to imagine that at one time he was under the management of Malcolm McLaren. I'm hurt, cos I liked them both very much. They're classic people I like to hang out with, and we're adrift because of all that.

Anne Beverley

Mother of Sid Vicious, also known as Simon Beverley and John Ritchie – she referred to him as 'Sime'. Was present at his death in February 1979. I arrived at Mrs Beverley's house in Swadlincote, Derbyshire, at midnight, and talked to her – with her long-time partner Charlie present – throughout the night. It was an emotional and troubling experience. I set off for London at dawn.

I was born in Manchester, and after the age of eight I lived everywhere. Mother was manageress of a sweets-and-paper-and-everything shop, worked from five in the morning to nine at night, seven days a week. My father died suddenly when I was two. He'd never had much illness, and then he died of double pneumonia in three days. Mother was absolutely devastated, has remained devastated. Never remarried.

I was brought up in a triangle of three ladies: mother, sister and self. A really vicious triangle, mother doted on sister and hated me, cos I was the rebel. She had to pick on somebody, and she picked on me. My sister is fifteen months older than me, and I hated her. When I was seventeen we moved to Edinburgh, and in the space of eighteen months we changed flats in Edinburgh five times. And guess who lugged the suitcases, on the bus. That's the early life.

When did you leave home?

When I was eighteen, just. I joined the Air Force, anything to get away from my mum. I was fifteen months in the Air Force, then I got pregnant and got married. Big career. My first husband was called Geoff Brown, who was gorgeous, but his conversational capacity was minus fifty. He was an athlete and a footballer, and I had to go and shout on the touchline every Saturday in the freezing cold.

Then I jumped into the arms of John Ritchie, who was a part-time trombonist. What was wrong with him was he'd got no self-confidence.

Instead of going for it, he wanted to be a big fish in a little pond. He was professional standard. John came from hick Chelmsford, he was married. We commiserated with each other. I was married at nineteen and felt trapped.

When did you start travelling?

1960. Again because of John Ritchie, cos he was in a group that played a jazz club in Redcliffe Street, near Earls Court. They went to Ibiza. He came back saying, 'Oh, you must go, it's marvellous there.' He was working for a company that made cigarette-rolling machines, and they gave him a yearly bonus, so he said, 'You have the bonus, you go out there and spend it.' But when it came, the bonus was sixteen quid. So we went to the bank, and you should have seen me laying it on, weeping to the bank manager. We got enough for a one-way ticket for me and Simon, and a week's food money, and he said, 'I'll send you a fiver every week.' Of course when I was gone, not a ha'penny. He was into nurses. I lived on credit, here, there and everywhere. At one time I earned money rolling joints for people.

When did you encounter dope?

In Ibiza. It was definitely a beatnik scene. I'd never had anything like it before. I loved it, we used to get smashed out of our minds, every night, fresh from Morocco. Kif, no rubbish. Laughing gas. I brought some back when I came back to England, and smoked it on the back of a bus, and nobody knew what it was.

How long did you spend in Ibiza?

Fifteen months. I typed scripts for people. There were lots of writers out there. It really opened me out. I cried when I had to leave. My friends came and said to me, 'Look, you're in debt all over the place', and they were going to nick me. My friends rallied round, and chipped in a bit, and I hitched back with Simon, and a fiver. Simon was marvellous, he was just about four.

When you got back had you finished with John Ritchie?

Yeah, I never wanted to see him again. He really left me in the lurch. Maybe twice in the whole fifteen months he'd send me a fiver. Simon would never leave my side. One time, apropos of nothing he said to me, 'Mum, if you got run over by a car, what would happen to me?' He was aware of his situation.

Where did Simon first go to school?

Great Windmill Street, St Peter and Paul's. He was bullied by a huge Jewish child called Lionel. He was really unhappy at school. I did eventually get a flat in Balham. I paid for a half-day at Rudolf Steiner kindergarten. Two quid out of the seven, and he loved it, he was really happy.

In 1961, in London, there was I, with a little kid, with hair an inch long, when everybody else had a great big beehive, and everybody else's dress was two inches below the knee and mine was two inches above. I got every remark you could think of thrown at me, and Simon was constantly with me, so he heard all this, and I had to say to him, 'I don't care what they say, I like my hair like this', and that's where he got this total idea.

I tried to inculcate into his psyche: you are you, you can do anything you like providing you don't hurt anybody else while doing it. You should be able to do what the fuck you like. That was my whole thing. At four, five, six years old, that's gone in. He saw all these remarks being made, and me just walking through it all.

Did he go to many schools between six and ten?

After Shaftesbury Avenue the next one was in Mayfair, then I was ill, I had to go into hospital, and from there I moved to Oxford, where I met my second husband, Chris. I met him, we wooed, married, and he was dead within a year. Kidney failure. He got on with Simon really well. Simon hated school, but then so did I. Couldn't stand it, not academically minded.

After Chris died, I moved down to Tunbridge Wells, where Chris came from. I didn't want to stay in London on my own. Chris's mother employed this nanny-cum-tutor to look after the two boys and two girls. Mam'selle. Subsequently, when the kids grew up, Mam'selle bought a private school, and that's where Simon went to school, in Tunbridge. That lasted from '65 to '71. I think that was the longest period we ever stayed in one spot. He changed schools in

Tunbridge Wells, from junior to secondary school. He got on quite well there. Then we moved to Clevedon, just outside Bristol. I then met Mike Hands, who was pretty . . . vacant. After I lived with him for a while – we ran a pub – I found he was a pathological liar. We had to leave the pub.

Did Simon make many friends?

Friends of a nine-day's-wonder kind. He was never in a stable situation, and it was like a mirror of my own early life. You don't do these things by choice, it's just circumstance. He was lovely as a kid. He never cried for anything. He'd ask for things when we were shopping, can I have this or that, and I'd say, 'If I had the money darling, with pleasure I'd buy it, but I just don't have the money', and he used to accept that. He was marvellous.

His last school was Albion Road, off Stoke Newington Church Street. We lived in Evering Road. He bunked off school. His story to me was that he'd slagged some girl off, coming out of school, and her older brother was waiting for him. He was scared shitless, and wouldn't go into school. Simon left school at fifteen, against my wishes, but I knew that school wasn't really for him.

He went and worked at Simpson's, the factory that makes the DAKS slacks, in Redland Road. He was so funny, perceptive, a good mimic. He could pick up the funny parts of a personality. He'd come home and tell me about these people he worked with, he had me in stitches. He had a go at people's pretensions, but that was later, when he realised how pretentious people could be. That was when he started to dress up.

He always liked clothes?

Yes, in fact he started talking about clothes when he was thirteen, it used to really get on my nerves. It got boring. He met John Lydon when he went back to full-time education. They met at Hackney College of Further Education. My nephew was at Kingsway, and Simon went down there and decided he didn't like Hackney, and just moved there.

What did you think of John Lydon when you first met him?

The first time he came round he had hair down to here, a beautiful head of hair. He was shy. If I just looked at him, he went beetroot red. Couldn't say a word. I'd never met anyone that shy before. He wouldn't eat anything. He wouldn't have devilled kidney, or spaghetti, he'd have egg and chips. Wouldn't eat foreign food.

What was Simon doing at Hackney?

He did a course in photography, and he produced that painting while he was there. He loved the art classes, they showed him how to paint and then let them do what they wanted to do, but he quit after the second term, cos they tried to make him do particular subjects. It turned him off. He was always the person who could not be told what to do, he had to do his own thing. I always lost all the arguments.

Were you aware that he was going down the King's Road?

Oh yeah. One of the best days of my life, about '74, I was riding a 750 motorbike, and the first time I took Simon on the back, on my work route, which entailed the Old Street roundabout, and we zoomed around the roundabout and the pillion pedal raised sparks, and his comment was, 'Wow, mum, you ride just like a fella!', which meant, I really thought you were going to hog the kerb, be a typical lady driver. Terrific.

The other great comment was on my birthday, when he took me down the King's Road and introduced me to some of his friends, and bought me a birthday present. We went to some place where they did vegetarian lunches and burgers, and he knew everybody in there. 'Hello, everybody, this is Anne.' To a woman with an eighteen-year-old son, to be taken in his company to his haunts, that was one of the biggest compliments I've ever been paid.

When did he first cut his hair, and get into punk?

In a way, he was a punk before Malcolm ever came on the scene. Right from '75 when he first dyed his hair. He was punk. He carried it all the way through.

He lived away from home then?

He left home for a while when he was fifteen. He lived in some squat in Bethnal Green, but after a couple of months he came back home. Then when he was about seventeen, again, we had a row. Over the years I've tried to remember what the row was about, and I cannot remember. It was so irrelevant.

Obviously he left the house, came back a while later and said he'd met somebody and there was a squat in Elgin Avenue or somewhere that they were waiting for, but they weren't moving in until next week, so can I stay for the week? So I said, 'Okay, but for Christ's sake, make it a decent week, I don't want a week of rows.' Well, it was terrific, but the dice had been thrown.

Didn't he squat with John in Hampstead?

That was afterwards. Elgin Avenue was first, and they got turfed out by the police, and they moved up to a disused block of flats in Glass Walk in Hampstead. Then I think John went back home, and then Simon had a collection of really weird ladies, and the one that moved in with him was something of a witch, into witchcraft. Daubing each other with syrup, stuff like that. She was weird.

Were you aware of the Sex Pistols?

Well, yes, Simon came home one Saturday. He used to stay weekends, and he'd come over for a meal. When he left I said, 'Take the key with you, this is still your home.' Anyway, he came back this Saturday and he looked really down. 'What's the matter, Simon, anything wrong?' 'I think that's a bit much', he said, 'after I took him down there in the first place. He would never have gone there if I hadn't forced him to go down the King's Road'.

John had been forced to go down King's Road by Simon, who was a King's Road-ite, long before punk started. Simon was working in Portobello Road market that afternoon and John had gone down there on his own and was in Malcolm McLaren's shop, and Malcolm McLaren said, can you sing? And he's gone, 'Er, yeah.' 'Right, so you're a singer in a group.' Now that should have been Simon, and he was really pipped at that.

That must have started a rivalry between them?

705

Well, no, he was put out but he got over it. Then the group took off, they were called the Sex Pistols and they got their first songs together, and Simon thought they were the dog's bleedin' dinner. 'Aw, mum', he said, 'I've been to listen to them, and they're fucking brilliant!' He was big enough for that. He wasn't a mean-minded, petty person at all. He even dragged me down. 'You've got to come and listen to them.'

Where did you see them?

The 100 Club, Oxford Street.

Did you like them?

Oh yeah! It was a real live band. The energy that was created. It was Paul's drumming and Steve's guitar which was so raw. John was just the singer with the band. I thought he was gauche and had no presence, and was odd, weird. But of course he made that his thing in the end, didn't he? The bass guitarist didn't impinge at all.

Were you aware that Sid was in Ashford, after that trouble with the glass?

Yes, but that was all a bit unfortunate, cos I'd just met Charles, and his mum was away, so he invited me down to his mum's house, and for that week I was out of my flat. For some reason I came back and found a telegram from a reporter with one of the music papers, Jonh Ingham, and he'd been in since the previous Saturday. I felt awful, that I'd been off enjoying myself, and I didn't happen to be at home when the telegram came.

That was his first real brush with trouble?

Absolutely.

Did he throw the glass?

No. He was wrongfully arrested, and because of that he tried to resist arrest, and they beat hell out of him. A week later when I went down to Ashford – as soon as I got the telegram I was on the bike and straight down to Ashford – he was still black and blue then. I should have demanded that a photograph be taken, really.

Did he ever talk to you about The Flowers of Romance?

No, that was very short-lived, wasn't it?

He was a natural musician almost from the day he was born. When he was eight months old, the thing he liked to hold was his dad's trombone mouthpiece. At two years old he was out in the garden singing, 'That old black magic has me in its spell . . . !' – with all the inflections, the lot. He'd drum away for hours, with a saucepan and two sticks.

Did he meet Nancy before he joined the Sex Pistols or after?

Just before. He was known in the States before he joined the Pistols. He told me one day, I think Jonh Ingham had gone to meet some band coming in from the States, and they were asking if he knew a guy called Sid Vicious.

Did he ever tell you how he got that name?

Rotten had said to him, 'Ooh you're a vicious person.' And that was where the Vicious came from. And I have names . . . for jokes I'd say, want a chucky-egg, Clarence? or, Oswald? This was a standing joke in the household, and one day it was Sidney. He probably carried my joke on with him – because he hated the name Sidney – to John. He must have said to John, 'At least you're not called Sidney.'

And John had a pet mouse or hamster he called Sidney, so that came from there. Simon had probably been saying, 'Aw, Sidney, what a dreadful name to call a hamster!' And John would retort by calling him Sidney, because he knew he hated it. It was one of those.

What did you think of Nancy?

I thought she was dreadful, quite honestly, I couldn't stand her. The first time I met her, she sat on the sofa next to me and tried to tell me her life-story in two seconds flat. Like she was vomiting, it was all about how badly she'd been treated, how rich her father was, how much better her brother and sister had been treated than her, she'd been this and done that, so full of herself. It set my teeth on edge straight away.

Where were you living then?

Dalston, in an eleventh-floor flat, which was wonderful.

707

So she took Sid away, and you didn't see much of him after that?

No. Like any mother, I would have liked a better person for him than her. It could have been the same with anybody, but I know a nice girl when I see one, and I didn't think she was.

They did seem very fond of each other, though.

They were absolutely head-over-heels in love with each other. I don't think she was, at first. I think at first she used him, but he loved her because she needed him. She needed somebody, without a doubt. And she loved him because he was willing to need her.

Were you proud of him, in the group?

Oh yes, cos his charisma just shone above everybody else's. When we went to see the film, *The Great Rock'n'Roll Swindle*, every time that Simon appeared, the audience applauded, it was just amazing. I noticed that every time there were photographers taking pictures of the group, their cameras would automatically steer towards Sid, he was so photogenic.

Did his personality change?

When he'd been drinking, when he was on drugs, when he was on downers. They used to drop Tuinal. A side effect of Tuinal is aggression. If Simon had a drink he could get very aggressive, but when he hadn't had anything, he was the nicest person. Everybody who met Sid and Nancy jointly didn't like Nancy. I don't think I've ever met anybody who had met Sid and didn't like him, for whatever reason, because he was funny, or because he was sweet.

Sid and Nancy subsequently led a very dull and insular life, because every time they went out they would be stopped by ten policemen in the space of an hour, and searched. John probably the same. They weren't allowed to have a life.

Can you remember what happened on the boat trip?

There was this photographer really bothering Wobble, and he wouldn't leave it out, and Wobble warned him, but he wouldn't stop, and he just knocked the camera out of his hands. It was brilliant until the police over-reacted. I've never seen so many policemen in my life.

When the boat pulled in, and the word went out that the trip had been stopped, I knew it would be sorted out, cos there was nothing serious, this guy had been baiting Wobble, and all he'd done was knock the camera out of his hands.

Do you think this society really penalises people if they're different?

Oh, absolutely. You try and be different. If you're different and you're harming somebody then society has got every right to turn on you, every right. Society has got to protect itself. But if you're just different and you doing no-one any harm, they have no right to turn on you, and make your life a misery.

Punk was a group of misfits standing together.

They were allowed to be misfits because somebody had instigated that you were allowed to be a misfit. Here we are, in public, misfits, and we're not ashamed, and you can be a misfit as well, if you want to.

They paid a penalty for that bravery.

They certainly did. But Simon eventually became disillusioned with John Rotten, because John really thought he was the star. The singer in the band, kind of thing. He got to hate him in the end.

Did he get disillusioned with Malcolm?

I don't think he ever did, no. It was always a love-hate relationship with Malcolm. Simon thought Malcolm was funny; weird and funny. And Malcolm would have loved to have been Sid. If he could have jumped into Sid's skin . . . so he'd do anything for Sid, he gave Sid more money than anybody else.

Is that because Sid acted out, whereas McLaren was too much of a thinker?

Yes, yes. Malcolm was too calculating, Sid never calculated anything. He was never a calculating person. He would do it for a laugh. He was once in a taxi with Malcolm, and Sid had a sneezing fit and pulled a hanky out of his pocket, and a load of loose change with it, and he said Malcolm was helping him pick up the money and putting it in his bleeding pocket!

That tickled Sid, it was one of the things that he found endearing in Malcolm. Anybody else would have thought, rotten bastard, but Sid thought, I can't believe anybody would have the nerve to be so blatantly rotten!

People say Malcolm destroyed him but I think Malcolm was genuinely fond of Sid . . .

No way. Malcolm didn't destroy anyone. I think Malcolm tried to look out for Sid. He brought him home, Easter Saturday morning. We were just about to set off somewhere and there's a knock on the door, and it's Malcolm. 'Sid's not well, and I've brought him home. I think you ought to look after him.' I was quite impressed. He had been given the impression by Simon that he, Simon, wasn't welcome in my house.

It was tonsillitis. The hepatitis came later. They'd been sleeping on floors, and of course he with Nancy. She didn't come. She just got her claws into him. He was using an excuse not to come home because he wanted to be with Nancy.

That weekend I was torn, I had a new lover, and here was Simon suddenly making demands on me, and he was going, 'You're not going to spoil our weekend.' So I told Simon, 'You're in the warm, you've got a bed, you're not going to die, and you're eighteen.' I got him tins of soup and bottles of milk and eggs, but I know Nancy stayed with him, I know he phoned Nancy and said, 'Right, they've gone.' They slept in our bed. They were happy.

Did he ever tell you about the American tour?

[long silence . . .] He was very secretive, subsequently, about his stint with the Pistols. After he and Nancy got really entrenched together, were living together. I didn't see very much of him. I used to go round; I wasn't going to let him go, just wave goodbye.

Would you have wanted to get him away from Nancy, or did you just want to see him?

I just wanted to see him. I knew there was nothing I could say. Simon was the type of person you would alienate yourself from if you tried. He was loyal. If you tried to point out that so-and-so wasn't a good person to hang around with, he would stick up for them through thick and thin – 'This is my friend you're talking about' – and he was like that all the more with Nancy.

When did you see him next, after she died?

After Nancy died, yes. All my friends were really good, they forked out whatever they could afford, and I was on the first plane I could catch, cos when you're in that kind of trouble, you need somebody with you.

Did he ever tell you the story of what happened that night when she died?

No. I never asked him, and he never told me. But I do know what happened. Long afterwards, maybe I'm kidding myself that I didn't know before then, but it was a suicide-pact note, in his handwriting, in his pocket. I think I'm trying to tell myself that I didn't find it until afterwards, because if you had tried to take your own life, by your-self, alone, and it doesn't come off, it's no longer a criminal offence. It used to be.

But it is still a criminal offence if you make a suicide pact with another person; if you survive and they don't, it's manslaughter. So although I knew what happened, there was no way I could, or would say anything. On the night in question, he told me he dropped nine Tuinals, which should have killed a horse.

And I really do think Nancy stabbed herself, I really do believe that. She wasn't a well person, she was always getting bladder infec-tions, I think she had kidney trouble, and in pain quite a lot. If you're intent on doing something like that, it's quite easy to do. If she told me once, she told me fifty times that she would die before she was twenty-one. It was a fixation with her.

Was Simon self-destructive before he met her?

No, not at all. He latched into hers. If there was two people in the whole goddamn world who should never ever have met, it was those two. People liken them to Romeo and Juliet. It was an absolute tragedy, but they did; and meeting, met self-destruction.

What happened when you got to the States? Did you have to organise lawyers?

711

Malcolm did it all, he really was wonderful. I was just there. He was amazing.

What state was Simon in?

He was very down. Perhaps I was the most unfortunate person for him to be with, because I'm really good at advice in a way that people can act on, for somebody who's in deep trouble, to someone who doesn't matter that much to me. I can communicate if I'm not involved. If I love someone, I can't talk, I can hold them, stroke their hair, but I can't talk, cos I'm so frightened of saying the wrong thing, I don't know why.

It was an absolute nightmare. I was rushing round, cos when people make a statement it has to be signed by a notary, and I was gathering statements. People were very good to me. I found New York rather depressing, but that could have been the state I was in. I could hear people screaming at night, and thinking, somebody's being murdered, practically every night. But I met nothing but kindness, from all and sundry.

It took hours to visit anybody. Visiting day would come around and you'd get out there at ten o'clock in the morning and you were lucky if you got to see your visitor by three in the afternoon.

Was he having a rough time in Rikers Island?

I don't think so, I think he was all right. I was very worried, cos being called Sid Vicious, somebody's going to want to have a go. But there again, they used to let him sit in the corridor under a light, and read a book, cos he couldn't sleep at night. Things like that. He made me laugh once – he said the governor wanted his autograph, for his daughter.

Was Malcolm going to make an album with him?

Yeah, Malcolm wanted to bring Steve and Paul and John across, to some studios in Florida, and make an album, yeah. By that time, he wanted to cash in on the money. He'd spent all the money the Pistols had made on the film, and he was brassic. He needed an earner.

Malcolm could never be a friend of mine, I didn't like the guy, but I could never put him down the way other people have, cos I think he was as much carried along as everyone else. He couldn't handle it. One ought to feel sorry for him rather than castigate him. Sid knew he was selfish and careless, and he loved him for it.

Can I ask you what happened the last night of his life.

We got back to Michelle Robinson's flat in Greenwich Village. I'd invited about eight people. I was going to do a spaghetti bolognese in celebration of Simon getting out. I went out and bought the ingredients, did the washing-up, cooked the meal. Simon had had a fix early in the day, supplied by this guy called Martin, which had so little in it that it didn't do anything.

Then later on this Martin said he could get some stuff, and I said to Simon, 'Look, you've already had some today, I know it didn't do anything for you but you're only out on bail, and if they decide to take a blood test and you come up positive, you could be inside again.'

He was a well-known person. Everybody would recognise him. If I had said no, he would have just walked out, gone and got it himself. So if he did that, he was going to get nicked, because he was Sid. So I had to go along with it. What are you gonna do, put a collar and a lead on somebody, lock them in a room? You can't.

So the guy left. I cooked the meal, the guy came back, we all had the meal. Whoever was going to do it went out into the bedroom, and about a quarter of an hour later, they all walked back in, and Simon had a rose-pink aura around his whole body. I went, 'Whaat?' I said, 'Jesus, son, that must have been a good hit', or whatever. He was elated, quietly so. Elated on the inside, coming out, creating the aura. I've never seen anything like it before.

This aura, are you saying it was something other than the drug?

No, I think he'd just been taken hold of by the drug. Five minutes later he went back into the bedroom and someone said, 'Simon's collapsed.' I went in, he was sliding down the bed, what should I do? Should I take him to the hospital, which was just up the road, and say, I think he's OD'd, he's had a fix, can you do anything for him? Next day, he's back in Rikers Island? Do I sit it out and hope he comes around? What do I do?

713

We put him on his side. Hope he slept it off, which he did. He came round. 'Oh fuck, I was so worried about you.' 'I'm fine, Mum, I'm all right.' He didn't want to go for a walk, and he had to report to the nick in the morning, so I said, 'If you don't want to go for a walk, I think we should just go to bed.' So they went to bed. I slept on the couch in the sitting room.

I can only think it was some sort of relapse, really. That night, after they'd taken it, I said, 'I'll have the rest of it, thank you very much, I don't want you taking any more', and I put it in my back pocket, and the next day when the police came in, I saw them turning the place over, I watched them doing it, and it didn't penetrate at all.

It wasn't until hours later when I was in the police station, when they said, 'Do you think he took some more?' And I said, 'No, he couldn't have.' 'How do you know?' 'Cos I've got it here.' 'We've turned the place inside-out looking for that.' They nearly did their nuts. They took it for analysis, and it was 93 per cent pure. You never get that on the street. It had come from before adulteration. Martin knew the person who had got it first. The head of the chain.

Do you think he would have got off, with the case?

I really can't say. It would have come out that it was a suicide pact, and she died and he didn't, which made him guilty of manslaughter, and sorry, here's five years, you'll be out in three. Three years in a hard nick in the States? Forget it. He couldn't have done that, cos he was not a hard man, he was too sweet and soft. He would never have survived.

I'm glad he died, in view of what happened. Nothing can hurt him any more. And where could he have gone, from where he was at? He couldn't have backed down and done something different, like John Lydon has. There was no way he could have reverted, and been a pop singer. He was in a corner. The rug was pulled out from under his feet, and he would never have survived in an English jail, let alone an American one.

What happened with the final court case, the Sex Pistols one?

I'd been involved with a solicitor all along. Sid's estate got nothing until after the court case. Then we got the film; Glitterbest, Matrixbest – the two companies; we got everything. Malcolm got nothing.

714

Do you think that was the right result?

In a way, yes. The only fault that I have with Malcolm is that he used the Sex Pistols' earnings to make a film which subsequently turned out to be a film by Malcolm for Malcolm about Malcolm. The Sex Pistols were incidental to it. Without any agreements or consulting them, he spent all their money. Everything was gone. So it was fair, and in the long run it was of benefit to Malcolm, cos he was cut out of it, gone.

Was it Lydon's solicitor who contacted you and got you all together again?

No, Lydon wouldn't talk to anybody. He wouldn't talk to his solicitor, my solicitor, their solicitors, anybody, but he brought the action in the first place, in '78. I was working as a security officer, and my boss had a cousin who was a barrister, and my solicitor was doing nothing, they were just piling up paper. But my boss talked to his cousin, who knew a lawyer who was the catalyst who got it all going. He charged me £30,000 for doing it, but he did it.

How much did the whole trial cost?

I've no idea. The Inland Revenue took £254,000 from us, jointly. They wrote quite a lot off. That was another thing, Malcolm never paid any tax on anything. I was legal-aided, so my lawyer's bill went to taxation, and I think they subsequently refunded me something like £12,000, which went back into the kitty.

So you should each have got about £100,000.

Before tax, yeah. There was something like a million and a half in the kitty. Lydon's lawyer was so expensive it isn't true. I was brought up to believe implicitly in doctors, lawyers and policemen. A bad upbringing.

Is it all settled now?

Yeah. There were two payments. I suppose there was something like £90,000. It's in a high-interest cheque account. I think the others got about £120,000, but Paul Cook got the least.

715

What do you feel now about your Simon being Sid, this icon?

I think he deserves to be a cult figure. He epitomises so much of what people really want to be, but until he came along hadn't had the guts to go out and be it. I don't know if I instigated that – it's what I've always believed.

Afterword: where are they now?

Chapter 1: The Shop

Malcolm McLaren

Since the release of his last solo long-player, *Paris* (1994), McLaren has been involved with various projects in the film, media, television and culture industries as well as the art world. He contributed a track to Quentin Tarantino's *Kill Bill Vol. 2*, and was a co-producer of the feature film *Fast Food Nation* (2006).

Robin Scott

In 1979 Robin Scott had a worldwide hit under the name of M with 'Pop Muzik', a pop classic featured by U2 in their Popmart tour and remixed by Junior Vasquez, amongst others. He has since returned to painting, and his digitally inspired Life Class collection can be found online at www.robinscott.org.

Helen Wallington-Lloyd

Appeared alongside Malcolm McLaren, as Helen of Troy, in *The Great Rock'n'Roll Swindle*. In recent years she has gained recognition as the designer of many early Sex Pistols' handbills. She sold some of her Sex Pistols collection at Sotheby's in 2001.

Jordan

After taking a lead role in *Jubilee* – as Amyl Nitrate – and managing both Adam and the Ants and Wide Boy Awake (the group formed by Ants' bass player Kevin Mooney), Jordan left the music and media industries for her current occupation as a veterinary nurse and a breeder of pedigree cats. She lives on the south coast.

Alan Jones

An internationally recognised film writer, specialising in fantasy, horror and science fiction. A member of the London Critics' Circle, he has written for the *Guardian*, *GQ* and many others. He has published *The Rough Guide to Horror Movies* and, with Jussi Kantonen, *Saturday Night Forever* – a great history of disco.

Chrissie Hynde
Formed the Pretenders in 1978 and has since become one of the most acclaimed female rock stars in the world. Among many other music projects, she provided the vocals for the 2004 US number-one dance hit, Tube and Berger's 'Straight Ahead'. A passionate campaigner for animal rights, in 2007 she opened a vegan restaurant called the Veg-iTerranean in her home town of Akron, Ohio.

Chapter 2: New York

Sylvain Sylvain
After the demise of the New York Dolls, Sylvain formed the Criminals before dropping out of music to drive a cab in NYC. In 2004 he re-formed the New York Dolls, with David Johansen and Arthur Kane, to great acclaim: the group – minus Kane, who died of leukaemia in 2004 – have released two albums and have toured constantly. Their next record will be produced by Todd Rundgren.

Leee Black Childers
Returned to the US after the end of The Heartbreakers, where he managed Levi and the Rockats, among others. A tireless photographer and witty raconteur, he has recently performed at the South Bank and is planning to publish a book of his many candid and historical photos. His website is at www.leeechilders.com.

Roberta Bayley
Has exhibited her work in many shows, both in America and Europe. She featured in the 1997 book edited by Stephanie Chernikowski, *Blank Generation Revisited: The Early Days of Punk Rock*, and in 2007 published *Blondie: Unseen 1976–80*. For more, go to www.robertabayley.com.

John Holmstrom
After *Punk* ceased publication for the first time in 1979, Holmstrom went on to work freelance for *High Times* and *Heavy Metal*, among other magazines, gaining acclaim for his comic character Bosko. He has

successfully relaunched *Punk* magazine at www.punkmagazine.com. His own website can be found at www.johnholmstrom.com.

Legs McNeil
Worked as a senior editor at *Spin* magazine before publishing – with Gillian McCain – the highly entertaining *Please Kill Me: The Uncensored Oral History of Punk* in 1997. Since then he has published *The Other Hollywood: The Uncensored Oral History of the Porn Film Industry* with Jennifer Osborne and Peter Pavia.

Mary Harron
Now an internationally renowned film director. Wrote for *Melody Maker* and the *Observer* in the early/mid-1980s before returning to New York, where she worked in television, directing episodes of *Six Feet Under* and *Homicide: Life on the Street*, among others. In 1996 she directed her first feature film, *I Shot Andy Warhol*, following it up with *American Psycho* (2000) and *The Notorious Bettie Page* (2007).

Chapter 3: Sex Pistols

Sex Pistols
Have toured regularly since their 1996 re-formation with the original four members: John Lydon, Steve Jones, Paul Cook and Glen Matlock. In 2008 their Combine Harvester tour included thirty-one dates in the UK, US, Russia, Japan and several European countries. In 2002 they released *Sex Pistols Box Set*, three CDs with many rarities, including the Mike Thorne demos and out-takes from *Never Mind the Bollocks*. In 2008 they released a live DVD from their November 2007 Brixton Academy show, *There'll Always Be an England*. In autumn 2008 the Sex Pistols' re-recorded version of 'Pretty Vacant' appeared in the new edition of the Guitar Hero video game, 'Guitar Hero World Tour'. 'Anarchy in the UK' was previously featured in 'Guitar Hero III: Legends of Rock'. For updates, there is an official site – www.sexpistolsofficial.com – and more can be found at www.sex-pistols.net and also at www.punk77.co.uk/groups/sex.htm.

Warwick Nightingale

Continued to live in the Wormholt Estate, but dropped out of the music industry. Was jailed in the early 1980s for 'drug-related offences'. Died in 1996.

Steve Jones

From 2004 to January 2009 Jones hosted a daily programme on Indie103.1 called 'Jonesy's Jukebox'. He has also continued to do studio sessions and has appeared on various music documentaries, including the BBC's *The Roxy Music Story*. For more, visit the joint Cook/Jones website, www.cookandjones.co.uk/kickdown.htm.

Paul Cook

Apart from touring with the Sex Pistols, Cook has continued to play with Edwyn Collins and appeared in the 2007 BBC documentary about Collins' rehabilitation after his serious illness, *Home Again*. In 2004 Cook formed a new band, Man Raze, who released their first album, *Surreal*, in June 2008.

Glen Matlock

As well as the Sex Pistols, Matlock has played with the Philistines and the Flying Padovanis during the last few years. In 2007 he formed Slinky Vagabond with former Bowie guitarist Earl Slick, Blondie drummer Clem Burke and designer Keanan Duffty. For more, go to his official website at www.glenmatlock.com.

Johnny Rotten/John Lydon

After 1997's *Psycho's Path*, Lydon has concentrated on a media career, appearing in the 2004 edition of *I'm a Celebrity . . . Get Me Out of Here!*, as well as fronting several programmes about wildlife for the Discovery Channel. In October 2008 he appeared in two advertisements for Country Life butter, shown on British TV. For more, go to the official website: www.johnlydon.com.

Chapter 4: The City

Roger Armstrong

Worked with many groups on the Chiswick label – including the Count Bishops and The Damned – before forming Ace Records with Ted Carroll in 1984. This is now one of the UK's longest established and best reissue labels, with a huge and well-researched catalogue. For more, go to www.acerecords.co.uk.

Joe Strummer

After disbanding The Clash in 1985, Strummer appeared in films by Alex Cox (*Walker, Straight to Hell*), Jim Jarmusch (*Mystery Train*) and Aki Kaurismaki (*I Hired a Contract Killer*). He also released a solo album, *Earthquake Weather*, and fronted for the Pogues on their 1991 tour. He formed the Mescaleros and released two well-received albums.

Joe Strummer died in December 1992, from a congenital heart defect. His legacy includes the institution of the Carbon Neutral Company, an organisation dedicated to planting trees in order to combat the effects of global warning, and the Strummerville Foundation, which promotes new music. He has been celebrated in two documentaries: *Let's Rock Again* (Dick Rude) and *Joe Strummer: The Future Is Unwritten* (Julien Temple). For more, go to www.joestrummer.com.

Adam Ant

Became a superstar in the early 1980s with hits like 'Antmusic' and 'Prince Charming'. After appearing at Live Aid, he concentrated on an acting career. Adam hit the headlines in 2002, when he threatened pub patrons with an imitation firearm. Since then, he has overseen the successful reissue of all the Ants albums and, in 2006, published his autobiography, *Stand and Deliver*. In 2008 he was granted the Q Music Icon Award.

Tony James

Found success with both Generation X and, in the mid-1980s, with Sigue Sigue Sputnik. He has since teamed up with Mick Jones in the well-received Carbon/Silicon, who since 2004 have released several download and hard-copy albums, including *Western Front, The Crackup Suite* and *The Last Post*. See www.carbonsiliconinc.com.

Viv Albertine

Made three albums with The Slits before leaving the group in 1981. Since then she has raised a family, before working for a while as a TV director. She has since returned to music. In late 2008 she rejoined

The Slits on guitar for two shows. See her MySpace page at www.myspace.com/albertine.

Jah Wobble

Since leaving Public Image in 1981, Wobble has pursued a prolific career, pioneering a fusion of dub and world music. He has worked with Holger Czukay and Jaki Liebezeit of Can, Brian Eno, Massive Attack and many others. In the early 1990s he found success with the Invaders of the Heart, before releasing a stream of solo albums on his own label, 30Hertz Records.

In 2008 he toured his new project, *Chinese Dub*, to great acclaim. He is publishing his autobiography, *Memoirs of a Geezer*, through Serpent's Tail in autumn 2009. For more, go to www.30hertzrecords.com.

Chapter 5: The Suburbs

Shanne Hasler

Played with Shane MacGowan in the Nipple Erectors (later the Nips) before forming the Men They Couldn't Hang in 1983. They released several albums in a hard-edged folk/protest style, including 1989's well-received *Silvertown*. After splitting up in 1990, the Men They Couldn't Hang re-formed in the mid-1990s.

Captain Sensible

The Damned re-formed in 1978 and went on to release a series of well-received albums, such as *The Black Album*, where the Captain's love of psychedelia came to the fore. He scored a massive solo hit in 1982 with his number-one cover of 'Happy Talk'. He also recorded for the Crass label. In late 2008 The Damned released their tenth studio LP, *So, Who's Paranoid?*. For more, go to www.captainsensible.com; and for Damned info, www.officialdamned.com.

Siouxsie Sioux

The Banshees recorded eleven LPs before finally splitting up in 1996. Siouxsie continued to record with long-term collaborator Budgie as The Creatures: their last album, *Hai!*, was released in 2003. Having moved to France, she took a few years out from music, before returning with the solo album *MantaRay* in 2007. Most recently Siouxsie worked with Angelo Badalamenti on the soundtrack for the film *The Edge of Love*. For more: www.vamp.org/Siouxsie.

Berlin

Appeared in the 1995 *Arena* documentary 'Punk and the Pistols' and published his first book, the novel *Psychoboys*, in 1997. In 2006 his unflinching memoir of the punk period, *Berlin Bromley*, came out to considerable acclaim. He lives in East London and is currently writing and planning a play, *The Bench*. For more, go to www.myspace.com/berlinbromley

Marco Pirroni

After playing with The Models and Rema Rema, Pirroni joined Adam and the Ants and co-wrote their huge early-1980s hits. In the mid-1980s he began a long creative association with Sinead O'Connor, which resulted in several albums, including *I Do Not Want What I Haven't Got*. He has formed his own label, Only Lovers Left Alive (named after the 1964 Dave Wallis teenage horror novel), and has released excellent compilations of the music played in 430 King's Road (*SEX: Too Fast to Live Too Young to Die*) and Biba (*Champagne and Novocaine*). He has also formed the Wolfmen (www.thewolfmen.net), who released their first album, *Modernity Killed Every Night*, in autumn 2008.

Vic Godard

Recorded two albums with Subway Sect and a solo record, *Songs for Sale*, before retiring from the music industry and working as a postman. He returned in the early 1990s with a record on Alan Horne's Postcard label, *The Revenge of the Surrey People* (featuring Paul Cook on drums), and has since released several records, including *Sansend* (2002) and *Singles Anthology* (2005). In 2007 he re-recorded all the tracks from the legendary lost 1978 Gooseberry LP. For more, visit www.motionrecords.com.

Steve Walsh

Moved to Manchester in 1978 and formed Manicured Noise, who played the first dates at the Factory Club and released two well-received 45s before splitting in 1980. Walsh continued to release singles on a number of labels, before returning to work as a graphic designer. In 2006 Caroline True Records released the Manicured Noise compilation *Northern Stories 1978/80*. For more information, go to www.myspace.com/manicurednoise.

Debbi Wilson

Also known as Debbi Juvenile. Wrote stories for *Mayfair* magazine in the early 1980s. Worked as researcher and production assistant on Alex Cox's *Love Kills*, where she did her best to ensure the film's period fidelity. Her current whereabouts are unknown.

Chapter 6: The Team

Nils Stevenson

Managed Siouxsie and the Banshees until 1982, after which he resumed working with Malcolm McLaren. He assisted on the *Duck Rock* LP and was involved with the careers of Neneh Cherry and Electribe 101. After publishing his visual autobiography, *Vacant: A Diary of the Punk Years 1976–79* with photos by his brother Ray Stevenson, he worked with Marco Pirroni until his death in 2002.

Ray Stevenson

Published several books of his photographs, including *Sex Pistols File* (1978), *Siouxsie and the Banshees* (1983) and *Photo Past* (1988). Stevenson's great Sex Pistols pix have been exhibited at the National Centre for Pop Music and the Heavenly Social Clubs. His classic portrait of Johnny Rotten in bondage gear and beret was included in the National Portrait Gallery's 1999–2000 'Faces of the Century' exhibition. For more, go to www.raystevenson.co.uk.

Dave Goodman

After many semi-legal Sex Pistols releases throughout the 1980s, his contribution was finally recognised in the appearance of the *Sex Pistols Box Set* in 2002, which included material from the 7/76, 10/76 and 1/77 demo sessions. Goodman died in 2005 of a heart attack, at his home in Malta. In 2007 Omnibus published his autobiography, *My Amazing Adventures with the Sex Pistols*.

Sophie Richmond
Worked for Penguin Books after leaving Glitterbest, before going freelance to raise a family. She now works as a copy-editor, principally on anthropological publications like David Moss and David Evans' *The Aid Effect* (2005).

Jamie Reid
Published a full account of his artworks (from 1966 to 1986) in *Up They Rise* (with Jon Savage). During the 1990s he produced sleeve artwork for the Afro Celt Sound System – which sourced his Druidic/Celtic roots. In 2007 he held a major retrospective at the Aquarium Gallery. Visit www.isisgallery.org/artists/jamie_reid.html.

John Tiberi
After the Sex Pistols Tiberi resumed his former occupation as an art dealer. He has continued to be involved with the Sex Pistols heritage industry, as a commentator and as an artist. His input into *Sex Pistols Number 1* is now recognised. In 2007 he appeared in the DVD *Never Mind the Sex Pistols: An Alternative History*.

Chapter 7: The Propagandists

Neil Spencer
Was editor of the *NME* from 1978 to 1985, when it was at the height of its influence. Subsequently he was a founding editor of the men's magazine *Arena*. He now contributes a weekly sun-sign column to the *Observer Magazine*. He is the author of *True As the Stars Above, Adventures in Modern Astrology* (Gollancz 2000), and the screenwriter for Jeremy Gooding's 2003 feature, *Bollywood Queen*. For more, visit www.neilspencer.co.uk.

Caroline Coon
Returned to her first love, painting, after managing The Clash and publishing her punk book, *1988: the New Wave Punk Rock Explosion*. Her excellent paintings can be seen at www.carolinecoon.com. As the founder of RELEASE, she remains an activist and a polemicist.

Jonh Ingham

Moved to Los Angeles in 1978, where he managed the Weirdos. He returned to the UK in the early 1990s, and has since worked in IT. Many of his seminal articles from the punk period are now exhibited on *Rock's Backpages*. As well as articles for *Mojo*, he writes a regular blog at mog.com/Jonh_Ingham.

Mark Perry

Has continued to write, sing and play with Alternative TV. In 2000 all thirteen issues of his fanzine were reprinted in *Sniffin' Glue: The Essential Fanzine Accessory*. In 2004 Perry finally recorded a version of The Ramones' 'Now I Wanna Sniff Some Glue'. For more, visit www.markperry.freeuk.com.

Chapter 8: The North-West

Howard Devoto

Magazine split up in 1981, after four well-received albums. Devoto released one solo record, *Jerky Versions of the Dream*, before teaming up with Noko for two LPs as Luxuria in the later 1980s. He then left the music industry to work at a photo archive. In 2001 he teamed up again with Pete Shelley and released *Buzzkunst*. In 2008 Magazine's back catalogue was released by Virgin, and they re-formed to play several UK shows in early 2009. For more, go to www.myspace.com/magazineofficial.

Pete Shelley

Pursued a solo career in the early 1980s, releasing electro classics like 'Homosapien'. Buzzcocks re-formed full-time in 1993, and played on Nirvana's last-ever tour. They have since released five studio LPs. In 2005 'Ever Fallen in Love' was re-recorded by artists including Roger Daltrey and Peter Hook and released as a tribute single after the death of the DJ John Peel. In 2008 the three classic EMI albums were re-released and the group also issued *30*, a live summary of their career. For more, go to the official site at www.buzzcocks.com.

Richard Boon
Ran the New Hormones label until 1982, after which he worked for Rough Trade. He now works as a librarian, and his informed and trenchant comments have enlivened many a period history – most recently the documentary film *Joy Division*. For more, go to the New Hormones website: www.newhormonesinfo.com.

Tony Wilson
Was a director of Factory Records until the label collapsed in late 1992 (for a musical history, see the four-CD box set *Factory Records: Communications 1978–1992*). Although Factory was later revived, Wilson concentrated on his broadcasting career and on the international music conference, In the City, which he co-launched in 1992. In the early twenty-first century he was fictionally portrayed in two films about Factory: *24 Hour Party People* and *Control*. A passionate supporter of regionalism and a fervent booster of Manchester and Salford, he died in August 2007. In December 2008 he was made an Honorary Freeman of the City of Manchester. For more: www.cerysmaticfactory.info.

Linder
Has concentrated on a successful artistic career since the demise of Ludus in 1983. As well as providing sleeve photographs for several Morrissey records, she has conducted several performance pieces, including *Salt Shrine* (1998) and *Requiem: Clint Eastwood, Clare Offreduccio and Me* (2001). Solo exhibitions of her multimedia work have been held in London, Prague and Geneva, and she has been part of group shows throughout Europe. In 2006 she published a career overview, *Linder Works 1976–2006*.

Chapter 9: 1977/1: The Roxy

Andy Czezowski and Susan Carrington
Ran the Fridge nightclub in Brixton from the mid-1980s on. In 2007 Paul Marko published his well-researched and entertaining history of the Roxy, *Roxy London WC2*.

Poly Styrene

Released one solo album, *Translucence*, in 1980, but subsequently devoted herself to a spiritual life. She re-formed X-Ray Spex for one mid-1990s album, *Conscious Consumer*. In 2008 she played at the 30th Anniversary of the Rock Against Racism concert in Victoria Park, and re-formed X-Ray Spex for a show at the Roundhouse. For more: www.x-rayspex.com.

Don Letts

After directing videos for the Pretenders, The Slits and Musical Youth, he made a feature, *Dancehall Queen* (1997), as well as several documentaries, including *The Clash: Westway to the World* (2000) and *Punk: Attitude* (2005). He has also curated several successful compilations, including *Dread Meets Punk Rockers Uptown: The Soundtrack to London's Legendary Roxy Club* (2001). In 2006 he published his autobiography, *Culture Clash: Dread Meets Punk Rockers*. He currently has a regular show on BBC Radio 6 Music.

Wire

Re-formed in the mid-1980s for several well-received albums, including *A Bell Is a Cup Until It Is Struck*. After the Britpop era of thievery, their three EMI albums have been reissued several times. Wire re-formed for a second time in 2000, and have released several new records, including three editions of *Read and Burn*, *The Scottish Play* and *Object 47*. In early 2009 they conducted a European tour. For more, go to www.pinkflag.com.

TV Smith

Has continued to perform since the end of the Adverts in 1979, both with TV Smith's Explorers and Cheap, before emerging as a solo artist in 1992. He has remained true to his punk ideals on albums like *Immortal Rich* (1995) and *Generation Y* (1999). His latest record, *In the Arms of My Enemy*, has a great cover picture of an owl, and was released in 2008. For more: www.tvsmith.com.

Pauline Murray

Made an album with Martin Hannett, *Pauline Murray and the Invisible Girls*, after Penetration split in 1980. Murray established the successful Polestar Studios, located in the Ouseburn Valley,

Newcastle-upon-Tyne. In 2008 Penetration issued two live shows from 1978/9 and a new single, 'Our World/Sea Song'. The official website is at www.loversofoutrage.com.

Chapter 10: 1977/2: The Jubilee

Al Clark
Moved to Australia in 1990 after a stint as the editor of *The Film Yearbook*. He also worked at Virgin Films, where he co-produced the film of *Nineteen Eighty-Four* (1984), among others. His subsequent producer credits include *The Adventures of Priscilla, Queen of the Desert* (1994), *Siam Sunset* (1999), *The Book of Revelation* (2006) and *Blessed* (2009).

Dennis Morris
Formed 'black punk band' Basement Five in the late 1970s. In 2002 he published his book of classic Sex Pistols photographs, *Destroy: Sex Pistols 1977*, and the next year, *Bob Marley: A Rebel Life*. He has held exhibitions in the UK, Japan and Canada, and his photographs have appeared in *Rolling Stone*, *Time*, *People* magazine, and the *Sunday Times*. Go to www.dennismorris.com.

Derek Jarman
Directed ten feature films after *Jubilee*, as well as several shorts and pop videos for artists like Marc Almond and The Smiths. His filmography includes: *The Tempest* (1979), *Caravaggio* (1986), *The Last of England* (1988), *The Garden* (1990), *Edward II* (1991) and *Blue* (1993). He also wrote several books, including *Dancing Ledge* (1984), *Modern Nature* (1991) and *Chroma: A Book of Colour* (1993). He continued to paint until his death in early 1994. He is perhaps best remembered for his garden at Dungeness, the subject of the book *Derek Jarman's Garden*, with photos by Howard Sooley. In 2007 Isaac Julien, Tilda Swinton and Colin MacCabe collaborated on a tribute, the film documentary *Derek*. Go to www.slowmotionangel.com.

Barbara Harwood
Studied under Chief Druid Dr Thomas Maughan and qualified as a homeopathic practitioner in the early 1980s. Harwood later became

principal of the London College of Homeopathy in Regent's Park, and is a member of the Society of Homeopaths.

Chapter 11: Sid Vicious

Joe Stevens

Remains, as Chris Salewicz has written, 'one of the very greatest of all rock'n'roll photographers'. In 2005 some of his CBGB's photos of the CBGB scene were published in Hilly Kristal's book, *CBGB & OMFUG – Thirty Years from the Home of Underground Rock*. To contact him, go to www.myspace.com/joestevens2008.

Anne Beverley

Continued to be involved with Sex Pistols business as the legatee of Sid Vicious: she attended the 1996 court case that vested control of Glitterbest in the four ex-Pistols and received an estimated six-figure sum in the settlement that followed. In the run-up to the Sex Pistols reunion in summer 1996, she committed suicide from an overdose of alcohol and painkillers.

Acknowledgments

Many thanks to my agent Tony Peake, to Lee Brackstone at Faber and Faber, to Marc Issue Robinson for his sterling work in doing the transcribing, and to all the interviewees for their time and generosity in the first place. The actual tapes used for the book are now contained in England's Dreaming: The Jon Savage Archive held at Liverpool John Moores University.

Index